Jack Hinton
The Guardsman

by
Charles James Lever

Jack Hinton
The Guardsman
by Charles James Lever

Copyright © 2024

All Rights reserved.

No part of this publication may be reproduced, stored in a retrieval system, or transmitted in any form or by any means, electronic, mechanical, photocopying or Otherwise, without the written permission of the publisher.
The author/editor asserts the moral right to be identified as the author/editor of this work.

ISBN: 978-93-62202-86-4

Published by
DOUBLE 9 BOOKS
2/13-B, Ansari Road
Daryaganj, New Delhi – 110002
info@double9books.com
www.double9books.com
Tel. 011-40042856

This book is under public domain

ABOUT THE AUTHOR

Charles James Lever was an Irish author and storyteller who lived from August 31, 1806 to June 1, 1872. Anthony Trollope said that Lever's books were like his conversations. Lever was born on Amiens Street in Dublin. He was the second son of architect and builder James Lever and went to special schools. He had many adventures at Trinity College, Dublin, from 1823 to 1828. It was there that he got his medical degree in 1831. Some of the stories of his books are based on these experiences. The character of Frank Webber in the book Charles O'Malley was based on Robert Boyle, a friend from college who later became a priest. Lever and Boyle made extra money by singing original songs in the streets of Dublin. They also pulled off a lot of other jokes, which Lever wrote about in more detail in his books O'Malley, Con Cregan, and Lord Kilgobbin. Before he really started studying medicine, Lever went to Canada on an emigrant ship as an untrained surgeon. He has used some of what he learned in Con Cregan, Arthur O'Leary, and Roland Cashel. When he got to Canada, he went into the woods and joined a Native American group. But he had to leave because his life was in danger, just like his character Bagenal Daly did in his book The Knight of Gwynne.

CONTENTS

PREFACE 9

CHAPTER I
A FAMILY PARTY 11

CHAPTER II
THE IRISH PACKET 16

CHAPTER III
THE CASTLE 23

CHAPTER IV
THE BREAKFAST 33

CHAPTER V
THE REVIEW IN THE PHOENIX 46

CHAPTER VI
THE SHAM BATTLE 51

CHAPTER VII
THE ROONEYS 60

CHAPTER VIII
THE VISIT 68

CHAPTER IX
THE BALL 74

CHAPTER X
A FINALE TO AN EVENING 85

CHAPTER XI
A NEGOTIATION 99

CHAPTER XII
A WAGER 104

CHAPTER XIII
A NIGHT OF TROUBLE 113

CHAPTER XIV
    THE PARTING 124
CHAPTER XV
    THE LETTER FROM HOME 128
CHAPTER XVI
    A MORNING IN TOWN 133
CHAPTER XVII
    AN EVENING IN TOWN 142
CHAPTER XVIII
    A CONFIDENCE 157
CHAPTER XIX
    THE CANAL-BOAT 164
CHAPTER XX
    SHANNON HARBOUR 171
CHAPTER XXI
    LOUGHREA 181
CHAPTER XXII
    A MOONLIGHT CANTER 192
CHAPTER XXIII
    MAJOR MAHON AND HIS QUARTERS 199
CHAPTER XXIV
    THE DEVIL'S GRIP 204
CHAPTER XXV
    THE STEEPLECHASE 213
CHAPTER XXVI
    THE DINNER-PARTY AT MOUNT BROWN 225
CHAPTER XXVII
    THE RACE BALL 230
CHAPTER XXVIII
    THE INN FIRE 240
CHAPTER XXIX
    THE DUEL 250
CHAPTER XXX
    A COUNTRY DOCTOR 256

CHAPTER XXXI
THE LETTER-BAG 261

CHAPTER XXXII
BOB MAHON AND THE WIDOW 267

CHAPTER XXXIII
THE PRIEST'S GIG 273

CHAPTER XXXIV
THE MOUNTAIN PASS 278

CHAPTER XXXV
THE JOURNEY 289

CHAPTER XXXVI
MURRANAKILTY 301

CHAPTER XXXVII
SIR SIMON 307

CHAPTER XXXVIII
ST. SENAN'S WELL 315

CHAPTER XXXIX
AN UNLOOKED-FOR MEETING 324

CHAPTER XL
THE PRIEST'S KITCHEN 333

CHAPTER XLI
TIPPERARY JOE 339

CHAPTER XLII
THE HIGHROAD 343

CHAPTER XLIII
THE ASSIZE TOWN 349

CHAPTER XLIV
THE BAD DINNER 353

CHAPTER XLV
THE RETURN 357

CHAPTER XLVI
FAREWELL TO IRELAND 361

CHAPTER XLVII
LONDON 368

CHAPTER XLVIII
AN UNHAPPY DISCLOSURE 374

CHAPTER XLIX
THE HORSE GUARDS 380

CHAPTER L
THE RETREAT FROM BURGOS 388

CHAPTER LI
A MISHAP 393

CHAPTER LII
THE MARCH 402

CHAPTER LIII
VITTORIA 406

CHAPTER LIV
THE RETREAT 411

CHAPTER LV
THE FOUR-IN-HAND 423

CHAPTER LVI
ST. DENIS 428

CHAPTER LVII
PARIS IN 1814 432

CHAPTER LVIII
THE RONI FÊTE 444

CHAPTER LIX
FRESCATI'S 457

CHAPTER LX
DISCLOSURES 468

CHAPTER LXI
NEW ARRIVALS 478

CHAPTER LXII
CONCLUSION 482

PREFACE

Very few words of preface will suffice to the volume now presented to my readers. My intention was to depict, in the early experiences of a young Englishman in Ireland, some of the almost inevitable mistakes incidental to such a character. I had so often myself listened to so many absurd and exaggerated opinions on Irish character, formed on the very slightest acquaintance with the country, and by persons, too, who, with all the advantages long intimacy might confer, would still have been totally inadequate to the task of a rightful appreciation, that I deemed the subject one where a little "reprisal" might be justifiable.

Scarcely, however, had I entered upon my story, than I strayed from the path I had determined on, and, with very little reference to my original intention, suffered Jack Hinton to "take his chance amongst the natives," and with far too much occupation on his hands to give time for reflecting over their peculiarities, or recording their singular traits, I threw him into the society of the capital, under the vice-royalty of a celebrated Duke, all whose wayward eccentricities were less marked than the manly generosity and genuine honesty of his character. I introduced him into a set where, whatever purely English readers may opine, I have wonderfully little exaggerated; and I led him down to the West to meet adventures which every newspaper, some twenty-five years ago, would show were by no means extravagant or strange.

As for the characters of the story, there is not one for which I did not take a "real sitter;" at the same time, I have never heard one single correct guess as to the types that afforded them. To Mrs. Paul Rooney, Father Tom Loftus, Bob Mahon, O'Grady, Tipperary Joe, and even Corny himself, I have scarcely added a touch which nature has not given them, while assuredly I have failed to impart many a fine and delicate tint far above the "reach of—'*my*—art," and which might have presented them in stronger light and shadow than I have dared to attempt. Had I desired to caricature English ignorance as to Ireland in the person of my Guardsman, nothing would have been easier; but I preferred merely exposing him to such errors as might throw into stronger relief the peculiarities of Irishmen, and, while offering something to laugh at, give no offence to either. The volume amused me while I was writing it,—less, perhaps, by what I recorded, than what I abstained from inditing; at all events, it was the work of some of the pleasantest hours of my life, and if it can ever impart to any of my readers a portion of the amusement some of the real characters afforded myself, it will not be all a failure. That it may succeed so far is the hope of the reader's

Very devoted servant,

CHARLES LEVER.

Casa Capponi, Florence, March, 1857.

CHAPTER I
A FAMILY PARTY

It was on a dark and starless night in February, 181—, as the last carriage of a dinner-party had driven from the door of a large house in St. James's-square, when a party drew closer around the drawing-room fire, apparently bent upon that easy and familiar chit-chat the presence of company interdicts.

One of these was a large and fine-looking man of about five-and-forty, who, dressed in the full uniform of a general officer, wore besides the ribbon of the Bath; he leaned negligently upon the chimney-piece, and, with his back towards the fire, seemed to follow the current of his own reflections: this was my Father.

Beside him, but almost concealed in the deep recess of a well-cushioned arm-chair, sat, or rather lay, a graceful figure, who with an air of languid repose was shading her fine complexion as well from the glare of the fire as from the trying brilliancy of an Argand lamp upon the mantelpiece. Her rich dress, resplendent with jewels, while it strangely contrasted with the careless ease of her attitude, also showed that she had bestowed a more than common attention that day upon her toilette: this, fair reader, was my Mother.

Opposite to her, and disposed in a position of rather studied gracefulness, lounged a tall, thin, fashionable-looking man, with a dark olive complexion, and a short black moustache. He wore in the button-hole of his blue coat the ribbon of St. Louis. The Count de Grammont, for such he was, was an *émigré* noble, who, attached to the fortunes of the Bourbons, had resided for some years in London, and who, in the double capacity of adviser of my father and admirer of my lady-mother, obtained a considerable share of influence in the family and a seat at its councils.

At a little distance from the rest, and apparently engaged with her embroidery, sat a very beautiful girl, whose dark hair and long lashes deepened the seeming paleness of features a Greek sculptor might have copied. While nothing could be more perfect than the calm loveliness of her face and the delicate pencilling of her slightly-arched eyebrows, an accurate observer could detect that her tremulous lip occasionally curled with a passing expression of half scorn, as from time to time she turned her eyes towards each speaker in turn, while she herself maintained a perfect silence. My cousin, Lady Julia Egerton, had indeed but that one fault: shall I venture to call by so harsh a name that spirit of gentle malice which loved to look for the ludicrous features of everything around her, and inclined her to indulge what the French call the *"esprit moqueur"* even on occasions where her own feelings were interested?

The last figure of the group was a stripling of some nineteen years, who, in the uniform of the Guards, was endeavouring to seem perfectly easy and unconcerned, while it was evident that his sword-knot divided his attention with some secret thoughts that rendered him anxious and excited: this was Myself!

A silence of some moments was at length broken by my mother, who, with a kind of sigh Miss O'Neill was fond of, turned towards the Count, and said,

"Do confess, Count, we were all most stupid to-day. Never did a dinner go off so heavily. But it's always the penalty one pays for a royal Duke. *A propos*, General, what did he say of Jack's appointment?"

"Nothing could be more kind, nothing more generous than his Royal Highness. The very first thing he did in the room was to place this despatch in my hands. This, Jack," said my father, turning to me, "this is your appointment as an extra aide-de-camp."

"Very proper indeed," interposed my mother; "I am very happy to think you'll be about the Court. Windsor, to be sure, is stupid."

"He is not likely to see much of it," said my father, dryly.

"Oh, you think he'll be in town then?"

"Why, not exactly that either."

"Then what can you mean?" said she, with more of animation than before.

"Simply, that his appointment is on the staff in Ireland."

"In Ireland!" repeated my mother, with a tragic start. "In Ireland!"

"In Ireland!" said Lady Julia, in a low, soft voice.

"*En Irlande!*" echoed the Count, with a look of well got up horror, as he elevated his eyebrows to the very top of his forehead; while I myself, to whom the communication was as sudden and as unexpected, assumed a kind of soldier-like indifference, as though to say, "What matters it to me?

what do I care for the rigours of climate? the snows of the Caucasus, or the suns of Bengal, are quite alike; even Ireland, if his Majesty's service require it."

"Ireland!" repeated my mother once more; "I really never heard anything so very shocking. But, my dear Jack, you can't think of it. Surely, General, you had presence of mind to decline."

"To accept, and to thank most gratefully his Royal Highness for such a mark of his favour, for this I had quite presence of mind," said my father, somewhat haughtily.

"And you really will go, Jack?"

"Most decidedly," said I, as I put on a kind of Godefroy de Bouillon look, and strutted about the room.

"And pray what can induce you to such a step?"

"*Oui, que diable allait-il faire dans cette galère?*'" said the Count.

"By Jove!" cried my father, hastily, "you are intolerable; you wished your boy to be a Guardsman in opposition to my desire for a regiment on service. You would have him an aide-de-camp: now he is both one and the other. In Heaven's name, what think ye of getting him made a lady of the bedchamber? for it's the only appointment I am aware of——"

"You are too absurd, General," said my mother, pettishly. "Count, pray touch the bell; that fire is so very hot, and I really was quite unprepared for this piece of news."

"And you, Julia," said I, leaning over the back of my cousin's chair, "what do you say to all this?"

"I've just been thinking what a pity it is I should have wasted all my skill and my worsted on this foolish rug, while I could have been embroidering a gay banner for our young knight bound for the wars. '*Partant pour la Syrie,*'" hummed she, half pensively, while I could see a struggling effort to suppress a laugh. I turned indignantly away, and walked towards the fire, where the Count was expending his consolations on my mother.

"After all, *Miladi*, it is not so bad as you think in the provinces; I once spent three weeks in Brittany, very pleasantly indeed: *oui, pardieu,* it's quite true. To be sure, we had Perlet, and Mademoiselle Mars, and got up the *Précieuse Ridicules* as well as in Paris."

The application of this very apposite fact to Ireland was clearly satisfactory to my mother, who smiled benignly at the speaker, while my father turned upon him a look of the most indescribable import.

"Jack, my boy!" said he, taking me by the arm, "were I your age, and had no immediate prospect of active service, I should prefer Ireland to any country in the world. I have plenty of old friends on the staff there. The Duke himself was my schoolfellow— —"

"I hope he will be properly attentive," interrupted my mother. "Dear Jack, remind me to-morrow to write to Lady Mary."

"Don't mistake the country you are going to," continued my father; "you will find many things very different from what you are leaving; and, above all, be not over ready to resent, as an injury, what may merely be intended as a joke: your brother officers will always guide you on these points."

"And above all things," said my mother, with great earnestness, "do not adopt that odious fashion of wearing their hair. I've seen members of both Houses, and particularly that little man they talk so much of, Mr. Grattan, I believe they call him— —"

"Make your mind perfectly easy on that head, my lady," said my father, dryly, "your son is not particularly likely to resemble Henry Grattan."

My cousin Julia alone seemed to relish the tone of sarcasm he spoke in, for she actually bestowed on him a look of almost grateful acknowledgment.

"The carriage, my lady," said the servant. And at the same moment my mother, possibly not sorry to cut short the discussion, rose from her chair.

"Do you intend to look in at the Duchess's, General?"

"For half an hour," replied my father; "after that I have my letters to write. Jack, you know, leaves us to-morrow."

"'Tis really very provoking," said my mother, turning at the same time a look towards the Count.

"*A vos ordres, Madame,*" said he, bowing with an air of most deferential politeness, while he presented his arm for her acceptance.

"Good night, then," cried I, as the party left the room; "I have so much to do and to think of, I shan't join you." I turned to look for Lady Julia, but she was gone, when and how I knew not; so I sat down at the fire to ruminate alone over my present position, and my prospects for the future.

These few and imperfect passages may put the reader in possession of some, at least, of the circumstances which accompanied my outset in life; and if they be not sufficiently explicit, I can only say, that he knows fully as much of me as at the period in question I did of myself.

At Eton, I had been what is called rather a smart boy, but incorrigibly idle; at Sandhurst, I showed more ability, and more disinclination to learn. By the favour of a royal Duke (who had been my godfather), my commission in a marching regiment was exchanged for a lieutenancy in the Guards; and at the time I write of I had been some six months in the service, which I spent in all the whirl and excitement of London society. My father, who, besides being a distinguished officer, was one of the most popular men among the clubs, my mother, a London beauty of some twenty years' standing, were claims sufficient to ensure me no common share of attention, while I added to the number what, in my own estimation at least were, certain very decided advantages of a purely personal nature.

To obviate, as far as might be, the evil results of such a career, my father secretly asked for the appointment on the staff of the noble Duke then Viceroy of Ireland, in preference to what my mother contemplated—my being attached to the royal household. To remove me alike from the enervating influence of a mother's vanity, and the extravagant profusion and voluptuous abandonment of London habits, this was his object. He calculated, too, that by new ties, new associations, and new objects of ambition, I should be better prepared, and more desirous of that career of real service to which in his heart he destined me. These were his notions, at least; the result must be gleaned from my story.

CHAPTER II
THE IRISH PACKET

A few nights after the conversation I have briefly alluded to, and pretty much about the same hour, I aroused myself from the depression of nearly thirty hours' sea-sickness, on hearing that at length we were in the bay of Dublin. Hitherto I had never left the precincts of the narrow den denominated my berth; but now I made my way eagerly on deck, anxious to catch a glimpse, however faint, of that bold coast I had more than once heard compared with, or even preferred to, Naples. The night, however, was falling fast, and, worse still, a perfect down-pour of rain was falling with it; the sea ran high, and swept the little craft from stem to stern; the spars bent like whips, and our single topsail strained and stretched as though at every fresh plunge it would part company with us altogether. No trace or outline of the coast could I detect on any side; a deep red light appearing and disappearing at intervals, as we rode upon or sank beneath the trough of the sea, was all that my eye could perceive: this the dripping helmsman briefly informed me was the "Kish," but, as he seemed little disposed for conversation, I was left to my unassisted ingenuity to make out whether it represented any point of the capital we were approaching or not.

The storm of wind and rain increasing at each moment, drove me once more back to the cabin, where, short as had been the period of my absence, the scene had undergone a most important change. Up to this moment my sufferings and my seclusion gave me little leisure or opportunity to observe my fellow travellers. The stray and scattered fragments of conversation that reached me, rather puzzled than enlightened me. Of the topics which I innocently supposed occupied all human attention, not a word was dropped; Carlton House was not once mentioned; the St. Leger and the Oaks not even alluded to; whether the Prince's breakfast was to come off at Knights-bridge or Progmore, no one seemed to know, or even care; nor was a hint dropped as to the fashion of the new bearskins the Guards were to sport at the review on Hounslow. The price of pigs, however, in Ballinasloe, they were perfect in. Of a late row in Kil—something, where one half of the population had massacred the other, they knew everything, even to the names of the defunct. A few of the better dressed chatted over country matters, from which I could glean that game and gentry were growing gradually scarcer; but a red-nosed, fat old gentleman, in rusty black and high boots, talked down the others by an eloquent account of the mawling that he, a certain Father Tom Loftus, had given the Reverend Paul Strong, at a late controversial meeting in the Rotunda.

The Packet.

Through all this "bald, disjointed chat," unceasing demands were made for bottled porter, "matarials," or spirits and wather, of which, were I to judge from the frequency of the requests, the consumption must have been awful.

There would seem something in the very attitude of lying down that induces reflection, and, thus stretched at full length in my berth, I could not help ruminating upon the land I was approaching, in a spirit which, I confess, accorded much more with my mother's prejudices than my father's convictions. From the few chance phrases dropped around me, it appeared that even the peaceful pursuits of a country market, or the cheerful sports of the field, were followed up in a spirit of recklessness and devilment; so that many a head that left home without a care, went back with a crack in it. But to return once more to the cabin. It must be borne in mind that some thirty odd years ago the passage between Liverpool and Dublin was not, as at present, the rapid flight of a dozen hours, from shore to shore; where, on one evening, you left the thundering din of waggons, and the iron crank of cranes and windlasses, to wake the next morning with the rich brogue of Paddy floating softly around you. Far from it! the thing was then a voyage. You took a solemn leave of your friends, you tore yourself from the embraces of your family, and, with a tear in your eye and a hamper on your arm, you betook yourself to the pier to watch, with an anxious and a beating heart, every step of the three hours' proceeding that heralded your departure. In those days there was some honour in being a traveller, and the man who had crossed the Channel a couple of times became a kind of Captain Cook among his acquaintances.

The most singular feature of the whole, however, and the one to which I am now about to allude, proceeded from the fact that the steward in those days, instead of the extensive resources of the present period, had little to offer you, save some bad brandy and a biscuit, and each traveller had to look to his various wants with an accuracy and foresight that required both tact and habit. The mere demands of hunger and thirst were not only to be considered in the abstract, but a point of far greater difficulty, the probable length of the voyage, was to be taken into consideration; so that you bought your beefsteaks with your eye upon the barometer, and laid in your mutton by the age of the moon. While thus the agency of the season was made to react upon your stomach, in a manner doubtless highly conducive to the interests of science, your part became one of the most critical nicety.

Scarcely were you afloat, and on the high seas, when your appetite was made to depend on the aspect of the weather. Did the wind blow fresh and fair, you eat away with a careless ease and a happy conscience, highly beneficial to your digestion. With a glance through the skylight at the blue heaven, with a sly look at the prosperous dog-vane, you helped yourself to the liver wing, and took an extra glass of your sherry. Let the breeze fall, however, let a calm come on, or, worse still, a trampling noise on deck, and a certain rickety motion of the craft betoken a change of wind, the knife and fork fell listlessly from your hand, the unlifted cutlet was consigned to your plate, the very spoonful of gravy you had devoured in imagination was dropped upon the dish, and you replaced the cork in your bottle, with the sad sigh of a man who felt that, instead of his income, he has been living on the principal of his fortune.

Happily, there is a reverse to the medal, and this it was to which now my attention was directed. The trip as occasionally happened, was a rapid one; and while under the miserable impression that a fourth part of the journey had not been accomplished, we were blessed with the tidings of land. Scarcely was the word uttered, when it flew from mouth to mouth; and I thought I could trace the elated look of proud and happy hearts, as home drew near. What was my surprise, however, to see the enthusiasm take another and very different channel. With one accord a general rush was made upon the hampers of prog. Baskets were burst open on every side. Sandwiches and sausages, porter bottles, cold punch, chickens, and hard eggs, were strewn about with a careless and reckless profusion; none semed too sick or too sore for this general epidemic of feasting. Old gentlemen sat up in their beds and bawled for beef; children of tender years brandished a drumstick. Individuals who but a short half-hour before seemed to have made a hearty meal, testified by the ravenous exploits of their appetites to their former forbearance and abstemiousness. Even the cautious little man in the brown spencer, who wrapped up the remnant of his breakfast in the *Times*, now opened his whole store, and seemed bent upon a day of rejoicing. Never was such a scene of riotous noise and tumultuous mirth. Those who scowled at each other till now, hob-nobbed across the table; and simpering old maids cracked merry thoughts with gay bachelors, without even a passing fear for the result. "Thank Heaven," said I, aloud, "that I see all this with my sense and my intellects clear about me." Had I suddenly awoke to such a prospect from the disturbed slumber of sickness" the chances were ten to one I had jumped overboard, and swam for my life. In fact, it could convey but one image to the mind, such as we read of, when some infuriated and reckless men, despairing of safety, without a hope left, resolve upon closing life in the mad orgies of drunken abandonment.

Here were the meek, the tranquil, the humble-minded, the solitary, the seasick, all suddenly converted into riotous and roystering feasters. The lips that scarcely moved, now blew the froth from a porter cup with the blast of a Boreas: and even the small urchin in the green face and nankeen jacket, bolted hard eggs with the dexterity of a clown in a pantomime. The end of all things (eatable) had certainly come. Chickens were dismembered like felons, and even jokes and witticisms were bandied upon the victuals. "What, if even yet," thought I, "the wind should change!" The idea was a malicious one, too horrible to indulge in. At this moment the noise and turmoil on deck apprised me that our voyage was near its termination.

The Landing

The night, as I have said, was dark and stormy. It rained too—as it knows only how to rain in Ireland. There was that steady persistence, that persevering monotony of down-pour, which, not satisfied with wetting you to the skin, seems bent upon converting your very blood into water. The wind swept in long and moaning gusts along the bleak pier, which, late and inclement as it was, seemed crowded with people. Scarcely was a rope thrown ashore, when we were boarded on every side, by the rigging, on the shrouds, over the bulwarks, from the anchor to the taffrail; the whole population of the island seemed to flock in upon us; while sounds of welcome and recognition resounded on all sides—

"How are you, Mister Maguire?" "Is the mistress with you?" "Is that you, Mr. Tierney?" "How are you, ma'am?" "And yourself, Tim?" "Beautiful, glory be to God!" "A great passage, entirely, ma'am." "Nothing but rain since I seen you." "Take the trunks up to Mrs. Tun-stall; and, Tim, darling, oysters and punch for four."

"Great mercy!" said I, "eating again!"

"Morrisson, your honour," said a ragged ruffian, nudging me by the elbow.

"Reilly, sir; isn't it? It's me, sir—the Club. I'm the man always drives your honour."

"Arrah, howld your prate," said a deep voice, "the gentleman hasn't time to bless himself."

"It's me, sir; Owen Daly, that has the black horse."

"More by token, with a spavin," whispered another; while a roar of laughter followed the joke.

"A car, sir—take you up in five minutes."

"A chaise, your honour—do the thing dacently."

Now, whether my hesitation at this moment was set down by the crowd of my solicitors to some doubt of my solvency or not, I cannot say; but true it is, their tone of obsequious entreaty gradually changed into one of rather caustic criticism.

"Maybe it's a gossoon you'd like to carry the little trunk."

"Let him alone; it's only a carpet-bag; he'll carry it himself."

"Don't you see the gentleman would rather walk; and as the night is fine, 'tis pleasanter—and—cheaper."

"Take you for a fipp'ny bit and a glass of sparits," said a gruff voice in my ear.

By this time I had collected my luggage together, whose imposing appearance seemed once more to testify in my favour, particularly the case of my cocked-hat, which to my ready-witted acquaintances proclaimed me a military man. A general rush was accordingly made upon my luggage; and while one man armed himself with a portmanteau, another laid hands on a trunk, a third a carpet-bag, a fourth a gun-case, and so on until I found myself keeping watch and ward over my epaulet-case and my umbrella, the sole remnant of my effects. At the same moment a burst of laughter and a half shout broke from the crowd, and a huge, powerful fellow jumped on the deck, and, seizing me by the arm, cried out,

"Come along now, Captain, it's all right. This way—this way, sir."

"But why am I to go with you?" said I, vainly struggling to escape his grasp.

"Why is it?" said he, with a chuckling laugh; "reason enough—didn't we toss up for ye, and didn't I win ye."

"Win me!"

"Ay; just that same."

By this time I found myself beside a car, upon which all my luggage was already placed.

"Get up, now," said he.

"It's a beautiful car, and a dhry cushion," added a voice near, to the manifest mirth of the bystanders.

Delighted to escape my tormentors, I sprang up opposite to him, while a cheer, mad and wild enough for a tribe of Iroquois, yelled behind us. Away We rattled over the pavement, without lamp or lantern to guide our path, while the sea dashed its foam across our faces, and the rain beat in torrents upon our backs.

"Where to, Captain?" inquired my companion, as he plied his whip without ceasing.

"The Castle; you know where that is?"

"Faix I ought," was the reply. "Ain't I there at the levees. But howld fast, your honour; the road isn't good; and there is a hole somewhere hereabouts."

"A hole! For Heaven's sake, take care. Do you know where it is?"

"Begorra! you're in it," was the answer; and, as he spoke, the horse went down head foremost, the car after him; away flew the driver on one side, while I myself was shot some half-dozen yards on the other, a perfect avalanche of trunks, boxes, and portmanteaus rattling about my doomed head. A crashing shower of kicks, the noise of the flying splinters, and the imprecations of the carman, were the last sounds I heard, as a heavy imperial full of books struck me on the head, and laid me prostrate.

Through my half-consciousness, I could still feel the rain as it fell in sheets; the heavy plash of the sea sounded in my ears; but, somehow, a feeling like sleepiness crept over me, and I became insensible.

CHAPTER III
THE CASTLE

When I next came to my senses, I found myself lying upon a sofa in a large room, of which I appeared the only occupant. A confused and misty recollection of my accident, some scattered fragments of my voyage, and a rather aching sensation in my head, were the only impressions of which I was well conscious. The last evening I spent at home was full in my memory, and I could not help thinking over my poor mother's direful anticipations in my vain endeavours to penetrate what I felt had been a misfortune of some kind or other. The mystery was, however, too deep for my faculties; and so, in despair of unravelling the past, I set myself to work to decipher the present. The room, I have already said, was large; and the ceiling, richly stuccoed and ornamented, spoke of a day whose architecture was of a grand and massive character. The furniture, now old and time-worn, had once been handsome, even magnificent — rich curtains of heavy brocaded silk, with deep gold fringes, gorgeously carved and gilded chairs, in the taste of Louis XV.; marble consoles stood between the windows, and a mirror of gigantic proportions occupied the chimney-breast. Years and neglect had not only done their worst, but it was evident that the hand of devastation had also been at work. The marbles were cracked; few of the chairs were available for use; the massive lustre, intended to shine with a resplendent glare of fifty wax-lights, was now made a resting-place for chakos, bearskins, and foraging caps; an ominous-looking star in the looking-glass bore witness to the bullet of a pistol; and the very Cupids carved upon the frame, who once were wont to smile blandly at each other, were now disfigured with cork moustaches, and one of them even carried a short pipe in his mouth. Swords, sashes, and sabretasches, spurs and shot-belts, with guns, fishing-tackle, and tandem whips, were hung here and there upon the walls, which themselves presented the strangest spectacle of all, there not being a portion of them unoccupied by caricature sketches, executed in every imaginable species of taste, style, and colouring. Here was a field-day in the Park, in which it was easy to see the prominent figures were portraits: there an enormous nose, surmounted by a grenadier cap, was passing in review some trembling and terrified soldiers. In another, a commander of the forces was seen galloping down the lines, holding on by the pommel of the saddle. Over the sofa I occupied, a levee at the Castle was displayed, in which, if the company were not villanously libelled, the Viceroy had little reason to be proud of his guests. There were also dinners at the Lodge; guards relieved by wine puncheons dressed up like field-officers; the whole accompanied by doggrel verses explanatory of the views.

The owner of this singular chamber had, however, not merely devoted his walls to the purposes of an album, but he had also made them perform the part of a memorandum-book. Here were the "meets" of the Kildare and the Dubber for the month of March; there, the turn of duty for the garrison of Dublin, interspersed with such fragments as the following:—"Mem. To dine at Mat Kean's on Tuesday, 4th.—Not to pay Hennesy till he settles about the handicap.—To ask Courtenay—for Fanny Burke's fan; the same Fanny has pretty legs of her own.—To tell Holmes to have nothing to do with Lanty Moore's niece, in regard to a reason!—Five to two on Giles's two-year-old, if Tom likes. N.B. The mare is a roarer.—A heavenly day; what fun they must have!—may the devil fire Tom O'Flaherty, or I would not be here now." These and a hundred other similar passages figured on every side, leaving me in a state of considerable mystification, not as to the character of my host, of which I could guess something, but as to the nature of his abode, which I could not imagine to be a barrack-room.

As I lay thus pondering, the door cautiously opened, and a figure appeared, which, as I had abundant leisure to examine it, and as the individual is one who occasionally turns up in the course of my history, I may as well take the present opportunity of presenting to my reader. The man who entered, scarcely more than four feet and a half high, might be about sixty years of age. His head, enormously disproportioned to the rest of his figure, presented a number of flat surfaces, as though nature had originally destined it for a crystal. Upon one of these planes the eyes were set; and although as far apart as possible, yet upon such terms of distance were they, that they never, even by an accident, looked in the same direction. The nose was short and snubby; the nostrils wide and expanded, as if the feature had been pitched against the face in a moment of ill-temper, and flattened by the force. As for the mouth, it looked like the malicious gash of a blunt instrument, jagged, ragged, and uneven. It had not even the common-place advantage of being parallel to the horizon, but ran in an oblique direction from right to left, enclosed between a parenthesis of the crankiest wrinkles that ever human cheek were creased by. The head would have been bald but for a scanty wig, technically called a "jasy," which, shrunk by time, now merely occupied the apex of the scalp, where it moved about with every action of the forehead and eyebrows, and was thus made to minister to the expression of a hundred emotions that other men's wigs know nothing about. Truly, it was the strangest peruke that ever covered a human cranium. I do not believe that another like it ever existed. It had nothing in common with other wigs. It was like its owner, perfectly *sui generis*. It had not the easy flow and wavy curl of the old beau. It had not the methodical precision and rectilinear propriety of the elderly gentleman. It was not full, like a lawyer's, nor horse-shoed, like a bishop's. No. It was a cross-grained, ill-tempered, ill-conditioned old scratch, that looked like nothing under heaven save the husk of a hedgehog.

The dress of this strange figure was a suit of very gorgeous light brown livery, with orange facings, a green plush waistcoat and shorts, frogged, flapped, and embroidered most lavishly with gold lace, silk stockings, with shoes, whose enormous buckles covered nearly the entire foot, and rivalled, in their paste brilliancy, the piercing brightness of the wearer's eye. Having closed the door carefully behind him, he walked towards the chimney, with a certain air of solemn and imposing dignity that very nearly overcame all my efforts at seriousness; his outstretched and expanded hands, his averted toes and waddling gait, giving him a most distressing resemblance to the spread eagle of Prussia, had that respectable bird been pleased to take a promenade in a showy livery. Having snuffed the candles, and helped himself to a pinch of snuff from a gold box on the mantelpiece, he stuck his arms, nearly to the elbows, in the ample pockets of his coat, and with his head a little elevated, and his under-lip slightly protruded, seemed to meditate upon the mutability of human affairs, and the vanity of all worldly pursuits.

I coughed a couple of times to attract his attention, and, having succeeded in catching his eye, I begged, in my blandest imaginable voice, to know where I was.

"Where are ye, is it?" said he, repeating my question in a tone of the most sharp and querulous intonation, to which not even his brogue could lend one touch of softness, — "where are ye? and where would you like to be? or where would any one be that was disgracing himself, or blackguarding about the streets till he got his head cut and his clothes torn, but in Master Phil's room: devil other company it's used to. Well, well! It is more like a watchhouse nor a gentleman's parlour, this same room. It's little his father, the Jidge"—here he crossed himself piously—"it is little he thought the company his son would be keeping; but it is no matter. I gave him warning last Tuesday, and with the blessin' o' God——"

The remainder of this speech was lost in a low muttering grumble, which I afterwards learnt was his usual manner of closing an oration. A few broken and indistinct phrases being only audible, such as—"Sarve you right"—"Fifty years in the family"—"Slaving like a negur"—"Oh, the Turks! the haythins!"

Having waited what I deemed a reasonable time for his honest indignation to evaporate, I made another effort to ascertain who my host might be.

"Would you favour me," said I, in a tone still more insinuating, "with the name of——"

"It's my name, ye want? Oh, sorrow bit I am ashamed of it! Little as you think of me, Cornelius Delany is as good a warrant for family as many a one of the dirty spalpeens about the Coort, that haven't a civiler word in their mouth than Cross Corny! Bad luck to them for that same."

This honest admission as to the world's opinion of Mister Delany's character was so far satisfactory as it enabled me to see with whom I had to deal; and, although for a moment or two it was a severe struggle to prevent myself bursting into laughter, I fortunately obtained the mastery, and once more returned to the charge.

"And now, Mister Delany, can you inform me how I came here? I remember something of an accident on my landing; but when, where, and how, I am totally ignorant."

"An accident!" said he, turning up his eyes; "an accident, indeed! that's what they always call it when they wring off the rappers, or bate the watch: ye came here in a hackney-coach, with the police, as many a one came before you."

"But where am I?" said I, impatiently.

"In Dublin Castle; bad luck to it for a riotous, disorderly place."

"Well, well," said I, half angrily, "I want to know whose room is this?"

"Captain O'Grady's. What have you to say agin the room? Maybe you're used to worse. There now, that's what you got for that. I'm laving the place next week, but that's no rayson——"

Here he went off, *diminuendo*, again, with a few flying imprecations upon several things and persons unknown.

Mr. Delany now dived for a few seconds into a small pantry at the end of the room, from which he emerged with a tray between his hands, and two decanters under his arms.

"Draw the little table this way," he cried, "more towards the fire, for, av coorse, you're fresh and fastin'; there now, take the sherry from under my arm—the other's port: that was a ham, till Captain Mills cut it away, as ye see—there's a veal pie, and here's a cold grouse—and, maybe, you've eat worse before now—and will again, plaze God."

I assured him of the truth of his observation in a most conciliating tone.

"Oh, the devil fear ye," was the reply, while he murmured somewhat lower, "the half of yees isn't used to meat twice in the week."

"Capital fare this, Mr. Delany," said I, as, half famished with long fasting, I helped myself a second time.

"You're eating as if you liked it," said he, with a shrug of his shoulders.

"Upon my word," said I, after throwing down a bumper of sherry, "that's a very pleasant glass of wine; and, on the whole, I should say, there are worse places than this in the world."

A look of unutterable contempt—whether at me for my discovery, or at the opinion itself, I can't say—was the sole reply of my friend; who, at the same moment, presuming I had sufficient opportunities for the judgment I pronounced, replaced the decanters upon the tray, and disappeared with the whole in the most grave and solemn manner.

Repressing a very great inclination to laughter, I sat still; and a silence of a few moments ensued, when Mr. Delany walked towards the window, and, drawing aside the curtains, looked out. All was in darkness save on the opposite side of the court-yard, where a blaze of light fell upon the pavement from over the half shutters of an apparently spacious apartment. "Ay, ay, there you go; hip, hip, hurrah! you waste more liquor every night than would float a lighter; that's all you're good for. Bad luck to your Grace—making fun of the people, laughing and singing as if the potatoes wasn't two shillings a stone."

"What's going on there?" said I.

"The ould work, nather more nor less. The Lord-Liftinnant, and the bishops, and the jidges, and all the privy councillors roaring drunk. Listen to them. May I never, if it isn't the Dean's voice I hear—the ould beast; he is singing 'The Night before Larry was stretched.'"

"That's a good fellow, Corny—Mr. Delany I mean—do open the window for a little, and let's hear them."

"It's a blessed night you'd have the window open to listen to a set of drunken devils: but here's Master Phil; I know his step well It's long before his father that's gone would come tearing up the stairs that way as if the bailiffs was after him; rack and ruin, sorrow else, av I never got a place—the haythins! the Turks!"

Mr. Delany, who, probably from motives of delicacy, wished to spare his master the pain of an interview, made his exit by one door as he came in at the other. I had barely time to see that the person before me was in every respect the very opposite of his follower, when he called out in a rich, mellow voice,

"All right again, I hope, Mr. Hinton; it's the first moment I could get away; we had a dinner of the Privy Council, and some of them are rather late sitters; you're not hurt, I trust?"

"A little bruised or so, nothing more; but pray, how did I fall into such kind hands?"

"Oh! the watchmen, it seems, could read, and, as your trunks were addressed to the Castle, they concluded you ought to go there also. You have despatches, haven't you?"

"Yes," said I, producing the packet; "when must they be delivered?"

"Oh, at once. Do you think you could make a little change in your dress, and manage to come over? his Grace always likes it better; there's no stiffness, no formality whatever; most of the dinner-party have gone home; there are only a few of the government people, the Duke's friends, remaining, and, besides, he's always kind and good-natured."

"I'll see what I can do," replied I, as I rose from the sofa; "I put myself into your hands altogether."

"Well, come along," said he; "you'll find everything ready in this room. I hope that old villain has left hot water. Corny! Corny, I say! Confound him, he's gone to bed, I suppose."

Having no particular desire for Mr. Delany's attentions, I prevailed on his master not to disturb him, and proceeded to make my toilette as well as I was able.

"Didn't that stupid scoundrel come near you at all?" cried O'Grady.

"Oh yes, we have had a long interview; but, somehow, I fear I did not succeed in gaining his good graces."

"The worst-tempered old villain in Europe."

"Somewhat of a character, I take it."

"A crab-tree planted in a lime-kiln, cranky and cross-grained; but he is a legacy, almost the only one my father left me. I've done my best to part with him every day for the last twelve years, but he sticks to me like a poor relation, giving me warning every night of his life, and every morning kicking up such a row in the house that every one is persuaded I am beating him to a jelly before turning him out to starve in the streets."

"Oh, the haythins! the Turks!" said I, slyly.

"Confound it!" cried he, "the old devil has been opening upon you already; and Jet, with all that, I don't know how I should get on without Corny; his gibes, his jeers, his everlasting ill-temper, his crankiness that never sleeps, seem to agree with me: the fact is, one enjoys the world from all its contrasts. The olive is a poor thing in itself, but it certainly improves the smack of your Burgundy. In this way Corny Delany does me good service. Come, by Jove, you have not been long dressing. This way: now follow' me." So saying, Captain O'Grady led the way down the stairs to the colonnade, following which to the opposite side of the quadrangle we arrived at a brilliantly lighted hall, where several servants in full-dress liveries were in waiting. Passing hastily through this, we mounted a handsome staircase, and, traversing several ante-chambers, at length arrived at one whose contiguity to the dinner-room I could guess at from the loud sound of many voices. "Wait one moment here," said my companion, "until I speak to his Grace." He disappeared as he spoke, but before a minute had elapsed he was again beside me. "Come this way; it's all right," said he. The next moment I found myself in the dinner-room.

The scene before me was altogether so different from what I had expected, that for a moment or two I could scarce do aught else than stand still to survey it. At a table which had been laid for about forty persons, scarcely more than a dozen were now present. Collected together at one end of the board, the whole party were roaring with laughter at some story of a strange, melancholy-looking man, whose whining voice added indescribable ridicule to the drollery of his narrative. Grey-headed general officers, grave-looking divines, lynx-eyed lawyers, had all given way under the irresistible impulse, and the very table shook with laughter.

"Mr. Hinton, your Excellency," said O'Grady for the third time, while the Duke wiped his eye with his napkin, and, pushing his chair a little back from the table, motioned me to approach.

"Ah, Hinton, glad to see you; how is your father?—a very old friend of mine, indeed; and Lady Charlotte—well, I hope? O'Grady tells me you've had an accident—something slight, I trust. So these are the despatches." Here he broke the seal of the envelope, and ran his eye over the contents. "There, that's your concern." So saying, he pitched a letter across the table to a shrewd-looking personage in a horse-shoe wig. "They won't do it, Dean, and we must wait. Ah!—so they don't like my new commissioners; but, Hinton, my boy, sit down. O'Grady, have you room there? A glass of wine with you."

"Nothing the worse of your mishap, sir?" said the melancholy-looking man who sat opposite to me.

I replied by briefly relating my accident.

"Strange enough," said he, in a compassionate tone, "your head should have suffered; your countrymen generally fall upon their legs in Ireland." This was said with a sly look at the Viceroy, who, deep in his despatches, paid no attention to the allusion.

"A very singular thing, I must confess," said the Duke, laying down the paper. "This is the fourth time the bearer of despatches has met with an accident. If they don't run foul of a rock in the Channel, they are sure to have a delay on the pier."

"It is so natural, my Lord," said the gloomy man, "that the carriers should stop at the Pigeon-house."

"Do be quiet, Curran," cried the Duke, "and pass round the decanter. They'll not take the duty off claret, it seems."

"And Day, my Lord, won't put the claret on duty; he has kept the wine at his elbow for the last half-hour. Upon my soul, your Grace ought to knight him."

"Not even his Excellency's habits," said a sharp, clever-looking man, "would excuse his converting Day into Knight."

Amid a shower of smart, caustic, and witty sayings, droll stories, retort and repartee, the wine circulated freely from hand to hand; the presence of the Duke adding fresh impulse to the sallies of fun and merriment around him. Anecdotes of the army, the bench, and the bar, poured in unceasingly, accompanied by running commentaries of the hearers, who never let slip an opportunity for a jest or a rejoinder. To me, the most singular feature of all this was, that no one seemed too old or too dignified, too high in station, or too venerable from office, to join in this headlong current of conviviality. Austere churchmen, erudite chief-justices, profound politicians, privy councillors, military officers of high rank and standing, were here all mixed up together into one strange medley, apparently bent on throwing an air of ridicule over the graver business of life, and laughing alike at themselves and the world. Nothing was too grave for a jest, nothing too solemn for a sarcasm. All the soldier's experience of men and manners, all the lawyer's acuteness of perception and readiness of wit, all the politician's practised tact and habitual subtlety, were brought to bear upon the common topics of the day with such promptitude, and such power, that one knew not whether to be more struck by the mass of information they possessed, or by that strange fatality which could make men, so great and so gifted, satisfied to jest where they might be called on to judge.

Play and politics, wine and women, debts and duels, were discussed, not only with an absence of all restraint, but with a deep knowledge of the world and a profound insight into the heart, which often imparted to the careless and random speech the sharpness of the most cutting sarcasm. Personalities, too, were rife; no one spared his neighbour, for he did not expect mercy for himself; and the luckless wight who tripped in his narrative, or stumbled in his story, was assailed on every side, until some happy expedient of his own, or some new victim being discovered, the attack would take another direction, and leave him once more at liberty. I feel how sadly inadequate I am to render even the faintest testimony to the talents of those, any one of whom, in after life, would have been considered to have made the fortune of a dinner-party, and who now were met together, not in the careless ease and lounging indifference of relaxation, but in the open arena where wit met wit, and where even the most brilliant talker, the happiest relater, the quickest in sarcasm, and the readiest in reply, felt he had need of all his weapons to defend and protect him. This was a *mêlée* tournament, where each man rode down his neighbour, with no other reason for attack than detecting a rent in his armour. Even the Viceroy himself, who, as judge of the lists, might be supposed to enjoy an immunity, was not safe here, and many an arrow, apparently shot at an adversary, was sent quivering into his corslet.

As I watched, with all the intense excitement of one to whom such a display was perfectly new, I could not help feeling how fortunate it was that the grave avocations and the venerable pursuits of the greater number of the party should prevent this firework of wit from bursting into the blaze of open animosity. I hinted as much to my neighbour, O'Grady, who at once broke into a fit of laughter at my ignorance; and I now learnt to my amazement that the Common Pleas had winged the Exchequer, that the Attorney-General had pinked the Bolls, and, stranger than all, that the Provost of the University himself had planted his man in the Phoenix.

"It is just as well for us," continued he, in a whisper, "that the churchmen can't go out; for the Dean, yonder, can snuff a candle at twenty paces, and is rather a hot-tempered fellow to boot. But come, now, his Grace is about to rise. We have a field-day to-morrow in the Park, and break up somewhat earlier in consequence."

As it was now near two o'clock, I could see nothing to cavil at as to the earliness of the hour, although, I freely confess, tired and exhausted as I felt, I could not contemplate the moment of separation without a sad foreboding that I ne'er should look upon the like again. The party rose at this moment, and the Duke, shaking hands cordially with each person as he passed down, wished us all a good night. I followed with O'Grady and some others of the household, but when I reached the ante-chamber, my new friend volunteered his services to see me to my quarters.

On traversing the lower castle-yard, we mounted an old-fashioned and rickety stair, which conducted to a gloomy, ill-lighted corridor. I was too much fatigued, however, to be critical at the moment, and so, having thanked O'Grady for all his kindness, I threw off my clothes hastily, and, before my head was well upon the pillow, was sound asleep.

CHAPTER IV
THE BREAKFAST

There are few persons so unreflective as not to give way to a little self-examination on waking for the first time in a strange place. The very objects about are so many appeals to your ingenuity or to your memory, that you cannot fail asking yourself how you became acquainted with them: the present is thus made the herald of the past, and it is difficult, when unravelling the tangled web of doubt that assails you, not to think over the path by which you have been travelling.

As for me, scarcely were my eyes opened to the light, I had barely thrown one glance around my cold and comfortless chamber, when thoughts of home came rushing to my mind. The warm earnestness of my father, the timid dreads of my poor mother, rose up before me, as I felt myself, for the first time, alone in the world. The elevating sense of heroism, that more or less blends with every young man's dreams of life, gilds our first journey from our father's roof. There is a feeling of freedom in being the arbiter of one's actions, to go where you will and when you will. Till that moment the world has been a comparative blank; the trammels of school or the ties of tutorship have bound and restrained you. You have been living, as it were, within the rules of court—certain petty privileges permitted, certain small liberties allowed; but now you come forth disenchanted, disenthralled, emancipated, free to come as to go—a man in all the plenitude of his volition; and, better still, a man without the heavy, depressing weight of responsibility that makes manhood less a blessing than a burden. The first burst of life is indeed a glorious thing; youth, health, hope, and confidence have each a force and vigour they lose in after years: life is then a splendid river, and we are swimming with the stream—no adverse waves to weary, no billows to buffet us, we hold on our course rejoicing.

The sun was peering between the curtains of my window, and playing in fitful flashes on the old oak floor, as I lay thus ruminating and dreaming over the future. How many a resolve did I then make for my guidance—how many an intention did I form—how many a groundwork of principle did I lay down, with all the confidence of youth! I fashioned to myself a world after my own notions; in which I conjured up certain imaginary difficulties, all of which were surmounted by my admirable tact and consummate cleverness. I remembered how, at both Eton and Sandhurst, the Irish boy was generally made the subject of some jest or quiz, at one time for his accent, at another for his blunders. As a Guardsman, short as had been my experience of the service, I could plainly see that a certain indefinable tone of superiority was ever asserted towards our friends across the sea. A wide-sweeping prejudice, whose limits were neither founded in reason, justice, or common sense, had thrown a certain air of undervaluing import over every one and every thing from that country. Not only were its faults and its follies heavily visited, but those accidental and trifling blemishes—those slight and scarce perceptible deviations from the arbitrary standard of fashion—were deemed the strong characteristics of the nation, and condemned accordingly; while the slightest use of any exaggeration in speech—the commonest employment of a figure or a metaphor—the casual introduction of an anecdote or a repartee, were all heavily censured, and pronounced "so very Irish!" Let some fortune-hunter carry off an heiress— let a lady trip over her train at the drawing-room—let a minister blunder in his mission—let a powder-magazine explode and blow up one-half of the surrounding population, there was but one expression to qualify all—"How Irish! how very Irish!" The adjective had become one of depreciation; and an Irish lord, an Irish member, an Irish estate, and an Irish diamond, were held pretty much in the same estimation.

Reared in the very hot-bed, the forcing-house, of such exaggerated prejudice, while imbibing a very sufficient contempt for everything in that country, I obtained proportionably absurd notions of all that was Irish. Our principles may come from our fathers; our prejudices certainly descend from the female branch. Now, my mother, notwithstanding the example of the Prince Regent himself, whose chosen associates were Irish, was most thoroughly exclusive on this point. She would admit that a native of that country could be invited to an evening party under extreme and urgent circumstances—that some brilliant orator, whose eloquence was at once the dread and the delight of the House—that some gifted poet, whose verses came home to the heart alike of prince and peasant—that the painter, whose canvas might stand unblushingly amid the greatest triumphs of art—could be asked to lionise for those cold and callous votaries of fashion, across the lake of whose stagnant nature no breath of feeling stirred, esteeming it the while, that in her card of invitation he was reaping the proudest proof of his success; but that such could be made acquaintances or companions, could be regarded in the light of equals or intimates, the thing never entered into her imagination, and she would as soon have made a confidant of the King of Kongo as a gentleman from Connaught.

Less for the purposes of dwelling upon my lady-mother's "Hibernian horrors," than of showing the school in which I was trained, I have made this somewhat lengthened *exposé*. It may, however, convey to my reader some faint impression of the feelings which animated me at the outset of my career in Ireland.

I have already mentioned the delight I experienced with the society at the Viceroy's table. So much brilliancy, so much wit, so much of conversational power, until that moment I had no conception of. Now, however, while reflecting on it, I was actually astonished to find how far the whole scene contributed to the support of my ancient prejudices. I well knew that a party of the highest functionaries—bishops and law-officers of the crown—would not have conducted themselves in the same manner in England. I stopped not to inquire whether it was more the wit or the will that was wanting; I did not dwell upon the fact that the meeting was a purely convivial one, to which I was admitted by the kindness and condescension of the Duke; but, so easily will a warped and bigoted impression find food for its indulgence, I only saw in the meeting an additional evidence of my early convictions. How far my theorising on this point might have led me—whether eventually I should have come to the conclusion that the Irish nation were lying in the darkest blindness of barbarism, while, by a special intervention of Providence, I, was about to be erected into a species of double revolving light—it is difficult to say, when a tap at the door suddenly aroused me from my musings.

"Are ye awake, yet?" said a harsh, husky voice, like a bear in bronchitis, which I had no difficulty in pronouncing to be Corny's.

"Yes, come in," cried I; "what hour is it?"

"Somewhere after ten," replied he, sulkily; "you're the first I ever heerd ask the clock, in the eight years I have lived here. Are ye ready for your morning?"

"My what?" said I, with some surprise.

"Didn't I say it, plain enough? Is it the brogue that bothers you?"

As he said this with a most sarcastic grin he poured, from a large jug he held in one hand, a brimming goblet full of some white compound, and handed it over to me. Preferring at once to explore, rather than to question the intractable Corny, I put it to my lips, and found it to be capital milk punch, concocted with great skill, and seasoned with what O'Grady afterwards called "a notion of nutmeg."

"Oh! devil fear you, that he'll like it. Sorrow one of you ever left as much in the jug as 'ud make a foot-bath for a flea."

"They don't treat you over well, then, Corny," said I, purposely opening the sorest wound of his nature.

"Trate me well! faix, them that 'ud come here for good tratement, would go to the devil for divarsion. There's Master Phil himself, that I used to bate, when he was a child, many's the time, when his father, rest his sowl, was up at the coorts—ay, strapped him, till he hadn't a spot that wasn't sore an him—and look at him now; oh, wirra! you'd think I never took a ha'porth of pains with him. Ugh!—the haythins!—the Turks!"

"This is all very bad, Corny; hand me those boots."

"And thim's boots!" said he, with a contemptuous expression on his face that would have struck horror to the heart of Hoby. "Well, well." Here he looked up as though the profligacy and degeneracy of the age were transgressing all bounds. "When you're ready, come over to the master's, for he's waiting breakfast for you. A beautiful hour for breakfast, it is! Many's the day his father sintenced a whole dockful before the same time!"

With the comforting reflection that the world went better in his youth, Corny drained the few remaining drops of the jug, and, muttering the while something that did not sound exactly like a blessing, waddled out of the room with a gait of the most imposing gravity.

I had very little difficulty in finding my friend's quarters; for, as his door lay open, and as he himself was carolling away, at the very top of his lungs, some popular melody of the day, I speedily found myself beyond the threshold.

"Ah! Hinton, my hearty, how goes it? your headpiece nothing the worse, I hope, for either the car or the claret? By-the-by, capital claret that is! you've nothing like it in England."

I could scarce help a smile at the remark, as he proceeded,

"But come, my boy, sit down; help yourself to a cutlet, and make yourself quite at home in Mount O'Grady."

"Mount O'Grady!" repeated I. "Ha! in allusion, I suppose, to these confounded two flights one has to climb up to you."

"Nothing of the kind; the name has a very different origin. Tea or coffee? there's the tap! Now, my boy, the fact is, we O'Gradys were once upon a time very great folk in our way; lived in an uncouth old barrack, with battlements and a keep, upon the Shannon, where we ravaged the country for miles round, and did as much mischief, and committed as much pillage upon the peaceable inhabitants, as any respectable old family in the province. Time, however, wagged on; luck changed; your countrymen came pouring in upon us with new-fangled notions of reading, writing, and road-making; police and petty sessions, and a thousand other vexatious contrivances followed, to worry and puzzle the heads of simple country gentlemen; so that, at last, instead of taking to the hill-side for our mutton, we were reduced to keep a market-cart, and employ a thieving rogue in Dublin to supply us with poor claret, instead of making a trip over to Galway, where a smuggling craft brought us our liquor, with a bouquet fresh from Bordeaux. But the worst wasn't come; for you see, a litigious spirit grew up in the country, and a kind of vindictive habit of pursuing you for your debts. Now, we always contrived, somehow or other, to have rather a confused way of managing our exchequer. No tenant on the property ever precisely knew what he owed; and, as we possessed no record of what he paid, our income was rather obtained after the maimer of levying a tribute, than receiving a legal debt. Meanwhile, we pushed our credit like a new colony: whenever a loan was to be, obtained, it was little we cared for ten, twelve, or even fifteen per cent.; and as we kept a jolly house, a good cook, good claret, and had the best pack of beagles in the country, he'd have been a hardy creditor who'd have ventured to push us to extremities. Even sheep, however, they say, get courage when they flock together, and so this contemptible herd of tailors, tithe-proctors, butchers, barristers, and bootmakers, took heart of grace, and laid siege to us in all form. My grandfather, Phil,—for I was called after him,—who always spent his money like a gentleman, had no notion of figuring in the Four Courts; but he sent Tom Darcy, his cousin, up to town, to call out as many of the plaintiffs as would fight, and to threaten the remainder that, if they did not withdraw their suits, they'd have more need of the surgeon than the attorney-general; for they shouldn't have a whole bone in their body by Michaelmas-day. Another cutlet, Hinton? But I am tiring you with all these family matters."

"Not at all; go on, I beg of you. I want to hear how your grandfather got out of his difficulties."

"Faith, I wish you could! it would be equally pleasant news to myself; but, unfortunately, his beautiful plan only made bad worse, for they began fresh actions. Some, for provocation to fight a duel; others, for threats of assault and battery; and the short of it was, as my grandfather wouldn't enter a defence, they obtained their verdicts, and got judgment, with all the costs."

"The devil they did! That must have pushed him hard."

"So it did; indeed it got the better of his temper, and he that was one of the heartiest, pleasantest fellows in the province, became, in a manner, morose and silent; and, instead of surrendering possession, peaceably and quietly, he went down to the gate, and took a sitting shot at the sub-sheriff, who was there in a tax-cart."

"Bless my soul! Did he kill him?"

"No; he only ruffled his feathers, and broke his thigh; but it was bad enough, for he had to go over to France till it blew over. Well, it was either vexation or the climate, or, maybe, the weak wines, or, perhaps, all three, undermined his constitution, but he died at eighty-four—the only one of the family ever cut off early, except such as were shot, or the like."

"Well, but your father—"

"I am coming to him. My grandfather sent for him from school when he was dying, and he made him swear he would be a lawyer. 'Morris will be a thorn in their flesh, yet,' said he; 'and look to it, my boy,' he cried, 'I leave you a Chancery suit that has nearly broke eight families and the hearts of two chancellors;—see that you keep it goings—sell every stick on the estate—put all the beggars in the barony on the property—beg, borrow, and steal them—plough up all the grazing-land; and I'll tell you a better trick than all——' Here a fit of coughing interrupted the pious old gentleman, and, when it was over, so was he!"

"Dead!" said I.

"As a door-nail! Well, my father was dutiful; he kept the suit moving till he got called to the Bar! Once there, he gave it all his spare moments; and when there was nothing doing in the Common Pleas or King's Bench, he was sure to come down with a new bill, or a declaration, before the Master, or a writ of error, or a point of law for a jury, till at last, when no case was ready to come on, the sitting judge would call out, 'Let us hear O'Grady/ in appeal, or in error, or whatever it was. But, to make my story short, my father became a first-rate lawyer, by the practice of his own suit—rose to a silk-gown—was made solicitor and attorney-general—afterwards, chief-justice——"

"And the suit?"

"Oh! the suit survived him, and became my property; but, somehow, I didn't succeed in the management quite as well as my father; and I found that my estate cost me somewhere about fifteen hundred a year—not to mention more oaths than fifty years of purgatory could pay off. This was a high premium to pay for figuring every term on the list of trials, so I raised a thousand pounds on my commission, gave it to Nick M'Namara, to take the property off my hands, and as my father's last injunction was, 'Never rest till you sleep in Mount O'Grady,'—why, I just baptised my present abode by that name, and here I live with the easy conscience of a dutiful and affectionate child that took the shortest and speediest way of fulfilling his father's testament."

"By Jove! a most singular narrative. I shouldn't like to have parted with the old place, however."

"Faith, I don't know! I never was much there. It was a rackety, tumble-down old concern, with rattling windows, rooks, and rats, pretty much like this; and, what between my duns and Corny Delany, I very often think I am back there again. There wasn't as good a room as this in the whole house, not to speak of the pictures. Isn't that likeness of Darcy capital? You saw him last night. He sat next Curran. Come, I've no curaçoa to offer you, but try this usquebaugh."

"By-the-by, that Corny is a strange character. I rather think, if I were you, I should have let him go with the property."

"Let him go! Egad, that's not so easy as you think. Nothing but death will ever part us."

"I really cannot comprehend how you endure him; he'd drive me mad."

"Well, he very often pushes me a little hard or so; and, if it wasn't that, by deep study and minute attention, I have at length got some insight into the weak parts of his nature, I frankly confess I couldn't endure it much longer."

"And, pray, what may these amiable traits be?"

"You will scarcely guess"

"Love of money, perhaps?"

"No."

"Attachment to your family, then?"

"Not that either."

"I give it up."

"Well, the truth is, Corny is a most pious Catholic. The Church has unbounded influence and control over all his actions. Secondly, he is a devout believer in ghosts, particularly my grandfather's, which, I must confess, I have personated two or three times myself, when his temper had nearly tortured me into a brain fever; so that between purgatory and apparitions, fears here and hereafter, I keep him pretty busy. There's a friend of mine, a priest, one Father Tom Loftus——"

"I've heard that name before, somewhere."

"Scarcely, I think; I'm not aware that he was ever in England; but he's a glorious fellow; I'll make you known to him, one of these days; and when you have seen a little more of Ireland, I am certain you'll like him. But I'm forgetting; it must be late; we have a field-day, you know, in the Park."

"What am I to do for a mount? I've brought no horses with me."

"Oh, I've arranged all that. See, there are the nags already. That dark chesnut I destine for you; and, come along, we have no time to lose; there go the carriages, and here comes our worthy colleague and fellow aide-de-camp. Do you know him?"

"Who is it, pray?"

"Lord Dudley de Vere, the most confounded puppy, and the emptiest ass— But here he is."

"De Vere, my friend Mr. Hinton—one of ours."

His Lordship raised his delicate-looking eyebrows as high as he was able, letting fall his glass at the same moment from the corner of his eye; and while he adjusted his stock at the glass, lisped out,

"Ah—yes—very happy. In the Guards, I think. Know Douglas, don't you?"

"Yes, very slightly."

"When did you come—to-day?"

"No; last night."

"Must have got a buffeting; blew very fresh. You don't happen to know the odds on the Oaks?"

"Hecate, they say, is falling. I rather heard a good account of the mare."

"Indeed," said he, while his cold, inanimate features brightened up with a momentary flush of excitement. "Take you five to two, or give you the odds, you don't name the winner on the double event."

A look from O'Grady decided me at once on declining the proffered wager; and his Lordship once more returned to the mirror and his self-admiration.

"I say, O'Grady, do come here for a minute. What the deuce can that be?"

Here an immoderate fit of laughter from his Lordship brought us both to the window. The figure to which his attention was directed was certainly not a little remarkable. Mounted upon an animal of the smallest possible dimensions, sat, or rather stood, the figure of a tall, gaunt, raw-boned looking man, in a livery of the gaudiest blue and yellow, his hat garnished with silver lace, while long tags of the same material were festooned gracefully from his shoulder to his breast; his feet nearly touched the ground, and gave him rather the appearance of one progressing with a pony between his legs, than of a figure on horseback; he carried under one arm a leather pocket, like a despatch bag; and, as he sauntered slowly about, with his eyes directed hither and thither, seemed like some one in search of an unknown locality.

The roar of laughter which issued from our window drew his attention to that quarter, and he immediately touched his hat, while a look of pleased recognition played across his countenance. "Holloa, Tim!" cried O'Grady, "what's in the wind now?"

Tim's answer was inaudible, but inserting his hand into the leathern con-veniency already mentioned, he drew forth a card of most portentous dimensions. By this time Corny's voice could be heard joining the conversation.

"Arrah, give it here, and don't be making a baste of yourself. Isn't the very battle-axe Guards laughing at you? I'm sure I wonder how a Christian would make a merry-andrew of himself by wearing such clothes; you're more like a play-actor nor a respectable servant."

With these words he snatched rather than accepted the proffered card; and Tim, with another flourish of his hat, and a singularly droll grin, meant to convey his appreciation of Cross Corny, plunged the spurs till his legs met under the belly of the little animal, and cantered out of the court-yard amid the laughter of the bystanders, in which even the sentinels on duty could not refrain from participating.

"What the devil can it be?" cried Lord Dudley; "he evidently knows you, O'Grady."

"And you, too, my Lord; his master has helped you to a cool hundred or two more than once before now."

"Eh—what—you don't say so! Not our worthy friend Paul—eh? Why, confound it, I never should have known Timothy in that dress."

"No," said O'Grady, slyly; "I acknowledge it is not exactly his costume when he serves a latitat."

"Ha, ha!" cried the other, trying to laugh at the joke, which he felt too deeply; "I thought I knew the pony, though. Old three-and-fourpence; his infernal canter always sounds in my ears like the jargon of a bill of costs."

"Here comes Corny," said O'Grady. "What have you got there?"

"There, 'tis for you," replied he, throwing, with an air of the most profound disdain, a large card upon the table; while, as he left the room, he muttered some very sagacious reflections about the horrors of low company—his father the Jidge—the best in the land—riotous, disorderly life; the whole concluding with an imprecation upon heathens and Turks, with which he managed to accomplish his exit.

"Capital, by Jove!" said Lord Dudley, as he surveyed the card with his glass.

"'Mr. and Mrs. Paul Rooney presents'—the devil they does—'presents their compliments, and requests the honour of Captain O'Grady's company at dinner on Friday, the 8th, at half-past seven o'clock.'"

"How good! glorious, by Jove! eh, O'Grady? You are a sure ticket there—*l'ami de la maison!*"

O'Grady's cheek became red at these words; and a flashing expression in his eyes told how deeply he felt them. He turned sharply round, his lip quivering with passion; then, checking himself suddenly, he burst into an affected laugh,

"You'll go too, wont you?"

"I? No, faith, they caught me once; but then the fact was, a protest and an invitation were both served on me together. I couldn't accept one, so I did the other."

"Well, I must confess," said O'Grady, in a firm, resolute tone, "there may be many more fashionable people than our friends; but I, for one, scruple not to say I have received many kindnesses from them, and am deeply, sincerely grateful."

"As far as doing a bit of paper now and then, when one is hard up," said Lord Dudley, "why, perhaps, I'm somewhat of your mind; but if one must take the discount out in dinners, it's an infernal bore."

"And yet," said O'Grady, maliciously, "I've seen your Lordship tax your powers to play the agreeable at these same dinners; and I think your memory betrays you in supposing you have only been there once. I myself have met you at least four times."

"Only shows how devilish hard up I must have been," was the cool reply; "but now, as the governor begins to behave better, I think I'll cut Paul."

"I'm certain you will," said O'Grady, with an emphasis that could not be mistaken. "But come, Hinton, we had better be moving; there's some stir at the portico yonder, I suppose they're coming."

At this moment the tramp of cavalry announced the arrival of the guard of honour; the drums beat, the troops stood to arms, and we had barely time to mount our horses, when the viceregal party took their places in the carriages, and we all set out for the Phoenix.

"Confess, Hinton, it is worth while being a soldier to be in Ireland." This was O'Grady's observation as we rode down Parliament-street, beside the carriage of the Viceroy. It was the first occasion of a field-day since the arrival of his Excellency, and all Dublin was on the tiptoe of expectation at the prospect. Handkerchiefs were waved from the windows; streamers and banners floated from the house-tops; patriotic devices and allegoric representations of Erin sitting at a plentiful board, opposite an elderly gentleman with a ducal coronet, met us at every turn of the way. The streets were literally crammed with people. The band played Patrick's-day; the mob shouted, his Grace bowed; and down to Phil O'Grady himself, who winked at the pretty girls as he passed, there did not seem an unoccupied man in the whole procession. On we went, following the line of the quays, threading our way through a bare-legged, ragged population, bawling themselves hoarse with energetic desires for prosperity to Ireland. "Yes," thought I, as I looked upon the worn, dilapidated houses, the faded and bygone equipages, the tarnished finery of better days—"yes, my father was right, these people are very different from their neighbours; their very prosperity has an air quite peculiar to itself." Everything attested a state of poverty, a lack of trade, a want of comfort and of cleanliness; but still there was but one expression prevalent in the mass—that of unbounded good humour and gaiety. With a philosophy quite his own, poor Paddy seemed to feel a reflected pleasure from the supposed happiness of those around him, the fine clothes, the gorgeous equipages, the prancing chargers, the flowing plumes—all, in fact, that forms the appliances of wealth—constituting in his mind a kind of paradise on earth. He thought their possessors at least ought to be happy, and, like a good-hearted fellow, he was glad of it for their sakes.

There had been in the early part of the day an abortive effort at a procession. The Lord Mayor and the Sheriffs, in their state liveries, had gone forth with a proud following of their fellow-citizens; but a manouvre, which hitherto has been supposed exclusively the province of the navy, was here employed with unbounded success; and the hackney coachmen, by "cutting the line" in several places, had completely disorganised the procession, which now presented the singular spectacle of an aldermanic functionary with emblazoned panels and bedizened horses, followed by a string of rackety jaunting-cars, or a noddy with its fourteen insides. Horsemen there were, too, in abundance. Were I to judge from the spectacle before me, I should say that the Irish were the most equestrian people of the globe; and at what a pace they went! Caring little or nothing for the foot-passengers, they only drew rein when their blown steeds were unable to go further, and then dashed onwards like a charge, amid a shower of oaths, curses, and imprecations, half drowned in the laughter that burst on every side. Deputations there were also from various branches of trade, entreating their Graces to wear and to patronise the manufacture of the country, and to conform in many respects to its habits and customs: by all of which, in my then ignorance, I could only understand the vehement desire of the population that the viceregal court should go about in a state of nature, and limit their diet to poteen and potatoes.

"Fine sight this, Hinton! Isn't it cheering?" said O'Grady, as his eye beamed with pleasure and delight.

"Why, yes," said I, hesitatingly; "but don't you think if they wore shoes——"

"Shoes!" repeated he, contemptuously, "they'd never suffer such restrictions on their liberties. Look at them! they are the fellows to make soldiers of! The only fear of half-rations with them would be the risk of indigestion."

On we went, a strange and motley mass, the only grave faces being a few of those who sat in gilded coaches, with embroidered hammercloths, while every half-naked figure that flitted past had a countenance of reckless jollity and fun. But the same discrepancy that pervaded the people and the procession was visible even in their dwellings, and the meanest hovels stood side by side with the public and private edifices of elegance and beauty.

"This, certainly," thought I, "is a strange land." A reflection I had reason to recur to more than once in my after experience of Ireland.

CHAPTER V
THE REVIEW IN THE PHOENIX

Winding along the quays, we crossed an old and dilapidated bridge; and after traversing some narrow and ruinous-looking streets, we entered the Park, and at length reached the Fifteen Acres.

The carriages were drawn up in a line; his Grace's led horses were ordered up, and staff-officers galloped right and left to announce the orders for the troops to stand to arms.

As the Duke descended from his carriage he caught my eye, and turning suddenly towards the Duchess, said, "Let me present Mr. Hinton to your Grace."

While I was making my bows and acknowledgments, his Grace put his hand upon my arm.

"You know Lady Killimore, Hinton? Never mind, it's of no consequence. You see her carriage yonder—they have made some blunder in the road, and the dragoons, it seems, wont let them pass. Just canter down and rescue them."

"Do, pray, Mr. Hinton," added the Duchess. "Poor Lady Killimore is so very nervous she'll be terrified to death if they make any fuss. Her carriage can come up quite close; there is plenty of room."

"Now, do it well," whispered O'Grady: "there is a pretty girl in the case; it's your first mission; acquit yourself with credit."

An infernal brass band playing "Rule Britannia" within ten paces of me, the buzz of voices, the crowd, the novelty of the situation, the excitement of the moment, all conspired to addle and confuse me; so that when I put spurs to my horse and struck out into a gallop, I had no very precise idea of what I was to do, and not the slightest upon earth of where I was to do it.

A pretty girl in a carriage beset by dragoons was to be looked for—Lady Kil—somebody's equipage—— "Oh! I have it; there they are," said I, as a yellow barouche, with four steaming posters, caught my eye in a far part of the field. From the number of dragoons that surrounded the carriage, no less than their violent gestures, I could perceive that an altercation had taken place; pressing my horse to the top of his speed, I flew across the plain, and arrived flushed, heated, and breathless beside the carriage.

A large and strikingly handsome woman in a bonnet and plumes of the most gaudy and showy character, was standing upon the front seat, and carrying on an active, and, as it seemed, acrimonious controversy with the sergeant of the horse police.

"You must go back—can't help it, ma'am—nothing but the members of the household can pass this way."

"Oh dear! where's Captain O'Grady?—sure it's not possible I could be treated this way. Paul, take that man's name, and mind you have him dismissed in the morning. Where are you, Paul? Ah! he's gone. It is the way with him always; and there you sit, Bob Dwyer, and you are no more good than a stick of sealing-wax!" Here a suppressed titter of laughter from the back of the carriage induced me to turn my eyes in that direction, and I beheld one of the most beautiful girls I ever looked at, holding her handkerchief to her month to conceal her laughter. Her dark eyes flashed, and her features sparkled, while a blush, at being so discovered, if possible, added to her beauty.

"All right," said I to myself, as taking off my hat I bowed to the very mane of my horse.

"If your Ladyship will kindly permit me," said I, "his Grace has sent me to show you the way."

The dragoons fell back as I spoke; the horse police looked awfully frightened; while the lady whose late eloquence manifested little of fear or trepidation, threw herself back in the carriage, and, covering her face with a handkerchief, sobbed violently.

"Ah, the Duchess said she was nervous. Poor Lady Kil——"

"Speak to me, Louisa dear. Who is it? Is it Mr. Wellesley Pole? Is it——"

I did not wait for a further supposition, but in a most insinuating voice, added,

"Mr. Hinton, my lady, extra aide-de-camp on his Excellency's staff. The Duchess feared you would be nervous, and hopes you'll get as close to her as possible."

"Where's Paul?" said the lady, once more recovering her animation. "If this is a hoax, young gentleman——"

"Madam," said I, bowing stiffly, "I am really at a loss to understand your meaning."

"Oh, forgive me, Mr. Hilton."

"Hinton, my Lady."

"Yes, Hinton," said she. "I am a beast to mistrust you, and you so young and so artless; the sweetest blue eyes I ever looked at."

This was said in a whisper to her young friend, whose mirth now threatened to burst forth.

"And was it really his Royal Highness that sent you?"

"His Grace, my lady, I assure you, despatched me to your aid. He saw your carriage through his glass, and, guessing what had occurred, directed me to ride over and accompany your Ladyship to the viceregal stand."

Poor Lady Kil——'s nervousness again seized her, and, with a faint cry for the ever-absent Paul, she went off into rather smart hysterics. During this paroxysm I could not help feeling somewhat annoyed at the young lady's conduct, who, instead of evincing the slightest sympathy for her mother, held her head down, and seemed to shake with laughter. By this time, however, the postilions were again under way, and, after ten minutes' sharp trotting, we entered the grand stand, with whips cracking, ribbons fluttering, and I myself caracoling beside the carriage with an air of triumphant success.

A large dusky travelling carriage had meanwhile occupied the place the Duchess designed for her friend. The only thing to do, therefore, was, to place them as conveniently as I could, and hasten back to inform her Grace of the success of my mission. As I approached her carriage I was saluted by a burst of laughter from the staff, in which the Duke himself joined most extravagantly; while O'Grady, with his hands on his sides, threatened to fall from the saddle.

"What the deuce is the matter?" thought I; "I didn't bungle it?"

"Tell her Grace," said the Duke, with his hand upon his mouth, unable to finish the sentence with laughter.

I saw something was wrong, and that I was in some infernal scrape, still, resolved to go through with it, I drew near, and said,

"I am happy to inform your Grace that Lady Kil——"

"Is here," said the Duchess, bowing haughtily, as she turned towards a spiteful-looking dowager beside her.

Here was a mess! So, bowing and backing, I dropped through the crowd to where my companions still stood convulsed with merriment.

"What, in the devil's name, is it?" said I to O'Grady "Whom have I been escorting this half-hour?"

"You've immortalised yourself," said O'Grady, with a roar of laughter. "Your bill at twelve months for five hundred pounds is as good this moment as bank paper."

"What is it?" said I, losing all patience. "Who is she?"

"Mrs. Paul Rooney, my boy, the gem of attorneys' wives, the glory of Stephen's-green, with a villa at Bray, a box at the theatre, champagne suppers every night in the week, dinners promiscuously, and lunch *à discrétion*: there's glory for you. You may laugh at a latitat, sneer at the King's Bench, and snap your fingers at any process-server from here to Kilmainham!"

"May the devil fly away with her!" said I, wiping my forehead with passion and excitement.

"The Heavens forbid!" said O'Grady, piously. "Our exchequer may be guilty of many an extravagance, but it could not permit such a flight as that. It is evident, Hinton, that you did not see the pretty girl beside her in the carriage."

"Yes, yes, I saw her," said I, biting my lip with impatience, "and she seemed evidently enjoying the infernal blunder I was committing. And Mrs. Paul—oh, confound her! I can never endure the sight of her again!"

"My dear young friend," replied O'Grady, with an affected seriousness, "I see that already the prejudices of your very silly countrymen have worked their effect upon you. Had not Lord Dudley de Vere given you such a picture of the Rooney family, you would probably be much more lenient in your judgment: besides, after all, the error was yours, not hers. You told her that the Duke had sent you; you told her the Duchess wished her carriage beside her own."

"You take a singular mode," said I, pettishly, "to bring a man back to a good temper, by showing him that he has no one to blame for his misfortunes but himself. Confound them! look how they are all laughing about us. Indeed, from the little I've seen, it is the only thing they appear to do in this country."

At a signal from the Duke, O'Grady put spurs to his horse and cantered down the line, leaving me to such reflections as I could form, beneath the gaze of some forty persons, who could not turn to look without laughing at me.

"This is pleasant," thought I; "this is really a happy *début*: that I, whose unimpeachable accuracy of manner and address should have won for me, at the Prince's levee, the approbation of the first gentleman of Europe, should here, among these semi-civilised savages, become an object of ridicule and laughter. My father told me they were very different; and my mother— — —" I had not patience to think of the frightful effects my absurd situation might produce upon her nerves. "Lady Julia, too—ah! there's the rub—my beautiful cousin, who, in the slightest solecism of London manners, could find matter for sarcasm and raillery. What would she think of me now? And this it is they persuaded me to prefer to active service! What wound to a man's flesh could equal one to his feelings? I would rather be condoled with than scoffed at any day; and see! by Jove, they're laughing still. I would wager a fifty that I furnish the dinner conversation for every table in the capital this day."

The vine twig shows not more ingenuity, as it traverses some rocky crag in search of the cool stream, at once its luxury and its life, than does our injured self-love, in seeking for consolation from the inevitable casualties of fate, and the irresistible strokes of fortune! Thus I found comfort in the thought that the ridicule attached to me rather proceeded from the low standard of manners and habits about me than from anything positively absurd in my position; and, in my warped and biassed imagination, I actually preferred the insolent insipidity of Lord Dudley de Vere to the hearty raciness and laughter-loving spirit of Phil O'Grady.

My reflections were now cut short by the order for the staff to mount, and, following the current of my present feelings, I drew near to Lord Dudley, in whose emptiness and inanity I felt a degree of security from sarcasm, that I could by no means be so confident of in O'Grady's company.

Amid the thunder of cannon, the deafening roll of drums, the tramp of cavalry, and the measured footfall of the infantry columns, these thoughts rapidly gave way to others, and I soon forgot myself in the scene around me. The sight, indeed, was an inspiring one; for, although but the mockery of glorious war, to my unpractised eye the deception was delightful: the bracing air, the bright sky, the scenery itself, lent their aid, and, in the brilliant panorama before me, I soon regained my light-heartedness, and felt happy as before.

CHAPTER VI
THE SHAM BATTLE

I have mentioned in my last chapter how very rapidly I forgot my troubles in the excitement of the scene around me. Indeed, they must have been much more important, much deeper woes, to have occupied any place in a head so addled and confused as mine was. The manoeuvres of the day included a sham battle; and scarcely had his Excellency passed down the line, when preparations for the engagement began. The heavy artillery was seen to limber up, and move slowly across the field, accompanied by a strong detachment of cavalry; columns of infantry were marched hither and thither with the most pressing and eager haste; orderly dragoons and staff-officers galloped to and fro like madmen; red-faced plethoric little colonels bawled out the word of command till one feared they might burst a bloodvessel; and already two companies of light infantry might be seen stealing cautiously along the skirts of the wood, with the apparently insidious design of attacking a brigade of guns. As for me, I was at one moment employed carrying despatches to Sir Charles Asgill, at another conveying intelligence to Lord Harrington; these, be it known, being the rival commanders, whose powers of strategy were now to be tested before the assembled and discriminating citizens of Dublin. Not to speak of the eminent personal hazard of a service which required me constantly to ride between the lines of contending armies, the fatigue alone had nigh killed me. Scarcely did I appear, breathless, at head-quarters on my return from one mission, when I was despatched on another. Tired and panting, I more than once bungled my directions, and communicated to Sir Charles the secret intentions of his Lordship, while with a laudable impartiality I disarranged the former's plans by a total misconception of the orders. Fatigue, noise, chagrin, and incessant worry had so completely turned my head, that I became perfectly incapable of the commonest exercises of reason. Some of the artillery I ordered into a hollow, where I was told to station a party of riflemen. Three squadrons of cavalry I desired to charge up a hill, which the 71st Highlanders were to have scrambled up if they were able. Light dragoons I posted in situations so beset with brushwood and firs, that all movement became impossible; and, in a word, when the signal-gun announced the commencement of the action, my mistakes had introduced such a new feature into tactics, that neither party knew what his adversary was at, nor, indeed, had any accurate notion of which were his own troops. The Duke, who had watched with the most eager satisfaction the whole of my proceedings, sat laughing upon his horse till the very tears coursed down his cheeks; and, as all the staff were more or less participators in the secret, I found myself once more the centre of a grinning audience, perfectly convulsed at my exploits. Meanwhile, the guns thundered, the cavalry charged, the infantry poured in a rattling roar of small arms; while the luckless commanders, unable to discover any semblance of a plan, and still worse, not knowing where one half of their forces were concealed, dared not adventure upon a movement, and preferred trusting to the smoke of the battle as a cover for their blunders. The fusilade, therefore, was hotly sustained; all the heavy pieces were brought to the front; and while the spectators were anxiously looking for the manoeuvres of a fight, the ammunition was waxing low, and the day wearing apace. Dissatisfaction at length began to show itself on every side; and the Duke assuming, as well as he was able, somewhat of a disappointed look, the unhappy generals made a final effort to retrieve their mishaps, and aides-de-camp were despatched through all the highways and byways, to bring up whoever they could find as quickly as possible. Now then began such a scene as few even of the oldest campaigners ever witnessed the equal of. From every dell and hollow, from every brake and thicket, burst forth some party or other, who up to this moment believed themselves lying in ambush. Horse, foot, and dragoons, artillery, sappers, light infantry, and grenadiers, rushed forward wherever chance or their bewildered officers led them. Here might be seen one half of a regiment blazing away at a stray company of their own people, running like devils for shelter; here some squadrons of horse, who, indignant at their fruitless charges and unmeaning movements, now doggedly dismounted, were standing right before a brigade of twelve-pounders, thundering mercilessly amongst them. Never was witnessed such a scene of riot, confusion, and disorder. Colonels lost their regiments, regiments their colonels. The Fusiliers captured the band of the Royal Irish, and made them play through the heat of the engagement. Those who at first expressed *enmui* and fatigue at the sameness and monotony of the scene, were now gratified to the utmost by its life, bustle, and animation. Elderly citizens in drab shorts and buff waistcoats explained to their listening wives and urchins the plans and intentions of the rival heroes, pronouncing the whole thing the while the very best field-day that ever was seen in the Phoenix.

In the midst of all this confusion, a new element of discord suddenly displayed itself. That loyal corps, the Cork militia, who were ordered up to attack close to where the Duke and his staff were standing, deemed that no better moment could be chosen to exhibit their attachment to church and state than when marching on to glory, struck up, with all the discord of their band, the redoubted air of "Protestant Boys." A cheer burst from the ranks as the loyal strains filled the air; but scarcely had the loud burst subsided, when the Louth militia advanced with a quick step, their fifes playing "Vinegar-hill."

For a moment or two the rivalry created a perfect roar of laughter; but this very soon gave way, as the two regiments, instead of drawing up at a reasonable distance for the interchange of an amicable blank cartridge, rushed down upon each other with the fury of madmen. So sudden, so impetuous was the encounter, all effort to prevent it was impracticable. Muskets were clubbed or bayonets fixed, and in a moment really serious battle was engaged; the musicians on each side encouraging their party, as they racked their brains for party-tunes of the most bitter and taunting character; while cries of "Down with King William I." "To hell with the Pope?" rose alternately from either side.

How far this spirit might have extended, it is difficult to say, when the Duke gave orders for some squadrons of cavalry to charge down upon them, and separate the contending forces. This order was fortunately in time; for scarcely was it issued, when a west country yeomanry corps came galloping up to the assistance of the brave Louth.

"Here we are, boys!" cried Mike Westropp, their colonel—"here we are! lave the way! lave the way for us! and we'll ride down the murthering Orange villains, every man of them!"

The Louth fell back, and the yeomen came forward at a charge; Westropp standing high in his stirrups, and flourishing his sabre above his head. It was just then that a heavy brigade of artillery, unconscious of the hot work going forward, was ordered to open their fire upon the Louth militia. One of the guns, by some accident, contained an undue proportion of wadding, and to this casual circumstance may, in a great degree, be attributed the happy issue of what threatened to be a serious disturbance; for, as Westropp advanced, cheering and encouraging his men, he received this wadding slap in his face. Down he tumbled at once, rolling over and over with the shock; while, believing that he had got his death-wound, he bellowed out,

"Oh! blessed Virgin! there's threason in the camp! hit in the face by a four-pounder, by Jove! Oh! Duke darling! Oh! your Grace! Oh! holy Joseph, look at this! Oh! bad luck to the arthillery, for spoiling a fair fight! Peter"—

this was the major of the regiment—"Peter Darcy, gallop into town and lodge informations against the brigade of guns. I'll be dead before you come back."

A perfect burst of laughter broke from the opposing ranks, and while his friends crowded round the discomfited leader, the rival bands united in a roar of merriment that for a moment caused a suspension of hostilities. For a moment, I say; for scarcely had the gallant Westropp been conveyed to the rear, when once more the bands struck up their irritating strains, and preparations for a still more deadly encounter were made on every side. The matter now assumed so serious an aspect, that the Duke was obliged himself to interfere, and order both parties off the ground; the Cork deploying towards the lodge, while the brave Louth marched off with banners flying and drums beating in the direction of Knockmaroon.

These movements were conducted with a serio-comic solemnity of the most ludicrous kind; and although the respect for viceregal authority was great, and the military devotion of each party strong, yet neither one nor the other was sufficient to prevent the more violent on both sides from occasionally turning, as they went, to give expression to some taunting allusion or some galling sarcasm, well calculated, did the opportunity permit, to renew the conflict.

A hearty burst of laughter from the Duke indicated pretty clearly how he regarded the matter; and, however the grave and significant looks of others might seem to imply that there was more in the circumstance than mere food for mirth, he shook his sides merrily; and, as his bright eye glistened with satisfaction, and his cheek glowed, he could not help whispering his regret that his station compelled him to check the very best joke he ever witnessed in his life.

"This is hot work, Sir Charles," said he, wiping his forehead as he spoke; "and, as it is now past three o'clock, and we have a privy council at four, I fear I must leave you."

"The troops will move past in marching order," replied Sir Charles, pompously: "will your Grace receive the salute at this point?"

"Wherever you like, Sir Charles; wherever you like. Would to Heaven that some good Samaritan could afford me a little brandy-and-water from his canteen. I say, Hinton, they seem at luncheon yonder in that carriage: do you think your diplomacy could negotiate a glass of sherry for me?"

"If you'll permit me, my Lord, I'll try," said I, as, disengaging myself from the crowd, I set off in the direction he pointed.

As I drew near the carriage—from which the horses had been taken—drawn up beside a clump of beech-trees for the sake of shelter—I was not long in perceiving that it was the same equipage I had so gallantly rescued in the morning from the sabres of the horse police. Had I entertained any fears for the effects of the nervous shock upon the tender sensibilities of Mrs. Paul Rooney, the scene before me must completely have dispelled my uneasiness. Never did a merrier peal of laughter ring from female lungs than hers as I rode forward. Seated in the back of the carriage, the front cushion of which served as a kind of table, sat the lady in question. One hand, resting upon her knee, held a formidable carving-fork, on the summit of which vibrated the short leg of a chicken; in the other she grasped a silver vessel, which, were I to predicate from the froth, I fear I should pronounce to be porter. A luncheon on the most liberal scale, displayed, in all the confusion and disorder inseparable from such a situation, a veal-pie, cold lamb, tongue, chickens, and sandwiches; drinking vessels of every shape and material; a smelling bottle full of mustard, and a newspaper paragraph full of salt. Abundant as were the viands, the guests were not wanting: crowds of infantry officers, flushed with victory or undismayed by defeat, hob-nobbed from the rumble to the box; the steps, the springs, the very splinter-bar had its occupant; and, truly, a merrier party, or a more convivial, it were difficult to conceive.

So environed was Mrs. Rooney by her friends, that I was enabled to observe them some time, myself unseen.

"Captain Mitchell, another wing? Well, the least taste in life of the breast? Bob Dwyer, will ye never have done drawing that cork?"

Now this I must aver was an unjust reproach, inasmuch as to my own certain knowledge he had accomplished three feats of that nature in about as many minutes; and, had the aforesaid Bob been reared from his infancy in drawing corks, instead of declarations, his practice could not have been more expert. Pop, pop, they went; ghig, glug, glug, flowed the bubbling liquor, as sherry, shrub, cold punch, and bottled porter succeeded each other in rapid order. Simpering ensigns, with elevated eyebrows, insinuated nonsense, soft, vapid, and unmeaning as their own brains, as they helped themselves to ham or dived into the pasty; while a young dragoon, who seemed to devote his attention to Mrs. Rodney's companion, amused himself by constant endeavours to stroke down a growing moustache, whose downy whiteness resembled nothing that I know of save the ill-omened fur one sees on an antiquated apple-pie.

As I looked on every side to catch a glance at him whom I should suppose to Mr. Rooney, I was myself detected by the watchful eye of Bob

Dwyer, who, at that moment having his mouth full of three hard eggs, was nearly asphyxiated in his endeavours to telegraph my approach to Mrs. Paul.

"The edge-du-cong, by the mortial!" said he, sputtering out the words, as his bloodshot eyes nearly bolted out of his head.

Had I been a Bengal tiger, my advent might have caused less alarm. The officers not knowing if the Duke himself were coming, wiped their lips, resumed their caps and chakos, and sprang to the ground in dismay and confusion: as Mrs. Rooney herself, with an adroitness an Indian juggler might have envied, plunged the fork, drumstick and all, into the recesses of her muff; while with a back hand she decanted the XX upon a bald major of infantry, who was brushing the crumbs from his facings. One individual alone seemed to relish and enjoy the discomfiture of the others: this was the young lady whom I before remarked, and whose whole air and appearance seemed strangely at variance with everything around her. She gave free current to her mirth; while Mrs. Paul, now suddenly restored to a sense of her nervous constitution, fell back in her carriage, and appeared bent upon a scene.

"You caught us enjoying ourselves, Mr. Stilton?"

"Hinton, if you'll allow me, madam."

"Ay, to be sure—Mr. Hinton. Taking a little snack, which I am sure you'd be the better for after the fatigues of the day."

"Eh, au au! a devilish good luncheon," chimed in a pale sub, the first who ventured to pluck up his courage.

"Would a sandwich tempt you, with a glass of champagne?" said Mrs. Paul, with the blandest of smiles.

"I can recommend the lamb, sir," said a voice behind.

"Begad, I'll vouch for the porter," said the Major. "I only hope it is a good cosmetic."

"It is a beautiful thing for the hair," said Mrs. Rooney, half venturing upon a joke.

"No more on that head, ma'am," said the little Major, bowing pompously.

By this time, thanks to the assiduous attentions of Bob Dwyer, I was presented with a plate, which, had I been an anaconda instead of an aide-decamp, might have satisfied my appetite. A place was made for me in the carriage; and the faithful Bob, converting the skirt of his principal blue into a glass-cloth, polished a wine-glass for my private use.

"Let me introduce my young friend, Mr. Hinton," said Mrs. Paul, with a graceful wave of her jewelled hand towards her companion. "Miss Louisa Bellew, only daughter of Sir Simon Bellew, of — — —" what the place was I could not well hear, but it sounded confoundedly like Killhimansmotherum—"a beautiful place in the county Mayo. Bob, is it punch you are giving?"

"Most excellent, I assure you, Mrs. Rooney."

"And how is the Duke, sir? I hope his Grace enjoys good health. He is a darling of a man."

By-the-by, it is perfectly absurd the sympathy your third or fourth-rate people feel in the health and habits of those above them in station, pleased as they are to learn the most common-place and worthless trifles concerning them, and happy when, by any chance, some accidental similitude would seem to exist even between their misfortunes.

"And the dear Duchess," resumed Mrs. Rooney, "she's troubled with the nerves like myself. Ah! Mr. Hinton, what an affliction it is to have a sensitive nature; that's what I often say to my sweet young friend here. It's better for her to be the gay, giddy, thoughtless, happy thing she is, than— —" Here the lady sighed, wiped her eyes, flourished her cambric, and tried to look like Agnes in the "Bleeding Nun." "But here they come. You don't know Mr. Rooney? Allow me to introduce him to you."

As she spoke, O'Grady cantered up to the carriage, accompanied by a short, pursy, round-faced little man, who, with his hat set knowingly on one side, and his top-boots scarce reaching to the middle of the leg, bestrode a sharp, strong-boned hackney, with cropped ears and short tail. He carried in his hand a hunting-whip, and seemed, by his seat in the saddle and the easy finger upon the bridle, no indifferent horseman.

"Mr. Rooney," said the lady, drawing herself up with a certain austerity of manner, "I wish you to make the acquaintance of Mr. Hinton, the aide-de-camp to his Grace."

Mr. Rooney lifted his hat straight above his head, and replaced it a little more obliquely than before over his right eye.

"Delighted, upon my honour—faith, quite charmed—hope you got something to eat—there never was such a murthering hot day—Bob Dwyer, open a bottle of port—the Captain is famished."

"I say, Hinton," called out O'Grady, "you forgot the Duke, it seems; he told me you'd gone in search of some sherry, or something of the kind; but I can readily conceive how easily a man may forget himself in such a position as yours."

Here Mrs. Paul dropped her head in deep confusion, Miss Bellew looked saucy, and I, for the first time remembering what brought me there, was perfectly overwhelmed with shame at my carelessness.

"Never mind, boy, don't fret about it, his Grace is the most forgiving man in the world; and when he knows where you were — —"

"Ah, Captain!" sighed Mrs. Rooney.

"Master Phil, it's yourself can do it," murmured Paul, who perfectly appreciated O'Grady's powers of "blarney," when exercised on the susceptible temperament of his fair spouse.

"I'll take a sandwich," continued the Captain. "Do you know, Mrs. Rooney, I've been riding about this half-hour to catch my young friend, and introduce him to you; and here I find him comfortably installed, without my aid or assistance. The fact is, these English fellows have a nattering, insinuating way of their own there's no coming up to. Isn't that so, Miss Bellew?"

"Very likely," said the young lady, who now spoke for the first time; "but it is so very well concealed that I for one could never detect it."

This speech, uttered with a certain pert and saucy air, nettled me for the moment; but as no reply occurred to me, I could only look at the speaker a tacit acknowledgment of her sarcasm; while I remembered, for the first time, that, although seated opposite my very attractive neighbour, I had hitherto not addressed to her a single phrase of even common-place attention.

"I suppose you put up in the Castle, sir?" said Mr. Rooney.

"Yes, two doors lower down than Mount O'Grady," replied the Captain for me. "But come, Hinton, the carriages are moving, we must get back as quick as we can. Good-by, Paul Adieu, Mrs. Rooney, Miss Bellew, good morning."

It was just at the moment when I had summoned up my courage to address Miss Bellew, that O'Grady called me away: there was nothing for it, however, but to make my adieus; while, extricating myself from the *débris* of the luncheon, I once more mounted my horse, and joined the viceregal party as they drove from the ground.

"I'm delighted you know the Rooneys," said O'Grady, as we drove along; "they are by far the best fun going. Paul good, but his wife superb!"

"And the young lady?" said I.

"Oh, a different kind of thing altogether. By-the-by, Hinton, you took my hint, I hope, about your English manner?"

"Eh—why—how—what did you mean?"

"Simply, my boy, that your Coppermine-river kind of courtesy may be a devilish fine thing in Hyde Park or St. James's, but will never do with us poor people here. Put more warmth into it, man. Dash the lemonade with a little maraschino; you'll feel twice as comfortable yourself, and the girls like you all the better. You take the suggestion in good part, I'm sure."

"Oh, of course," said I, somewhat stung that I should get a lesson in manner where I had meant to be a model for imitation; "if they like that kind of thing, I must only conform."

CHAPTER VII
THE ROONEYS

I cannot proceed further in this my veracious history without dwelling a little longer upon the characters of the two interesting individuals I have already presented to my readers as Mr. and Mrs. Rooney.

Paul Rooney, attorney-at-law, 42, Stephen's-green, north, was about as well known in his native city of Dublin as Nelson's Pillar. His reputation, unlimited by the adventitious circumstances of class, spread over the whole surface of society; and, from the chancellor down to the carman, his claims were confessed.

It is possible that, in many other cities of the world, Mr. Rooney might have been regarded as a common-place, every-day personage, well to do in the world, and of a free-and-easy character, which, if it left little for reproach, left still less for remark: but in Ireland, whether it was the climate or the people, the potteen or the potatoes, I cannot say, but certainly he "came out," as the painters call it, in a breadth of colour quite surprising.

The changeful character of the skies has, they tell us, a remarkable influence in fashioning the ever-varying features of Irish temperament; and, certainly, the inconstant climate of Dublin had much merit if it produced in Mr. Rooney the versatile nature he rejoiced in.

About ten o'clock, on every morning during term, might be seen a shrewd, cunning-looking, sly little fellow, who, with pursed-up lips and slightly elevated nose, wended his way towards the Four Courts, followed by a ragged urchin with a well-filled bag of purple stuff. His black coat, drab shorts, and gaiters, had a plain and business-like cut; and the short, square tie of his white cravat had a quaint resemblance to a flourish on a deed; the self-satisfied look, the assured step, the easy roll of the head—all bespoke one with whom the world was thriving; and it did not need the additional evidence of a certain habit he had of jingling his silver in his breeches-pocket as he went, to assure you that Rooney was a warm fellow, and had no want of cash.

Were you to trace his steps for the three or four hours that ensued, you would see him bustling through the crowded hall of the Four Courts—

now, whispering some important point to a leading barrister, while he held another by the gown lest he should escape him; now, he might be remarked seated in a niche between the pillars, explaining some knotty difficulty to a western client, whose flushed cheek and flashing eye too plainly indicated his impatience of legal strategy, and how much more pleased he would feel to redress his wrongs in his own fashion; now brow-beating, now cajoling, now encouraging, now condoling, he edged his way through the bewigged and dusty throng, not stopping to reply to the hundred salutations he met with, save by a knowing wink, which was the only civility he did not put down at three-and-fourpence. If his knowledge of law was little, his knowledge of human nature—at least of such of it as Ireland exhibits—was great; and no case of any importance could come before a jury, where Paul's advice and opinion were not deemed of considerable importance. No man better knew all the wiles and twists, all the dark nooks and recesses of Irish character. No man more quickly could ferret out a hoarded secret; no one so soon detect an attempted imposition. His was the secret *police* of law: he read a witness as he would a deed, and detected a flaw in him to the full as easily.

As he sat near the leading counsel in a cause, he seemed a kind of middle term between the lawyer and the jury. Marking by some slight but significant gesture every point of the former, to the latter he impressed upon their minds every favourable feature of his client's cause; and twelve deaf men might have followed the pleadings in a cause through the agency of Paul's gesticulations. The consequence of these varied gifts was, business flowed in upon him from every side, and few members of the bar were in the receipt of one-half his income.

Scarcely, however, did the courts rise, when Paul, shaking from his shoulders the learned dust of the Exchequer, would dive into a small apartment which, in an obscure house in Mass-lane, he dignified by the name of his study. Short and few as were his moments of seclusion, they sufficed to effect in his entire man a complete and total change. The shrewd little attorney, that went in with a *nisi prius* grin, came out a round, pleasant-looking fellow, with a green coat of jockey cut, a buff waistcoat, white cords, and tops; his hat set jauntily on one side, his spotted neckcloth knotted in bang-up mode,—in fact, his figure the *beau idéal* of a west-country squire taking a canter among his covers before the opening of the hunting.

His grey eyes, expanded to twice their former size, looked the very soul of merriment; his nether lip, slightly dropped, quivered with the last joke it uttered. Even his voice partook of the change, and was now a rich, full, mellow Clare accent, which, with the recitative of his country, seemed to Italianise his English. While such was Paul, his *accessoires*—as the French would call them—were in admirable keeping: a dark chesnut cob, a perfect model of strength and symmetry, would be led up and down by a groom, also mounted upon a strong hackney, whose flat rib and short pastern showed his old Irish breeding; the well-fitting saddle, the well-balanced stirrup, the plain but powerful snaffle, all looked like the appendages of one whose jockeyism was no assumed feature; and, indeed, you had only to see Mr. Rooney in his seat, to confess that he was to the full as much at home there as in the Court of Chancery.

From this to the hour of a late dinner, the Phoenix Park became his resort. There, surrounded by a gay and laughing crowd, Paul cantered along, amusing his hearers with the last *mot* from the King's Bench, or some stray bit of humour or fun from a case on circuit. His conversation, however, principally ran on other topics: the Curragh Meeting, the Loughrea Steeplechase, the Meath Cup, or Lord Boyne's Handicap; with these he was thoroughly familiar. He knew the odds of every race, could apportion the weights, describe the ground, and, better than all, make rather a good guess at the winner. In addition to these gifts, he was the best judge of a horse in Ireland; always well mounted, and never without at least two hackneys in his stable, able to trot their fifteen Irish miles within the hour. Such qualities as these might be supposed popular ones in a country proverbially given to sporting; but Mr. Rooney had other and very superior powers of attraction,—he was the Amphitryou of Dublin. It was no figurative expression to say that he kept open house. *Déjeuners*, dinners, routs, and balls followed each other in endless succession. His cook was French, his claret was Sneyd's; he imported his own sherry and Madeira, both of which he nursed with a care and affection truly parental. His venison and blackcock came from Scotland; every Holyhead packet had its consignment of Welsh mutton; and, in a word, whatever wealth could purchase, and a taste, nurtured as his had been by the counsel of many who frequented his table, could procure, such he possessed in abundance, his greatest ambition being to outshine in splendour, and surpass in magnificence, all the other dinner-givers of the day, filling his house with the great and titled of the land, who ministered to his vanity with singular good-nature, while they sipped his claret, and sat over his Burgundy. His was indeed a pleasant house. The *bons vivants* liked it for its excellent fare, the perfection of its wines, the certainty of finding the first rarity of the season before its existence was heard of at other tables; the lounger liked it for its ease and informality; the humorist, for the amusing features of its host and hostess; and not a few were attracted by the gracefulness and surpassing loveliness of one who, by some strange fatality of fortune, seemed to have been dropped down into the midst of this singular *ménage*.

Of Mr. Rooney, I have only further to say that, hospitable as a prince, he was never so happy as at the head of his table; for, although his natural sharpness could not but convince him of the footing which he occupied among his high and distinguished guests, yet he knew well there are few such levellers of rank as riches, and he had read in his youth that even the lofty Jove himself was accessible by the odour of a hecatomb.

Mrs. Rooney—or, as she wrote herself upon her card, Mrs. Paul Rooney (there seemed something distinctive in the prenom.)—was a being of a very different order. Perfectly unconscious of the ridicule that attaches to vulgar profusion, she believed herself the great source of attraction of her crowded staircase and besieged drawing-room. True it was, she was a large and very handsome woman. Her deep, dark, brown eyes, and brilliant complexion, would have been beautiful, had not her mouth somewhat marred their effect, by that coarse expression which high living and a voluptuous life is sure to impress upon those not born to be great. There is no doubt of it, the mouth is your thorough-bred feature. You will meet eyes as softly beaming, as brightly speaking, among the lofty cliffs of the wild Tyrol, or in the deep valleys of the far west; I have seen, too, a brow as fairly pencilled, a nose no Grecian statue could surpass, a skin whose tint was fair and transparent as the downy rose-leaf, amid the humble peasants of a poor and barren land; but never have I seen the mouth whose clean-cut lip and chiselled arch betokened birth. No; that feature would seem the prerogative of the highly born; fashioned to the expression of high and holy thoughts; moulded to the utterance of ennobling sentiment, or proud desire. Its every lineament tells of birth and blood.

Now, Mrs. Rooney's mouth was a large and handsome one, her teeth white and regular withal, and, when at rest, there was nothing to find fault with; but let her speak—was it her accent?—was it the awful provincialism of her native city?—was it that strange habit of contortion any *patois* is sure to impress upon the speaker?—I cannot tell, but certainly it lent to features of very considerable attraction a vulgarising character of expression.

It was truly provoking to see so handsome a person mar every effect of her beauty by some extravagant display. Dramatising every trivial incident in life, she rolled her eyes, looked horror-struck or happy, sweet or sarcastic, lofty or languishing, all in one minute. There was an eternal play of feature of one kind or other; there was no rest, no repose. Her arms—and they were round, and fair, and well-fashioned—were also enlisted in the service; and to a distant observer Mrs. Rooney's animated conversation appeared like a priest performing mass.

And that beautiful head, whose fair and classic proportions were balanced so equally upon her white and swelling throat, how tantalising to know it full of low and petty ambitions, of vulgar tastes, of contemptible rivalries, of insignificant triumph. To see her, amid the voluptuous splendour and profusion of her gorgeous house, resplendent with jewellery, glistening in all the blaze of emeralds and rubies; to watch how the poisonous venom of innate vulgarity had so tainted that fair and beautiful form, rendering her an object of ridicule who should have been a thing to worship. It was too bad; and, as she sat at dinner, her plump but taper fingers grasping a champagne glass, she seemed like a Madonna enacting the part of Moll Flagon.

Now, Mrs. Paul's manner had as many discrepancies as her features. She was by nature a good, kind, merry, coarse personage, who loved a joke not the less if it were broad as well as long. Wealth, however, and its attendant evils, suggested the propriety of a very different line; and catching up as she did at every opportunity that presented itself such of the airs and graces as she believed to be the distinctive traits of high life, she figured about in these cast-off attractions, like a waiting-maid in the abandoned finery of her mistress.

As she progressed in fortune, she "tried back" for a family, and discovered that she was an O'Toole by birth, and consequently of Irish blood-royal; a certain O'Toole being king of a nameless tract, in an unknown year, somewhere about the time of Cromwell, who, Mrs. Rooney had heard, came over with the Romans.

"Ah, yes, my dear," as she would say when, softened by sherry and sorrow, she would lay her hand upon your arm—"ah, yes, if every one had their own, it isn't married to an attorney I'd be, but living in regal splendour in the halls of my ancestors. Well, well!" Here she would throw up her eyes with a mixed expression of grief and confidence in Heaven, that if she hadn't got her own, in this world, Oliver Cromwell, at least, was paying off, in the other, his foul wrongs to the royal house of O'Toole.

I have only one person more to speak of ere I conclude my rather prolix account of the family. Miss Louisa Bellew was the daughter of an Irish baronet, who put the keystone upon his ruin by his honest opposition to the passing of the Union. His large estates, loaded with debt and encumbered by mortgage, had been for half a century a kind of battle-field for legal warfare at every assizes. Through the medium of his difficulties he became acquainted with Mr. Rooney, whose craft and subtlety had rescued him from more than one difficulty, and whose good-natured assistance had done still more important service by loans upon his property.

At Mr. Rooney's suggestion, Miss Bellew was invited to pass her winter with them in Dublin. This proposition which, in the palmier days of the baronet's fortune, would in all probability never have been made, and would certainly never have been accepted, was now entertained with some consideration, and finally acceded to, on prudential motives. Rooney had lent him large sums; he had never been a pressing, on the contrary, he was a lenient creditor; possessing great power over the property, he had used it sparingly, even delicately, and showed himself upon more than one occasion not only a shrewd adviser, but a warm friend. "'Tis true," thought Sir Simon, "they are vulgar people, of coarse tastes and low habits, and those with whom they associate laugh at, though they live upon them; yet, after all, to refuse this invitation may be taken in ill part; a few months will do the whole thing. Louisa, although young, has tact and cleverness enough to see the difficulties of her position; besides, poor child, the gaiety and life of a city will be a relief to her, after the dreary and monotonous existence she has passed with me."

This latter reason he plausibly represented to himself as a strong one for complying with what his altered fortunes and ruined prospects seemed to render no longer a matter of choice.

To the Rooneys, indeed, Miss Bellew's visit was a matter of some consequence; it was like the recognition of some petty state by one of the great powers of Europe. It was an acknowledgment of a social existence, an evidence to the world not only that there was such a thing as the kingdom of Rooney, but also that it was worth while to enter into negotiation with it, and even accredit an ambassador to its court.

Little did that fair and lovely girl think, as with tearful eyes she turned again and again to embrace her father, as the hour arrived, when for the first time in her life she was to leave her home, little did she dream of the circumstances under which her visit was to be paid. Less a guest than a hostage, she was about to quit the home of her infancy, where, notwithstanding the inroads of poverty, a certain air of its once greatness still lingered; the broad and swelling lands, that stretched away with wood and coppice, far as the eye could reach—the woodland walks—the ancient house itself, with its discordant pile, accumulated at different times by different masters—all told of power and supremacy in the land of her fathers. The lonely solitude of those walls, peopled alone by the grim-visaged portraits of long-buried ancestors, were now to be exchanged for the noise and bustle, the glitter and the glare of second-rate city life; profusion and extravagance, where she had seen but thrift and forbearance; the gossip, the scandal, the tittle-tattle of society, with its envies, its jealousies, its petty rivalries, and its rancours, were to supply those quiet evenings beside the winter hearth, when reading aloud some old and valued volume she learned to prize the treasures of our earlier writers under the guiding taste of one whose scholarship was of no mean order, and whose cultivated mind was imbued with all the tenderness and simplicity of a refined and gentle nature.

When fortune smiled, when youth and wealth, an ancient name and a high position, all concurred to elevate him, Sir Simon Bellew was courteous almost to humility; but when the cloud of misfortune lowered over his house, when difficulties thickened around him, and every effort to rescue seemed only to plunge him deeper, then the deep-rooted pride of the man shone forth: and he who in happier days was forgiving even to a fault, became now scrupulous about every petty observance, exacting testimonies of respect from all around him, and assuming an almost tyranny of manner totally foreign to his tastes, his feelings, and his nature; like some mighty oak of the forest, riven and scathed by lightning, its branches leafless and its roots laid bare, still standing erect, it stretches its sapless limbs proudly towards heaven, so stood he, reft of nearly all, yet still presenting to the adverse wind of fortune his bold, unshaken front.

Alas and alas! poverty has no heavier evil in its train than its power of perverting the fairest gifts of our nature from their true channel,—making the bright sides of our character dark, gloomy, and repulsive. Thus the high-souled pride that in our better days sustains and keeps us far above the reach of sordid thoughts and unworthy actions, becomes, in the darker hour of our destiny, a misanthropic selfishness, in which we wrap ourselves as in a mantle. The caresses of friendship, the warm affections of domestic love, cannot penetrate through this; even sympathy becomes suspect, and then commences that terrible struggle against the world, whose only termination is a broken heart.

Notwithstanding, then, all Mr. Rooney's address in conveying the invitation in question, it was not without a severe struggle that Sir Simon resolved on its acceptance; and when at last he did accede, it was with so many stipulations, so many express conditions, that, thad they been complied with *de facto*, as they were acknowledged by promise, Miss Bellew would, in all probability, have spent her winter in the retirement of her own chamber in Stephen's-green, without seeing more of the capital and its inhabitants than a view from her window presented. Paul, it is true, agreed to everything; for, although, to use his own language, the codicil revoked the entire body of the testament, he determined in his own mind to break the will. "Once in Dublin," thought he, "the fascinations of society, the pleasures of the world, with such a guide as Mrs. Rooney"—and here let me mention, that for his wife's tact and social cleverness Paul had the most heartfelt admiration—"with advantages like these, she will soon forget the humdrum life of Kilmorran Castle, and become reconciled to a splendour and magnificence unsurpassed by even the viceregal court."

Here, then, let me conclude this account of the Rooneys, while I resume the thread of my own narrative. Although I feel for and am ashamed of the prolixity in which I have indulged, yet, as I speak of real people, well known at the period of which I write, and as they may to a certain extent convey an impression of the tone of one class in the society of that day, I could not bring myself to omit their mention, nor even dismiss them more briefly.

CHAPTER VIII
THE VISIT

I have already recorded the first twenty-four hours of my life in Ireland; and, if there was enough in them to satisfy me that the country was unlike in many respects that which I had left, there was also some show of reason to convince me that, if I did not conform to the habits and tastes of those around me, I should incur a far greater chance of being laughed at by them than be myself amused by their eccentricities. The most remarkable feature that struck me was the easy, even cordial manner with which acquaintance was made. Every one met you as if he had in some measure been prepared for the introduction; a tone of intimacy sprang up at once; your tastes were hinted, your wishes guessed at, with an unaffected kindness that made you forget the suddenness of the intimacy: so that, when at last you parted with your dear friend of some half an hour's acquaintance, you could not help wondering at the confidences you had made, the avowals you had spoken, and the lengths to which you had gone in close alliance with one you had never seen before, and might possibly never meet again. Strange enough as this was with men, it was still more singular when it extended to the gentler sex. Accustomed as I had been all my life to the rigid observances of etiquette in female society, nothing surprised me so much as the rapid steps by which Irish ladies passed from acquaintance to intimacy, from intimacy to friendship. The unsuspecting kindliness of woman's nature has certainly no more genial soil than in the heart of Erin's daughters. There is besides, too, a winning softness in their manner towards the stranger of another land that imparts to their hospitable reception a tone of courteous warmth I have never seen in any other country.

The freedom of manner I have here alluded to, however delightful it may render the hours of one separated from home, family, and friends, is yet not devoid of its inconveniences. How many an undisciplined and uninformed youth has misconstrued its meaning and mistaken its import How often have I seen the raw subaltern elated with imaginary success— flushed with a fancied victory—where, in reality, he had met with nothing save the kind looks and the kind words in which the every-day courtesies of life are couched, and by which, what, in less favoured lands, are the cold and chilling observances of ceremony, are here the easy and familiar intercourse of those who wish to know each other.

The coxcomb who fancies that he can number as many triumphs as he has passed hours in Dublin, is like one who, estimating the rich production of a southern clime by their exotic value in his own colder regions, dignifies by the name of luxury what are in reality but the every-day productions of the soil: so he believes peculiarly addressed to himself the cordial warmth and friendly greeting which make the social atmosphere around him.

If I myself fell deeply into this error, and if my punishment was a heavy one, let my history prove a beacon to all who follow in my steps; for Dublin is still a garrison city, and I have been told that lips as tempting and eyes as bright are to be met there as heretofore. Now to my story.

Life in Dublin, at the time I write of, was about as gay a thing as a man can well fancy. Less debarred than in other countries from partaking of the lighter enjoyments of life, the members of the learned professions mixed much in society; bringing with them stores of anecdote and information unattainable from other sources, they made what elsewhere would have proved the routine of intercourse a season of intellectual enjoyment. Thus, the politician, the churchman, the barrister, and the military man, shaken as they were together in dose intimacy, lost individually many of the prejudices of their caste, and learned to converse with a wider and more extended knowledge of the world. While this was so, another element, peculiarly characteristic of the country, had its share in modelling social life—that innate tendency to drollery, that bent to laugh with every one and at everything, so eminently Irish, was now in the ascendant. From the Viceroy downwards, the island was on the broad grin. Every day furnished its share, its quota of merriment. Epigrams, good stories, repartees, and practical jokes rained in showers over the land. A privy council was a *conversazione* of laughing bishops and droll chief-justices. Every trial at the bar, every dinner at the court, every drawing-room, afforded a theme for some ready-witted absurdity; and all the graver business of life was carried on amid this current of unceasing fun and untiring drollery, just as we see the serious catastrophe of a modern opera assisted by the crash of an orchestral accompaniment.

With materials like these society was made up; and into this I plunged with all the pleasurable delight of one who, if he could not appreciate the sharpness, was at least dazzled by the brilliancy of the wit that flashed around him. My duties as aide-de-camp were few, and never interfered with my liberty: while in my double capacity of military man and *attaché* to the court, I was invited everywhere, and treated with marked courtesy and kindness. Thus passed my life pleasantly along, when a few mornings after the events I have mentioned, I was sitting at my breakfast, conning over my invitations for the week, and meditating a letter, home, in which I should describe my mode of life with as much reserve as might render the record of my doings a safe disclosure for the delicate nerves of my lady-mother. In order to accomplish this latter task with success, I scribbled with some notes a sheet of paper that lay before me. "Among other particularly nice people, my dear mother," wrote I, "there are the Rooneys. Mr. Rooney—a member of the Irish bar, of high standing and great reputation—is a most agreeable and accomplished person. How much I should like to present him to you." I had got thus far, when a husky, asthmatic cough, and a muttered curse on the height of my domicile, apprised me that some one was at my door. At the same moment a heavy single knock, that nearly stove in the panel, left no doubt upon my mind.

"Are ye at home, or is it sleeping ye are? May I never, if it's much else the half of ye's fit for. Ugh, blessed hour! three flights of stairs, with a twist in them instead of a landing. Ye see he's not in the place. I tould you that before I came up. But if s always the same thing. Corny, run here; Corny, fly there; get me this, take that. Bad luck to them! One would think they badgered me for bare diversion, the haythins, the Turks!"

A fit of coughing, that almost convinced me that Corny had given his last curse, followed this burst of eloquence, just as I appeared at the door.

"What's the matter, Corny?"

"The matter?—ugh, ain't I coughing my soul out with a wheezing and whistling in my chest like a creel of chickens. Here's Mr. Rooney wanting to see ye; and faith," as he added in an under tone, "if s not long you wor in making his acquaintance. That's his room," added he, with a jerk of his thumb. "Now lave the way if you plase, and let me got a howld of the banisters."

With these words Corny began his descent, while I, apologising to Mr. Rooney for not having sooner perceived kirn, bowed him into the room with all proper ceremony.

"A thousand apologies, Mr. Hinton, for the unseasonable hour of my visit, but business——"

"Pray not a word," said I; "always delighted to see you. Mrs. Rooney is well, I hope?"

"Charming, upon my honour. But, as I was saying, I could not well come later; there is a case in the King's Bench—Rex *versus* Ryves—a heavy record, and I want to catch the counsel to assure him that all's safe. God knows, it has cost me an anxious night. Everything depended on one witness, an obstinate beast that wouldn't listen to reason. We got hold of him last night; got three doctors to certify he was out of his mind; and, at this moment, with his head shaved, and a grey suit on him, he is the noisiest inmate in Glassnevin madhouse."

"Was not this a very bold, a very dangerous expedient?"

"So it was. He fought like a devil, and his outrageous conduct has its reward, for they put him on low diet and handcuffs the moment he went in. But excuse me, if I make a hurried visit. Mrs. Rooney requests that—that—but where the devil did I put it?"

Here Mr. Rooney felt his coat-pockets, dived into those of his waistcoat, patted himself all over, then looked into his hat, then round the room, on the floor, and even outside the door upon the lobby.

"Sure it is not possible I've lost it."

"Nothing of consequence, I hope?" said I.

"What a head I have," replied he, with a knowing grin, while at the same moment throwing up the sash of my window, he thrust out the head in question, and gave a loud shrill whistle.

Scarcely was the casement closed when a ragged urchin appeared at the door, carrying on his back the ominous stuff-bag containing the record of Mr. Rooney's rogueries.

"Give me the bag, Tim," quoth he; at the same moment he plunged his hand deep among the tape-tied parcels, and extricated a piece of square pasteboard, which, having straightened and flattened upon his knee, he presented to me with a graceful bow, adding, jocosely, "an ambassador without his credentials would never do."

It was an invitation to dinner at Mr. Rooney's for the memorable Friday for which my friend O'Grady had already received his card.

"Nothing will give me more pleasure——"

"No, will it though? how very good of you! a small cosy party—Harry Burgh, Bowes Daley, Barrington, the judges, and a few more. There now, no ceremony, I beg of you. Come along, Joe. Good morning, Mr. Hinton: not a step further."

So saying, Mr. Rooney backed and shuffled himself out of my room, and, followed by his faithful attendant, hurried down stairs, muttering a series of self-gratulations, as he went, on the successful result of his mission.

Scarcely had he gone, when I heard the rapid stride of another visitor, who, mounting four steps at a time, came along chanting, at the top of his voice,

> "My two back teeth I will bequeath
> To the Reverend Michael Palmer;
> His wife has a tongue that'll match them well,
> She's a devil of a scold, God d—n her!"

"How goes it, Jack my hearty?" cried he, as he sprang into the room, flinging his sabre into the corner, and hurling his foraging cap upon the sofa.

"You have been away, O'Grady? What became of you for the last two days?"

"Down at the Curragh, taking a look at the nags for the Spring Meeting. Dined with the bar at Naas; had a great night with them; made old Moore gloriously tipsy, and sent him into court the next morning with the overture to Mother Goose in his bag instead of his brief. Since daybreak I have been trying a new horse in the Park, screwing him over all the fences, and rushing him at the double rails in the pathway, to see if he can't cross the country."

"Why the hunting season is nearly over."

"Quite true; but it is the Loughrea Steeple-chase I am thinking of. I have promised to name a horse, and I only remembered last night that I had but twenty-four hours to do it. The time was short, but by good fortune I heard of this grey on my way up to town."

"And you think he'll do?"

"He has a good chance, if one can only keep on his back; but what between bolting, plunging, and rushing through his fences, he is not a beast for a timid elderly gentleman. After all, one must have something: the whole world will be there; the Rooneys are going; and that pretty little girl with them. By-the-by, Jack, what do you think of Miss Bellew?"

"I can scarcely tell you; I only saw her for a moment, and then that Hibernian hippopotamus, Mrs. Paul, so completely overshadowed her, there was no getting a look at her."

"Devilish pretty girl, that she is; and one day or other, they say, will have an immense fortune. Old Rooney always shakes his head when the idea is thrown out, which only convinces me the more of her chance."

"Well, then, Master Phil, why don't you do something in that quarter?"

"Well, so I should; but somehow, most unaccountably, you'll say, I don't think I made any impression. To be sure, I never went vigorously to work: I couldn't get over my scruples of making up to a girl who may have a large fortune, while I myself am so confoundedly out at the elbows; the thing would look badly, to say the least of it; and so, when I did think I was making a little running, I only 'held in' the faster, and at length gave up the race. *You* are the man, Hinton. *Your* chances, I should say—"

"Ah, I don't know."

Just at this moment the door opened, and Lord Dudley de Vere entered, dressed in coloured clothes, cut in the most foppish style of the day, and with his hands stuck negligently behind in his coat-pockets. He threw himself affectedly into a chair, and eyed us both without speaking.

"I say, messieurs, Rooney or not Rooney? that's the question. Do we accept this invitation for Friday?"

"I do, for one," said I, somewhat haughtily.

"Can't be, my boy," said O'Grady; "the thing is most unlucky: they have a dinner at court that same day; our names are all on the list; and thus we lose the Rooneys, which, from all I hear, is a very serious loss indeed. Daley, Barrington, Harry Martin, and half a dozen others, the first fellows of the day, are all to be there."

"What a deal they will talk," yawned out Lord Dudley. "I feel rather happy to have escaped it. There's no saying a word to the woman beside you, as long as those confounded fellows keep up a roaring fire of what they think wit. What an idea! to be sure; there is not a man among them that can tell you the odds upon the Derby, nor what year there was a dead heat for the St. Léger. That little girl the Rooneys have got is very pretty, I must confess; but I see what they are at: won't do, though. Ha! O'Grady, you know what I mean?"

"Faith, I am very stupid this morning; can't say that I do."

"Not see it! It is a hollow thing; but perhaps you are in the scheme too. There, you needn't look angry; I only meant it in joke—ha! ha! ha! I say, Hinton, do you take care of yourself: Englishers have no chance here; and when they find it won't do with *me*, they'll take you in training."

"Anything for a *pis-aller*" said O'Grady, sarcastically; "but let us not forget there is a levee to-day, and it is already past twelve o'clock."

"Ha! to be sure, a horrid bore."

So saying, Lord Dudley lounged one more round the room, looked at himself in the glass, nodded familiarly to his own image, and took his leave. O'Grady soon followed; while I set about my change of dress with all the speed the time required.

CHAPTER IX
THE BALL

As the day of Mr. Rooney's grand entertainment drew near, our disappointment increased tenfold at our inability to be present. The only topic discussed in Dublin was the number of the guests, the splendour and magnificence of the dinner, which was to be followed by a ball, at which above eight hundred guests were expected. The band of the Fermanagh militia, at that time the most celebrated in Ireland, was brought up expressly for the occasion. All that the city could number of rank, wealth, and beauty had received invitations, and scarcely a single apology had been returned.

'Is there no possible way.' said I, as I chatted with O'Grady on the morning of the event; 'is there no chance of our getting away in time to see something of the ball at least?'

'None whatever,' replied he despondingly; 'as ill-luck would have it, it's a command-night at the theatre. The duke has disappointed so often, that he is sure to go now, and for the same reason he 'll sit the whole thing out. By that time it will be half-past twelve, we shan't get back here before one; then comes supper; and —— in fact, you know enough of the habits of this place now to guess that after that there is very little use of thinking of going anywhere.'

'It is devilish provoking,' said I.

'That it is: and you don't know the worst of it. I 've got rather a heavy book on the Loughrea race, and shall want a few hundreds in a week or so; and, as nothing renders my friend Paul so sulky as not eating his dinners, it is five-and-twenty per cent, at least out of my pocket, from this confounded *contretemps*. There goes De Vere. I say, Dudley, whom have we at dinner to-day?'

'Harrington and the Asgills, and that set,' replied he, with an insolent shrug of his shoulder.

'More of it, by Jove,' said O'Grady, biting his lip. 'One must be as particular before these people as a young sub. at a regimental mess. There's not a button of your coat, not a loop of your aiguillette, not a twist of your sword-knot, little Charley won't note down; and as there is no orderly-book in the drawing-room, he will whisper to his grace before coffee.'

'Whatabore!'

'Ay, and to think that all that time we might have been up to the very chin in fun. The Rooneys to-day will outdo even themselves. They've got half-a-dozen new lords on trial; all the judges; a live bishop; and, better than all, every pretty woman in the capital. I've a devil of a mind to get suddenly ill, and slip off to Paul's for the dessert.'

'No, no, that's out of the question; we must only put up with our misfortunes as well as we can. As for me, the dinner here is, I think, the worst part of the matter.'

'I estimate my losses at a very different rate. First, there is the three hundred, which I should certainly have had from Paul, and which now becomes a very crooked contingency. Then there's the dinner and two bottles—I speak moderately—of such burgundy as nobody has but himself. These are the positive *bonâ fide* losses: then, what do you say to my chance of picking up some lovely girl, with a stray thirty thousand, and the good taste to look out for a proper fellow to spend it with? Seriously, Jack, I must think of something of that kind one of these days. It's wrong to lose time; for, by waiting, one's chances diminish, while becoming more difficult to please. So you see what a heavy blow this is to me: not to mention my little gains at short-whist, which in the half-hour before supper I may fairly set down as a fifty.'

'Yours is a very complicated calculation; for, except the dinner, and I suppose we shall have as good a one here, I have not been able to see anything but problematic loss or profit.'

'Of course you haven't: your English education is based upon grounds far too positive for that; but we mere Irish get a habit of looking at the possible as probable, and the probable as most likely. I don't think we build castles more than our neighbours, but we certainly go live in them earlier; and if we do, now and then, get a chill for our pains, why we generally have another building ready to receive us elsewhere for change of air.'

'This is, I confess, somewhat strange philosophy.'

'To be sure it is, my boy; for it is of pure native manufacture. Every other people I ever heard of deduce their happiness from their advantages and prosperity. As we have very little of one or the other, we extract some fun out of our misfortunes; and, what between laughing occasionally at ourselves, and sometimes at our neighbours, we push along through life right merrily after all. So now, then, to apply my theory: let us see what we can do to make the best of this disappointment. Shall I make love to Lady Asgill? Shall I quiz Sir Charles about the review? Or can you suggest anything in the way of a little extemporaneous devilry, to console us for our disappointment? But, come along, my boy, we'll take a canter; I want to show you Moddiridderoo. He improves every day in his training; but they tell me there is only one man can sit him across a country, a fellow I don't much fancy, by-the-bye; but the turf, like poverty, leads us to form somewhat strange acquaintances. Meanwhile, my boy, here come the nags; and now for the park till dinner.'

During our ride O'Grady informed me that the individual to whom he so slightly alluded was a Mr. Ulick Burke, a cousin of Miss Bellew. This individual, who by family and connections was a gentleman, had contrived by his life and habits to disqualify himself from any title to the appellation in a very considerable degree. Having squandered the entire of his patrimony on the turf, he had followed the apparently immutable law on such occasions, and ended by becoming a hawk, where he had begun as a pigeon. For many years past he had lived by the exercise of those most disreputable sources, his own wits. Present at every racecourse in the kingdom, and provided with that undercurrent of information obtainable from jockeys and stable-men, he understood all the intrigue, all the low cunning of the course: he knew when to back the favourite, when to give, when to take the odds; and, if upon any occasion he was seen to lay heavily against a well-known horse, the presumption became a strong one, that he was either 'wrong' or withdrawn. But his qualifications ended not here; for he was also that singular anomaly in our social condition—a gentleman-rider, ready upon any occasion to get into the saddle for any one that engaged his services; a flat race, or a steeplechase, all the same to him. His neck was his livelihood, and to support, he must risk it. A racing-jacket, a pair of leathers and tops, a heavy-handled whip, and a shot-belt, were his stock-in-trade, and he travelled through the world a species of sporting Dalgetty, minus the probity which made the latter firm to his engagements, so long as they lasted. At least, report denied the quality to Mr. Burke; and those who knew him well scrupled not to say that fifty pounds had exactly twice as many arguments in its favour as five-and-twenty.

So much then in brief concerning a character to whom I shall hereafter have occasion to recur; and now to my own narrative.

O'Grady's anticipations as to the Castle dinner were not in the least exaggerated; nothing could possibly be more stiff or tiresome; the entertainment being given as a kind of *ex officio* civility, to the commander-of-the-forces and his staff, the conversation was purely professional, and never ranged beyond the discussion of military topics, or such as bore in any way upon the army. Happily, however, its duration was short. We dined at six, and by half-past eight we found ourselves at the foot of the grand staircase of the theatre in Crow Street, with Mr. Jones in the full dignity of his managerial costume waiting to receive us.

'A little late, I fear, Mr. Jones,' said his grace with a courteous smile. 'What have we got?'

'Your Excellency selected the *Inconstant*, said the obsequious manager; while a lady of the party darted her eyes suddenly towards the duke, and with a tone of marked sarcastic import, exclaimed—

'How characteristic!'

'And the after-piece, what is it?' said the duchess, as she fussed her way upstairs.

'*Timour the Tartar*, your grace.'

The next moment the thundering applause of the audience informed us that their Excellencies had taken their places. Cheer after cheer resounded through the building, and the massive lustre itself shook under the deafening acclamations of the audience. The scene was truly a brilliant one. The boxes presented a perfect blaze of wealth and beauty; nearly every person in the pit was in full dress; to the very ceiling itself the house was crammed. The progress of the piece was interrupted, while the band struck up 'God Save the King,' and, as I looked upon the brilliant dress-circle, I could not but think that O'Grady had been guilty of some exaggeration when he said that Mrs. Rooney's ball was to monopolise that evening the youth and the beauty of the capital The National Anthem over, 'Patrick's Day' was called for loudly from every side, and the whole house beat time to the strains of their native melody, with an energy that showed it came as fully home to their hearts as the air that preceded it. For ten minutes at least the noise and uproar continued; and, although his grace bowed repeatedly, there seemed no prospect to an end of the tumult, when a voice from the gallery called out, 'Don't make a stranger of yourself, my lord; take a chair and sit down.' A roar of laughter, increased as the duke accepted the suggestion, shook the house; and poor Talbot, who all this time was kneeling beside Miss Walstein's chair, was permitted to continue his ardent tale of love, and take up the thread of his devotion where he had left it twenty minutes before.

While O'Grady, who sat in the back of the box, seemed absorbed in his chagrin and disappointment, I myself became interested in the play, which was admirably performed; and Lord Dudley, leaning affectedly against a pillar, with his back towards the stage, scanned the house with his vapid, unmeaning look, as though to say they were unworthy of such attention at his hands.

The comedy was at length over, and her grace, with the ladies of her suite, retired, leaving only the Asgills and some members of the household in the box with his Excellency. He apparently was much entertained by the performance, and seemed most resolutely bent on staying to the last. Before the first act, however, of the after-piece was over, many of the benches in the dress-circle became deserted, and the house altogether seemed considerably thinner.

'I say, O'Grady,' said he, 'what are these good people about? There seems to be a general move among them. Is there anything going on?'

'Yes, your grace,' said Phil, whose impatience now could scarcely be restrained, 'they are going to a great ball in Stephen's Green; the most splendid thing Dublin has witnessed these fifty years.'

'Ah, indeed! Where is it? Who gives it?' 'Mr. Rooney, sir, a very well-known attorney, and a great character in the town.'

'How good! And he does the thing well?' 'He flatters himself that he rivals your grace.' 'Better still! But who has he? What are his people?' 'Every one; there is nothing too high, nothing too handsome, nothing too distinguished for him. His house, like the Holyhead packet, is open to all comers, and the consequence is, his parties are by far the pleasantest thing going. One has such strange rencontres, sees such odd people, hears such droll things; for, besides having everything like a character in the city, the very gravest of Mr. Rooney's guests seems to feel his house as a place to relax and unbend in. Thus, I should not be the least surprised to see the Chief-Justice and the Attorney-General playing small plays, nor the Bishop of Cork dancing Sir Roger de Coverley.'

'Glorious fun, by Jove! But why are you not there, lads? Ah, I see; on duty. I wish you had told me. But come, it is not too late yet. Has Hinton got a card?'

'Yes, your grace.'

'Well, then, don't let me detain you any longer. I see you are both impatient; and 'faith, if I must confess it, I half envy you; and mind and give me a full report of the proceedings to-morrow morning.'

'How I wish your grace could only witness it yourself!'

'Eh? Is it so very good, then?'

'Nothing ever was like it; for, although the company is admirable, the host and hostess are matchless.'

'Egad! you've quite excited my curiosity. I say, O'Grady, would they know me, think ye? Have you no uncle or country cousin about my weight and build?'

'Ah, my lord, that is out of the question; you are too well known to assume an incognito. But still, if you wish to see it for a few minutes, nothing could be easier than just to walk through the rooms and come away. The crowd will be such, the thing is quite practicable, done in that way.'

'By Jove, I don't know; but if I thought— — To be sure, as you say, for five minutes or so one might get through. Come, here goes; order up the carriages. Now mind, O'Grady, I am under your management. Do the thing as quietly as you can.'

Elated at the success of his scheme, Phil scarcely waited for his grace to conclude, but sprang down the box-lobby to give the necessary orders, and was back again in an instant.

'Don't you think I had better take this star off?'

'Oh no, my lord, it will not be necessary. By timing the thing well, we'll contrive to get your grace into the midst of the crowd without attracting observation. Once there, the rest is easy enough.'

Many minutes had not elapsed ere we reached the corner of Grafton Street. Here we became entangled with the line of carriages, which extended more than half-way round Stephen's Green, and, late as was the hour, were still thronging and pressing onwards towards the scene of festivity. O'Grady, who contrived entirely to engross his grace's attention by many bits of the gossip and small-talk of the day, did not permit him to remark that the viceregal liveries and the guard of honour that accompanied us enabled us to cut the line of carriages, and taking precedence of all others, arrive at the door at once. Indeed, so occupied was the duke with some story at the moment, that he was half provoked as the door was flung open, and the clattering clash of the steps interrupted the conversation.

'Here we are, my lord,' said Phil.

'Well, get out, O'Grady. Lead on. Don't forget it is my first visit here; and you, I fancy, know the map of the country.'

The hall in which we found ourselves, brilliantly lighted and thronged with servants, presented a scene of the most strange confusion and tumult; for, such was the eagerness of the guests to get forward, many persons were separated from their friends: turbaned old ladies called in cracked voices for their sons to rescue them, and desolate daughters seized distractedly the arm nearest them, and implored succour with an accent as agonising as though on the eve of shipwreck. Mothers screamed, fathers swore, footmen laughed, and high above all came the measured tramp of the dancers overhead, while fiddles, French horns, and dulcimers scraped and blew their worst, as if purposely to increase the inextricable and maddening confusion that prevailed.

'Sir Peter and Lady Macfarlane!' screamed the servant at the top of the stairs.

'Counsellor and Mrs. Blake!'

'Captain O'Ryan of the Rifles!'

'Lord Dumboy———-'

'Dunboyne, you villain!'

'Ay, Lord Dunboyne and five ladies!'

Such were the announcements that preceded us as we wended our way slowly on, while I could distinguish Mr. Rooney's voice receiving and welcoming his guests, for which purpose he used a formula, in part derived from the practice of an auction-room.

'Walk in, ladies and gentlemen, walk in. Whist, tea, dancing, negus, and blind-hookey—delighted to see you—walk in'; and so, *da capo*, only varying the ritual when a lord or a baronet necessitated a change of title.

'You're quite right, O'Grady; I wouldn't have lost this for a great deal,' whispered the duke.

'Now, my lord, permit me,' said Phil. 'Hinton and I will engage Mr. Rooney in conversation, while your grace can pass on and mix with the crowd.'

'Walk in, walk in, ladies and — — Ah! how are you, Captain? This is kind of you — — Mr. Hinton, your humble servant — — Whist, dancing, blind-hookey, and negus — walk in — and, Captain Phil,' added he in a whisper, 'a bit of supper by-and-by below-stairs.'

'I must tell you an excellent thing, Rooney, before I forget it,' said O'Grady, turning the host's attention away from the door as he spoke, and inventing some imaginary secret for the occasion; while I followed his grace, who now was so inextricably jammed up in the dense mob that any recognition of him would have been very difficult, if not actually impossible.

For some time I could perceive that the duke's attention was devoted to the conversation about him. Some half-dozen ladies were carrying on a very active and almost acrimonious controversy on the subject of dress; not, however, with any artistic pretension of regulating costume or colour, not discussing the rejection of an old or the adoption of a new mode, but with a much more practical spirit of inquiry they were appraising and valuing each other's finery, in the most sincere and simple way imaginable.

'Seven-and-sixpence a yard, my dear; you 'll never get it less, I assure you.' 'That's elegant lace, Mrs. Mahony; was it run, ma'am?' Mrs. Mahony bridled at the suggestion, and replied that, though neither her lace nor her diamonds were Irish — — 'Six breadths, ma'am, always in the skirt,' said a fat, little, dumpy woman, holding up her satin petticoat in evidence.

'I say, Hinton,' whispered the duke, 'I hope they won't end by an examination of us. But what the deuce is going on here?'

This remark was caused by a very singular movement in the room. The crowd which had succeeded to the dancers, and filled the large drawing-room from end to end, now fell back to either wall, leaving a space of about a yard wide down the entire centre of the room, as though some performance was about to be enacted or some procession to march there.

'What can it be?' said the duke; 'some foolery of O'Grady's, depend upon it; for look at him up there talking to the band.'

As he spoke, the musicians struck up the grand march in *Blue Beard*, and Mrs. Paul Rooney appeared in the open space, in all the plenitude of her charms — a perfect blaze of rouge, red feathers, and rubies — marching in solemn state. She moved along in time to the music, followed by Paul, whose cunning eyes twinkled with more than a common shrewdness, as he peered here and there through the crowd. They came straight towards where we were standing; and while a whispered murmur ran through the room, the various persons around us drew back, leaving the duke and myself completely isolated. Before his grace could recover his concealment, Mrs. Rooney stood before him. The music suddenly ceased; while the lady, disposing her petticoats as though the object were to conceal all the company behind her, curtsied down to the very floor.

'Ah, your grace,' uttered in an accent of the most melting tenderness, were the only words she could speak, as she bestowed a look of still more speaking softness. 'Ah, did I ever hope to see the day when your Highness would honour— —'

'My dear madam,' said the duke, taking her hand with great courtesy, 'pray don't overwhelm me with obligations. A very natural, I hope a very pardonable desire, to witness hospitality I have heard so much of, has led me to intrude thus uninvited upon you. Will you allow me to make Mr. Rooney's acquaintance?'

Mrs. Rooney moved gracefully to one side, waving her hand with the air of a magician about to summons an attorney from the earth, when suddenly a change came over his grace's features; and, as he covered his mouth with his handkerchief, it was with the greatest difficulty he refrained from an open burst of laughter. The figure before him was certainly not calculated to suggest gravity.

Mr. Paul Rooney for the first time in his life found himself the host of a viceroy, and, amid the fumes of his wine and the excitement of the scene, entertained some very confused notion of certain ceremonies observable on such occasions. He had read of curious observances in the East, and strange forms of etiquette in China, and probably, had the Khan of Tartary dropped in on the evening in question, his memory would have supplied him with some hints for his reception; but, with the representative of Britannic Majesty, before whom he was so completely overpowered, he could not think of, nor decide upon anything. A very misty impression flitted through his mind, that people occasionally knelt before a Lord Lieutenant; but whether they did so at certain moments, or as a general practice, for the life of him he could not tell. While, therefore, the dread of omitting a customary etiquette weighed with him on the one hand, the fear of ridicule actuated him on the other; and thus he advanced into the presence with bent knees and a supplicating look eagerly turned towards the duke, ready at any moment to drop down or stand upright before him as the circumstances might warrant.

Mr. Paul Rooney's introduction to the Duke

Entering at once into the spirit of the scene, the duke bowed with the most formal courtesy, while he vouchsafed to Mr. Rooney some few expressions of compliment. At the same time, drawing Mrs. Rooney's arm within his own, he led her down the room, with a grace and dignity of manner no one was more master of than himself. As for Paul, apparently unable to stand upright under the increasing load of favours that fortune was showering upon his head, he looked over his shoulder at Mrs. Rooney, as she marched off in triumph, with the same exuberant triumph Young used to throw into Othello, as he passionately exclaims—

'Excellent wench I perdition catch my soul, but I do love thee!'

Not but that, at the very moment in question, the object of it was most ungratefully oblivious of Mr. Rooney and his affection.

Had Mrs. Paul Rooney been asked on the morning after her ball, what was her most accurate notion of Elysian bliss, she probably would have answered—leaning upon a viceroy's arm in her own ball-room, under the envious stare and jealous gaze of eight hundred assembled guests. Her flushed look, her flashing eye, the trembling hand with which she waved her fan, the proud imperious step, all spoke of triumph. In fact, such was the halo of reverence, such the reflected brightness the representative of monarchy then bore, she felt it a prouder honour to be thus escorted, than if the Emperor of all the Russias had deigned to grace her mansion with his presence. How she loved to run over every imaginable title she conceived applicable to his rank, 'Your Royal Highness,' 'Your Grace,' 'Your noble Lordship,' varying and combining them like a a child who runs his erring fingers over the keys of a pianoforte, and is delighted with the efforts of his skill.

While this kingly scene was thus enacting, the ballroom resumed its former life and vivacity. This indeed was owing to O'Grady. No sooner had his scheme succeeded of delivering up the duke into the hands of the Rooneys, than he set about restoring such a degree of turmoil, tumult, noise, and merriment, as, while it should amuse his grace, would rescue him from the annoyance of being stared at by many who never had walked the boards with a live viceroy.

'Isn't it gloriously done, Hinton?' he whispered in my ear as he passed. 'Now lend me your aid, my boy, to keep the whole thing moving. Get a partner as quick as you can, and let us try if we can't do the honours of the house, while the master and mistress are basking in the sunshine of royal favour.'

As he spoke, the band struck up 'Haste to the Wedding!' The dancers assumed their places—Phil himself flying hither and thither, arranging, directing, ordering, countermanding, providing partners for persons he had never seen before, and introducing individuals of whose very names he was ignorant.

'Push along, Hinton,' said he; 'only set them going. Speak to every one—half the men in the room answer to the name of "Bob," and all the young ladies are "Miss Magees." Then go it, my boy; this is a great night for Ireland!'

This happy land, indeed, which, like a vast powder-magazine, only wants but the smallest spark to ignite it, is always prepared for an explosion of fun. No sooner than did O'Grady, taking out the fattest woman in the room, proceed to lead her down the middle to the liveliest imaginable country-dance, than at once the contagious spirit flew through the room, and dancers pressed in from every side. Champagne served round in abundance, added to the excitement; and, as eight-and-thirty couple made the floor vibrate beneath them, such a scene of noise, laughter, uproar, and merriment ensued, as it were difficult to conceive or describe.

CHAPTER X
A FINALE TO AN EVENING

A ball, like a battle, has its critical moment: that one short and subtle point, on which its trembling fate would seem to hesitate, ere it incline to this side or that. In both, such is the time for generalship to display itself— and of this my friend O'Grady seemed well aware; for, calling up his reserve for an attack in force, he ordered strong negus for the band; and ere many minutes, the increased vigour of the instruments attested that the order had been attended to.

'Right and left!' 'Hands across!' 'Here we are!' 'This way, Peter!' 'Ah! Captain, you 're a droll crayture!' 'Move along, alderman!' 'That negus is mighty strong!' 'The Lord grant the house is——-'

Such and such like phrases broke around me, as, under the orders of the irresistible Phil, I shuffled down the middle with a dumpy little school-girl, with red hair and red shoes; which, added to her capering motion, gave her a most unhappy resemblance to a cork fairy.

'You are a trump, Jack,' said Phil. 'Never give in. I never was in such spirits in my life. Two bottles of champagne under my belt, and a cheque for three hundred Paul has just given me without a scrape of my pen; it might have been five if I had only had presence of mind.'

'Where is Miss Bellew all this time?' inquired I.

'I only saw her a moment; she looks saucy, and won't dance.'

My pride, somewhat stimulated by a fact which I could not help interpreting in Miss Bellew's favour, I went through the rooms in search of her, and at length discovered her in a boudoir, where a whist-party were assembled. She was sitting upon a sofa, beside a tall, venerable-looking old man, to whom she was listening with a semblance of the greatest attention as I entered. I had some time to observe her, and could not help feeling struck how much handsomer she was than I had formerly supposed. Her figure, slightly above the middle size, and most graceful in all its proportions, was, perhaps, a little too much disposed to embonpoint; the character of her features, however, seemed to suit, if not actually to require as much. Her eyes of deep blue, set well beneath her brow, had a look of intensity in them that evidenced thought; but the other features relieved by their graceful softness this strong expression, and a nose short and slightly, very slightly *retroussé*, with a mouth, the very perfection of eloquent and winning softness, made ample amends to those who prefer charms purely feminine to beauty of a severer character. Her hair, too, was of that deep auburn through which a golden light seems for ever playing; and this, contrary to the taste of the day, she wore simply braided upon her temple and cheeks, marking the oval contour of her face, and displaying, by this graceful coquetry, the perfect chiselling of her features. Let me add to this, that her voice was low and soft in all its tones; and, if the provincialism with which she spoke did at first offend my ear, I learned afterwards to think that the breathing intonations of the west lent a charm of their own to all she said, deepening the pathos of a simple story, or heightening the drollery of a merry one. Yes, laugh if you will, ye high-bred and high-born denizens of a richer sphere, whose ears, attuned to the rhythm of Metastasio, softly borne on the strains of Donizetti, can scarce pardon the intrusion of your native tongue in the everyday concerns of life—smile if it so please ye; but from the lips of a lovely woman, a little, *a very little* of the brogue is most seductive. Whether the subject be grave or gay, whether mirth or melancholy be the mood, like the varnish upon a picture, it brings out all the colour into strong effect, brightening the lights, and deepening the shadows; and then, somehow, there is an air of *naïveté*, a tone of simplicity about it, that appeals equally to your heart as your hearing.

Seeing that the conversation in which she was engaged seemed to engross her entire attention, I was about to retire without addressing her, when suddenly she turned round and her eyes met mine. I accordingly came forward, and, after a few of the commonplace civilities of the moment, asked her to dance.

'Pray, excuse me, Mr. Hinton; I have declined already several times. I have been fortunate enough to meet with a very old and dear friend of my father——'

'Who is much too attached to his daughter to permit her to waste an entire evening upon him. No, sir, if you will allow me, I will resign Miss Bellew to your care.'

She said something in a low voice, to which he muttered in reply. The only words which I could catch—'No, no; very different, indeed; this is a most proper person'—seemed, as they were accompanied by a smile of much kindness, in some way to concern me; and the next moment Miss Bellew took my arm and accompanied me to the ball-room.

As I passed the sofa where the duke and Mrs. Rooney were still seated, his grace nodded familiarly to me, with a gesture of approval; while Mrs. Paul clasped both her hands before her with a movement of ecstasy, and seemed about to bestow upon us a maternal blessing. Fearful of incurring a scene, Miss Bellew hastened on, and, as her arm trembled within mine, I could perceive how deeply the ridicule of her friend's position wounded her own pride.

Meanwhile, I could just catch the tones of Mrs. Rooney's voice, explaining to the duke Miss Bellow's pedigree. 'One of the oldest families of the land, your grace; came over with Romulus and Remus; and, if it were not for Oliver Cromwell and the Danes— —' The confounded fiddles lost the rest, and I was left in the dark, to guess what these strange allies had inflicted upon the Bellew family.

The dancing now began, and only between the intervals of the cotillon had I an opportunity of conversing with my partner. Few and brief as these occasions were, I was delighted to find in her a tone and manner quite different from anything I had ever met before. Although having seen scarcely anything of the world, her knowledge of character seemed an instinct, and her quick appreciation of the ludicrous features of many of the company was accompanied by a naïve expression, and at the same time a witty terseness of phrase, that showed me how much real intelligence lay beneath that laughing look. Unlike my fair cousin, Lady Julia, her raillery never wounded: hers were the fanciful combinations which a vivid and sparkling imagination conjures up, but never the barbed and bitter arrows of sarcasm. Catching up in a second any passing absurdity, she could laugh at the scene, yet seem to spare the actor. Julia, on the contrary, with what the French call *l'esprit moqueur*, never felt that her wit had hit its mark till she saw her victim writhing and quivering beneath her.

There is always something in being the partner of the belle of a ball-room. The little bit of envy and jealousy, whose limit is to be the duration of a waltz or quadrille, has somehow its feeling of pleasure. There is the reflective flattery in the thought of a fancied preference, that raises one in his own esteem; and, as the muttered compliments and half-spoken praises of the bystanders fall upon your ears, you seem to feel that you are a kind of shareholder in the company, and ought to retire from business with your portion of the profits. Such, I know, were some of my feelings at the period in question; and, as I pulled up my stock and adjusted my sash, I looked upon the crowd about me with a sense of considerable self-satisfaction, and began really for the first time to enjoy myself.

Scarcely was the dance concluded, when a general movement was perceptible towards the door, and the word 'supper,' repeated from voice to voice, announced that the merriest hour in Irish life had sounded. Delighted to have Miss Bellew for my companion, I edged my way into the mass, and was borne along on the current.

The view from the top of the staircase was sufficiently amusing: a waving mass of feathers of every shape and hue, a crowd of spangled turbans, bald and powdered heads, seemed wedged inextricably together, swaying backwards and forwards with one impulse, as the crowd at the door of the supper-room advanced or receded. The crash of plates and knives, the jingling of glasses, the popping of champagne corks, told that the attack had begun, had not even the eager faces of those nearer the door indicated as much. *Nulli oculi retrorsum,* seemed the motto of the day, save when some anxious mother would turn a backward and uneasy glance towards the staircase, where her daughter, preferring a lieutenant to a lobster, was listening with elated look to his tale of love and glory. 'Eliza, my dear, sit next me.'—'Anna, my love, come down here.' These brief commands, significantly as they were uttered, would be lost to those for whom intended, and only served to amuse the bystanders, and awaken them to a quicker perception of the passing flirtation. Some philosopher has gravely remarked, that the critical moments of our life are the transitions from one stage or state of our existence to another; and that our fate for the future depends in a great measure upon those hours in which we emerge from infancy to boyhood, from boyhood to manhood, from manhood to maturer years. Perhaps the arguments of time might be applied to place, and we might thus be enabled to show how a staircase is the most dangerous portion of a building. I speak not here of the insecurity of the architecture, nor, indeed, of any staircase whose well-tempered light shines down at noonday through the perfumed foliage of a conservatory; but of the same place, a blaze of lamplight, about two in the morning, crowded, crammed, and creaking by an anxious and elated throng pressing towards a supper-room. Whether it is the supper or the squeeze, the odour of balmy lips, or the savoury smell of roast ducks—whether it be the approach to silk tresses, or *sillery mousseux*—whatever the provocation, I cannot explain it; but the fact remains: one is tremendously given in such a place, at such a time, to the most barefaced and palpable flirtation. So strongly do I feel on this point, that, were I a lawgiver, I would never award damages for a breach of contract, where the promise was made on a staircase.

As for me, my acquaintance with Miss Bellew was not of more than an hour's standing. During that time we had contrived to discuss the ball-room, its guests, its lights, its decorations, the music, the dancers—in a word, all the commonplaces of an evening party; thence we wandered on to Dublin, society in general, to Ireland, and Irish habits, and Irish tastes; quizzed each other a little about our respective peculiarities, and had just begun to discuss the distinctive features which characterise the softer emotions in the two nations, when the announcement of supper brought us on the staircase. À propos, or *mal à propos'*, this turn of our conversation, let the reader decide by what I have already stated; so it was, however, and in a little nook of the landing I found myself with my fair companion's arm pressed closely to my side, engaged in a warm controversy on the trite subject of English coldness of manner. Advocating my country, I deemed that no more fitting defence could be entered, than by evidencing in myself the utter absence of the frigidity imputed. Champagne did something for me; Louisa's bright eyes assisted; but the staircase, the confounded staircase, crowned all. In fact, the undisguised openness of Miss Bellew's manner, the fearless simplicity with which she had ventured upon topics a hardened coquette would not dare to touch upon, led me into the common error of imputing to flirtation what was only due to the untarnished freshness of happy girlhood.

Finding my advances well received, I began to feel not a little proud of my success, and disposed to plume myself upon the charm of my eloquence, when, as I concluded a high-flown and inflated phrase of sentimental absurdity, she suddenly turned round, fixed her bright eyes upon me, and burst out into a fit of laughter.

'There, there! pray don't try that! No one but an Irishman ever succeeds in blarney. It is our national dish, and can never be seasoned by a stranger.'

This pull-up, for such it most effectually was, completely unmanned me. I tried to stammer out an explanation, endeavoured to laugh, coughed, blundered, and broke down; while, merciless in her triumph, she only laughed the more, and seemed to enjoy my confusion.

With such a failure hanging over me, I felt happy when we reached the supper-room; and the crash, din, and confusion about us once more broke in upon our conversation. It requires far less nerve for the dismounted jockey, whose gay jacket has been rolled in the mud of a racecourse, resuming his saddle, to ride in amid the jeers and scoffs of ten thousand spectators, than for the gallant who has blundered in the full tide of a flirtation, to recover his lost position, and sustain the current of his courtship. The sarcasm of our sex is severe enough, Heaven knows; but no raillery, no ridicule, cuts half so sharp or half so deep as the bright twinkle of a pretty girl's eye, when, detecting some exhibition of dramatised passion, some false glitter of pinchbeck sentiment, she exchanges her look of gratified attention for the merry mockery of a hearty laugh. No tact, no *savoir faire*, no knowledge of the world, no old soldierism that ever I heard of, was proof against this. To go back is bad; to stand still, worse; to go on, impossible.

The best—for I believe it is the only thing to do—is to turn approver on your own misdeeds, and join in the laughter against yourself. Now this requires no common self-mastery, and an *aplomb* few young gentlemen under twenty possess—hence both my failure and its punishment.

That staircase which, but a moment before, I wished might be as long as a journey to Jerusalem, I now escaped from with thankfulness. Concealing my discomfiture as well as I was able, I bustled about, and finally secured a place for my companion at one of the side-tables. We were too far from the head of the table, but the clear ringing of his grace's laughter informed me of his vicinity; and, as I saw Miss Bellew shrank from approaching that part of the room, I surrendered my curiosity to the far more grateful task of cultivating her acquaintance.

All the ardour of my attentions—and I had resumed them with nearly as much warmth, although less risk of discomfiture, for I began to feel what before I had only professed—all the preoccupation of my mind, could not prevent my hearing high above the crash and clatter of the tables the rich roundness of Mrs. Rooney's brogue, as she recounted to the duke some interesting trait of the O'Toole family, or adverted to some classical era in Irish history, when, possibly, Mecænas was mayor of Cork, or Diogenes an alderman of Skinner's Alley.

'Ah, my dear!—the Lord forgive me! I mean your grace.'

'I shall never forgive you, Mrs. Rooney, if you change the epithet.'

'Ah, your grace's worship, them was fine times; and the husband of an O'Toole, in them days, spent more of his time harrying the country with his troops at his back, than driving about in an old gig full of writs and latitats, with a process-server behind him.'

Had Mr. Rooney, who at that moment was carving a hare in total ignorance of his wife's sarcasm, only heard the speech, the chances are ten to one he would have figured in a steel breastplate and an iron head-piece before the week was over. I was unable to hear more of the conversation, notwithstanding my great wish to do so, as a movement of those next the door implied that a large instalment of the guests who had not supped would wait no longer, but were about to make what Mr. Rooney called a forcible entry on a summary process, and eject the tenant in possession.

The Finale to an Evening.

We accordingly rose, and all (save the party around the viceroy) along with us, once more to visit the ball-room, where already dancing had begun. While I was eagerly endeavouring to persuade Miss Bellew that there was no cause or just impediment to prevent her dancing the next set with me, Lord Dudley de Vere lounged affectedly forward, and mumbled out some broken indistinct phrases, in which the word da-ance was alone audible. Miss Bellew coloured slightly, turned her eyes towards me, curtsied, took his arm, and the next moment was lost amid the crowd.

I am not aware of any readier method of forming a notion of perpetual motion than watching the performance of Sir Roger de Coverley at an evening party in Dublin. It seems to be a point of honour never to give in; and thus the same complicated figures, the same mystic movements that you see in the beginning, continue to succeed each other in a never-ending series. You endeavour in vain to detect the plan, to unravel the tangled web of this strange ceremony; but somehow it would seem as if the whole thing was completely discretionary with the dancers, there being only one point of agreement among them, which is, whenever blown out of breath, to join in a vigorous hands-round; and, the motion being confined to a shuffling of the feet, and a shaking of the elbows, little fatigue is incurred. To this succeeds a capering forward movement of a gentleman, which seemingly magnetises an opposite lady to a similar exhibition; then, after seizing each other rapturously by the hands, they separate to run the gauntlet in and out down the whole line of dancers, to meet at the bottom, when, apparently reconciled, they once more embrace. What follows, the devil himself may tell. As for me, I heard only laughing, tittering, now and then a slight scream, and a cry of 'Behave, Mr. Murphy!' etc.; but the movements themselves were conic sections to me, and I closed my eyes as I sat alone in my corner, and courted sleep as a short oblivion to the scene. Unfortunately I succeeded; for, wild and singular as the gestures, the looks, and the voices were before, they now became to my dreaming senses something too terrible. I thought myself in the centre of some hobgoblin orgie, where demons, male and female, were performing their fantastic antics around me, grinning hideously, and uttering cries of menacing import. Tarn O'Shanter's vision was a respectable tea-party of Glasgow matrons compared to my imaginings; for so distorted were the pictures of my brain, that the leader of the band, a peaceable-looking old man in shorts and spectacles, seemed to me like a grim-visaged imp, who flourished his tail across the strings of his instrument in lieu of a bow.

I must confess that the dancers, without any wish on my part to detract from their efforts, had not the entire merit of this transmutation. Fatigue, for the hour was late, chagrin at being robbed of my partner, added to the heat and the crowd, had all their share in the mystification. Besides, if I must confess it, Mr. Rooney's champagne was strong. My friend O'Grady, however, seemed but little of my opinion; for, like the master-spirit of the scene, he seemed to direct every movement and dictate every change—no touch of fatigue, no semblance of exhaustion about him. On the contrary, as the hour grew later, and the pale grey of morning began to mingle with the glare of wax-lights, the vigour of his performance only increased, and several new steps were displayed, which, like a prudent general, he seemed to have kept in reserve for the end of the engagement. And what a sad thing is a ball as it draws towards the close! What an emblem of life at a similar period!

How much freshness has faded! how much of beauty has passed away! how many illusions are dissipated! how many dreams the lamplight and chalk floors have called into life fly like spirits with the first beam of sunlight! The eye of proud bearing is humbled now; the cheek, whose downy softness no painter could have copied, looks pale, and wan, and haggard; the beaming looks, the graceful bearing, the elastic step, where are they? Only to be found where youth—bright, joyous, and elastic youth—unites itself to beauty.

Such were my thoughts as the dancers flew past, and many whom I had remarked at the beginning of the evening as handsome and attractive, seemed now without a trace of either—when suddenly Louisa Bellew came by, her step as light, her every gesture as graceful, her cheek as blooming, and her liquid eye as deeply beaming as when first I saw her. The excitement of the dance had slightly flushed her face, and heightened the expression its ever-varying emotions lent it.

Handsome as I before had thought her, there was a look of pride about her now that made her lovely to my eyes. As I continued to gaze after her, I did not perceive for some time that the guests were rapidly taking their leave, and already the rooms were greatly thinned. Every moment now, however, bore evidence of the fact: the unceasing roll of carriages to the door, the clank of the steps, the reiterated cry to drive on, followed by the call for the next carriage, all betokened departure. Now and then, too, some cloaked and hooded figure would appear at the door of the drawing-room, peering anxiously about for a daughter, a sister, or a friend who still lingered in the dance, averring it 'was impossible to go, that she was engaged for another set.' The disconsolate gestures, the impatient menaces of the shawled spectres—for, in truth, they seemed like creatures of another world come back to look upon the life they left—are of no avail: the seductions of the 'major' are stronger than the frowns of mamma, and though a rowing may come in the morning, she is resolved to have a reel at night.

An increased noise and tumult below-stairs at the same moment informed me that the supper-party were at length about to separate. I started up at once, wishing to see Miss Bellew again ere I took my leave, when O'Grady seized me by the arm and hurried me away.

'Come along, Hinton! Not a moment to lose; the duke is going.'

'Wait an instant,' said I, 'I wish to speak to——'

'Another time, my dear fellow; another time. The duke is delighted with the Rooneys, and we are going to have Paul knighted!'

With these words he dragged me along, dashing down the stairs like a madman. As we reached the door of the dining-room we found his grace, who, with one hand on Lord Dudley's shoulder, was endeavouring to steady himself by the other.

'I say, O'Grady, is that you? Very powerful Burgundy this—— It's not possible it can be morning!'

'Yes, your grace—half-past seven o'clock.'

'Indeed, upon my word, your friends are very charming people. What did you say about knighting some one? Oh, I remember: Mr. Rooney, wasn't it? Of course, nothing could be better!'

'Come, Hinton, have you got a sword?' said O'Grady; 'I've mislaid mine somehow. There, that'll do. Let us try and find Paul now.'

Into the supper-room we rushed; but what a change was there! The brilliant tables, resplendent with gold plate, candelabras, and flowers, were now despoiled and dismantled. On the floor, among broken glasses, cracked decanters, pyramids of jelly, and pagodas of blancmange, lay scattered in every attitude the sleeping figures of the late guests. Mrs. Rooney alone maintained her position, seated in a large chair, her eyes closed, a smile of Elysian happiness playing upon her lips. Her right arm hung gracefully over the side of the chair, where lately his grace had kissed her hand at parting. Overcome, in all probability, by the more than human happiness of such a moment, she had sunk into slumber, and was murmuring in her dreams such short and broken phrases as the following:—'Ah, happy day!—What will Mrs. Tait say?—The lord mayor, indeed!—Oh, my poor head! I hope it won't be turned.—Holy Agatha, pray for us! your grace, pray for us I—Isn't he a beautiful man? Hasn't he the darling white teeth?'

The Finale to an Evening

'Where's Paul?' said O'Grady; 'where's Paul, Mrs. Rooney?' as he jogged her rather rudely by the arm.

'Ah, who cares for Paul?' said she, still sleeping; 'don't be bothering me about the like of him.'

'Egad! this is conjugal, at any rate,' said Phil

'I have him!' cried I; 'here he is!' as I stumbled over a short, thick figure, who was propped up in a corner of the room. There he sat, his head sunk upon his bosom, his hands listlessly resting on the floor. A large jug stood beside him, in the concoction of whose contents he appeared to have spent the last moments of his waking state. We shook him, and called him by his name, but to no purpose; and, as we lifted up his head, we burst out a-laughing at the droll expression of his face; for he had fallen asleep in the act of squeezing a lemon in his teeth, the half of which not only remained there still, but imparted to his features the twisted and contorted expression that act suggests.

'Are you coming, O'Grady?' now cried the duke impatiently.

'Yes, my lord,' cried Phil, as he rushed towards the door. 'This is too bad, Hinton: that confounded fellow could not possibly be moved. I'll try and carry him.' As he spoke, he hurried back towards the sleeping figure of Mr. Rooney, while I made towards the duke.

As Lord Dudley had gone to order up the carriages, his grace was standing alone at the foot of the stairs, leaning his back against the banisters, his eyes opening and shutting alternately as his head nodded every now and then forward, overcome by sleep and the wine he had drunk. Exactly in front of him, but crouching in the attitude of an Indian monster, sat Corny Delany. To keep himself from the cold, he had wrapped himself up in his master's cloak, and the only part of his face perceptible was the little wrinkled forehead, and the malicious-looking fiery eyes beneath it, firmly fixed on the duke's countenance.

'Give me your sword,' said his grace, turning to me, in a tone half sleeping, half commanding; 'give me your sword, sir!'

Drawing it from the scabbard, I presented it respectfully.

'Stand a little on one side, Hinton. Where is he? Ah! quite right. Kneel down, sir; kneel down, I say!' These words, addressed to Corny, produced no other movement in him than a slight change in his attitude, to enable him to extend his expanded hand above his eyes, and take a clearer view of the duke.

'Does he hear me, Hinton? Do you hear me, sir?'

'Do you hear his grace?' said I, endeavouring with a sharp kick of my foot to assist his perceptions.

'To be sure I hear him,' said Corny; 'why wouldn't I hear him?'

'Kneel down, then,' said I.

'Devil a bit of me'll kneel down. Don't I know what he's after well enough? *Ach na bocklish!* Sorrow else he ever does nor make fun of people.'

'Kneel down, sir!' said his grace, in an accent there was no refusing to obey. 'What is your name?'

'Oh, murther! Oh, heavenly Joseph!' cried Corny, as I hurled him down upon his knees, 'that I 'd ever live to see the day!'

'What is his d——d name?' said the duke passionately.

'Corny, your grace—Corny Delany.'

'There, that'll do,' as with a hearty slap of the sword, not on his shoulder, but on his bullet head, he cried out, 'Rise, Sir Corny Delany!'

'Och, the devil a one of me will ever get up out of this same spot. Oh, wirra, wirra! how will I ever show myself again after this disgrace?'

The Duke Knighting Corny Delany

Leaving Corny to his lamentations, the duke walked towards the door. Here above a hundred people were now assembled, their curiosity excited in no small degree by a picket of light dragoons, who occupied the middle of the street, and were lying upon the ground, or leaning on their saddles, in all the wearied attitudes of a night-watch. In fact, the duke had forgotten to dismiss his guard of honour, who had accompanied him to the theatre, and thus had spent the dark hours of the night keeping watch and ward over the proud dwelling of the Rooneys. A dark frown settled on the duke's features as he perceived the mistake, and muttered between his teeth, 'How they will talk of this in England!' The next moment, bursting into a hearty fit of laughter, he stepped into the carriage, and amid a loud cheer from the mob, by whom he was recognised, drove rapidly away.

Seated beside his grace, I saw nothing more of O'Grady, whose efforts to ennoble the worthy attorney only exposed him to the risk of a black eye; for no sooner did Paul perceive that he was undergoing rough treatment than he immediately resisted, and gave open battle.

O'Grady accordingly left him, to seek his home on foot, followed by Corny, whose cries and heart-rending exclamations induced a considerable crowd of well-disposed citizens to accompany them to the Castle gate. And thus ended the great Rooney ball.

CHAPTER XI
A NEGOTIATION

From what I have already stated, it may be inferred that my acquaintance with the Rooneys was begun under favourable auspices. Indeed, from the evening of the ball the house was open to me at all hours; and, as the hour of luncheon was known to every lounger about town, by dropping in about three o'clock one was sure to hear all the chit-chat and gossip of the day. All the dinners and duels of the capital, all its rows and runaway matches, were there discussed, while future parties of pleasure were planned and decided on, the Rooney equipages, horses, servants, and cellar being looked upon as common property, the appropriation of which was to be determined on by a vote of the majority.

At all these domestic parliaments O'Grady played a prominent part. He was the speaker and the whipper-in; he led for both the government and the opposition; in fact, since the ever-memorable visit of the viceroy his power in the house was absolute. How completely they obeyed, and how implicitly they followed him, may be guessed, when I say that he even persuaded Mrs. Rooney herself not only to abstain from all triumph on the subject of their illustrious guest, but actually to maintain a kind of diplomatic silence on the subject; so that many simple-minded people began to suspect his grace had never been there at all, and that poor Mrs. Rooney, having detected the imposition, prudently held her tongue and said nothing about the matter. As this influence might strike my reader as somewhat difficult in its exercise, and also as it presents a fair specimen of my friend's ingenuity, I cannot forbear mentioning the secret of its success.

When the duke awoke late in the afternoon that followed Mrs. Rooney's ball, his first impression was one bordering on irritation with O'Grady. His quick-sightedness enabled him at once to see how completely he had fallen into the trap of his worthy aide-de-camp; and although he had confessedly spent a very pleasant evening, and laughed a great deal, now that all was over, he would have preferred if the whole affair could be quietly consigned to oblivion, or only remembered as a good joke for after dinner. The scandal and the éclat it must cause in the capital annoyed him considerably; and he knew that before a day passed over, the incident of the guard of honour lying in bivouac around their horses would furnish matter for every caricature-shop in Dublin. Ordering O'Grady to his presence, and with a severity of manner in a great degree assumed, he directed him to remedy, as far as might be, the consequences of this blunder, and either contrive to give a totally different version of the occurrence, or else by originating some new subject of scandal to eclipse the memory of this unfortunate evening.

O'Grady promised and pledged himself to everything; vowed that he would give such a turn to the affair that nobody would ever believe a word of the story; assured the duke (God forgive him!) that however ridiculous the Rooneys at night, by day they were models of discretion; and at length took his leave to put his scheme into execution, heartily glad to discover that his grace had forgotten all about Corny and the knighthood, the recollection of which might have been attended with very grave results to himself.

So much for his interview with the duke. Now for his diplomacy with Mrs. Rooney!

It was about five o'clock on the following day when O'Grady cantered up to the door. Giving his horse to his groom, he dashed boldly upstairs, passed through the ante-chamber and the drawing-room, and tapping gently at the door of a little boudoir, opened it at the same moment and presented himself before Mrs. Paul.

That amiable lady, reclining *à la* Princess OToole, was gracefully disposed on a small sofa, regarding with fixed attention a little plaster bust of his grace, which, with considerable taste and propriety, was dressed in a blue coat and bright buttons, with a star on the breast, a bit of sky-blue satin representing the ribbon of the Bath. Nothing was forgotten; and a faint attempt was even made to represent the colouring of the viceregal nose, which I am bound to confess was not flattered in the model.

'Ah, Captain, is it you?' said Mrs. Paul, with a kind of languishing condescension very different from her ordinary reception of a Castle aide-de-camp. 'How is his grace this evening?'

Drawing his chair beside her, Phil proceeded to reply to her questions and assure her that whatever her admiration for the duke, the feeling was perfectly mutual. 'Egad,' said he, 'the thing may turn out very ill for me when the duchess finds out that it was all my doing. Speaking in confidence to you, my dear Mrs. Paul, I may confess that although without exception she is the most kind, amiable, excellent soul breathing, yet she has one fault. We all have our faults.'

'Ah!' sighed Mrs. Rooney, as she threw down her eyes as though to say, 'That's very true, but you will not catch me telling what mine is.'

'As I was observing, there never was a more estimable being save in this one respect— — You guess it? I see you do.'

'Ah, the creature, she drinks!'

The captain found it not a little difficult to repress a burst of laughter at Mrs. Rooney's suggestion. He did so, however, and proceeded: 'No, my dear madam, you mistake. Jealousy is her failing; and when I tell you this, and when I add, that unhappily for her the events of last night may only afford but too much cause, you will comprehend the embarrassment of my present position.'

Having said this, he walked up and down the room for several minutes as if sunk in meditation, while he left Mrs. Rooney to ruminate over an announcement, the bare possibility of which was ecstasy itself. To be the rival of a peeress; that peeress a duchess; that duchess the lady of the viceroy! These were high thoughts indeed. What would Mrs. Riley say now? How would the Maloneys look? Wouldn't Father Glynn be proud to meet her at the door of Liffey Street Chapel in full pontificals as she drove up, who knows but with a guard of honour beside her? Running on in this way, she had actually got so far as to be discussing with herself what was to be done with Paul—not that her allegiance was shaken towards that excellent individual—not a single unworthy thought crossed her mind—far from it. Poor Mrs. Rooney was purity herself; she merely dreamed of those outward manifestations of the viceroy's preference, which were to procure for her consideration in the world, a position in society, and those attentions from the hands of the great and the titled, which she esteemed at higher price than the real gifts of health, wealth, and beauty, so bounteously bestowed upon her by Providence.

She had come then to that difficult point in her mind as to what was to be done with Paul; what peculiar course of training could he be submitted to, to make him more presentable in the world; how were they to break him off whisky-and-water and small jokes? Ah,' she was thinking, 'it's very hard to make a real gentleman out of such materials as grog and drab gaiters,' when suddenly O'Grady, wiping his forehead with his handkerchief, and then flourishing it theatrically in the air, exclaimed—

'Yes, Mrs. Rooney, everything depends on you. His grace's visit—I have just been with him talking the whole thing over—must be kept a profound secret. If it ever reach the ears of the duchess we are ruined and undone.'

Here was a total overthrow to all Mrs. Paul's speculations; here was a beautiful castle uprooted from its very foundation. All her triumph, all her vaunted superiority over her city acquaintances was vanishing like a mirage before her! What was the use of his coming after all? What was the good of it, if not to be spoken of, if not talked over at tea, written of in notes, discussed at dinner, and displayed in the morning papers? Already was her brow contracted, and a slight flush of her cheek showed the wily captain that resistance was in preparation.

'I know, my dear Mrs. Paul, how gratifying it would be for even the highest of the land to speak of his grace's condescension in such terms as you might speak; but then, after all, how very fleeting such a triumph! Many would shrug their shoulders, and not believe the story. Some of those who believed would endeavour to account for it as a joke: one of those odd wild fancies the duke is ever so fond of'—here she reddened deeply. 'In fact, the malevolence and the envy of the world will give a thousand turns to the circumstance. Besides that, after all, they would seem to have some reason on their side; for the publicity of the affair must for ever prevent a repetition of the visit; whereas, on the other side, by a little discretion, by guarding our own secret'—here Phil looked knowingly in her eyes, as though to say they had one—'not only will the duke be delighted to continue his intimacy, but from the absence of all mention of the matter, all display on the subject, the world will be ten times more disposed to give credence to the fact than if it were paragraphed in every newspaper in the kingdom.'

This was hitting the nail on the head with a vengeance. Here was a picture, here a vision of happiness! Only to think of the duke dropping in, as a body might say, to take his bit of dinner, or his dish of tea in the evening, just in a quiet, homely, family way! She thought she saw him sitting with his feet on the fender, talking about the king and the queen, and the rest of the royal family, just as he would of herself and Paul; and her eyes involuntarily turned towards the little bust, and two round full tears of pure joy trickled slowly down her cheeks.

Yielding at length to these and similar arguments, Mrs. Rooney gave in her adhesion, and a treaty was arranged and agreed upon between the high contracting parties, which ran somewhat to this effect:—

In the first place, for the enjoyment of certain advantages to be hereafter more fully set forth, the lady was bound to maintain in all large companies, balls, dinners, drums, and déjeuners, a rigid silence regarding the duke's visit to her house, never speaking of, nor alluding to it, in any manner whatever, and, in fact, conducting herself in all respects as if such a thing had never taken place.

Secondly, she was forbidden from making any direct inquiries in public respecting the health of the duke or the duchess, or exercising any overt act of personal interest in these exalted individuals.

Thirdly, so long as Mrs. Rooney strictly maintained the terms of the covenant, nothing in the foregoing was to preclude her from certain other privileges—namely, blushing deeply when the duke's name was mentioned, throwing down her eyes, gently clasping her hands, and even occasionally proceeding to a sigh; neither was she interdicted from regarding any portion of her domicile as particularly sacred in consequence of its viceregal associations. A certain arm-chair might be selected for peculiar honours, and preserved inviolate, etc.

And lastly, nevertheless, notwithstanding that in all large assemblies Mrs. Rooney was to conduct herself with the reserve and restrictions aforesaid, yet in small *réunions de famille*—this O'Grady purposely inserted in French, for, as Mrs. Paul could not confess her ignorance of that language, the interpretation must rest with himself—she was to enjoy a perfect liberty of detailing his grace's advent, entering into all its details, discussing, explaining, expatiating, inquiring with a most minute particularity concerning his health and habits, and, in a word, conducting herself in all respects, to use her own expressive phrase, 'as if they were thick since they were babies.'

Armed with this precious document, formally signed and sealed by both parties, O'Grady took his leave of Mrs. Rooney—not, indeed, in his usual free-and-easy manner, but with the respectful and decorous reserve of one addressing a favourite near the throne. Nothing could be more perfect than Phil's profound obeisance, except perhaps the queenly demeanour of Mrs. Rooney herself; for, with the ready tact of a woman, she caught up in a moment the altered phase of her position, and in the reflective light of O'Grady's manner she learned to appreciate her own brilliancy.

'From this day forward,' muttered O'Grady, as he closed the door behind him and hurried downstairs—'from this day forward she 'll be greater than ever. Heaven help the lady mayoress that ventures to shake hands with her, and the attorney's wife will be a bold woman that asks her to a tea-party henceforth!'

With these words he threw himself upon his horse and cantered off towards the park to inform the duke that all was happily concluded, and amuse him with a sight of the great Rooney treaty, which he well knew would throw the viceroy into convulsions of laughter.

CHAPTER XII
A WAGER

In a few weeks after the events I have mentioned, the duke left Ireland to resume his parliamentary duties in the House of Lords, where some measure of considerable importance was at that time under discussion. Into the hands of the lords justices, therefore, the government *ad interim* was delivered; while upon Mrs. Paul Rooney devolved the more pleasing task of becoming the leader of fashion, the head and fountain of all the gaieties and amusements of the capital. Indeed, O'Grady half hinted that his grace relied upon her to supply his loss, which manifestation of his esteem, so perfectly in accordance with her own wishes, she did not long hesitate to profit by.

Had a stranger, on his first arrival in Dublin, passed along that part of Stephen's Green in which the 'Hotel Rooney,' as it was familiarly called, was situated, he could not have avoided being struck, not only with the appearance of the house itself, but with that of the strange and incongruous assembly of all ranks and conditions of men that lounged about its door. The house, large and spacious, with its windows of plate-glass, its Venetian blinds, its gaudily gilt and painted balcony, and its massive brass knocker, betrayed a certain air of pretension, standing as it did among the more sombre-looking mansions where the real rank of the country resided. Clean windows and a bright knocker, however—distinctive features as they were in the metropolis of those days—would not have arrested the attention of the passing traveller to the extent I have supposed, but that there were other signs and sights than these.

At the open hall door, to which you ascended by a flight of granite steps, lounged some half-dozen servants in powdered heads and gaudy liveries—the venerable porter in his leather chair, the ruddy coachman in his full-bottomed wig, tall footmen with bouquets in their button-holes, were here to be seen reading the morning papers, or leisurely strolling to the steps to take a look at the weather, and cast a supercilious glance at the insignificant tide of population that flowed on beneath them; a lazy and an idle race, they toiled not, neither did they spin, and I sincerely trust that Solomon's costume bore no resemblance to theirs.

More immediately in front of the house stood a mixed society of idlers, beggars, horseboys, and grooms, assembled there from motives of curiosity or gain. Indeed, the rich odour of savoury viands that issued from the open kitchen windows and ascended through the area to the nostrils of those without, might in its appetising steam have brought the dew upon the lips of greater gourmands than they were. All that French cookery could suggest to impart variety to the separate meals of breakfast, luncheon, dinner, and supper, here went forward unceasingly; and the beggars who thronged around the bars, and were fed with the crumbs from the rich man's table, became by degrees so habituated to the delicacies and refinements of good living, that they would have turned up their noses with contempt at the humble and more homely fare of the respectable shopkeeper. Truly, it was a strange picture to see these poor and ragged men as they sat in groups upon the steps and on the bare flagway, exposed to every wind of heaven, the drifting rain soaking through their frail and threadbare garments, yet criticising, with practical acumen, the savoury food before them. Consommés, ragouts, pâtés, potages, jellies, with an infinity of that smaller grapeshot of epicurism with which fine tables are filled, all here met a fair and a candid appreciation.

A little farther off, and towards the middle of the street, stood another order of beings, who, with separate and peculiar privileges, maintained themselves as a class apart; these were the horseboys, half-naked urchins, whose ages varied from eight to fourteen, but whose looks of mingled cunning and drollery would defy any guess as to their time of life, who here sported in all the wild, untrammelled liberty of African savages. The only art they practised was to lead up and down the horses of the various visitors whom the many attractions of the Hotel Rooney brought daily to the house. And here you saw the proud and pampered steed, with fiery eye and swelling nostrils, led about by this ambulating mass of rags and poverty, whose bright eye wandered ever from his own tattered habiliments to the gorgeous trappings and gold embroidery of the sleek charger beside him. In the midst of these, such as were not yet employed, amused themselves by cutting summersets, standing on their heads, walking crab-fashion, and other classical performances, which form the little distractions of life for this strange sect.

Jaunting-cars there were too, whose numerous fastenings of rope and cordage looked as though they were taken to pieces every night and put together in the morning; while the horse, a care-worn and misanthropic-looking beast, would turn his head sideways over the shaft to give a glance of compassionating scorn at the follies and vanities of a world he was sick of. Not so the driver: equally low in condition, and fully as ragged in coat, the droll spirit that made his birthright was, with him, a lamp that neither poverty nor penury could quench. Ever ready with his joke, never backward with his repartee, prepared to comfort you by assurances of the strength of his car and the goodness of his horse, while his own laughing look gave the lie to his very words, he would persuade you that with him alone there was safety, while it was a risk of life and limb to travel with his rivals.

These formed the ordinary *dramatis persono*, while every now and then some flashy equipage, with armorial bearings and showy liveries, would scatter the crowd right and left, set the led horses lashing among the bystanders, and even break up the decorous conviviality of a dinner-party gracefully disposed upon the flags. Curricles, tandems, tilburies, and dennets were constantly arriving and departing. Members of Daly's with their green coats and buff waistcoats, whiskered dragoons and plumed aides-de-camp, were all mixed up together, while on the open balcony an indiscriminate herd of loungers telegraphed the conversation from the drawing-room to the street, and thus all the *bons mots*, all the jests, all the witticisms that went forward within doors, found also a laughing auditory without; for it is a remarkable feature of this singular country, that there is no turn of expression whose raillery is too delicate, no repartee whose keenness is too fine, for the appreciation of the poorest and meanest creature that walks the street. Poor Paddy, if the more substantial favours of fortune be not your lot, nature has linked you by a strong sympathy with tastes, habits, and usages which, by some singular intuition, you seem thoroughly to comprehend. One cannot dwell long among them without feeling this, and witnessing how generally, how almost universally, poverty of condition and wealth of intellect go hand in hand together; and, as it is only over the bleak and barren surface of some fern-clad heath the wildfire flashes through the gloom of night, so it would seem the more brilliant firework of fancy would need a soil of poverty and privation to produce it.

But, at length, to come back, the Rooneys now were installed as the great people of the capital. Many of the *ancien régime*, who held out sturdily before, and who looked upon the worthy attorney in the light of a usurper, now gave in their allegiance, and regarded him as the true monarch. What his great prototype effected by terror, he brought about by turtle; and, if Napoleon consolidated his empire and propped his throne by the bayonets of the grand army, so did Mr. Rooney establish his claims to power by the more satisfactory arguments which, appealing not only to the head, but to the stomach, convince while they conciliate. You might criticise his courtesy, but you could not condemn his claret. You might dislike his manners, but you could not deny yourself his mutton. Besides, after all, matters took pretty much the same turn in Paris as in Dublin; public opinion ran strong in both cases. The mass of the world consists of those who receive benefits, and he who confers them deserves to be respected. We certainly thought so; and among those of darker hue who frequented Mr. Rooney's table, three red-coats might daily be seen, whose unchanged places, added to their indescribable air of at-homeishness, bespoke them as the friends of the family.

O'Grady, at Mrs. Rooney's right hand, did the honours of the soup; Lord Dudley, at the other end of the table, supported Mr. Rooney, while to my lot Miss Bellew fell. But, as our places at table never changed, there was nothing marked in my thus every day finding myself beside her, and resuming my place on our return to the drawing-room. To me, I confess, she formed the great attraction of the house. Less imbued than my friend O'Grady with the spirit of fun, I could not have gone on from day to day to amuse myself with the eccentricities of the Rooneys, while I could not, on the other hand, have followed Lord Dudley's lead, and continued to receive the hospitalities of a house while I sneered at the pretensions of its owner.

Under any circumstances Louisa Bellew might be considered a very charming person; but, contrasted with those by whom she was surrounded, her attractions were very great. Indeed, her youth, her light-heartedness, and the buoyancy of her spirit, concealed to a great degree the sorrow it cost her to be associated with her present hosts; for, although they were kind to her, and she felt and acknowledged their kindness, yet the humiliating sense of a position which exposed her to the insolent familiarity of the idle, the dissipated, or the underbred visitors of the house, gradually impressed itself upon her manner, and tempered her mild and graceful nature with a certain air of hauteur and distance. A circumstance, slight in itself, but sufficiently indicative of this, took place some weeks after what I have mentioned.

Lord Dudley de Vere, who, from his rank and condition, was looked upon as a kind of privileged person in the Rooney family, sitting rather later than usual after dinner, and having drunk a great deal of wine, offered a wager that, on his appearance in the drawing-room, not only would he propose for, but be accepted by, any unmarried lady in the room. The puppyism and coxcombry of such a wager might have been pardoned, were it not that the character of the individual, when sober, was in perfect accordance with this drunken boast. The bet, which was for three hundred guineas, was at once taken up; and one of the party running hastily up to the drawing-room, obtained the names of the ladies there, which, being written on slips of paper, were thrown into a hat, thus leaving chance to decide upon whom the happy lot was to fall.

'Mark ye, Upton,' cried Lord Dudley, as he prepared to draw forth his prize—'mark ye, I didn't say I'd marry her.'

'No, no,' resounded from different parts of the room; 'we understand you perfectly.'

'My bet,' continued he, 'is this: I have booked it.' With these words he opened a small memorandum-book and read forth the following paragraph:—'Three hundred with Upton that I don't ask and be accepted by any girl in Paul's drawing-room this evening, after tea; the choice to be decided by lottery. Isn't that it?'

'Yes, yes, quite right, perfectly correct,' said several persons round the table. 'Come, my lord, here is the hat.'

'Shake them up well, Upton.'

'So here goes,' said Herbert, as affectedly tucking up the sleeve of his coat, he inserted two fingers and drew forth a small piece of paper carefully folded in two. 'I say, gentlemen, this is your affair; it doesn't concern me.' With these words he threw it carelessly on the table, and resuming his seat, leisurely filled his glass, and sipped his wine.

'Come, read it, Blake; read it up! Who is she?'

'Gently, lads, gently; patience for one moment. How are we to know if the wager be lost or won? Is the lady herself to declare it?'

'Why, if you like it; it is perfectly the same to me.'

'Well, then,' rejoined Blake, 'it is—Miss Bellew!'

No sooner was the name read aloud, than, instead of the roar of laughter which it was expected would follow the announcement, a kind of awkward and constrained silence settled on the party. Mr. Rooney himself, who felt shocked beyond measure at this result, had been so long habituated to regard himself as nothing at the head of his own table, accepting, not dictating, its laws, that, much as he may have wished to do so, did not dare to interfere to stay any further proceedings. But many of those around the table who knew Sir Simon Bellew, and felt how unsuitable and inadmissible such a jest as this would be, if practised upon *his* daughter, whispered among themselves a hope thai the wager would be abandoned, and never thought of more by either party.

'Yes, yes,' said Upton, who was an officer in a dragoon regiment, and although of a high family and well connected, was yet very limited in his means. 'Yes, yes, I quite agree. This foolery might be very good fun with some young ladies we know, but with Miss Bellew the circumstances are quite different; and, for *my* part, I withdraw from the bet.'

'Eh—aw! Pass down the claret, if you please. You withdraw from the bet, then? That means you may pay me three hundred guineas; for d—n me, if I do! No, no; I am not so young as that. I haven't lost fifteen thousand on the Derby without gaining some little insight into these matters. Every bet is a p. p., if not stated to be the reverse. I leave it to any gentleman in the room.'

'Come, come, De Vere,' said one, 'listen to reason, my boy!'

'Yes, Dudley,' cried another, 'only think over the thing. You must see—'

'I only wish to see a cheque for three hundred. And I 'll not be done,'

'Sir!' said Upton, springing from his chair, as the blood mounted to his face and temples, 'did you mean that expression to apply to me?'

'Sit down, Mr. Upton, for the love of Heaven! Sit down; do, sir; his lordship never meant it at all. See, now, I'll pay the money myself. Give me a pen and ink. I'll give you a cheque on the bank this minute. What the devil signifies a trifle like that!' stammered out poor Paul, as he wiped his forehead with his napkin, and looked the very picture of terror. 'Yes, my lord and gentlemen of the jury, we agree to pay the whole costs of this suit.'

A perfect roar of laughter interrupted the worthy attorney, and as it ran from one end of the table to the other, seemed to promise a happier issue to this unpleasant discussion.

'There, now,' said honest Paul, 'the Lord be praised, it is all settled! So let us have another cooper up, and then we 'll join the ladies.'

'Then I understand it thus,' said Lord Dudley: 'you pay the money for Mr. Upton, and I may erase the bet from my book?'

'No, sir!' cried Upton passionately. 'I pay my own wagers; and if you still insist— —'

'No, no, no!' cried several voices; while, at the same time, to put an end at once to any further dispute, the party suddenly rose to repair to the drawing-room.

On passing through the hall, chance, or perhaps design, on Lord Dudley's part, brought him beside Upton. 'I wish you to understand, once more,' said he, in a low whisper, 'that I consider this bet to hold.'

'Be it so,' was the brief reply, and they separated.

O'Grady and myself, having dined that day in the country, only arrived in the Rooneys' drawing-room as the dinner-party was entering it. Contrary to their wont, there was less of loud talking, less of uproarious and boisterous mirth, as they came up the stairs, than usual O'Grady remarked this to me afterwards. At the time, however, I paid but little attention to it. The fact was, my thoughts were principally running in another channel Certain innuendoes of Lord Dudley de Vere, certain broad hints he had ventured upon even before Mrs. Rooney, had left upon my mind a kind of vague, undecided impression that, somehow or other, I was regarded as their dupe. Miss Bellow's manner was certainly more cordial, more kind to me than to any of the others who visited the house. The Rooneys themselves omitted nothing to humour my caprices, and indulge my fancies, affording me, at all times, opportunities of being alone with Louisa, joining in her walks, and accompanying her on horseback. Could there be anything in all this? Was this the quarter in which the mine was to explode? This painful doubt hanging upon my mind I entered the drawing-room.

The drawing-room of 42 Stephen's Green had often afforded me an amusing study. Its strange confusion of ranks and classes; its *mélange* of lordly loungers and city beauties; the discordant tone of conversation, where each person discussed the very thing he knew least of; the blooming daughters of a lady mayoress talking 'fashion and the musical glasses'; while the witless scion of a noble house was endeavouring to pass himself as a sayer of good things. These now, however, afforded me neither interest nor pleasure; bent solely upon one thought, eager alone to ascertain how far Louisa Bellow's manner towards me was the fruit of artifice, or the offspring of an artless and unsuspecting mind, I left O'Grady to entertain a whole circle of turbaned ladies, while I directed my course towards the little boudoir where Louisa usually sat.

In a house where laxity of etiquette and a freedom of manner prevailed to the extent I have mentioned, Miss Bellow's more cautious and reserved demeanour was anything but popular; and, as there was no lack of beauty, men found it more suitable to their lounging and indolent habits to engage those in conversation who were less *exigeante* in their demands for amusement, and were equally merry themselves, as mercifully disposed when the mirth became not only easy but free.

Miss Bellew, therefore, was permitted to indulge many of her tastes unmolested; and as one of these was to work at embroidery in the small room in question, few persons intruded themselves upon her—and even they but for a short time, as if merely paying their required homage to a member of the family.

As I approached the door of the boudoir, my surprise was not a little to hear Lord Dudley de Vere's voice, the tones of which, though evidently subdued by design, had a clear distinctness that made them perfectly audible where I stood.

'Eh! you can't mean it, though. 'Pon my soul, it is too bad! You know I shall lose my money if you persist.'

'I trust Lord Dudley de Vere is too much of a gentleman to make my unprotected position in this house the subject of an insolent wager. I'm sure nothing in my manner could ever have given encouragement to such a liberty.'

'There, now, I knew you didn't understand it. The whole thing was a chance; the odds were at least eighteen to one against you—ha, ha! I mean in your favour. Devilish good mistake that of mine. They were all shaken up in a hat. You see there was no collusion—could be none.'

'My lord, this impertinence becomes past enduring; and if you persist——'

'Well, then, why not enter into the joke? It'll be a devilish expensive one to me if you don't; that I promise you. What a confounded fool I was not to draw out when Upton wished it! D—n it! I ought to have known there is no trusting to a woman.' As he said this, he walked twice or thrice hurriedly to and fro, muttering as he went, with ill-suppressed passion: 'Laughed at, d—n me! that I shall be, all over the kingdom. To lose the money is bad enough; but the ridicule of the thing, that's the devil! Stay, Miss Bellew, stop one minute; I have another proposition to make. Begad, I see nothing else for it. This, you know, was all a humbug—mere joke, nothing more. Now, I can't stand the way I shall be quizzed about it at all. So, here goes! hang me, if I don't make the proposition in real earnest! There, now, say yes at once, and we'll see if I can't turn the laugh against them.'

There was a pause for an instant, and then Miss Bellew spoke. I would have given worlds to have seen her at that moment; but the tone of her voice, firm and unshaken, sank deep into my heart.

'My lord,' said she, 'this must now cease; but, as your lordship is fond of a wager, I have one for your acceptance. The sum shall be your own choosing. Whatever it be, I stake it freely, that, as I walk from this room, the first gentleman I meet—you like a chance, my lord, and you shall have one—will chastise you before the world for your unworthy, unmanly insult to a weak and unoffending girl.'

As she spoke, she sprang from the room, her eyes flashing with indignant fire, while her cheek, pale as death, and her heaving bosom, attested how deep was her passion. As she turned the corner of the door, her eyes met mine. In an instant the truth flashed upon her mind. She knew I had overheard all that passed. She gasped painfully for breath; her lips moved with scarce a sound; a violent trembling shook her from head to foot, and she fell fainting to the ground.

I followed her with my eyes as they bore her from the room; and then, without a thought for anything around me, I hurriedly left the room, dashed downstairs, and hastened to my quarters in the Castle.

CHAPTER XIII
A NIGHT OF TROUBLE

Until the moment when I reached the room and threw myself into a chair, my course respecting Lord Dudley de Vere seemed to present not a single difficulty. The appeal so unconsciously made to me by Miss Bellew, not less than my own ardent inclination, decided me on calling him out. No sooner, however, did calm reflection succeed to the passionate excitement of the moment, than at once I perceived the nicety of my position. Under what possible pretext could I avow myself as her champion, not as of her own choosing? for I knew perfectly well that the words she uttered were merely intended as a menace, without the slightest idea of being acted on. To suffer her name, therefore, to transpire in the affair would be to compromise her in the face of the world. Again, the confusion and terror she evinced when she beheld me at the door proved to me that, perhaps of all others, I was the last person she would have wished to have been a witness to the interview.

What was to be done? The very difficulty of the affair only made my determination to go through with it the stronger. I have already said my inclination also prompted me to this course. Lord Dudley's manner to me, without being such as I could make a plea for resenting, had ever been of a supercilious and almost offensive character. If there be anything which more deeply than another wounds our self-esteem, it is the assumed superiority of those whom we heartily despise. More than once he ventured upon hinting at the plans of the Rooneys respecting me, suggesting that their civilities only concealed a deeper object; and all this he did with a tone of half insolence that irritated me ten times more than an open affront. Often and often had I promised myself that a day of retribution must come. Again and again did I lay this comfort to my heart—that, one time or other, his habitual prudence would desert him; that his transgression would exceed the narrow line that separates an impertinent freedom from an insult, and then—— Now this time had come at last. Such a chance might not again present itself, and must not be thrown away.

My reasonings had come to this point, when a tremendous knocking at my door, and a loud shout of 'Jack! Jack Hinton!' announced O'Grady. This was fortunate. He was the only man whom I knew well enough to consult in such a matter; and of all others, he was the one on whose advice and counsel I could place implicit reliance.

'What the deuce is all this, my dear Hinton?' said he, as he grasped my hand in both of his. 'I was playing whist with the tabbies when it occurred, and saw nothing of the whole matter. She fainted, didn't she? What the deuce could you have said or done?'

'Could I have said or done! What do you mean, O'Grady?'

'Come, come, be frank with me; what was it? If you are in a scrape, I am not the man to leave you in it.'

'First of all,' said I, assuming with all my might a forced and simulated composure, 'first of all, tell me what you heard in the drawing-room.'

'What I heard? Egad, it was plain enough. In the beginning, a young lady came souse down upon the floor; screams and smelling-bottles followed; a general running hither and thither, in which confusion, by-the-bye, our adversaries contrived to manage a new deal, though I had four by honours in my hand. Old Miss Macan upset my markers, drank my negus, and then fainted off herself, with a face like an apothecary's rose.'

'Yes, yes; but,' said I impatiently, 'what of Miss Bellew?'

'What of her! that you must know best. You know, of course, what occurred between you.'

'My dear O'Grady,' said I, with passionate eagerness, 'do be explicit. What did they say in the drawing-room? What turn has been given to this affair?'

''Faith, I can't tell you; I am as much in the dark as my neighbours. After the lady was carried out and you ran away, they all began talking it over. Some said you had been proposing an elopement: others said you hadn't. The Rileys swore you had asked to have your picture back again; and old Mrs. Ram, who had planted herself behind a curtain to overhear all, forgot, it seems, that the window was open, and caught such a cold in her head, and such a deafness, that she heard nothing. She says, however, that your conduct was abominable; and in fact, my dear Hinton, the whole thing is a puzzle to us all.'

'And Lord Dudley de Vere,' said I, 'did he offer no explanation?'

'Oh yes, something pretty much in his usual style; pulled up his stock, ran his fingers through his hair, and muttered some indistinct phrases about lovers' quarrels.'

'Capital!' exclaimed I with delight; 'nothing could be better, nothing more fortunate than this! Now, O'Grady, listen to my version of the matter, and then tell me how to proceed in it.'

I here detailed to my friend every circumstance that had occurred from the moment of my entering to my departure from the drawing-room. 'As to the wager,' said I, 'what it was when made, and with whom, I know not.'

'Yes, yes; I know all that,' interrupted O'Grady; 'I have the whole thing perfectly before me. Now let us see what is to be done: and first of all, allow me to ring the bell for some sherry and water—that's the head and front of a consultation.'

When O'Grady had mixed his glass, sipped, corrected, and sipped again, he beat the bars of the grate a few moments contemplatively with the poker, and then turning to me, gravely said: 'We must parade him, Jack, that's certain. Now for the how. Our friend Dudley is not much given to fighting, and it will be rather difficult to obtain his consent. Indeed, if it had not been for the insinuation he threw out, after you had left the room, I don't well see how you could push him to it.'

'Why, my dear O'Grady, wasn't there quite cause enough?'

'Plenty, no doubt, my dear Jack, as far as feeling goes; but there are innumerable cases in this life which, like breaches of trust in law, escape with slight punishment. Not but that, when you owe a man a grudge, you have it always in your power to make him sensible of it; and among gentlemen there is the same intuitive perception of a contemplated collision as you see at a dinner-party, when one fellow puts his hand on a decanter; his friend at the end of the table smiles, and cries, "With pleasure my boy!" There is one thing, however, in your favour.'

'What is that?' said I eagerly.

'Why, he has lost his wager; that's pretty clear; and, as that won't improve his temper, it's possible—mind, I don't say more, but it's possible he may feel better disposed to turn his irritation into valour; a much more common process in metaphysical chemistry than the world wots of. Under these circumstances the best thing to do, as it strikes me, is to try the cause, as our friend Paul would say, on the general issue; that is, to wait on Herbert; tell him we wish to have a meeting; that, after what has passed—that 's a sweet phrase isn't it? and has got more gentlemen carried home on a door than any other I know—that after what has passed, the thing is unavoidable, and the sooner it comes off the better. He can't help referring me to a friend, and he can scarcely find any one that won't see the thing with our eyes. It's quite clear Miss Bellow's name must be kept out of the matter; and now, my boy, if you agree with me, leave the whole affair in my hands, tumble into bed, and go to sleep as fast as you can.'

'I leave it all to you, Phil,' said I, shaking his hand warmly, 'and to prove my obedience, I'll be in bed in ten minutes.'

O'Grady finished the decanter of sherry, buttoned up his coat, and slapping his boots with his cane, sauntered downstairs, whistling an Irish quick step as he went.

When I had half accomplished my undressing, I sat down before the fire, and, unconsciously to myself, fell into a train of musing about my present condition. I was very young; knew little of the world: the very character of my education had been so much under the eye and direction of my mother, that my knowledge was even less than that of the generality of young men of my own time of life. It is not surprising, then, if the events which my new career hurried so rapidly one upon another, in some measure confused me. Of duelling I had, of course, heard repeatedly, and had learned to look upon the necessity of it as more or less imperative upon every man in the outset of his career. Such was, in a great measure, the tone of the day; and the man who attained a certain period of life, without having had at least one affair of honour, was rather suspected of using a degree of prudent caution in his conduct with the world than of following the popular maxim of the period, which said, 'Be always ready with the pistol.'

The affair with Lord De Vere, therefore, I looked upon rather as a lucky hit; I might as well make my début with him as with any other. So much, then, for the prejudice of the period. Now, for my private feelings on the subject, they were, I confess, anything but satisfactory. Without at all entering into any anticipation I might have felt as to the final result, I could not avoid feeling ashamed of myself for my total ignorance about the whole matter; not only, as I have said, had I never seen a duel, but I never had fired a pistol twice in my life. I was naturally a nervous fellow, and the very idea of firing at a word, would, I knew, render me more so. My dread that the peculiarity of my constitution might be construed into want of courage, increased my irritability; while I felt that my endeavour to acquit myself with all the etiquette and punctilio of the occasion would inevitably lead me to the commission of some mistake or blunder.

And then, as to my friends at home, what would my father say? His notions on the subject I knew were very rigid, and only admitted the necessity of an appeal to arms as the very last resort. What account could I give him, sufficiently satisfactory, of my reasons for going out? How would my mother feel, with all her aristocratic prejudices, when she heard of the society where the affair originated, when some glowing description of the

Rooneys should reach her? and this some kind friend or other was certain to undertake. And, worse than all, Lady Julia, my high-born cousin, whose beauty and sarcasm had inspired me with a mixture of admiration and dread—how should I ever bear the satirical turn she would give the whole affair? Her malice would be increased by the fact that a young and pretty girl was mixed up in it; for somehow, I must confess, a kind of half-flirtation had always subsisted between my cousin and me. Her beauty, her wit, her fascinating manner, rendered me at times over head and ears in love with her; while, at others, the indifference of her manner towards me, or, still worse, the ridicule to which she exposed me, would break the spell and dissipate the enchantment.

Thoughts like these were far from assuring me, and contributed but little towards that confidence in myself I stood so much in need of. And, again, what if I were to fall? As this thought settled on my mind, I resolved to write home. Not to my father, however: I felt a kind of constraint about unburdening myself to him at such a moment. My mother was equally out of the question; in fact, a letter to her could only be an apologetic narrative of my life in Ireland—softening down what she would call the atrocities of my associates, and giving a kind of Rembrandt tint to the Rooneys, which might conceal the more vivid colouring of their vulgarity. At such a moment I had no heart for this: such trifling would ill suit me now. To Lady Julia, then, I determined to write: she knew me well. Besides, I felt that, when I was no more, the kindliness of her nature would prevail, and she would remember me but as the little lover that brought her bouquets from the conservatory; who wrote letters to her from Eton; who wore her picture round his neck at Sandhurst, and, by-the-bye, that picture I had still in my possession: this was the time to restore it. I opened my writing-desk and took it out. It was a strange love-gift, painted when she was barely ten years old. It represented a very lovely child, with blue eyes, and a singular regularity of feature, like a Grecian statue. The intensity of look that after years developed more fully, and the slight curl of the lip that betrayed the incipient spirit of mockery, were both there; still was she very beautiful I placed the miniature before me and fixed my eyes upon it. Carried away by the illusion of the moment, I burst into a rhapsody of proffered affection, while I vindicated myself against any imputation my intimacy with Miss Bellew might give rise to. As I proceeded, however, I discovered that my pleading scarce established my innocence even to myself; so I turned away, and once more sat down moodily before the fire.

The Castle clock struck two. I started up, somewhat ashamed of myself at not having complied with O'Grady's advice, and at once threw myself on my bed, and fell sound asleep. Some confused impression upon my mind of a threatened calamity gave a gloomy character to all my dreams, and more than once I awoke with a sudden start and looked about me. The flickering and uncertain glare of the dying embers threw strange goblin shapes upon the wall and on the old oak floor. The window-curtains waved mournfully to and fro, as the sighing night wind pierced the openings of the worn casements, adding, by some unknown sympathy, to my gloom and depression; and although I quickly rallied myself from these foolish fancies, and again sank into slumber, it was always again to wake with the same unpleasant impressions, and with the same sights and sounds about me. Towards morning, however, I fell into a deep, unbroken sleep, from which I was awakened by the noise of some one rudely drawing my curtains. I looked up, as I rubbed my eyes: it was Corny Delany, who, with a mahogany box under his arm, and a little bag in his hand, stood eyeing me with a look, in which his habitual ill-temper was dashed with a slight mixture of scorn and pity.

'So you are awake at last!' said he; ''faith, and you sleep sound, and'— this he muttered between his teeth—'and maybe it's sounder you'll sleep to-morrow night! The Captain bid me call you at seven o'clock, and it's near eight now. That blaguard of a servant of yours wouldn't get up to open the door till I made a cry of fire outside, and puffed a few mouthfuls of smoke through the keyhole!'

'Well done, Corny! But where's the Captain?' 'Where is he? Sorrow one o'me knows! Maybe at the watch-house, maybe in George's Street barrack, maybe in the streets, maybe—— Och, troth! there's many a place he might be, and good enough for him any of them. Them's the tools, well oiled; I put flints in them.'

'And what have you got in the bag, Corny?'

'Maybe you'll see time enough. It's the lint, the sticking-plaster and the bandages, and the turn-an'-twist.' This, be it known, was the Delany for tourniquet. 'And, 'faith, it's a queer use to put the same bag to; his honour the judge had it made to carry his notes in. Ugh, ugh, ugh! a bloody little bag it always was! Many's the time I seen the poor craytures in the dock have to hould on by the spikes, when they'd see him put his hands in it! It's not lucky, the same bag! Will you have some brandy-and-water, and a bit of dry toast? It's what the Captain always gives them the first time they go out. When they're used to it, a cup of chocolate with a spoonful of whisky is a fine thing for the hand.'

I could scarce restrain a smile at the notion of dieting a man for a duel, though, I confess, there seemed something excessively bloodthirsty about it. However, resolved to give Corny a favourable impression of my coolness, I said, 'Let me have the chocolate and a couple of eggs.'

He gave a grin a demon might have envied, as he muttered to himself, 'He wants to try and die game, ugh, ugh!' With these words he waddled out of the room to prepare my breakfast, his alacrity certainly increased by the circumstance in which he was employed.

No sooner was I alone than I opened the pistol-case to examine the weapons. They were, doubtless, good ones; but a ruder, more ill-fashioned, clumsy pair it would be impossible to conceive. The stock, which extended nearly to the end of the barrel, was notched with grooves for the fingers to fit in, the whole terminating in an uncouth knob, inlaid with small pieces of silver, which at first I imagined were purely ornamental On looking closer, however, I perceived that each of them contained a name and a date, with an ominous phrase beneath, which ran thus: 'Killed!' or thus: 'Wounded!'

'Egad,' thought I, 'they are certainly the coolest people in the world in this island, and have the strangest notions withal of cheering a man's courage!'

It was growing late, meanwhile; so that without further loss of time I sprang out of bed, and set about dressing, huddling my papers and Julia's portrait into my writing-desk. I threw into the fire a few letters, and was looking about my room lest anything should have escaped me, when suddenly the quick movement of horses' feet on the pavement beneath drew me to the window. As I looked out, I could just catch a glimpse of O'Grady's figure as he sprang from a high tandem; I then heard his foot as he mounted the stairs, and the next moment he was knocking at my door. 'Holloa!' cried he, 'by Jove, I have had a night of it! Help me off with the coat, Jack, and order breakfast, with any number of mutton-chops you please; I never felt so voracious in my life. Early rising must be a bad thing for the health, if it makes a man's appetite so painful.'

While I was giving my necessary directions, O'Grady stirred up the fire, drew his chair close to it, and planting his feet upon the fender, and expanding his hands before the blaze, called out—

'Yes, yes, quite right—cold ham and a devilled drumstick by all means; the mulled claret must have nothing but cloves and a slice of pine-apple in it; and, mind, don't let them fry the kidneys in champagne; they are fifty times better in moselle: we'll have the champagne *au naturel*, There, now, shut the door; there's a confounded current of air comes up that cold staircase. So, come over, my boy; let me give you all the news, and to begin:—

'After I parted with you, I went over to De Vere's quarters, and heard that he had just changed his clothes and driven over to Clare Street. I followed immediately; but, as ill-luck would have it, he left that just five minutes before, with Watson of the Fifth, who lives in one of the hotels near.

This, you know, looked like business; and, as they told me they were to be back in half an hour, I cut into a rubber of whist with Darcy and the rest of them, where, what between losing heavily, and waiting for those fellows, I never got up till half-past four; when I did, it was minus Paul's cheque, all the loose cash about me, and a bill for one hundred and thirty to Vaughan. Pleasant, all that wasn't it? Monk, who took my place, told me that Herbert and Watson were gone out together to the park, where I should certainly find them. Off, then, I set for the Phoenix, and, just as I was entering the gate of the Lodge, a chaise covered with portmanteaus and hat-boxes drove past me. I had just time to catch a glimpse of De Vere's face as the light fell suddenly upon it; I turned as quickly as possible, and gave chase down Barrack Street. We flew, he leading, and I endeavouring to keep up; but my poor hack was so done up, between waiting at the club and the sharp drive, that I found we couldn't keep up the pace. Fortunately, however, a string of coal-cars blocked up Essex Bridge, upon which my friend came to a check, and I also. I jumped out immediately, and running forward, just got up in the nick, as they were once more about to move forward, "Ah, Dudley," cried I, "I've had a sharp run for it, but by good fortune have found you at last" I wish you had seen his face as I said these words; he leaned forward in the carriage, so as completely to prevent Watson, who was with him, overhearing what passed?

"May I ask," said he, endeavouring to get up a little of his habitual coolness; "may I ask, what so very pressing has sent you in pursuit of me?"

"'Nothing which should cause your present uneasiness," replied I, in a tone and a look he could not mistake.

"'Eh—aw! don't take you exactly; anything gone wrong?"

"'You 've a capital memory, my lord, when it suits you; pray call it to your aid for a few moments, and it will save us both a deal of trouble. My business with you is on the part of Mr. Hinton, and I have to request you will, at once, refer me to a friend."

"'Eh! you want to fight? Is that it? I say, Watson, they want to make a quarrel out of that foolish affair I told you of."

"'Is Major Watson your friend on this occasion, my lord?"

"'No; oh no; that is, I didn't say—— I told Watson how they walked into me for three hundred at Rooney's. Must confess I deserved it richly for dining among such a set of fellows; and, as I have paid the money and cut the whole concern, I don't see what more's expected of me."

"'We have very little expectation, my lord, but a slight hope, that you'll not disgrace the cloth you wear and the profession you follow."

'"I say, Watson, do you think I ought to take notice of these words?"

'"Would your lordship like them stronger?"

'"One moment, if you please, Captain O'Grady," said Major Watson, as, opening the door of the chaise, he sprang out. "Lord Dudley de Vere has detailed to me, and of course correctly, the whole of his last night's proceedings. He has expressed himself as ready and anxious to apologise to your friend for any offence he may have given him—in fact, that their families are in some way connected, and any falling out would be a very unhappy thing between them; and, last of all, Lord Dudley has resigned his appointment as aide-de-camp, and resolved on leaving Ireland; in two hours more he will sail from this. So I trust, that under every circumstance, you will see the propriety of not pressing the affair any further."

'"With the apology——"

'"That" of course," said Watson.

'"I say," cried Herbert, "we shall be late at the Pigeon-house; it's half-past seven."

'Watson whispered a few words into his ear; he was silent for a second, and a slight crimson flush settled on his cheek.

'"It won't do for me if they talk of this afterwards; but tell him—I mean Hinton—that I am sorry; that is, I wish him to forgive——"

'"There, there," said I impatiently, "drive on! that is quite enough!"

'The next moment the chaise was out of sight, and I leaned against the balustrade of the bridge, with a sick feeling at my heart I never felt before. Vaughan came by at the moment with his tandem, so I made him turn about and set me down; and here I am, my boy, now that my qualmishness has passed off, ready to eat you out of house and home, if the means would only present themselves.'

Here ended O'Gradys narrative, and as breakfast very shortly after made its appearance, our conversation dropped into broken, disjointed sentences; the burden of which, on his part, was that, although no man would deserve more gratitude from the household and the garrison generally than myself for being the means of exporting Lord De Vere, yet that under every view of the case all effort should be made to prevent publicity, and stop the current of scandal such an event was calculated to give rise to in the city.

'No fear of that, I hope,' said I.

'Every fear, my dear boy. We live in a village here: every man hears his friend's watch tick, and every lady knows what her neighbour paid for her paste diamonds. However, be comforted! your reputation will scarcely stretch across the Channel; and one's notoriety must have strong claims before it pass the custom-house at Liverpool.'

'Well, that is something; but hang it, O'Grady, I wish I had had a shot at him.'

'Of course you do: nothing more natural, and at the same time, if you care for the lady, nothing more *mal à propos*. Do what you will, her name will be mixed up in the matter; but had it gone further she must have been deeply compromised between you. You are too young, Jack, to understand much of this; but take my word for it—fight about your sister, your aunt, your maternal grandmother, if you like, but never for the girl you are about to marry. It involves a false position to both her and yourself. And now that I am giving advice, just give me another cutlet. I say, Corny, any hot potatoes?'

'Thim was hot awhile ago,' said Corny, without taking his hands from his pockets.

'Well, it is pleasant to know even that. Put that pistol-case back again. Ah! there goes Vaughan; I want a word with him.'

So saying, he sprang up, and hastened downstairs.

'What did he say I was to do with the pistols?' said Corny, as he polished the case with the ample cuff of his coat.

'You are to put them by: we shan't want them this morning.'

'And there is to be no devil after all,' said he with a most fiendish grin. 'Ugh, ugh! didn't I know it? Ye's come from the wrong side of the water for that. It's little powder ye blaze, for all your talking.'

Taking out one of the pistols as he spoke, he examined the lock for a few minutes patiently, and then muttered to himself: 'Wasn't I right to put in the ould flints? The devil a more ye 'd he doing I guessed nor making a flash in the pan!'

It was rather difficult, even with every allowance for Mr. Delany's temper, to submit to his insolence patiently. After all, there was nothing better to be done; for Corny was even greater in reply than attack, and any rejoinder on my part would unquestionably have made me fare the worse. Endeavouring, therefore, to hum a tune, I strolled to the window and looked out; while the imperturbable Corny, opening the opposite sash, squibbed off both pistols previous to replacing them in the box.

I cannot say what it was in the gesture and the action of this little fiend; but somehow the air of absurdity thus thrown over our quarrel by this ludicrous termination hurt me deeply; and Corny's face as he snapped the trigger was a direct insult. All my self-respect, all my self-approval gave way in a moment, and I could think of nothing but cross Corny's commentary on my courage.

'Yes,' said I, half aloud, 'it is a confounded country! If for nothing else, that every class and condition of man thinks himself capable to pronounce upon his neighbour. Hard drink and duelling are the national pénates; and Heaven help him who does not adopt the religion of the land! My English servant would as soon have thought of criticising a chorus of Euripides as my conduct; and yet this little wretch not only does so, but does it to my face, superadding a sneer upon my country!'

This, like many other of my early reflections on Ireland, had its grain of truth and its bushel of fallacy; and before I quitted the land I learned to make the distinction.

CHAPTER XIV
THE PARTING

From motives of delicacy towards Miss Bellew I did not call that day at the Rooneys. For many months such an omission on my part had never occurred. Accordingly, when O'Grady returned at night to the Castle, he laughingly told me that the house was in half-mourning. Paul sat moodily over his wine, scarce lifting his head, and looking what he himself called nonsuited. Mrs. Paul, whose grief was always in the active mood, sobbed, hiccupped, gulped, and waved her arms as if she had lost a near relative. Miss Bellew did not appear at all, and Phil discovered that she had written home that morning, requesting her father to send for her without loss of time.

'The affair, as you see,' continued O'Grady, 'has turned out ill for all parties. Dudley has lost his post, you your mistress, and I my money—a pretty good illustration how much mischief a mere fool can at any moment make in society.'

It was about four o'clock in the afternoon when I mounted my horse to ride over to Stephen's Green. As I passed slowly along Dame Street my attention was called to a large placard, which, in front of a house opposite the lower Castle gate, had attracted a considerable crowd around it. I was spared the necessity of stopping to read by the hoarse shout of a ragged ruffian who elbowed his way through the mob, carrying on one arm a mass of printed handbills; the other hand he held beside his mouth to aid the energy of his declamation. 'Here's the full and true account,' cried he, 'of the bloody and me-lan-chc-ly duel that tuk place yesterday morning in the Phaynix Park, between Lord Dudley de Vere and Mr. Hinton, two edge-du-congs to his Grace the Lord Liftinint, wid all the particulars, for one ha'penny.'

'Here's the whole correspondence between the Castle bucks,' shouted a rival publisher—the Colburn to this Bentley—'wid a beautiful new song to an old tune—

"Bang it up, bang it up, to the lady in the Green."'

'Give me one, if you please,' said a motherly-looking woman, in a grey cloak.

'No, ma'am, a penny,' responded the vendor. 'The bloody fight for a halfpenny! What!' said he; 'would you have an Irish melody and the picture of an illigint female for a copper?'

'Sing us the song, Peter,' called out another.

'This is too bad!' said I passionately, as, driving the spurs into my horse, I dashed through the ragged mob, upsetting and overturning all before me. Not, however, before I was recognised; and, as I cantered down the street, a shout of derision, and a hailstorm of offensive epithets followed me.

It was, I confess, some time before I recovered my equanimity enough to think of my visit. For myself, individually, I cared little or nothing; but who could tell in what form these things might reach my friends in England?—how garbled! how exaggerated! how totally perverted! And then, too, Miss Bellew! It was evident that she was alluded to. I trembled to think that her name, polluted by the lips of such wretches as these, should be cried through the dark alleys and purlieus of the capital; a scoff and a mockery among the very outcasts of vice.

As I turned the corner of Grafton Street a showy carriage with four grey horses passed me by. I knew it was the Rooney equipage, and although for a moment I was chagrined that the object of my visit was defeated, on second thoughts I satisfied myself that, perhaps, it was quite as well; so I rode on to leave my card. On reaching the door, from which already some visitors were turning away, I discovered that I had forgotten my ticket-case; so I dismounted to write my name in the visiting-book; for this observance among great people Mrs. Rooney had borrowed, to the manifest horror and dismay of many respectable citizens.

'A note for you, sir,' said the butler, in his most silvery accent, as he placed a small sealed billet in my hand.

I opened it hastily. It contained but two lines:

'Miss Bellew requests Mr. Hinton will kindly favour her with a few moments' conversation at an early opportunity.'

'Is Miss Bellew at home?'

'Yes, sir,' said the servant, who stood waiting to precede me upstairs, and announce me.

'Mr. Hinton,' said the man; and the words echoed in the empty drawing-room, as he closed the door behind me. The next moment I heard the rustle of a silk dress, and Miss Bellew came out of the boudoir and walked towards me. Contrary to her usual habit—which was to hold out her hand to me—she now came timidly, hesitatingly forward, her eyes downcast, and her whole air and appearance indicating, not only the traces of sorrow, but of physical suffering.

'Mr. Hinton,' said she, in a voice every accent of which vibrated on my heart, 'I have taken the liberty to ask a few moments' interview with you; for, although it is not only probable, but almost certain, we shall not meet again, yet I wish to explain certain portions of my conduct, and, indeed, to make them the reason of a favour I have to ask at your hands.'

'Permit me to interrupt you for a moment,' said I. 'It is evident how painful the matter you would speak of is to you; you have no need of explanation, least of all to me. By accident, I overheard that which, however high my esteem for Miss Bellew before, could but elevate her in my eyes. Pass then at once, I beseech you, to what you call a favour; there is no service you can seek for— —'

'I thank you,' replied she, in a voice scarcely articulate; 'you have, indeed, spared me much in not asking me to speak of what it is misery enough to remember. But it is not the first time my unprotected position in this house has exposed me to outrage: though assuredly it shall be the last.' The tone of indignation she spoke in supplied her with energy, as she hurriedly continued: 'Already, Mr. Hinton, persons have dared to build a scandal upon the frail foundation of this insolent wager. Your name has been mixed up with it in such a way that no possible intercourse could exist between us without being construed into evidence of a falsehood; therefore, I have made up my mind to ask you to discontinue your visits here, for the few days I may yet remain. I have already written home; the answer may arrive the day after to-morrow; and, while I feel that I but ill repay the hospitality and kindness I have received, and have met with, in closing the door to a most valued guest, I am assured you will understand and approve my motives, and not refuse me my request.'

Delighted at the prospect of being in some way engaged in a service, I had listened with a throbbing heart, up to the moment she concluded. Nothing could so completely overthrow all my hopes as these last few words. Seeing my silence and my confusion—for I knew not what to say—she added, in a slightly tremulous voice—

'I am sorry, Mr. Hinton, that my little knowledge of the world should have led me into this indiscretion. I perceive from your manner that I have asked a sacrifice you are unwilling to make. I ought to have known that habits have their influence, as well as inclinations; and that this house, being the resort of your friends— —'

'Oh, how much, how cruelly you have mistaken me! Not on this account, not for such reasons as you suppose did I hesitate in my reply; far from it. Indeed, the very cause which made me a frequent visitor of this house, is that which now renders me unable to answer you.' A slight flush upon her cheek and a tremulous motion of her lip, prevented my adding more. 'Fear not, Miss Bellew,' said I, 'fear not from me; however different the feeling that would prompt it, no speech of mine shall cause you pain to listen to, however the buried thought may rack my own bosom. You shall have your request; good-bye.'

'Nay, nay, not so,' said she, as she raised her handkerchief to her eyes, and gave a soft but sickly smile; 'you mustn't go without my thanking you for all your kindness. It may so chance that one day or other you will visit the wild west; if so, pray don't forget that my father, of whom you have heard me speak so much, would be but too happy to thank one who has been so kind to his daughter. And, if that day should come'—here a slight gleam of animation shot across her features—' I beseech you not to think, from what you will see of me there, that I have forgotten all your good teaching, and all your lessons about London manners, though I sadly fear that neither my dress nor deportment will testify in my favour; and so, good-bye.'

She drew her glove from her hand as she spoke. I raised the taper fingers, respectfully, to my lips, and, without venturing another look, muttered 'good-bye,' and left the room.

As step by step I loitered on the stairs, I struggled with myself against the rising temptation to hurry back to her presence, and tell her that, although hitherto the fancied security of meeting her every day had made me a stranger to my own emotions, the hour of parting had dispelled the illusion; the thought of separation had unveiled the depth of my heart, and told me that I loved her. Was this true?

CHAPTER XV
THE LETTER FROM HOME

Feigning illness to O'Grady as the reason of my not going to the Rooneys, I kept my quarters for several days, during which time it required all my resolution to enable me to keep my promise; and scarcely an hour of the day went over without my feeling tempted to mount my horse and try if, perchance, I could not catch even a passing look at her once more. Miss Bellew was the first woman who had ever treated me as a man; this, in itself, had a strong hold on my feelings; for after all, what flattery is there so artful as that which invests us with a character to which we feel in our hearts our pretension is doubtful? Why has college life, why has the army, such a claim upon our gratitude at our outset in the world? Is it not the acknowledgment of our manhood? And for the same reason the man who first accepts our bill, and the woman who first receives our addresses, have an unqualified right to our regard for evermore.

It is the sense of what we seem to others that moulds and fashions us through life; and how many a character that seems graven in letters of adamant took its type, after all, from some chance or casual circumstance, some passing remark, some hazarded expression! We begin by simulating a part, and we end by dovetailing it into our nature; thence the change which a first passion works in every young mind. The ambition to be loved and the desire to win affection teach us those ways of pleasing, which, whether real or affected, become part and parcel of ourselves. Little know we that in the passion we believe to be the most disinterested how much of pure egoism is mixed up; and well is it for us that such is the case. The imaginary standard we set up before ourselves is a goal to strive for, an object of high hope before us; and few, if any, of our bolder enterprises in after-life have not their birth in the cradle of first love. The accolade, that in olden days by its magic touch converted the humble squire into the spurred and belted knight, had no such charm as the first beam from a bright eye, when, falling upon the hidden depths of our heart, it has shown us a mine of rich thoughts, of dazzling hopes, of bright desires. This indeed is a change; and who is there, having felt it, has not walked forth a prouder and a nobler spirit?

Thoughts like these came rushing on my mind as I reflected on my passion for Louisa Bellew; and as I walked my room my heart bounded with elation, and my step grew firm in its tread, for I felt that already a new influence was beaming on me, a new light was shining upon my path in life. Musing thus, I paid but little attention to my servant who had just left a letter upon my table; my eye, at length, glanced at the address, which I perceived was in my mother's handwriting. I opened it somewhat carelessly, for somehow my dear mother's letters had gradually decreased in their interest as my anti-Irish prejudices grew weaker by time; her exclusively English notions I could no longer respond to so freely as before; and as I knew the injustice of some of her opinions, I felt proportionably dispose to mistrust the truth of many others.

The letter, as usual, was crossed and recrossed; for nothing, after all, was so thorough a criterion of fashion as a penurious avoidance of postage, and in consequence scarcely a portion of the paper was uncovered by ink. The detail of balls and dinners, the gossip of the town, the rumoured changes in the ministry—who was to come in and who to go out; whether Lord Arthur got a regiment, or Lady Mary a son—had all become comparatively uninteresting to me. What we know and what we live in, is the world to us; and the arrival of a new bear is as much a matter of interest in the prairies of the far west as the first night of a new ballet in the circles of Paris. In all probability, therefore, after satisfying myself that my friends were well, I should have been undutiful enough to put my mother's letter to bed in a card-rack without any very immediate intention of disturbing its slumbers, when suddenly the word 'Rooney' attracted my eye, and at once awakened my curiosity. How the name of these people should have come to my mother's aristocratic ears I could not conceive; for although I had myself begun a letter about them, yet, on second thoughts, I deemed it better to consign it to destruction than risk a discovery, by no means necessary.

I now sat patiently down before the fire, resolved to spell over the letter from beginning to end, and suffer nothing to escape me. All her letters, like the preamble of a deed, began with a certain formula—-a species of lamentation over her wretched health; the difficulty of her case, which, consisting in the absence of all symptoms, had puzzled the Faculty for years long; the inclemency of the weather, which by some fatality of fortune was sure to be rainy when Dr. Y——— said it ought to be fine, and oppressively hot when he assured her she required a bracing element; besides, it was evident the medical men mistook her case, and what chance had she, with Providence and the College of Physicians against her! Then every one was unkind—nobody believed her sick, or thought her valuable life in danger, although from four o'clock in the afternoon to the same hour the next morning she was continually before their eyes, driving in the park, visiting, dining, and even dancing, too; in fact, exerting herself in every imaginable shape and form for the sake of an ungrateful world that had nothing but hollow civilities to show her, instead of tears for her sufferings. Skimming my eye rapidly over this, I came at length to the well-known paragraph which always concluded this exordium, and which I could have repeated by heart—the purport of it being simply a prophetic menace of what would be the state, and what the feelings, of various persons unknown, when at her demise they discovered how unjustly, how ungenerously, how cruelly, they had once or twice complimented her upon her health and looks, during her lifetime. The undying remorse of those unfeeling wretches, among whom it was very plain my father was numbered, was expatiated upon with much force and Christian charity; for as certain joint-stock companies contrive in their advertisements to give an apparent stability to their firm, by quoting some well-known Coutts or Drummond as their banker, so my poor mother, by simply introducing the word 'Providence' into all her worldly transactions, thought she was discharging the most rigid of Christian duties, and securing a happy retreat for herself when that day should arrive when neither rouge nor false hair would supply the deficiencies of youth, and death should unlock the jaw the dentist had furnished.

After this came the column of court gossip, the last pun of the prince, and a *mot* of Mr. Canning. 'We hope,' continued she, 'poor Somerset will go to Madrid as ambassador: to refuse him would be a great cruelty, as he has been ordered by his medical men to try a southerly climate.' Hum; ah!—'Lady Jane to replace Miss Barclay with the Landgravine.' Very stupid all this. But come, here we have it, the writing too changes as if a different spirit had dictated it.

'Two o'clock. I've just returned from the Grevilles, seriously ill from the effect of the news that has reached me. Wretched boy! what have you done? What frightful career of imprudence have you entered upon? Write to me at once; for although I shall take immediate steps for your recall, I shall be in a fever of impatience till you tell me all about it. Poor dear Lord Dudley de Vere, how I love him for the way he speaks of you! for although, evidently, your conduct to him has been something very gross, yet his language respecting you is marked not only by forbearance, but by kindness. Indeed, he attributes the spirit you have manifested to the instigation of another member of the staff, whose name, with his habitual delicacy, we could not prevail upon him to disclose. His account of that wretched country is distressing indeed; the frightful state of society, the barbarism of the natives, and the frequency of bloodshed. I shall not close my eyes to-night thinking of you; though he has endeavoured to reassure me, by telling us, that as the Castle is a strong place, and a considerable military force always there, you are in comparative safety. But, my dear child, who are these frightful Rooneys, with the odious house where all this gambling and ruin goes forward? How feelingly poor Lord Dudley spoke of the trials young men are exposed to! His parents have indeed a treasure in him. Rooney appears to be a money-lender, a usurer—most probably a Jew. His wretched wife, what can she be? And that designing minx, niece, daughter, or whatever this Miss Belloo—what a shocking name!—may be? To think you should have fallen among such people! Lord George's debts are, they say, very considerable, all owing, as he assures me, to his unfortunate acquaintance with this Rooney, with whom he appears to have had bill transactions for some time past. If your difficulties were only on the score of money I should think little of it; but a quarrelsome, rancorous spirit, a taste for low company, and vulgar associates, and a tendency to drink—these, indeed, are very shocking features, and calculated to inflict much misery on your parents.

'However, let us, as far as possible, endeavour to repair the mishap. I write by this post to this Mr. Rooney, requesting him to send in his account to your father, and that in future any dinners, or wine, you may have at his house will not be paid for, as you are under age. I shall also let him know that the obscurity of his rank in life, and the benighted state of the country he lives in, shall prove no safeguard to him from our vigilance; and as the chancellor dines with us to-morrow, I think of asking him if he couldn't be punished some way. Transportation, they tell me, has already nearly got rid of the gypsies. As for yourself, make your arrangements to return immediately; for, although your father knows nothing about it, I intend to ask Sir Henry Gordon to call on the Duke of York, and contrive an exchange for you. How I hate this secret adviser of yours! how I detest the Rooneys! how I abhor the Irish! You have only to come back with long hair, and the frightful accent, to break the heart of your affectionate but afflicted mother.

'Your cousin Julia desires her regards. I must say she has not shown a due respect to my feelings since the arrival of this sad intelligence; it is only this minute she has finished a caricature of you making love to a wild Irish girl with wings. This is not only cruel towards me, but an unbecoming sarcasm towards a wretched people, to whom the visitations of Providence should not be made matters of reproach.'

Thus concluded this famous epistle, at which, notwithstanding that every line offended me deeply, I could not refrain from bursting into laughter. My opinion of Lord Dudley had certainly not been of the highest; but yet was I totally unprepared for the apparent depth of villainy his character possessed. But I knew not, then, how strong an alloy of cunning exists in every fool; and how, almost invariably, a narrow intellect and a malevolent disposition are associated in the same individual.

There is no prejudice more popular, nor is there any which is better worth refuting, than that which attributes to folly certain good qualities of heart, as a kind of compensation for the deficiency in those of the head. Now, although there are of course instances to the contrary, yet will the fact be found generally true, that mediocrity of mind has its influence in producing a mischievous disposition. Unable to carry on any lengthened chain of reasoning, the man of narrow intellect looks for some immediate result; and in his anxiety to attain his object, forgetful of the value of both character and credit, he is prepared to sacrifice the whole game of life, provided he secure but the odd trick. Besides, the very insufficiency of his resources leads him out of himself for his enjoyments and his occupations. Watching, therefore, the game of life, he gradually acquires a certain low and underhand cunning, which, being mistaken by himself for ability, he omits no occasion to display; and hence begins the petty warfare of malice he wages against the world with all the spiteful ingenuity and malevolence of a monkey.

I could trace through all my mother's letter the dexterity with which Lord Dudley avoided committing himself respecting me, while his delicacy regarding O'Grady's name was equally conspicuous to a certain extent. He might have been excused if he bore no good-will to one or other of us; but what could palliate his ingratitude to the Rooneys? What could gloss over the base return he made them for all their hospitalities and attention? for nothing was more clear than that the light in which he represented them to my mother made them appear as low and intriguing adventurers.

This was all bad enough; but what should I say of the threatened letter to them? In what a position would it place *me*, before those who had been uniformly kind and good-natured towards me! The very thought of this nearly drove me to distraction, and I confess it was in no dutiful mood I crushed up the epistle in my hand, and walked my room in an agony of shame and vexation.

CHAPTER XVI
A MORNING IN TOWN

The morning after the receipt of the letter, the contents of which I have in part made known to the reader, O'Grady called on me to accompany him into the city.

'I am on a borrowing expedition, Jack,' cried he; 'and there's nothing like having a new face with one. Cavendish, Hopeton, and the rest of them, are so well known, it's of no use having them. But you, my boy, you're fresh; your smooth chin does not look like a protested bill, and you've got a *dégagé*, careless manner, a kind of unsuspicious look about you, a man never has, after a bailiff has given him an epaulette of five dirty fingers.'

'But, Phil,' said I, 'if you really want money——'

'My very excellent young friend,' interrupted he, in a kind of sermon voice, 'don't finish it, I beseech you; that is the very last thing in the way of exchequer a gentleman is ever driven to—borrowing from a friend. Heaven forbid! But even supposing the case that one's friend has money, why, the presumption is, that he must have borrowed it himself; so that you are sponging upon his ingenuity, not his income. Besides, why riddle one's own ships, while there is an enemy before us to fight? Please to remember the money-lenders, the usurers, the stockbroking knaves at fifty per cent, that the world is glutted with; these are the true game for a sporting gentleman, who would rather harpoon a shark any day, than spear a salmon.'

'But what's become of Paul? Is he not available.'

'Don't you know what has happened there? But I was forgetting you 've kept the house this week past. In the first place, La Belle Louise has gone home, Paul has taken his departure for the circuit, and Mrs. Paul, after three days' sharp hysterics, has left town for her villa, near Bray—old Harvey finding it doubtless more convenient to visit her there, with twenty guineas for his fee, than to receive one for his call at Stephen's Green.'

'And what is supposed to be the cause of all this?' said I, scarce able to conceal my agitation.

'The report goes,' replied he, 'that some bank has broke in Calcutta or the Caucasus, or somewhere, or that some gold-mine in Peru, in which Paul had a share, has all turned out to be only plated goods; for it was on the receipt of a letter, on the very morning of Paul's departure, that she took so dangerously ill; and as Paul, in his confusion, brought the attorney, instead of the surgeon-general, the case became alarming, and they gave her so much ether and sal-volatile that it required the united strength of the family to keep her from ascending like a balloon. However, the worst of it all is, the house is shut, the windows closed, and where lately on the door-steps a pair of yellow plush breeches figured bright and splendent as the glorious sun, a dusky-looking planet in threadbare black now informs you that the family are from home, and not expected back for the summer.'

'Perhaps I can explain the mystery,' said I, as a blush of shame burned on my cheek. Read this.'

So saying, I handed O'Grady the letter, doubled down at the part where Lord Dudley's mention of the Rooneys began. Grieved as I felt thus to expose the absurd folly of my mother's conduct, yet I felt the necessity of having at least one friend to advise with, and that, to render his counsel of any value, a perfect candour on my part was equally imperative.

While his eye glanced over the lines, I walked towards the window, expecting at each moment some open burst of indignation would escape him—some outbreak of passionate warmth, at the cold-blooded ingratitude and malevolence of one whom previously we had regarded but as a fool. Not so; on the contrary, he read the letter to the end with an unchanged countenance, folded it up with great composure, and then turning his back to the fire, he burst out into a fit of the most immoderate laughter.

'Look ye, Jack,' cried he, in a voice almost suffocated with the emotion, 'I am a poor man, have scarcely a guinea I can call my own, yet I 'd have given the best hack in my stable to have seen the Rooneys reading that letter. There, there! don't talk to me, boy, about villainy, ingratitude, and so forth. The fun of it, man, covers all the rest. Only to think of Mr. Paul Rooney, the Amphytrion of viceroys, chancellors, bishops, major-generals, and lord mayors, asked for his bill—to score up all your champagne and your curacoa, your turtle, your devilled kidneys; all the heavy brigade of your grand dinners, and all the light infantry of luncheons, breakfasts, grilled bones, and sandwiches! The Lord forgive your mother for putting it in his head! *My* chalk would be a fearful one, not to speak of the ugly item of "cash advanced." Oh, it 'll kill me, I know that! Don't look so serious, man;

you may live fifty years, and never have so good a joke to laugh at. Tell me, Jack, do you think your mother has kept a copy of the letter? I would give my right eye for it. What a fearful temper Paul will be in, on circuit! and as to Mrs. Rooney, it will go hard with her but she cuts the whole aristocracy for at least a week. There never was anything like it. To hint at transporting the Princess O'Toole, whose ancestor was here in the time of Moses. Ah, Jack, how little respect your mother appears to have for an old family! She evidently has no classical associations to hallow her memory withal.'

'I confess,' said I, somewhat tartly, 'had I anticipated the spirit with which you have taken up this matter, I doubt whether I should have shown you the letter.'

'And if you had not,' replied he, 'I 'd not have forgiven you till the day of my death. Next to a legacy, a good laugh is the best thing I know; indeed, sometimes it is better, for you can't be choused out of it by your lawyer.'

'Laughing is a very excellent practice, no doubt, but I looked for some advice— —-'

'Advice! to be sure, my boy; and so you shall have it. Only give me a good training canter of a hearty laugh, and you 'll see what running I' ll make, when it comes to sound discretion afterwards. The fun of a man's temperament is like the froth on your champagne; while it gives a zest to the liquor of life by its lightness and its sparkle, it neither detracts from the flavour nor the strength of the beverage. At the same time, when I begin to froth up, don't expect me to sober down before twenty-four hours. So take your hat, come along into town, and thank your stars that you have been able to delight the heart of a man who's trying to get a bill discounted. Now hear me, Jack,' said he, as we descended the stairs; 'if you expect me to conduct myself with becoming gravity and decorum, you had better avoid any mention of the Rooneys for the rest of the day. And now to business!'

As we proceeded down Dame Street my friend scientifically explained to me the various modes there were of obtaining money on loan.

'I don't speak,' said he, 'of those cases where a man has landed security, or property of one kind or other, or even expectations, because all these are easy—the mere rule of three in financial arithmetic What I mean are the decimal fractions of a man's difficulties, when, with as many writs against him as would make a carpet for his bedroom, he can still go out with an empty pocket in the morning and come back with it furnished at night. And now to begin. The maxims of the sporting world are singularly applicable to the practice before us. You're told that before you enter a preserve your first duty is to see that your gun is properly loaded—all the better if it be a double-barrelled one. Now, look here'—as he spoke he drew from his sabretache five bills for one hundred pounds each; 'you see I am similarly prepared. The game may get up at any moment, and not find me at half-cock; and although I only go out for a single bird—that is, but one hundred, yet, if by good-luck I flush a covey, you see I am ready for them all. The doctrine of chances shows us that five to one is better than an even bet; so, by scattering these five bills in different directions, the odds are exactly so many in my favour that I raise a hundred somewhere.' 'And now,' said I, 'where does the game lie?' 'I'm coming to that, Jack. Your rich preserves are all about the neighbourhood of Clare Street, Park Street, Merrion Street, and that direction. With them, alas! I have nothing to do. My broad acres have long since taken wings to themselves; and I fear a mortgage upon Mount O'Grady, as it at present exists, would be a poor remedy for an empty pocket. The rich money-lenders despise poor devils like me; they love not contingencies; and, as Macbeth says, "They have no speculation in their eyes." For them, my dear Jack, you must have messuages and tenements, and outhouses, townlands, and turbaries; corn, cattle, and cottages; pigs, potatoes, and peasantry. They love to let their eyes range over a rich and swelling scene of woodland and prairie; for they are the landscape-gardeners of usury—they are the Hobbimas and Berghems of the law.

'Others again, of smaller range and humbler practice, there are, to whom, upon occasion, you assign your grandfather's plate and the pictures of your grand-aunts for certain monied conveniences you stand in need of. These are a kind of Brobdingnag pawnbrokers, who have fine houses, the furniture of which is everlastingly changing, each creditor sending his representative, like a minister to a foreign court; with them, also, I have nothing to do. The family have had so little to eat for the last two generations that they trouble themselves but slightly on the score of silver dishes; and as to pictures, I possess but one in the world—a portrait of my father in his wig and robes. This, independent of other reasons, I couldn't part with, as it is one of the only means I possess of controlling Corny when his temper becomes more than usually untractable. Upon these occasions, I hang up the "jidge" over the chimney-piece, and the talisman has never failed yet.

'Now, Jack, my constituency live about fleet Street, and those small, obscure, dingy-looking passages that branch from it on either side. Here live a class of men who, having begun life as our servants or valets, are in perfect possession of all our habits of life, our wants, and our necessities. Having amassed enough by retail robbery of us while in our service, to establish some petty tavern, or some low livery-stable, they end by cheating us wholesale, for the loan of our own money, at their rate of interest. Well aware that, however deferred, we must pay eventually, they are satisfied— good, easy souls!—to renew and renew bills, whose current percentage varies from five-and-twenty to forty. And even, notwithstanding all this, Jack, they are difficult devils to deal with, any appearance of being hard up, any show of being out-at-elbows, rendering a negotiation as difficult as the assurance of a condemned ship for a China voyage. No, my boy; though your house be besieged by duns, though in every passenger you see a bailiff, and never nap after dinner without dreaming of the Marshalsea, yet still, the very moment you cross the precincts of their dwelling, you must put your care where your cash ought to be—in your pocket. You must wear the easy smile of a happy conscience, and talk of your want of a few hundreds as though it were a question of a pinch of snuff, or a glass of brandy-and-water, while you agree to the exorbitant demands they exact, with the careless indifference of one to whom money is no object, rather than with the despair of a wretch who looks for no benefit in life save in the act for insolvent debtors. This you 'll say is a great bore, and so I once thought too; now, however, I have got somewhat used to it, and sometimes don't actually dislike the fun. Why, man, I have been at it for three months at a time. I remember when I never blew my nose without pulling out a writ along with my pocket-handkerchief, and I never was in better spirits in all my life. But here we are. This is Bill Fagan's, a well-known drysalter; you'll have to wait for me in the front parlour for a moment while I negotiate with Billy.'

Elbowing our way through a squalid and miserable-looking throng of people that filled the narrow hall of a house in fleet Street, we forced on till we reached an inner door in which a sliding panel permitted those within to communicate with others on the outside. Tapping at this with his cane, O'Grady called out something which I could not catch, the panel at once flew back, a red carbuncled face appeared at the opening, the owner of which, with a grin of very peculiar signification, exclaimed—' Ah, it's yourself, Captain? Walk in, sir.' With these words the door was opened, and we were admitted into the inner hall. This was also crowded, but with a different class from what I had seen without. These were apparently men in business, shopkeepers and traders, who, reduced by some momentary pressure, to effect a loan, were content to prop up their tottering credit by sapping the very core of their prosperity. Unlike the others, on whom habitual poverty and daily misery had stamped its heavy impress, and whose faces too, inured to suffering, betrayed no shame at being seen—these, on the contrary, looked downward or aside; seemed impatient, fretful, and peevish, and indicated in a hundred ways how unused they were to exigencies of this nature, muttering to themselves in angry mood at being detained, and feigning a resolution to depart at every moment. O'Grady, after a conference of a few moments with the rubicund Cerberus I have mentioned, beckoned to me to follow him. We proceeded accordingly up a narrow creaking stair, into a kind of front drawing-room, in which about a dozen persons were seated, or listlessly lounging in every imaginable attitude—some on chairs, some on the window-sills, some on the tables, and one even on the mantel-piece, with his legs gracefully dangling in front of the fire. Perfectly distinct from the other two classes I have mentioned, these were all young men whose dress, look, and bearing bespoke them of rank and condition. Chatting away gaily, laughing, joking, and telling good stories, they seemed but little to care for the circumstances which brought them there; and, while they quizzed one another about their various debts and difficulties, seemed to think want of money as about the very best joke a gentleman could laugh at. By all of these O'Grady was welcomed with a burst of applause, as they eagerly pressed forward to shake hands with him.

'I say, O'Grady,' cried one, 'we muster strong this morning. I hope Fagan's bank will stand the run on it. What's your figure?'

'Oh, a couple of hundred,' said Phil carelessly; 'I have got rather a heavy book on the steeplechase.'

'So I hear,' said another; 'and they say Ulick Burke won't ride for you. He knows no one can sit the horse but himself; and Maher, the story goes, has given him a hundred and fifty to leave you in the lurch!'

'How good!' said Phil, smiling; for although this intelligence came upon him thus suddenly, he never evinced the slightest surprise nor the most trifling irritation.

'You'll pay forfeit, of course, Phil,' said the gentleman on the chimney.

'I fancy not.'

'Then will you take two fifties to one, against your horse?'

'Will you give it?' was the cool reply. 'Yes.'

'And I—and I also,' said different voices round the room.

'Agreed, gentlemen, with all of you. So, if you please, we'll book this. Jack, have you got a pencil?'

The Money Lender's Drawing-room.

As I drew forth my pocket-book I could not help whispering to O'Grady that there seemed something like a coalition among his opponents. Before I could conclude, the red face appeared at the door. O'Grady hastily muttered, 'Wait for me here,' and left the room.

During his absence I had abundant time to study those about me. Indeed, a perfect sameness in their characters as in their pursuits rendered it an easy process; for as with unguarded frankness they spoke of their several difficulties, their stories presented one uniform feature-reckless expenditure and wasteful extravagance, with limited means and encumbered fortunes. They had passed through every phase of borrowing, every mode of raising money, and were now reduced to the last rung of the ladder of expediency, to become the prey of the usurer, who meted out to them a few more months of extravagance at the cost of many a future year of sorrow and repining.

I was beginning to grow impatient as the door gently opened, and I saw my friend, as he emerged from the back drawing-room. Without losing a moment's time I joined him. We descended the stairs together, and walked out into the street.

'Are you fond of pickled herrings, Jack?' said O'Grady, as he took my arm.

'Pickled herrings! Why, what do you mean?'

'Probably,' resumed he, in the same dry tone of voice, 'you prefer ash bark, or asafetida?'

'Why, I can't say.'

'Ah, my boy, you're difficult to please, then. What do you say to whale oil and Welsh wigs?'

'Confound me if I understand you!'

'Nothing more easy after all, for of each of these commodities I'm now a possessor to the amount of some two hundred and twenty pounds. You look surprised, but such is the nature of our transactions here; and for my bill of five hundred, payable in six months, I have become a general merchant to the extent I've told you, not to mention paying eighty more for a certain gig and horse, popularly known in this city as the discount dennet. This,' continued he with a sigh, 'is about the tenth time I've been the owner of that vile conveyance; for you must know whenever Fagan advances a good round sum he always insists upon something of this kind forming part of it, and thus, according to the figure of your loan, you may drive from his door in anything, from a wheel-barrow to a stage-coach. As for the discount dennet, it is as well known as the black-cart that conveys the prisoners to Newgate, and the reputation of him who travels in either is pretty much on a par. From the crank of the rusty springs, to the limping amble of the malicious old black beast in the shafts, the whole thing has a look of beggary about it. Every jingle of the ragged harness seems to whisper in your ear, "Fifty per cent."; and drive which way you will, it is impossible to get free of the notion that you're not trotting along the road to ruin. To have been seen in it once is as though you had figured in the pillory, and the very fact of its being in your possession is a blow of a battering-ram to your credit for ever!'

'But why venture into it? If you must have it, let it be like the pickled herrings and the paving-stones—so much of pure loss.'

'The fact is, Jack, it is generally passed off on a young hand, the first time he raises money. He knows little of the town, less of its secret practices, and not until he has furnished a hearty laugh to all his acquaintances does he discover the blunder he has committed. Besides, sometimes you're hard up for something to carry you about.

I remember once keeping it an entire winter, and as I painted Latitat a good piebald, and had his legs whitewashed every morning, few recognised him, except such as had paid for their acquaintance. After this account, probably, you'll not like to drive with me; but as I am going to Loughrea for the races, I 've determined to take the dennet down, and try if I can't find a purchaser among the country gentlemen. And now let's think of dinner. What do you say to a cutlet at the club, and perhaps we shall strike out something there to finish our evening?'

CHAPTER XVII
AN EVENING IN TOWN

We dined at the club-house, and sat chatting over our wine till near ten o'clock. The events of the morning were our principal topics; for although I longed myself to turn the conversation to the Rooneys, I was deterred from doing so by the fear of another outbreak of O'Grady's mirth. Meanwhile the time rolled on, and rapidly too, for my companion, with an earnestness of manner and a force of expression I little knew he possessed, detailed to me many anecdotes of his own early career. From these I could glean that while O'Grady suffered himself to be borne along the current of dissipation and excess, yet in his heart he hated the life he led, and, when a moment of reflection came, felt sorrow for the past, and but little hope for the future.

'Yes, Jack,' said he, on concluding a narrative of continual family misfortune, 'there would seem a destiny in things; and if we look about us in the world we cannot fail to see that families, like individuals, have their budding spring of youth and hope, their manhood of pride and power, and their old age of feebleness and decay. As for myself, I am about the last branch of an old tree, and all my endeavour has been, to seem green and cheerful to the last. My debts have hung about my neck all through life; the extravagances of my early years have sat like a millstone upon me; and I who began the world with a heart brimful of hope, and a soul bounding with ambition, have lingered on my path like a truant schoolboy. And here I am, at the age of three-and-thirty, without having realised a single promise of my boyhood, the poorest of all imaginable things—a gentleman without fortune, a soldier without service, a man of energy without hope.'

'But why, Phil,' said I, 'how comes it that you never went out to the Peninsula?'

'Alas, my boy! from year to year I have gone on expecting my gazette to a regiment on service. Too poor to purchase, too proud to solicit, I have waited in anxious expectancy from some of those with whom, high as was their station, I've lived on terms of intimacy and friendship, that notice they extended to others less known than I was; but somehow the temperament that would seem to constitute my happiness, has proved my bane, and those qualities which have made me a boon companion, have left me a beggar. Handed over from one viceroy to another, like a state trumpeter or a butt of sherry, I have been left to linger out my best years a kind of court-jester; my only reward being, the hour of merriment over, that they who laughed with, should laugh at me.'

There was a tone of almost ferocity in the way he spoke these words; while the trembling lip, the flashing eye, and the swollen veins of his temple betrayed that the very bitterest of all human emotions—self-scorn—was racking his heart within him.

For some time we were both silent. Had I even known what to say at such a moment, there was that comfortless expression about his face, that look of riveted despair, which would have rendered any effort on my part to console him a vain and presumptuous folly.

'But come, Jack,' said he, filling his glass and pushing over the decanter to me, 'I have learned to put little faith in patrons; and although the information has been long in acquiring, still it has come at last, and I am determined to profit by it. I am now endeavouring to raise a little money to pay off the most pressing of my creditors, and have made an application to the Horse Guards to be appointed to any regiment on service, wherever it may be. If both these succeed, and it is necessary both should, then, Jack, I 'll try a new path, and even though it lead to nothing, yet, at least, it will be a more manly one to follow. And if I am to linger on to that period of life when to look back is nearly all that's left us—why, then, the retrospect will be less dashed with shame than with such a career as this is. Meanwhile, my boy, the decanter is with you, so fill your glass; I 'll join you presently.'

As he spoke, O'Grady sprang up and walked to the other end of the room, where a party of some half-dozen persons were engaged in putting on greatcoats, and buttoning up previous to departure. In an instant I could hear his voice high above the rest—that cheerful ringing tone that seemed the very tocsin of a happy heart—while at some observation he made, the whole party around him were convulsed with laughter. In the midst of all this he drew one of them aside, and conversing eagerly with him for a few seconds, pointed to me as he spoke.

'Thank you, my lord, thank you,' said he, as he turned away. 'I'll be answerable for my friend. Now, Hinton,' whispered he, as he leaned his hand upon my shoulder and bent over me, 'we 're in luck to-night, at all events, for I have just got permission to bring you with me where I am to spend the evening. It's no small favour if you knew but all; so finish your wine, for my friends there are moving already.'

All my endeavours to ascertain where we were going, or to whose house, were in vain; the only thing I could learn was, that my admission was a prodigious favour—while to satisfy my scruples about dress he informed me that no change of costume was necessary.

'I perceive,' said O'Grady, as he drew the curtain and looked out into the street, 'the night is fine and starlight; so what say you if we walk? I must tell you, however, our place of rendezvous is somewhat distant.'

Agreeing to the proposition with pleasure, I took his arm, and we sallied forth together. Our way led at first through a most crowded and frequented part of the capital We traversed Dame Street, passed by the Castle, and ascended a steep street beyond it; after this we took a turning to the left, and entered a part of the city, to me at least, utterly unknown. For about half an hour we continued to wander on, now to the right, now to the left, the streets becoming gradually narrower, less frequented, and less lighted; the shops were all closed, and few persons stirred in the remote thoroughfares.

'I fear I must have made a mistake,' said O'Grady, endeavouring to take a short cut; 'but here comes a watchman. I say, is this Kevin Street?'

'No, sir; the second turning to your right brings you into it.'

'Kevin Street!' said I, repeating the name half aloud to myself.

'Yes, Jack, so it is called; but all your ingenuity will prove too little in discovering whither you are going. So come along; leave time to tell you what guessing never will.'

By this time we arrived at the street in question, when very soon after O'Grady called out—

'All right—here we are!'

With these words he knocked three times in a peculiar manner at the door of a large and gloomy-looking house. An ill-trimmed lamp threw a faint and flickering light upon the old and ruined building, and I could trace here and there, through all the wreck of time, some remnants of a better day. The windows now, however, were broken in several places, those on the lower storey being defended on the outside by a strong iron railing; not a gleam of light shone through any one of them, but a darkness unrelieved, save by the yellow gleam of the street lamp, enveloped the entire building. O'Gradys summons was twice repeated ere there seemed any chance of its being replied to, when, at last, the step of a heavy foot descending the stairs announced the approach of some one. While I continued my survey of the house O'Grady never spoke, and, perceiving that he made a mystery of our visit, I resolved to ask no further questions, but patiently await the result;

my impression, however, was, that the place was the resort either of thieves or of some illegal association, of which more than one, at that time, were known to have their meetings in the capital. While I was thus occupied in my conjectures, and wondering within myself how O'Grady had become acquainted with his friends, the door opened, and a diminutive, mean-looking old man, shading the candle with his hand, stood at the entrance.

'Good-evening, Mickey,' cried O'Grady, as he brushed by him into the hall. 'Are they come?'

'Yes, Captain,' said the little man, as, snuffing the long wick with his fingers, he held the light up to O'Grady's face. 'Yes, Captain, about fifteen.'

'This gentleman's with me—come along, Jack—he is my friend, Mickey.'

'Oh, I can't do it by no means, Mister Phil,' said the dwarf, opposing himself as a barrier to my entrance. 'You know what they said the last night'—here he strained himself on his toes, and, as O'Grady stooped down, whispered some words I couldn't catch, while he continued aloud—'and you know after that, Captain, I daren't do it.'

'I tell you, you old fool, I've arranged it all; so get along there, and show us the light up these confounded stairs. I suppose they never mended the hole on the lobby?'

'Troth they didn't,' growled the dwarf; 'and it would be chaper for them nor breaking their shins every night.'

I followed O'Grady up the stairs, which creaked and bent beneath us at every step; the hand-rail, broken in many places, swung to and fro with every motion of the stair, and the walls, covered with green, and damp mould, looked the very picture of misery and decay. Still grumbling at the breach of order incurred by my admission, the old man shuffled along, wheezing, coughing, and cursing between times, till at length we reached the landing-place, where the hole of which I heard them speak permitted a view of the hall beneath. Stepping across this, we entered a large room lighted by a lamp upon the chimney-piece; around the walls were hung a variety of what appeared to be cloaks of a lightish drab colour, while over each hung a small skull-cap of yellow leather.

'Don't you hear the knocking below, Mickey? There's some one at the door,' said O'Grady.

The little man left the room, and as we were now alone, I expected some explanation from my friend as to the place we were in, and the people who frequented it. Not so, however. Phil merely detached one of the cloaks from its peg, and proceeded to invest himself in its folds; he placed the skull-cap on his head, after which, covering the whole with a hood, he fastened the garment around his waist with a girdle of rope, and stood before me the perfect picture of a monk of St. Benedict, as we see them represented in old pictures—the only irregularity of costume being, that instead of a rosary, the string from his girdle supported a corkscrew and a horn spoon of most portentous proportions.

'Come, my son,' said he reverently, 'indue thy garment.' So saying, he proceeded to clothe me in a similar manner, after which he took a patient survey of me for a few seconds. 'You'll do very well; wear the hood well forward; and mark me, Jack, I've but one direction to give you—never speak a word, not a syllable, so long as you remain in the house; if spoken to, cross your arms thus upon your breast, and bow your head in this manner. Try that—perfectly—you have your lesson; now don't forget it.'

O'Grady now, with his arms crossed upon his bosom, and his head bent slightly forward, walked slowly forth, with a solemn gravity well befitting his costume. Imitating him as well as I was able, I followed him up the stairs. On reaching the second landing, he tapped twice with his knuckles at a low door, whose pointed arch and iron grating were made to represent the postern of a convent.

'*Benedicite,*' said Phil, in a low voice.

'*Et tu quoque, frater,*' responded some one from within, and the door was opened.

Saluting a venerable-looking figure, who, with a long grey beard, bowed devoutly as we passed, we entered an apartment, where, so sudden was the change from what I had hitherto seen, I could scarcely trust my eyes. A comfortable, well-carpeted room, with curtained windows, cushioned chairs, and, not least inviting of all, a blazing fire of wood upon the hearth, were objects I was little prepared for; but I had little time to note them, my attention being directed with more curiosity to the living occupants of this strange dwelling. Some fifteen or sixteen persons, costumed like ourselves, either walked up and down engaged in conversation, or sat in little groups around the fire. Card-tables there were in different parts of the room, but one only was occupied. At this a party of reverend fathers were busily occupied at whist. In the corner next the fire, seated in a large chair of carved oak, was a figure, whose air and bearing bespoke authority; the only difference in his costume from the others being a large embroidered corkscrew, which he wore on his left shoulder.

'Holy Prior, your blessing,' said Phil, bowing obsequiously before him.

'You have it, my son: much good may it do you,' responded the superior, in a voice which, somehow or other, seemed not perfectly new to me.

While O'Grady engaged in a whispered conversation with the prior, I turned my eyes towards a large-framed paper which hung above the chimney. It ran thus:—

'Rules and regulations to be observed in the monastery of the venerable and pious brothers, the Monks of the Screw.'

Conceiving it scarcely delicate in a stranger to read over the regulations of a society of which he was not a member, I was turning away, when O'Grady, seizing me by the arm, whispered, 'Remember your lesson'; then added aloud, 'Holy Father, this is the lay brother of whom I spoke.'

The prior bowed formally, and extended his hands towards me with a gesture of benediction—

'*Accipe benedictionem — —*'

'Supper, by the Lord Harry!' cried a jolly voice behind me, and at the same moment a general movement was made by the whole party.

The prior now didn't wait to conclude his oration, but tucking up his garments, put himself at the head of the procession which had formed, two and two, in order of march. At the same moment, two fiddles from the supper-room, after a slight prelude, struck up the anthem of the order, which was the popular melody of, 'The Night before Larry was stretched!'

Marching in measured tread, we entered the supper-room, when, once having made the circuit of the table, at a flourish of the fiddles we assumed our places, the superior seating himself at the head in a chair of state, slightly elevated above the rest. A short Latin grace, which I was unfortunate enough not to catch, being said, the work of eating began; and, certainly, whatever might have been the feats of the friars of old, when the bell summoned them to the refectory, their humble followers, the Monks of the Screw, did them no discredit. A profusion of dishes covered the table; and although the entire service was of wood, and the whole 'equipage' of the most plain and simple description, yet the cookery was admirable, and the wines perfection itself.

While the supper proceeded, scarcely a word was spoken. By the skilful exercise of signs, with which they all seemed familiar, roast ducks, lobsters, veal-pies, and jellies flew from hand to hand; the decanters also paraded up and down the table with an alacrity and despatch I had seldom seen equalled. Still, the pious brethren maintained a taciturn demeanour that would have done credit to La Trappe itself. As for me, my astonishment and curiosity increased every moment. What could they be? What could they mean? There was something too farcical about it all to suppose that any political society or any dangerous association could be concealed under such a garb; and if mere conviviality and good fellowship were meant, their unbroken silence and grave demeanour struck me as a most singular mode of promoting either.

Supper at length concluded, the dishes were removed by two humble brethren of the order, dressed in a species of grey serge; after which, marching to a solemn tune, another monk appeared, bearing a huge earthenware bowl, brimful of steaming punch—at least so the odour and the floating lemons bespoke it. Each brother was now provided with a small, quaint-looking pipkin, after which the domestics withdrew, leaving us in silence as before. For about a second or two this continued, when suddenly the fiddles gave a loud twang, and each monk, springing to his legs, threw hack his cowl, and, bowing to the superior, reseated himself. So sudden was the action, so unexpected the effect, for a moment or two I believed it a dream. What was my surprise, what my amazement, that this den of thieves, this hoard of burglars, this secret council of rebels, was nothing more or less than an assemblage of nearly all the first men of the day in Ireland! And as my eye ran rapidly over the party, here I could see the Chief Baron, with a venerable dignitary of St. Patrick's on his right; there was the Attorney-General; there the Provost of Trinity College; lower down, with his skull-cap set jauntily on one side, was Wellesley Pole, the secretary of state; Yelverton, Day, Plunket, Parsons, Toler; in a word, all those whose names were a guarantee for everything that was brilliant, witty, and amusing, were there; while, conspicuous among the rest, the prior himself was no other than John Philpot Curran! Scarcely was my rapid survey of the party completed, when the superior, filling his pipkin from the ample bowl before him, rose to give the health of the order. Alas me! that time should have so sapped my memory! I can but give my impression of what I heard.

The speech, which lasted about ten minutes, was a kind of burlesque on speeches from the throne, describing in formal phrase the prosperous state of their institution, its amicable foreign relations, the flourishing condition of its finances—brother Yelverton having paid in the two-and-sixpence he owed for above two years—concluding all with the hope that by a rigid economy, part of which consisted in limiting John Toler to ten pipkins, they would soon be enabled to carry into effect the proposed works on the frontier, and expend the sum of four shillings and nine-pence in the repair of the lobby. Winding up all with a glowing eulogium on monastic institutions in general, he concluded with recommending to their special devotion and unanimous cheers 'the Monks of the Screw.' Never, certainly, did men compensate for their previous silence better than the worthy brethren in question. Cheering with an energy I never heard the like of, each man finished his pipkin with just voice enough left to call for the song of the order.

Motioning with his hand to the fiddlers to begin, the prior cleared his throat, and, to the same simple but touching melody they had marched in to supper, sang the following chant:—

GOOD-LUCK TO THE FRIARS OF OLD

'Of all trades that flourished of old,
Before men knew reading and writing,
The friars' was best I am told,
If one wasn't much given to fighting;
For, rent free, you lived at your ease—
You had neither to work nor to labour—
You might eat of whatever you please,
For the prog was supplied by your neighbour.
Oh, good-luck to the friars of old!

'Your dress was convenient and cheap—
A loose robe like this I am wearing:
It was pleasant to eat in or sleep,
And never much given to tearing.
Not tightened nor squeezed in the least—
How of modern days you might shame us!
With a small bit of cord round your waist—
With what vigour you'd chant the oremus!
Oh, good-luck to the friars of old!

'What miracles then, too, you made!
The fame to this hour is lasting;
But the strangest of all, it is said,
You grew mighty fat upon fasting!
And though strictly forbid to touch wine,

How the fact all your glory enhances!
You well knew the taste of the vine—
Some miraculous gift of St. Francis!
Oh, good-luck to the friars of old!

'To trace an example so meek,
And repress all our carnal desires,
We mount two pair stairs every week,
And put on the garment of friars;
And our order itself it is old—
The oldest between me and you, sir;
For King David, they say, was enrolled,
And a capital Monk of the Screw, sir.
So, good-luck to the friars of old!'

The song over, and another cheer given to the brethren of the Screw, the pipkins were replenished, and the conversation, so long pent up, burst forth in all its plenitude. Nothing but fun, nothing but wit, nothing but merriment, was heard on either side. Here were not only all the bright spirits of the day, but they were met by appointment; they came prepared for the combat, armed for the fight; and, certainly, never was such a joust of wit and brilliancy. Good stories rained around; jests, repartees, and epigrams flew like lightning; and one had but time to catch some sparkling gem as it glittered, ere another and another succeeded.

But even already I grow impatient with myself while I speak of these things. How poor, how vapid, and how meagre is the effort to recall the wit that set the table in a roar! Not only is memory wanting, but how can one convey the incessant roll of fun, the hailstorm of pleasantry, that rattled about our ears; each good thing that was uttered ever suggesting something still better; the brightest fancy and the most glowing imagination stimulated to their utmost exercise; while powers of voice, of look, and of mimicry unequalled, lent all their aid to the scene.

While I sat entranced and delighted with all I saw and all I heard, I had not remarked that O'Grady had been addressing the chair for some time previous.

'Reverend brother,' replied the prior, 'the prayer of thy petition is inadmissible. The fourth rule of our faith says, *de confessione:* No subject, mirthful, witty, or jocose, known to, or by, any member of the order, shall be withheld from the brotherhood under a penalty of the heaviest kind. And it goes on to say, that whether the jest involve your father or your mother, your wife, your sister, or the aunt from whom you expect a legacy, no exception can be made. What you then look for is clearly impossible; make a clean breast of it, and begin.'

This being a question of order, a silence was soon established, when, what was my horror to find that Phil O'Grady began the whole narrative of my mother's letter on the subject of the Rooneys! Not limiting himself, however, to the meagre document in question, but colouring the story with all the force of his imagination, he displayed to the brethren the ludicrous extremes of character personated by the London fine lady and the Dublin attorney's wife. Shocked as I was at first, he had not proceeded far, when I was forced to join the laughter. The whole table pounced upon the story. The Rooneys were well known to them all; and the idea of poor Paul, who dispensed his hospitalities with a princely hand, having his mansion degraded to the character of a chop-house, almost convulsed them with laughter.

'I am going over to London next week,' said Parsons, 'with old Lambert; and if I thought I should meet this Lady Charlotte Hinton, I'd certainly contrive to have him presented to her as Mr. Paul Rooney.'

This observation created a diversion in favour of my lady-mother, to which I had the satisfaction of listening without the power to check.

'She has,' said Dawson, 'most admirable and original views about Ireland; and were it only for the fact of calling on the Rooneys for their bill, she deserves our gratitude. I humbly move, therefore, that we drink to the health of our worthy sister, Lady Charlotte Hinton.'

The next moment found me hip-hipping, in derision, to my mother's health, the only consolation being that I was escaping unnoticed and unknown.

'Well, Barrington, the duke was delighted with the corps; nothing could be more soldierlike than their appearance, as they marched past.'

'Ah, the attorneys', isn't it—the Devil's Own, as Curran calls them?'

'Yes, and remarkably well they looked. I say, Parsons, you heard what poor Rooney said when Sir Charles Asgill read aloud the general order complimenting them: "May I beg, Sir Charles," said he, "to ask if the document in your hand be an attested copy?"'

'Capital, 'faith! By-the-bye, what's the reason, can any one tell me, Paul has never invited me to dine for the last two years?'

'Indeed!' said Curran; 'then your chance is a bad one, for the statute of limitations is clearly against you.'

'Ah, Kellar, the Rooneys have cut all their low acquaintances, and your prospects look very gloomy. You know what took place between Paul and Lord Manners?'

'No, Barrington; let's hear it, by all means!'

'Paul had met him at Kinnegad, where both had stopped to change horses. "A glass of sherry, my lord?" quoth Paul, with a most insinuating look.

'"No, sir, thank you," was the distant reply.

'"A bowl of gravy, then, my lord?" rejoined he. '"Pray, excuse me," more coldly than before.

'"Maybe a chop and a crisped potato would tempt your lordship?"

'"Neither, sir, I assure you."

'"Nor a glass of egg-flip?" repeated Paul, in an accent bordering on despair.

'"Nor even the egg-flip," rejoined his lordship, in the most pompous manner.

'"Then, my lord," said Paul, drawing himself up to his full height, and looking him firmly in the face, "I've only to say, the 'onus' is now on you." With which he stalked out of the room, leaving the chancellor to his own reflections.'

'Brethren, the saint!' cried out the prior, as he rose from the chair.

'The saint! the saint!' re-echoed from lip to lip; and at the same moment the door opened, and a monk appeared, bearing a silver image of St. Patrick, about a foot and a half high, which he deposited in the middle of the table with the utmost reverence. All the monks rose, filling their pipkins, while the junior of the order, a fat little monk with spectacles, began the following ditty, in which all the rest joined, with every energy of voice and manner:—

I

'When St. Patrick our order created,
And called us the Monks of the Screw,
Good rules he revealed to our abbot
To guide us in what we should do.

II

'But first he replenished his fountain
With liquor the best in the sky,
And he swore by the word of his saintship
That fountain should never run dry.

III

'My children, be chaste, till you 're tempted;
While sober, be wise and discreet;
And humble your bodies with fasting
Whene'er you 've nothing to eat.

IV

'Then be not a glass in the convent,
Except on a festival, found;
And this rule to enforce, I ordain it
A festival all the year round.'

A hip, hip, hurrah! that made the very saint totter on his legs, shook the room; and once more the reverend fathers reseated themselves to resume their labours.

Again the conversation flowed cm in its broader channel; and scarcely was the laughter caused by one anecdote at an end when another succeeded, the strangest feature of all this being that he who related the story was, in almost every instance, less the source of amusement to the party than they who, listening to the recital, threw a hundred varied lights upon it, making even the tamest imaginable adventure the origin of innumerable ludicrous situations and absurd fancies. Besides all this, there were characteristic differences in the powers of the party, which deprived the display of any trace or appearance of sameness: the epigrammatic terseness and nicety of Curran; the jovial good-humour and mellow raciness of Lawrence Parsons; the happy facility of converting all before him into a pun or a repartee, so eminently possessed by Toler; and, perhaps more striking than all, the caustic irony and piercing sarcasm of Plunket's wit—relieved and displayed one another, each man's talent having only so much of rivalry as to excite opposition and give interest to the combat, yet never by any accident originating a particle of animosity, or even eliciting a shade of passing irritation.

With what pleasure could I continue to recount the stories, the songs, the sayings, I listened to! With what satisfaction do I yet look back upon that brilliant scene, nearly all the actors in which have since risen to high rank and eminence in the country! How often, too, in their bright career, when I have heard the warm praise of the world bestowed upon their triumphs and their successes, has my memory carried me back to that glorious night, when with hearts untrammelled by care, high in hope, and higher in ambition, these bright spirits sported in all the wanton exuberance of their genius, scattering with profusion the rich ore of their talent, careless of the depths to which the mine should be shafted hereafter! Yes, it is true there were giants in those days. However much one may be disposed to look upon the eulogist of the past, as one whose fancy is more ardent than his memory is tenacious, yet with respect to this, there is no denial of the fact, that great convivial gifts, great conversational power, no longer exist as they did some thirty or forty years ago. I speak more particularly of the country where I passed my youth—of Ireland. And who that remembers those names I have mentioned; who that can recall the fascination, and charm, which almost every dinner-party of the day could boast; who that can bring to mind the brilliancy of Curran, the impetuous power of Plunket, or the elegance of manner and classical perfection of wit that made Burke the Cicero of his nation; who, I say, with all these things before his memory, can venture to compare the society of that period with the present? No, no; the grey hairs that mingle with our brown may convict us of being a prejudiced witness, but we would call into court every one whose testimony is available, and confidently await the verdict.

'And so they ran away!' said the prior, turning towards a tall, gaunt-looking monk, who with a hollow voice and solemn manner was recording the singular disappearance of the militia regiment he commanded on the morning they were to embark for England. 'The story we heard,' resumed the prior, 'was, that when drawn up in the Fifteen Acres, one of the light company caught sight of a hare, and flung his musket at it; that the grenadiers followed the example, and that then the whole battalion broke loose, with a loud yell, and set off in pursuit——'

'No, sir,' said the gaunt man, waving his hand to suppress the laughter around him. 'They were assembled on the lighthouse wall, as it might be here, and we told them off by tallies as they marched on board, not perceiving, however, that as fast as they entered the packet on one side they left it on the opposite, there being two jolly-boats in waiting to receive them; and as it was dusk at the time, the scheme was undetected, until the corporal of a flank company shouted out to them to wait for him, that being his boat. At this time we had fifty men of our four hundred and eighty.'

'Ay, ay, holy father,' cried the prior, as he helped himself to a devilled bone, 'your fellows were like the grilled bone before me—when they were mustered, they would not wait to be peppered?'

This sally produced a roar of laughter, not the less hearty that the grim-visaged hero it was addressed to never relaxed a muscle of his face.

It was now late, and what between the noise, the wine, and the laughter, my faculties were none of the clearest. Without having drunk much, I felt all the intoxication of liquor, and a whirlwind of confusion in my ideas, that almost resembled madness. To this state one part of their proceedings in a great measure contributed; for every now and then, on some signal from the prior, the whole party would take hands and dance round the table to the measure of an Irish jig, wilder and even more eccentric than their own orgies. Indeed, I think this religious exercise finished me; for after the third time of its performance, the whole scene became a confused and disturbed mass, and amid the crash of voices, the ringing of laughter, the tramping of feet, I sank into something which, if not sleep, was at least unconsciousness; and thus is a wet sponge drawn over the immediately succeeding portion of my history.

A Monk of the Screw unscrews Mr. Delany's courage

Some faint recollection I have of terrifying old Corny by my costume; but what the circumstances, or how they happened, I cannot remember. I can only call to mind one act in vindication of my wisdom—I went to bed.

CHAPTER XVIII
A CONFIDENCE

I slept late on the morning after my introduction to the Monks of the Screw, and probably should have continued to indulge still longer, had not O'Grady awoke me.

'Come, Jack,' he cried, 'this is the third time I have been here to-day. I can't have mercy on you any longer; so rub your eyes, and try if you can't wake sufficiently to listen to me. I have just received my appointment as captain in the Forty-first, with an order to repair immediately to Chatham to join the regiment, which is under orders for foreign service.'

'And when do you go, Phil?'

'To-night at eight o'clock. A private note from a friend at the Horse Guards tells me not to lose a moment; and as I shall have to wait on the duke to thank him for his great kindness to me, I have no time to spare.'

This news so stunned me that for a moment or two I couldn't reply. O'Grady perceived it, and, patting me gaily on the shoulder, said—

'Yes, Jack, I am sorry we are to separate. But as for me, no other course was open; and as to you, with all your independence from fortune, and with all your family influence to push your promotion, the time is not very distant when you will begin to feel the life you are leading vapid and tiresome. You will long for an excitement more vigorous and more healthy in its character; and then, my boy, my dearest hope is that we may be thrown once more together.'

Had my friend been able at the moment to have looked into the secret recesses of my heart and read there my inmost thoughts, he could not more perfectly have depicted my feelings, nor pictured the impressions that, at the very moment he spoke, were agitating my mind. The time he alluded to had indeed arrived. The hour had come when I wished to be a soldier in more than the mere garb; but with that wish came linked another even stronger still; and this was, that, before I went on service, I should once more see Louisa Bellew, explain to her the nature and extent of my attachment to her, and obtain, if possible, some pledge on her part that, with the distinction I hoped to acquire, I should look to the possession of her love as my reward and my recompense. Young as I was, I felt ashamed at avowing to O'Grady the rapid progress of my passion. I had not courage to confess upon what slight encouragement I built my hopes, and at the same time was abashed at being compelled to listen tamely to his prophecy, when the very thoughts that flashed across me would have indicated my resolve.

While I thus maintained an awkward silence, he once more resumed—

'Meanwhile, Jack, you can serve me, and I shall make no apologies for enlisting you. You've heard me speak of this great Loughrea steeplechase: now, somehow or other, with my usual prudence, I have gone on adding wager to wager, until at last I find myself with a book of some eight hundred pounds—to lose which at a moment like this, I need not say, would almost ruin all my plans. To be free of the transaction, I this morning offered to pay half forfeit, and they refused me. Yes, Hinton, they knew every man of them the position I stood in. They saw that not only my prospects but my honour was engaged; that before a week I should be far away, without any power to control, without any means to observe them. They knew well that, thus circumstanced, I must lose; and that if I lost, I must sell my commission, and leave the army beggared in character and in fortune.'

'And now, my dear friend,' said I, interrupting, 'how happens it that you bet with men of this stamp? I understood you it was a friendly match, got up at a dinnerparty.'

'Even so, Jack. The dinner was in my own rooms, the claret mine, the men my *friends*. You may smile, but so the world is pleased to call those with whom from day to day we associate, with no other bond of union than the similarity of a pursuit which has nothing more reprehensible in it than the character of the intimacies it engenders. Yes, Hinton, these are my sporting friends, sipping my wine while they plot my ruin. Conviviality with them is not the happy abandonment to good fellowship and enjoyment, but the season of cold and studied calculation—the hour when, unexcited themselves, they trade upon the unguarded and unwary feelings of others. They know how imperative is the code of honour as regards a bet, and they make a virtue to themselves in the unflinching firmness of their exaction, as a cruel judge would seek applause for the stern justice with which he condemns a felon. It is usual, however, to accept half forfeit in circumstances like these of mine: the condition did not happen to be inserted, and they rejected my offer.'

'Is this possible,' said I, 'and that these men call themselves your friends?'

'Yes, Jack; a betting-book is like Shylock's bond, and the holder of one pretty much about as merciful as the worthy Israelite. But come, come! it is but boyish weakness in one like me to complain of these things; nor, indeed, would I speak of them now, but with the hope that my words may prove a warning to you, while they serve to explain the service I look for from you, and give you some insight into the character of those with whom you 'll have to deal.'

'Only tell me,' said I, 'only explain, my dear O'Grady, what I can do, and how; it is needless for me to say I 'm ready.'

'I thought as much. Now listen to me. When I made this unlucky match it was, as I have said, over a dinnerparty, when, excited by wine and carried away by the enthusiasm of the moment, I made a proposition which, with a calmer head, I should never have ventured. For a second or two it was not accepted, and Mr. Burke, of whom you 've heard me speak, called out from the end of the table, "A sporting offer, by Jove! and I'll ride for you myself." This I knew was to give me one of the first horsemen in Ireland; so, while filling my glass and nodding to him, accepted his offer, I cried out, "Two to one against any horse named at this moment!" The words were not spoken when I was taken up, at both sides of the table; and as I leaned across to borrow a pencil from a friend, I saw that a smile was curling every lip, and that Burke himself endeavoured with his wine-glass to conceal the expression of his face. I needed no stronger proof that the whole match had been a preconcerted scheme between the parties, and that I had fallen into a snare laid purposely to entrap me. It was too late, however, to retract; I booked my bets, drank my wine, congeed my friends, went to bed, and woke the next morning to feel myself a dupe.

'But come, Jack; at this rate I shall never have done. The match was booked, the ground chosen, Mr. Burke to be my jockey, and, in fact, everything arranged, when, what was my surprise, my indignation, to find that the horse I destined for the race (at the time in possession of a friend) was bought up for five hundred and sent off to England! This disclosed to me how completely I was entrapped. Nothing remained for me then but to purchase one which offered at the moment! and this one, I 've told you already, has the pleasant reputation of being the most wicked devil and the hardest to ride in the whole west; in fact, except Burke himself, nobody would mount him on a road, and as to crossing a country with him, even *he*, they say, has no fancy for it. In any case, he made it the ground of a demand which I could not refuse—that, in the event of my winning, he was to claim a third of the stakes. At length the horse is put in training, improves every hour, and matters seem to be taking a favourable turn. In the midst of this, however, the report reaches me, as you heard yourself yesterday morning, that Burke will not ride. However I affected to discredit it at the moment, I had great difficulty to preserve the appearance of calm. This morning settles the question by this letter:—

'"Red House, Wednesday Morning."

'"Dear Sir,—A friendly hint has just reached me that I am to be arrested on the morning of the Loughrea race for a trifle of a hundred and eighteen pounds and some odd shillings. If it suits your convenience to pay the money, or enter into bail for the amount, I'll be very happy to ride your horse; for, although I don't care for a double ditch, I've no fancy to take the wall of the county jail, even on the back of as good a horse as Moddiridderoo.—Yours truly, Ulick Burke."'

'Well,' said I, as, after some difficulty, I spelled through this ill-written and dirty epistle, 'and what do you mean to do here?'

'If you ask me,' said Phil, 'what I'd like to do, I tell you fairly it would be to horsewhip my friend Mr. Burke as a preliminary, pay the stakes, withdraw my horse, and cut the whole concern; but my present position is, unhappily, opposed to each of these steps. In the first place, a rencontre with Burke would do me infinite disservice at the Horse Guards, and as to the payment of eight hundred pounds, I don't think I could raise the money, unless some one would advance five hundred of it for a mortgage on Corny Delany. But to be serious, Jack—and, as time passes, I must be serious—I believe the best way on this occasion is to give Burke the money (for as to the bill, that's an invention); yet as I must start to-night for England, and the affair will require some management, I must put the whole matter into your hands, with full instructions how to act.'

'I am quite ready and willing,' said I; 'only give me the *carte du pay*.'

'Well, then, my boy, you'll go down to Loughrea for me the day before the race, establish yourself as quietly as you can in the hotel, and, as the riders must be named on the day before the running, contrive to see Mr. Burke, and inform him that his demand will be complied with. Have no delicacy with him—-it is a mere money question; and although by the courtesy of the turf he is a gentleman, yet there is no occasion to treat him with more of ceremony than is due to yourself in your negotiation. This letter contains the sum he mentions. In addition to that, I have inclosed a bank cheque for whatever you like to give him; only remember one thing, Hinton—*he* must ride, and *I* must win.'

All the calmness with which O'Grady had hitherto spoken deserted him at this moment; his face became scarlet, his brow was bent, and his lip quivered with passion, while, as he walked the room with hurried steps he muttered between his teeth—

'Yes, though it cost my last shilling, I'll win the race! They thought to ruin me; the scheme was deeply laid and well planned too, but they shall fail. No, Hinton,' resumed he in a louder tone—'no, Hinton; believe me, poor man that I am, this is not with me a question of so many pounds: it is the wounded *amour propre* of a man who, all through his life, held out the right hand of fellowship to those very men who now conspire to be his ruin. And such, my dear boy, such, for the most part, are the dealings of the turf. I do not mean to say that men of high honour and unblemished integrity are not foremost in the encouragement of a sport which, from its bold and manly character, is essentially an English one; but this I would assert, that probity, truth, and honour are the gifts of but a very small number of those who make a traffic of the turf, and are, what the world calls, "racing men." And oh how very hard the struggle, how nice the difficulty, of him who makes these men his daily companions, to avoid the many artifices which the etiquette of the racecourse permits, but which the feelings of a gentleman would reject as unfair and unworthy! How contaminating that laxity of principle that admits of every stratagem, every trick, as legitimate, with the sole proviso that it be successful! And what a position is it that admits of no alternative save being the dupe or the blackleg! How hard for the young fellow entering upon life with all the ardour, all the unsuspecting freshness of youth about him, to stop short at one without passing on to the other stage! How difficult, with offended pride and wounded self-love, to find himself the mere tool of sharpers! How very difficult to check the indignant spirit, that whispers retaliation by the very arts by which he has been cheated! Is not such a trial as this too much for any boy of twenty? and is it not to be feared that, in the estimation he sees those held in whose blackguardism is their pre-eminence, a perverted ambition to be what is called a sharp fellow may sap and undermine every honourable feeling of the heart, break down the barriers of rigid truth and scrupulous fidelity, teaching him to exult at what formerly he had blushed, and to recognise no folly so contemptible as that of him who believes the word of another? Such a career as this has many a one pursued, abandoning bit by bit every grace, every virtue, and every charm of his character, that, at the end, he should come forth a "sporting gentleman."'

He paused for a few seconds, and then, turning towards me, added, in a voice tremulous from emotion, 'And yet, my boy, to men like this I would now expose you! No, no, Jack; I'll not do it. I care not what turn the thing may take; I'll not embitter my life with this reflection.' He seized the letter, and crushing it in his hand, walked towards the window.

'Come, come, O'Grady,' said I, 'this is not fair; you first draw a strong picture of these men, and then you deem me weak enough to fall into their snares. That would hardly say much for my judgment and good sense; besides, you have stimulated my curiosity, and I shall be sadly disappointed if I'm not to see them.'

'Be it so, Jack!' said he with a sigh. 'I shall give you a couple of letters to some friends of mine down there; and I know but one recompense you'll have for all the trouble and annoyance of this business—your pretty friend, Miss Bellew, is on a visit in the neighbourhood, and is certain to be at the race.'

Had O'Grady looked at me while he spoke he would have seen how deeply this intelligence affected me, while I myself could with difficulty restrain the increased interest I now felt in all about the matter, questioning him on every particular, inquiring into a hundred minute points, and, in fact, displaying an ardour on the subject that nothing short of my friend's preoccupation could have failed in detecting the source of. My mind now fixed on one object, I could scarcely follow him in his directions as to travelling down, secrecy, etc.

I heard something about the canal-boat, and some confused impression was on my mind about a cross-road and a jaunting-car; but the prospect of meeting Louisa, the hope of again being in her society, rendered me indifferent to all else; and as I thrust the letters he gave me into my coat-pocket, and promised an implicit observance of all his directions, I should have been sorely puzzled had he asked me to repeat them.

'Now,' continued O'Grady, at the end of about half-an-hour's rapid speaking, 'I believe I've put you in possession of all the bearings of this case. You understand, I hope, the kind of men you have to deal with, and I trust Mr. Ulick Burke is thoroughly known to you by this time?'

'Oh, perfectly,' said I, half mechanically.

'Well, then, my boy, I believe I had better say good-bye. Something tells me we shall meet ere long; meanwhile, Jack, you have my best wishes.' He paused for a moment and turned away his head, evidently affected, then added, 'You'll write to me soon, of course; and as that old fool Corny follows me in a week——'

'And is Corny going abroad?'

'Ay, confound him! like the old man in Sindbad, there's no getting him off one's shoulders. Besides, he has a kind of superstition that he ought to close the eyes of the last of the family; and as he has frankly confessed to me this morning he knows I am in that predicament, he esteems it a point of duty to accompany me. Poor fellow, with all his faults, I can't help feeling attached to him; and were I to leave him behind me, what would become of him? No, Jack, I am fully sensible of all the inconvenience, all the ridicule of this step, but, 'faith, I prefer both to the embittering reflection I should have did I desert him.'

'Why does he remain after you, Phil? He 'll never find his way to London.'

'Oh, trust him! What with scolding, cursing, and abusing every one he meets, he'll attract notice enough on the road never to be forgotten, or left behind. But the fact is, it is his own proposition; and Corny has asked for a few days' leave of absence, for the first time for seven-and-twenty years!'

'And what the deuce can that be for?'

'You 'd never guess if you tried until to-morrow — to see his mother.'

'Corny's mother! Corny Delany's mother!'

'Just so — his mother. Ah, Hinton! you still have much to learn about us all here. And now, before we part, let me instruct you on this point; not that I pretend to have a reason for it, nor do I know that there is any, but somehow I'll venture to say that whenever you meet with a little cross-grained, ill-conditioned, ill-thriven old fellow, with a face as if carved in the knot of a crab-tree, the odds are about fifteen to one that the little wretch has a mother alive. Whether it is that the tenacity of life among such people is greater, or whether Nature has any peculiar objects of her own in view in the matter, I can't say, but trust me for the fact. And now, I believe, I have run myself close to time; so once more, Jack, good-bye, and God bless you!'

He hurried from the room as he spoke, but, as the door was closing, I saw that his lip trembled and his cheek was pale; while I leaned against the window-shutter and looked after him with a heavy and oppressed heart, for he was my first friend in the world.

CHAPTER XIX
THE CANAL-BOAT

In obedience to O'Grady's directions, of which, fortunately for me, he left a memorandum in writing, I started from Portobello in the canal-boat on the afternoon of the day after his departure. The day was dark and lowering, with occasional showers of cold and sleety rain. However, the casual glance I took of the gloomy cell, denominated cabin, deterred me from seeking shelter there, and buttoned up in my greatcoat and with my travelling-cap drawn firmly over my eyes, I walked the deck for several hours, my own thoughts affording me sufficient occupation; and even had the opportunity presented itself, I should not have desired any other. On this score, however, there was no temptation; and as I looked at my fellow-passengers, there was nothing either in their voice, air, or appearance to induce me to care for any closer intimacy.

The majority of them were stout, plain-looking countryfolk, with coats of brown or grey frieze, leather gaiters, and thick shoes, returning, as I could guess from some chance expressions they dropped, from the Dublin market, whither they had proceeded with certain droves of bullocks, wethers, and hoggets, the qualities of which formed the staple of conversation. There were also some lady passengers—one a rather good-looking woman, with a certain air of half gentility about her, which enabled her at times to display to her companion her profound contempt for the rest of the company. This companion was a poor subdued-looking girl of about eighteen or twenty years, who scarcely ventured to raise her haggard eyes, and spoke with an accent painful from agitation; her depressed look and her humble manner did not conceal, however, a certain air of composed and quiet dignity, which spoke of happier days. A host of ill-bred, noisy, and unmannerly children accompanied them; and I soon discovered that the mother was the wife of the great shopkeeper in Loughrea, and her pale companion a governess she had just procured in Dublin, to initiate the promising offspring in the accomplished acquirements of French, Italian, music, and painting. Their only acquaintance on board seemed to be a jolly-looking man who, although intimate with every one, seemed somehow not to suffer in the grand lady's esteem from the familiarities he dispensed on all sides. He was a short, florid-looking little fellow, with a round bullet head, the features of which seemed at first sight so incongruous that it was difficult to decide on their prevailing expression; his large grey eyes, which rolled and twinkled with fun, caught a character of severity from his heavy overhanging eyebrows, and there was a stern determination in his compressed lips that every moment gave way to some burst of jocular good-humour, as he accosted one or other of his friends. His voice, however, was the most remarkable thing about him; for while at one moment he would declaim in the full round tone of a person accustomed to speak in public, in the next he would drop down into an easy and familiar accent, to which the mellowness of his brogue imparted a raciness quite peculiar. His dress was a suit of rusty black, with leather breeches of the same colour, and high boots. This costume, which pronounced him a priest, might also, had I known more of the country, have explained the secrets of that universal understanding he maintained with all on board. He knew every one's business, whither they were going, where they had been, what success had attended them in the market, how much the black heifer brought, what the pigs were sold for; he asked why Tim didn't come to his duties, and if Molly's child was well of the measles; he had a word too for the shopkeeper's wife, but that was said in a whisper; and then producing a copper snuff-box, about the size of a saucer, he presented it to me with a graceful bow, saying—

'This is not the first time I have had the honour of being your fellow-traveller, Captain. We came over from Liverpool together.'

I now remembered that this was the same priest whose controversial powers had kept me awake for nearly half the night, and whose convivial ones filled up the remainder. I was delighted, however, to renew my acquaintance, and we soon cemented an intimacy, which ended in his proposing that we should sit together at dinner, to which I at once assented.

'Dacent people, dacent people, Captain; but *bastes*, after all, in the ways of the world—none of the *usage de société*, as we used to say at St. Omer's. No, no; *feræ naturæ*, devil a more. But here comes the dinner; the ould story—leg of mutton and turnips, boiled chickens and ham, a cod and potatoes! By the Mass, they would boil one's father if they had him on board,' while he added in a whisper—'by rason they can't roast! So now, will you move down, if you please?'

'After your reverence, if you'll permit. *Arma cedant togæ*.'

'Thrue for you, my son, *sacerdotes priores*; and though I am only a priest——'

'More's the pity,' said I, interrupting.

'You're right,' said he, with a slight pinch of my arm, 'whether you are joking or not.'

The dinner was not a very appetising one, nor indeed the company over seductive, so that I disappeared with the cloth, glad to find myself once more in the open air, with the deck to myself; for my fellow-travellers had, one and all, begun a very vigorous attack upon sundry jugs of hot water and crucibles full of whisky, the fumes of which, added to the heat, the smoke, and other disagreeables, made me right happy to escape.

As the evening wore late, the noise and uproar grew louder and more vociferous, and, had not frequent bursts of laughter proclaimed the spirit of the conviviality, I should have been tempted to believe the party were engaged in deadly strife. Sometimes a single narrator would seem to hold the company in attentive silence; then a general chorus of the whole would break in, with shouts of merriment, knocking of knuckles on the table, stamping of feet, and other signs of approbation and applause. As this had now continued for some time, and it was already verging towards midnight, I began to grow impatient; for as sleep stole over my eyelids, I was desirous of some little quiet, to indulge myself in a nap. Blessings on my innocent delusion! the gentlemen below-stairs had as much notion of swimming as sleeping. Of this a rapid glance through a little window, at the extremity of the cabin, soon satisfied me. As well as the steamed and heated glass would permit my seeing, the scene was a strange one.

About forty persons were seated around a narrow table, so closely packed that any attitude but the bolt upright was impracticable. There they were, of every age and sex; some asleep with Welsh wigs and red pocket-handkerchiefs screening their heads from cold, and their ears as well as might be from uproar; some were endeavouring to read by the light of mutton candles, with wicks like a light infantry feather, with a nob at the head; others, with their heads bent down together, were confidentially exchanging the secrets of the last market; while here and there were scattered about little convivial knots of jolly souls, whose noisy fun and loud laughter indicated but slight respect for their drowsy neighbours.

The group, however, which attracted most of my attention was one near the fire at the end. This consisted of his reverence Father Tom, a stout, burly-looking old farmer opposite him, the austere lady from Loughrea, and a little dried-up, potted-herring of a man, who, with a light-brown coat and standing collar, sat up perpendicularly on his seat and looked about him with an eye as lively and an accent as sharp as though it were only noonday. This little personage, who came from that Irish Pennsylvania called Moate, was endeavouring to maintain a controversy with the worthy priest, who, in addition to his polemics, was deep in a game of spoiled five with the farmer, and carrying on besides another species of warfare with his fair neighbour. The diversity of all these occupations might possibly have been overmuch for him, were it not for the aid of a suspicious-looking little kettle that sat hissing and rocking on the hob, with a look of pert satisfaction that convinced me its contents were something stronger than water.

Perceiving a small space yet unoccupied in the party, I made my way thither by the stair near it, and soon had the satisfaction to find myself safely installed, without attracting any other notice from the party than a proud stare from the lady, as she removed a little farther from beside the priest.

As to his reverence, far too deeply interested in his immediate pursuits to pay any attention to me, he had quite enough on his hands with his three antagonists, none of whom did he ever for a moment permit to edge in even a word. Conducting his varied warfare with the skill of a general, who made the artillery, the infantry, and the cavalry of mutual aid and assistance to one another, he continued to keep the church, the courtship, and the cards all moving together, in a manner perfectly miraculous—the vehemence with which he thumped down a trump upon the table serving as a point in his argument, while the energy of the action permitted a squeeze of the lady's hand with the other.

'There ye go, six of spades! Play a spade, av ye have one, Mr. Larkins— — For a set of shrivelled-up craytures, with nothing but thee and thou for a creed to deny the real ould ancient faith, that Saint Peter and— — The ace of diamonds! *that* tickled you under the short ribs— —- Not you, Mrs. Carney; for a sore time you have of it, and an angel of a woman ye are; and the husband that could be cruel to you, and take— — The odd trick out of you, Mr. Larkins— —

No, no, I deny it—*nego in omnibus, Domine*. What does Origen say? The rock, says he, is Peter; and if you translate the passage without— — Another kettleful, if you please. I go for the ten, Misther Larkins. Trumps! another— another—hurroo! By the tower of Clonmacnoise, I'll beggar the bank to-night. *Malhereux au jeux, heureux en amour,* as we used to say formerly. God forgive us!'

Whether it was the French, or the look that accompanied it, I cannot aver, but certainly the lady blushed and looked down. In vain did the poor Quaker essay a word of explanation. In vain did Mrs. Carney herself try to escape from the awkward inferences some of his allusions seemed to lead to. Even the old farmer saw his tricks confiscated, and his games estreated, without a chance of recovery; for, like Coeur de Lion with his iron mace, the good priest laid about him, smashing, slaying, and upsetting all before him, and never giving his adversaries a moment to recover from one blow, ere he dealt another at their heads.

'To be sure, Mrs. Carney, and why not? It's as mild as mother's milk. Come, ould square-toes, take a thimbleful of it, and maybe it'll lead you to a better understanding. I play the five fingers, Mr. Larkins. There goes Jack, my jewel! Play to that—the trick is mine. Don't be laughing; I've a bit of fat in the heel of my fist for you yet. There now, what are you looking at? Don't you see the cards? Troth, you 're as bad as the Quaker; you won't believe your own eyes— — And ye see, ma'am'—here he whispered something in the lady's ear for a few seconds, adding as he concluded—'and thim, Mrs. Carney, thim's the rights of the Church. Friends, indeed! ye call yourselves friends! Faix, ye're the least social friends I ever forgathered with, even if the bare look of you wasn't an antidote to all kinds of amusements— — Cut, Mr. Larkins— — And it's purgatory ye don't like? Ye know what Father O'Leary said, "Some of ye may go farther and fare worse," not to speak of what a place heaven would be, with the likes of you in it— — Av it was Mrs. Carney, indeed. Yes, Mary, your own beautiful self, that's fit to be an angel any day, and discoorse with angels— — Howld, av you please, I've a club for that— — Don't you see what nonsense you're talking—the little kettle is laughing at you— — What's that you 're mumbling about my time of life? Show me the man that'll carry twelve tumblers with me; show me the man that'll cross a country; show me the man that 'll— — Never mind, Mrs. Carney— — Time of life, indeed! Faix, I'll give you a song.'

With these words, the priest pushed the cards aside, replenished the glasses, and began the following melody to an air much resembling 'Sir Roger de Coverley':—

> 'To-morrow I 'll just be three-score;
> May never worse fortune betide me
> Than to have a hot tumbler before,
> And a beautiful crayture beside me!
> If this world 's a stage, as they say,
> And that men are the actors, I 'm certain,
> In the after-piece I 'd like to play,
> And be there at the fall of the curtain.
> Whack! fol lol.

'No, no, Mrs. Carney, I'll take the vestment on it, nothing of the kind—the allusion is most discreet; but there is more.

'For the pleasures of youth are a flam;
To try them again, pray excuse me;
I 'd rather be priest that I am,
With the rights of the Church to amuse me.
Sure, there's naught like a jolly old age,
And the patriarchs knew this, it said is;
For though they looked sober and sage,
'Faith, they had their own fun with the ladies!
Whack! fol lol.

'Come now, Captain, you are a man that knows his humanities; 'I be judged by you.'

'I protest,' said I laughingly, 'I'd rather pronounce on your punch than your polemics.'

'No, would you though?' said the priest, with a joyous twinkle in his eye, that showed which controversy had more attraction for him. 'Faix, then, you shall have a fair trial. Beach me that glass, Mr. Larkins; and if it isn't sweet enough, maybe Mrs. Carney would stir it for you with her finger. There, now, we'll be comfortable and social, and have no more bother about creeds, nor councils; for although it is only child's play for me to demolish a hundred like you, I'd rather be merciful, and leave you, like Alexander the coppersmith, to get the reward of your works.'

Whether it was the polite attention bestowed upon me by his reverence, or that the magical word 'Captain,' so generic for all things military in Ireland, had its effect, or that any purely personal reasons were the cause, I cannot aver; but, certainly, Mrs. Carney's manner became wonderfully softened. She smiled at me slyly when the priest wasn't looking, and vouchsafed an inquiry as to whether I had ever served in the Roscommon yeomanry.

The kettle once more sent forth its fragrant steam, the glasses were filled, the vanquished Quaker had extinguished both himself and his argument beneath his broad beaver; and Father Tom, with a glance of pleasure at the party, pronounced our arrangements perfect, and suggested a round game, by way of passing the time.

'We are now,' said he, 'on the long level for eighteen miles; there's neither a lock nor a town to disturb us. Give Mrs. Carney the cards.'

The proposition was met with hearty approval; and thus did I, Lieutenant Hinton, of the Grenadier Guards, extra aide-de-camp to the viceroy, discover myself at four in the morning engaged at a game of loo, whose pecuniary limits were fourpence, but whose boundaries as to joke and broad humour were wide as the great Atlantic. Day broke, and I found myself richer by some tumblers of the very strongest whisky punch, a confounded headache, and two-and-eightpence in bad copper jingling in my pocket.

CHAPTER XX
SHANNON HARBOUR

Little does he know who voyages in a canal-boat, dragged along some three miles and a half per hour, ignominiously at the tails of two ambling hackneys, what pride, pomp, and circumstance await him at the first town he enters. Seated on the deck, watching with a Dutchman's apathy the sedgy banks, whose tall naggers bow their heads beneath the ripple that eddies from the bow—now lifting his eyes from earth to sky, with nothing to interest, nothing to attract him, turning from the gaze of the long dreary tract of bog and moorland, to look upon his fellow-travellers, whose features are perhaps neither more striking nor more pleasing—the monotonous jog of the postillion before, the impassive placidity of the helmsman behind; the lazy smoke that seems to lack energy to issue from the little chimney; the brown and leaden look of all around—have something dreamy and sleep-compelling, almost impossible to resist. And, already, as the voyager droops his head, and lets fall his eyelids, a confused and misty sense of some everlasting journey, toilsome, tedious, and slow, creeps over his besotted faculties; when suddenly the loud bray of the horn breaks upon his ears—the sound is re-echoed from a distance—the far-off tinkle of a bell is borne along the water, and he sees before him, as if conjured up by some magician's wand, the roofs and chimneys of a little village. Meanwhile the excitement about him increases: the deck is lumbered with hampers and boxes, and parcels—the note of departure to many a cloaked and frieze-coated passenger has rung; for, strange as it may seem, in that little assemblage of mud hovels, with their dunghills and duck-pools around them, with its one-slated house and its square chapel, there are people who live there; and, stranger still, some of those who have left it, and seen other places, are going back there again, to drag on life as before. But the plot is thickening: the large brass bell at the stern of the boat is thundering away with its clanging sound; the banks are crowded with people; and as if to favour the melodramatic magic of the scene, the track-rope is cast off, the weary posters trot away towards their stable, and the stately barge floats on to its destined haven without the aid of any visible influence. He who watches the look of proud, important bearing that beams upon 'the captain's' face at a moment like this, may philosophise upon the charms of that power which man wields above his fellow-men. Such, at least, were some of my reflections; and I could not help muttering to myself, if a man like this feel pride of station, what a glorious service must be the navy!

Watching with interest *the* nautical skill with which, having fastened a rope to the stern, the boat was swung round, with her head in the direction from whence she came, intimating thereby the monotonous character of her avocations, I did not perceive that one by one the passengers were taking their departure.

'Good-bye, Captain,' cried Father Tom, as he extended his ample hand to me; 'we'll meet again in Loughrea. I'm going on Mrs. Carney's car, or I'd be delighted to join you in a conveyance; but you'll easily get one at the hotel.'

I had barely time to thank the good father for his kind advice, when I perceived him adjusting various duodecimo Carneys in the well of the car, and then having carefully included himself in the frieze coat that wrapped Mrs. Carney, he gave the word to drive on.

As the day following was the time appointed for naming the horses and the riders, I had no reason for haste. Loughrea, from what I had heard, was a commonplace country town, in which, as in all similar places every new-comer was canvassed with a prying and searching curiosity. I resolved, therefore, to stop where I was; not, indeed, that the scenery possessed any attractions. A prospect more bleak, more desolate, and more barren, it would be impossible to' conceive—a wide river with low and reedy banks, moving sluggishly on its yellow current, between broad tracts of bog or callow meadow-land; no trace of cultivation, not even a tree was to be seen.

Such is Shannon Harbour. No matter, thought I, the hotel at least looks well. This consolatory reflection of mine was elicited by the prospect of a large stone building of some storeys high, whose granite portico and wide steps stood in strange contrast to the miserable mud hovels that flanked it on either side. It was a strange thought to have placed such a building in such a situation. I dismissed the ungrateful notion, as I remembered my own position, and how happy I felt to accept its hospitality.

A solitary jaunting-car stood on the canal side—the poorest specimen of its class I had ever seen. The car—a few boards cobbled up by some country carpenter—seemed to threaten disunion even with the coughing of the wretched beast that wheezed between its shafts; while the driver, an emaciated creature of any age from sixteen to sixty, sat shivering upon the seat, striking from time to time with his whip at the flies that played about the animal's ears, as though anticipating their prey.

'Banagher, yer honour? Loughrea, sir? Bowl ye over in an hour and a half. Is it Portumna, sir?'

'No, my good friend,' replied I, 'I stop at the hotel.'

Had I proposed to take a sail down the Shannon on my portmanteau, I don't think the astonishment could have been greater. The bystanders, and they were numerous enough by this time, looked from one to the other with expressions of mingled surprise and dread; and indeed had I, like some sturdy knight-errant of old, announced my determination to pass the night in a haunted chamber, more unequivocal evidences of their admiration and fear could not have been evoked.

'In the hotel!' said one.

'He is going to stop at the hotel!' cried another.

'Blessed hour!' said a third, 'wonders will never cease!'

Short as had been my residence in Ireland, it had at least taught me one lesson—never to be surprised at anything I met with. So many views of life peculiar to the land met me at every turn, so many strange prejudices, so many singular notions, that were I to apply my previous knowledge of the world, such as it was, to my guidance here, I should be like a man endeavouring to sound the depths of the sea with an instrument intended to ascertain the distance of a star. Leaving, therefore, to time the explanation of the mysterious astonishment around me, I gathered together my baggage, and left the boat.

The first impressions of a traveller are not uncommonly his best. The finer and more distinctive features of a land require deep study and long acquaintance, but the broader traits of nationality are caught in an instant, or not caught at all Familiarity destroys them, and it is only at first blush that we learn to appreciate them with force. Who that has landed at Calais, at Rotterdam, or at Leghorn, has not felt this? The Flemish peasant, with her long-eared cap and heavy sabots—the dark Italian, basking his swarthy features in the sun, are striking objects when we first look on them; but days and weeks roll on, the wider characteristics of human nature swallow up the smaller and more narrow features of nationality, and in a short time we forget that the things which have surprised us at first are not what we have been used to from our infancy.

Gifted with but slender powers of observation, such as they were, this was to me always a moment of their exercise. How often in the rural districts of my own country had the air of cheery comfort and healthy contentment spoken to my heart; how frequently, in the manufacturing ones, had the din of hammers, the black smoke, or the lurid flame of furnaces, turned my thoughts to those great sources of our national wealth, and made me look on every dark and swarthy face that passed as on one who ministered to his country's weal! But now I was to view a new and very different scene.

Scarcely had I put foot on shore when the whole population of the village thronged around me. What are these, thought I? What art do they practise? what trade do they profess? Alas! their wan looks, their tattered garments, their outstretched hands, and imploring voices, gave the answer—they were all beggars! It was not as if the old, the decrepit, the sickly, or the feeble, had fallen on the charity of their fellow-men in their hour of need; but here were all—all—the old man and the infant, the husband and the wife, the aged grandfather and the tottering grandchild, the white locks of youth, the whiter hairs of age—pale, pallid, and sickly—trembling between starvation and suspense, watching with the hectic eye of fever every gesture of him on whom their momentary hope was fixed; canvassing, in muttered tones, every step of his proceeding, and hazarding a doubt upon its bearing oh their own fate.

'Oh, the heavens be your bed, noble gentleman! look at me! The Lord reward you for the little sixpence that you have in your fingers there! I'm the mother of ten of them.'

'Billy Cronin, yer honour; I'm dark since I was nine years old.'

'I'm the ouldest man in the town-land,' said an old fellow with a white beard, and a blanket strapped round him.

Joe the mighty hunter.

While bursting through the crowd came a strange, odd-looking figure, in a huntsman's coat and cap, but both so patched and tattered, it was difficult to detect their colour. 'Here's Joe, your honour,' cried he, putting his hand to his mouth at the same moment. 'Tally-ho! ye ho! ye yo!' he shouted, with a mellow cadence I never heard surpassed. 'Yow! yow! yow!' he cried, imitating the barking of dogs, and then uttering a long, low wail, like the bay of a hound, he shouted out, 'Hark away t hark away!' and at the same moment pranced into the thickest of the crowd, upsetting men, women, and children as he went—the curses of some, the cries of others, and the laughter of nearly all ringing through the motley mass, making their misery look still more frightful.

Corny's Mamma

Throwing what silver I had about me amongst them, I made my way towards the hotel—not alone, however, but heading a procession of my ragged friends, who, with loud praises of my liberality, testified their gratitude by bearing me company. Arrived at the porch, I took my luggage from the carrier, and entered the house. Unlike any other hotel I had ever seen, there was neither stir nor bustle, no burly landlord, no buxom landlady, no dapper waiter with napkin on his arm, no pert-looking chambermaid with a bedroom candlestick. A large hall, dirty and unfurnished, led into a kind of bar, upon whose unpainted shelves a few straggling bottles were ranged together, with some pewter measures and tobacco-pipes; while the walls were covered with placards, setting forth the regulations for the Grand Canal Hotel, with a list, copious and abundant, of all the good things to be found therein, with the prices annexed; and a pressing entreaty to the traveller, should he not feel satisfied with his reception, to mention it in a 'book kept for that purpose by the landlord.' I cast my eye along the bill of fare so ostentatiously put forth—I read of rump-steaks and roast-fowls, of red rounds and sirloins, and I turned from the spot resolved to explore farther. The room opposite was large and spacious, and probably destined for the coffee-room, but it also was empty; it had neither chair nor table, and save a pictorial representation of a canal-boat, drawn by some native artist with a burnt stick upon the wall, it had no decoration. Having amused myself with the *Lady Caher*—such was the vessel called—I again set forth on my voyage of discovery, and bent my steps towards the kitchen. Alas! my success was no better there. The goodly grate, before which should have stood some of that luscious fare of which I had been reading, was cold and deserted; in one corner, it was true, three sods of earth, scarce lighted, supported an antiquated kettle, whose twisted spout was turned up with a misanthropic curl at the misery of its existence. I ascended the stairs, my footsteps echoed along the silent corridor, but still no trace of human habitant could I see, and I began to believe that even the landlord had departed with the larder.

At this moment the low murmur of voices caught my ear. I listened, and could distinctly catch the sound of persons talking together at the end of the corridor. Following along this, I came to a door, at which, having knocked twice with my knuckles, I waited for the invitation to enter. Either indisposed to admit me, or not having heard my summons, they did not reply; so turning the handle gently, I opened the door, and entered the room unobserved. For some minutes I profited but little by this step; the apartment, a small one, was literally full of smoke, and it was only when I had wiped the tears from my eyes three times that I at length began to recognise the objects before me.

Seated upon two low stools, beside a miserable fire of green wood, that smoked, not blazed, upon the hearth, were a man and a woman. Between them a small and rickety table supported a tea equipage of the humblest description, and a plate of fish whose odour pronounced them red herrings.

Of the man I could see but little, as his back was turned toward me; but had it been otherwise, I could scarcely have withdrawn my looks from the figure of his companion. Never had my eyes fallen on an object so strange and so unearthly. She was an old woman, so old, indeed, as to have numbered nearly a hundred years; her head, uncovered by cap, or quoif, displayed a mass of white hair that hung down her back and shoulders, and even partly across her face, not sufficiently, however, to conceal two dark orbits, within which her dimmed eyes faintly glimmered; her nose was thin and pointed, and projecting to the very mouth, which, drawn backwards at the angles by the tense muscles, wore an expression of hideous laughter. Over her coarse dress of some country stuff she wore, for warmth, the cast-off coat of a soldier, giving to her uncouth figure the semblance of an aged baboon at a village-show. Her voice, broken with coughing, was a low, feeble treble, that seemed to issue from passages where lingering life had left scarce a trace of vitality; and yet she talked on, without ceasing, and moved her skinny fingers among the tea-cups and knives upon the table, with a fidgety restlessness, as though in search of something.

Corny's Mamma

'There, acushla, don't smoke; don't now! Sure it is the ruin of your complexion. I never see boys take to tobacco this way when I was young.'

'Whisht, mother, and don't be bothering me,' was the cranky reply, given in a voice which, strange to say, was not quite unknown to me.

'Ay, ay,' said the old crone; 'always the same, never mindin' a word I say; and maybe in a few years I won't be to the fore to look after you and watch you.'

Here the painful thought of leaving a world, so full of its seductions and sweets, seemed too much for her feelings, and she began to cry. Her companion, however, appeared but little affected, but puffed away his pipe at his ease, waiting with patience till the paroxysm was past.

'There, now,' said the old lady, brightening up, 'take away the tay-things, and you may go and take a run on the common; but mind you don't be pelting Jack Moore's goose; and take care of Bryan's sow, she is as wicked as the devil now that she has boneens after her. D'ye hear me, darlin', or is it sick you are? Och, wirra! wirra! What's the matter with you, Corny mabouchal?'

'Corny!' exclaimed I, forgetful of my incognito.

'Ay, Corny, nayther more nor less than Corny himself,' said that redoubted personage, as, rising to his legs, he deposited his pipe upon the table, thrust his hands into his pockets, and seemed prepared to give battle.

'Oh, Corney,' said I, 'I am delighted to find you here. Perhaps you can assist me. I thought this was an hotel.'

'And why wouldn't you think it an hotel? hasn't it a bar and a coffee-room? Isn't the regulations of the house printed, and stuck up on all the walls? Ay, that's what the directors did—put the price on everything, as if one was going to cheat the people. And signs on it, look at the place now! Ugh! the Haythins! the Turks!'

'Yes, indeed, Corny, look at the place now,' glad to have an opportunity to chime in with my friend's opinions.

'Well, and look at it,' replied he, bristling up; 'and what have you to say agin it? Isn't it the Grand Canal Hotel?'

'Yes; but,' said I conciliatingly, 'an hotel ought at least to have a landlord, or a landlady.'

'And what do you call my mother there?' said he, with indignant energy.

'Don't bate Corny, sir! don't strike the child!' screamed the old woman, in an accent of heart-rending terror. 'Sure he doesn't know what he is saying.'

'He is telling me it isn't the Grand Canal Hotel, mother,' shouted Corny in the old lady's ears, while at the same moment he burst into a fit of the most discordant laughter. By some strange sympathy the old woman joined in, and I myself, unable to resist the ludicrous effect of a scene which still had touched my feelings, gave way also, and thus we all three laughed on for several minutes.

Suddenly recovering himself in the midst of his cachin-nations, Corny turned briskly round, fixed his fiery eyes upon me, and said—

'And did you come all the way from town to laugh at my mother and me?'

I hastened to exonerate myself from such a charge, and in a few words informed him of the object of my journey, whither I was going, and under what painful delusion I laboured, in supposing the internal arrangements of the Grand Canal Hotel bore any relation to its imposing exterior.

'I thought I could have dined here?'

'No, you can't,' was the reply, 'av ye're not fond of herrins.'

'And had a bed too?'

'Nor that either, av ye don't like straw.'

'And has your mother nothing better than that?' said I, pointing to the miserable plate of fish.

'Whisht, I tell you, and don't be putting the like in her head: sometimes she hears as well as you or me.' Here he dropped his voice to a whisper. 'Herrins is so cheap that we always make her believe it's Lent—this is nine years now she's fasting.' Here a fit of laughing at the success of this innocent ruse again broke from Corny, in which, as before, his mother joined.

'Then what am I to do,' asked I, 'if I can get nothing to eat here? Is there no other house in the village?'

'No, devil a one.'

'How far is it to Loughrea?'

'Fourteen miles and a bit.'

'I can get a car, I suppose?'

'Ay, if Mary Doolan's boy is not gone back.'

The old woman, whose eyes were impatiently fixed upon me during this colloquy, but who heard not a word of what was going forward, now broke in—

'Why doesn't he pay the bill and go away? Devil a farthing I'll take off it. Sure, av ye were a raal gentleman ye'd be givin' a fippenny-bit to the gossoon there, that sarved you. Never mind, Corny dear, I'll buy a bag of marbles for you at Banagher.'

Fearful of once more giving way to unseasonable mirth I rushed from the room and hurried downstairs; the crowd that had so lately accompanied me was now scattered, each to his several home. The only one who lingered near the door was the poor idiot (for such he was) that wore the huntsman's dress.

'Is the Loughrea car gone, Joe?' said I, for I remembered his name.

'She is, yer honour, she's away.'

'Is there any means of getting over to-night?'

'Barrin' walkin', there's none.'

'Ay; but,' said I, 'were I even disposed for that, I have got my luggage.'

'Is it heavy?' said Joe.

'This portmanteau and the carpet-bag you see there.'

'I'll carry them,' was the brief reply.

'You 'll not be able, my poor fellow,' said I.

'Ay, and you on the top of them.'

'You don't know how heavy I am,' said I laughingly.

'Begorra, I wish you was heavier.'

'And why so, Joe?'

'Because one that was so good to the poor is worth his weight in goold any day.'

I do not pretend to say whether it was the flattery, or the promise these words gave me of an agreeable companion *en route*; but, certain it is, I at once closed with his proposal, and, with a ceremonious bow to the Grand Canal Hotel, took my departure, and set out for Loughrea.

CHAPTER XXI
LOUGHREA

With the innate courtesy of his country, my humble companion endeavoured to lighten the road by song and story. There was not a blackened gable, not a ruined tower, not even a well we passed, without its legend. The very mountains themselves, that reared their mighty peaks towards the clouds, had their tale of superstitious horror; and, though these stories were simple in themselves, there was something in the association of the scene, something in the warm fervour of his enthusiasm that touched and thrilled my heart.

Like a lamp, whose fitful glare flickers through the gloomy vault of some rocky cavern, too feeble to illumine it, but yet calling up wild and goblin shapes on every side, and peopling space with flickering spectres, so did the small modicum of intellect this poor fellow possessed enable him to look at life with strange, distorted views. Accustomed to pass his days in the open air—the fields, the flowers, the streams, his companions—he had a sympathy in the eddying current that flowed on beneath—in the white cloud that rolled above him. Happy—for he had no care—he journeyed about from one county to another. In the hunting season he would be seen lounging about a kennel, making or renewing his intimacy with the dogs, who knew and loved him; then he was always ready to carry a drag, to stop an earth, or do a hundred other of those minor services that are ever wanted. Many who lived far from a post-town knew the comfort of falling in with poor 'Tipperary Joe.' for such was he called. Not more fleet of foot than honest in heart, oftentimes was a letter intrusted to his keeping that with any other messenger would have excited feelings of anxiety. His was an April-day temperament—ever varying, ever changing. One moment would he tell, with quivering lip and broken voice, some story of wild and thrilling interest; the next, breaking suddenly off, he would burst out into some joyous rant, generally ending in a loud 'tally-ho,' in which all his enthusiasm would shine forth, and in his glistening eye and flushed cheek one could mark the pleasure that stirred his heart He knew every one, not only in this, but in the surrounding counties; and they stood severally classed in his estimation by their benevolence to the poor, and their prowess in the hunting-field. These, with him, were the two great qualities of mankind. The kind man, and the bold rider, made his beau-ideal of all that was excellent, and it was strange to watch with what ingenuity he could support his theory.

'There's Burton Pearse—that's the darling of a man!

It's he that's good to the poor, and takes his walls flying. It isn't a lock of bacon or a bag of meal he cares for—be-gorra, it's not that, nor a double ditch would ever stop him. Hurroo! I think I'm looking at him throwing up his whip-hand this way, going over a gate and calling out to the servant, "Make Joe go in for his dinner, and give him half-a-crown"—devil a less! And then there's Mr. Power of Kilfane—maybe your honour knows him? Down in Kilkenny, there. He's another of them—one of the right sort. I wish you see him facing a leap—a little up in his stirrups, just to look over and see the ground, and then—hoo! he's across and away. A beautiful place he has of it, and an elegant pack of dogs, fourteen hunters in the stable, and as pleasant a kitchen as ever I broke my fast in. The cook's a mighty nice woman—a trifle fat, or so; but a good sowl, and a raal warrant for an Irish stew.' 'And Mr. Ulick Burke, Joe, do you know him?' 'Is it blazing Burke? Faix, I do know him! I was as near him as I am to you when he shot Matt Callanan at the mills. "There, now," says he, when he put a ball in his hip, and lamed him for life, "you were always fond of your trade, and I'll make you a hopper." And sure enough, this is the way he goes ever since.'

'He is a good horseman, they tell me, Joe?' 'The best in Ireland; for following the dogs, flat race, or steeplechase, show me his equal. Och! it's himself has the seat in a saddle. Mighty short he rides with his knees up, this way, and his toes out. Not so purty to look at, till you are used to it; but watch him fingering his baste—feeling his mouth with the snaffle—never tormenting, but just letting him know who is on his back. It's raal pleasure to look at him; and then to see him taking a little canter before he sets off, with his hand low, and just tickling the flanks with his spurs, to larn the temper of the horse. May I never! if it isn't a heavenly sight!' 'You like Mr. Burke, then, I see, Joe?' 'Like him! Who wouldn't like him a-horseback? Isn't he the moral of a rider, that knows his baste better than I know my Hail Mary? But see him afoot, he's the greatest divil from here to Croaghpatrick—nothing civiller in his mouth than a curse and a "bloody end" to ye! Och! it's himself hates the poor, and they hate him; the beggars run away from him as if he was the police; and the blind man that sits on Banagher Bridge takes up his bags, and runs for the bare life the minit he hears the trot of his horse. Isn't it a wonder how he rides so bowld with all the curses over him? Faix, myself wouldn't cross that little stream there, if I was like him. Well, well, he'll have a hard reckoning at last. He's killed five men already, and wounded a great many more; but they say he won't be able to go on much further, for when he kills another the divil's to come for him. The Lord be about us! by rason he never let's any one kill more nor six.'

Thus chatting away, the road passed over; and as the sun was setting we came in sight of the town, now not above a mile distant.

'That's Loughrea you see there—it's a mighty fine place,' said Joe. 'There's slate houses, and a market and a barrack; but you 'll stop a few days in the town?'

'Oh, certainly; I wish to see this race.'

'That will be the fine race. It is a great country entirely—every kind of fence, gates, ditches, and stone walls, as thick as they can lie. I'll show you all the course, for I know it well, and tell you the names of all the gentlemen, and the names of their horses, and their servants; and I'll bring you where you 'll see the whole race, from beginning to end, without stirring an inch. Are you going to bet any money?'

'I believe not, Joe; but I'm greatly interested for a friend.'

'And who is he?'

'Captain O'Grady.'

'Master Phil! Tare-an'-ages! are you a friend of Master Phil's? Arrah, why didn't you tell me that before? Why didn't you mintion his name to me? Och! isn't myself proud this evening to be with a friend of the Captain's. See now, what's your name?'

'Hinton,' said I.

'Ay, but your Christian name?'

'They who know me best call me Jack Hinton.'

'Musha! but I'd like to call you Jack Hinton just for this once. Now, will you do one thing for me?'

'To be sure, Joe; what is it?'

'Make them give me a half-pint to drink your health and the Captain's; for, faix, you must be the right sort, or he wouldn't keep company with you. It's just like yesterday to me the day I met him, down at Bishop's Loch. The hounds came to a check, and a hailstorm came on, and all the gentlemen went into a little shebeen house for shelter. I was standing outside, as it may be here, when Master Phil saw me. "Come in, Joe," says he; "you 're the best company, and the pleasantest fellow over a mug of egg-nip." And may I never! if he didn't make me sit down fornint him at a little table, and drink two quarts of as beautiful flip as ever I tasted. And Master Phil has a horse here, ye tell me—what's his name?'

'That, Joe, I am afraid I can't pronounce for you; it's rather beyond my English tongue; but I know that his colour's grey, and that he has one cropped ear.'

'That's Moddiridderoo!' shouted Joe, as throwing my portmanteau to the ground, he seated himself leisurely on it, and seemed lost in meditation.

'Begorra,' said he at length, 'he chose a good-tempered one, when he was about it! there never was such a horse foaled in them parts. Ye heard what he did to Mr. Shea, the man that bred him? He threw him over a wall, and then jumped after him; and if it wasn't that his guardian-angel made his leather breeches so strong, he'd have ate him up entirely! Sure, there's no one can ride him barrin' the man I was talkin' of.'

'Well, Joe, I believe Mr. Burke is to ride him.'

'Musha! but I am sorry for it!'

'And why so? You seem to think highly of his horsemanship.'

'There's no mistaken that, ay it was fair; but then, you see, he has as many tricks in him as the devil. Sometimes he 'll break his stirrup leather, or he 'll come in a pound too heavy, or he'll slip the snaffle out of the mouth; for he doesn't care for his neck. Once I see him stake his baste, and bring him in dead lame.'

Here ended our conversation; for by this time we entered the town, and proceeded to Mrs. Doolan's. The house was full, or the apartments bespoke; and I was turning away in disappointment, when I accidentally overheard the landlady mention the two rooms ordered by Captain O'Grady. A little explanation ensued, and I discovered, to my delight, that these were destined for me by my friend, who had written sometime before to secure them. A few minutes more saw me comfortably installed in the little inn, whose unpretending exterior and cheerful comfort within doors were the direct antithesis to the solemn humbug I had left at Shannon Harbour.

Under Joe's auspices—for he had established himself as my own man—tea and rashers made their appearance. My clothes were unpacked and put by; and as he placed my dressing-gown and slippers in readiness before the fire, I could not help observing the servant-like alacrity of his manner, perfect in everything, save in his habit of singing to himself as he went, which I can't say, however, that I disliked, and certainly never dreamed of checking. Having written a few lines to Mr. Burke, expressing my desire for a few minutes' interview the following morning, I despatched the note, and prepared for bed.

I had often listened with apathy to the wise saws of people who, never having felt either hunger or fatigue, are so fond of pronouncing a glowing eulogium on such luxuries, when the period of their gratification has arrived; but, I confess, as I lay down that night in bed, and drew the clothes around me, I began to believe that they had underrated the pleasures they spoke of. The house clock ticked pleasantly in the room without; the cheerful turf-fire threw its mild red light across the room; the sounds from the street were those of happy voices and merry laughter, and when I ceased to hear them I had fallen into a sound and peaceful sleep.

It was after about a dozen efforts, in which I had gone through all the usual formula on such occasions—rubbing my eyes, stretching, and even pinching myself—before I could awake on the following morning. I felt somewhat stiffened from the unaccustomed exertions of the day before, but, somehow, my spirits were unusually high, and my heart in its very lightest mood. I looked about me through the little room, where all was order, neatness, and propriety. My clothes carefully brushed and folded, my boots resplendent in their blacking, stood basking before the fire; even my hat, placed gently on one side, with my gloves carefully flattened, were laid out in true valet fashion. The door into my little sitting-room lay open, and I could mark the neat and comfortable preparations for my breakfast, while at a little distance from the table, and in an attitude of patient attention, stood poor Joe himself, who, with a napkin across his arm, was quietly waiting the moment of my awaking.

I know not if my reader will have any sympathy with the confession; but I own I have always felt a higher degree of satisfaction from the unbought and homely courtesy chance has thrown in my way, than from the more practised and dearly-paid-for attentions of the most disciplined household. There is something nattering in the personal devotion which seems to spring from pure good-will, that insensibly raises one in his own esteem. In some such reflection as this was I lost, when the door of my outer room was opened, and a voice inquired if Mr. Hinton stopped there.

'Yes, sir,' replied Joe; 'he is in bed and asleep.'

'Ah! it is you, Joe?' replied the other. 'So you are turned footman, I see. If the master be like the man, it ought to be a shrewd establishment.'

'No,' replied Joe carelessly; 'he's not very like anything down in these parts, for he appears to be a gentleman.'

'Tell him I am here, and be d——d to you,' was the indignant reply, as the speaker threw himself into his chair and stirred the fire with his foot.

Suspecting at once who my visitor was, I motioned to Joe to leave the room, and proceeded to dress myself with all despatch. During the operation, however, my friend without manifested several symptoms of impatience: now walking the room with rapid strides, as he whistled a quick step; now beating the bars of the grate with a poker, and occasionally performing that popular war-dance, 'The Devil's Tattoo,' with his knuckles upon the table. At length his endurance seemed pushed to its limit, and he knocked sharply at the door, calling out at the same moment—

'I say, sir, time's up, if you please.'

The next moment I was before him.

Mr. Ulick Burke—for I need not say it was he—was a well-looking man, of about eight-and-twenty or thirty years of age. Although his height was below the middle size, he was powerfully and strongly made; his features would have been handsome, were it not for a certain expression of vulgar suspicion that played about the eyes, giving him a sidelong look when he spoke; this, and the loss of two front teeth from a fall, disfigured a face originally pleasing. His whiskers were large, bushy, and meeting beneath his chin. As to his dress, it was in character with his calling—a green coat cut round in jockey fashion, over which he wore a white 'bang-up,' as it was called, in one pocket of which was carelessly thrust a lash-whip; a belcher handkerchief, knotted loosely about his neck, buckskin breeches, reaching far down upon the leg, and top-boots completed his costume. I had almost forgotten a hat, perhaps the most characteristic thing of all. This, which once had been white, was now, by stress of time and weather, of a dirty drab colour, its crown dinged in several places, and the leaf jagged and broken, bespoke the hard usage to which it was subjected. While speaking, he held it firmly clutched in his ungloved hand, and from time to time struck it against his thigh, with an energy of manner that seemed habitual His manner was a mixture of timid embarrassment and vulgar assurance, feeling his way, as it were, with one, while he forgot himself with the other. With certain remnants of the class he originally belonged to, he had associated the low habitudes and slang phraseology of his daily associates, making it difficult for one, at first sight, to discover to which order he belonged. In the language of his companions, Click Burke 'could be a gentleman when he pleased it.'

How often have we heard this phrase, and with what a fatal mistake is it generally applied! He who can be a gentleman when he pleases, never pleases to be anything else. Circumstances may, and do, every day in life, throw men of cultivated minds and refined habits into the society of their inferiors; but while, with the tact and readiness that is their especial prerogative, they make themselves welcome among those with whom they have few, if any, sympathies in common, yet never by any accident do they derogate from that high standard that makes them gentlemen. So, on the other hand, the man of vulgar tastes and coarse propensities may simulate, if he be able, the outward habitudes of society, speaking with practised intonation and bowing with well-studied grace; yet is he no more a gentleman in his thought or feeling than is the tinselled actor, who struts the board, the monarch his costume would bespeak him. This being the 'gentleman when he likes' is but the mere performance of the character. It has all the smell of the orange-peel and the footlights about it, and never can be mistaken by any one who knows the world.

But to come back to Mr. Burke. Having eyed me for a second or two, with a look of mingled distrust and impertinence, he unfolded my note, which he held beneath his fingers, and said—

'I received this from you last night, Mr. — — —'

'Hinton,' said I, assisting him.

'Mr. Hinton,' repeated he slowly.

'Won't you be seated?' said I, pointing to a chair, and taking one myself.

He nodded familiarly, and placing himself on the window-sill, with one foot upon a chair, resumed—

'It's about O'Gradys business I suppose you've come down here. The Captain has treated me very ill.'

'You are quite right,' said I coolly, 'in guessing the object of my visit; but I must also let you know, that in any observations you make concerning Captain O'Grady, they are made to a friend, who will no more permit his name to be slightingly treated than his own.'

'Of course,' pronounced with a smile of the most insulting coolness, was the only reply. 'That, however, is not the matter in hand: *your friend*, the Captain, never condescended to answer my letter.'

'He only received it a few days ago.'

'Why isn't he here himself? Is a gentleman-rider to be treated like a common jockey that's paid for his race?'

I confess the distinction was too subtle for me, but I said nothing in reply.

'I don't even know where the horse is, nor if he is here at all. Will you call that handsome treatment Mr. Hinton?'

'One thing I am quite sure of, Mr. Burke—Captain O'Grady is incapable of anything unworthy or unbecoming a gentleman; the haste of his departure for foreign service may have prevented him observing certain matters of etiquette towards you, but he has commissioned me to accept your terms. The horse is here, or will be here to-night; and I trust nothing will interrupt the good understanding that has hitherto subsisted between you.'

'And will he take up the writ?' 'He will,' said I firmly.

'He must have a heavy book on the race.' 'Nearly a thousand pounds.'

'I'm sorry for it for his sake,' was the cool reply, 'for he'll lose his money.'

'Indeed!' said I; 'I understand that you thought well of his horse, and that with your riding — —'

'Ay; but I won't ride for him.'

'You won't ride! — not on your own terms?'

'No; not even on my own terms. Don't be putting yourself into a passion, Mr. Hinton — you've come down to a country where that never does any good; we settle all our little matters here in a social, pleasant way of our own. But, I repeat it, I won't ride for your friend; so you may withdraw his horse as soon as you like; except,' added he, with a most contemptuous sneer, 'you have a fancy for riding him yourself.'

Resolving that whatever course I should follow I would at least keep my temper for the present, I assumed as much calmness as I could command, and said —

'And what is there against O'Gradys horse?'

'A chestnut mare of Tom Molloy's, that can beat him over any country. The rest are withdrawn; so that I'll have a "ride over" for my pains.'

'Then you ride for Mr. Molloy?' said I.

'You've guessed it,' replied he with a wink, as throwing his hat carelessly on one side of his head he gave me an insolent nod and lounged out of the room.

I need not say that my breakfast appetite was not improved by Mr. Burke's visit; in fact, never was a man more embarrassed than I was. Independent of the loss of his money, I knew how poor Phil would suffer from the duplicity of the transaction; and in my sorrow for his sake I could not help accusing myself of ill-management in the matter. Had I been more conciliating or more blunt — had I bullied, or bid higher, perhaps a different result might have followed. Alas! in all my calculations, I knew little or nothing of him with whom I had to deal. Puzzled and perplexed, uncertain how to act — now resolving on one course, now deciding on the opposite, I paced my little room for above an hour, the only conviction I could come to being the unhappy choice that poor O'Grady had made when he selected me for his negotiator.

The town clock struck twelve. I remembered suddenly that was the hour when the arrangements for the race were to be ratified; and without a thought of what course I should pursue, what plan I should adopt, I took my hat and sallied forth.

The main street of the little town was crowded with people, most of them of that class which, in Irish phrase, goes by the appellation of squireen—a species of human lurcher, without any of the good properties of either class from which it derives its origin, but abounding in the bad traits of both. They lounged along, followed by pointers and wire-haired greyhounds, their hands stuck in their coat-pockets, and their hats set well back on their heads. Following in the train of this respectable cortege, I reached the market-house, upon the steps of which several 'sporting gentlemen' of a higher order were assembled. Elbowing my way with some difficulty through these, I mounted a dirty and sandy stair to a large room, usually employed by the magistrates for their weekly sessions; here, at a long table, sat the race committee, an imposing display of books, pens, and papers before them. A short little man, with a powdered head, and a certain wheezing chuckle when he spoke that voluntarily suggested the thought of apoplexy, seemed to be the president of the meeting.

The room was so crowded with persons of every class that I could with difficulty catch what was going forward. I looked anxiously round to see if I could not recognise some friend or acquaintance, but every face was strange to me. The only one I had ever seen before was Mr. Burke himself, who with his back to the fire was edifying a select circle of his friends by what I discovered, from the laughter of his auditory, was a narrative of his visit to myself. The recital must have owed something to his ingenuity in telling, for indeed the gentlemen seemed convulsed with mirth; and when Mr. Burke concluded, it was plain to see that he stood several feet higher in the estimation of hie acquaintances.

'Silence!' wheezed the little man with the white head: 'it is a quarter past twelve o'clock, and I'll not wait any longer.'

'Read the list, Maurice,' cried some one. 'As it is only "a walk over," you needn't lose any time.'

'Here, then, No. 1—Captain Fortescue's Tramp.' 'Withdrawn,' said a voice in the crowd. 'No. 2—Harry Studdard's Devil-may-care.'

'Paid forfeit,' cried another.

'No. 3—Sir George O'Brien's Billy-the-bowl.' 'Gone home again,' was the answer. 'No. 4—Tom Molloy's Cathleen.'

'All right!' shouted Mr. Burke, from the fireplace" 'Who rides?' asked the president.

'Ulick!' repeated half-a-dozen voices together.

'Eleven stone eight,' said the little man.

'And a pound for the martingale,' chimed in Mr. Burke.

'Well, I believe that's all. No; there's another horse-Captain O'Grady's Moddiridderoo.'

'Scratch him out with the rest,' said Mr. Burke.

'No!' said I, from the back of the room.

The word seemed electric; every eye was turned towards the quarter where I stood; and as I moved forward towards the table the crowd receded to permit my passage.

'Are you on the part of Mr. O'Grady, sir?' said the little man, with a polite smile.

I bowed an affirmative.

'He does not withdraw his horse, then?' said he.

'No,' said I again.

'But you are aware, sir, that Mr. Burke is going to ride for my friend, Mr. Molloy, here. Are you prepared with another gentleman?'

I nodded shortly.'

'His name, may I ask?' continued he. 'Mr. Hinton.'

By this time Mr. Burke, attracted by the colloquy, had approached the table, and, stooping down, whispered some words in the president's ear.

'You will forgive me, I'm sure,' said the latter, addressing me, 'if I ask, as the name is unknown to me, if this be a gentleman-rider?'

The blood rushed to my face and temples. I knew at once from whom this insult proceeded. It was no time, however, to notice it, so I simply replied—

'Mr. Hinton is an officer of the Guards, an aide-de-camp to the Lord Lieutenant, and I beg leave respectfully to present him to you.'

The obsequious civility exhibited by the party as I pronounced these few words were an ample *amende* for what I had suffered a few minutes before. Meanwhile, Mr. Burke had resumed his place at the fire, once more surrounded by his admiring satellites.

Being accommodated with a chair at the table, I proceeded to read over and sign the usual papers, by which I bound myself to abide by the regulations of the course, and conform in all things to the decision of the stewards. Scarcely had I concluded, when Mr. Burke called out—

'Who'll take eight to one on the race?'

Not a word was spoken in reply.

'Who'll take fifty to five?' cried he again.

'I will,' said a voice from the door.

'Who is that takes my bet? What is his name?' 'Tom Loftus, P.P. of Murranakilty.'

'A better fellow nor an honester couldn't do it, said the president.

'Book your bet, sir,' said Mr. Burke; 'or if it is equally convenient for you, you can pay it at present.'

'I never make a memorandum of such trifles,' said the priest; 'but I'll stake the money in some decent man's hands.'

A roar of laughter followed the priest's proposition, than which nothing could be less to Mr. Burke's taste. This time, however, he was in funds; and while the good father disengaged his five-pound note from the folds of a black leather pocket-book as large as a portfolio, his antagonist threw a fifty on the table, with an air of swaggering importance. I turned now to shake hands with my friend; but to my surprise and astonishment he gave me a look of cold and impressive import, that showed me at once he did not wish to be recognised, and the next moment left the room. My business there was also concluded, and having promised to be forthcoming the following day at two o'clock, I bowed to the chairman and withdrew.

CHAPTER XXII
A MOONLIGHT CANTER

I was not quite satisfied with the good priest for his having cut me, no matter what his reasons. I was not overmuch pleased with the tone of the whole meeting itself, and certainly I was very little satisfied with the part I had myself taken therein; for as cooler judgment succeeded to hot excitement, I perceived in what a mesh of difficulties I had involved myself, and how a momentary flush of passionate indignation had carried me away beyond the bounds of reason and sense, to undertake what but half an hour previously I should have shrunk from with shame, and the very thought of which now filled me with apprehension and dread—not indeed as to the consequences to myself, physically considered, for most willingly would I have compounded for a fractured limb, or even two, to escape the ridicule I was almost certain of incurring. This it was which I could not bear, and my *amore propre* recoiled from the thought of being a laughing-stock to the underbred and ill-born horde that would assemble to witness me.

When I arrived at the inn poor Joe was there awaiting me; he had been down to see the horse, which for precaution's sake was kept at a mill a little distance from the town, and of whose heart and condition he spoke in glowing terms.

'Och! he is a raal beauty—a little thick in fat about the crest, but they say he always trains fleshy, and his legs are as clean as a whistle. Sorra bit, but it will give Mr. Ulick as much as he can do to ride him to-morrow. I know by the way he turns his eyes round to you in the stable he's in the devil's temper.'

'But it is not Mr. Burke, Joe—I am going to ride him.'

'You are going to do it! You! Oh! by the powers! Mr. Ulick wasn't far out when he said the master was as mad as the man. "Tell me your company," says the old proverb; and you see there it is. What comes of it? If you lie down with dogs, you'll get up with fleas; and that's the fruits of travelling with a fool.'

I was in no temper for badinage at the moment, and replied to the poor fellow in a somewhat harsher tone than I should have used; and as he left the room without speaking, I felt ashamed and angry with myself for thus banishing the only one that seemed to feel an interest in my fortunes.

I sat down to my dinner discontented and unhappy. But a few hours previous, and I awoke high in heart and hope; and now without any adverse stroke of fortune, without any of those casualties of fate which come on us unlooked for and unthought of, but simply by the un-guided exercise of a passionate temperament, I found myself surrounded by embarrassments and environed by difficulties, without one friend to counsel or advise me.

Yes—I could not conceal it from myself—my determination to ride the steeplechase was the mere outbreak of passion. The taunting insolence of Burke had stung me to adopt a course which I had neither previously considered, nor, if suggested by another, could ever have consented to. True, I was what could be called a good horseman. In the two seasons I had spent in Leicestershire, on a visit to a relative, I had acquitted myself with credit and character; but a light weight splendidly mounted on a trained hunter, over his accustomed country, has no parallel with the same individual upon a horse he has never crossed, over a country he has never seen. These and a hundred similar considerations came rushing on me now when it was too late. However, the thing was done, and there being no possible way of undoing it, there was but one road, the straightforward, to follow in the case. Alas! half of our philosophy in difficulties consists in shutting our eyes firmly against consequences, and, *tête baissée*, rushing headlong at the future. Though few may be found willing to admit that the bull in the china-shop is the model of their prudence, I freely own it was mine, and that I made up my mind to ride the horse with the unspeakable name as long as he would permit me to ride him, at everything, over everything, or through everything before me. This conclusion at length come to, I began to feel more easy in my mind. Like the felon that feels there is no chance of a reprieve, I could look my fate more steadily in the face.

I had no great appetite for my dinner, but I sat over an excellent bottle of port, sipping and sipping, each glass I swallowed lending a rose tint to the future. The second bottle had just been placed on the table before me, when O'Gradys groom came in to receive his instructions. He had heard nothing of my resolution to ride, and certainly looked aghast when I announced it to him. By this time, however, I had combated my own fears, and I was not going to permit his to terrify me. Affecting the easy nonchalance of that excellent type Mr. Ulick Burke, I thrust my hands into my coat-pockets, and standing with my back to the fire, began questioning him about the horse. Confound it! there's no man so hard to humbug as an Irishman, but if he be a groom, I pronounce the thing impossible. The fellow saw through me in a moment; and as he sipped the glass of wine I had filled out for him, he approached me confidentially, while he said in a low tone—

'Did you say you 'd ride him?'

'Yes, to be sure I did.'

'You did! well, well! there's no helping it, since you said it. There's only one thing to be done'—he looked cautiously about the room, lest any one should overhear him. 'There's but one thing I know of—-let him throw you at the first leap. Mind me now, just leave it to himself; hell give you no trouble in life; and all you have to do is to choose the soft side. It's not your fault after that, you know, for I needn't tell you he won't be caught before night.'

I could not help laughing at this new receipt for riding a steeplechase, although I confess it did not raise my courage regarding the task before me.

'But what does he do?' said I—'this infernal beast; what trick has he?'

'It isn't one, but a hundred that he has. First of all, it isn't so easy to get on his back, for he is as handy with his hind foot as a fiddler; and if you are not mighty quick in mounting, he 'll strike you down with it. Then, when you are up, maybe he won't move at all, but stand with his forelegs out, his head down, and his eyes turned back just like a picture, hitting his flanks between times with his long tail You may coax him, pet him, and pat him—'faith, you might as well be tickling a milestone; for it's laughing at you he 'll be all the time. Maybe at last you 'll get tired, and touch him with the spur. Hurroo! begorra, you 'll get it then!'

'Why—what happens then?'

'What happens, is it? Maybe it's your neck is broke, or your thigh, or your collar-bone at least. He 'll give you a straight plunge up in the air, about ten feet high, throw his head forward till he either pulls the reins out of your hands or lifts you out of the saddle, and at the same moment he'll give you a blow with his hind-quarters in the small of the back. Och, murther!' said he, placing both hands upon his loins, and writhing as he spoke, 'it'll be six weeks to-morrow since he made one of them buck-leaps with me, and I never walked straight since. But that is not all.'

'Come, come,' said I impatiently, 'this is all nonsense; he only wants a man with a little pluck to bully him out of all this.'

As I said these valorous words I own that to my own heart I didn't exactly correspond to the person I described; but as the bottle of port was now finished, I set forth with my companion to pay my first visit to this redoubted animal.

The mill where the stable lay was about a mile from the town; but the night was a fine moonlight one, with not an air of wind stirring, and the walk delightful When we reached the little stream that turned the mill, over which a plank was thrown as a bridge, we perceived that a country lad was walking a pair of saddle-horses backwards and forwards near the spot. The suspicion of some trickery, some tampering with the horse, at once crossed me; and I hinted as much to the groom.

'No, no,' said he, laughing, 'make your mind easy about that. Mr. Ulick Burke knows the horse well, and he'll leave it all to himself.'

The allusion was a pleasant one; but I said nothing, and walked on.

Having procured a lantern at the mill, the groom preceded me to the little outhouse, which acted as stable. He opened the door cautiously, and peeped in.

'He's lying down,' said he to me in a whisper, and at the same moment taking the candle from the lantern, he held it up to permit my obtaining a better view. 'Don't be afeard,' continued he, 'he 'll not stir now, the thief of the earth! When once he's down that way, he lies as peaceable as a lamb.'

As well as I could observe him, he was a magnificent horse—a little too heavy perhaps about the crest and forehand, but then so strong behind, such powerful muscle about the haunches, that his balance was well preserved. As I stood contemplating him in silence, I felt the breath of some one behind me. I turned suddenly around; it was Father Tom Loftus himself. There was the worthy priest, mopping his forehead with a huge pocket-handkerchief and blowing like a rhinoceros.

'Ugh!' said he at length, 'I have been running up and down the roads this half-hour after you, and there's not a puff left in me.'

'Ah, father! I hoped to have seen you at the inn.' 'Whisht! I darn't. I thought I'd do it better my own way; but, see now, we've no time to lose. I knew as well as yourself you never intended to ride this race. No matter; don't say a word, but listen to me. I know the horse better than any one in these parts; and it isn't impossible, if you can keep the saddle over the first two or three fences, that you may win. I say, if you can—for 'faith it's not in a "swing-swong" you'll be! But, come now, the course was marked out this evening. Burke was over it before dinner; and, with a blessing, we will be before supper. I've got a couple of hacks here that'll take us over every bit of it; and perhaps it is not too much to say you might have a worse guide.'

''Faith, your reverence,' chimed in the groom, 'he'd find it hard to have a better.'

Thanking the kind priest for his good-natured solicitude, I followed him out upon the road, where the two horses were waiting us.

'There, now,' said he, 'get up; the stirrups are about your length. He looks a little low in flesh, but you'll not complain of him when he's under you.'

The next moment we were both in the saddle. Taking a narrow path that led off from the highroad, we entered a large tilled field; keeping along the headlands of which, we came to a low stone wall, through a gap of which we passed, and came out upon an extensive piece, of grassland, that gently sloped away from where we were standing to a little stream at its base, an arm of that which supplied the mill.

'Here, now,' said the priest, 'a little to the left yonder is the start. You come down this hill; you take the water there, and you keep along by Freney's house, where you see the trees there. There's only a small stone wall and a clay ditch between this and that; afterwards you turn off to the right. But, come now, are you ready? We'll explore a bit.'

As he spoke, the good priest, putting spurs to his hackney, dashed on before me, and motioning me to follow, cantered down the slope. Taking the little mill-stream at a fly, he turned in his saddle to watch my performance.

'Neat! mighty neat!' cried he, encouraging me. 'Keep your hand a little low. The next is a wall— —'

Scarcely had he spoke when we both came together at a stone-fence, about three feet high. This time I was a little in advance, as my horse was fresher, and took it first.

'Oh, the devil a better!' said Father Tom. 'Burke himself couldn't beat that! Here, now: keep this way out of the deep ground, and rush him at the double ditch there.'

Resolved on securing his good opinion, I gripped my saddle firmly with my knees, and rode at the fence. Over we went in capital style; but lighting on the top of a rotten ditch, the ground gave way, and my horse's hind legs slipped backwards into the gripe. Being at full stretch, the poor animal had no power to recover himself, so that, disengaging his forelegs, I pulled him down into the hollow, and then with a vigorous dash of the spur and a bold lift carried him clean over it into the field.

'Look, now!' said the priest; 'that pleases me better than all you did before. Presence of mind—that's the real gift for a horseman when he's in a scrape; but, mind me, it was your own fault, for here's the way to take the fence.' So saying, he made a slight semicircle in the field, and then, as he headed his horse towards the leap, rushed him at it furiously, and came over like the bound of a stag.

'Now,' said Father Tom, pointing with his whip as he spoke, 'we have a beautiful bit of galloping-ground before us; and if you ever reach this far, and I don't see why you shouldn't, here's where you ought to make play. Listen to me now,' said he, dropping his voice: 'Tom Molloy s mare isn't thoroughbred, though they think she is. She has got a bad drop in her. Now, the horse is all right, clean bred, sire and dam, by reason he 'll be able to go through the dirt when the mare can't; so that all you 've to do, if, as I said before, you get this far, is to keep straight down to the two thorn-bushes—there, you see them yonder. Burke won't be able to take that line, but must keep upon the headlands, and go all round yonder; look, now, you see the difference—so that before he can get over that wide ditch you'll be across it, and making for the stone wall After that, by the powers, if you don't win, I, can't help you!'

'Where does the course turn after, father?' said I.

'Oh! a beautiful line of flat country, intersprinkled with walls, ditches, and maybe a hedge or two; but all fair, and only one rasping fence—the last of all. After that, you have a clean gallop of about a quarter of a mile, over as nice a sod as ever you cantered.'

'And that last fence, what is it like?'

"Faith, it is a rasper! It's a wide gully, where there was a *boreen* once, and they say it is every inch of sixteen feet—that'll make it close upon twenty when you clear the clay on both sides. The grey horse, I'm told, has a way of jumping in and jumping out of these narrow roads; but take my advice, and go it in a fly. And now, Captain, what between the running, and the riding, and the talking altogether, I am as dry as a limekiln; so what do you say if we turn back to town, and have a bit of supper together? There's a kind of a cousin of mine, one Bob Mahon, a Major in the Roscommon, and he has got a grouse-pie, and something hot to dilute it with, waiting for us.'

'Nothing will give me more pleasure, father; and there's only one thing more—indeed I had nearly forgotten it altogether——"

'What's that?' said the priest, with surprise.

'Not having any intention to ride, I left town without any racing equipment; breeches and boots I have, but as to a cap and a jacket——'

'I 've provided for both,' said Father Tom. 'You saw the little man with a white head that sat at the head of the table—Tom Dillon of Mount Brown; you know him?'

'I am not acquainted with him.'

'Well, he knows you; that's all the same. His son, that's just gone to Gibraltar with his regiment, was about your size, and he had a new cap and jacket made for this very race, and of course they are lying there and doing nothing. So I sent over a little gossoon with a note, and I don't doubt but they are all at the inn this moment.'

'By Jove, father!' said I, 'you are a real friend, and a most thoughtful one, too.'

'Maybe I'll do better than that for you,' said he, with a sly wink of his eye, that somehow suggested to my mind that he knew more of and took a deeper interest in me than I had reason to believe.

CHAPTER XXIII
MAJOR MAHON AND HIS QUARTERS

The Major's quarters were fixed in one of the best houses in the town, in the comfortable back-parlour of which was now displayed a little table laid for three persons. A devilled lobster, the grouse-pie already mentioned, some fried ham, and crisped potatoes were the viands; but each was admirable in its kind, and with the assistance of an excellent bowl of hot punch and the friendly welcome of the host, left nothing to be desired.

Major Bob Mahon was a short, thickset little man, with round blue eyes, a turned-up nose, and a full under lip, which he had a habit of protruding with an air of no mean pretension; a short crop of curly black hair covered a head as round as a billiard-ball. These traits, with a certain peculiar smack of his mouth, by which he occasionally testified the approval of his own eloquence, were the most remarkable things about him. His great ambition was to be thought a military man; but somehow his pretensions in this respect smacked much more of the militia than the line. Indeed, he possessed a kind of adroit way of asserting the superiority of the former to the latter, averring that they who fought *pro aris et focis*—the Major was fond of Latin—stood on far higher ground than the travelled mercenaries who only warred for pay. This peculiarity, and an absurd attachment to practical jokes, the result of which had frequently through life involved him in lawsuits, damages, compensations, and even duels, formed the great staple of his character—of all which the good priest informed me most fully on our way to the house.

'Captain Hinton, I believe,' said the Major, as he held out his hand in welcome.

'Mr. Hinton,' said I, bowing.

'Ay, yes; Father Tom, there, doesn't know much about these matters. What regiment, pray?'

'The Grenadier Guards.'

'Oh, a very good corps—mighty respectable corps; not that, between ourselves, I think overmuch of the regulars; between you and me, I never knew foreign travel do good to man or beast. What do they bring back with them, I'd like to know?—French cookery and Italian licentiousness. No, no; give me the native troops! You were a boy at the time, but maybe you have heard how they behaved in the west, when Hoche landed. Egad! if it wasn't for the militia the country was sacked. I commanded a company of the Roscommon at the time. I remember well we laid siege to a windmill, held by a desperate fellow, the miller—a resolute character, Mr. Hinton; he had two guns in the place with him.'

'I wish to the Lord he had shot you with one of them, and we 'd have been spared this long story!' said the priest.

'I opened a parallel——'

'Maybe you 'd open the pie?' said the priest, as he drew his chair, and sat down to the table. 'Perhaps you forget, Bob, we have had a sharp ride of it this evening?'

'Upon my conscience, so I did,' replied the Major good-humouredly. 'So let us have a bit of supper now, Mr. Hinton, and I'll finish my story by-and-by.'

'The Heavens forbid!' piously ejaculated the priest, as he helped himself to a very considerable portion of the lobster.

'Is this a fast, Father Loftus?' said I slyly.

'No, my son, but we'll make it one. That reminds me of what happened to me going up in the boat. It was a Friday, and the dinner, as you may suppose, was not over-good; but there was a beautiful cut of fried salmon just before me—about a pound and a half, maybe two pounds; this I slipped quietly on my plate, observing to the company, in this way, "Ladies and gentlemen, this is a fast day with me"—when a big fellow, with red whiskers, stooped across the table, cut my bit of fish in two halves, calling out as he carried off one, "Bad scran to ye! d'ye think nobody has a soul to be saved but yourself?"'

'Ah, they're a pious people, are the Irish!' said the Major solemnly, 'and you'll remark that when you see more of them. And now, Captain, how do you like us here?'

'Exceedingly,' said I, with warmth. 'I have had every reason to be greatly pleased with Ireland.'

'That's right! and I'm glad of it! though, to be sure, you have not seen us in our holiday garb. Ah, if you were here before the Union; if you saw Dublin as I remember it—and Tom there remembers it—"that was a pleasant place."

It was not trusting to balls and parties, to dinners and routs, but to all kinds of fun and devilment besides. All the members of Parliament used to be skylarking about the city, playing tricks on one another, and humbugging the Castle people. And, to be sure, the Castle was not the grave, stupid place it is now—they were convivial, jovial fellows——'

'Come, come, Major,' interrupted I; 'you are really unjust—the present court is not the heavy——'

'Sure, I know what it is well enough. Hasn't the duke all the privy council and the bishops as often to dinner as the garrison and the bar? Isn't he obliged to go to his own apartment when they want to make a night of it, and sing a good chorus? Don't tell me! Sure, even as late as Lord Westmorland's time it was another thing—pleasant and happy times they were, and the country will never be the same till we have them back again!'

Being somewhat curious to ascertain in what particular our degeneracy consisted—for in my ignorance of better, I had hitherto supposed the present regime about as gay a thing as need be—I gradually led the Major on to talk of those happier days when Ireland kept all its fun for home consumption, and never exported even its surplus produce.

'It was better in every respect,' responded the Major. 'Hadn't we all the patronage amongst us? There's Jonah, there—Harrington, I mean; well, he and I could make anything, from a tide-waiter to a master in Chancery. It's little trouble small debts gave us then; a pipe of sherry never cost me more than a storekeeper in the ordnance, and I kept my horses at livery for three years with a washwoman to Kilmainham Hospital And as for fun—look at the Castle now! Don't I remember the times when we used to rob the coaches coming from the drawing-rooms; and pretty girls they were inside of them.'

'For shame, for shame!' cried Father Tom, with a sly look in the corner of his eye that by no means bespoke a suitable degree of horror at such unwarrantable proceedings.

'Well, if it was a shame it was no sin,' responded the Major; 'for we never took anything more costly than kisses. Ah, dear me! them was the times! And, to be sure, every now and then we got a pull-up from the Lady lieutenant, and were obliged to behave ourselves for a week or two together. One thing she never could endure was a habit we had of leaving the Castle before they themselves left the ball-room. I'm not going to defend it—it was not very polite, I confess; but somehow or other there was always something going on we couldn't afford to lose—maybe a supper at the barrack, or a snug party at Daly's, or a bit of fun elsewhere. Her Excellency, however, got angry about it, and we got a quiet hint to reform our manners. This, I need not tell you, was a hopeless course; so we hit on an expedient that answered to the full as well. It was by our names being called out, as the carriages drove up, that our delinquency became known. So Matt Fortescue suggested that we should adopt some feigned nomenclature, which would totally defy every attempt at discovery; the idea was excellent, and we traded on it for many a day with complete success. One night, however, from some cause or other, the carriages were late in arriving, and we were all obliged to accompany the court into the supper-room. Angry enough we were; but still there was no help for it; and so, "smiling through tears," as the poet says, in we went. Scarcely, however, had we taken our places when a servant called out something from the head of the stairs; another re-echoed it at the ante-chamber, and a third at the supper-room shouted out, "Oliver Cromwell's carriage stops the way!" The roar of laughter the announcement caused shook the very room; but it had scarcely subsided when there was another call for "Brian Boru's coach," quickly followed by "Guy Fawkes" and "Paddy O'Rafferty's jingle," which latter personage was no other than the Dean of Cork. I need not tell you that we kept our secret, and joined in the universal opinion of the whole room, "that the household was shamefully disguised in drink"; and indeed there was no end to the mistakes that night, for every now and then some character in heathen or modern history would turn up among the announcements; and as the laughter burst forth, the servants would grow ashamed for a while, and refuse to call any carriage where the style and title was a little out of the common. Ah, Mr. Hinton, if you had lived in those days! Well, well, no matter—here's a glass to their memory, anyway. It is the first time you 've been in these parts, and I suppose you haven't seen much of the country?'

'Very little indeed,' replied I; 'and even that much only by moonlight.'

'I'm afraid,' said Father Tom, half pensively, 'that many of your countrymen take little else than a "dark view" of us.'

'See now,' said the Major, slapping his hand on the table with energy, 'the English know as much about Pat as Pat knows of purgatory—no offence to you, Mr. Hinton. I could tell you a story of a circumstance that once happened to myself.'

No, no, Bob,' said the priest; 'it is bad taste to tell a story *en petit comité*. I'll leave it to the Captain.'

'If I am to be the judge,' said I laughingly, 'I decide for the story.'

'Let's have it, then,' said the priest. 'Come, Bob, a fresh brew, and begin your tale.'

'You are a sensual creature, Father Tom,' said the Major, 'and prefer drink to intellectual discussion; not but that you may have both here at the same time. But in honour of my friend beside me, I'll not bear malice, but give you the story; and let me tell you, it is not every day in the week a man hears a tale with a moral to it, particularly down in this part of the country.'

CHAPTER XXIV
THE DEVIL'S GRIP

'The way of it was this. There was a little estate of mine in the county of Waterford that I used now and then to visit in the shooting season. In fact, except for that, there was very little inducement to go there; it was a bleak, ugly part of the country, a bad market-town near it, and not a neighbour within twelve miles. Well, I went over there—it was, as well as I remember, December two years. Never was there such weather; it rained from morning till night, and blew and rained from night till morning; the slates were flying about on every side, and we used to keep fellows up all night, that in case the chimneys were blown away we 'd know where to find them in the morning. This was the pleasant weather I selected for my visit to the "Devil's Grip"—that was the name of the town-land where the house stood; and no bad name either, for, 'faith, if he hadn't his paw on it, it might have gone in law,-like the rest of the property. However, down I went there, and only remembered on the evening of my arrival that I had ordered my gamekeeper to poison the mountain, to get rid of the poachers; so that, instead of shooting, which, as I said before, was all you could do in the place, there I was, with three brace of dogs, two guns, and powder enough to blow up a church, walking a big dining-parlour, all alone by myself, as melancholy as may be.

'You may judge how happy I was, looking out upon the bleak country-side, with nothing to amuse me except when now and then the roof of some cabin or other would turn upside down, like an umbrella, or watching an old windmill that had gone clean mad, and went round at such a pace that nobody dare go near it. All this was poor comfort. However, I got out of temper with the place; and so I sat down and wrote a long advertisement for the English papers, describing the Devil's Grip as a little terrestrial paradise, in the midst of picturesque scenery, a delightful neighbourhood, and an Arcadian peasantry, the whole to be parted with—-a dead bargain—as the owner was about to leave the country. I didn't add that he had some thought of blowing his brains out with sheer disgust of his family residence. I wound up the whole with a paragraph to the effect that if not disposed of within the month, the proprietor would break it up into small farms. I said this because I intended to remain so long there; and, although I knew no purchaser would treat after he saw the premises, yet still some one might be fool enough to come over and look at them, and even that would help me to pass the Christmas. My calculation turned out correct; for before a week was over, a letter reached me, stating that a Mr. Green, of No. 196 High Holborn, would pay me a visit as soon as the weather moderated and permitted him to travel If he waits for that, thought I, he 'll not find me here; and if it blows as hard for the next week, he 'll not find the house either; so I mixed another tumbler of punch, and hummed myself to sleep with the "Battle of Ross."

'It was about four or five evenings after I received this letter that old Dan M'Cormick—a kind of butler I have, a handy fellow; he was a steward for ten years in the Holyhead packet—burst into the room about ten o'clock, when I was disputing with myself whether I took six tumblers or seven—I said one, the decanter said the other.

'"It's blowing terrible, Mr. Bob," said Dan.

'"Let it blow! What else has it to do?"

'"The trees is tumbling about as if they was drunk; there won't be one left before morn."

'"They're right," says I, "to leave that, for the soil was never kind for planting."

'"Two of the chimneys is down," says he.

'"Devil mend them!" said I, "they were always smoking."

'"And the hall door," cried he, "is blown flat into the hall."

'"It's little I care," said I; "if it couldn't keep out the sheriff it may let in the storm, if it pleases."

'"Murther! murther!" said he, wringing his hands, "I wish we were at say! It's a cruel thing to have one's life perilled this way."

'While we were talking, a gossoon burst into the room with the news that the Milford packet had just gone ashore somewhere below the Hook Tower, adding, as is always the case on such occasions, that they were all drowned.

'I jumped up at this, put on my shooting-shoes, buttoned up my frieze coat, and followed by Dan, took a short cut over the hills towards Passage, where I now found the packet had been driven in. Before we had gone half a mile I heard the voices of some country-people coming up the road towards me; but it was so dark you couldn't see your hand.

'"Who's there?" said I.

'"Tim Molloy, your honour," was the answer.

'"What's the matter, Tim?" said I. "Is there anything wrong?"

'"Nothing, sir, glory be to God—it's only the corpse of the gentleman that was drowned there below."

'"I ain't dead, I tell you; I'm only faint," called out a shrill voice.

'"He says he's better," said Tim; "and maybe it's only the salt water that's in him; and, faix, when we found him, there was no more spark in him than in a wet sod."

'Well, the short of it was, we brought him up to the house, rubbed him with gunpowder before the fire, gave him about half a pint of burnt spirits, and put him to bed, he being just able to tell me, as he was dropping asleep, that he was my friend from No. 196 High Holborn.

'The next morning I sent up Dan to ask how he was, and he came down with the news that he was fast asleep. "The best thing he could do," said I; and I began to think over what a mighty load it would be upon my conscience if the decent man had been drowned. "For, maybe, after all," thought I, "he is in earnest, maybe he wished to buy a beautiful place like that I have described in the papers"; and so I began to relent, and wonder with myself how I could make the country pleasant for him during his stay. "It'll not be a day or two at farthest, particularly after he sees the place. Ay, there's the rub—the poor devil will find out then that I have been hoaxing him." This kept fretting me all day; and I was continually sending up word to know if he was awake, and the answer always was—still sleeping.

'Well, about four o'clock, as it was growing dark, Oakley of the Fifth and two of his brother officers came bowling up to the door, on their way to Carrick. Here was a piece of luck! So we got dinner ready for the party, brought a good store of claret at one side of the fireplace, and a plentiful stock of bog-fir at the other, and resolved to make a night of it; and just as I was describing to my friends the arrival of my guest above-stairs, who should enter the room but himself. He was a round little fellow, about my size, with a short, quick, business-like way about him. Indeed, he was a kind of a drysalter, or something of that nature, in London, had made a large fortune, and wished to turn country gentleman. I had only time to learn these few particulars, and to inform him that he was at that moment in the mansion he had come to visit, when dinner was announced.

'Down we sat; and, 'faith, a jollier party rarely met f together. Poor Mr. Green knew but little of Ireland; but we certainly tried to enlighten him; and he drank in wonders with his wine at such a rate that by eleven o'clock he was carried to his room pretty much in the same state as on his arrival the night before, the only difference being, it was Sneyd, not saltwater, this time that filled him.

'"I like the cockney," said Oakley; "that fellow's good fun. I say, Bob, bring him over with you to-morrow to dinner. We halt at Carrick till the detachment comes up."

'"Could you call it breakfast?" said I. "There's a thought just strikes me: we'll be over in Carrick with you about six o'clock; well have our breakfast, whatever you like to give us, and dine with you about eleven or twelve afterwards."

'Oakley liked the project well; and before we parted the whole thing was arranged for the next day.

'Towards four o'clock in the afternoon of the following day Mr. Green was informed by Daniel that, as we had made an engagement to take an early breakfast some miles off, he ought to be up and stirring; at the same time a pair of candles were brought into the room, hot water for shaving, etc; and the astonished cockney, who looked at his watch, perceived that it was but four.

'"These are very early people," thought he. "However, the habits of the country must be complied with." So saying, he proceeded with his toilette, and at last reached the drawing-room, just as my drag dashed up to the door—the lamps fixed and shining, and everything in readiness for departure.

'"We'll have a little shooting, Mr. Green," said I. "After breakfast, we'll see what my friend's preserves offer. I suppose you're a good shot?"

'"I can't say much for my performance; but I'm passionately fond of it."

'"Well," added I, "I believe I can answer for it, you 'll have a good day here."

'So chatting, we rolled along, the darkness gradually thickening round us, and the way becoming more gloomy and deserted.

'"It's strange," says Mr. Green, after a while; "it's strange, how very dark it grows before sunrise; for I perceive it's much blacker now than when we set out."

'"Every climate has its peculiarities," said I; "and now that we 're used to this, we like it better than any other. But see there, yonder, where you observe the light in the valley—that's Carrick. My friend's house is a little at the side of the town. I hope you 've a good appetite for breakfast."

'"Trust me, I never felt so hungry in my life."

'"Ah, here they come!" said Oakley, as he stood with a lantern in his hand at the barrack-gate; "here they are! Good-morning, Mr. Green. Bob, how goes it? Heavenly morning!"

'"Delightful indeed," said poor Green, though evidently not knowing why.

'"Come along, boys, now," said Oakley; "we've a great deal before us; though I am afraid, Mr. Green, you will think little of our Irish sporting after your English preserves. However, I have kept a few brace of pheasants, very much at your service, in a snug clover-field near the house. So now to breakfast."

'There were about half a dozen of the Fifth at that time in the barrack, who all entered heart and hand into the scheme, and with them we sat down to a capital meal, which, if it was not for a big tea-pot and an urn that figured in the middle of the table, might very well have been called dinner. Poor Mr. Green, who for old prejudice' sake began with his congo and a muffin, soon afterwards, and by an easy transition, glided into soup and fish, and went the pace with the rest of us. The claret began to circulate briskly, and after a couple of hours the whisky made its appearance. The Englishman, whose attention was never suffered to flag with singular anecdotes of a country, whose eccentricities he already began to appreciate, enjoyed himself to the utmost. He laughed, he drank, he even proposed to sing; and with one hand on Oakley's shoulder, and the other on mine, he registered a vow to purchase an estate and spend the rest of his days in Ireland. It was now about eleven o'clock, when I proposed that we should have a couple of hours at the woodcocks before luncheon.

'"Ah, yes," said Green, rubbing his hands, "let us not forget the shooting. I'm passionately fond of sport."

'It took some time to caparison ourselves for the field. Shot-bags, flasks, and powder-horns were distributed about, while three brace of dogs caracoled round the room, and increased the uproar. We now sallied forth. It was a dark and starless night—the wind still Mowing a hurricane from the north-east, and not a thing to be seen two yards from where you stood.

'"Glorious weather!" said Oakley.

'"A delicious morning!" cried another. "When those clouds blow over we shall have no rain."

'"That's a fine line of country, Mr. Green," said I.

'"Eh? what? a fine what? I can see nothing—it's pitch dark."

'"Ah, I forgot," said I. "How stupid we were, Oakley, not to remember that Mr. Green was not used to our climate! We can see everything, you know; but come along, you'll get better by-and-by."

'With this we hurried him down a lane, through a hedge, and into a ploughed field; while on every side of him pop, pop went the guns, accompanied by exclamations of enthusiastic pleasure and delight.

'"There they go—mark! That's yours, Tom! Well done—cock pheasant* by Jove! Here, Mr. Green! this way, Mr. Green! that dog is pointing—there, there! don't you see there?" said I, almost lifting the gun to his shoulder, while poor Mr. Green, almost in a panic of excitement and trepidation, pulled both triggers, and nearly fell back with the recoil.

Irish Sport — with a Cockney

'"Splendid shot, begad!—killed both," said Oakley. "Ah, Mr. Green, we have no chance with you. Give him another gun at once."

'"I should like a little brandy," said Mr. Green, "for my feet are wet."

'I gave him my flask, which he emptied at a pull; while, at the same time, animated with fresh vigour, he tramped manfully forward, without fear or dread. The firing still continued hotly around us; and as Mr. Green discharged his piece whenever he was bid, we calculated that in about an hour and a half he had fired above a hundred and fifty times. Wearied and fatigued by his exertions, at length he sat down upon a bank, while one of the gamekeepers covered the ground about him with ducks, hens, and turkey-cocks, as the spoils of his exertions.

'At Oakley's proposal we now agreed to go back to luncheon, which I need not tell you was a hot supper, followed by mulled claret and more punch. Here the cockney came out still better than before. His character as a sportsman raised him in his own esteem, and he sang "The Poacher" for two hours, until he fell fast asleep on the carpet. He was then conveyed to bed, where, as on the former day, he slept till late in the afternoon.

'Meanwhile, I had arranged another breakfast-party at Ross, where we arrived about seven o'clock in the evening—and so on for the rest of the week, occasionally varying the amusement by hunting, fishing, or coursing.

'At last poor Mr. Green, when called on one morning to dress, sent down Dan with his compliments that he wished to speak to me. I went to him at once, and found him sitting up in his bed.

'"Ah, Mr. Manon," said he, "this will never do; it's a pleasant life, no doubt, but I never could go On with it. Will you tell me one thing—do you never see the sun here?"

'"Oh, bless you! yes," said I; "repeatedly. He was out for two hours on last Patrick's Day, and we have him now and then, promiscuously!"

'"How very strange, how very remarkable," said he, with a sigh, "that we in England should know so little of all this! But, to tell you the truth, I don't think I ever could get used to Lapland—it's Ireland I mean; I beg your pardon for the mistake. And now, may I ask you another question—Is this the way you always live?"

'"Why, pretty much in this fashion; during the hazy season we go about to one another's houses, as you see; and one gets so accustomed to the darkness——"

'"Ah, now, don't tell me that! I know I never could—it's no use my trying it. I 'm used to the daylight; I have seen it, man and boy, for about fifty years, and I never could grope about this way. Not but that I am very grateful to you for all your hospitality; but I had rather go home."

'"You'll wait for morning, at all events," said I; "you will not leave the house in the dead of the night?"

'"Oh, indeed, for the matter of that, it doesn't signify much; night and day is much about the same thing in this country."

'And so he grew obstinate, and notwithstanding all I could say, insisted on his departure; and the same evening he sailed from the quay of Waterford, wishing me every health and happiness, while he added, with a voice of trembling earnestness—

'"Yes, Mr. Mahon, pardon me if I am wrong, but I wish to heaven *you had a little more light in Ireland!*"'

I am unable to say how far the good things of Major Mahon's table seasoned the story I have just related; but I confess I laughed at it loud and long, a testimony on my part which delighted the Major's heart; for, like all anecdote-mongers, he was not indifferent to flattery.

'The moral particularly pleases me,' said I.

'Ah, but the whole thing's true as I am here. Whisht! there's somebody at the door. Come in, whoever you are.'

At these words the door cautiously opened, and a boy of about twelve years of age entered. He carried a bundle under one arm, and held a letter in his hand.

'Oh, here it is,' said Father Tom. 'Come here, Patsey, my boy, here's the penny I promised you. There, now, don't make a bad use of your money.'

The little fellow's eyes brightened, and with a happy smile and a pull of his forelock for a bow, left the room delighted.

'Twelve miles—ay, and long miles too—in less than three hours! Not bad travelling, Captain, for a bit of a gossoon like that.'

'And for a penny!' said I, almost startled with surprise.

'To be sure,' said the priest, as he cut the cord of the package, and opened it on the table. 'Here we are! as nate a jacket as ever I set my eyes on, green and white, with a cap of the same.' So saying, he unfolded the racing-costume, which, by the desire of both parties, I was obliged immediately to try on. 'There, now,' resumed he; 'turn about; it fits you like your skin.'

'It looks devilish well, upon my word,' said the Major. 'Put on the cap; and see too, he has sent a whip—that was very thoughtful of Dillon. But what's this letter here? for you, I think, Mr. Hinton.'

The letter was in a lady's hand; I broke the seal and read as follows:—

'Mount Brown, Wednesday Evening.'

'Dear Sir,—My uncle Dillon requests that you will give us the pleasure of your company to dinner to-morrow at six o'clock. I have taken the liberty to tell him that as we are old acquaintances you will perhaps kindly overlook his not having visited you to-day; and I shall feel happy if, by accepting the invitation, you will sustain my credit on this occasion.

'He desires me to add that the racing-jacket, etc, are most perfectly at your service, as well as any articles of horse-gear you may be in want of.—-Believe me, dear sir, truly yours, Louisa Bellow.'

A thrill of pleasure ran through me as I read these lines; and, notwithstanding my efforts to conceal my emotion from my companions, they but too plainly saw the excitement I felt.

'Something agreeable there! You don't look, Mr. Hinton, as if that were a latitat or a bill of costs you were reading.'

'Not exactly,' said I, laughing. 'It is an invitation to dinner from Mount Brown—wherever that may be.'

'The best house in the county,' said the Major; 'and a good fellow he is, Hugh Dillon. When is it for?'

'To-morrow at six.'

'Well, if he has not asked me to meet you, I'll invite myself, and we'll go over together.'

'Agreed,' said I. 'But how shall I send back the answer?'

The Major promised to send his servant over with the reply, which I penned at once.

'Just tell Hugh,' said the Major, 'that I'll join you.'

I blushed, stammered, and looked confused. 'I am not writing to Mr. Dillon,' said I, 'for the invitation came through a lady of the family, Miss Bellew—his niece, I believe.'

'Whew!' said the Major, with a long whistle. 'Is it there we are! Oh, by the powers, Mr. Hinton! that's not fair—to come down here not only to win our money in a steeplechase, but to want to carry off the belle of our county besides. That'll never do.'

'She doesn't belong to you at all,' said Father Tom; 'she is a parishioner of mine, and so were her father and grandfather before her. And moreover than that, she is the prettiest girl, and the best too, in the county she lives in—and that's no small praise, for it's Galway I'm talking of. And now here's a bumper to her, and who'll refuse it?'

'Not I, certainly.'

'Nor I,' said the Major, as we drank to her health with all the honours.

'Now for another jug,' quoth the Major, as he moved towards the fireplace in search of the kettle.

'After that toast, not another drop,' said I resolutely.

'Well said!' chimed in the priest; 'may I never, if that wasn't very Irish!'

Firmly resisting all the Major's solicitations to resume my place at the table, I wished both my friends goodnight; and having accepted Bob Mahon's offer of a seat in his tax-cart to the race, I shook their hands warmly, and took my leave.

CHAPTER XXV
THE STEEPLECHASE

I did not awake till past noon the next day, and had only completed my dressing when Major Mahon made his appearance. Having pronounced my costume accurate, and suggested that instead of carrying my racing-cap in my hat I should tie the string round my neck and let it hang down in front, he assisted me on with my greatcoat, in which, notwithstanding that the season was summer, and the day a hot one, he buttoned me up to the chin and down to the knees.

'There, now,' said he, 'you look mighty like the thing. Where's your whip? We have no time to lose, so jump into the tax-cart, and let us be off.'

As my reader may remember, the race-ground lay about a mile from the town; but the road thither, unlike the peaceful quiet of the preceding night, was now thronged with people on foot and horseback. Vehicles, too, of every description were there—barouches and landaus, hack-chaises, buggies, and jaunting-cars, whiskys, noddies, and, in fact, every species of conveyance pronounced capable of rolling upon its wheels, was put into requisition. Nor was the turn-out of cavalry of a character less mixed. Horses of every shape and colour—some fat from grass; others lean, like anatomical specimens; old and young; the rich and the poor; the high-sheriff of the county, with his flashy four-in-hand; the mendicant on his crutches—all pressed eagerly forward. And as I surveyed the motley mass I felt what pleasure I could take in the scene, were I not engaged as a principal performer.

On reaching the course we found it already occupied by numerous brilliant equipages, and a strong cavalcade of horsemen; of these the greater number were well mounted, and amused themselves and the bystanders by leaping the various fences around—a species of pastime which occasionally afforded food for laughter, many a soiled coat and broken hat attesting the colour and consistence of the clayey ground. There were also refreshment-booths, stalls for gaming on a humble scale, tables laid out with beer, hard eggs, and gingerbread—in a word, all the ordinary and extraordinary preparations which accompany any great assemblage of people whose object is amusement.

A temporary railing of wood, rudely and hastily put together, inclosed a little space reserved as a weighing-stand; here the stewards of the course were assembled, along with 'the dons' of the country; and into this privileged sanctum was I introduced by the Major, in due form. All eyes were turned on me as I entered; and whether from the guardianship of him who acted as my chaperon, or that the costume of my coat and overalls had propitiated their favour, I cannot say; but somehow I felt that there was more courtesy in their looks, and an air of greater civility in their bearing, than I had remarked the preceding day at the Town-hall. True, these were, for the most part, men of better stamp—the real gentry of the country—who, devotedly attached to field-sports, had come, not as betting characters, but to witness a race. Several of them took off their hats as I approached, and saluted me with politeness. While returning their courtesy, I felt my arm gently touched, and on looking around perceived Mr. Dillon, of Mount Brown, who, with a look of most cordial greeting, and an outstretched hand, presented himself before me.

'You 'll dine with us, Mr. Hinton, I hope?' said he. 'No apology, pray. You shall not lose the hall, for my girls insist on going to it, so that we can all come in together. There, now, that is settled. Will you permit me to introduce you to a few of my friends? Here's Mr. Barry Connolly wishes much to know you. You 'll pardon me, Mr. Hinton, but your name is so familiar to me through my niece, I forget that we are not old acquaintances.'

So saying, the little man took my arm and led me about through the crowd, introducing me right and left. Of the names, the rank, and the residences of my new friends, I knew as much as I did of the domestic arrangements of the King of Congo; but one thing I can vouch for—more unbounded civility and hospitable attention never did man receive. One gentleman begged me to spend a few days with him at his shooting-lodge in the mountains—another wanted to make up a coursing-party for me—a third volunteered to mount me if I'd come down in the hunting season; one and all gave me most positive assurance that if I remained in the country I should neither lack bed nor board for many a day to come.

But a few days before, and in my ignorance I had set down this same class as rude, underbred, and uncivilised; and had I left the country on the preceding evening, I should have carried away my prejudices with me. The bare imitation of his better that the squireen presents was the source of this blunder; the spurious currency had, by its false glitter, deteriorated the sterling coin in my esteem; but now I could detect the counterfeit from the genuine metal.

'The ladies are on this side,' said Mr. Dillon. 'Shall we make our bow to them?'

'You'll not have time, Dillon,' said a friend who overheard his remark: 'here come the horses.'

As he spoke, a distant cheer rose from the bottom of the hill, which, gradually taken up by those nearer, grew louder and louder, till it filled the very air.

'What is it?' said I eagerly.

'It's Jug of Punch,' said a person beside me. 'The mare was bred in the neighbourhood, and excites a great interest among the country-people.'

The crowd now fell back rapidly, and Mr. Burke, seated in a high tandem, dashed up to the weighing-stand, and, giving the reins to his servant, sprang to the ground. His costume was a loose coat of coarse drab cloth, beset on every side by pockets of various shapes and dimensions; long gaiters of the same material incased his legs, and the memorable white hat, set most rakishly on his head, completed his equipment.

Scarcely had he put foot to the ground when he was surrounded by a number of his obsequious followers; but, paying little or no attention to their proffered civilities, he brushed rudely through them, and walked straight up to where I was standing. There was an air of swaggering insolence in his manner which could not be mistaken; and I could mark that, in the sidelong glance he threw about him, he intended that our colloquy should be for the public ear. Nodding familiarly, while he touched his hat with one finger, he addressed me.

'Good-morning, sir; I am happy to have met you so soon. There is a report that we are to have no race: may I ask you if there be any ground for it?'

'Not so far as I am concerned,' replied I, in a tone of quiet indifference.

'At least,' resumed he, 'there would seem some colour for the rumour. Your horse is not here—I understand he has not left the stable—and your groom is among the crowd below. I only asked the question, as it affects my betting-book; there are doubtless here many gentlemen among your friends who would wish to back you.'

This was said with an air of sneering mockery so palpable as to call forth an approving titter from the throng of satellites at his back.

Without deigning any reply to his observation, I whispered a few words to the Major, who at once, taking a horse from a farmer, threw himself into the saddle and cantered off to the mill.

'In fifteen minutes the time will be up,' said Mr. Burke, producing his watch. 'Isn't that so, Dillon? You are the judge here.'

'Perfectly correct,' replied the little man, with a hasty confused manner that showed me in what awe he stood of his redoubted relative.

'Then in that time I shall call on you to give the word to start; for I believe the conditions require me to ride over the course, with or without a competitor.'

So saying, Mr Burke proceeded leisurely to unbutton his greatcoat, which, with the assistance of his friends, he drew off. Two sedulous familiars were meanwhile unbuttoning his gaiters, and in a few seconds he stood forth what even my most prejudiced judgment could not deny—the very beau-ideal of a gentleman-rider. His jacket, of black and yellow, bore the stains of more than one race; but his whole carriage, not less than his costume, looked like one who felt every inch the jockey. His mare was led within the ropes to be saddled—a proceeding conducted under his own eye, and every step of which he watched with critical nicety. This done, he sat down upon a bench, and, with watch in hand, seemed to count the minutes as they flew past.

'Here we are! here we are! all right, Hinton!' shouted the Major, as he galloped up the hill. 'Jump into the scale, my lad; your saddle is beside you. Don't lose a moment.'

'Yes, off with your coat,' said another, 'and jump in!'

Divesting myself of my outer garments with a speed not second to that of Mr. Burke, I took my saddle under my arm, and seated myself in the scale. The groom fortunately had left nothing undone, and my saddle being leaded to the required weight, the operation took not a minute.

'Saddle now as quickly as you can,' whispered Dillon; 'for Burke, being overweight, won't get into the scale.'

While he was yet speaking, the gallant grey was led in, covered with clothing from head to tail.

'All was quite right,' said Mahon, in a low whisper—'your horse won't bear a crowd, and the groom kept him stabled to the last moment. You are in luck besides,' continued he: 'they say he is in a good temper this morning—and, indeed, he walked up from the mill as gently as a lamb.'

'Mount, gentlemen!' cried Mr. Dillon, as, with watch in hand, he ascended a little platform in front of the weighing-stand.

I had but time to throw one glance at my horse when the Major gave me his hand to lift me into the saddle.

'After you, sir,' said Mr. Burke, with a mock politeness, as he drew back to permit me to pass out first.

I touched my horse gently with the snaffle, but he stood stock-still; I essayed again, but with no better success. The place was too crowded to permit of any attempt to bully him, so I once more tried gentle means. It was of no use—he stood rooted to the ground. Before I could determine what next to do, Mahon sprang forward and took him by the head, when the animal walked quietly forward without a show of restiveness.

'He's a droll devil,' said the groom, 'and in one of his odd humours this morning, for that's what I never saw him do before.'

I could see as I passed out that this little scene, short as it was, had not impressed the bystanders with any exalted notion of my horsemanship; for although there was nothing actually to condemn, my first step did not seem to augur well. Having led me forth before the stand, the Major pointed with his finger to the line of country before me, and was repeating the priest's injunctions, when Mr. Burke rode up to my side, and, with a smile of very peculiar meaning, said—

'Are you ready *now*, sir?'

I nodded assent. The Major let go the bridle.

'We are all ready, Dillon!' cried Burke, turning in his saddle.

'All ready!' repeated Dillon; 'then away!'

As he spoke, the hell rang, and off we went.

For about thirty yards we cantered side by side—the grey horse keeping stroke with the other, and not betraying the slightest evidence of bad temper. Whatever my own surprise, the amazement of Burke was beyond all bounds. He turned completely round in his saddle to look, and I could see, in the workings of his features, the distrustful expression of one who suspected he had been duped. Meanwhile, the cheers of the vast multitude pealed high on every side; and, as the thought flashed across me that I might still acquit myself with credit, my courage rose, and I gripped my saddle with double energy.

At the foot of the slope there was, as I have already mentioned, a small fence; towards this we were now approaching at the easy sling of a hand-gallop, when suddenly Burke's features—which I watched from time to time with intense anxiety—changed their expression of doubt and suspicion for a look of triumphant malice. Putting spurs to his horse, he sprang a couple of lengths in advance, and rode madly at the fence; the grey stretched out to follow, and already was I preparing for the leap, when

Burke, who had now reached the fence, suddenly swerved his horse round, and, affecting to baulk, cantered back towards the hill. The manoeuvre was perfectly successful. My horse, who up to that moment was going on well, threw his forelegs far out, and came to a dead stop. In an instant the trick was palpable to my senses; and, in the heat of my passion, I dashed in both spurs, and endeavoured to lift him by the rein. Scarcely had I done so, when, as if the very ground beneath had jerked us upwards, he sprang into the air, dashing his head forward between the forelegs, and throwing up his haunches behind, till I thought we should come clean over in the somersault. I kept my seat, however; and thinking that boldness alone could do at such a moment, I only waited till he reached the ground, when I again drove the spurs up to the rowels in his flanks. With a snort of passion he bounded madly up, and pawing the air for some moments with his forelegs, lit upon the earth, panting with rage, and trembling in every limb.

Modirideroo

The shouts which now filled my ears seemed but like mockery and derision; and stung almost to madness, I fixed myself in my seat, pulled my cap upon my brows, and with clenched teeth gathered up the reins to renew the conflict. There was a pause now for a few seconds; both horse and man seemed to feel that there was a deadly strife before them, and each seemed to collect his energy for the blow. The moment came; and driving in the spurs with all my force, I struck him with the whip between the ears. With something like a yell, the savage animal sprang into the air, writhing his body like a fish. Bound after bound he made, as though goaded on to madness; and, at length, after several fruitless efforts to unseat me, he dashed straight upwards, struck out with his forelegs, poised for a second or two, and then with a crash fell back upon me, rolling me to the ground, bruised, stunned, and senseless.

How long this state lasted I cannot tell; but when half consciousness returned to me, I found myself standing in the field, my head reeling with the shock, my clothes torn and ragged. My horse was standing beside me, with some one at his head; while another, whose voice I thought I could recognise, called out—

'Get up, man, get up! you 'll do the thing well yet. There, don't lose time.'

'No, no,' said another voice, 'it's a shame; the poor fellow is half killed already—and there, don't you see Burke's at the second fence?'

Thus much I heard, amid the confusion around me; but more I know not. The next moment I was in the saddle, with only sense enough left to feel reckless to desperation. I cried out to leave the way, and turned towards the fence.

A tremendous cut of a whip fell upon the horse's quarter from some one behind, and, like a shell from a mortar, he leaped wildly out. With one fly he cleared the fence, dashed across the field, and, before I was firm in my seat, was over the second ditch. Burke had barely time to look round him ere I had passed. He knew that the horse was away with me, but he also knew his bottom, and that, if I could but keep my saddle, the chances were now in my favour.

Then commenced a terrible struggle. In advance of him, about four lengths, I took everything before me, my horse flying straight as an arrow. I dared not turn my head, but I could mark that Burke was making every effort to get before me. We were now approaching a tall hedge, beyond which lay the deep ground of which the priest had already spoken. So long as the fences presented nothing of height, the tremendous pace I was going was all in my favour; but now there was fully five feet of a hedge standing before me. Unable to collect himself, my horse came with his full force against it, and chesting the tangled branches, fell head-foremost into the field. Springing to my legs unhurt, I lifted him at once; but ere I could remount, Burke came bounding over the hedge, and lit safely beside me. With a grin of malice he turned one look towards me, and dashed on.

For some seconds my horse was so stunned he could scarcely move, and as I pressed him forward the heavy action of his shoulder and his drooping head almost filled me with despair. By degrees, however, he warmed up and got into his stride. Before me, and nearly a hundred yards in advance, rode Burke, still keeping up his pace, but skirting the headlands to my right. I saw now the force of the priest's remark, that were I to take a straight line through the deep ground the race was still in my favour. But dare I do so with a horse so dead beat as mine was? The thought was quick as lightning; it was my only chance to win, and I resolved to take it. Plunging into the soft and marshy ground before me, I fixed my eye upon the blue flag which marked the course. At this moment Burke turned and saw me, and I could perceive that he immediately slackened his pace. Yes, thought I, he thinks I am pounded; but it is not come to that yet. In fact, my horse was improving at every stride, and although the ground was trying, his breeding began to tell, and I could feel that he had plenty of running still in him. Affecting, however, to lift him at every stroke, and seeming to labour to help him through, I induced Burke to hold in, until I gradually crept up to the fence before he was within several lengths of it. The grey no sooner caught sight of the wall than he pricked up his ears and rushed towards it; with a vigorous lift I popped him over, without touching a stone. Burke followed in splendid style, and in an instant was alongside of me.

Now began the race in right earnest. The cunning of his craft could avail him little here, except as regarded the superior management of his own horse; so Burke, abandoning every ruse, rode manfully on. As for me, my courage rose at every moment; and so far from feeling any fear, I only wished that the fences were larger; and like a gambler who would ruin his adversary at one throw, I would have taken a precipice if he pledged himself to follow. For some fields we rode within a few yards of each other, side by side, each man lifting his horse at the same moment to his leap, and alighting with the same shock beyond it. Already our heads were turned homewards, and I could mark on the distant hill the far-off crowds whose echoing shouts came floating towards us. But one fence of any consequence remained; that was the large gripe that formed the last of the race. We had cleared a low stone wall, and now entered the field that led to the great leap. It was evident that Burke's horse, both from being spared the shocks that mine had met with, and from his better riding, was the fresher of the two; we had neither of us, however, much to boast of on that score, and perhaps at a calmer moment would have little fancied facing such a leap as that before us. It was evident that the first over must win; and as each man measured the other's stride, the intense anxiety of the moment nearly rose to madness.

From the instant of entering the field I had marked out with my eye where I meant to take the leap. Burke had evidently done this also; and we now slightly diverged, each to his allotted spot. The pace was awful. All thought of danger lost, or forgotten, we came nearer and nearer with knitted brow and clenched lip—I, the first. Already I was on the side; with a loud cry and a cut of my whip I rose my horse to it. The noble beast sprang forward, but his strength was spent, and he fell downwards on his head. Recovering him without losing my seat, I scrambled up the opposite bank and looked round. Burke, who had pressed the pace so hotly before, had only done so to blow my horse and break him down at his leap; and I saw him now approaching the fence with his mare fully in hand, and her haunches well under her. Unable to move forward, save at a walk, I turned in my saddle to watch him. He came boldly to the brink of the fence; his hand was up prepared to strike; already the mare was collecting herself for the effort, when from the bottom of the gripe a figure sprang wildly up, and as the horse rose into the air, he jumped at the bridle, pulling down both the horse and the rider with a crash upon him, a loud cry of agony rising amid the struggle.

As they disappeared from my sight I felt like one in a trance. All thoughts, however, were lost in the desire to win; and collecting my energies for a last struggle, I lifted the gallant grey with both hands, and by dint of spurring and shaking, pressed him to a canter, and rode in, the winner, amid the deafening cheers and cries of thousands.

'Keep back! keep back!' cried Mahon, restraining with his whip the crowd that bore down upon me. 'Hinton, take care that no one touches your horse; ride inside, take off your saddle and get into the scale.'

Moving onwards like one in a dream, I mechanically obeyed the direction, while the cries and shouts around me grew each moment louder and wilder.

'Here he comes! here he comes!' shouted several voices; and Burke galloped up, and without drawing rein rode into the weighing-stand.

'Foul play!' roared he in a tone hoarse with passion. 'I protest against the race! Holloa, sir!' he shouted, turning towards me.

'There, there!' said Mahon, as he hurried me along towards the scale, 'you have nothing to do with him.' And at the same moment a number of others pressed eagerly forward to shake my hand and wish me joy.

'Look here, Dillon,' cried the Major, 'mark the weight—twelve stone two, and two pounds over, if he wanted it. There, now,' whispered he, in a voice which though not meant for my hearing I could distinctly catch— 'there, now, Dillon, take him into your carriage and get him off the ground as fast as you can.'

Just at this instant Burke, who had been talking with loud voice and violent gesticulation, burst through the crowd, and stood before us.

'Do you say, Dillon, that I have lost this race?'

'Yes, yes, to be sure!' cried out full twenty voices.

'My question was not addressed to you, sirs,' said he, boiling with passion; 'I ask the judge of this course, have I lost?'

'My dear Ulick——' said Dillon, in a voice scarce audible from agitation.

'No cursed palaver with me,' said he, interrupting. 'Lost or won, sir—one word.'

'Lost, of course,' replied Dillon, with more of firmness than I believed him capable.

'Well, sir,' said Burke, as he turned towards me, his teeth clenched with passion, 'it may be some alloy to your triumph to know that your accomplice has smashed his thigh-bone in your service; and yet I can tell you you have not come to the end of this matter.'

Before I could reply, Burke's friends tore him from the spot and hurried him to a carriage; while I, still more than ever puzzled by the words I had heard, looked from one to the other of those around for an explanation.

'Never mind, Hinton,' said Mahon, as, half breathless with running, he rushed up and seized me by the hand. 'The poor fellow was discharging a double debt in his own rude way—gratitude on your score, vengeance on his own.'

'Tally-ho, tally-ho!—hark, there—stole away!' shouted a wild cry from without, and at the same instant four countrymen came forward, carrying a door between them, on which was stretched the pale and mangled figure of Tipperary Joe. 'A drink of water—spirits—tay—anything, for the love of the Virgin! I'm famished, and I want to drink Captain Phil's health. Ah, darling!' said he, as he turned his filmy eyes up towards me, 'didn't I do it beautifully; didn't I pay him off for this?' With these words he pointed to a blue welt that stretched across his face, from the mouth to the ear. 'He gave me that yesterday for saying long life and success to you!'

'Oh! this is too horrible,' said I, gasping for breath. 'My poor fellow! and I who had treated you so harshly!' I took his hand in mine, but it was cold and clammy; his features were sunken too—he had fainted.

'Come, Hinton,' said the Major, 'we can do no good here; let us move down to the inn at once, and see after this poor boy.'

'You are coming with us, Mr. Hinton?' cried Dillon.

'Not now, not now,' said I, while my throat was swelling with repressed emotion. Without suffering me to say more, Mahon almost lifted me into the tax-cart, and putting his horse to the gallop, dashed towards the town, the cheers of the people following us as we went; for, to their wild sense of justice, Joe was a genuine martyr, and I shared in the glory of his self-devotion.

The whole way towards Loughrea, Mahon continued to talk; but not a word could I catch. My thoughts were fixed on the poor fellow who had suffered for my sake; and I would have given all I possessed in the world to have lost the race, and seen him safe and sound before me.

'There, there!' said the Major, as he shook me by the arm; 'don't take it to heart this way. You know little of Ireland, that's plain; that poor fellow will be prouder for the feeling you have shown towards him this night than many a king upon his throne. To have served a gentleman, to have put him under an obligation—*that* has a charm you can't estimate the extent of. Beware, only beware of one thing—do not by any offer of money destroy the illusion; do what you like for him, but take care of that.'

We now reached the little inn; and Mahon—for I was incapable of all thought or exertion—got a room in readiness for Joe, and summoning the doctor of the place, provided everything for his care and accommodation.

'Now, Hinton,' said he, as he burst into my room, 'all's right. Joe is comfortable in bed; the fracture turns out not to be a bad one. So rouse yourself, for Dillon's carriage with all its ladies is waiting these ten minutes.'

'No, no!' cried I; 'I can't go to this dinner-party! I'll not quit——'

'Nonsense, man!' said he, interrupting me; 'you can only do harm here; the doctor says he must be left quite quiet" and alone. Besides, Dillon has behaved so well to-day—so stoutly for *him*, that you mustn't forget it. There, now, where are your clothes? I'll pack them for you.'

I started up to obey him, but a giddiness came over me, and I sank into my chair, weak and sick.

'This will never do,' said Mahon; 'I had better tell them I'll drive you over myself. And now, just lie down for an hour or two, and keep quiet.'

This advice I felt was good; and thanking my kind friend with a squeeze of the hand, for I could not speak, I threw myself upon my bed, and strange enough, while such contending emotions disturbed my brain, fell asleep almost immediately.

CHAPTER XXVI
THE DINNER-PARTY AT MOUNT BROWN

I awoke refreshed after half-an-hour's doze, and then every circumstance of the whole day was clear and palpable before me. I remembered each minute particular, and could bring to my mind all the details of the race itself, notwithstanding the excitement they had passed in, and the rapidity with which they succeeded one another.

My first thought was to visit poor Joe; and creeping stealthily to his room, I opened the door. The poor fellow was fast asleep. His features had already become coloured with fever, and a red hectic spot on either cheek told that the work of mischief had begun; yet still his sleep was tranquil, and a half smile curled; his bloodless lips. On his bed his old hunting-cap was placed, a bow of white and green ribbons—the colours I wore—fastened gaudily in the front; upon this, doubtless, he had been gazing to the last moment of his waking. I now stole noiselessly back, and began a letter to O'Grady, whose anxiety as to the result would, I knew, be considerable.

It was not without pride, I confess, that I narrated the events of the day; yet when I came to that part of my letter in which Joe was to be mentioned, I could not avoid a sense of shame in acknowledging the cruel contrast between *my* conduct and *his* gratitude. I did not attempt to theorise upon what he had done, for I felt that O'Grady's better knowledge of his countrymen would teach him to sound the depths of a motive, the surface of which I could but skim. I told him frankly that the more I saw of Ireland the less I found I knew about it; so much of sterling good seemed blended with unsettled notions and unfixed opinions; such warmth of heart, such frank cordiality, with such traits of suspicion and distrust, that I could make nothing of them. Either, thought I, these people are born to present the anomaly of all that is most opposite and contradictory in human nature, or else the fairest gifts that ever graced manhood have been perverted and abused by mismanagement and misguidance.

I had just finished my letter when Bob Mahon drove up, his honest face radiant with smiles and good-humour.

'Well, Hinton,' cried he, 'the whole thing is properly settled. The money is paid over; and if you are writing to O'Grady, you may mention that he can draw on the Limerick bank, at sight if he pleases. There's time enough, however, for all this; so get up beside me. We've only half an hour to do our five miles, and dress for dinner.'

I took my place beside the Major; and as we flew fast through the air, the cool breeze and his enlivening conversation rallied and refreshed me. Such was our pace that we had ten minutes to spare, as we entered a dark avenue of tall beech-trees, and a few seconds after arrived at the door of a large old-fashioned-looking manor-house, on the steps of which stood Hugh Dillon himself, in all the plenitude of a white waistcoat and black-silk tights. While he hurried me to a dressing-room, he overwhelmed me with felicitations on the result of the day.

'You'll think it strange, Mr. Hinton,' said he, 'that I should congratulate you, knowing that Mr. Burke is a kind of relation of mine; but I have heard so much of your kindness to my niece Louisa, that I cannot but rejoice in your success.'

'I should rather,' said I, 'for many reasons, had it been more legitimately obtained; and, indeed, were I not acting for another, I doubt how far I should feel justified in considering myself a winner.'

'My dear sir,' interrupted Dillon, 'the laws of racing are imperative in the matter; besides, had you waived your right, all who backed you must have lost their money.'

'For that matter,' said I, laughing, 'the number of my supporters was tolerably limited.'

'No matter for that; and even if you had not a single bet upon you, Ulick's conduct, in the beginning, deserved little favour at your hands.'

'I confess,' said I, 'that there you have touched on the saving clause to my feeling of shame. Had Mr. Burke conducted himself in a different spirit towards my friend and myself, I should feel sorely puzzled this minute.'

'Quite right, quite right,' said Dillon; 'and now try if you can't make as much haste with your toilette as you did over the clover-field.'

Within a quarter of an hour I made my appearance in the drawing-room, now crowded with company, the faces of many among whom I remembered having seen in the morning. Mr. Dillon was a widower, but his daughters—three fine, tall, handsome-looking girls—did the honours. While I was making my bows to them, Miss Bellew came forward, and with an eye bright with pleasure held out her hand towards me.

'I told you, Mr. Hinton, we should meet in the west. Have I been as good a prophetess in saying that you would like it?'

'If it afforded me but this one minute,' said I, in a half-whisper.

'Dinner!' said the servant, and at the same moment that scene of pleasant confusion ensued that preludes the formal descent of a party to the dining-room.

The host had gracefully tucked a large lady under his arm, beside whose towering proportions he looked pretty much like what architects call 'a lean-to,' superadded to a great building. He turned his eye towards me to go and do likewise, with a significant glance at a heaving mass of bugles and ostrich feathers that sat panting on a sofa. I parried the stroke, however, by drawing Miss Bellow's arm within mine, while I resigned the post of honour to my little friend the Major.

The dinner passed off like all other dinners. There was the same routine of eating and drinking, and pretty much the same ritual of table-talk. As a kind of commentary on the superiority of natural gifts over the affected and imitated graces of society, I could not help remarking that those things which figured on the table of homely origin were actually luxurious, while the exotic resources of the cookery were, in every instance, miserable failures. Thus the fish was excellent, and the mutton perfect, while the *fricandeau* was atrocious, and the *petits pâtés* execrable.

Should my taste be criticised, that with a lovely girl beside me, for whom I already felt a strong attachment, I could thus set myself to criticise the cookery, in lieu of any other more agreeable occupation, let my apology be, that my reflection was an apropos, called forth by comparing Louisa Bellow with her cousins the Dillons. I have said they were handsome girls; they were more—they were beautiful. They had all that fine pencilling of the eyebrow, that deep, square orbit, so characteristically Irish, which gives an expression to the eye, whatever be its colour, of inexpressible softness; their voices too, albeit the accent was provincial, were soft and musical, and their manners quiet and ladylike—yet, somehow, they stood immeasurably apart from her.

I have already ventured on one illustration from the cookery, may I take another from the cellar? How often in wines of the same vintage, of even the same cask, do we find one bottle whose bouquet is more aromatic, whose flavour is richer, whose colour is more purely brilliant! There seems to be no reason why this should be so, nor is the secret appreciable to our senses; however, the fact is incontestable. So among women. You meet some half-dozen in an evening party, equally beautiful, equally lovely; yet will there be found one among the number towards whom, without any assignable cause, more eyes are turned, and more looks bent; around whose chair more men are found to linger, and in whose slightest word some cunning charm seems ever mingled. Why is this so? I confess I cannot tell you; but trust me for the fact. If, however, it will satisfy you that I adduce an illustration — Louisa Bellew was one of these. With all the advantages of a cultivated mind, she possessed that fearlessness that only girls really innocent of worldly trickery and deceit ever have; and thus, while her conversation ranged far beyond the limits the cold ordeal of fashion would prescribe to a London beauty, the artless enthusiasm of her manner was absolutely captivating.

In Dublin the most marked feature about her was an air of lofty pride and hauteur, by which, in the mixed society of Rooney's house, was she alone enabled to repel the obtrusive and impertinent attentions it was the habit of the place to practise. Surrounded by those who resorted there for a lounge, it was a matter of no common difficulty for her, a young and timid girl, to assert her own position, and exact the respect that was her due. Here, however, in her uncle's house, it was quite different. Relieved from all performance of a part, she was natural, graceful, and easy; and her spirits, untrammelled by the dread of misconstruction, took their own free and happy flight without fear and without reproach.

When we returned to the drawing-room, seated beside her, I entered into an explanation of all my proceedings since my arrival in the country, and had the satisfaction to perceive that not only did she approve of everything I had done, but, assuming a warmer interest than I could credit in my fortunes, she counselled me respecting the future. Supposing that my success might induce me to further trials of my horsemanship, she cautioned me about being drawn into any matches or wagers.

'My cousin Ulick,' said she, 'is one of those who rarely let a prey escape them. I speak frankly to you, for I know I may do so; therefore, I would beseech you to take care of him, and, above all things, do not come into collision with him. I have told you, Mr. Hinton, that I wish you to know my father. For this object, it is essential you should have no misunderstanding with my cousin; for although his whole conduct through life has been such as to grieve and afflict him, yet the feeling for his only sister's child has sustained him against all the rumours and reports that have reached him, and even against his own convictions.'

'You have, indeed,' said I, 'suggested a strong reason for keeping well with your cousin. My heart is not only bent on being known to your father, but, if I dare hope it, on being liked by him also.'

'Yes, yes,' said she quickly, blushing while she spoke, 'I am sure he'll like you — and I know you'll like him. Our house, perhaps I should tell you, is not a gay one. We lead a secluded and retired life; and this has had its effect upon my poor father, giving a semblance of discontent—only a semblance, though—to a nature mild, manly, and benevolent.'

She paused an instant, and, as if fearing that she had been led away to speak of things she should not have touched upon, added with a more lively tone—

'Still, we may contrive to amuse you. You shall have plenty of fishing and coursing, the best shooting in the west, and, as for scenery, I'll answer for it you are not disappointed.'

While we chatted thus, the time rolled on, and at last the clock on the mantel-piece apprised us that it was time to set out for the ball. This, as it may be believed, was anything but a promise of pleasure to me. With Louisa Bellew beside me, talking in a tone of confidential intimacy she had never ventured on before, I would have given worlds to have remained where I was. However, the thing was impossible; 'the ball! the ball!' passed from lip to lip, and already the carriages were assembled before the door, and cloaks, hoods, and mantles were distributed on all sides.

Resolving, at all events, to secure Miss Bellew as my fellow-traveller, I took her arm to lead her downstairs.

'Holloa, Hinton!' cried the Major, 'you 're coming with me, ain't you?'

I got up a tremendous fit of coughing, as I stammered out an apology about night-air, etc.

'Ah, true, my poor fellow,' said the simple-hearted Bob; 'you must take care of yourself—this has been a severe day's work for you.'

'With such a heavy cold,' said Louisa, laughing, as her bright eyes sparkled with fun, 'perhaps you 'll take a seat in our carriage.'

I pressed her arm gently and murmured my assent, assisted her in, and placed myself beside her.

CHAPTER XXVII
THE RACE BALL

Fast as had been the pace in the Major's tax-cart, it seemed to me as though the miles flew much more quickly by as I returned to the town. How, indeed, they passed I cannot well say; but, from the instant that I quitted Mr. Dillon's house to that of my arrival in Loughrea, there seemed to be but one brief, delightful moment. I have already said that Miss Bellew's manner was quite changed; and, as I assisted her from the carriage, I could not but mark the flashing brilliancy of her eye and the sparkling animation of her features, lending, as they did, an added loveliness to her beauty.

'Am I to dance with you, Mr. Hinton?' said she laughingly, as I led her up the stairs. 'If so, pray be civil enough to ask me at once—otherwise, I must accept the first partner that offers himself.'

'How very stupid I have been! Will you, pray, let me have the honour?'

'Yes, yes—you shall have the honour; but, now that I think of it, you mustn't ask me a second time. We countryfolk are very prudish about these things; and, as you are the lion of the party, I should get into a sad scrape were I to appear to monopolise you.'

'But you surely will have compassion on me,' said I, in a tone of affected bashfulness. 'You know I am a stranger here—neither known to nor by any one save you.'

'*Ah, trêve de modestie!*' said she coquettishly. 'My cousins will be quite delighted; and indeed, you owe them some *amende* already.'

'As how?' said I. 'What have I done?'

'Rather, what have you left undone? I'll tell you. You have not come to the ball in your fine uniform, with your aiguillette and your showy feathers, and all the pride, pomp, and circumstance of your dignity as aide-de-camp. Learn, that in the west we love the infantry, doat on the dragoons, but we adore the staff. Now, a child would find it as difficult to recognise a plump gentleman without a star on his breast as a king, as we western ladies would to believe in the military features of a person habited in quiet black. You should, at least, have some symbol of your calling. A little bit of moustache like a Frenchman, a foreign order at your button-hole, your arm in a sling—from a wound, as it were—even a pair of brass spurs would redeem you. Poor Mary here won't believe that you wear a great sword, and are the most warlike-looking person imaginable on occasions.'

'Dearest Louisa, how silly you are!' said her cousin, blushing deeply. 'Pray, Mr. Hinton, what do you think of the rooms?'

This question happily recalled me to myself, for up to that very moment, forgetful of everything save my fair companion, I had not noticed our entrance into the ballroom, around which we were promenading with alow steps. I now looked up, and discovered that we were in the Town-hall, the great room of which building was generally reserved for occasions like the present. Nothing could be more simple than the decorations of the apartment. The walls, which were whitewashed, were tastefully ornamented with strings and wreaths of flowers suspended between the iron chandeliers, while over the chimney-piece were displayed the colours of the marching regiment then quartered in the town. Indeed, to do them justice, the garrison were the main contributors to the pleasure of the evening. By *them* were the garlands so gracefully disposed; by *them* were the rat-holes and other dangerous crevices in the floor caulked with oakum; *their* band was now blowing 'God Save the King' and 'Rule Britannia' alternately for the last hour, and *their* officers, in all the splendour of scarlet, were parading the room, breaking the men's hearts with envy and the women's with admiration.

O'Grady was quite right—it is worth while being a soldier in Ireland; and, if such be the case in the capital, how much more true is it in Connaught? Would that some minute anatomist of human feeling could demonstrate that delicate fibre in an Irishwoman's heart that vibrates so responsively to everything in the army-list! In this happy land you need no nitrous oxide to promote the high spirits of your party; I had rather have a sub. in a marching regiment than a whole gasometer full of it. How often have I watched the sleepy eye of languid loveliness brighten up—how often have I seen features almost plain in their character assume a kind of beauty, as some red-coat drew near! Don't tell me of your insurrection acts, of your nightly outrages, your outbreaks, and your burnings, as a reason for keeping a large military force in Ireland—nothing of the kind. A very different object, indeed, is the reason—Ireland is garrisoned to please the ladies. The War Office is the most gallant of public bodies; and, with a true appreciation of the daughters of the west, it inundates the land with red-coats.

These observations were forced upon me as I looked about the room, and saw on every side how completely the gallant Seventy-something had cut out the country gentry. Poor fellows! you are great people at the assizes—you are strong men at a road-sessions—but you're mighty small folk indeed before your wives and daughters when looked at to the music of 'Paddy Carey,' and by the light of two hundred and fifty mutton-candles.

The country-dance was at length formed, and poor Mr. Harkin, the master of the ceremonies and Coryphaeus-in-ordinary of Loughrea, had, by dint of scarce less fatigue than I experienced in my steeplechase, by running hither and thither, imploring, beseeching, wheedling, coaxing, and even cursing, at length succeeded in assembling sixty-four souls in a double file upon the floor. Poor fellow! never was there a more disorderly force. Nobody would keep his own place, but was always trying to get above his neighbour. In vain did he tell the men to stand at their own side. Alas! they thought that side their own where the ladies were also. Then the band added to his miseries; for scarcely had he told them to play 'The Wind that shakes the Barley,' when some changed it to 'The Priest in his Boots,' and afterwards to 'The Dead March in Saul.' These were heavy afflictions; for be it known that he could not give way, as other men would in such circumstances, to a good outbreak of passion—for Mr. Harkin was a public functionary, who, like all other functionaries, had a character to sustain before the world. When kings are angry, we are told by Shakespeare, Schiller, and others, they rant it in good royal style. Now, when a dancing-master is excited by passion, he never loses sight of the unities. If he flies down the floor to chide the little fat man that is talking loudly, he contrives to do it with a step, a spring, and a hop, to the time of one, two, three. Is there a confusion in the figure, he advances to rectify it with a *chassé* rigadoon. Does Mr. Somebody turn his toes too much out, or is Miss So-and-so holding her petticoats too high, he fugles the correction in his own person—first imitating the deformity he would expose, and then displaying the perfection he would point to.

On the evening in question, this gentleman afforded me by far the most of the amusement of the ball. Nearly half the company had been in time of yore his pupils, or were actually so at the very moment; so that, independent of his cares as conductor of the festivities, he had also the *amour propre* of one who saw his own triumphs reflected in the success of his disciples.

At last the dances were arranged. A certain kind of order was established in the party; and Mr. Harkin, standing in the fifth position, with all his fingers expanded, gave three symbolic claps of his hand, and cried out, 'Begin!' Away went the band at once, and down the middle I flew with my partner, to the measure of a quick country-dance that no human legs could keep time to. Two others quickly followed, more succeeding them like wave after wave. Nothing was too fat, nothing too short, nothing too long, to dance. There they were, as ill-paired as though, instead of treading a merry measure, they had been linked in the very bonds of matrimony — old and young, the dwarf and the brobdingnag, the plump and the lean, each laughing at the eccentricities of his neighbour, and happily indifferent to the mirth he himself afforded. By-the-bye, what a glorious thing it would be if we could carry out this principle of self-esteem into all our reciprocity-treaties, and, while we enjoyed what we derive from others, be unconscious of the loss we sustained ourselves!

Unlike our English performance, the dance here was as free-and-easy a thing as needs be. Down the middle you went, holding, mayhap squeezing your partner's hand, laughing, joking, flirting, venturing occasionally on many a bolder flight than at other times you could have dared; for there was no time for the lady to be angry, as she tripped along to 'The Hare in the Corn'; and besides, but little wisdom could be expected from a man while performing more antics than Punch in a pantomime. With all this, there was a running fire of questions, replies, and recognitions, from every one you passed—

'That's it, Captain: push along! begad, you're doing it well!'— 'Don't forget to-morrow!'—'Hands round!'—'Hasn't she a leg of her own!'—'Keep it up!'—'This way I—turn, Miss Malone!'—'You'll come to breakfast!'— 'How are ye, Joe?' etc.

Scarcely was the set concluded, when Miss Bellew was engaged by another partner; while I, at her suggestion, invited her cousin Mary to become mine. The ball-room was now crowded with people; the mirth and fun grew fast and furious. The country-dance occupied the whole length of the room; and round the walls were disposed tables for whist or loo, where the elders amused themselves with as much pleasure, and not less noise.

I fear that I gave my fair partner but a poor impression of an aide-de-camp's gallantry—answering at random, speaking vaguely and without coherence, my eyes fixed on Miss Bellew, delighted when by chance I could catch a look from her, and fretful and impatient when she smiled at some remark of her partner. In fact, love has as many stages as a fever; and I was in that acute period of the malady when the feeling of devotion, growing every moment stronger, is checkered by a doubt lest the object of your affections should really be indifferent to you—thus suggesting all the torturing agonies of jealousy to your distracted mind. At such times as these a man can scarcely be very agreeable even to the girl he loves; but he is a confounded bore to a chance acquaintance. So, indeed, did poor Mary Dillon seem to think; and as, at the conclusion of the dance, I resigned her hand to a lieutenant somebody, with pink cheeks, black eyebrows, and a most martial air, I saw she looked upon her escape as a direct mercy from Providence.

Just at this moment, Mr. Dillon, who had only been waiting for the propitious moment to pounce upon me, seized me by the arm, and led me down the room. There was a charming woman dying to know me in one corner; the best cock-shooting in Ireland wished to make my acquaintance in another; thirty thousand pounds, and a nice little property in Leitrim, was sighing for me near the fire; and three old ladies, the *gros bonnets* of the land, had kept the fourth place at the whist table vacant for *my* sake, and were at length growing impatient at my absence.

Non sunt mea verba, good reader. Such was Mr. Dillon's representation to me, as he hurried me along, presenting me as he went to every one we met—a ceremony in which I soon learned to perform my part respectably, by merely repeating a formula I had adopted for my guidance: 'Delighted to know you, Mr. Burke!' or, 'Charmed to make your acquaintance, Mrs. French!' for, as nine-tenths of the men were called by the one, and nearly all the ladies by the other appellation, I seldom blundered in my addresses.

The evening wore on, but the vigour of the party seemed unabated. The fatigues of fashionable life seemed to be as little known in Ireland as its apathy and its ennui Poor, benighted people! you appear to enjoy society, not as a refuge for your own weariness, not as an escape-valve for your own vapours, but really as a source of pleasurable emotions—an occasion for drawing closer the bonds of intimacy, for being agreeable to your friends, and for making yourselves happy. Alas! you have much to learn in this respect; you know not yet how preferable is the languid look of *blasé* beauty to the brilliant eye and glowing cheek of happy girlhood; you know not how superior is the cutting sarcasm, the whispered equivoque, to the kind welcome and the affectionate greeting; and while enjoying the pleasure of meeting your friends, you absolutely forget to be critical upon their characters or their costume!

What a pity it is that good-nature is underbred, and good-feeling is vulgarity; for, after all, while I contrasted the tone of everything around me with the supercilious cant and unimpassioned coldness of London manners, I could not but confess to myself that the difference was great and the interval enormous. To which side my own heart inclined, it needed not my affection for Louisa Bellew to tell me; yes, I had seen enough of life to learn how far are the real gifts of worth and excellence preferable to the adventitious polish of high society. While these thoughts rushed through my mind, another flashed across it. What if my lady-mother were here! What if my proud cousin! How would her dark eyes brighten as some absurd or ludicrous feature of the company would suggest its *mot* of malice or its speech of sarcasm! how would their air, their carriage, their deportment, appear in *her* sight! I could picture to myself the cold scorn of her manner towards the men, the insulting courtesy of her demeanour to the women; the affected *naïveté* with which she would question them as to their everyday habits, and habitudes, their usages and their wants, as though she were inquiring into the manners and customs of South Sea Islanders! I could imagine the ineffable scorn with which she would receive what were meant to be kind and polite attentions; and I could fashion to myself her look, her manner, and her voice when escaping, as she would call it, from her *Nuit parmi les sauvages*, she would caricature every trait, every feature of the party, converting into food for laughter their frank and hospitable bearing, and making their very warmth of heart the groundwork of a sarcasm.

The ball continued with unabated vigour, and as, in obedience to Miss Bellew's request, I could not again ask her to dance, I myself felt little inclination to seek for another partner. The practice of the place seemed, however, as imperatively to exclude idleness as the discipline of a man-of-war. If you were not dancing you ought to be playing cards, making love, drinking negus, or exchanging good stories with some motherly, fat, old lady, too heavy for a reel, too stupid for loo. In this dilemma I cut into a round game, which I remember often to have seen at Rooney's, technically called 'speculation.' A few minutes before, and I was fancying to myself what my mother would think of all this; and now, as I drew my chair to the table, I muttered a prayer to my own heart that she might never hear of my doings. How strange it is that we would much rather be detected in some overt act of vice than caught in any ludicrous situation or absurd position! I could look my friends and family steadily enough in the face while standing amid all the blacklegs of Epsom and the swindlers of Ascot, exchanging with them the courtesies of life, and talking on terms of easy and familiar intercourse; yet would I rather have been seen with the veriest pickpocket in fashionable life, than seated amid that respectable and irreproachable party who shook their sides with laughter around the card-table!

Truly, it was a merry game, and well suited for a novice, as it required no teaching. Each person had his three cards dealt him, one of which was displayed to the company in rotation. Did this happen to be a knave or some other equally reproachful character, the owner was mulcted to the sum of fivepence; and he must indeed have had a miser's heart who could regret a penalty so provocative of mirth. Often as the event took place, the fun never seemed to grow old; and from the exuberance of the delight, and the unceasing flow of the laughter, I began to wonder within myself if these same cards had not some secret and symbolic meaning unknown to the neophyte. But the drollery did not end here: you might sell your luck and put up your hand to auction. This led to innumerable droll allusions and dry jokes, and, in fact, if ever a game was contrived to make one's sides ache, this was it.

A few sedate and sober people there were, who, with bent brow and pursed-up lip, watched the whole proceeding. They were the secret police of the card-table; it was in vain to attempt to conceal your luckless knave from their prying eyes; with the glance of a tax-collector they pounced upon the defaulter, and made him pay. Barely or never smiling themselves, they really felt all the eagerness, all the excitement of gambling; and I question if, after all, their hard looks and stern features were not the best fun of the whole.

After about two hours had been thus occupied, during which I had won the esteem and affection of several elderly ladies by the equanimity and high-mindedness with which I bore up against the loss of two whole baskets of counters, amounting to the sum of four-and-sixpence, I felt my shoulder gently touched, and at the same moment Bob Mahon whispered in my ear—'The Dillons are going, and he wants to speak a word with you; so give me your cards, and slip away.'

Resigning my place to the Major, whose advent was received with evident signs of dissatisfaction, inasmuch as he was a shrewd player, I hurried through the room to find out Dillon.

'Ah, here he is!' said Miss Bellew to her uncle, while she pointed to me. 'How provoking to go away so early—isn't it, Mr. Hinton?'

'You, doubtless, feel it so,' said I, with something of pique in my manner; 'your evening has been so agreeably passed.'

'And yours, too, if I am to judge from the laughter of your card-table. I am sure I never heard so noisy a party. Well, Mary, does he consent?'

'No; papa is still obstinate, and the carriage is ordered. He says we shall have so much gaiety this week that we must go home early to-night.'

'There! there! now be good girls; get on your muffling, and let us be off. Ah, Mr. Hinton!—the very man I wanted. Will you do us the very great favour of coming over for a few days to Mount Brown? We shall have the partridge-shooting after to-morrow, and I think I can show you some sport. May I send in for you in the morning? What hour will suit you? You will not refuse me, I trust?'

'I need not say, my dear sir, how obliged I feel for and with what pleasure I should accept your kind invitation; but the truth is, I've come away without leave of absence. The duke may return any day, and I shall be in a sad scrape.'

'Do you think a few days— —'

A look from Louisa Bellew, at this moment, came most powerfully in aid of her uncle's eloquence. I hesitated, and looked uncertain how to answer.

'There, girls! now is your time. He is half persuaded to do a kind thing; do try and convince him the whole way. Come, Mary! Fanny! Louisa!'

A second look from Miss Bellew decided the matter; and as a flush of pleasure coloured my cheek, I shook Dillon warmly by the hand, and promised to accept his invitation.

'That is like a really good fellow,' said the little man, with a face sparkling with pleasure. 'Now, what say you, if we drive over for you about two o'clock? The girls are coming in to make some purchases, and we shall all drive out together.'

This arrangement, so very palatable to me, was agreed upon, and I now took Miss Bellow's arm to lead her to the carriage. On descending to the hall a delay of a few minutes ensued, as the number of vehicles prevented the carriage coming up. The weather appeared to have changed; and it was now raining heavily, and blowing a perfect storm.

As the fitful gusts of wind howled along the dark corridors of the old building, dashing the rain upon our faces even where we stood, I drew my fair companion closer to my side, and held her cloak more firmly round her. What a moment was that! Her arm rested on mine; her very tresses were blown each moment across my cheek. I know not what I said, but I felt that in the tones of my voice they were the utterings of my heart that fell from my lips. I had not remembered that Mr. Dillon had already placed his daughters in the carriage, and was calling to us loudly to follow.

'No, no, I pray you not!' said Louisa, in reply to I know not what. 'Don't you hear my uncle?'

In her anxiety to press forward she had slightly disengaged her arm from mine as she spoke. At this instant a man rushed forward, and catching her hand, drew it rudely within his arm, calling out as he did so—

'Never fear, Louisa! you shall not be insulted while your cousin is here to protect you.'

She sprang round to reply: 'You are mistaken, Ulick! It is Mr. Hinton!' She could say no more, for he lifted her into the carriage, and, closing the door with a loud bang, desired the coachman to drive on.

Stupefied with amazement, I stood quite motionless. My first impulse was to strike him to the ground; for although a younger and a weaker man, I felt within me at the moment the strength to do it. My next thought was of Louisa's warning not to quarrel with her cousin. The struggle was indeed a severe one, but I gained the victory over my passion. Unable, however, to quit the spot, I stood with my arms folded, and my eyes riveted upon him. He returned my stare, and with a sneer of insufferable insolence passed me by and walked upstairs. Not a word was spoken on either side; but there are moments in one's life in which a look or passing glance rivets an undying hate. Such a one did we exchange and nothing that the tongue could speak could compass that secret instinct by which we ratified our enmity.

With slow, uncertain steps I mounted the stairs. Some strange fascination led me, as it were, to dog his steps; and although in my heart I prayed that no collision should ever come between us, yet I could not resist the headlong impulse to follow and to watch him. Like that unexplained temptation that leads the gazer over some lofty precipice to move on, step by step, yet nearer to the brink, conscious of his danger, yet unable to recede; so did I track this man from place to place, following him as he passed from one group to the other of his friends, till at length he seated himself at a table, around which a number of persons were engaged in noisy and boisterous conversation. He filled a tumbler to the brim with wine, and drinking it off at a draught, refilled again.

'You are thirsty, Ulick,' said some one.

'Thirsty! On fire, by G——! You'll not believe me when I tell you—I can't do it; no, by Heaven! there is nothing in the way of provocation——'

As he said thus much, some lady passing near induced him to drop his voice, and the remainder of the sentence was inaudible to me. Hitherto I had been standing beside his chair; I now moved round to the opposite side of the table, and, with my arms folded and my eyes firmly fixed, stood straight before him. For an instant or two he did not remark me, as he continued to speak with his head bent downwards. Suddenly lifting up his eyes, he started—pushed his chair slightly back from the table—

'And look! see!' cried he, as with outstretched finger he pointed toward me—'see! if he isn't there again!'

Then suddenly changing the tone of his voice to one of affected softness, he continued, addressing me—

'I have been explaining, sir, as well as my poor powers will permit, the excessive pains I have taken to persuade you to prove yourself a gentleman. One half the trouble you have put me to would have told an Irish gentleman what was looked for at his hands; you appear, however, to be the best-tempered fellows in the world at your side of the Channel. Come now, boys! if any man likes a bet, I'll wager ten guineas that even this won't ruffle his amiable nature. Pass the sherry here, Godfrey! Is that a clean glass beside you?'

So saying, he took the decanter, and, leisurely filling the glass, stood up as if to present it, but when he attained the erect position, he looked at me fixedly for a second, and then dashed the wine in my face. A roar of laughter burst around me, but I saw and heard no more. The moment before, and my head was cool, my senses clear, my faculties unclouded; but now, as if derangement had fallen upon me, I could see nothing but looks of mockery and scorn, and hear nothing save the discordant laugh and the jarring accent of derision.

CHAPTER XXVIII
THE INN FIRE

How I escaped from that room, and by what means I found myself in the street, I know not. My first impulse was to tear off my cravat, that I might breathe more freely; still a sense of suffocation oppressed me, and I felt stunned and stupefied.

'Come along, Hinton—rouse yourself, my boy! See, your coat is drenched with rain,' said a friendly voice behind me; while, grasping me forcibly by the arm, the Major led me forward.

'What have I done?' cried I, struggling to get free. 'Tell me—oh, tell me, have I done wrong? Have I committed any dreadful thing? There is an aching pain here—here in my forehead, as though——- I dare not speak my shame.'

'Nothing of the kind, my boy,' said Mahon: 'you've conducted yourself admirably. Matt Keane saw it all, and he says he never witnessed anything finer; and he's no bad judge, let me tell you. So, there now, be satisfied, and take off your wet clothes.'

There was something imperative in the tone in which he spoke; besides, the Major was one of those people who somehow or other always contrive to have their own way in the world; so that I yielded at once, feeling, too, that any opposition would only defer my chance of an explanation.

While I was thus occupied in my inner room, I could overhear my friend without engaged in the preparation of a little supper, mingling an occasional soliloquy with the simmering of the grilled bone that browned upon the fire—the clink of glasses and plates, and all the evidences of punch-making, breaking every now and then amid such reflections as these:—

'A mighty ugly business! nothing for it but meeting him. Poor lad, they'll say we murdered him among us! Och, he's far too young for Galway. Holloa, Hinton, are you ready? Now you look something reasonable; and when we've eaten a bit, well talk this matter over coolly and sensibly. And to make your mind easy, I may tell you at once, I have arranged a meeting for you with Burke at five to-morrow morning.'

I grasped his hand convulsively within mine, as a gleam of savage satisfaction shot through me.

'Yes, yes,' said he, as if replying to my look, 'it's all as it ought to be. Even his own friends are indignant at his conduct; and indeed I may say it's the first time a stranger has met with such in our country.'

'I can well believe it, Major,' said I; 'for, unless from the individual in question, I have met with nothing but kindness and good feeling amongst you. He indeed would seem an exception to his countrymen.'

'Therefore the sooner you shoot him the better. But I wish I could Father Tom.'

'*Adest, domine,*' cried the priest, at the same moment, as he entered the room, throwing his wet greatcoat into a corner and giving himself a shake a Newfoundland dog might have envied. 'Isn't this pretty work, Bob?' said he, turning to his cousin with a look of indignant reproach: 'he is not twenty-four hours in the town, and you've got him into a fight already! And sure it's my own fault that ever brought you together. *Nec fortunam nec gratiam habes*—no indeed, you have neither luck nor grace. *Mauvaise tête*, as the French say—-always in trouble. Arrah, don't be talking to me at all, at all! reach me over the spirits. Sorra better I ever saw you!—disturbing me out of my virtuous dreams at two in the morning. True enough, *dic mihi societatem tuam*; but little I thought he'd be getting you shot before you left the place.'

I endeavoured to pacify the good priest as well as I was able; the Major too made every explanation; but what between his being called out of bed, his anger at getting wet, and his cousin's well-known character for affairs of this nature, it was not before he had swallowed his second tumbler of punch that he would 'listen to rayson.'

'Well, well, if it is so, God's will be done,' said he with a sigh. '*Un bon coup d'épee,* as we used to say formerly, is beautiful treatment for bad blood; but maybe you're going to fight with pistols? Oh, murther, them's dreadful things!'

'I begin to suspect,' said the Major slyly, 'that Father Tom's afraid if you shoot Ulick he'll never get that fifty pounds he won. *Hinc illo lacrymo*—eh, Tom?'

'Ah, the spalpeen,' said the priest, with a deep groan, 'didn't he do me out of that money already?'

'How so, father?' said I, scarce able to repress my laughter at the expression of his face.

'I was coming down the main street yesterday evening with Doctor Plunkett, the bishop, beside me, discoursing a little theology, and looking as pious and respectable as may be, when that villain Burke came running out of a shop, and pulling out his pocket-book, cried—

'"Wait a bit, Father Tom, you know I'm a little in your debt about that race; and as you're a sporting character, it's only fair to book up at once."

'"What is this I hear, Father Loftus?" says the bishop.

'"Oh, my lord," say I, "he's a *jocosus puer*—a humbugging bla-guard; a *farceur*, your reverence, and that's the way he is always cutting his jokes upon the people."

'"And so he does not owe you this money?" said the bishop, looking mighty hard at us both.

'"Not a farthing of it, my lord."

'"That's comfortable, anyhow," says Burke, putting up his pocket-book; "and 'faith, my lord," said he with a wink, "I wish I had a loan of you for an hour or two every settling day, for troth you're a trump!" And with that he went off laughing, till ye'd have thought he'd split his sides—and I am sure I wish he had.'

I don't think Mr. Burke himself could have laughed louder or longer at his scheme than did we in hearing it, The priest at length joined in the mirth, and I could perceive, as the punch made more inroads upon him and the evening wore on, that his holy horror of duelling was gradually melting away before the warmth of his Hibernian propensities, like a wet sponge passed across the surface of a dark picture, bringing forth from the gloom many a figure and feature indistinct before, and displaying touches of light not hitherto appreciable, so whisky seems to exercise some strange power of displaying its votaries in all their breadth of character, divesting them of the adventitious clothes in which position or profession has invested them. Thus a tipsy Irishman stands forth in the exuberance of his nationality, *Hibernicis Hibernior*. Forgetting all his moral declamation on duelling, oblivious of his late indignation against his cousin, he rubbed his hands pleasantly, and related story after story of his own early experiences, some of them not a little amusing.

The Major, however, seemed not fully to enjoy the priest's anecdotical powers, but sipped his glass with a grave and sententious air. 'Very true, Tom,' said he at length, breaking silence; 'you have seen a fair share of these things for a man of your cloth. But where's the man living—show him to me, I say—that has had my experience, either as principal or second? Haven't I had my four men out in the same morning?'

'Why, I confess,' said I meekly, 'that does seem an extravagant allowance.'

'Clear waste, downright profusion, *du luxe, mon cher,* nothing else,' observed Father Tom.

Meanwhile, the Major rolled his eyes fearfully at me, and fidgeted in his chair with impatience to be asked for his story; and as I myself had some curiosity on the subject, I begged him to relate it.

'Tom, here, doesn't like a story at supper,' said the Major pompously; for, perceiving our attitude of attention, he resolved on being a little tyrannical before telling it.

The priest made immediate submission; and, slyly hinting that his objection only lay against stories he had been hearing for the last thirty years, said he could listen to the narration in question with much pleasure.

'You shall have it, then,' said the Major, as he squared himself in his chair, and thus began:—

'You have never been in Castle Connel, Hinton? Well, there is a wide bleak line of country there, that stretches away to the westward, with nothing but large round-backed mountains, low boggy swamps, with here and there a miserable mud hovel, surrounded by, maybe, half an acre of lumpers, or bad oats; a few small streams struggle through this on their way to the Shannon, but they are brown and dirty as the soil they traverse; and the very fish that swim in them are brown and smutty also.

'In the very heart of this wild country, I took it into my head to build a house. A strange notion it was, for there was no neighbourhood and no sporting; but, somehow, I had taken a dislike to mixed society some time before that, and I found it convenient to live somewhat in retirement; so that, if the partridges were not in abundance about me, neither were the process-servers; and the truth was, I kept a much sharper look-out for the sub-sheriff than I did for the snipe.

'Of course, as I was over head and ears in debt, my notion was to build something very considerable and imposing; and, to be sure, I had a fine portico, and a flight of steps leading up to it; and there were ten windows in front, and a grand balustrade at the top; and 'faith, taking it all in all, the building was so strong, the walls so thick, the windows so narrow, and the stones so black, that my cousin Darcy Mahon called it Newgate; and not a bad name either—and the devil another it ever went by. And even that same had its advantages; for when the creditors used to read that at the top of my letters, they'd say, "Poor devil! he has enough on his hands: there's no use troubling him any more." Well, big as Newgate looked from without, it had not much accommodation when you got inside. There was, 'tis true, a fine hall, all flagged; and, out of it, you entered what ought to have been the dinner-room, thirty-eight feet by seven-and-twenty, but which was used for herding sheep in winter. On the right hand, there was a cosy little breakfast-room, just about the size of this we are in. At the back of the hall, but concealed by a pair of folding-doors, there was a grand staircase of old Irish oak, that ought to have led up to a great suite of bedrooms, but it only conducted to one—a little crib I had for myself. The remainder were never plastered nor floored; and, indeed, in one of them, that was over the big drawing-room, the joists were never laid—which was all the better, for it was there we used to keep our hay and straw. Now, at the time I mention, the harvest was not brought in, and instead of its being full, as it used to be, it was mighty low; so that, when you opened the door above the stairs, instead of finding the hay up beside you, it was about fourteen feet down beneath you.

'I can't help boring you with all these details; first, because they are essential to my story; and next, because, being a young man, and a foreigner to boot, it may lead you to a little better understanding of some of our national customs. Of all the partialities we Irish have, after lush and the ladies, I believe our ruling passion is to build a big house, spend every shilling we have, or that we have not, as the case may be, in getting it half finished, and then live in a corner of it, "just for grandeur," as a body may say. It's a droll notion, after all; but show me the county in Ireland that hasn't at least six specimens of what I mention.

'Newgate was a beautiful one; and although the she lived in the parlour, and the cows were kept in the blue drawing-room, Darby Whaley slept in the boudoir, and two bull-dogs and a buck goat kept house in the library—'faith, upon the outside it looked very imposing; and not one that saw it, from the highroad to Ennis—and you could see it for twelve miles in every direction—didn't say, "That Mahon must be a snug fellow: look what a beautiful place he has of it there!" Little they knew that it was safer to go up the "Reeks" than my grand staircase, and it was like rope-dancing to pass from one room to the other.

'Well, it was about four o'clock in the afternoon of a dark lowering day in December that I was treading homewards in no very good-humour; for except a brace and a half of snipe, and a grey plover, I had met with nothing the whole day. The night was falling fast; so I began to hurry on as quickly as I could, when I heard a loud shout behind me, and a voice called out—

'"It's Bob Mahon, boys! By the Hill of Scariff, we are in luck!"

'I turned about, and what should I see but a parcel of fellows in red coats—they were the Blazers. There was Dan Lambert, Tom Burke, Harry Eyre, Joe M'Mahon, and the rest of them—fourteen souls in all. They had come down to draw a cover of Stephen Blake's about ten miles from me; but, in the strange mountain country, they lost the dogs, they lost their way and their temper; in truth, to all appearance, they lost everything but their appetites. Their horses were dead beat too, and they looked as miserable a crew as ever you set eyes on.

'"Isn't it lucky, Bob, that we found you at home?" said Lambert.

'"They told us you were away," says Burke.

'"Some said that you were grown so pious that you never went out except on Sundays," added old Harry, with a grin.

'"Begad," said I, "as to the luck, I won't say much for it; for here's all I can give you for your dinner"; and so I pulled out the four birds and shook them at them; "and as to the piety, troth, maybe you'd like to keep a fast with as devoted a son of the Church as myself."

'"But isn't that Newgate up there?" said one.

'"That same."

'"And you don't mean to say that such a house as that hasn't a good larder and a fine cellar?"

'"You're right," said I; "and they're both full at this very moment—the one with seed-potatoes, and the other with Whitehaven coals."

'"Have you got any bacon?" said M'Mahon.

'"Oh yes!" said I, "there's bacon."

'"And eggs?" said another.

'"For the matter of that, you might swim in batter."

'"Come, come," said Dan Lambert, "we're not so badly off after all."

'"Is there whisky?" cried Eyre.

'"Sixty-three gallons, that never paid the king sixpence!"

'As I said this, they gave three cheers you'd have heard a mile off.

'After about twenty minutes' walking, we got up to the house, and when poor Darby opened the door, I thought he'd faint; for, you see, the red coats made him think it was the army, coming to take me away; and he was for running off to raise the country, when I caught him by the neck.

'"It's the Blazers, ye old fool!" said I, "The gentlemen are come to dine here."

'"Hurroo!" said he, clapping his hands on his knees—"there must be great distress entirely, down about Nenagh, and them parts, or they'd never think of coming up here for a bit to eat."

'"Which way lie the stables, Bob?" said Burke.

'"Leave all that to Darby," said I; for ye see he had only to whistle and bring up as many people as he liked. And so he did too; and as there was room for a cavalry regiment, the horses were soon bedded down and comfortable; and in ten minutes' time we were all sitting pleasantly round a big fire, waiting for the rashers and eggs.

'"Now, if you'd like to wash your hands before dinner, Lambert, come along with me."

'"By all means," said he.

'The others were standing up too; but I observed that as the house was large, and the ways of it unknown to them, it was better to wait till I'd come back for them.

'"This was a real piece of good-luck, Bob," said Dan, as he followed me upstairs. "Capital quarters we've fallen into; and what a snug bedroom ye have here."

'"Yes," said I carelessly; "it's one of the small rooms. There are eight like this, and five large ones, plainly furnished, as you see; but for the present, you know——"

'"Oh, begad! I wish for nothing better. Let me sleep here—the other fellows may care for your four-posters with satin hangings."

'"Well," said I, "if you are really not joking, I may tell you that the room is one of the warmest in the house"—and this was telling no lie.

'"Here I 'll sleep," said he, rubbing his hands with satisfaction, and giving the bed a most affectionate look. "And now let us join the rest."

'When I brought Dan down, I took up Burke, and after him M'Mahon, and so on to the last; but every time I entered the parlour, I found them all bestowing immense praises on my house, and each fellow ready to bet he had got the best bedroom.

'Dinner soon made its appearance; for if the cookery was not very perfect, it was at least wonderfully expeditious. There were two men cutting rashers, two more frying them in the pan, and another did nothing but break the eggs, Darby running from the parlour to the kitchen and back again, as hard as he could trot.

'Do you know, now, that many a time since, when I have been giving venison, and Burgundy and claret enough to swim a lifeboat in, I often thought it was a cruel waste of money; for the fellows weren't half as pleasant as they were that evening on bacon and whisky!

'I've a theory on that subject, Hinton, I'll talk to you more about another time; I'll only observe now, that I'm sure we all overfeed our company. I've tried both plans; and my honest experience is, that as far as regards conviviality, fun, and good-fellowship, it is a great mistake to provide too well for your guests. There is something heroic in eating your mutton-chop, or your leg of a turkey, among jolly fellows; there is a kind of reflective flattering about it that tells you you have been invited for your drollery, and not for your digestion; and that your jokes and not your flattery have been your recommendation. Lord bless you! I 've laughed more over red-herrings and poteen than I ever expect to do again over turtle and toquay.

'My guests were, to do them justice, a good illustration of my theory. A pleasanter and a merrier party never sat down together. We had good songs, good stories, plenty of laughing, and plenty of drink; until at last poor Darby became so overpowered, by the fumes of the hot water I suppose, that he was obliged to be carried up to bed, and so we were compelled to boil the kettle in the parlour. This, I think, precipitated matters; for, by some mistake, they put punch into it instead of water, and the more you tried to weaken the liquor, it was only the more tipsy you were getting.

'About two o'clock, five of the party were under the table, three more were nodding backwards and forwards like insane pendulums, and the rest were mighty noisy, and now and then rather disposed to be quarrelsome.

'"Bob," said Lambert to me, in a whisper, "if it's the same thing to you, I'll slip away and get into bed."

'"Of course, if you won't take anything more. Just make yourself at home; and as you don't know the way here, follow me."

'"I 'm afraid," said he, "I 'd not find my way alone."

'"I think," said I, "it's very likely. But come along!"

'I walked upstairs before him; but instead of turning to the left, I went the other way, till I came to the door of the large room that I have told you already was over the big drawing-room. Just as I put my hand on the lock, I contrived to blow out the candle, as if it was the wind.

'"What a draught there is here," said I; "but just step in, and I'll go for a light."

'He did as he was bid; but instead of finding himself on my beautiful little carpet, down he went fourteen feet into the hay at the bottom. I looked down after him for a minute or two, and then called out—

"'As I am doing the honours of Newgate, the least I could do was to show you the drop. Good-night, Dan! but let me advise you to get a little farther from the door, as there are more coming."

'Well, sir, when they missed Dan and me out of the room, two or three more stood up, and declared for bed also. The first I took up was Ffrench, of Green Park; for indeed he wasn't a cute fellow at the best of times; and if it wasn't that the hay was so low, he'd never have guessed it was not a feather-bed till he woke in the morning. Well, down he went. Then came Eyre; then Joe M'Mahon—two-and-twenty stone—no less! Lord pity them!—this was a great shock entirely! But when I opened the door for Tom Burke, upon my conscience you'd think it was Pandemonium they had down there. They were fighting like devils, and roaring with all their might.

'"Good-night, Tom," said I, pushing Burke forward. "It's the cows you hear underneath."

'"Cows!" said he. "If they're cows, begad they must have got at that sixty-three gallons of poteen you talked of; for they're all drunk."

'With that, he snatched the candle out of my hand and looked down into the pit. Never was such a sight seen before or since. Dan was pitching into poor Ffrench, who, thinking he had an enemy before him, was hitting out manfully at an old turf-creel, that rocked and creaked at every blow, as he called out—

'"I'll smash you! I'll ding your ribs for you, you' infernal scoundrel!"

'Eyre was struggling in the hay, thinking he was swimming for his life; and poor Joe M'Mahon was patting him on the head, and saying, "Poor fellow! good dog!" for he thought it was Towzer, the bull-terrier, that was prowling round the calves of his legs.

'"If they don't get tired, there will not be a man of them alive by morning!" said Tom, as he closed the door. "And now, if you'll allow me to sleep on the carpet, I'll take it as a favour."

'By this time they were all quiet in the parlour; so I lent Tom a couple of blankets and a bolster, and having locked my door, went to bed with an easy mind and a quiet conscience. To be sure, now and then a cry would burst forth, as if they were killing somebody below-stairs, but I soon fell asleep and heard no more of them.

'By daybreak next morning they made their escape; and when I was trying to awake at half-past ten, I found Colonel M'Morris, of the Mayo, with a message from the whole four.

'"A bad business this, Captain Mahon," said he; "my friends have been shockingly treated."

'"It's mighty hard," said I, "to want to shoot me because I hadn't fourteen feather-beds in the house."

'"They will be the laugh of the whole country, sir."

'"Troth!" said I, "if the country is not in very low spirits, I think they will."

'"There's not a man of them can see!—their eyes are actually closed up!"

'"The Lord be praised!" said I. "It's not likely they'll hit me."

'But to make a short story of it—out we went. Tom Burke was my friend. I could scarce hold my pistol with laughing; for such faces no man ever looked at. But for self-preservation's sake, I thought it best to hit one of them; so I just pinked Ffrench a little under the skirt of the coat. '"Come, Lambert!" said the Colonel, "it's your turn now."

'"Wasn't that Lambert," said I, "that I hit?"

'"No," said he, "that was Ffrench."

'"Begad, I'm sorry for it. Ffrench, my dear fellow, excuse me; for you see you're all so like each other about the eyes this morning——"

'With this there was a roar of laughing from them all, in which, I assure you, Lambert took not a very prominent part; for somehow he didn't fancy my polite inquiries after him. And so we all shook hands, and left the ground as good friends as ever—though to this hour the name of Newgate brings less pleasant recollections to their minds than if their fathers had been hanged at its prototype.'

CHAPTER XXIX
THE DUEL

When morning broke, I started up and opened the window. It was one of those bright and beauteous daybreaks which would seem to be the compensation a northern climate possesses for its want of the azure sky of noon and the silvery moonlight of night, the gifts of happier climes. The pink hue of the sky was gradually replacing the paler tints, like a deep blush mantling the cheek of beauty; the lark was singing high in heaven, and the deep note of the blackbird came mellowed from the leafy grove; the cattle were still at rest, and seemed half unwilling to break the tranquil stillness of the scene, as they lay breathing the balmy odours from the wild flowers that grew around them. Such was the picture that lay on one side of me. On the other was the long street of a little town, on which yet the shadows of night were sleeping; the windows were closed; not a smoke-wreath rose from any chimney, but all was still and peaceful.

In my little parlour I found the good priest and the Major fast asleep in their chairs, pretty much in the same attitudes I had left them in some hours before. The fire had died away; the square decanter of whisky was emptied to its last drop, and the kettle lay pensively on one side, like some shipwrecked craft high and dry upon the shore. I looked at my watch; it was but four o'clock. Our meeting was appointed for half-past five; so I crept noiselessly back to my room, not sorry to have half an hour to myself of undisturbed reflection. When I had finished my dressing, I threw up the sash and sprang out into the garden. It was a wild, uncultivated spot; but still there was something of beauty in those old trees whose rich blossoms scented the air, while the rank weeds of many a gay and gaudy hue shot up luxuriantly about their trunks, the pink marsh-mallow and the taper foxglove mingling their colours with the sprayey meadowsweet and the wild sweet-brier. There was an air of solitude in the neglect around me that seemed to suit the habit of my soul; and I strolled along from one walk to another, lost in my own thoughts.

There were many things at a moment like that I would fain have written, fain have said; but so it is, in the wealth of our emotions we can give nothing, and I could not bring myself to write to my friends even to say farewell Although I felt that in every stage of this proceeding I had nothing to reproach myself with, this duel being thrust on me by one who had singled me out for his hatred, yet I saw as its result nothing but the wreck of all my hopes. Already had *she* intimated how strong was her father's attachment to his nephew, and with an expressive fear cautioned me against any collision with him. How vain are all our efforts, how fruitless are all our endeavours, to struggle against the current of our fate. We may stem for a short time the full tide of fortune, we may breast with courage high and spirit fierce the rough billows as they break upon us, but we are certain to succumb in the end. With some men failure is a question of fear; some want the persevering courage to drag on amid trials and difficulties; and some are deficient in the temper which, subduing our actions to a law, governs and presides over every moment of our lives, rendering us, even in our periods of excitement and irritation, amenable to the guidance of our reason. This was my case; and I felt that notwithstanding all my wishes to avoid a quarrel with Burke, yet in my heart a lurking spirit urged me to seek him out and offer him defiance.

While these thoughts were passing through my mind, I suddenly heard a voice which somehow seemed half familiar to my ear. I listened; it came from a room of which the window was partly open. I now remembered that poor Joe lay in that part of the house, and the next moment I knew it to be his. Placing a ladder against the wall, I crept quietly up till I could peep into the room. The poor fellow was alone, sitting up in his bed, with his hunting-cap on, an old whip in his hand, which he flourished from time to time with no small energy; his cheek was flushed, and his eye, prominent and flashing, denoted the access of high fever. It was evident that his faculties, clouded as they were even in their happiest moments, were now under the wilder influence of delirium. He was speaking rapidly to himself in a quick undertone, calling the dogs by name, caressing this one, scolding that; and then, bursting forth into a loud tally-ho, his face glowed with an ecstatic pleasure, and he broke forth into a rude chant, the words of which I have never forgotten, for as he sang them in a voice of wild and touching sweetness, they seemed the very outpourings of his poor simple heart:—

> 'I never yet owned a horse or hound,
> I never was lord of a foot of ground;
> Yet few are richer, I will be bound,
> Than me of a hunting morning.

> 'I 'm far better off nor him that pays,
> For though I 've no money, I live at my aise,
> With hunting and shooting whenever I plase,
> And a tally-high-ho in the morning.
>
> 'As I go on foot, I don't lose my sate,
> As I take the gaps, I don't break a gate;
> And if I'm not first, why I'm seldom late,
> With my tally-high-ho in the morning.
>
> 'And there's not a man, be he high or low,
> In the parts down here, or wherever you go,
> That doesn't like poor Tipperary Joe,
> With his tally-high-ho in the morning.'

A loud view-holloa followed this wild chant; and then the poor fellow, as if exhausted by his efforts, sank back in the bed muttering to himself in a low broken voice, but with a look so happy, and a smile so tranquil, he seemed more a thing to envy than one to commiserate and pity.

'I say, Hinton!' shouted the Major from the window of my bedroom, 'what the deuce are you doing up that ladder there? Not serenading Mrs. Doolan, I hope. Are you aware it is five o'clock?'

I descended with all haste, and joining my friend, took his arm, and set out towards the rendezvous.

'I didn't order the horses,' said Mahon, 'for the rumour of such a thing as this always gets abroad through one's servants.'

'Ah, yes,' said I; 'and then you have the police.'

'The police!' repeated he, laughing—'not a bit of it, my boy; don't forget you're in glorious old Ireland, where no one ever thinks of spoiling a fair fight. It is possible the magistrate might issue his warrant if you would not come up to time, but for anything else——'

'Well,' said I, 'that certainly does afford me another glimpse of your habits. How far have we to go, Major?'

'You remember the grass-field below the sunk fence, to the left of the mill?'

'Where the stream runs?'

'Exactly; that's the spot. It was old Pigott chose it, and no man is a better judge of these things. By-the-bye, it is very lucky that Burke should have pitched upon a gentleman for his friend—I mean a real gentleman, for there are plenty of his acquaintances who under that name would rob the mail.'

Thus chatting as we went, Mahon informed me that Pigott was an old half-pay Colonel, whose principal occupation for thirteen years had been what the French would call 'to assist' at affairs of honour. Even the Major himself looked up to him as a last appeal in a disputed or a difficult point; and many a reserved case was kept for his opinion, with the same ceremonious observance as a knotty point of law for the consideration of the twelve judges. Crossing the little rivulet near the mill, we held on by a small bypath which brought us over the starting-ground of the steeplechase, by the scene of part of my preceding day's exploits. While I was examining with some curiosity the ground cut up and trod by the horses' feet, and looking at the spot where we had taken the fence, the sharp sound of two pistol-shots quickly aroused me, and I eagerly asked what it was.

'Snapping the pistols,' said Mahon. 'Ah, by-the-bye, all this kind of thing is new to you. Never mind; put a careless, half-indifferent kind of face on the matter. Do you take snuff? It doesn't signify; put your hands in your pockets, and hum "Tatter Jack Walsh!"'

As I supposed there was no specific charm in the melody he alluded to, nor if there had been, had I any time to acquire it, I consoled myself by observing the first part of his direction, and strolled after him into the field with a nonchalance only perhaps a little too perfect.

Mr. Burke and his friends, to the number of about a dozen persons, were already assembled; and were one to judge from their loud talking and hearty laughter as we came forward, it would seem difficult to believe the occasion that brought them there was that of mortal combat. So, at least, I thought. Not so, however, the Major; for with a hop, step, and a jump, performed by about the shortest pair of legs in the barony, he sprang into the midst of the party, with some droll observation on the benefits of early rising which once more called forth their merriment. Seating myself on a large moss-covered stone, I waited patiently for the preliminaries to be settled. As I threw my eye among the group, I perceived that Burke was not there; but on turning my head, I remarked two men walking arm-in-arm on the opposite side of the hedge. As they paced to and fro, I could see, by the violence of his gesticulations and the energy of his manner, that one was Burke. It seemed as though his companion was endeavouring to reason with and dissuade him from some course of proceeding he appeared bent on following; but there was a savage earnestness in his manner that would not admit of persuasion; and at last, as if wearied and vexed by his friend's importunities, he broke rudely from him, and springing over the fence, called out—

'Pigott, are you aware it is past six?' Then pulling out his watch, he added, 'I must be at Ballinasloe by eleven o'clock.'

'If you speak another word, sir,' said the old Colonel, with an air of offended dignity, 'I leave the ground. Major Mahon, a word, if you please.'

They walked apart from the rest for a few seconds; and then the Colonel, throwing his glove upon the grass, proceeded to step off the ground with a military precision and formality that I am sure at any other time would have highly amused me.

After a slight demur from the Major, to which I could perceive the Colonel readily yielded, a walking-stick was stuck at either end of the measured distance; while the two seconds, placing themselves beside them, looked at each other with very great satisfaction, and mutually agreed it was a sweet spot.

'Would you like to look at these?' said Pigott, taking up the pistols from where they lay on the grass.

'Ah, I know them well,' replied the Major, laughing; 'these were poor Tom Casey's, and a better fellow, and a handier with his iron, never snapped a trigger. These are ours, Colonel'; presenting, as he spoke, two splendid-looking Mortimers, in all the brilliancy of their maiden freshness. A look of contempt from the Colonel, and a most expressive shrug of his shoulders, was his reply.

'Begad, I think so,' said Mahon, as if appreciating the gesture; 'I had rather have that old tool with the cracked stock—not but this is a very sweet instrument, and elegantly balanced in the hand.'

'We are ready now,' said Pigott; 'bring up your man, Major.'

As I started up to obey the summons, a slight bustle near attracted me. Two or three of Burke's friends were endeavouring as it were to pacify and subdue him; but his passion knew no bounds, and as he broke from them, he said in a voice perfectly audible where I stood—

'Won't I, by G——! then I'll tell you, if I don't shoot him——.'

'Sir,' said the Colonel, turning on him a look of passionate indignation, 'if it were not that you were here to answer the appeal of wounded honour, I'd leave you to your fate this moment; as it is, another such expression as that you've used, and I abandon you on the spot.'

Doggedly and without speaking, Burke drew his hat far down upon his eyes, and took the place marked out for him.

'Mr. Hinton,' said the Colonel, as he touched his hat with most courteous politeness, 'will you have the goodness to stand there?'

Mahon, meanwhile, handed each man his pistol, and whispering in my ear, 'Aim low,' retired.

'The word, gentlemen,' said the Colonel, 'will be, "One, two, three." Mr. Hinton, pray observe, I beg of you, you 'll not reserve your fire after I say "three."' With his eyes fixed upon us he walked back about ten paces. 'Are you ready? Are you both ready?'

'Yes, yes,' said Burke impatiently.

'Yes,' said I.

'One, two, three.'

I lifted my pistol at the second word, and as the last dropped from the Colonel's lips one loud report rang through the air, and both pistols went off together. A quick sharp pang shot through my cheek as though it had been seared by a hot instrument. I put up my hand, but the ball had only touched the flesh, and a few drops of blood were all the damage. Not so Burke; my ball had entered above the hip, and already his trousers were stained with blood, and notwithstanding his endeavours he could not stand up straight.

'Is he hit, Pigott?' cried he, in a voice harsh from agony. 'Is he hit, I say?'

'Only grazed,' said I tranquilly, as I wiped the stain from my face.

'Another pistol, quick! Do you hear me, Pigott?'

'We are not the arbiters in this case,' replied the Colonel coolly. 'Major Mahon, is your friend satisfied?'

'Perfectly satisfied on our own account,' said the Major; 'but if the gentleman desires another shot——'

'I do, I do!' screamed Burke, as, writhing with pain, he pressed both hands to his side, from which the blood, now gushing in torrents, formed a pool about his feet. 'Be quick there, Pigott! I am getting faint.' He staggered forward as he spoke, his face pale and his lips parted; then suddenly clutching his pistol by the barrel, he fixed his eyes steadily on me, while with a curse he hurled the weapon at my head, and fell senseless to the earth. His aim was true; for straight between the eyes the weapon struck me, and felled me to the ground. Although stunned for the moment, I could hear the cry of horror and indignant shame that broke from the bystanders; but the next instant a dreamy confusion came over me, and I became unconscious of what was passing around.

CHAPTER XXX
A COUNTRY DOCTOR

Should my reader feel any interest concerning that portion of my history which immediately followed the events of my last chapter, I believe I must refer him to Mrs. Doolan, the amiable hostess of the Bonaveen Arms. She could probably satisfy any curious inquiry as to the confusion produced in her establishment by the lively sallies of Tipperary Joe in one quarter, and the more riotous madness of myself in another. The fact is, good reader, my head was an English one; and although its contents were gradually acclimating themselves to the habits of the country, the external shell had not assumed that proper thickness and due power of resistance which Irish heads would appear to be gifted with. In plain words, the injury had brought on delirium.

It was somewhere in the third week after this unlucky morning that I found myself lying in my bed with a wet cloth upon my temples, while over my whole frame was spread that depressing sense of great debility more difficult to bear than acute bodily suffering. Although unable to speak, I could distinctly hear the conversation about me, and recognise the voices of both Father Tom and the Major as they conversed with a third party, whom I afterwards learned was the Galen of Loughrea.

Dr. Mopin, surgeon of the Roscommon militia, had been for forty years the terror of the sick of the surrounding country; for, independent of a naturally harsh and disagreeable manner, he had a certain slangy and sneering way of addressing his patients that was perfectly shocking. Amusing himself the while at their expense, by suggesting the various unhappy and miserable consequences that might follow on their illness, he appeared to take a diabolical pleasure in the terror he was capable of eliciting. There was something almost amusing in the infernal ingenuity he had acquired in this species of torture. There was no stage of your illness, no phase of your constitution, no character or condition of your malady, that was not the immediate forerunner of one or more afflicting calamities. Were you getting weaker, it was the way they always died out; did you gain strength, it was a rally before death; were you despondent, it was the best for you to know your state; were you sanguine, he would rebuke your good spirits and suggest the propriety of a priest. However, with all these qualifications people put up with him; and as he had a certain kind of rude skill, and never stuck at a bold method, he obtained the best practice of the country and a widespread reputation.

'Well,' said Father Tom, in a low voice—'well, Doctor, what do you think of him this evening?'

'What do I think of him? Just what I thought before—congestion of the membranes. This is the low stage he is in now; I wouldn't be surprised if he'd get a little better in a few days, and then go off like the rest of them.'

'Go off! eh? Now you don't mean——'

'Don't I? Maybe not. The ould story—coma, convulsions, and death.'

'Damn the fellow!' said the Major, in a muttered voice, 'I feel as if I was in a well. But I say, Doctor, what are we to do?'

'Anything you plase. They say his family is mighty respectable, and have plenty of money. I hope so; for here am I coming three times a day, and maybe when he dies it will be a mourning ring they'll be sending me instead of my fee. He was a dissipated chap I am sure: look at the circles under his eyes!'

'Ay, ay,' said the priest, 'but they only came since his illness.'

'So much the worse,' added the invincible Doctor; 'that's always a symptom that the base of the brain is attacked.'

'And what happens then?' said the Major.

'Oh, he might recover. I knew a man once get over it, and he is alive now, and in Swift's Hospital.'

'Mad?' said the priest.

'Mad as a March hare,' grinned the Doctor; 'he thinks himself the post-office clock, and chimes all the hours and half-hours day and night.'

'The heavens be about us!' said Father Tom, crossing himself piously. 'I had rather be dead than that.'

'When did you see Burke?' inquired the Major, wishing to change the conversation.

'About an hour ago; he is going fast.'

'Why, I thought he was better,' said Father Tom; 'they told me he ate a bit of chicken, and took a little wine and water.'

'Ay, so he did; I bid them give him whatever he liked, as his time was so short. So, after all, maybe it is as well for this young chap here not to get over it.'

'How so?' said the Major. 'What do you mean by that?'

'Just that it is as good to die of a brain fever as be hanged; and it won't shock the family.'

'I'd break his neck,' muttered Bob Mahon, 'if there was another doctor within forty miles.'

Of all his patients, Tipperary Joe was the only one of whom the Doctor spoke without disparagement. Whether that the poor fellow's indifference to his powers of terrorising had awed or conciliated him, I know not; but he expressed himself favourably regarding his case, and his prospects of recovery.

'Them chaps always recover,' drawled out the Doctor in a dolorous cadence.

'Is it true,' said the Major, with a malicious grin—'is it true that he changed all the splints and bandages to the sound leg, and that you didn't discover the mistake for a week afterwards? Mary Doolan told me.'

'Mrs. Doolan,' said the Doctor, 'ought to be thinking of her own misfortunes; and with an acute inflammation of the pericardium, she might be making her sowl.'

'She ill?—that fine, fat, comfortable-looking woman!'

'Ay, just so; they're always fat, and have a sleepy look about the eyes, just like yourself. Do you ever bleed at the nose?'

'Never without a blow on it. Come, come, I know you well, Doctor; you shall not terrify me.'

'You're right not to fret; for it will take you off suddenly, with a giddiness in your head, and a rolling in your eyes, and a choking feeling about your throat——'

'Stop, and be d——d to you!' said the Major, as he cleared his voice a couple of times, and loosed the tie of his cravat. 'This room is oppressively hot.'

'I protest to God,' said Father Tom, 'my heart is in my mouth, and there isn't a bone in my body that's not aching.'

'I don't wonder,' chimed in the Doctor; 'you are another of them, and you are a surprising man to go on so long. Sure, it is two years ago I warned your niece that when she saw you fall down she must open a vein in your neck, if it was only with a carving-knife.'

'The saints in heaven forbid!' said the priest, cutting the sign of the cross in the air; 'it's maybe the jugular she'd cut!'

'No,' drawled out the Doctor, 'she needn't go so deep; and if her hand doesn't shake, there won't be much danger. Good-evening to you both.'

So saying, with his knees bent, and his hands crossed under the skirts of his coat, he sneaked out of the room; while the others, overcome, with fear, shame, and dismay, sat silently, looking misery itself, at each side of the table.

'That fellow would kill a regiment,' said the Major at length. 'Come, Tom, let's have a little punch; I've a kind of a trembling over me.'

'Not a drop of anything stronger than water will cross my lips this blessed night. Do you know, Bob, I think this place doesn't agree with me? I wish I was back in Murranakilty: the mountain air, and regular habits of life, that's the thing for me.'

'We are none of us abstemious enough,' said the Major; 'and then we bachelors—to be sure you have your niece.'

'Whisht!' said the priest, 'how do you know who is listening? I vow to God I am quite alarmed at his telling that to Mary; some night or other, if I take a little too much, she'll maybe try her anatomy upon me!'

This unhappy reflection seemed to weigh upon the good priest's mind, and set him a-mumbling certain Latin offices between his teeth for a quarter of an hour.

'I wish,' said the Major, 'Hinton was able to read his letters, for here is a whole bundle of them—some from England, some from the Castle, and some marked "On His Majesty's service."'

'I'll wait another week anyhow for him,' said the priest. 'To go back to Dublin in the state he is now would be the ruin of him, after the shake he has got. The dissipation, the dining-out, and all the devilment would destroy him entirely; but a few weeks' peace and quietness up at Murranakilty will make him as sound as a bell.'

'You are right, Tom, you are right,' said the Major; 'the poor fellow mustn't be lost for the want of a little care; and now that Dillon has gone, there is no one here to look after him. Let us go down and see if the post is in; I think a walk would do us good.'

Assenting to this proposition, the priest bent over me mournfully for a moment, shook his head, and having muttered a blessing, walked out of the room with the Major, leaving me in silence to think over all I had overheard.

Whether it was that youth suggested the hope, or that I more quickly imbibed an appreciation of the Doctor's character from being the looker-on at the game, I am not exactly sure; but certainly I felt little depressed by his gloomy forebodings respecting me, and greatly lightened at my heart by the good news of poor Tipperary Joe.

Of all the circumstances which attended my illness, the one that most impressed me was the warm, affectionate solicitude of my two friends, the priest and his cousin. There was something of kindness and good feeling in their care of me that spoke rather of a long friendship than of the weaker ties of chance and passing acquaintance. Again I thought of home; and while I asked myself if the events which beset my path in Ireland could possibly have happened to me there, I could not but acknowledge that if they had so, I could scarcely have hoped to suddenly conjure up such faithful and benevolent friends, with no other claim, nor other recommendation, save that of being a stranger.

The casual observation concerning my letters had, by stimulating my curiosity, awakened my dormant energy; and by a great effort I stretched out my hand to the little bell beside my bed, and rang it. The summons was answered by the barelegged girl who acted as waiter in the inn. When she had sufficiently recovered from her astonishment to comprehend my request, I persuaded her to place a candle beside me; and having given me the packet of letters that lay on the chimney-piece, I desired her on no account to admit any one, but say that I had fallen into a sound sleep, and should not be disturbed.

CHAPTER XXXI
THE LETTER-BAG

The package of letters was a large one, of all sizes. From all quarters they came—some from home; some from my brother officers of the Guards; some from the Castle; and even one from O'Grady.

The first I opened was a short note from Horton, the private secretary to the viceroy. This informed me that Major Mahon had written a statement to the duke of all the circumstances attending my duel; and that his grace had not only expressed himself highly satisfied with my conduct, but had ordered a very polite reply to be addressed to the Major, thanking him for his great kindness, and saying with what pleasure he found that a member of his staff had fallen into such good hands.

'His grace desires me to add,' continued the writer, 'that you need only consult your own health and convenience with respect to your return to duty; and, in fact, your leave of absence is perfectly discretionary.'

My mind relieved of a weighty load by the contents of this letter, I recovered my strength already so far that I sat up in bed to peruse the others. My next was from my father; it ran thus:—

'Dear Jack,—Your friend Major Mahon, to whom I write by this post, will deliver this letter to you when he deems fit. He has been most good-natured in conveying to me a narrative of your late doings; and I cannot express how grateful we all are to him for the truly friendly part he has taken towards you. After the strictest scrutiny, for I confess to you I feared lest the Major's might be too partial an account, I rejoice to say that your conduct meets with my entire approbation. An older and a wiser head might, it is possible, have avoided some of the difficulties you have met with; but this I will add, that once in trouble, no one could have shown better temper or a more befitting spirit than you did. While I say this, my dear Jack, understand me clearly that I speak of you as a young, inexperienced man, thrown, at his very outset of life, not only among strangers, but in a country where, as I remarked to you at first, everything was different from those in your own. You have now shown yourself equal to any circumstances in which you may be placed. I therefore not only expect that you will meet with fewer embarrassments in future, but that, should they arise, I shall have the satisfaction of finding your character and your habits will be as much your safeguard against insult as your readiness to resent any will be sure and certain.

'I have seen the duke several times, and he expresses himself as much pleased with you. From what he mentions, I can collect that you are well satisfied with Ireland, and therefore I do not wish to remove you from it. At the same time, bear in mind, that by active service alone can you ever attain to, or merit, rank in the army; and that hitherto you have only been a soldier by name.'

After some further words of advice respecting the future, and some few details of family matters, he concluded by entrusting to my mother the mention of what she herself professed to think lay more in her peculiar province.

As usual, her letter opened with some meteorological observations upon the climate of England for the preceding six weeks; then followed a journal of her own health, whose increasing delicacy, and the imperative necessity of being near Doctor Y———, rendered a journey to Ireland too dangerous to think of.

'Yes, my dearest boy,' wrote she, 'nothing but this would keep me from you a moment; however, I am much relieved at learning that you are now rapidly recovering, and hope soon to hear of your return to Dublin. It is a very dreadful thing to think of, but perhaps, upon the whole, it is better that you did kill this Mr. Burke. De Grammont tells me that a *mauvaise tête* like that must be shot sooner or later. It makes me nervous to dwell on this odious topic, so that I shall pass on to something else.

'The horrid little man that brought your letters, and who calls himself a servant of Captain O'Grady, insisted on seeing me yesterday. I never was more shocked in my life. From what he says, I gather that he may be looked on as rather a favourable specimen of the natives. They must indeed be a very frightful people; and although he assured me he would do me no injury, I made Thomas stay in the room the entire time, and told Chubbs to give the alarm to the police if he heard the slightest noise. The creature, however did nothing, and I have quite recovered from my fear already.

'What a picture, my dear boy, did he present to me of your conduct and habits! Your intimacy with that odious family I mentioned in my last seems the root of all your misfortunes. Why will such people thrust themselves forward? What do they mean by inviting you to their frightful parties? Have they not their own peculiar horrors?—not but I must confess that they are more excusable than you; and I cannot conceive how you could so soon have forgotten the lessons instilled into you from your earliest years. As your poor dear grandfather, the admiral, used to say, a vulgar acquaintance is a shifting sand; you can never tell where you won't meet it—always at the most inopportune moment; and then, if you remark, your underbred people are never content with a quiet recognition, but they must always indulge in a detestable cordiality there is no escaping from. Oh, John, John! when at ten years of age you made the banker's son at Northampton hold your stirrup as you mounted your pony, I never thought I should have this reproach to make you.

'The little fiend who calls himself Corny something, also mentions your continued familiarity with the young woman I spoke of before. What her intentions are is perfectly clear; and should she accomplish her object your position in society and future fortune might possibly procure her large damages; but pause, my dear boy, before you go any further. I do not speak of the moral features of the case, for you are of an age to judge of them yourself; but think, I beseech you, of the difficulties it will throw around your path in life, and the obstacles it will oppose to your success. There is poor Lord Henry Effingham; and since that foolish business with the clergyman's wife or daughter, where somebody went mad, and some one else drowned or shot himself, they have never given him any appointment whatever. The world is a frightful and unforgiving thing, as poor Lord Henry knows; therefore beware!

'The more I think of it, the more strongly do I feel the force of my first impressions respecting Ireland; and were it not that we so constantly hear of battles and bloodshed in the Peninsula, I should even prefer your being there. There would seem to be an unhappy destiny over everything belonging to me. My poor dear father, the admiral, had a life of hardship, almost unrewarded. For eleven years he commanded a guardship in the Nore; many a night have I seen him, when I was a little girl, come home dripping with wet, and perfectly insensible from the stimulants he was obliged to resort to, and be carried in that state to his bed; and after all this he didn't get his blue ribbon till he was near sixty.

'De Vere is constantly with us, and is, I remark, attentive to your cousin Julia. This is not of so much consequence, as I hear that her Chancery suit is taking an unhappy turn; should it be otherwise, your interests will, of course, be looked to. De Vere is most amusing, and has a great deal of wit; but for him and the Count we should be quite dreary, as the season is over, and we can't leave town for at least three weeks. [The epistle concluded with a general summing up of its contents, and an affectionate entreaty to bear in mind her caution regarding the Rooneys.] Once more, my dear boy, remember that vulgar people are a part of our trials in this life. As that delightful man, the Dean of St. George's, says, they are snares for our feet; and their subservient admiration of us is a dangerous and a subtle temptation. Read this letter again, and believe me, my dearest John, your affectionate and unhappy mother,

'Charlotte Hinton.'

I shall not perform so undutiful a task as to play the critic on my excellent mother's letter. There were, it is true, many new views of life presented to me by its perusal, and I should feel sadly puzzled were I to say at which I was more amused or shocked — at the strictness of her manners, or the laxity of her morals; but I confess that the part which most outraged me of all was the eulogy on Lord Dudley de Vere's conversational gifts. But a few short months before, and it is possible I should not only have credited but concurred in the opinion; brief, however, as had been the interval, it had shown me much of life; it had brought me into acquaintance, and even intimacy, with some of the brightest spirits of the day; it had taught me to discriminate between the unmeaning jargon of conventional gossip and the charm of a society where force of reasoning, warmth of eloquence, and brilliancy of wit contested for the palm; it had made me feel that the intellectual gifts reserved in other countries for the personal advancement of their owner by their public and ostentatious display, can be made the ornament and the delight of the convivial board, the elegant accompaniment to the hours of happy intercourse, and the strongest bond of social union. So gradually had this change of opinion crept over me that I did not recognise in myself the conversion; and indeed had it not been for my mother's observations on Lord Dudley, I could not have credited how far my convictions had gone round. I could now understand the measurement by which Irishmen were estimated in the London world. I could see that if such a character as De Vere had a reputation for ability, how totally impossible it was for those who appreciated him to prize the great and varied gifts of such men as Grattan and Curran, and many more.

Lost in such thoughts, I forgot for some moments that O'Grady's letter lay open before me. It was dated Chatham, and written the night before he sailed. The first few lines showed me that he knew nothing of my duel, having only received my own letter with an account of the steeplechase. He wrote in high spirits. The Commander-in-chief had been most kind to him, appointing him to a vacant Majority—not, as he anticipated, in the Forty-first, but in the Ninth light Dragoons.

'I am anxiously looking out for Corny,' said he, 'and a great letter-bag from Ireland—the only bit of news from which, except your own, is that the Rooneys have gone into deep mourning, themselves and their whole house. Various rumours are afloat as to whether any money speculations of Paul's may have suggested the propriety of retrenchment, or whether there may not have been a death in the royal family of OToole. Look to this for me, Hinton; for even in Canada I shall preserve the memory of that capital house, its excellent *cuisine*, its charming hostess. Cultivate them, my dear Jack, for your sake and for mine. One Rembrandt is as good as a gallery; so sit down before them, and make a study of the family.'

The letter concluded as it began, by hearty thanks for the service I had rendered him, begging me to accept of Moddiridderoo as a souvenir of his friendship. And in a postscript, to write which the letter had evidently been reopened, was a warning to me against any chance collision with Ulick Burke.

'Not, my dear boy, because he is a dead shot—although that same is something—but that a quarrel with him could scarcely be reputable in its commencement, and must be bad whatever the result.'

After some further cautioning on this matter, the justice of which was tolerably evident from my own experience, O'Grady concluded with a hurried postscript:—

'Corny has not yet arrived, and we have received our orders for embarkation within twenty-four hours. I begin half to despair of his being here in time. Should this be the case, will you, my dear Hinton, look after the old villain for me, at least until I write to you again on the subject?'

While I was yet pondering on these last few lines, I perceived that a card had fallen from my father's letter. I took it up, and what was my astonishment to find that it contained a correct likeness of Corny Delany, drawn with a pen, underneath which was written, in my cousin Julia's hand, the following few lines:—

'The dear old thing has waited three days, and I think I have at length caught something like him. Dear Jack, if the master be only equal to the man, we shall never forgive you for not letting us see him.—Yours, Julia.'

This, of course, explained the secret of Corny's delay—my cousin, with her habitual wilfulness, preferring the indulgence of a caprice to anything resembling a duty; and I now had little doubt upon my mind that O'Grady's fears were well founded, and that he had been obliged to sail without his follower.

The exertion it cost me to read my letters, and the excitement produced by their perusal, fatigued and exhausted me, and as I sank back upon my pillow I closed my eyes and fell sound asleep, not to wake until late on the following day. But strange enough, when I did so, it was with a head clear and faculties collected, my mind refreshed by rest unbroken by a single dream; and so restored did I feel, that, save in the debility from long confinement to bed, I was unconscious of any sense of malady.

From this hour my recovery dated. Advancing every day with rapid steps, my strength increased; and before a week elapsed, I so far regained my lost health that I could move about my chamber, and even lay plans for my departure.

CHAPTER XXXII
BOB MAHON AND THE WIDOW

It was about eight or ten days after the events I have mentioned, when Father Tom Loftus, whose care and attention to me had been unceasing throughout, came in to inform me that all the preparations for our journey were properly made, and that by the following morning at sunrise we should be on the road.

I confess that I looked forward to my departure with anxiety. The dreary monotony of each day, spent either in perambulating my little room or in a short walk up and down before the inn door, had done more to depress and dispirit me than even the previous illness. The good priest, it is true, came often to see me; but then there were hours spent quite alone, without the solace of a book or the sight of even a newspaper. I knew the face of every man, woman, and child in the village; I could tell their haunts, their habits, and their occupations. Even the very hours of the tedious day were marked in my mind by various little incidents, that seemed to recur with unbroken precision; and if when the pale apothecary disappeared from over the half-door of his shop I knew that he was engaged at his one o'clock dinner, so the clink of the old ladies' pattens, as they passed to an evening tea, told me that the day was waning, when the town-clock should strike seven. There was nothing to break the monotonous jog-trot of daily life save the appearance of a few raw subalterns, who, from some cause or other, less noticed than others of the regiment by the neighbouring gentry, strolled about the town, quizzing and laughing at the humble townsfolk, and endeavouring, by looks of most questionable gallantry, to impress the female population with a sense of their merits.

After all, mankind is pretty much the same in every country and every age—some men ambitioning the credit of virtues the very garb of which they know not; others, and a large class too, seeking for the reputation of vices the world palliates with the appellation of 'fashionable.' We laugh at the old courtier of Louis xiv.'s time, who in the flattery of the age he lived in preferred being called a *scélérat*, an *infâme scélérat*, that by the excesses *he* professed the vicious habits of the sovereign might seem less striking; and yet we see the very same thing under our own eyes every day we live.

But to return. There was nothing to delay me longer at Loughrea. Poor Joe was so nearly recovered that in a few days more it was hoped he might leave his bed. He was in kind hands, however, and I had taken every precaution that he should want for nothing in my absence. I listened, then, with pleasure to Father Tom's detail of all his preparations; and although I knew not whither we were going, nor how long the journey was likely to prove, yet I looked forward to it with pleasure, and only longed for the hour of setting out.

As the evening drew near, I looked anxiously out for the good father's arrival. He had promised to come in early with Major Mahon, whom I had not seen for the two days previous—the Major being deeply engaged in consultations with his lawyer regarding an approaching trial at the assizes. Although I could gather from his manner, as well as from the priest's, that something of moment impended, yet as neither of them more than alluded to the circumstance, I knew nothing of what was going forward.

It was eight o'clock when Father Tom made his appearance. He came alone, and by his flurried look and excited manner I saw there was something wrong.

'What is it, father?' said I. 'Where is the Major?'

'Och, confound him! they have taken him at last,' said he, wiping his forehead with agitation.

'Taken him!' said I. 'Why, was he hiding?'

'Hiding! to be sure he was hiding, and masquerading and disguising himself! But, 'faith, those Clare fellows, there's no coming up to them; they have such practice in their own county, they would take the devil himself if there was a writ out against him. And, to be sure, it was a clever trick they played old Bob.'

Here the good priest took such a fit of laughing that he was obliged to wipe his eyes.

'May I never,' said he, 'if it wasn't a good turn they played him, after what he did himself!'

'Come, father, let's hear it.'

'This was the way of it. Maybe you never remarked—of course you didn't, for you were only up there a couple of times—that opposite Bob's lodgings there was a mighty sweet-looking crayture, a widow-woman; she was dressed in very discreet black, and had a sorrowful look about her that somehow or other, I think, made her even more interesting.

'"I'd like to know that widow," said Bob; "for now that the fellows have a warrant against me, I could spend my days so pleasantly over there, comforting and consoling her."

'"Whisht," said I, "don't you see that she is in grief?"

'"Not so much in grief," said he, "but she lets down two beautiful braids of her brown hair under her widow's cap; and whenever you see that, Father Tom, take my word for it, the game's not up."

Bob Mahon and the Widdy

'I believe there was some reason in what he said, for the last time I went up to see him he had the window open, and he was playing "Planxty Kelly" with all his might on an old fiddle; and the widow would come now and then to the window to draw the little muslin curtain, or she would open it to give a halfpenny to the beggars, or she would hold out her hand to see if it was raining—and a beautiful lily-white hand it was; but all the time, you see, it was only exchanging looks they were. Bob was a little ashamed when he saw me in the room, but he soon recovered.

'"A very charming woman that Mrs. Moriarty is," said he, closing the window. "It's a cruel pity that her fortune is all in the Grand Canal—I mean Canal debentures. But indeed it comes pretty much to the same thing."

'And so he went on raving about the widow; for by this time he knew all about her. Her maiden name was Cassidy, and her father a distiller; and, in fact, Bob was quite delighted with his beautiful neighbour. At last I bid him good-bye, promising to call for him at eight o'clock to come over here to you; for you see there was a backdoor to the house that led into a small alley, by which Mahon used to make his escape in the evening. He was sitting, it seems, at his window, looking out for the widow, who for some cause or other hadn't made her appearance the entire of the day. There he sat with his hand on his heart, and a heavenly smile upon him for a good hour, sipping a little whisky-and-water between times, to keep up his courage.

'"She must be out," said Bob to himself. "She's gone to pass the day somewhere. I hope she doesn't know any of these impudent vagabonds up at the barracks. Maybe, after all, it's sick she is."

'While he was ruminating this way, who should he see turn the corner but the widow herself. There she was, coming along in deep weeds, with her maid after her—a fine slashing-looking figure, rather taller than her though, and lustier every way; but it was the first time he saw her in the streets. As she got near to her door, Bob stood up to make a polite bow. Just as he did so, the widow slipped her foot, and fell down on the flags with a loud scream. The maid ran up, endeavouring to assist her, but she couldn't stir; and as she placed her hand on her leg, Bob perceived at once she had sprained her ankle. Without waiting for his hat, he sprang downstairs, and rushed across the street. '"Mrs. Moriarty, my angel!" said Bob, putting his arm round her waist. "Won't you permit me to assist you?"

'She clasped his hand with fervent gratitude, while the maid, putting her hand into her reticule, seemed fumbling for a handkerchief.

'"I am a stranger to you, ma'am," said Bob; "but if Major Mahon, of the Roscommon——"

'"The very man we want!" said the maid, pulling a writ out of the reticule; for a devil a thing else they were but two bailiffs from Ennis.

'"The very man we want!" said the bailiffs.

'"I am caught!" said Bob.

'"The devil a doubt of it!"

'At the same moment the window opened overhead, and the beautiful widow looked out to see what was the matter.

'"Good-evening to you, ma'am," says Bob; "and I'd like to pay my respects if I wasn't particularly engaged to these ladies here." And with that he gave an arm to each of them and led them down the street, as if it was his mother and sister.'

'The poor Major!' said I. 'And where is he now?'' On his way to Ennis in a post-chaise; for it seems the ladies had a hundred pounds for their capture. Ah, poor Bob! But there is no use fretting; besides it would be sympathy thrown away, for he'll give them the slip before long. And now, Captain, are you ready for the road? I have got a peremptory letter from the bishop, and must be back in Murranakilty as soon as I can.'

'My dear father, I am at your disposal I believe we can do no more for poor Joe; and as to Mr. Burke—and, by-the-bye, how is he?'

'Getting better, they say. But I believe you've spoiled a very lucrative source of his income. He was the best jumper in the west of Ireland; and they tell me you've lamed him for life. He is down at Milltown, or Kilkee, or somewhere on the coast; but sure well have time enough to talk of these things as we go along. I'll be with you by seven o'clock. We must start early, and get to Portumna before night.'

Having promised implicit obedience to the worthy priest's directions, be they what they might, I pledged myself to make up my luggage in the smallest possible space, and have breakfast ready for him before starting. After a few other observations and some suggestions as to the kind of equipment he deemed suitable to the road, he took his leave, and I sat down alone to a little quiet reckoning with myself as to the past, the present, and the future.

From my short experience of Ireland, the only thing approaching to an abstract principle I could attain to was the utter vanity, the perfect impossibility, of any man's determining on a given line of action or the steady pursuit of any one enterprise. No; the inevitable course of fate seems to have chosen this happy island to exhibit its phenomena. Whether your days be passed in love or war, or your evenings in drink or devotion, not yours be the glory; for there would seem to be a kind of headlong influence at work, impelling you ever forward. Acquaintances grow up, ripen, and even bear fruit before in other lands their roots would have caught the earth; by them your tastes are regulated, your habits controlled, your actions fashioned.

You may not, it is true, lisp in the *patois* of blarney; you may weed your phraseology of its tropes and figures; but trust me, that if you live in Ireland, if you like the people (and who does not?), and if you are liked by them (and who would not be?), then do I say you will find yourself, without knowing or perceiving it, going the pace with the natives—courtship, fun, frolic, and devilment filling up every hour of your day, and no inconsiderable portion of your night also. One grand feature of the country seemed to me, that, no matter what particular extravagance you were addicted to, no matter what strange or absurd passion to do or seem something remarkable, you were certain of always finding some one to sympathise with if not actually to follow you. Nothing is too strange, nothing too ridiculous, nothing too convivial, nothing too daring for Paddy. With one intuitive bound he springs into your confidence and enters into your plans. Only be open with him, conceal nothing, and he's yours heart and hand; ready to endorse your bill, to carry off a young lady, or carry a message; to burn a house for a joke, or jeopardy his neck for mere pastime; to go to the world's end to serve you, and on his return shoot you afterwards out of downright good-nature.

As for myself, I might have lived in England to the age of Methuselah, and yet never have seen as much of life as in the few months spent in Ireland. Society in other lands seems a kind of free-masonry, where for lack of every real or important secret men substitute signs and passwords, as if to throw the charm of mystery where, after all, nothing lies concealed; but in Ireland, where national character runs in a deep or hidden channel, with cross currents and backwater ever turning and winding—where all the incongruous and discordant elements of what is best and worst seem blended together—there, social intercourse is free, cordial, warm, and benevolent. Men come together disposed to like one another; and what an Irishman is disposed to, he usually has a way of effecting. My brief career had not been without its troubles; but who would not have incurred such, or as many more, to have evoked such kind interest and such warm friendship? From Phil O'Grady, my first, to Father Tom, my last friend, I had met with nothing but almost brotherly affection; and yet I could not help acknowledging to myself, that, but six short months before, I would have recoiled from the friendship of the one and the acquaintance of the other, as something to lower and degrade me. Not only would the outward observances of their manner have deterred me, but in their very warm and earnest proffers of good-nature, I would have seen cause for suspecting and avoiding them. Thank Heaven! I now knew better, and felt deeper. How this revolution became effected in me I am not myself aware. Perhaps—I only say perhaps—Miss Bellew had a share in effecting it.

Such were some of my thoughts as I betook myself to bed, and soon after to sleep.

CHAPTER XXXIII
THE PRIEST'S GIG

I am by no means certain that the prejudices of my English education were sufficiently overcome to prevent my feeling a kind of tingling shame as I took my place beside Father Tom Loftus in his gig. Early as it was, there were still some people about; and I cast a hurried glance around to see if our equipage was not as much a matter of amusement to them as of affliction to me.

When Father Tom first spoke of his 'dennet,' I innocently pictured to myself something resembling the indigenous productions of Loughrea. 'A little heavy or so,' thought I; 'strong for country roads; mayhap somewhat clumsy in the springs, and not over-refined about the shafts.' Heaven help my ignorance! I never fancied a vehicle whose component parts were two stout poles, surmounting a pair of low wheels, high above which was suspended, on two lofty C springs, the body of an ancient buggy—the lining of a bright scarlet, a little faded and dimmed by time, bordered by a lace of the most gaudy pattern; a flaming coat-of-arms, with splendid blazonry and magnificent quarterings, ornamented each panel of this strange-looking tub, into which, for default of steps, you mounted by a ladder.

'Eh, father,' said I, 'what have we here? This is surely not the— —'

'Ay, Captain,' said the good priest, as a smile of proud satisfaction curled his lip, 'that's "the convaniency"; and a pleasanter and an easier never did man sit in. A little heavy, to be sure; but then one can always walk up the hills; and if they're very stiff ones entirely, why it's only throwing out the ballast.'

'The ballast! What do you mean?'

'Just them,' said he, pointing with his whip to some three or four huge pieces of limestone rock that lay in the bottom of the gig; 'there's seven, maybe eight, stone weight, every pound of it.'

'And for heaven's sake,' said I, 'why do you carry that mass of rubbish along with you?'

'I'll just tell you then. The road has holes in it you could bury your father in; and when the convaniency gets into one of them, she has a way of springing up into the air, that, if you're not watching, is sure to pitch you out—maybe into the bog at the side, maybe on the beast's back. I was once actually thrown into a public-house window, where there was a great deal of fun going on, and the bishop came by before I extricated myself. I assure you I had hard work to explain it to his satisfaction.' There was a lurking drollery in his eye, as he said these last few words, that left me to the full as much puzzled about the accident as his worthy diocesan. 'But look at the springs,' he continued; 'there's metal for you! And do you mind the shape of the body? It's for all the world like the ancient *curriculus*. And look at Bathershin himself—the ould varmint! Sure, he's classical too! Hasn't he a Roman nose; and ain't I a Roman myself? So get up, Captain—*ascendite ad currum*; get into the shay. And now for the *doch-aiv-dhurrss*—the stirrup-cup, Mrs. Doolan: that's the darlin'. Ah, there's nothing like it!

"*Sit mihi lagena, Ad summum plena.*"

Here, Captain, take a pull—beautiful milk-punch!'

Draining the goblet to the bottom, which I confess was no unpleasant task, I pledged my kind hostess, who, curtsying deeply refilled the vessel for Father Tom.

'That's it, Mary; froth it up, acushla! Hand it here, my darlin'—my blessing on ye.'

As he spoke, the worthy father deposited the reins at his feet, and lifted the cup with both hands to his mouth; when suddenly the little window over the inn door was burst open, and a loud tally-ho was shouted out, in accents the wildest I ever listened to. I had barely time to catch the merry features of poor Tipperary Joe, when the priest's horse, more accustomed to the hunting-field than the highroad, caught up the welcome sound, gave a wild toss of his head, cocked up his tail, and, with a hearty bang of both hind legs against the front of the chariot, set off down the street as if the devil were after him. Feeling himself at liberty, as well as favoured by the ground, which was all down hill, the pace was really terrific. It was some time before I could gather up the reins, as Father Tom, jug and all, had been thrown at the first shock on his knees to the bottom of the convaniency, where, half suffocated by fright and the milk-punch that went wrong with him, he bellowed and coughed with all his might.

Father Tom's Curriculum

'Howld him tight I—ugh, ugh, ugh!—not too hard; don't chuck him for the love of—ugh, ugh, ugh!—the reins is rotten and the traces no better—ugh, ugh, ugh! Bad luck to the villains, why didn't they catch his head? And the *stultus execrabilis!*—the damned fool! how he yelled!'

Almost fainting with laughter, I pulled my best at the old horse, not, however, neglecting the priest's caution about the frailty of the harness. This, however, was not the only difficulty I had to contend with; for the curriculus, participating in the galloping action of the horse, swung upwards and downwards, backwards and forwards, and from one side to the other—all at once too—in a manner so perfectly addling that it was not before we reached the first turnpike that I succeeded in arresting our progress. Here a short halt was necessary for the priest to recover himself, and to examine whether either his bones or any portion of the harness had given way. Both had happily been found proof against mishaps, and drew from the reverend father strong encomiums upon their merits; and after a brief delay we resumed our road, but at a much more orderly and becoming pace than before.

Once more *en route*, I bethought me it was high time to inquire about the direction we were to travel, and the probable length of our journey; for I confess I was sadly ignorant as to the geography of the land we were travelling, and the only point I attempted to keep in view was the number of miles we were distant from the capital The priest's reply was, however, anything but instructive to me, consisting merely of a long catalogue of names, in which the syllables 'kill,' 'whack,' 'nock,' 'shock,' and 'bally' jostled and elbowed one another in the rudest fashion imaginable—the only intelligible portion of his description being, that a blue mountain scarcely perceptible in the horizon lay about half-way between us and Murranakilty.

My attention was not, however, permitted to dwell on these matters; for my companion had already begun a narrative of the events which had occurred during my illness. The Dillons, I found, had left for Dublin soon after my mishap. Louisa Bellew returned to her father; and Mr. Burke, whose wound had turned out a more serious affair than was at first supposed, was still confined to his bed, and a lameness for life anticipated as the inevitable result of the injury.

'Sir Simon, for once in his life,' said the priest, 'has taken a correct view of his nephew's character, and has, now that all danger to life is past, written him a severe letter, reflecting on his conduct. Poor Sir Simon! his life has been one tissue of trial and disappointment throughout. Every buttress that supported his venerable house giving way, one by one, the ruin seems to threaten total downfall, ere the old man exchanges the home of his fathers for his last narrow rest beside them in the churchyard. Betrayed on every hand, wronged and ruined, he seems merely to linger on in life—like the stern-timbers of some mighty wreck, that marks the spot where once the goodly vessel perished, and are now the beacon of the quicksand to others. You know the sad story, of course, that I alluded to——'

'No; I am completely ignorant of the family history,' said I.

The priest blushed deeply, as his dark eyebrows met in a heavy frown; then turning hastily towards me, he said, in a voice whose thick, low utterance bespoke his agitation—

'Do not ask me, I beseech you, to speak further of what, had I been more collected, I had never alluded to! An unhappy duel, the consequence of a still more unhappy event, has blasted every hope in life for my poor friend. I thought—that is, I feared lest the story might have reached you. As I find this is not so, you will spare my recurring to that the bare recollection of which comes like a dark cloud over the happiest day of my existence. Promise me this, or I shall not forgive myself.'

I readily gave the pledge he required; and we pursued our road—not, however, as before, but each sunk in his own reflections, silent, reserved, and thoughtful.

'In about four days,' said Father Tom, at last breaking the silence, 'perhaps five, we'll be drawing near Murranakilty. He then proceeded, at more length, to inform me of the various counties through which we were to pass, detailing with great accuracy the several seats we should see, the remarkable places, the ruined churches, the old castles, and even the very fox-covers that lay on our route. And although my ignorance was but little enlightened by the catalogue of hard names that fell as glibly from his tongue as Italian from a Roman, yet I was both entertained and pleased with the many stories he told—some of them legends of bygone days, some of them the more touching and truth-dealing records of what had happened in his own time. Could I have borrowed any portion of his narrative power, were I able to present in his strong but simple language any of the curious scenes he mentioned, I should perhaps venture on relating to my reader one of his stories; but when I think how much of the interest depended on his quaint and homely but ever-forcible manner, as, pointing with his whip to some ruined house with blackened walls and fallen chimneys, he told some narrative of rapine and of murder, I feel how much the force of reality added power to a story that in repetition might be weak and ineffective.

CHAPTER XXXIV
THE MOUNTAIN PASS

On the whole, the journey was to me a delightful one, and certainly not the least pleasant portion of my life in Ireland. Endowed—partly from his individual gifts, partly from the nature of his sacred functions—with influence over all the humble ranks in life, the good priest jogged along with the assurance of a hearty welcome wherever he pleased to halt—the only look of disappointment being when he declined some proffered civility, or refused an invitation to delay his journey. The chariot was well known in every town and village, and scarcely was the rumble of its wheels heard coming up the 'street' when the population might be seen assembling in little groups and knots, to have a word with 'the father,' to get his blessing, to catch his eye, or even obtain a nod from him. He knew every one and everything, and with a tact which is believed to be the prerogative of royalty, he never miscalled a name nor mistook an event. Inquiring after them, for soul and body, he entered with real interest into all their hopes and plans, their fears and anticipations, and talked away about pigs, penances, purgatory, and potatoes in a way that showed his information on any of these matters to be of no mean or common order.

By degrees our way left the more travelled highroad, and took by a mountain tract through a wild, romantic line of country beside the Shannon. No villages now presented themselves, and indeed but little trace of any habitation whatever; large misshapen mountains, whose granite sides were scarce concealed by the dark fern, the only vegetation that clothed them, rose around and about us. In the valleys some strips of bog might be seen, with little hillocks of newly-cut turf, the only semblance of man's work the eye could rest on. Tillage there was none. A dreary silence, too, reigned throughout. I listened in vain for the bleating of a lamb or the solitary tinkle of a sheep-bell; but no—save the cawing of the rooks or the mournful cry of the plover, I could hear nothing. Now and then, it is true, the heavy flapping of a strong wing would point the course of a heron soaring towards the river; but his low flight even spoke of solitude, and showed he feared not man in his wild and dreamy mountains. At intervals we could see the

Shannon winding along, far, far down below us, and I could mark the islands in the bay of Scariff, with their ruined churches and one solitary tower; but no sail floated on the surface, nor did an oar break the sluggish current of the stream. It was, indeed, a dreary scene, and somehow my companion's manner seemed coloured by its influence; for scarcely had we entered the little valley that led to this mountain track than he became silent and thoughtful, absorbed in reflection, and when he spoke, either doing so at random or in a vague and almost incohérent way that showed his ideas were wandering.

I remarked that as we stopped at a little forge shortly after daybreak, the smith had taken the priest aside and whispered to him a few words, at which he seemed strangely moved; and as they spoke together for some moments in an undertone, I perceived by the man's manner and gesture, as well as by the agitation of the good father himself, that something of importance was being told. Without waiting to finish the little repair to the carriage which had caused our halt, he remounted hastily, and beckoning me to take my place, drove on at a pace that spoke of haste and eagerness. I confess that my curiosity to know the reason was great; but as I could not with propriety ask, nor did my companion seem disposed to give the information, I soon relapsed into a silence unbroken as his own, and we travelled along for some miles without speaking. Now and then the priest would make an effort to relieve the weariness of the way by some remark upon the scenery, or some allusion to the wild grandeur of the pass; but it was plain he spoke only from constraint, and that his mind was occupied on other and very different thoughts.

It was now wearing late, and yet no trace of any house or habitation could I see, where to rest for the night. Not wishing, however, to interrupt the current of my friend's thoughts I maintained my silence, straining my eyes on every side—from the dark mountains that towered above me, to the narrow gloomy valley that lay several hundred feet beneath our track—but all in vain. The stillness was unbroken, and not a roof, not even a smoke-wreath, could be seen far as the view extended. The road by which we travelled was scarped from the side of a mountain, and for some miles pursued a gradually descending course. On suddenly turning the angle of a rocky wall that skirted us for above a mile, we came in sight of a long reach of the Shannon upon which the sun was now setting in all its golden lustre. The distant shore of Munster, rich in tillage and pasture-land, was lit up too with cornfield and green meadow, leafy wood and blue mountain, all glowing in their brightest hue. It was a vivid and a gorgeous picture, and I could have looked on it long with pleasure, when suddenly I felt my arm grasped by a strong finger. I turned round, and the priest, relaxing his hold, pointed down into the dark valley below us, as he said in a low and agitated voice—

'You see the light? It is there—there.'

Quickening our pace by every effort, we began rapidly to descend the mountain by a zigzag road, whose windings soon lost us the view I have mentioned, and left nothing but the wild and barren mountains around us. Tired as our poor horse was, the priest pressed him forward; and regardless of the broken and rugged way he seemed to think of nothing but his haste, muttering between his teeth with a low but rapid articulation, while his face grew flushed and pale at intervals, and his eye had all the lustrous glare and restless look of fever. I endeavoured, as well as I was able, to occupy my mind with other thoughts; but with that invincible fascination that turns us ever to the side we try to shun, I found myself again and again gazing on my companion's countenance. Every moment now his agitation increased; his lips were firmly closed, his brow contracted, his cheek flattened and quivering with a nervous spasm, while his hand trembled violently as he wiped the big drops of sweat that rolled from his forehead.

At last we reached the level, where a better road presented itself before us, and enabled us so to increase our speed that we were rapidly coming up with the light, which, as the evening closed in, seemed larger and brighter than before. It was now that hour when the twilight seems fading into night—a grey and sombre darkness colouring every object, but yet marking grass and rock, pathway and river, with some seeming of their noonday hues, so that as we came along I could make out the roof and walls of a mud cabin built against the very mountainside, in the gable of which the light was shining. A rapid, a momentary thought flashed across my mind as to what dreary and solitary man could fix his dwelling-place in such a spot as this, when in an instant the priest suddenly pulled up the horse, and, stretching out one hand with a gesture of listening, whispered—

'Hark! Did you not hear that?'

As he spoke, a cry, wild and fearful, rose through the gloomy valley—at first in one prolonged and swelling note; then broken as if by sobs, it altered, sank, and rose again wilder and madder, till the echoes, catching up the direful sounds, answered and repeated them as though a chorus of unearthly spirits were calling to one another through the air.

'O God! too late—too late!' said the priest, as he bowed his face upon his knees, and his strong frame shook in agony. 'O Father of Mercy!' he cried, as he lifted his eyes, bloodshot and tearful, toward heaven, 'forgive me this; and if unshriven before Thee—'

Another cry, more frantic than before, here burst upon us, and the priest, muttering with rapid utterance, appeared lost in prayer. But at him I looked no longer, for straight before us on the road, and in front of the little cabin, now not above thirty paces from us, knelt the figure of a woman, whom, were it not for the fearful sounds we had heard, one could scarcely believe a thing of life. Her age was not more than thirty years; she was pale as death; not a tinge, not a ray of colour streaked her bloodless cheek; her black hair, long and wild, fell upon her back and shoulders, straggling and disordered; while her hands were clasped, as she held her stiffened arms straight before her. Her dress bespoke the meanest poverty, and her sunken cheek and drawn-in lips betokened famine and starvation. As I gazed on her almost breathless with awe and dread, the priest leaped out, and hurrying forward, cried out to her in Irish; but she heard him not, she saw him not— dead to every sense, she remained still and motionless. No feature trembled, no limb was shaken; she knelt before us like an image of stone; and then, as if by some spell that worked within her, once more gave forth the heart-rending cry we heard at first. Now low and plaintive, like the sighing night-wind, it rose fuller and fuller, pausing and continuing at intervals; and then breaking into short and fitful efforts, it grew wilder and stronger, till at last with one outbreak, like the overflowing of a heart of misery, it ceased abruptly.

The priest bent over her and spoke to her; he called her by her name, and shook her several times—but all in vain. Her spirit, if indeed present with her body, had lost all sympathy with things of earth.

'God help her!' said he; 'God comfort her! This is sore affliction.'

As he spoke he walked towards the little cabin, the door of which now stood open. All was still and silent within its walls. Unused to see the dwellings of the poor in Ireland, my eye ranged over the bare walls, the damp and earthen floor, the few and miserable pieces of furniture, when suddenly my attention was called to another and a sadder spectacle. In one corner of the hovel, stretched upon a bed whose poverty might have made it unworthy of a dog to lie in, lay the figure of a large and powerfully-built man, stone dead. His eyes were closed, his chin bound up with a white cloth, and a sheet, torn and ragged, was stretched above his cold limbs, while on either side of him two candles were burning. His features, though rigid and stiffened, were manly and even handsome—the bold character of the face heightened in effect by his beard and moustache, which appeared to have been let grow for some time previous, and whose black and waving curl looked darker from the pallor around it.

Some lines there were about the mouth that looked like harshness and severity, but the struggle of departing life might have caused them.

Gently withdrawing the sheet that covered him, the priest placed his hand upon the man's heart. It was evident to me, from the father's manner, that he still believed the man living; and as he rolled back the covering, he felt for his hand. Suddenly starting, he fell back for an instant; and as he moved his fingers backwards and forwards, I saw that they were covered with blood. I drew near, and now perceived that the dead man's chest was laid open by a wound of several inches in extent. The ribs had been cut across, and some portion of the heart or lung seemed to protrude. At the slightest touch of the body, the blood gushed forth anew, and ran in streams upon him. His right hand, too, was cut across the entire palm, the thumb nearly severed at the joint. This appeared to have been rudely bound together; but it was evident, from the nature and the size of the other wound, that he could not have survived it many hours.

As I looked in horror at the frightful spectacle before me, my foot struck at something beneath the bed. I stooped down to examine, and found it was a carbine, such as dragoons usually carry. It was broken at the stock and bruised in many places, but still seemed not unserviceable. Part of the butt-end was also stained with blood. The clothes of the dead man, clotted and matted with gore, were also there, adding by their terrible testimony to the dreadful fear that haunted me. Yes, everything confirmed it—murder had been there.

A low, muttering sound near made me turn my head, and I saw the priest kneeling beside the bed, engaged in prayer. His head was bare, and he wore a kind of scarf of blue silk, and the small case that contained the last rites of his Church was placed at his feet. Apparently lost to all around, save the figure of the man that lay dead before him, he muttered with ceaseless rapidity prayer after prayer—stopping ever and anon to place his hand on the cold heart, or to listen with his ear upon the livid lips; and then resuming with greater eagerness, while the big drops rolled from his forehead, and the agonising torture he felt convulsed his entire frame.

'O God!' he exclaimed, after a prayer of some minutes, in which his features worked like one in a fit of epilepsy—'O God, is it then too late?'

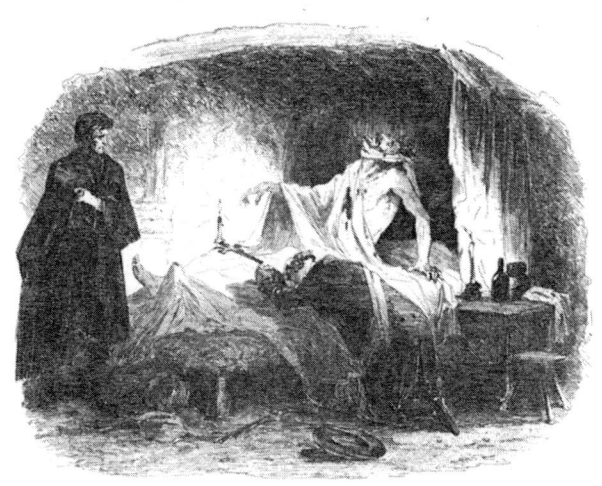

Death of Shaun

He started to his feet as he spoke, and bending over the corpse, with hands clasped above his head, he poured forth a whole torrent of words in Irish, swaying his body backwards and forwards, as his voice, becoming broken by emotion, now sank into a whisper, or broke into a discordant shout. 'Shaun, Shaun!' cried he, as, stooping down to the ground; he snatched up the little crucifix and held it before the dead man's face; at the same time he shook him violently by the shoulder, and cried, in accents I can never forget, some words aloud, among which alone I could recognise one word, 'Thea'—the Irish word for God. He shook the man till his head rocked heavily from side to side, and the blood oozed from the opening wound, and stained the ragged covering of the bed.

At this instant the priest stopped suddenly, and fell upon his knees, while with a low, faint sigh he who seemed dead lifted his eyes and looked around him; his hands grasped the sides of the bed, and, with a strength that seemed supernatural, he raised himself to a sitting posture. His lips were parted and moved, but without a sound, and his filmy eyes turned slowly in their sockets from one object to another, till at length they fell upon the little crucifix that had dropped from the priest's hand upon the bed. In an instant the corpse-like features seemed inspired with life; a gleam of brightness shot from his eyes; the head nodded forward a couple of times, and I thought I heard a discordant, broken sound issue from the open mouth; but a moment after the head dropped upon the chest, and the hands relaxed, and he fell back with a crash, never to move more.

Overcome with horror, I staggered to the door and sank upon a little bench in front of the cabin. The cool air of the night soon brought me to myself, and while in my confused state I wondered if the whole might not be some dreadful dream, my eyes once more fell upon the figure of the woman, who still knelt in the attitude we had first seen her. Her hands were clasped before her, and from time to time her wild cry rose into the air and woke the echoes of that silent valley. A faint moonlight lay in broken patches around her, and mingled its beams with the red glare of the little candles within, as their light fell upon her marble features. From the cabin I could hear the sounds of the priest's voice, as he continued to pray without ceasing.

As the hours rolled on, nothing changed; and when, prompted by curiosity, I looked within the hovel, I saw the priest still kneeling beside the bed, his face pale and sunk and haggard, as though months of sickness and suffering had passed over him. I dared not speak; I dared not disturb him; and I sat down near the door in silence.

It is one of the strange anomalies of our nature that the feelings which rend our hearts with agony have a tendency, by their continuance, to lull us into slumber. The watcher by the bedside of his dying friend, the felon in his cell but a few hours before death, sleep—and sleep soundly. The bitterness of grief would seem to blunt sensation, and the mind, like the body, can only sustain a certain amount of burden, after which it succumbs and yields. So I found it amid this scene of horror and anguish, with everything to excite that can operate upon the mind—the woman stricken motionless and senseless by grief; the dead man, as it were, recalled to life by the words that were to herald him into life everlasting; the old man, whom I had known but as a gay companion, displayed now before my eyes in all the workings of his feeling heart, called up by the afflictions of one world and the terrors of another—and this in a wild and dreary valley, far from man's dwelling. Yet amid all this, and more than all, the harassing conviction that some deed of blood, some dark hour of crime, had been here at work, perhaps to be concealed for ever, and go unavenged save of Heaven—with this around and about me, I slept. How long I know not; but when I woke, the mist of morning hung in the valley, or rolled in masses of cloudlike vapour along the mountain-side. In an instant the whole scene of the previous night was before me, and the priest still knelt beside the bed and prayed. I looked for the woman, but she was gone.

The noise of wheels, at some distance, could now be heard on the mountain-road; and as I walked stealthily from the door, I could see three figures descending the pass, followed by a car and horse. As they came along, I marked that beneath the straw on the car something protruded itself on either side, and this, I soon saw, was a coffin. As the men approached the angle of the road they halted, and seemed to converse in an eager and anxious manner, when suddenly one of them broke from the others, and springing to the top of a low wall that skirted the road, continued to look steadily at the house for some minutes together. The thought flashed on me at the moment that perhaps my being a stranger to them might have caused their hesitation; so I waved my hat a couple of times above my head. Upon this they resumed their march, and in a few minutes more were standing beside me. One of them, who was an old man with hard, weather-beaten features, addressed me, first in Irish, but correcting himself, at once asked, in a low, steady voice—

'Was the priest in time? Did he get the rites?'

I nodded in reply; when he muttered, as if to himself—'God's will be done! Shaun didn't tell of Hogan——'

'Whisht, father! whisht!' said one of the younger men as he laid his hand upon the old man's arm, while he added something in Irish, gesticulating with energy as he spoke.

'Is Mary come back, sir?' said the third, as he touched his hat to me respectfully.

'The woman—his wife?' said I. 'I have not seen her to-day.'

'She was up with us, at Kiltimmon, at two o'clock this morning, but wouldn't wait for us. She wanted to get back at once, poor crayture! She bears it well, and has a stout heart. 'Faith, maybe before long she 'll make some others faint in their hearts that have stricken hers this night.'

'Was she calm, then?' said I.

'As you are this minute; and sure enough she helped me, with her own hands, to put the horse in the car, for you see I couldn't lift the shaft with my one arm.'

I now saw that his arm was bound up, and buttoned within the bosom of his greatcoat.

The priest now joined us, and spoke for several minutes in Irish; and although ignorant of all he said, I could mark in the tone of his voice, his look, his manner, and his gesture that his words were those of rebuke and reprobation. The old man heard him in silence, but without any evidence of feeling. The others, on the contrary, seemed deeply affected; and the younger of the two, whose arm was broken, seemed greatly moved, and the tears rolled down his hardy cheeks.

These signs of emotion were evidently displeasing to the old man, whose nature was of a sterner and more cruel mould; and as he turned away from the father's admonition he moved past me, muttering, as he went—

'Isn't it all fair? Blood for blood; and sure they dhruv him to it.'

After a few words from the priest, two of the party took their spades from the car, and began digging the grave; while Father Loftus, leading the other aside, talked to him for some time.

'Begorra,' said the old man, as he shovelled the earth to either side, 'Father Tom isn't like himself, at all, at all. He used to have pity and the kind word for the poor when they were turned out on the world to starve, without as much as a sheaf of straw to lie upon, or potatoes enough for the children to eat.'

'Whisht, father! or the priest will hear ye,' said the younger one, looking cautiously around.

'Sorrow bit o' me cares if he does! it's thruth I'm telling. You are not long in these parts, sir, av I may make so bowld?'

'No,' said I, 'I'm quite a stranger.'

'Well, anyhow, ye may understand that this isn't a fine soil for a potato-garden; and yet the devil a other poor Shaun had since they turned him out on the road last Michaelmas Day, himself and his wife and the little gossoon—the only one they had, too—with a fever and ague upon him. The poor child, however, didn't feel it long, for he died in ten days after. Well, well! the way of God there's no saying against it. But, sure, if the little boy didn't die Shaun was off to America; for he tuk his passage, and got a sea-chest of a friend, and was all ready to go. But you see, when the child died, he could not bring himself to leave the grave; and there he used to go and spend half of his days fixing it, and settling the sods about it, and wouldn't take a day's work from any of the neighbours. And at last he went off one night, and we never knew what was become of him, till a pedlar brought word that he and Mary was living in the Cluan Beg, away from everybody, without a friend to say "God save you!" It's deep enough now, Mickey; there's nobody will turn him out of this. And so, sir, he might have lived for many a year; but when he heerd that the boys was up, and going to settle a reckoning with Mr. Tarleton——'

'Come, you,' cried the priest, who joined us at the moment, and who I could perceive was evidently displeased at the old man's communicativeness—'come, you, the sooner you all get back the better. We must look after Mary, too; for God knows where she is wandering. And now let us put the poor boy in the earth.'

With slow and sullen steps the old man entered the house, followed by the others. I did not accompany them, but stood beside the grave, my mind full of all I heard. In a few minutes they returned, carrying the coffin, one corner of which was borne by the priest himself. Their heads were bare, and their features were pale and care-worn. They placed the body in the grave, and gazed down after it for some seconds. The priest spoke a few words in a low, broken voice, the very sounds of which, though their meaning was unknown to me, sank deep into my heart. He whispered for an instant to one of the young men, who went into the cabin and speedily returned, carrying with him some of the clothes of the deceased and the old carbine that lay beneath the bed.

'Throw them in the grave, Mickey—throw them in,' said the priest. 'Where's his coat?'

'It isn't there, sir,' said the man. 'That's everything that has a mark of blood upon it.'

'Give me that gun,' cried the priest; and at the same moment he took the carbine by the end of the barrel, and by one stroke of his strong foot snapped it at the breech. 'My curse be on you!' said he, as he kicked the fragments into the grave; 'there was peace and happiness in the land before men knew ye, and owned ye! Ah, Hugh,' said he, turning his eyes fiercely on the old man, 'I never said ye hadn't griefs and trials, and sore ones too, some of them; but God help you, if you think that an easy conscience and a happy home can be bought by murder.' The old man started at the words, and as his dark brow lowered and his lip trembled, I drew near to the priest, fearful lest an attack might be made on him. 'Ay, murder, boys! that's the word, and no less. Don't tell me about righting yourselves, and blood for blood, and all that. There's a curse upon the land where these things happen, and the earth is not lucky that is moistened with the blood of God's creatures.'

'Cover him up! cover him up!' said the old man, shovelling in the earth so as to drown the priest's words, 'and let us be going. We ought to be back by six o'clock, unless,' added he with a sarcastic bitterness that made him look like a fiend—'unless your reverence is going to set the police on our track.'

'God forgive you, Hugh, and turn your heart,' said the priest, as he shook his outstretched hands at the old man. As the father spoke these words he took me by the arm, and led me within the house. I could feel his hand tremble as it leaned upon me, and the big tears rolled down his cheeks in silence.

We sat down in the little cabin, but neither of us spoke. After some time we heard the noise of the cartwheels and the sound of voices, which grew fainter and fainter as they passed up the glen, and at length all became still.

'And the poor wife,' said I, 'what, think you, has become of her?'

'Gone home to her people, most likely,' answered the priest. 'Her misfortunes will make her a home in every cabin. None so poor, none so wretched, as not to succour and shelter her. But let us hence.'

We walked forth from the hovel, and the priest closing the door after him fastened it with a padlock that he had found within, and then, placing the key upon the door-sill, he turned to depart; but suddenly stopping, he took my hand in both of his, and said, in a voice of touching earnestness—

'This has been a sad scene. Would to God you had not witnessed it! Would to God, rather, that it might not have occurred! But promise me, on the faith of a man of honour and the word of a gentleman, that what you have seen this night you will reveal to no man, until I have passed away myself, and stand before that judgment to which we all are coming.'

'I promise you faithfully,' said I. 'And now let us leave a spot that has thrown a gloom upon my heart which a long life will never obliterate.'

CHAPTER XXXV
THE JOURNEY

As we issued from the glen the country became more open; patches of cultivation presented themselves, and an air of comfort and condition superior to what we had hitherto seen was observable in the dwellings of the country-people. The road lead through a broad valley bounded on one side by a chain of lofty mountains, and on the other separated by the Shannon from the swelling hills of Munster. Deeply engaged in our thoughts, we travelled along for some miles without speaking. The scene we had witnessed was of that kind that seemed to forbid our recurrence to it, save in our own gloomy reflections. We had not gone far when the noise of horsemen on the road behind us induced us to turn our heads. They came along at a sharp trot, and we could soon perceive that although the two or three foremost were civilians, they who followed were dragoons. I thought I saw the priest change colour as the clank of the accoutrements struck upon his ear. I had, however, but little time for the observation, as the party soon overtook us.

'You are early on the road, gentlemen,' said a strong, powerfully-built man, who, mounted upon a grey horse of great bone and action, rode close up beside us.

'Ah, Sir Thomas, is it you?' said the priest, affecting at once his former easy and indifferent manner. 'I'd rather see the hounds at your back than those beagles of King George there. Is there anything wrong in the country?'

'Let me ask you another question,' said the knight in answer. 'How long have you been in it, and where did you pass the night, not to hear of what has occurred?'

''Faith, a home question,' said the priest, summoning up a hearty laugh to conceal his emotion; 'but if the truth must out, we came round by the priory at Glenduff, as my friend here being an Englishman—may I beg to present him to you? Mr. Hinton, Sir Thomas Garland—he heard wonders of the monks' way of living up there, and I wished to let him judge for himself.'

'Ah, that accounts for it,' said the tall man to himself. 'We have had a sad affair of it, Father Tom. Poor Tarleton has been murdered.'

'Murdered!' said the priest, with an expression of horror in his countenance I could scarcely believe feigned.

'Yes, murdered! The house was attacked a little after midnight. The party must have been a large one, for while they forced in the hall door, the haggard and the stables were seen in a blaze. Poor George had just retired to bed, a little later than usual; for his sons had returned a few hours before from Dublin, where they had been to attend their college examination. The villains, however, knew the house well, and made straight for his room. He got up in an instant, and seizing a sabre that hung beside his bed, defended himself, with the courage of desperation, against them all. The scuffle and the noise soon brought his sons to the spot, who, although mere boys, behaved in the most gallant manner. Overpowered at last by numbers, and covered with wounds, they dragged poor Tarleton downstairs, shouting out as they went, "Bring him down to Freney's! Let the bloody villain see the black walls and the cold hearth he has made, before he dies!" It was their intention to murder him on the spot where, a few weeks before, a distress for rent had been executed against some of his tenants. He grasped the banisters with a despairing clutch, while fixing his eyes upon his servant, who had lived with him for some years past, he called out to him in his agony to save him; but the fellow came deliberately forward and held the flame of a candle beneath the dying man's fingers, until he relaxed his hold and fell back among his murderers. Yes, yes, father, Henry Tarleton saw it with his own eyes, for while his brother was stretched senseless on the floor, he was struggling with the others at the head of the staircase; and, strange enough too, they never hurt the boys, but when they had wreaked their vengeance on the father, bound them back to back, and left them.'

'Can you identify any of them?' said the priest, with intense emotion in his voice and manner.

'Scarcely, I fear; their faces were blackened, and they wore shirts over their coats. Henry thinks he could swear to two or three of the number; but our best chance of discovery lies in the fact that several of them were badly wounded, and one in particular, whom he saw cut down by his father's sabre, was carried downstairs by his comrades, bathed in blood.'

'He didn't recognise him?' said the priest eagerly.

'No; but here comes the poor boy, so I'll wish you good-morning.'

He put spurs to his horse as he spoke and dashed forward, followed by the dragoons; while at the same moment, on the opposite side of the road, a young man—pale, with his dress disordered, his arm in a sling—rode by. He never turned a look aside; his filmy eye was fixed, as it were, on some far-off object, and he seemed scarce to guide his horse as he galloped onward over the rugged road.

The priest relaxed his pace to permit the crowd of horsemen to pass on, while his countenance once more assumed its drooping and despondent look, and he relapsed into his former silence.

'You see that high mountain to the left there?' said he after a long pause. 'Well, our road lies around the foot of it; and, please God, by to-morrow evening we'll be some five-and-twenty miles on the other side, in the heart of my own wild country, with the big mountains behind you, and the great blue Atlantic rearing its frothing waves at your feet.' He stopped for an instant, and then grasping my arm with his strong hand, continued in a low, distinct voice: 'Never speak to me nor question me about what we saw last night, and try only to remember it as a dream. And now let me tell you how I intend to amuse you in the far west.'

Here the priest began a spirited and interesting description of the scenery and the people—their habits, their superstitions, and their pastimes. He sustained the interest of his account with legend and story, now grave, now gay—sometimes recalling a trait from the older history of the land; sometimes detailing an incident of the fair or the market, but always by his wonderful knowledge of the peasantry, their modes of thinking and reasoning, and by his imitation of their figurative and forcible expressions, able to carry me with him, whether he took the mountain's side for his path, sat beside some cotter's turf-fire, or skimmed along the surface of the summer sea in the frail bark of an Achill fisherman. I learned from him that in the wild region where he lived there were above fifteen thousand persons, scarce one of whom could speak or understand a word of English. Of these he was not only the priest, but the ruler and judge. Before him all their disputes were settled, all their differences reconciled. His word, in the strongest sense of the phrase, was law—not indeed to be enforced by bayonets and policemen, by constables and sheriffs' officers, but which in its moral force demanded obedience, and would have made him who resisted it an outcast among his fellows.

'We are poor,' said the priest, 'but we are happy. Crime is unknown among us, and the blood of man has not been shed in strife for fifty years within the barony. When will ye learn this in England? When will ye know that these people may be led, but never driven; that they may be persuaded, but never compelled? When will ye condescend to bend so far the prerogative of your birth, your riches, and your rank, as to reason with the poor and humble peasant that looks up to you for protection? Alas! my young friend, were you to ask me what is the great source of misery of this unhappy land, I should tell you the superior intelligence of its people. I see a smile, but hear me out. Unlike the peasantry of other countries, they are not content. Their characters are mistaken, their traits misconstrued—-partly from indifference, partly from prejudice, and in a great measure because it is the fashion to recognise in the tiller of the soil a mere drudge, with scarce more intelligence than the cattle in his plough or the oxen in his team. But here you really have a people quick, sharp-sighted, and intelligent, able to scan your motives with ten times the accuracy you can guess at theirs; suspicious, because their credulity has been abused; revengeful, because their wild nature knows no other vindicator than their own right arm; lawless, for they look upon your institutions as the sources of their misery and the instruments of your tyranny towards them; reckless, for they have nothing to lose; indolent, for they have nothing to gain. Without an effort to win their confidence or secure their good-will, you overwhelm them with your institutions, cumbrous, complicated, and unsuitable; and while you neglect or despise all appeal to their feelings or affections, you place your faith in your soldiery or a special commission. Heaven help you! you may thin them off by the gallows and transportation, but the root of the evil is as far from you as ever. You do not know them, you will not know them. More prone to punish than prevent, you are satisfied with the working of the law, and not shocked with the accumulation of crime; and when, broken by poverty and paralysed by famine, a gloomy desolation spreads over the land, you meet in terms of congratulation to talk over tranquilised Ireland.'

In this strain did the good priest continue to develop his views concerning his country—the pivot of his argument being, that, to a people so essentially different in every respect, English institutions and English laws were inadequate and unsuitable. Sometimes I could not only but agree with him. At others I could but dimly perceive his meaning and dissent from the very little I could catch.

Enough of this, however. In a biography so flimsy as mine, politics would play but an unseemly part; and even were it otherwise, my opportunities were too few and my own incapacity too great to make my opinions of any value on a subject so complicated and so vast. Still, the topic served to shorten the road, and when towards evening we found ourselves in the comfortable parlour of the little inn at Ballyhocsousth,* so far had we both regained our spirits that once more the priest's jovial good-humour irradiated his happy countenance; and I myself, hourly improving in health and strength, felt already the bracing influence of the mountain air, and that strong sense of liberty never more thoroughly appreciated than when regaining vigour after the sufferings of a sick-bed.

* *Town of the Fight of Flails.*

We were seated by an open window, looking out upon the landscape. It was past sunset, and the tall shadows of the mountains were meeting across the lake, like spirits who waited for the night-hour to interchange their embraces. A thin pale crescent of a new moon marked the blue sky, but did not dim the lustre of the thousand stars that glittered round it. All was hushed and still, save the deep note of the rail, or the measured plash of oars heard from a long distance. The rich meadows that sloped down to the water sent up their delicious odours in the balmy air, and there stole over the senses a kind of calm and peaceful pleasure as such a scene at such an hour can alone impart.

'This is beautiful—this is very beautiful, father,' said I.

'So it is, sir,' said the priest. 'Let no Irishman wander for scenery; he has as much right to go travel in search of wit and good fellowship. We don't want for blessings; all we need is, to know how to enjoy them. And, believe me, there is a plentiful feast on the table if gentlemen would only pass down the dishes. And, now, that reminds me: what are you drinking— negus? I wouldn't wish it to my greatest enemy. But, to be sure, I am always forgetting you are not one of ourselves. There, reach me over that square decanter. It wouldn't have been so full now if we had had poor Bob here— poor fellow! But one thing is certain—-wherever he is, he is happy. I believe I never told you how he got into his present scrape.'

'No, father; and that's precisely the very thing I wish to ask you.'

'You shall hear it, and it isn't a bad story in its way. But don't you think the night-air is a little too much for you? Shall we close the window?'

'If it depend on me, father, pray leave it open.'

'Ha, ha! I was forgetting again,' said the old fellow, laughing roguishly— *'Stella sunt amantium oculi*, as Pharis says. There now, don't be blushing, but listen to me.

'It was somewhere about last November that Bob got a quiet hint from some one at Daly's that the sooner he got out of Dublin the more conducive it would be to his personal freedom, as various writs were flying about the capital after him. He took the hint, and set off the same night, and reached his beautiful château of Newgate without let or molestation—which having victualled for the winter, he could, if necessary, sustain in it a reasonable siege against any force the law was likely to bring up. The house had an abundant supply of arms. There were guns that figured in '41, pikes that had done good service a little later, swords of every shape, from the two-handed weapon of the twelfth century to a Roman pattern made out of a scythe by a smith in the neighbourhood; but the grand terror of the country was an old four-pounder of Cromwell's time, that the Major had mounted on the roof, and whose effects, if only proportionately injurious to the enemy to the results nearer home, must indeed have been a formidable engine, for the only time it was fired—I believe to celebrate Bob's birthday—it knocked down a chimney with the recoil, blew the gardener and another man about ten feet into the air, and hurled Bob himself through a skylight into the housekeeper's room. No matter for that; it had a great effect in raising the confidence of the country-people, some of whom verily believed that the ball was rolling for a week after.

'Bob, I say, victualled the fortress; but he did more, for he assembled all the tenants, and in a short but pithy speech told them the state of his affairs, explaining with considerable eloquence what a misfortune it would be for them if by any chance they were to lose him for a landlord.

'"See, now, boys," said he, "there's no knowing what misfortune wouldn't happen ye; they'd put a receiver on the property—a spalpeen with bailiffs and constables after him—that would be making you pay up the rent, and 'faith I wouldn't say but maybe he'd ask you for the arrears."

'"Oh, murther, murther! did any one ever hear the like!" the people cried on every side; and Bob, like a clever orator, continued to picture forth additional miseries and misfortunes to them if such a calamitous event were to happen, explaining at the same time the contemptible nature of the persecution practised against him.

'"No, boys," cried he, "there isn't a man among them all that has the courage to come down and ask for his money, face to face; but they set up a pair of fellows they call John Doe and Richard Roe—there's names for you! Did you ever hear of a gentleman in the country with names like that? But that's not the worst of it, for you see even these two chaps can't be found. It's truth I'm telling you, and some people go so far as to say that there is no such people at all, and it's only a way they have to worry and annoy country gentlemen with what they call a fiction of the law; and my own notion is, that the law is nothing but lies and fiction from beginning to end."

'A very loud cheer from Bob's audience proclaimed how perfectly they coincided in his opinion; and a keg of whisky being brought into the lawn, each man drained a glass to his health, uttering at the same time a determination with respect to the law-officers of the crown that boded but little happiness to them when they made a tour in the neighbourhood.

'In about a week after this there was a grand drawing-home: that's, you understand, what we call in Ireland bringing in the harvest. And sure enough, the farmyard presented a very comely sight, with ricks of hay, and stacks of corn and oats and barley, and outhouses full of potatoes, and in fact everything the country produces, besides cows and horses, sheep, pigs, goats, and even turkeys; for most of the tenants paid their rents in kind, and as Bob was an easy landlord, very few came without a little present—a game-cock, a jackass, a ram, or some amusing beast or other. Well, the next day—it was a fine dry day with a light frost, and as the bog was hard, Bob sent them all away to bring in the turf. Why, then, but it is a beautiful sight, Captain, and I wish you saw it—maybe two or three hundred cars all going as fast as they can pelt, on a fine bright day, with a blue sky and a sharp air, the boys standing up in the kishes driving without rein or halter, always at a gallop—for all the world like Ajax, Ulysses, and the rest of them that we read of; and the girls, as pretty craytures as ever you threw an eye upon, with their short red petticoats, and their hair plaited and fastened up at the back of their heads: on my conscience the Trojan women was nothing to them!

'But to come back. Bob Mahon was coming home from the bog about five o'clock in the evening, cantering along on a little dun pony he had, thinking of nothing at all, except maybe the elegant rick of turf that he 'd be bringing home in the morning, when what did he see before him but a troop of dragoons, and at their head old Basset, the sub-sheriff, and another fellow whose face he had often seen in the Four Courts of Dublin. "By the mortial," said Bob, "I am done for!" for he saw in a moment that Basset had waited until all the country-people were employed at a distance, to come over and take him. However, he was no ways discouraged, but brushing his way through the dragoons, he rode up beside Basset's gig, and taking a long pistol out of the holster, he began to examine the priming as cool as may be.

'"How are you, Nick Basset?" said Bob; "and where are you going this evening?"

'"How are you, Major?" said Basset, with his eye all the while upon the pistol. "It is an unpleasant business, a mighty unpleasant business to me, Major Bob," says he; "but the truth is, there is an execution against you, and my friend here, Mr. Hennessy—Mr. Hennessy, Major Mahon—asked me to come over with him, because as I knew you——"

'"Well, well," said Bob, interrupting him. "Have you a writ against me? Is it me you want?"

'"Nothing of the kind, Major Mahon. God forbid we 'd touch a hair of your head. It's just a kind of a capias, as I may say, nothing more."

'"And why did you bring the dragoons with you?" said Bob, looking at him mighty hard.

'Basset looked very sheepish, and didn't know what to say; but Mahon soon relieved him—-

'"Never mind, Nick, never mind; you can't help your trade. But how would you look if I was to raise the country on ye?"

'"You wouldn't do the like, Major; but surely, if you did, the troops——"

'"The troops!" said Bob; "God help you! we'd be twenty, ay, thirty to one. See now, if I give a whistle, this minute——"

'"Don't distress yourself, Major," said Basset, "for the decent people are a good six miles off at the bog, and couldn't hear you if you whistled ever so loud."

'The moment he said this Bob saw that the old rogue was up to him, and he began to wonder within himself what was best to be done.

'"See now, Nick," said he, "it isn't like a friend to bring up all these redcoats here upon me, before my tenantry, disgracing me in the face of my people. Send them back to the town, and go up yourself with Mr. Hennessy there, and do whatever you have to do."

'"No, no!" screamed Hennessy, "I'll never part with the soldiers!"

'"Very well," said Bob, "take your own way, and see what will come of it."

'He put spurs to his pony as he said this, and was just striking into the gallop when Nick called out—

'"Wait a bit, Major! wait a bit! If we leave the dragoons where we are now, will you give us your word of honour not to hurt or molest us in the discharge of our duty, nor let any one else do so?"

'"I will," said Bob, "now that you talk reasonably; I'll treat you well."

'After a little parley it was settled that part of the dragoons were to wait on the road, and the rest of them in the lawn before the house, while Nick and his friend were to go through the ceremony of seizing Bob's effects, and make an inventory of everything they could find.

'"A mere matter of form, Major Mahon," said he. "We'll make it as short as possible, and leave a couple of men in possession; and as I know the affair will be arranged in a few days——"

'"Of course," says Bob, laughing; "nothing easier. So come along now and let me show you the way."

'When they reached the house, Bob ordered up dinner at once, and behaved as politely as possible, telling them it was early, and they would have plenty of time for everything in the evening. But whether it was that they had no appetite just then, or that they were not over-easy in their minds about Bob himself, they declined everything, and began to set about their work. To it they went with pen and ink, putting down all the chairs and tables, the cracked china, the fire-irons, and at last Bob left them counting over about twenty pairs of old top-boots that stood along the wall of his dressing-room.

'"Ned," said Bob to his own man, "get two big padlocks and put them on the door of the hayloft as fast as you can."

'"Sure it is empty, sir," said Ned. "Barrin' the rats, there's nothing in it."

'"Don't I know that as well as you?" said Bob; "but can't you do as you are bid? And when you've done it, take the pony and gallop over to the bog, and tell the people to throw the turf out of their carts and gallop up here as fast as they can."

'He'd scarcely said it when Nick called out, "Now, Major, for the farmyard, if you please." And so taking Hennessy's arm, Bob walked out, followed by the two big bailiffs, that never left them for a moment. To be sure it was a great sight when they got outside, and saw all the ricks and stacks as thick as they could stand; and so they began counting and putting them down on paper, and the devil a thing they forgot, not even the boneens and the bantams; and at last Nick fixed his eye upon the little door into the loft, upon which now two great big padlocks were hanging.

'"I suppose it's oats you have up there, Major?" said he.

'"No, indeed," said Bob, looking a little confused.

'"Maybe seed-potatoes?" said Hennessy.

'"Nor it neither," said he.

'"Barley, it's likely?" cried Nick; "it is a fine dry loft."

'"No," said Bob, "it is empty."

'And with that he endeavoured to turn them away and get them back into the house; but old Basset turned back, and fixing his eye upon the door, shook his head for a couple of minutes.

'"Well," said he, "for an empty loft it has the finest pair of padlocks I ever looked at. Would there be any objection, Major, to our taking a peep into it?"

'"None," said Bob; "but I haven't a ladder that long in the place."

'"I think this might reach," said Hennessy, as he touched one with his foot that lay close along the wall, partly covered with straw.

'"Just the thing," said Nick; while poor Bob hung down his head and said nothing. With that they raised the ladder and placed it against the door.

'"Might I trouble you for the key, Major Mahon?" said Hennessy.

'"I believe it is mislaid," said Bob, in a kind of sulky way, at which they both grinned at each other, as much as to say, "We have him now."

'"You "ll not take it amiss then, Major, if we break the door?" said Nick.

'"You may break it and be hanged!" said Bob, as he stuck his hands into his pockets and walked away.

'"This will do," cried one of the bailiffs, taking up a big stone as he mounted the ladder, followed by Nick, Hennessy, and the other.

Bob Mahon's elevation of the Sheriff

'It took some time to smash the locks, for they were both strong ones, and all the while Nick and his friend were talking together in great glee; but poor Bob stood by himself against a hayrick, looking as melancholy as might be. At last the locks gave way, and down went the door with a bang.

The bailiffs stepped in, and then Nick and the other followed. It took them a couple of minutes to satisfy themselves that the loft was quite empty; but when they came back again to the door, what was their surprise to discover that Bob was carrying away the ladder upon his shoulders to a distant part of the yard.

'"Holloa, Major!" cried Basset, "don't forget us up here!"

'"Devil a fear of that," said Bob; "few that know you ever forget you."

'"We are quite satisfied, sir," said Hennessy; "what you said was perfectly correct."

'"And why didn't you believe it before, Mr. Hennessy? You see what you have brought upon yourself."

'"You are not going to leave us up here, sir," cried Hennessy; "will you venture upon false imprisonment?"

'"I'd venture on more than that, if it were needful; but see now, when you get back, don't be pretending that I didn't offer to treat you well, little as you deserved it, I asked you to dinner, and would have given you your skinful of wine afterwards; but you preferred your own dirty calling, and so take the consequences."

'While he was speaking a great cheer was heard, and all the country-people came galloping into the yard with their turf cars.

'"Be alive now, my boys!" cried Bob. "How many cars have you?"

'"Seventy, sir, here; but there is more coming."

'"That'll do," said he; "so now set to work and carry away all the oats and the wheat, the hay, barley, and potatoes. Let some of you take the calves and the pigs, and drive the bullocks over the mountain to Mr. Bodkin's. Don't leave a turkey behind you, boys, and make haste; for these gentlemen have so many engagements I can scarcely prevail on them to pass more than a day or two amongst us."

'Bob pointed as he spoke to the four figures that stood trembling at the hayloft door. A loud cheer, and a roar of laughter to the full as loud, answered his speech; and at the same moment to it they went, loading their cars with the harvest or the live-stock as fast as they could. To be sure, such a scene was never witnessed—the sheep bleating, pigs grunting, fowls cackling, men and women all running here and there laughing like mad, and Nick Basset himself swearing like a trooper the whole time that he'd have them all hanged at the next assizes. Would you believe, the harvest it took nearly three weeks to bring home was carried away that night and scattered all over the country at different farms, where it never could be traced; all the cattle too were taken away, and before sunrise there wasn't as much as a sheep or a lamb left to bleat on the lawn.

'The next day Bob set out on a visit to a friend at some distance, leaving directions with his people to liberate the gentlemen in the hayloft in the course of the afternoon. The story made a great noise in the country; but before people were tired laughing at it an action was entered against Bob for false imprisonment, and heavy damages awarded against him. So that you may see there was a kind of poetic justice in the manner of his capture, for after all it was only trick for trick.'

The worthy priest now paused to mix another tumbler, which, when he had stirred and tasted and stirred again, he pushed gently before him on the table, and seemed lost in reverie.

'Yes,' said he half aloud, 'it is a droll country we live in; and there's not one of us doesn't waste more ingenuity and display more cunning in getting rid of his fortune than the cleverest fellows elsewhere evince in accumulating theirs. But you are looking a little pale, I think; these late hours won't suit you, so I 'll just send you to bed.'

I felt the whole force of my kind friend's advice, and yielding obedience at once, I shook him by the hand and wished him good-night.

CHAPTER XXXVI
MURRANAKILTY

If my kind reader is not already tired of the mountain-road and the wild west, may I ask him—dare I say her?—to accompany me a little farther, while I present another picture of its life?

You see that bold mountain, jagged and rugged in outline, like the spine of some gigantic beast, that runs far out into the Atlantic, and ends in a bold, abrupt headland, against which the waves, from the very coast of Labrador, are beating without one intervening rock to break their force? Carry your eye along its base, to where you can mark a little clump of alder and beech, with here and there a taper poplar interspersed, and see if you cannot detect the gable of a long, low, thatched house, that lies almost buried in the foliage. Before the door a little patch of green stretches down to the shore, where a sandy beach, glowing in all the richness of a morning sun, glitters with many a shell and brilliant pebble. That, then, is Murranakilty.

But approach, I beg you, a little nearer. Let me suppose that you have traced the winding of that little bay, crossing the wooden bridge over the bright trout stream, as it hastens on to mingle its waters with the ocean; you have climbed over the rude stile, and stopped for an instant to look into the holy well, in whose glassy surface the little wooden crucifix above is dimly shadowed, and at length you stand upon the lawn before the cottage. What a glorious scene is now before you! On the opposite side of the bay, the mountain, whose summit is lost among the clouds, seems as it were cleft by some earthquake force; and through its narrow gorge you can trace the blue water of the sea passing in, while each side of the valley is clothed with wood. The oak of a hundred years, here sheltered from the rude wind of the Atlantic, spreads its luxuriant arms, while the frothy waves are breaking at its feet. High, however, above their tops you may mark the irregular outline of a large building, with battlements and towers and massive walls, and one tall and loopholed turret, that rises high into the air, and around whose summit the noisy rooks are circling in their flight. That is Kilmorran Castle, the residence of Sir Simon Bellew. There, for centuries past, his ancestors were born and died; there, in the midst of that wild and desolate grandeur, the haughty descendants of an ancient house lived on from youth to age, surrounded by all the observances of feudal state, and lording it far and near, for many a mile, with a sway and power that would seem to have long since passed away.

You carry your eye seaward, and I perceive your attention is fixed upon the small schooner that lies anchored in the offing; her topsail is in the clews, and flaps lazily against the mast, as she rolls and pitches in the breaking surge. The rake of her low masts and the long boom that stretches out far beyond her taffrail have, you deem it, a somewhat suspicious look; and you are right. She is *La Belle Louise*, a smuggling craft from Dieppe, whose crew, half French, half Irish, would fight her to the gunwale, and sink with but never surrender her. You hear the plash of oars, and there now you can mark the eight-oared gig springing to the stroke, as it shoots from the shore and heads out to sea. Sir Simon loves claret, and like a true old Irish gentleman he drinks it from the wood; there may, therefore, be some reason why those wild-looking red-caps have pulled in shore.

But now I'll ask you to turn to an humbler scene, and look within that room where the window, opened to the ground, is bordered by blossoming honeysuckle. It is the priest's parlour. At a little breakfast-table, whose spotless cloth and neat but simple equipage has a look of propriety and comfort, is seated one whose gorgeous dressing-gown and lounging attitude seem strangely at variance with the humble objects around him. He seems endeavouring to read a newspaper, which ever and anon he lays down beside him, and turns his eyes in the direction of the fire; for although it is July, yet a keen freshness of the morning air makes the blazing turf by no means objectionable. He looks towards the fire, perhaps you would say, lost in his own thoughts and musings; but no, truth must out, and his attention is occupied in a very different way. Kneeling before the fire is a young and lovely country-girl, engaged in toasting a muffin for the priest's breakfast. Her features are flushed, partly with shame, partly with heat; and as now and then she throws back her long hair from her face with an impatient toss of her head, she steals a glance at the stranger from a pair of eyes so deeply blue that at first you were unjust enough to think them black.

Her dress is a low bodice, and a short skirt of that brilliant dye the Irish peasant of the west seems to possess the secret for. The jupe is short, I say; and so much the better for you, as it displays a pair of legs which, bare of shoe or stocking, are perfect in their symmetry — the rounded instep and the swelling ankle chiselled as cleanly as a statue of Canova.

And now, my good reader, having shown you all this, let me proceed with my narrative.

'And sure now, sir, wouldn't it be better for you, and you sickly, to be eating your breakfast, and not be waiting for Father Tom? Maybe he wouldn't come in this hour yet.'

'No, thank you, Mary; I had rather wait. I hope you are not so tired of my company that you want an excuse to get away?'

'Ah, be aisy now, if you plaze, sir! It's myself that's proud to be talking to you.' And as she spoke she turned a pair of blue eyes upon me with such a look that I could not help thinking if the gentlemen of the west be exposed to such, their blood is not as hot as is reputed. I suppose I looked as much; for she blushed deeply, and calling out, 'Here's Father Tom!' sprang to her legs and hurried from the room.

'Where are you scampering that way?' cried the good priest, as he passed her in the hall. 'Ah, Captain, Captain! behave yourself!'

'I protest, father——' cried I.

'To be sure you do! Why wouldn't you protest? But see now, it was your business brought me out this morning. Hand me over the eggs; I am as hungry as a hawk. The devil is in that girl—they are as hard as bullets! I see how it was, plain enough. It's little she was thinking of the same eggs. Well, well! this is an ungrateful world; and only think of me, all I was doing for you.'

'My dear father, you are quite wrong——'

'No matter. Another slice of bacon. And, after all, who knows if I have the worst of it? Do you know, now, that Miss Bellew has about the softest cheek——'

'What the devil do you mean?' said I, reddening. 'Why, just that I was saluting her *à la Française* this morning; and I never saw her look handsomer in my life. It was scarce seven o'clock when I was over at Kilmorran, but, early as it was, I caught her making breakfast for me; and, father and priest that I am, I couldn't help feeling in love with her. It was a beautiful sight just to watch her light step and graceful figure moving about the parlour—now opening the window to let in the fresh air of the morning; now arranging a bouquet of moss-roses; now busying herself among the breakfast things, and all the while stealing a glance at Sir Simon, to see if he were pleased with what she was doing. He'll be over here by-and-by, to call on you; and, indeed, it is an attention he seldom pays any one, for latterly, poor fellow, he is not over satisfied with the world—and if the truth were told, he has not had too much cause to be so.'

'You mentioned to him, then, that I was here?' 'To be sure I did; and the doing so cost me a scalded finger; for Miss Louisa, who was pouring out my tea at the moment, gave a jerk with her hand, and spilled the boiling water all over me.—Bad cess to you, Mary, but you've spoiled the toast this morning! half of it never saw the fire, and the other half is as black as my boot.—But, as I was saying, Sir Simon knows all about you, and is coming over to ask us to dine there—though I offered to give the invitation myself, and accept it first; but he is very punctilious about these things, and wouldn't hear of anything but doing it in the regular way.'

'Did he allude to Mr. Ulick Burke's affair?'

'Not a word. And even when I wished to touch on it for the sake of a little explanation, he adroitly turned the subject, and spoke of something else. But it is drawing late, and I have some people to see this morning; so come along now into my little library here, and I'll leave you for a while to amuse yourself.'

The priest led me, as he spoke, into a small room, whose walls were covered with books from the floor to the ceiling; even the very door by which we entered had its shelves, like the rest, so that when once inside you could see no trace of it. A single window looked seaward, towards the wide Atlantic, and presented a view of many miles of coast, indented with headland and promontory. Beneath, upon the placid sea, was a whole fleet of fishing-boats, the crews of which were busily engaged in collecting the sea-weed to manure the land. The sight was both curious and picturesque. The light boats, tossing on the heavy swell, were crowded with figures whose attitude evinced all the eagerness of a chase. Sometimes an amicable contest would arise between two parties, as their boat-hooks were fixed in the same mass of tangled weed. Sometimes two rival crews would be seen stretching upon their oars, as they headed out to sea in search of a new prize. The merry voices and the loud laughter, however, that rose above all other sounds, told that good-humour and goodwill never deserted them in all the ardour of the contest.

Long after the priest left me, I continued to watch them. At last I set myself to explore the good father's shelves, which I found, for the most part, were filled with portly tomes of divinity and polemics—huge folio copies of Saint Augustine, Origen, Eusebius, and others; innumerable volumes of learned tractates on disputed points in theology—none of which possessed any interest for me. In one corner, however, beside the fire, whose convenience to the habitual seat of Father Tom argued that they were not least in favour with his reverence, was an admirable collection of the French dramatists—Molière, Beaumarchais, Racine, and several more. These were a real treat; and seating myself beside the window, I prepared, for about the twentieth time in my life, to read *La Folle Journée*.

I had scarcely got to the end of the second act, when the door was gently opened, and Mary made her appearance—not in the deshabille of the morning, however, but with a trim cotton gown, and smart shoes and stockings; her hair, too, was neatly dressed, in the country fashion. Yet still I was more than half disposed to think she looked even better in her morning costume.

The critical scrutiny of my glance had evidently disconcerted her, and made her, for the moment, forget the object of her coming. She looked down and blushed; she fiddled with the corner of her apron, and at last, recollecting herself, she dropped a little curtsy, and, opening the door wide, announced Sir Simon Bellew.

'Mr. Hinton, I believe,' said Sir Simon, with a slight smile, as he bowed himself into the apartment; 'will you allow me to introduce myself—Sir Simon Bellew.'

The baronet was a tall, thin, meagre-looking old man, somewhat stooped by age, but preserving, both in look and gesture, not only the remains of good looks, but the evident traces of one habituated to the world. His dress was very plain; but the scrupulous exactitude of his powdered cue, and the massive gold-headed cane he carried, showed he had not abandoned those marks of his position so distinctive of rank in those days. He wore, also, large and handsome buckles in his shoes; but in every other particular his costume was simplicity itself. Conversing with an ease which evinced his acquaintance with all the forms of society, he touched shortly upon my former acquaintance with his daughter, and acknowledged in terms slight, but suitable, how she had spoken of me. His manner was, however, less marked by everything I had deemed to be Irish than that of any other person I had met with in the country; for while he expressed his pleasure at my visit to the west, and invited me to pass some days at his house, his manner of doing so had nothing whatever of the warmth and *empressement* I had so often seen. In fact, save a slight difference in accent, it was as English as need be.

Whether I felt disappointed at this, or whether I had myself adopted the habite and prejudices of the land, I am unable to say, but certainly I felt chilled and repulsed; and although our interview scarce lasted twenty minutes, I was delighted when he rose to take his leave, and say, good-morning.

'You are good enough, then, to promise you'll dine with us to-morrow, Mr. Hinton. I need scarcely remark that I can have no party to meet you, for this wild neighbourhood has denied us that; but as I am aware that your visit to the west is less for society than scenery, perhaps I may assure you you will not be disappointed. So now, *au revoir*.' Sir Simon bowed deeply as he spoke, and, with a wave of his hat that would have done honour to the court of Louis xv., he took his leave and departed.

I followed him with my eye, as mounted on his old gray pony, he ambled quietly down the little path that led to the shore. Albeit an old man, his seat was firm, and not without a certain air of self-possession and ease; and as he returned the salutations of the passing country-people, he did so with the quiet dignity of one who felt he conveyed an honour even in the recognition. There was something singular in the contrast of that venerable figure with the wild grandeur of the scene; and as I gazed after him, it set me thinking on the strange vicissitudes of life that must have made such as he pass his days in the dreary solitude of these mountains.

CHAPTER XXXVII
SIR SIMON

My journey had so far fatigued me that I wasn't sorry to have a day of rest; and as Father Tom spent the greater part of it from home, I was left to myself and my own reflections. The situation in which I found myself was singular enough—the guest of a man whose acquaintance I had made by chance, and who, knowing as little of me as I did of him, yet showed by many an act of kindness, not less than by many a chance observation, a deep interest in myself and my fortunes. Here, then, I was—far from the sphere of my duties, neglecting the career I had adopted, and suffering days, weeks, to pass over without bestowing a thought upon my soldier life.

Following on this train of thought, I could not help acknowledging to myself that my attachment to Miss Bellew was the cause of my journey, and the real reason of my wandering. However sanguine may be the heart when touched by the first passion, the doubts that will now and then shoot across it are painful and poignant; and now, in the calmness of my judgment, I could not but see the innumerable obstacles my family would raise to all my hopes. I well knew my father's predilection for a campaigning life, and that nothing would compensate him for the defeat of this expectation. I had but too many proofs of my mother's aristocratic prejudices to suppose that she ever could acknowledge as her daughter-in-law one whose pretensions to rank, although higher than her own, were yet neither trumpeted by the world nor blazoned by fashion. And lastly, changed as I was myself since my arrival in Ireland, there was yet enough of the Englishman left in me to see how unsuited was Louisa Bellew, in many respects, to be launched forth in the torrent of London life, while yet her experience of the world was so narrow and limited. Still, I loved her. The very artless simplicity of her manner, the untutored freshness of her mind, had taught me to know that even great personal attractions may be the second excellence of a woman. And besides, I was just at that time of life when ambition is least natural. One deems it more heroic to renounce all that is daring in enterprise, all that is great in promise, merely to be loved. My mind was therefore made up. The present opportunity was a good one to see her frequently and learn thoroughly to know her tastes and her dispositions. Should I succeed in gaining her affections, however opposed my family might prove at first, I calculated on their fondness for me as an only son, and knew that in regard to fortune I should be independent enough to marry whom I pleased.

In speculations such as these the time passed over; and although I waited with impatience for the hour of our visit to Kilmorran Castle, still, as the time drew near, many a passing doubt would flit across me—how far I had mistaken the promptings of my own affection for any return of my love. True it was, that more than once Louisa's look and manner testified I was not indifferent to her; still, when I remembered that I had ever seen her surrounded by persons she was anxious to avoid, a suspicion crossed me that perhaps I owed the little preference she showed me less to any qualities I possessed than to my own unobtrusiveness. These were galling and unpleasant reflections; and whither they might have led me I know not, when the priest tapped with his knuckles at my window, and called out—

'Captain, we shall be late if you don't hurry a bit; and I had rather be behind time with his gracious Majesty himself than with old Sir Simon.'

I opened the window at once, and jumped out into the lawn.

'My dear father, I've been ready this half-hour, but fell into a dreamy fit and forgot everything. Are we to walk it?'

'No, no; the distance is much greater than you think. Small as the bay looks, it is a good three miles from this to Kilmorran; but here comes your old friend the curriculus.'

I once more mounted to my old seat, and the priest, guiding the horse down to the beach, selected the strand, from which the waves had just receded, as the hardest road, and pressed on at a pace that showed his desire to be punctual.

'Get along there. Nabocklish! How lazy the devil is! 'Faith, we'll be late, do our best. Captain, darling, put your watch back a quarter of an hour, and I'll stand to it that we are both by Dublin time.'

'Is he, then, so very particular/ said I, 'as all that comes to?'

'Particular, is it? 'Faith he is. Why, man, there is as much ringing of bells before dinner in that house as if every room in it was crammed with company. And the old butler will be there, all in black, and his hair powdered, and beautiful silk stockings on his legs, every day in the week, although, maybe, it is a brace of snipe will be all that is on the table. Take the whip for a while, and lay into that baste—my heart is broke flogging him.'

Had Sir Simon only watched the good priest's exertions for the preceding quarter of an hour, he certainly would have had a hard heart if he had criticised his punctuality. Shouting one moment, cursing the next, thrashing away with his whip, and betimes striding over the splash-board to give a kick with his foot, he undoubtedly spared nothing in either voice or gesture.

'There, glory be to God!' cried he at last, as he turned sharp from the shady road into a narrow avenue of tall lime-trees; 'take the reins, Captain, till I wipe my face. Blessed hour, look at the state I am in! Lift him to it, and don't spare him. May I never, if that isn't the last bell, and he only gives five minutes after that!'

Although I certainly should have preferred that Father Tom had continued his functions as charioteer now that we were approaching the house, common humanity, however, compelled me to spare him, and I flogged and chucked the old beast with all my might up the rising ground towards the house. I had but just time to see that the building before us was a large embattled structure, which, although irregular and occasionally incongruous in detail, was yet a fine specimen of the castellated Gothic of the seventeenth century. Massive square towers flanked the angles, themselves surmounted by smaller turrets, that shot up into the air high above the dark woods around them. The whole was surrounded by a fosse, now dry, and overgrown with weeds; but the terrace, which lay between this and the castle, was laid out as a flower-garden, with a degree of taste and beauty that to my mind at least bespoke the fostering hand of Louisa Bellew. Upon this the windows of a large drawing-room opened, at one of which I could mark the tall and stately figure of Sir Simon, as he stood, watch in hand, awaiting our arrival. I confess, it was not without a sense of shame that I continued my flagellations at the moment. Under any circumstances, our turn-out was not quite unexceptionable; but when I thought of my own position, and of the good priest who sat beside me mopping his head and face with a huge red cotton handkerchief, I cursed my stars for the absurd exposure. Just at this instant the skirt of a white robe passed one of the windows, and I thought—I hope it was but a thought—I heard a sound of laughter.

'There, that will do. Phoebus himself couldn't do it better. I wouldn't wish my worst enemy to be in a pair of shafts before you.'

Muttering a curse on the confounded beast, I pulled short up and sprang out.

'Not late, Nicholas, I hope?' said the priest to a tall, thin old butler, who bore a most absurd resemblance to his master.

'Your reverence has a minute and a half yet; but the soup's on the table.' As he spoke, he drew from his pocket a small bit of looking-glass, in a wooden frame, and with a pocket-comb arranged his hair in a most orderly and decorous manner; which being done, he turned gravely round and said, 'Are ye ready, now, gentlemen?'

The priest nodded, and forward we went. Passing through a suite of rooms whose furniture, however handsome once, was now worm-eaten and injured by time, we at length reached the door of the drawing-room, when the butler, after throwing one more glance at us to assure himself that we were in presentable array, flung the door wide open, and announced, with the voice of a king-at-arms—

'The Reverend Father Loftus, and Mr. Hinton.'

'Serve!' said Sir Simon, with a wave of his hand. While, advancing towards us, he received us with most polished courtesy. 'You are most welcome to Kilmorran, Mr. Hinton. I need not present my daughter.'

He turned towards the priest, and the same moment I held Miss Bellow's hand in mine. Dressed in white, and with her hair plainly braided on her cheek, I thought she looked handsomer than I had ever seen her. There was an air of assured calmness in her manner that sat well upon her lovely features, as, with a tone of winning sweetness, she seconded the words of her father, and welcomed me to Kilmorran.

The first step in the knowledge of the female heart is to know how to interpret any constraint or reserve of manner on the part of the woman you are in love with. Your mere novice is never more tempted to despair than at the precise moment his hopes should grow stronger; nor is he ever so sanguine as when the prospect is gloomy before him. The quick perceptions of even a very young girl enable her to perceive when she is loved; and however disposed she may feel towards the individual, a certain mixture of womanly pride and coquetry will teach her a kind of reserve towards him. Now, there was a slight dash of this constrained tone through Miss Bellow's manner to me; and little experience as I had had in such matters, I knew enough to augur favourably from it. While doing the honours of her house, a passing timidity would seem every now and then to check her advances, and I could remark how carefully she avoided any allusion, however slight, to our past acquaintance.

The austerity of Sir Simon's manner at his first visit, as well as the remarks of my friend the priest, had led me to suspect that our dinner-party would prove cold, formal, and uncomfortable; indeed, the baronet's constrained and measured courtesy in the drawing-room gave me but little encouragement to expect anything better. Most agreeable, therefore, was my disappointment to find that before the soup was removed he had thawed considerably. The stern wrinkles of his haughty face relaxed, and a bland and good-humoured smile had usurped the place of his former fixed and determined look. Doing the honours of his table with the most perfect tact, he contrived, while almost monopolising the conversation, to appear the least obtrusive amongst us; his remarks being ever accompanied by some appeal to his daughter, the priest, or myself, seemed to link us in the interest of all he said, and make his very listeners deem themselves entertaining and agreeable. Unfortunately, I can present but a very meagre picture of this happy gift; but I remember well how insensibly my prejudices gave way, one by one, as I listened to his anecdotes, and heard him recount, with admirable humour, many a story of his early career. To be sure, it may be said that my criticism was not likely to be severe while seated beside his beautiful daughter, whose cheek glowed with pleasure, and whose bright eye glistened with added lustre as she remarked the impression her father's agree-ability was making on his guests. Such may, I doubt not, have increased the delight I felt; but Sir Simon's own claims were still indisputable.

I know not how far I shall meet my reader's concurrence in the remark, but it appears to me that conversational talent, like wine, requires age to make it mellow. The racy flavour that smacks of long knowledge of life, the reflective tone that deepens without darkening the picture, the freedom from exaggeration either in praise or censure, are not the gifts of young men, usually; and certainly they do season the intercourse of older ones, greatly to its advantage. There is, moreover, a pleasant flattery in listening to the narratives of those who were mixing with the busy world—its intrigues, its battles, and its byplay—while we were but boys. How we like to hear of the social everyday life of those great men of a bygone day, whose names have become already historical; what a charm does it lend to reminiscence, when the names of Burke, Sheridan, Grattan, and Curran start up amid memories of youthful pleasure; and how we treasure every passing word that is transmitted to us, and how much, in spite of all the glorious successes of their after days, do we picture them to ourselves, from some slight or shadowy trait of their school or college life!

Sir Simon Bellow's conversation abounded in features of this kind. His career had begun and continued for a long time in the brightest period of Ireland's history—when wealth and genius were rife in the land, and when the joyous traits of Irish character were elicited in all their force by prosperity and happiness. It was then shone forth in all their brilliancy the great spirits whose flashing wit and glittering fancy have cast a sunlight over their native country that even now, in the twilight of the past, continues to illumine it. Alas! they have had no heritors to their fame; they have left no successors behind them.

I have said that Miss Bellew listened with delight to all her father's stores of amusement—happy to see him once more aroused to the exertion of his abilities, and pleased to watch how successfully his manner had won over us. With what added loveliness she looked up to him as he narrated some circumstances of his political career, where his importance with his party was briefly alluded to; and how proudly her features glowed, as some passing sentiment of high and simple patriotism would break from him! At such moments, the resemblance between them both became remarkably striking, and I deemed her even more beautiful than when her face wore its habitual calm and peaceful expression.

Father Loftus himself seemed also to have undergone a change—no longer indulging in his accustomed free-and-easy manner, seasoning his conversation with droll allusions and sly jokes. He now appeared a shrewd, intelligent reasoner, a well-informed man of the world, and at times evidenced traits of reading and scholarship I was nowise prepared for. But how vain is it for one of any other country to fathom one half the depth of Irish character, or say what part is inapplicable to an Irishman! My own conviction is that we are all mistaken in our estimate of them; that the gay and reckless spirit, the wild fun, and frantic, impetuous devilment are their least remarkable features, and in fact only the outside emblem of the stirring nature within. Like the lightning that flashes over the thunder-cloud, but neither influences the breaking of the storm nor points to its course, so have I seen the jest break from lips pale with hunger, and heard the laugh come free and mellow when the heart was breaking in misery. But what a mockery of mirth!

When we retired to the drawing-room, Sir Simon, who had something to communicate to Father Tom, took him apart into one of the deep window recesses, and I was left for the first time alone beside Miss Bellew. There was something of awkwardness in the situation; for as neither of us could allude to the past without evoking recollections we both shunned to touch on, we knew not well of what to speak. The window lay open to the ground, displaying before us a garden in all the richness of fruit and blossom; the clustering honeysuckle and the dog-rose hung in masses of flower across the casement, and the graceful hyacinth and the deep carnation were bending to the night-air, scented with the odour of many a flower. I looked wistfully without. Miss Bellew caught my glance; a slight hesitation followed, and then, as if assuming more courage, she said—

'Are you fond of a garden? Would you like a walk?'

The haste with which I caught at the proposal half disconcerted her; but, with a slight smile, she stepped out into the walk.

How I do like a large, old-fashioned garden with its venerable fruit-trees, its shady alleys, its overgrown and tangled beds, in which the very luxuriance sets all effort of art at defiance, and where rank growth speaks of wild-ness rather than culture! I like those grassy walks, where the footstep falls unheard; those shady thickets of nut-trees, which the blackbird haunts in security, and where the thrush sings undisturbed. What a sense of quiet home-happiness there breathes in the leafy darkness of the spot, and how meet for reverie and reflection does it seem!

As I sauntered along beside my companion, these thoughts crowded on me. Neither spoke; but her arm was in mine, our footsteps moved in unison, our eyes followed the same objects, and I felt as though our hearts beat responsively. On turning from one of the darker walks we suddenly came upon an elevated spot, from which, through an opening in the wood, the coast came into view, broken into many a rocky promontory, and dotted with small islands. The sea was calm and waveless, and stretched away towards the horizon in one mass of unbroken blue, where it blended with the sky. An exclamation of 'How beautiful!' broke from me at once; and as I turned towards Louisa, I perceived that her eyes sparkled with pleasure, and a half blush was mantling her cheek.

'You are not, then, disappointed with the west?' said she, with animation.

'No, no! I did not look for anything like this; nor,' added I, in a lower tone, while the words trembled on my lips, 'did I hope to enjoy it thus.'

She seemed slightly confused, but with woman's readiness to turn the meaning of my speech, added—

'Your recovery from illness doubtless gives a heightened pleasure to everything like this. The dark hour of sickness is often needed to teach us to feel strongly as we ought the beauty of the fair world we live in.'

'It may be so; but still I find that every sorrow leaves a scar upon the heart, and he who has mourned much loses the zest for happiness.'

'Or, rather, his views of it are different. I speak, happily for me, in ignorance; yet it seems as though every trial in life was a preparation for some higher scale of blissful enjoyment; and that as our understandings mature in power, so do our hearts in goodness—chastening at each ordeal of life, till at last the final sorrow, death, bids us prepare for the eternity where there is no longer grief, and where the weary are at rest.'

'Is not your view of life rather derived from the happy experience of this quiet spot than suited for the collisions of the world, where, as men grow older, their consciences grow more seared, their hearts less open?'

'Perhaps; but is not my philosophy a good one that fits me for my station? My life has been cast here; I have no wish to leave it. I hope I never shall.'

'Never! Surely, you would like to see other countries,—to travel?'

'No, no! All the brilliant pleasures you can picture for me would never requite the fears I must suffer lest these objects should grow less dear to me when I came back to them. The Tyrol is doubtless grander in its wild magnificence; but can it ever come home to my heart with so many affections and memories as these bold cliffs I have gazed on in my infancy; or should I benefit in happiness if it did? Can your Swiss peasant, be his costume ever so picturesque, interest me one half as much as yonder poor fisherman, who is carrying up his little child in his arms from the beach? I know him, his home, his hearth; I have seen his grateful smile for some small benefit, and heard his words of thankfulness. And think you not that such recollections as these are all mingled in every glance I throw around me, and that every sunlit spot of landscape shines not more brightly in my heart for its human associations? These may be narrow prejudices—I see you smile at me.'

'No, no! Trust me, I do not undervalue your reasons.'

'Well, here comes Father Loftus, and he shall be judge between us. We were discussing the advantages of contrasting our home with other countries— —'

'Ahem! A very difficult point,' said the priest, interrupting her, and drawing himself up with a great air of judicial importance. '*Ubi bene, ibi patria*—which may be rendered, "There's potatoes everywhere." Not that I incline to the doctrine myself. Ireland is the only enjoyable country I know of. *Utamur creatura, dum possumus*—that means "a moderate use of creature comforts," Miss Louisa. But, troth, I'm so heated with an argument I had with Sir Simon, that I'm no ways competent— — Did I tell you he was waiting for his tea?'

'No, indeed you did not,' said Miss Bellew, giving vent to a laugh she had been struggling against for the last few minutes; and which I did not at the moment know was caused by her perceiving the priest's air of chagrin and discontent, the evident proofs of his being worsted by the old baronet, whose chief pleasure in life was to worry the father into a discussion, and either confuse or confute him. 'My father seems in such good spirits to-night! Don't you think so?' said she roguishly, looking over at the priest.

'Never saw him better; quite lively and animated, and'—dropping his voice to a whisper—-'as obstinate as ever.'

As we entered the house we found Sir Simon walking leisurely up and down the drawing-room, with his hands behind his back, his face radiant with smiles, and his eye gleaming with conscious triumph towards the corner where the priest stood tumbling over some books to conceal his sense of defeat. In a few minutes after we were seated round the tea-table; the little cloud was dispelled, and a happier party it was difficult to imagine.

CHAPTER XXXVIII
ST. SENAN'S WELL

How shall I trace this, the happiest period of my life, when days and weeks rolled on and left no trace behind, save in that delicious calm that stole over my senses gradually and imperceptibly! Each morning saw me on my way to Castle Bellew. The mountain path that led up from the little strand was well worn by my footsteps; I knew its every turn and winding; scarcely a dog-rose bloomed along the way with which I had not grown familiar. And how each object spoke to my heart! For I was happy. The clouds that moved above, the rippling tide that flowed beneath, the sunny shore, the shady thicket, were all to me as though I had known them from boyhood. For so it is, in our glad moments we cling to all things that surround us; and giving to external Nature the high colouring of our own hearts, we feel how beautiful is this world.

Yet was my mind not all tranquil; for often, as I hastened on, some passing thought would shoot across me. Where is this to end? Can I hope ever to overcome the deep-rooted prejudices of my family, and induce them to receive amongst them as my wife the beautiful and artless daughter of the wild west? Or could I dare to expose her, on whom all my affections were centred, to the callous criticism of my fine lady-mother, and her fashionable friends in London? What right had I to stake Louisa's happiness on such a chance—to take her from all the objects endeared to her by taste, by time, by long-hallowed associations, and place her amid those among whom the very charm of her untarnished nature would have made her their inferior? Is it that trait of rebellious spirit that would seem to leaven every portion of our nature which makes our love strongest when some powerful barrier has been opposed to our hopes and wishes; or is it, rather, that in the difficulties and trials of life we discover those deeper resources of our hearts, that under happier auspices had lain dormant and unknown? I scarcely know; but true it is, after such reflections as these I ever hurried on the faster to meet Louisa, more resolutely bent than ever, in weal or woe, to link my fortune with her own.

Though I returned each night to the priest's cottage, my days were entirely spent at Castle Bellew. How well do I remember every little incident that marked their tranquil course! The small breakfast-parlour, with its old Tudor window looking out upon the flower-garden—how often have I paced it, impatient for her coming; turning ever and anon to the opening door, where the old butler, with the invariable habitude of his kind, continually appeared with some portion of the breakfast equipage! How I started, as some distant door would shut or open, some far-off footstep sound upon the stair, and wonder within myself why she felt not some of this impatient longing! And when at last, tortured with anxiety and disappointment, I had turned away towards the window, the gentle step, the rustling dress, and, more than all, the indescribable something that tells us we are near those we love, bespoke her coming—oh, the transport of that moment! With what a fervid glow of pleasure I sprang to meet her, to touch her hand, to look upon her! How rapidly, too, I endeavoured to speak my few words of greeting, lest her father's coming might interfere with even this short-lived period of happiness; and, after all, how little meaning were in the words themselves, save in the tone I spoke them!

Then followed our rambles through the large but neglected garden, where the rich blossoming fruit-tree scented the air, loaded with all the fragrance of many a wild flower. Now strolling onwards, silent, but full of thought, we trod some dark and shaded alley; now we entered upon some open glade, where a view of the far-off mountains would break upon us, or where some chance vista showed the deep-blue sunny sea swelling with sullen roar against the rocky coast. How often, at such times as these, have I asked myself if I could look for greater happiness than thus to ramble on, turning from the stupendous majesty of Nature to look into her eyes whose glance met mine so full of tender meaning, while words would pass between us, few and low-voiced, but all so thrilling; their very accents spoke of love!

Yet, amid all this, some agonising doubt would shoot across me that my affection was not returned. The very frankness of her nature made me fear; and when we parted at night, and I held my homeward way towards the priest's cottage, I would stop from time to time, conning over every word she spoke, calling to mind each trivial circumstance; and if by accident some passing word of jest" some look of raillery, recurred to my memory, how have the warm tears rushed to my eyes, as with my heart full to bursting I muttered to myself, 'She loves me not!' These fears would then give way to hope, as in my mind's eye she stood before me, all beaming in smiles. And amid these alternate emotions, I trod my lonely path, longing for the morrow when we should meet again, when I vowed within my heart to end my life of doubt by asking if she loved me. But with that morrow came the same spell of happiness that lulled me; and like the gambler who had set his life upon the die, and durst not throw, so did I turn with trembling fear from tempting the chance that might in a moment dispel the bright dream of my existence, and leave life bleak and barren to me for ever.

The month of August was drawing to a close, as we sauntered one fine evening towards the sea-shore. There was a little path which wound round the side of a bold crag, partly by steps, partly by a kind of sloping way, defended at the sides by a rude wooden railing, which led down upon the beach exactly at the spot where a well of clear spring-water sprang up, and tracked its tiny stream into the blue ocean. This little spring, which was always covered by the sea at high-water, was restored, on the tide ebbing, to its former purity, and bubbled away as before; and from this cause it had obtained from the simple peasantry the reputation of being miraculous, and was believed to possess innumerable properties of healing and consoling.

I had often heard of it but never visited it before; and thither we now bent our steps, more intent upon catching the glorious sunset that was glowing on the Atlantic than of testing the virtues of St. Senan's Well, for so was it called. The evening, an autumnal one, was calm and still; not a leaf stirred; the very birds were hushed; and there was all that solemn silence that sometimes threatens the outbreak of a storm. As we descended the crag, however, the deep booming of the sea broke upon us, and between the foliage of the oak-trees we could mark the heavy rolling of the mighty tide, as wave after wave swelled on, and then was dashed in foam and spray upon the shore. There was something peculiarly grand and almost supernatural in the heavy swell of the great sea, rearing its white crest afar and thundering along the weather-beaten rocks, when everything else was calm and unmoved around; the deep and solemn roar, echoing from many a rocky cavern, rose amid the crashing spray that sent up a thin veil of mist, through which the setting sun was reflected in many a bright rainbow. It was indeed a glorious sight, and we stopped for several minutes gazing on it; when suddenly Louisa, letting go my arm, exclaimed, as she pointed downwards—

'See, see the swell beneath that large black rock yonder! The tide is making fast; we must get quickly down if you wish to test St. Senan's power.'

I had no time left me to ask what peculiar virtues the saint dispensed through the mediation of his well, when she broke from my side and hurried down the steep descent. In a moment we had reached the shore, upon which already the tide was fast encroaching, and had marked with its dark stain the yellow sand within a few feet of the well. As we drew nearer, I perceived the figure of an old woman bent with age, who seemed busily occupied sprinkling the water of the spring over something that, as I came closer, seemed like a sailor's jacket. She was repeating some words rapidly to herself; but on hearing our approach, she quickly collected her bundle together under her remnant of a cloak, and sat waiting our approach in silence.

'It's Molly Ban!' said Louisa suddenly, and growing pale as she spoke. 'Give her something, if you have any money, I beseech you.'

There was no opportunity for inquiring further about her now, for the old woman slowly rose from the stone by the aid of a stick, and stood confronting us. Her figure was singularly short, scarce four feet in height; but her head was enormously large, and her features, which were almost terrific in ugliness, were swarthy as a gypsy's. A man's hat was fastened upon her head by a red kerchief which was knotted beneath her chin; a short cloak of faded scarlet, like what the peasantry of the west usually wear, covered her shoulders, beneath which a patched and many-coloured petticoat appeared, that reached to the middle of her legs, which, as well as her feet, were completely naked, giving the old woman a look of wildness and poverty which I cannot attempt to convey. The most singular part of her costume, however, was a rude collar she wore round her neck of seashells, among which, here and there, I could detect some bits of painted and gilded carving, like fragments of a wreck. This strange apparition now stood opposite me, her dark eyes fixed steadily on my companion, to whom, unlike the people of the country, she never made the slightest reverence, or showed any semblance of respect.

'And was it to spy after me, Miss Loo, ye brought down yer sweetheart to the well this evening?' said the hag, in a harsh, grating voice, that seemed the very last effort of some suppressed passion.

Louisa's arm grasped mine, and I could feel it tremble with agitation as she whispered in my ear—

'Give her money quickly; I know her.'

'And is your father going to send me back to jail because the cattle's got the rot amongst them? Ha, ha, ha!' said she, breaking into a wild, discordant laugh. 'There will be more mourning than for that at Castle Bellew before long.'

Louisa leaned against me, faint and almost falling, while drawing out my purse hastily I held forth my hand full of silver. The old hag clutched at it eagerly, and as her dark eyes flashed fire, she thrust the money into a pocket at her side, and again broke out into a horrid laugh.

'So, you're beginnin' to know me, are ye? Ye won't mock Molly Ban now, eh? No, 'faith, nor Mary Lafferty either, that turned me from the door and shut it agin me. Where 'll her pride be to-morrow night, when they bring in her husband a corpse to her? Look at that!'

With these words she threw her cloak on one side, and showed the blue jacket of a fisherman which I had seen her sprinkling with the water as we came up.

'The blue water will be his winding-sheet this night, calm as it is now.'

'Oh, Molly dear, don't speak this way!'

'Molly dear!' echoed the beldame, in an accent of biting derision. 'Who ever heerd one of your name call me that? Or are ye come for a charm for that young man beside you? See, now! the sun's just gone; in a minit more the sea 'll be in, and it'll be too late. Here, come near me! kneel down there! kneel down, I say! or is it only my curse ye mind?'

'She's mad, poor thing,' said I, in my companion's ear. 'Let her have her way; do as she bids you.'

Sinking with terror, pale as death, and trembling all over, Louisa bent one knee upon the little rock beside the well, while the old hag took her fair hand within her own skinny fingers and plunged it rudely in the well.

'There, drink,' said the old woman, offering me the fair palm, through which the clear water was running rapidly, while she chanted rather than spoke the rude rhyme that follows—

'By the setting sun,
The flowing sea,
The waters that run,
I swear to thee
That my faith shall be true, at this moment now,
In weal or in woe, wherever or how:
So help me, Saint Senan, to keep my vow!'

The last words had scarcely been uttered when Louisa, who apparently had been too much overcome by terror to hear one word the hag had muttered, sprang up from the stone, her face and neck covered with a deep blush, her lip trembling with agitation, while her eyes were fixedly directed towards the old woman with an expression of haughty anger.

'Ay, ye may look as proud as ye like. It's little I mind ye, in love or in hate. Ye are well humbled enough now. And as for you,' said she, turning towards me a look of scornful pity—'you, I wish ye joy of your fair sweetheart; let her only keep her troth like her own mother, and ye'll have a happy heart to sit at your fireside with.'

St. Senan's Well.

The blood fled from Louisa's cheek as these words were uttered; a deadly paleness spread over her features; her lips were bloodless and parted; and her hands firmly clenched together and pressed against her side, bespoke the agony of the moment. It lasted not longer; for she fell back fainting and insensible into my arms. I bathed her face and temples from the well; I called upon her, rubbed her hands within my own, and endeavoured by every means to arouse her; but in vain. I turned to beg for aid from the woman, but she was gone. I again endeavoured to awake Louisa from her stupor, but she lay cold, rigid, and motionless; her features had stiffened like a corpse, and showed no touch of life. I shouted aloud for aid; but, alas! we were far from all human habitations, and the wild cries of the curlew were the only sounds that met my ear, or the deep rushing of the sea, as it broke nearer and nearer to where I stood. A sudden pang of horror shot across me as I looked around and below, and saw no chance of aid from any quarter. Already the sun was below the horizon, and the grey twilight gave but gloomy indications all around. The sea, too, was coming fast; the foam had reached us, and even now the salt tide had mingled its water with the little spring. No more time was to be lost. A projecting point of rock intervened between us and the little path by which we had descended to the beach; over this the spray was now splashing, and its base was only to be seen at intervals between the advancing or retiring wave. A low, wailing sound, like distant wind, was creeping over the water, which from time to time was curled along the round-backed wave with all the threatening aspect of a coming storm; the sea-birds wheeled round in circles, waking the echoes with their wild notes, and the heavy swell of the breaking sea roared through many a rocky cavern with a sad and mournful melody. I threw one last look above, where the tall beetling cliff was lost in the gloom of coming night, another on the broad bleak ocean, and then, catching up my companion in my arms, set forward.

For the first few moments I felt not my burden. My beating heart throbbed proudly, and as I pressed her to my bosom, how I nerved myself for any coming danger by the thought that all the world to me lay in my arms! Every step, however, brought me farther out; the sea, which at first washed only to my ankles, now reached my knees; my step became unsteady, and when for an instant I turned one look on her who lay still and insensible within my grasp, I felt my head reel and my sight wander as I again looked out on the dark water that rolled around us. We were now near the rocky point which, once passed, placed us in safely; and to reach this I summoned up every effort. Around this the waves had worn a deeper track, and against its side they heat and lashed themselves to foam, which boiled in broad sheets around. A loud cheer from some one on the cliff above us turned my glance upwards, and I could see lights moving backwards and forwards through the darkness; before I could reply to the voice, however, a large wave came mantling near, gathering force as it approached, and swelling its gigantic mass so as to shut out all besides. I fixed myself firmly to resist the shock, and slightly bending, opposed my shoulder to the mighty roll of water that now towered like a wall above us. On it came, till its dark crest frowned above our heads; for a second or two it seemed to pause, as the white curl tipped its breaking edge, and then, with a roll like thunder, broke over us. For an instant I held my footing; at length, however, my step tottered; I felt myself lifted up, and then hurled headlong beneath the swollen volume of water that closed above my head. Stunned, but not senseless, I grasped my burden closer to my heart, and struggled to regain my footing. The wave passed inwards as I rose to my feet, and a sea of boiling foam hissed around me. Beyond, all was dim and indistinct; a brooding darkness stretched towards the sea, and landward the tall cliffs were wrapped in deep shadow, except when the light that I had seen flitted from place to place, like the dancing wildfire. A loud cheer from on high made me suppose that we were perceived; but my attention was turned away by a low, moaning sound that came floating over the water; and as I looked, I could see that the black surface swelled upwards, as if by some mighty force beneath, and rose towering into the air. The wave that now approached us was much greater than the former one, and came thundering on as if impatient for its prey. My fear was of being carried out to sea, and I looked hastily around for some rocky point to hold on by; but in vain. The very sands beneath me seemed moving and shifting; the voice of thunder was in my ears; my senses reeled, and the thought of death by drowning, with all its agony, came over me.

'Oh, my father! my poor father!' said a low, plaintive voice beside my cheek; and the next instant the blood rushed warm to my heart. My courage rallied; my arm grew nerved and strong; my footsteps seemed to grasp the very ground, and with a bold and daring spirit I waited for the coming shock. On it came, a mighty flood, sweeping high above us as we struggled in the midst. The blue water moved on, unbroken; for a moment or two I felt we were borne along with a whirlwind speed; then suddenly we touched the strand—but only for a second, for the returning wave came thundering back, and carried us along with it. My senses now began to wander; the dark and gloomy sea stretched around us; the stars seemed to flit to and fro; the roar of water and the sounds of human voices were mingled in my ears; my strength, too, was failing me, and I buffeted the waves with scarcely consciousness. Just at that moment, when, all dread of danger past, the gloomy indifference to life was fast succeeding, I saw a bright gleam of light flying rapidly across the water; the shouts of voices reached me also, but the words I heard not. Now falling beneath, now rising above the foamy surface, I struggled on, with only strength to press home closer to my bosom the form of her my heart was filled by, when of a sudden I felt my arm rudely grasped on either side. A rope, too, was thrown around my waist, and I was hurried inwards towards the shore amid cries of 'All safe! all safe! not too fast, there!' A dreary indistinctness of what followed even still haunts my mind. A huge wood-fire upon the beach, the figures of the fishermen, the country-people passing hither and thither, the tumult of voices, and a rude chair in which lay a pale, half-fainting form. The rest I know not.

It was dark—so dark I could not see the persons that moved beside me. As we passed along the grassy turf in silence, I held a soft hand in mine, and a fair cheek rested on my shoulder, while masses of long and dripping hair fell on my neck and bosom. Carried by two stout peasant-fishermen in a chair, Louisa Bellew, faint but conscious of the danger past, was borne homeward. I walked beside her, my heart too full for words. A loud, wild cheer burst suddenly forth, and a bright gleam of light aroused me from my trance of happiness. The steps were crowded with people, the large hall so full we scarce could force our way. The door of the parlour was now thrown open, and there sat the pale, gaunt figure of Sir Simon Bellew—his eyes staring wildly, and his lips parted; his hands resting on each arm of his chair—motionless.

Bursting from those that carried her, Louisa sprang towards her father with a cry; but ere she reached his arms he had fallen from his seat to his knees, and with his hands clasped above his head, and upturned eyes, poured forth a prayer to God. Sinking to his side, she twined her hands with his; and as if moved by the magic of the scene, the crowd fell to their knees, and joined in the thanksgiving. It was a moment of deep and touching feeling to hear the slow, scarce articulate words of that old man, who turned from the sight of her his heart treasured to thank the great Father of Mercy, who had not left him childless in his age—to mark the low sobs of those around, as they strove to stifle them, while tears coursed down the hard and weather-beaten cheeks of humble poverty, as they muttered to themselves their heartfelt thanks for her preservation. There was a pause; the old man turned his eyes upon his child, and, like a dammed-up torrent breaking forth, the warm tears gushed out, and with a cry of 'My own—my only one!' he fell upon her neck and wept.

I could hear no more. Springing to my feet, I dashed through the hall, and resisting every effort to detain me, rushed down the steps and gained the lawn. Once there alone, I sank down upon the sward, and poured forth my heart in tears of happiness.

CHAPTER XXXIX
AN UNLOOKED-FOR MEETING

I made many ineffectual efforts to awake on the morning after my adventure. Fatigue and exhaustion, which seem always heaviest when incurred by danger, had completely worn me out, and scarcely had I succeeded in opening my eyes and muttering some broken words, ere again I dropped off to sleep, soundly, and without a dream. It was late in the afternoon when at length I sat up in my bed and looked about me. A gentle hand suddenly fell upon my shoulder, and a low voice, which I at once recognised as Father Tom's, whispered —

'There now, my dear fellow, lie down again. You must not stir for a couple of hours yet.'

I looked at him fixedly for a moment, and, as I clasped his hand in mine, asked —

'How is she, father?'

Scarcely were these words spoken when I felt a burning blush upon my cheek. It was the confidence of long months that found vent in one second — the pent-up secret of my heart that burst from me unconsciously, and I hid my face upon the pillow, and felt as though I had betrayed her.

'Well — quite well,' said the old man, as he pressed my hand forcibly in his own. 'But let us not speak now. You must take more rest, and then have your arm looked to. I believe you have forgotten all about it.'

'My arm!' repeated I, in some surprise; while, turning down the clothes, I perceived that my right arm was sorely bruised, and swollen to an immense size. 'The rocks have done this,' muttered I. 'And she, father — what of her, for heaven's sake?'

'Be calm, or I must leave you,' said the priest 'I said before that she was well. Poor boy!'

There was something so touching in the tone of the last words that without my knowing why, I felt a kind of creeping fear pass across me, and a dread of some unknown evil steal over me.

'Father,' said I, springing up, and grasping him with both my hands, while the pain of my wounded arm shot through my very heart, 'you are an honest man, and you are a man of God: you would not tell me a lie. Is she well?' The big drop fell from my brow as I spoke.

He clasped his hands fervently together as he replied, in a voice tremulous with agitation, 'I have not told you a lie!' He turned away as he spoke, and I lay down in my bed with a mind relieved, but not at rest.

Alas, how hard it is to be happy! The casualties of this world come on like waves, one succeeding the other. We may escape the heavy roll of the mighty ocean, and be wrecked in the still, smooth waters of the landlocked bay. We dread the storm and the hurricane, and we forget how many have perished within sight of shore. But yet a secret fear is ever present with us when danger hovers near; and this sense of some impending evil it was which now darkened me, and whispered me to be prepared.

I lay for some time sunk in my reflections, and when I looked up, the priest was gone. A letter had fallen on the floor, as if by accident" and I rose to place it on my table, when, to my surprise, I found it addressed to myself. It was marked 'On His Majesty's service,' and ran thus:—

'Dublin Castle.

'Sir,—*I have received his Excellency's orders to inform you that unless you, on receipt of the present letter, at once return to your duty as a member of the staff, your name will be erased from the list, and the vacancy immediately filled up.—I have the honour to be,* etc.,

'Henry Horton.'

What could have caused the great alteration in his Excellency's feelings that this order evinced I could not conceive, and I felt hurt and indignant at the tone of a letter which came on me so completely by surprise. I knew, however, how much my father looked to my strict obedience to every call of duty, and resolved that, come what would, I should at once resume my position on the duke's staff.

These were but momentary reflections. My thoughts recurred at once to where my heart was dwelling—-with her whose very image lived within me. Try how I would, I could think of no pleasure in which she took not part, imagine no scheme of life in which she was not concerned. Ambition had lost its charm; the path of glory I had longed to tread, I felt now as nothing beside that heather walk which led me towards her; and if I were to have chosen between the most brilliant career high station, influence, and fortune could bestow, and the lowly condition of a dweller in these wild mountain solitudes, I felt that not a moment of hesitation or doubt would mark my decision. There was a kind of heroism in the relinquishing all the blandishments of fortune, all the seductions of the brilliant world, for one whose peaceful and humble life strayed not beyond the limits of these rugged mountains; and this had its charm. There were times when I loved to ask myself whether Louisa Bellew would not, even amid all the splendour and display of London life, be as much admired and courted as the most acknowledged of beauty's daughters: now I turned rather to the thought of how far happier and better it was to know that a nature so unhackneyed, a heart so rich in its own emotions, was never to be exposed to the callous collision of society and all the hardened hypocrisy of the world. My own lot, too, how many more chances of happiness did it not present as I looked at the few weeks of the past, and thought of whole years thus gliding away, loving and beloved!

A kind of stir, and the sound of voices beneath my window, broke my musings, and I rose and looked out. It proceeded from the young girl and the country lad who formed the priest's household. They were talking together before the door, and pointing in the direction of the highroad, where a cloud of dust had marked the passage of some carriage—an event rare enough to attract attention in these wild districts.

'And did his reverence say that the Captain was to be kept in bed till he came back?'

'Ah, then, sure, he knew well enough,' said Mary, 'that the young man would be up and off to the castle the moment he was able to walk—ay, and maybe before it too. Troth, Patsey, it's what I'm thinking—there's nobody knows how to coort like a raal gentleman.'

'Och, botheration!' said Patsey, with an offended toss of his head, and a look of half malice.

'Faix, you may look how you like, but it's truth I'm telling ye. They know how to do it. It isn't winking at a body, nor putting their great rough arms round their neck; but it's a quiet, mannerly, dacent way they have, and soothering voice, and a look under their eyes, as much as to say, "Maybe ye wouldn't, now?"'

'Troth, Mary,' said Patsey sharply, 'it strikes me that you know more of their ways than is just convenient—eh, do you understand me now?'

'Well, and if I do,' replied Mary, 'there's no one can be evenin' it to you, for I'm sure it wasn't you taught me!'

'Ye want to provoke me,' said the young man, rising, and evidently more annoyed than he felt disposed to confess; 'but, faix, I'll keep my temper. It's not after spaking to his reverence, and buying a cow and a dresser, that I 'm going to break it off.'

'Heigh-ho!' said Mary, as she adjusted a curl that was most coquettishly half falling across her eyes; 'sure there's many a slip betune the cup and the lip, as the poor dear young gentleman will find out when he wakes.'

A cold fear ran through me as I heard these words, and the presentiment of some mishap, that for a few moments I had been forgetting, now came back in double force. I set about dressing myself in all haste, and, notwithstanding that my wounded arm interfered with me at each instant, succeeded at last in my undertaking. I looked at my watch; it was already six o'clock in the afternoon, and the large mountains were throwing their great shadows over the yellow strand. Collecting from what I had heard from the priest's servants that it was their intention to detain me in the house, I locked my door on leaving the room, and stole noiselessly down the stairs, crossed the little garden, and passing through the beech hedge, soon found myself upon the mountain path. My pace quickened as I breasted the hillside, my eyes firmly fixed upon the tall towers of the old castle, as they stood proudly topping the dense foliage of the oak-trees. Like some mariner who gazes on the long-wished-f or beacon that tells of home and friends, so I bent my steadfast looks to that one object, and conjured up many a picture to myself of the scene that might be at that moment enacting there. Now I imagined the old man seated, silent and motionless, beside the bed where his daughter, overcome with weakness and exhaustion, still slept, her pale face scarce coloured by a pinkish flush that marked the last trace of feverish excitement; now I thought of her as if still seated in her own drawing-room, at the little window that faced seaward, looking perhaps upon the very spot that marked our last night's adventure, and, mayhap, blushing at the memory.

As I came near the park I turned from the regular approach to a small path, which, opening by a wicket, led to a little flower-garden beside the drawing-room. I had not walked many paces when the sound of some one sobbing caught my ear. I stopped to listen, and could distinctly hear the low broken voice of grief quite near me. My mind was in that excited state when every breeze that rustled, every leaf that stirred, thrilled through my heart;

the same dread of something, I knew not what, that agitated me as I awoke came fresh upon me, and a cold tremor crept over me. The next moment I sprang forward, and as I turned the angle of the walk beheld—with what relief of heart!—that the cries proceeded from a little child, who, seated in the grass, was weeping bitterly. It was a boy of scarce five years old that Louisa used to employ about the garden—rather to amuse the little fellow, to whom she had taken a liking, than for the sake of services which at the best were scarcely harmless.

'Well, Billy,' said I, 'what has happened to you, my boy? Have you fallen and hurt yourself?'

'Na,' was the only reply; and sinking his head between his knees, he sobbed more bitterly than ever.

'Has Miss Loo been angry with you, then?'

'Na, na,' was the only answer, as he poured forth a flood of tears.

'Come, come, my little man, what is it? Tell me, and perhaps we can set it all to rights.'

'Gone! gone away for ever!' cried the child, as a burst of pent-up agony broke from him; and he cried as though his very heart would break.

Again the terrible foreboding crossed my mind, and without waiting to ask another question I rushed forward, cleared the little fence of the flower-garden at a spring and stood within a few yards of the window. It lay open as usual; the large china vase of moss-roses that she had plucked the evening before stood on the little table beside it. I stopped for an instant to breathe; the beating of my heart was so painful that I pressed my hand upon my side. At that instant I had given my life to have heard Louisa's voice; but for one single word I had bartered my heart's blood. But all was as hushed and still as midnight. I thought I did hear something like a sigh; yes, and now I could distinctly hear the rustling sound of some one as if turning in a chair. Sir Simon Bellew, for some cause, or other, I knew never came into that room. I listened again: yes, and now too I could see the shadow of a figure on the floor. I sprang forward to the window and cried out, 'Louisa!' The next instant I was in the room, and my eyes fell upon the figure of—Ulick Burke! Seated in a deep arm-chair, his leg resting on a low stool, he was reclining at half-length, his face pale as death, and his very lips blanched; but there rested on the mouth the same curl of insolent mockery that marked it when first we met.

'Disappointed, I fear, sir,' said he, in a tone which, however weakened by sickness, had lost nothing of its sneering bitterness.

'I confess, sir,' said I confusedly, 'that this is a pleasure I had not anticipated.'

'Nor I either, sir,' replied he, with a dark frown. 'Had I been able to ring the bell before, the letter that lies there should have been sent to you, and might have spared both of us this "pleasure," as you are good enough to call it.'

'A letter for me?' said I eagerly; then half ashamed at my own emotion, and not indifferent to the sickly and apparently dying form before me, I hesitated, and added, 'I trust that you are recovering from the effects of your wound.'

A warm reception!

'Damn the wound, sir; don't speak to me about it! You never came here for that, I suppose? Take your letter, sir!' A purple flush here coloured his features, as though some pang of agonising pain had shot through him, and his livid lip quivered with passion. 'Take your letter, sir!' and he threw it towards me as he spoke.

I stood amazed and thunderstruck at this sudden outbreak of anger, and for a second or two could not recover myself to speak. 'You mistake me,' said I.

'Mistake you? No, confound me! I don't mistake you; I know you well and thoroughly! But you mistake me, ay, and damnably too, if you suppose that because I 'm crippled here this insolence shall pass unpunished! Who but a coward, sir, would come thus to taunt a man like me? Yes, sir, a coward! I spoke it—I said it! Would you like to hear it over again? Or if you don't like it, the remedy is near you—nearer than you think. There are two pistols in that case, both loaded with ball; take your choice, and your own distance; and here, where we are, let us finish this quarrel! For, mark me!' and here his brow darkened, till the veins, swelled and knotted in his forehead, looked like indigo—'mark me, the account shall be closed one day or other!'

I saw at once that he had lashed his fury up to an ungovernable pitch, and that to speak to him was only to increase his passion; so I stooped down without saying a word, and took up the letter that lay at my feet.

'I am waiting your reply, sir,' said he, with a low voice, subdued by an inward effort into a seeming quietness of tone.

'You cannot imagine,' said I mildly, 'that I could accept of such a challenge as this, nor fight with a man who cannot leave his chair?'

'And who has made me so, sir? Who has made me a paralytic thing for life? But if that be all, give me your arm, and help me through that window; place me against that yew-tree, yonder. I can stand well enough. You won't?—you refuse me this? Oh, coward! coward! You grow pale and red again! Let your white lip mutter, and your nails eat into your hands with passion! Your heart is craven, and you know it!'

Shall I dare to own it? For an instant or two my resolution tottered, and involuntarily my eyes turned to the pistol-case upon the table beside me. He caught the look, and in a tone of triumphant exultation cried out—

'Bravo, bravo! What! you hesitate again? Oh, that this should not be before the world—in some open and public place—that men should not look on and see us here!'

'I leave you, sir,' said I sternly—'thankful, for *your* sake at least, that this is not before the world.'

'Stop, sir! stop!' cried he, hoarse with rage. 'Ring that bell!' I hesitated, and he called out again, 'Ring that bell, sir!'

I approached the chimney, and did as he desired. The butler immediately made his appearance.

'Nicholas,' cried the sick man, 'bring in the servants—bring them in here; you hear me well. I want to show them something they have never seen. Go!'

The man disappeared at once, and as I met the scowling look of hate that fixed its glare upon me, once more I felt myself to waver. The struggle was but momentary. I sprang to the window, and leaped into the garden. A loud curse broke from Burke as I did so; a cry of disappointed wrath, like the yell of a famished wolf, followed. The next moment I was beyond the reach of his insolence and his invective.

The passionate excitement of the moment over, my first determination was to gain the approach, and return to the house by the hall door; my next, to break the seal of the letter which I held in my hand, and see if its contents might not throw some light upon the events which somehow I felt were thickening around me, but of whose nature and import I knew nothing.

The address was written in a stiff, old-fashioned hand; but the large seal bore the arms of the Bellew family, and left no doubt upon my mind that it had come from Sir Simon. I opened it with a trembling and throbbing heart, and read as follows:—

'My dear Sir,—The event of last night has called back upon a failing and broken memory the darkest hour of a long and blighted life, and made the old man, whose steadfast gaze looked onward to the tomb, turn once backward to behold the deepest affliction of his days—misfortune, crime, remorse. I cannot even now, while already the very shadow of death is on me, recount the sad story I allude to; enough for the object I have in view if I say, that, where I once owed the life of one I held dearest in the world, the hand that saved lived to steal, and the voice that blessed me was perjured and forsworn. Since that hour I have never received a service of a fellow-mortal, until the hour when you rescued my child. And oh! loving her as I do, wrapped up as my soul is in her image, I could have borne better to see her cold and dripping corpse laid down beside me than to behold her, as I have done, in your arms. You must never meet more. The dreadful anticipation of long-suffering years is creeping stronger and stronger upon me; and I feel in my inmost heart that I am reserved for another and a last bereavement ere I die.

'We shall have left before this letter reaches you. You may perhaps hear the place of our refuge, for such it is; but I trust that to your feelings as a gentleman and a man of honour I can appeal, in the certain confidence that you will not abuse my faith—you will not follow us.

'I know not what I have written, nor dare I read it again. Already my tears have dimmed my eyes, and are falling on the paper; so let me bid you farewell—an eternal farewell. My nephew has arrived here. I have not seen him, nor shall I; but he will forward this letter to you after our departure.—Yours, S. Bellew.'

The first stunning feeling past, I looked round me to see if it were not some horrid dream, and the whole events but the frightful deception of a sleeping fancy. But bit by bit the entire truth broke upon me; the full tide of sorrow rushed in upon my heart. The letter I could not comprehend further than that some deep affliction had been recalled by my late adventure. But then, the words of the hag—the brief, half-uttered intimations of the priest—came to my memory. 'Her mother,' said I—'what of her mother?' I remembered Louisa had never mentioned or even alluded to her; and now a thousand suspicions crossed my mind, which all gave way before my own sense of bereavement and the desolation and desertion I felt, in my own heart. I threw myself upon the ground where she walked so often beside me, and burst into tears. But a few brief hours, and how surrounded by visions of happiness and lovet Now, bereft of everything, what charm had life for me! How valueless, how worthless did all seem! The evening sun I loved to gaze on, the bright flowers, the waving grass, the low murmur of the breaking surf that stole like music over the happy sense, were now but gloomy things or discordant sounds. The very high and holy thoughts that used to stir within me were changed to fierce and wrathful passions or the low drooping of despair. It was night, still and starry night, when I arose and wended my way towards the priest's cottage.

CHAPTER XL
THE PRIEST'S KITCHEN

The candles were burning brightly, and the cheerful bog-fire was blazing on the hearth, as I drew near the window of the priest's cottage; but yet there was no one in the room. The little tea-kettle was hissing on the hob, and the room had all that careful look of watchful attention bestowed upon it that showed, the zeal of his little household.

Uncertain how I should meet him, how far explain the affliction that had fallen on me, I walked for some time up and down before the door; at length I wandered to the back of the house, and passing the little stable, I remarked that the pony was absent. The priest had not returned perhaps since morning; perhaps he had gone some distance off—in all likelihood accompanied the Bellews; again the few words he had spoken that morning recurred to me, and I pondered in silence over their meaning. As I thus mused, a strong flood of mellow light attracted me as it fell in a broad stream across the little paved court, and I now saw that it came from the kitchen. I drew near the window in silence, and looked in. Before the large turf-fire were seated three persons; two of them, who sat in the shining light, I at once recognised as the servants; but the third was concealed in the shadow of the chimney, and I could only trace the outline of his figure against the blaze. I was not long, however, in doubt as to his identity.

'Seemingly, then, you're a great traveller,' said Patsey, the priest's man, addressing the unknown.

A long whiff of smoke, patiently emitted, and a polite wave of the hand in assent was the reply.

'And how far did you come to-day, av I might be so bould?' said Mary.

'From the cross of Kiltermon, beyond Gurtmore, my darlin'; and sure it is a real pleasure and a delight to come so far to see as pretty a crayture as yourself.' Here Patsey looked a little put out, and Mary gave a half smile of encouragement. 'For,' continued the other, breaking into a song—

'Though I love a fox in a cover to find,
When the clouds is low, with a sou'west wind,

> *Faix, a pretty girl is more to my mind*
> *Than the tally-high-ho of a morning.'*

I need scarcely say that the finale of this rude verse was given in a way that only Tipperary Joe could accomplish, as he continued—

> *'And just show me one with an instep high,*
> *A saucy look, and a roguish eye,*
> *Who 'd smile ten times for once she 'd sigh,*
> *And I'm her slave till morning.'*

'And that's yoursel', devil a less—ye ho, ye ho, tally-ho! I hope the family isn't in bed?'

'Troth, seemingly,' said Patsey, in a tone of evident pique, 'it would distress you little av they were; you seem mighty well accustomed to making yourself at home.'

'And why wouldn't the young man?' said Mary, apparently well pleased to encourage a little jealousy on the part of her lover, 'and no harm neither. And ye do be always with the hounds, sir?'

'Yes, miss, that's what I be doing. But I wonder what's keeping the Captain; I've a letter here for him that I know ought to have no delay. I run all the way for fourteen miles over Mey'nacurraghew mountain to be here quick with him.'

I opened the door as I heard this, and entered the kitchen.

'Hurroo! by the mortial,' cried Joe, with one of his wild shouts, 'it 's himself! Arrah, darlin', how is every bit in your skin?'

'Well, Joe, my poor fellow, I am delighted to see you safe and sound once more. Many a day have I reproached myself for the way you suffered for my sake, and for the manner I left you.'

'There's only one thing you have any rayson to grieve over,' said the poor fellow, as the tears started to his eyes, and rolled in heavy drops down his cheeks, 'and here it is.'

As he spoke, he drew from his bosom a little green-silk purse, half filled with gold.

'Ah, Captain, jewel, why wouldn't you let a poor fellow taste happiness his own way? Is it because I had no shoes on me that I hadn't any pride in my heart? And is it because I wasn't rich that you wouldn't let me be a friend to you, just to myself alone? Oh, little as we know of grand people and their ways, troth, they don't see our hearts half as plain. See, now I 'd rather you 'd have come up to the bed that morning and left me your curse—ay, devil a less—than that purse of money; and it wouldn't do me as much harm.'

He dropped his head as he spoke, and his arms fell listlessly to his side, while he stood mute and sorrow-struck before me.

'Come, Joe,' said I, holding out my hand to him—'come, Joe, forgive me. If I didn't know better, remember we were only new acquaintance at that time: from this hour we are more.'

The words seemed to act like a spell upon him; he stood proudly up, and his eyes flashed with their wildest glare, while, seizing my hand, he pressed it to his lips, and called out—

'While there's a drop in my heart, darlin'——'

'You have a letter for me,' said I, glad to turn the channel of both our thoughts. 'Where did you get it?'

'At the Curragh, sir, no less. I was standing beside the staff, among all the grand generals and the quality, near the Lord Liftinint, and I heard one of the officers say, "If I knew where to write to him, I'd certainly do so; but he has never written to any of us since his duel." "Ah," said another, "Binton's an odd fellow that way." The minit I heard the name, I up and said to him, "Write the letter, and I'll bring it, and bring you an answer besides, av ye want it."

'"And who the devil are you?" said he.

'"Troth," said I, "there's more on this race knows me nor yourself, fine as ye are." And they all began laughing at this, for the officer grew mighty red in the face, and was angry; and what he was going to say it's hard to tell, for just then Lord Clonmel called out—

'"Sure, it's Tipperary Joe himself; begad, every one knows him. Here, Joe, I owe you half-a-crown since last meeting at the lough."

'"Faix, you do," says I, "and ten shillings to the back of it for Lanty Cassan's mare that I hired to bring you home when you staked the horse; you never paid it since." And then there was another laugh; but the end of all was, he writ a bit of a note where he was on horseback, with a pencil, and here it is.'

So saying, he produced a small crumpled piece of paper, in which I could with some difficulty trace the following lines:—

'Dear Jack,—If the fool who bears this ever arrives with it, come back at once. Your friends in England have been worrying the duke to command your return to duty; and there are stories afloat about your western doings that your presence here can alone contradict.—Yours, J. Horton.'

It needed not a second for me to make up my mind as to my future course, and I said—

'How can I reach Limerick the shortest way?' 'I know a short cut,' said Joe, 'and if we could get a pony I'd bring you over the mountain before to-morrow evening.'

'And you,' said I—'how are you to go?' 'On my feet, to be sure; how else would I go?' Despatching Joe, in company with Patsey, in search of a pony to carry me over the mountain, I walked into the little parlour which I was now about to take my leave of for ever.

It was only then when I threw myself upon a seat, alone and in solitude, that I felt the full force of all my sorrow—the blight that had fallen on my dearest hopes, and the blank, bleak prospect of life before me. Sir Simon Bellew's letter I read over once more; but now the mystery it contained had lost all interest for me, and I had only thoughts for my own affliction. Suddenly, a deep burning spot glowed on my cheek as I remembered my interview with Ulick Burke, and I sprang to my legs, and for a second or two felt undecided whether I would not give him the opportunity he so longed for. It was but a second, and my better reason came back, and I blushed even deeper with shame than I had done with passion.

Calming myself with a mighty effort, I endeavoured to pen a few lines to my worthy and kind friend, Father Loftus. I dared not tell him the real cause of my departure, though indeed I guessed from his absence that he had accompanied the Bellews, and but simply spoke of my return to duty as imperative, and my regret that after such proofs of his friendship I could not shake his hand at parting. The continued flurry of my feelings doubtless made this a very confused and inexplicit document; but I could do no better. In fact, the conviction I had long been labouring under, but never could thoroughly appreciate, broke on me at the moment. It was this: the sudden vicissitudes of everyday life in Ireland are sadly unsuited to our English natures and habits of thought and action. These changes from grave to gay, these outbreaks of high-souled enthusiasm followed by dark, reflective traits of brooding thought, these noble impulses of good, these events of more than tragic horror, demand a changeful, even a forgetful temperament to bear them; and while the Irishman rises or falls with every emergency of his fate, with us impressions are eating deeper and deeper into our hearts, and we become sad and thoughtful, and prematurely old. Thus at least did I feel, and it seemed to me as though very many years had passed over me since I left my father's house.

The tramp of feet and the sounds of speaking and laughter outside interrupted my musings, and I heard my friend Joe carolling at the top of his voice—

> 'Sir Pat bestrode a high-bred steed,
> And the huntsman one that was broken-kneed,
> And Father Fitz had a wiry weed
> With his tally-high-ho in the morning.'

"Faith, and you're a great beast entirely; and one might dance a jig on your back, and leave room for the piper besides.'

I opened the window, and in the bright moonlight beheld the party leading up a short, rugged-looking pony, whose breadth of beam and square proportions fully justified all Joe's encomiums.

'Have you bought this pony for me, Joe?' cried I. 'No, sir, only borrowed him. He'll take you up to Wheley's mills, where we'll get Andy's mare to-morrow morning.'

'Borrowed him?' 'Yes.'

'Where 's his owner?'

'He 's in bed, where he ought to be. I tould him through the door who it was for, and that he needn't get up, as I 'd find the ways of the place myself; and ye see so I did.'

'Told him who it was for! Why, he never heard of me in his life.'

'Devil may care; sure you're the priest's friend, and who has a better warrant for everything in the place? Don't you know the song—

> "And Father Fitz had no cows nor sheep,
> And the devil a hen or pig to keep;
> But a pleasanter house to dine or sleep
> You 'd never find till morning."

> "For Molly, says he, if the fowls be few,
> I 've only one counsel to give to you:
> There's hens hard by—go kill for two,
> For I 've a friend till morning."

By the Rock of Cashel, it 'ud be a hard case av the priest was to want. Look how the ould saddle fits him! faix, ye 'd think he was made for it!'

I am not quite sure that I felt all Joe's enthusiasm for the beast's perfections; nor did the old yeomanry 'demi-pique,' with its brass mountings and holsters, increase my admiration. Too happy, however, to leave a spot where all my recollections were now turned to gloom and despondence, I packed my few traps, and was soon ready for the road.

It was not without a gulping feeling in my throat, and a kind of suffocating oppression at my heart, that I turned from the little room where in happier times I had spent so many pleasant hours, and bidding a last good-bye to the priest's household, told them to say to Father Tom how sad I felt at leaving before he returned. This done, I mounted the little pony, and escorted by Joe, who held the bridle, descended the hill, and soon found myself by the little rivulet that murmured along the steep glen through which our path was lying.

CHAPTER XLI
TIPPERARY JOE

I have already passingly alluded to Joe's conversational powers; and certainly they were exercised on this occasion with a more than common ability. Either taking my silence as a suggestion for him to speak, or perhaps, and more probably, perceiving that some deep depression was over me, the kind-hearted fellow poured forth his stores of song and legend without ceasing. Now amusing me by his wild and fitful snatches of old ballads, now narrating in his simple but touching eloquence some bygone story of thrilling interest, the long hours of the night passed over, and at daybreak we found ourselves descending the mountain towards a large and cultivated valley, in which I could faintly distinguish in the misty distance the little mill where our relay was to be found.

I stopped for a few minutes to gaze upon the scene before me. It was one of those peaceful landscapes of rural beauty which beam more of soothing influence upon the sorrow-struck heart than the softest voice of consolation. Unlike the works of man, they speak directly to our souls while they appeal to our reason; and the truth comes forced upon us, that we alone must not repine. A broad and richly cultivated valley was bounded by mountains whose sides were clothed with deep wood; a stream, whose wayward course watered every portion of the plain, was seen now flowing among the grassy meadows, now peeping from the alders that lined the banks. The heavy mist of morning was rolling lazily up the mountain-side; and beneath its grey mantle the rich green of pasture and meadow land was breaking forth, dotted with cattle and sheep. As I looked, Joe knelt down and placed his ear upon the ground, and seemed for some minutes absorbed in listening. Then suddenly springing up, he cried out—

'The mill isn't going to-day! I wonder what's the matter. I hope Andy isn't sick.'

A shade of sorrow came over his wild features as he muttered between his teeth the verse of some old song, of which I could but catch the last two lines—

> 'And when friends are crying around the dying,
> Who wouldn't wish he had lived alone!'

'Ay,' cried he aloud, as his eye glistened with an unnatural lustre, 'better be poor Tipperary Joe, without house or home, father or mother, sister or friend, and when the time comes, run to earth, without a wet eye after him.'

'Come, come, Joe, you have many a friend! and when you count them over, don't forget me in the reckoning.'

'Whisht, whisht!' he whispered in a low voice, as if fearful of being overheard, 'don't say that; them's dangerous words.'

I turned towards him with astonishment, and perceived that his whole countenance had undergone a striking change. The gay and laughing look was gone; the bright colour had left his cheek, and a cold, ghastly paleness was spread over his features; and as he cast a hurried and stealthy look around him, I could mark that some secret fear was working within him.

'What is it, Joe?' said I; 'what's the matter? Are you ill?'

'No,' said he, in a tone scarce audible—'no, but you frightened me just now when you called me your friend.'

'How could that frighten you, my poor fellow?'

'I'll tell you. That's what they called my father; they said he was friendly with the gentlemen, and sign's on it.' He paused, and his eye became rooted to the ground as if on some object there from which he could not turn his gaze. 'Yes, I mind it well; we were sitting by the fire in the guard-room all alone by ourselves—the troops was away, I don't know where—when we heard the tramp of men marching, but not regular, but coming as if they didn't care how, and horses and carts rattling and rumbling among them.

'"Thim's the boys," says my father. "Give me that ould cockade there, till I stick it in my cap; and reach me over the fiddle, till I rise a tune for them."

'I mind little more till we was marching at the head of them through the town, down towards the new college that was building—it's Maynooth, I'm speaking about—and then we turned to the left, my father scraping away all the time every tune he thought they'd like; and if now and then by mistake he'd play anything that did not plaze them, they'd damn and blast him with the dreadfullest curses, and stick a pike into him, till the blood would come running down his back; and then my father would cry out—

'"I'll tell my friends on you for this—divil a lie in it, but I will"

'At last we came to the duke's wall, and then my father sat down on the roadside, and cried out that he wouldn't go a step farther, for I was crying away with sore feet at the pace we were going, and asking every moment to be let sit down to rest myself.

'"Look at the child," said he, "his feet's all bleeding."

'"Ye have only a little farther to go," says one of them that had crossed belts on and a green sash about him.

'"The divil resave another step," says my father.

'"Tell Billy to play us 'The Parmer's Daughter' before he goes," says one in the crowd.

'"I 'd rather hear 'The Little Bowld Fox,'" says another.

'"No, no, 'Baltiorum! Baltiorum!'" says many more behind.

'"Ye shall have them all," says my father, "and that'll plaze ye."

'And so he set to, and played the three tunes as beautiful as ever ye heard; and when he was done, the man with the belts ups and says to him—

'"Ye're a fine hand, Billy, and it's a pity to lose you, and your friends will be sorry for you," and he said this with a grin; "but take the spade there and dig a hole, for we must be jogging, it's nigh day."

'Well, my father, though he was tired enough, took the spade, and began digging as they told him; for he thought to himself, "The boys is going to hide the pikes and the carbines before they go home." Well, when he worked half an hour, he threw off his coat, and set to again; and at last he grew tired and sat down on the side of the big hole, and called out—

'"Isn't it big enough now, boys?"

'"No," says the captain, "nor half."

'So my father set to once more, and worked away with all his might; and they all stood by, talking and laughing with one another.

'"Will it do now?" says my father; "for sure enough I'm clean beat."

'"Maybe it might," says one of them; "lie down, and see if it's the length."

'"Well, is it that it's for?" says my father; "faix, I never guessed it was a grave." And so he took off his cap and lay down his full length in the hole.

'"That's all right," says the others, and began with spades and shovels to cover him up. At first he laughed away as hearty as the rest; but when the mould grew heavy on him he began to screech out to let him up; and then his voice grew weaker and fainter, and they waited a little; then they worked harder, and then came a groan, and all was still; and they patted the sods over him and heaped them up. And then they took me and put me in the middle of them, and one called out, "March!" I thought I saw the green sod moving on the top of the grave as we walked away, and heard a voice half choking calling out, "There, boys, there!" and then a laugh. But sure I often hear the same still, when there's nobody near me, and I do be looking on the ground by myself.'

'Great God!' cried I, 'is this true?'

'True as you 're there,' replied he. 'I was ten years of age when it happened, and I never knew how time went since, nor how long it is ago; only it was in the year of the great troubles here, when the soldiers and the country-people never could be cruel enough to one another; and whatever one did to-day, the others would try to beat it out to-morrow. But it's truth every word of it; and the place is called "Billy the fool's grave" to this hour. I go there once a year to see it myself.'

This frightful story—told, too, with all the simple power of truth—thrilled through me with horror long after the impression seemed to have faded away from him who told it; and though he still continued to speak on, I heard nothing; nor did I mark our progress, until I found myself beside the little stream which conducted to the mill.

CHAPTER XLII
THE HIGHROAD

Joe was right; the mill was not at work, for 'Andy' had been summoned to Ennis, where the assizes were then going forward. The mare which had formed part of our calculations was also absent; and we sat down in the little porch to hold a council of war as to our future proceedings. After canvassing the question for some time, Joe left me for a few minutes, and returned with the information that the highroad to Ennis lay only a couple of miles distant, and that a stage-coach would pass there in about two hours, by which I could reach the town that evening. It was therefore decided that he should return with the pony to Murranakilty; while I, having procured a gossoon to carry my baggage, made the best of my way towards the Ennis road.

Joe soon found me an urchin to succeed him as my guide and companion; and with an affectionate leave-taking, and a faithful promise to meet me sometime and somewhere, we parted.

So long as I had journeyed along beside my poor, half-witted follower, the strange and fickle features of his wandering intellect had somehow interrupted the channels of my own feelings, and left me no room for reflection on my changed fortunes. Now, however, my thoughts returned to the past with all the force of some dammed-up current, and my blighted hopes threw a dark and sombre shadow over all my features. What cared I what became of me? Why did I hasten hither and thither? These were my first reflections. If life had lost its charm, so had misfortune lost its terror. There seemed something frivolous and contemptible in the return to those duties which in all the buoyant exhilaration of my former life had ever seemed unfitting and unmanly. No! rather let me seek for some employment on active service. The soldier's career I once longed for, to taste its glorious enthusiasm—that I wished for now, to enjoy its ceaseless movement and exertion.

As I thought over all I had seen and gone through since my arrival in Ireland—its varied scenes of mirth and woe; its reckless pleasures, its wilder despair—I believed that I had acquired a far deeper insight into my own heart in proportion as I looked more into those of others. A not unfrequent error this. The outstretched page of human nature that I had been gazing on had shown me the passions and feelings of other men laid bare before me, while my own heart was dark, enshrined, and unvisited within me. I believed that life had no longer anything to tie me to it—and I was not then twenty! Had I counted double as many years, I had had more reason for the belief, and more difficulty to think so.

Sometimes I endeavoured to console myself by thinking of all the obstacles that under the happiest circumstances must have opposed themselves to my union with Louisa Bellew. My mother's pride alone seemed an insurmountable one. But then I thought of what a noble part had lain before me, to prefer the object of my love—the prize of my own winning—to all the caresses of fortune, all the seductions of the world. Sir Simon Bellew, too—what could he mean? The secret he alluded to, what was it? Alas! what mattered it? My doom was sealed, my fate decided; I had no care how.

Such were my thoughts as I journeyed along the path that conducted towards the highroad; while my little guide—barelegged and barefooted, trotted on merrily before me—who, with none of this world's goods, had no room in his heart for sorrow or repining.

We at last reached the road, which, dusty and deserted, skirted the side of a bleak mountain for miles—not a house to be seen; not a traveller, nor scarce a wheel-track, to mark the course of any one having passed there. I had not followed it for more than half an hour when I heard the tramp of horses and the roll which announced the approach of an equipage. A vast cloud of dust, through which a pair of leaders were alone visible, appeared at a distance. I seated myself at the roadside to await its coming, my little gossoon beside me, evidently not sorry to have reached a resting-place; and once more my thoughts returned to their well-worn channel, and my head sank on my bosom. I forgot where I was, when suddenly the prancing of a pair of horses close to me aroused me from my stupor, and a postillion called out to me in no very subdued accent—

'Will ye hook on that trace there, avick, av ye 're not asleep?'

Whether it was my look of astonishment at the tone and the nature of the request, or delay in acceding to it, I know not; but a hearty curse from the fellow on the wheelers perfectly awakened me, and I replied by something not exactly calculated to appease the heat of the discussion.

'Begorra,' said he of the leaders, 'it's always the way with your shabby genteels!' and he swung himself down from the saddle to perform the required service himself.

During this operation I took the opportunity of looking at the carriage, which was a large and handsome barouche, surrounded by all the appurtenances of travel—cap-cases, imperials, etc.; a fat-looking, lazy footman was nodding sleepily on the box, and a well-tanned lady's-maid was reading a novel in the rumble. Within I saw the figure of a lady, whose magnificent style of dress but little accorded with the unfrequented road she was traversing and the wild inhabitants so thinly scattered through it. As I looked, she turned round suddenly; and, before I could recognise her, she called out my name. The voice in an instant reassured me: it was Mrs. Paul Rooney herself!

'Stop!' cried she, with a wave of her jewelled hand. 'Michael, get down. Only think of meeting you here, Captain!'

I stammered out some explanation about a cross-cut over the mountain to catch the stage, and my desire to reach Ennis; while the unhappy termination of our intimacy, and my mother's impertinent letter kept ever uppermost in my mind, and made me confused and uneasy. Mrs. Paul, however, had evidently no participation in such feelings, but welcomed me with her wonted cordiality, and shook my hand with a warmth that proved, if she had not forgotten, she had certainly forgiven, the whole affair.

'And so you are going to Ennis!' said she, as I assumed the place beside her in the barouche, while Michael was busily engaged in fastening on my luggage behind—the two movements seeming to be as naturally performed as though the amiable lady had been in the habit of taking up walking gentlemen with a portmanteau every day of her life. 'Well, how fortunate! I'm going there too. Pole [so she now designated her excellent spouse, it being the English for Paul] has some little business with the chief-justice— two murder cases, and a forcible abduction—and I promised to take him up on my return from Milltown, where I have been spending a few weeks. After that we return to our little place near Bray, where I hope you 'll come and spend a few weeks with us.'

'This great pleasure I fear I must deny myself,' said I, 'for I have already outstayed my leave, and have unfortunately somehow incurred the displeasure of his Excellency; and unless'—here I dropped my voice, and stole a half-timid look at the lady under my eyelashes—'some one with influence over his grace shall interfere on my behalf, I begin to fear lest I may find myself in a sad scrape.'

Mrs. Paul blushing, turned away her head; and while pressing my hand softly in her own, she murmured—

'Don't fret about it; it won't signify.'

I could scarce repress a smile at the success of my bit of flattery, for as such alone I intended it, when she turned towards me, and, as if desirous to change the topic, said—

'Well, we heard of all your doings—your steeplechase and your duel and your wound, and all that; but what became of you afterwards?'

'Oh,' said I hesitatingly, 'I was fortunate enough to make a most agreeable acquaintance, and with him I have been spending a few weeks on the coast—Father Tom Loftus.'

'Father Tom!' said Mrs. Rooney with a laugh—'the pleasantest crayture in Ireland! There isn't the like of him. Did he sing you the "Priest's Supper?"' The lady blushed as she said these words, as if carried away by a momentary excitement to speak of matters not exactly suitable; and then drawing herself up, she continued in a more measured tone: 'You know, Captain, one meets such strange people in this world.'

'To be sure, Mrs. Rooney,' said I encouragingly; 'and to one like yourself, who can appreciate character, Father Loftus is indeed a gem.'

Mrs. Rooney, however, only smiled her assent, and again changed the course of the conversation.

'You met the Bellews, I suppose, when down in the west?'

'Yes,' stammered I; 'I saw a good deal of Sir Simon when in that country.'

'Ah, the poor man!' said she with real feeling, 'what an unhappy lot his has been!'

Supposing that she alluded to his embarrassment as to fortune, the difficulties which pressed upon him from money causes, I merely muttered my assent.

'But I suppose,' continued she, 'you have heard the whole story, though the unhappy event occurred when you were a mere child.'

'I am not aware to what you allude,' said I eagerly, while a suspicion shot across my mind that the secret of Sir Simon Bellow's letter was at length to be cleared up.

'Ah,' said Mrs. Rooney with a sigh, 'I mean poor dear Lady Bellow's affair—when she went away with a major of dragoons; and to be sure an elegant young man he was, they said. Pole was on the inquest, and I heard him say he was the handsomest man he ever saw in his life.'

'He died suddenly, then?'

'He was shot by Sir Simon in a duel the very day-week after the elopement.'

'And she?' said I.

'Poor thing! she died of a consumption, or some say a broken heart, the same summer.'

'That is a sad story, indeed,' said I musingly; 'and I no longer wonder that the poor old man should be such as he is.'

'No, indeed; but then he was very much blamed after all, for he never had that Jerningham out of the house.'

'Horace Jerningham!' cried I, as a cold sickening fear crept over me.

'Oh, yes, that was his name. He was the Honourable Horace Jerningham, the younger son of some very high family in England; and, indeed, the elder brother has died since, and they say the title has become extinct.'

It is needless for me to attempt any description of the feelings that agitated my heart, when I say that Horace Jerningham was the brother of my own mother. I remembered when a child to have heard something of a dreadful duel, when all the family went into deep mourning, and my mother's health suffered so severely that her life was at one time feared for; but that fate should have ever thrown me into intimacy with those upon whom this grievous injury was inflicted, and by whom death and mourning were brought upon my house, was a sad and overwhelming affliction that rendered me stunned and speechless. How came it then, thought I, that my mother never recognised the name of her brother's antagonist when speaking of Miss Bellew in her letter to me? Before I had time to revolve this doubt in my mind Mrs. Rooney had explained it.

'And this was the beginning of all his misfortunes. The friends of the poor young man were people of great influence, and set every engine to work to ruin Sir Simon, or, as he then was, Mr. Simon Barrington. At last they got him outlawed; and it was only the very year he came to the title and estates of his uncle that the outlawry was taken off, and he was once more enabled to return to Ireland. However, they had their revenge if they wished for it; for what between recklessness and bad company, he took to gambling when abroad, contracted immense debts, and came into his fortune little better than a beggar. Since then the world has seen little of him, and indeed he owes it but little favour. Under Pole's management the property is now rapidly improving; but the old man cares little for this, and all I believe he wishes for is to have health enough to go over to the Continent and place his daughter in a convent before he dies.'

Little did she guess how every word sank deep into my heart. Every sentence of the past was throwing its shadow over all my future, and the utter wreck of my hopes seemed now inevitable.

While thus I sat brooding over my gloomiest thoughts, Mrs. Rooney, evidently affected by the subject, maintained a perfect silence. At last, however, she seemed to have summed up the whole case in her mind, as turning to me confidentially, with her hand pressed upon my arm, she added in a true moralising cadence, very different from that she had employed when her feelings were really engaged—

'And that's what always comes of it when a gallant, gay Lutherian gets admission into a family.'

Shall I confess, that, notwithstanding the deep sorrow of my heart, I could scarce repress an outbreak of laughter at these words! We now chatted away on a variety of subjects, till the concourse of people pressing onwards to the town, the more thickly populated country, and the distant view of chimneys apprised us we were approaching Ennis. Notwithstanding all my wishes to get on as fast as might be, I found it impossible to resist an invitation to dine that day with the Rooneys, who had engaged a small select party at the Head Inn, where Mrs. Rooney's apartments were already awaiting her.

It was dusk when we arrived, and I could only perceive that the gloomy and narrow streets were densely crowded with country-people, who conversed together in groups. Here and there a knot of legal folk were congregated, chatting in a louder tone; and before the court-house stood the carriage of the chief-justice, with a guard of honour of the county yeomanry, whose unsoldierlike attitudes and droll equipments were strongly provocative of laughter. The postillions, who had with true tact reserved a 'trot for the town,' whipped and spurred with all their might; and as we drove through the thronged streets a changed impression fled abroad that we were the bearers of a reprieve, and a hearty cheer from the mob followed us to our arrival at the inn door—a compliment which Mrs. Paul, in nowise attributing to anything save her own peculiar charms and deserts, most graciously acknowledged by a smile and a wave of her hand, accompanied by an unlimited order for small beer—which act of grace was, I think, even more popular than their first impression concerning us.

'Ah, Captain,' said the lady, with a compassionate smile, as I handed her out of the carriage, 'they are so attached to the aristocracy!'

CHAPTER XLIII
THE ASSIZE TOWN

When I had dressed, I found that I had above an hour to spare before dinner; so taking my hat I strolled out into the town. The streets were even more crowded now than before. The groups of country-people were larger, and as they conversed together in their native tongue, with all the violent gesticulation and energetic passion of their nature, an inexperienced spectator might well have supposed them engaged in active strife. Now and then a kind of movement, a species of suppressed murmur from the court-house, would turn every eye in that direction; and then every voice was hushed, not a man moved. It was evident that some trial of the deepest interest was going forward, and on inquiry I learned that it was a murder case, in which six men were concerned. I heard also that the only evidence against them was from one of their own party, who had turned, as the lawyers term it, 'approver.' I knew well that no circumstance was more calculated than this to call forth all that is best and worst in Irish character, and thought, as I walked along through the dense crowd, I could trace in the features around me the several emotions by which they were moved.

Here was an old grey-headed man leaning on a staff, his lack-lustre eyes gazing in wonder at some speaker who narrated a portion of the trial, his face all eagerness, and his hands tremulous with anxiety; but I felt I could read the deep sorrow of his heart as he listened to the deed of blood, and wondered how men would risk their tenure of a life which in a few days more, perhaps, he himself was to leave for ever. Here beside him was a tall and powerfully-built countryman, his hat drawn upon his eyes, that peered forth from their shadow dark, lustrous, and almost wild in their expression; his face, tanned by season and exposure, was haggard and care-worn, and in his firmly-clenched lips and fast-locked jaw you could read the resolute purpose of one who could listen to nothing save the promptings of the spirit of vengeance, and his determination that blood should have blood. Some there were whose passionate tones and violent gestures showed that all their sympathy for the prisoners was merged in the absorbing feeling of detestation for the informer; and you could mark in such groups as these that more women were mingled, whose bloodshot eyes and convulsed features made them appear the very demons of strife itself. But the most painful sight of all was the children who were assembled around every knot of speakers, their eyes staring and their ears eagerly drinking in each word that dropped; no trace of childhood's happy carelessness was there, no sign of that light-hearted youth that knows no lasting sorrow. No: theirs were the rigid features of intense passion, in which fear, suspicion, craft, but above all, the thirst for revenge, were writ. There were some whose clenched hand and darkened brow betokened the gloomy purpose of their hearts; there were others whose outpoured wrath heaped curses on him who had betrayed his fellows. There was grief, violent, wild, and frantic; there was mute and speechless suffering; but not a tear did I see, not even on the cheek of childhood or of woman. No! their seared and withered sorrow no dew of tears had ever watered; like a blighting simoon the spirit of revenge had passed over them, and scorched and scathed all the verdant charities of life. The law which in other lands is looked to for protection and security, was regarded by them as an instrument of tyranny; they neither understood its spirit nor trusted its decisions; and when its blow fell upon them, they bent their heads in mournful submission, to raise them when opportunity offered in wild and stern defiance. Its denunciations came to them sudden and severe; they deemed the course of justice wayward and capricious, the only feature of certainty in its operation being that its victim was ever the poor man. The passionate elements of their wild natures seemed but ill-adapted to the slow-sustained current of legal investigation; they looked upon all the details of evidence as the signs of vindictive malice, and thought that trickery and deceit were brought in arms against them. Hence each face among the thousands there bore the traces of that hardened, dogged suffering that tells us that the heart is rather steeled with the desire to avenge than bowed to weep over the doomed.

Before the court-house a detachment of soldiers was drawn up under arms, their unmoved features and fixed attitudes presenting a strange contrast to the excited expressions and changeful gestures of those about them. The crowd at this part was thickest, and I could perceive in their eager looks and mute expressions that something more than common had attracted their attention. My own interest was, however, directed in another quarter; for through the open window of the court-house I could hear the words of a speaker, whom I soon recognised as the counsel for the prisoners addressing the jury. My foraging-cap passed me at once through the ranks, and after some little crushing I succeeded in gaining admission to the body of the court.

Such was the crowd within, I could see nothing but the heads of a closely-wedged mass of people, save at the distant part of the court the judges, and to their right the figure of the pleader, whose back was turned towards me.

Little as I heard of the speech, I was overwhelmed with surprise at what I did hear. Touching on the evidence of the 'approver' but slightly, the advocate dwelt with a terrific force upon the degraded character of a man who could trade upon the blood of his former friends and associates. Scarce stopping to canvass how the testimony bore home upon the prisoners, he burst forth into an impassioned appeal to the hearts of the jury on faith betrayed and vows forsworn, and pictured forth the man who could thus surrender his fellows to the scaffold as a monster whose evidence no man could trust, no jury confide in; and when he had thus heightened the colouring of his description by every power of an eloquence that made the very building ring, he turned suddenly towards the informer himself, as, pale, wan, and conscience-stricken, he cowered beneath the lightning glance from an eye that seemed to pierce his secret soul within him, and apostrophising his virtues, he directed every glance upon the miserable wretch that writhed beneath his sarcasm. This seemed, indeed, the speakers forte. Never did I hear anything so tremendous as the irony with which he described the credit due to one who had so often been sworn and forsworn—'who took an oath of allegiance to his king, and an oath of fealty to his fellows, and now is here this day with a third oath, by which, in the blood of his victim, he is to ratify his perjury to both, and secure himself an honourable independence.' The caustic satire verged once—only once—on something that produced a laugh, when the orator suddenly stopped:—

'I find, my lord, I have raised a smile. God knows, never did I feel less merriment. Let me not be condemned. Let not the laugh be mistaken. Few are those events that are produced by folly and vice that fire the hearts with indignation, but something in them will shake the sides with laughter. So, when the two famous moralists of old beheld the sad spectacle of Life, the one burst into laughter, the other melted into tears. They were each of them right, and equally right. But these laughs are the bitter, rueful laughs of honest indignation, or they are the laughs of hectic melancholy and despair. But look there, and tell me where is your laughter now!'

With these words he turned fully round and pointed his finger to the dock, where the six prisoners side by side leaned their haggard, deathlike faces upon the rail, and gazed with stupid wonder at the scene before them. Four of the number did not even know the language, but seemed by the instinct of their position to feel the nature of the appeal their advocate was making, and turned their eyes around the court as if in search of some one look of pity or encouragement that should bring comfort to their hearts.

The whole thing was too dreadful to bear longer, so I forced my way through the crowd, and at last reached the steps in front of the building. But here a new object of horror presented itself, and one which to this hour I cannot chase from before me. In the open space between the line formed by the soldiers and the court knelt a woman, whose tattered garments scarce covered a figure emaciated nearly to starvation; her cheeks, almost blue with famine, were pinched inwards, and her hands, which she held clasped with outstretched arms before her, were like the skinny claws of some wild animal. As she neither spoke nor stirred, there was no effort made to remove her; and there she knelt, her eyes, bloodshot and staring, bent upon the door of the building. A vague fear took possession of me. Somewhere I had seen that face before. I drew near, and as a cold thrill ran through my blood, I remembered where. She was the wife of the man by whose bedside I had watched in the mountains. A half dread of being recognised by her kept me back for a moment; then came the better feeling that perhaps I might be able to serve her, and I walked towards her. But though she turned her eyes towards me as I approached, her look had no intelligence in it, and I could plainly see that reason had fled, and left nothing save the poor suffering form behind it. I endeavoured to attract her attention, but all in vain. At last I tried by gentle force to induce her to leave the place; but a piercing shriek, like one whose tones had long dwelt in my heart, broke from her, with a look of such unutterable anguish, that I was obliged to desist and leave her. The crowd made way for me as I passed out, and I could see in their looks and demeanour the expression of grateful acknowledgment for even this show of feeling on my part; while some muttered as I went by, 'God reward ye,' 'the Lord be good to ye,' as though at that moment they had nothing in their hearts save thoughts of kindness and words of blessing.

I reached my room, and sat down a sadder, perhaps a wiser man; and yet I know not this. It would need a clearer head than mine to trace all the varying and discordant elements of character I had witnessed to their true source; to sift the evil from the good; to know what to cherish, what to repress, whereon to build hope or what to fear. Such was this country once! Has it changed since?

CHAPTER XLIV
THE BAD DINNER

At nine o'clock the jury retired, and a little afterwards the front drawing-room of the Head Inn was becoming every moment more crowded, as the door opened to admit the several members of the bar, invited to partake of Mrs. Rooney's hospitalities. Mrs. Rooney's, I say; for the etiquette of the circuit forbidding the attorney to entertain the dignitaries of the craft, Paul was only present at his own table on sufferance, and sought out the least obtrusive place he could find among the juniors and side-dishes.

No one who could have seen the gay, laughing, merry mob of shrewd, cunning-looking men that chatted away there would have imagined them a few moments previously engaged in a question where the lives of four of their fellow-men hung in the balance, and where at the very moment the deliberation was continuing that should, perhaps, sentence them to death upon the scaffold.

The instincts of a profession are narrow and humiliating things to witness. The surgeon who sees but in the suffering agony of his patient the occasional displacement of certain anatomical details is little better than a savage; the lawyer who watches the passions of hope and fear, distrust, dread, and suspicion, only to take advantage of them in his case, is far worse than a savage. I confess, on looking at these men, I could never divest myself of the impression that the hired and paid-for passion of the advocate, the subtlety that is engaged special, the wit that is briefed, the impetuous rush of indignant eloquence that is bottled up from town to town in circuit, and like soda-water grows weaker at every corking, make but a poor *ensemble* of qualities for the class who, *par excellence*, stand at the head of professional life.

One there was, indeed, whose haggard eye and blanched cheek showed no semblance of forgetting the scene in which so lately he had been an actor. This was the lawyer who had defended the prisoners. He sat in a window, resting his head upon his hand—fatigue, exhaustion, but more than all, intense feeling, portrayed in every lineament of his pale face.

'Ah,' said the gay, jovial-looking attorney-general, slapping him familiarly on the shoulder—'ah, my dear fellow; not tired, I hope. The court was tremendously hot; but come, rally a bit: we shall want you. Bennet and O'Grady have disappointed us, it seems; but you are a host in yourself.'

'Maybe so,' replied the other faintly, and scarce lifting his eyes; 'but you can't depend on my elevation.'

The ease and readiness of the reply, as well as the tones of the voice, struck me; and I perceived that it was no other than the prior of the Monks of the Screw who had spoken. Mrs. Rooney made her appearance at the moment, and my attention was soon taken away by the announcement of dinner.

One of the judges arrived in time to offer his arm, and I could not help feeling amused at the mock-solemnity of the procession, as we moved along. The judge, I may observe, was a young man, lately promoted, and one whose bright eye and bold, dashing expression bore many more traces of the outer bar than it smacked of the dull gravity of the bench. He took the end of the table beside Mrs. Paul, and the others soon seated themselves promiscuously along the table.

There is a species of gladiatorial exhibition in lawyers' society which is certainly very amusing. No one speaks without the foreknowledge that he is to be caught up, punned up, or ridiculed, as the case may be. The whole conversation is therefore a hailstorm of short stories, quips, and retorts, intermingled with details of successful bar-stratagems, and practical jokes played off upon juries. With less restraint than at a military mess, there is a strong professional feeling of deference for the seniors, and much more tact and knowledge of the world to unite them. While thus the whole conversation ran on topics of the circuit, I was amazed at Mrs. Rooney's perfect intimacy with all the niceties of a law joke, or the fun of a *nisi prius* story. She knew the chief peculiarities of the several persons alluded to, and laughed loud and long at the good things she listened to. The judge alone, above all others, had the lady's ear. His bold but handsome features, his rich commanding voice (nothing the worse that it was mellowed by a little brogue), his graceful action and manly presence, stamped him as one well suited to be successful wherever good looks, ready tact, and consummate conversational powers have a field for their display. His stories were few, but always pertinent and well told; and frequently the last joke at the table was capped by him, when no one else could have ventured to try it, while the rich roll of his laugh was a guarantee for mirth that never failed.

It was just when my attention was drawn off by Mrs. Booney to some circumstance of our former intimacy, that a hearty burst of laughing from the end of the table told that something unusually absurd was being related.

'Yes, sir,' said a shrewd-looking, thin old fellow in spectacles, 'we capitulated, on condition of leaving the garrison with all the honours of war; and, 'faith, the sheriff was only too glad to comply.'

'Bob Mahon is certainly a bold fellow, and never hard pushed, whatever you may do with him.'

'Bob Mahon!' said I: 'what of him?'

'Keatley has just been telling how he held the jail of Ennis for four weeks against the sheriff. The jailer was an old tenant of his, and readily came into his plans. They were victualled for a long siege, and as the place was strong they had nothing to fear. When the garrison was summoned to surrender, they put a charge of No. 4 into the sub-sheriff, that made him move to the rear; and as the prisoners were all coming from the assizes, they were obliged to let him have his own terms if he 'd only consent to come out. So they gave him twelve hours' law, and a clear run for it? and he's away.'

This was indeed a very quick realisation of Father Tom's prediction, and I joined in the mirth the story elicited—not the less readily that I was well acquainted with the principal actor in it.

While the laughter still continued, the door opened, and a young barrister stole into the room and whispered a few words into the ear of the counsel for the prisoners. He leaned back in his chair, and pushed his wine-glass hurriedly before him.

'What, Collinson!' cried the attorney-general, 'have they agreed?' 'Yes, sir—a verdict of guilty.'

'Of course; the evidence was too home for a doubt,' said he, filling his glass from the decanter.

A sharp glance from the dark eye of the opposite counsel was the only reply, as he rose and left the room.

'Our friend has taken a more than common interest in this case,' was the cool observation of the last speaker; 'but there was no getting over Hanlon's testimony.' Here he entered into some detail of the trial, while the buzz and confusion of voices became greater than ever. I took this opportunity of making my escape, and joined Mrs. Rooney, who a short time before had retired to the drawing-room.

Mrs. Paul had contrived, even in the short space since her arrival, to have converted the drawing-room into a semblance of something like an apartment in a private house—books, prints, and flowers, judiciously disposed, as well as an open pianoforte, giving it an air of comfort and propriety far different from its ordinary seeming. She was practising

Moore's newly-published song of, 'My from this world, dear Bessy, with me,' as I entered.

'Pray, continue, my dear Mrs. Rooney,' said I: 'I will take it as the greatest possible favour——'

'Ah,' said Mrs..Paul, throwing up her eyes in the most languishing ecstasy—'ah, you have a soul, I know you have!'

Protesting that I had strong reasons to believe so, I renewed my entreaty.

'Yes,' said she, musing, and in a Siddons tone of soliloquy, 'yes, the poet is right—

"Music hath charms to *smooth* the savage *beast*."

But I really can't sing the melodies—they are too much for me. The allusion to former times, when King O'Toole and the rest of the royal family—— Ah, you are aware, I believe, that family reasons——'

Here she pressed her embroidered handkerchief to her eyes with one hand, while she pressed mine convulsively with the other.

'Yes, yes,' said I hurriedly, while a strong temptation to laugh outright seized me; 'I have heard that your descent——'

'Yes, my dear; if it wasn't for the Danes, and the cruel battle of the Boyne, there's no saying where I might not be seated now.'

She leaned on the piano as she spoke, and seemed overpowered with sorrow. At this instant the door opened, and the judge made his appearance.

'A thousand pardons for the indiscretion,' said he, stepping back as he saw me sitting with the lady's hand in mine. I sprang up, confused and ashamed, and rushing past him hurried downstairs.

I knew how soon my adventure, for such it would grow into, would be the standing jest of the bar mess; and not feeling disposed to be present at their mirth, I ordered a chaise, and before half an hour elapsed was on my road to Dublin.

CHAPTER XLV
THE RETURN

We never experience to the full how far sorrow has made its inroad upon us until we come back, after absence, to the places where we have once been happy, and find them lone and tenantless. While we recognise each old familiar object, we see no longer those who gave them all their value in our eyes; every inanimate thing about speaks to our senses, but where are they who were wont to speak to our hearts? The solitary chamber is then, indeed, but the body of all our pleasure, from which the soul has departed for ever.

These feelings were mine as I paced the old well-worn stairs, and entered my quarters in the Castle. No more I heard the merry laugh of my friend O'Grady, nor his quick step upon the stair. The life, the stir, the bustle of the place itself seemed to have all fled; the court echoed only to the measured tread of the grenadier, who marched backwards and forwards beside the flagstaff in the centre of the open space. No cavalcade of joyous riders, no prancing horses led about by grooms, no showy and splendid equipages; all was still, sad, and neglected-looking. The dust whirled about in circling eddies, as the cold wind of an autumnal day moaned through the arched passages and gloomy corridors of the old building. A care-worn official, or some slatternly inferior of the household, would perhaps pass from time to time; but except such as these, nothing stirred. The closed shutters and drawn-down blinds showed that the viceroy was absent and I found myself the only occupant of the building.

It requires the critical eye of the observant resident of great cities to mark the changes which season and fashion effect in their appearance. To one unaccustomed to their phases it seems strange to hear, 'How empty the town is! how very few people are in London!'—while the heavy tide of population pours incessantly around him, and his ear is deafened with the ceaseless roll of equipage. But in such a city as Dublin the alteration is manifest to the least observant. But little frequented by the country gentry, and never except for the few months when the court is there; still less visited by foreigners; deserted by the professional classes, at least such of them as are independent enough to absent themselves—the streets are actually empty. The occupations of trade, the bustle of commerce, that through every season continue their onward course in the great trading cities such as Liverpool, Hamburg, Frankfort, and Bourdeaux, scarce exist here; and save that the tattered garments of mendicancy, and the craving cries of hunger are ever before you, you might fall into a drowsy reverie as you walked, and dream yourself in Palmyra.

I had strolled about for above an hour, in the moody frame of mind my own reflections and the surrounding objects were well calculated to suggest, when, meeting by accident a subaltern with whom I was slightly acquainted, I heard that the court had that morning left the Lodge in the Park for Kilkenny, where the theatricals of that pleasant city were going forward—a few members of the household alone remaining, who were to follow in a day or two.

For some days previous I had made up my mind not to remain in Ireland. Every tie that bound me to the country was broken. I had no heart to set about forming new friendships while the wounds of former ones were still fresh and bleeding; and I longed for change of scene and active occupation, that I might have no time to reflect or look back.

Resolving to tender my resignation on the duke's staff without any further loss of time, I set out at once for the Park. I arrived there in the very nick of time; the carriages were at the entrance, waiting for the private secretary of his grace and two of the aides-de-camp, who were eating a hurried luncheon before starting. One of the aides-de-camp I knew but slightly, the other was a perfect stranger to me; but the secretary, Horton, was an intimate acquaintance. He jumped up from his chair as my name was announced, and a deep blush covered his face as he advanced to meet me.

'My dear Hinton, how unfortunate! Why weren't you here yesterday? It's too late now.'

'Too late for what? I don't comprehend you.'

'Why, my dear fellow,' said he, drawing his arm within mine, and leading me towards a window, as he dropped his voice to a whisper, 'I believe you heard from me that his grace was provoked at your continued absence, and expected at least that you would have written to ask an extension of your leave. I don't know how it was, but it seemed to me that the duchess came back from England with some crotchet in her head, about something she heard in London. In any case, they ordered me to write.'

'Well, well,' said I impatiently; 'I guess it all. I have got my dismissal. Isn't that the whole of it?'

He nodded twice, without speaking.

'It only anticipates my own wishes,' said I coolly, 'as this note may satisfy you.' I placed the letter I had written for the purpose of my resignation in his hand, and continued: 'I am quite convinced in my own mind that his grace, whose kindness towards me has never varied, would never have dreamed of this step on such slight grounds as my absence. No, no; the thing lies deeper. At any other time I should certainly have wished to trace this matter to its source; now, however, chiming as it does with my own plans, and caring little how fortune intends to treat me, I'll submit in silence.'

'And take no notice of the affair further?'

'Such is my determination,' said I resolutely.

'In that case,' said Horton, 'I may tell you that some story of a lady had reached the duchess, when in London—some girl that it was reported you endeavoured to seduce, and had actually followed for that purpose to the west of Ireland. There, there! don't take the matter up that way, for heaven's sake! My dear fellow, hear me out!' But I could hear no more; the rushing blood that crowded on my brain stunned and stupefied me, and it took several minutes before I became sufficiently collected to ask him to go on.

'I heard the thing so confusedly,' said he, 'that I cannot attempt anything like connection in relating it. But the story goes that your duel in Loughrea did not originate about the steeplechase at all, but in a quarrel about this girl, with her brother or her cousin, who, having discovered your intentions regarding her, you wished to get rid of, as a preliminary. No one but a fool could credit such a thing.'

'None but such could have invented it,' said I, as my thoughts at once recurred to Lord Dudley de Vere.

'The duke, however, spoke to General Hinton——'

'To my father! And how did he——'

'Oh, behaved as only he could have done: "Stop, my lord!" said he; "I'll spare you any further relation of this matter. If it be true, my son is unworthy of remaining on your staff. If it be false, I'll not permit him to hold an appointment where his reputation has been assailed without affording him an opportunity of defence." High words ensued, and the end was that if you appeared before to-day, you were to hear the charge and have an opportunity for reply. If not, your dismissal was to be made out, and another appointed in your place. Now that I have told you what I feel the indiscretion of my ever having spoken of, promise me, my dear Hinton, that you will take no step in the matter. The intrigue is altogether beneath you, and your character demands no defence on your part.'

'I almost suspect I know the person,' said I gloomily.

'No, no; I'm certain you can't. It is some woman's story; some piece of tea-table gossip, depend on it—in any case, quite unworthy of caring about.'

'At all events, I am too indifferent at this moment to feel otherwise about anything,' said I. 'So, good-bye; Horton. My regards to all our fellows; good-bye!'

'Good-bye, my boy,' said he, warmly shaking my hand. 'But, stop a moment, I have got some letters for you; they arrived only a few days since.'

He took a packet from a drawer as he spoke, and once more bidding him adieu, I set out on my return to the Castle.

CHAPTER XLVI
FAREWELL TO IRELAND

My first care on reaching my quarters was to make preparations for my departure by the packet of the same evening; my next was to sit down and read over my letters. As I turned them over, I remarked that there were none from my father or Lady Charlotte; there was, however, one in Julia's hand, and also a note from O'Grady. The others were the mere commonplace correspondence of everyday acquaintants, which I merely threw my eyes carelessly over ere I consigned them to the fire. My fair cousin's possessed—I cannot explain why—a most unusual degree of interest for me; and throwing myself back in my chair, I gave myself up to its perusal.

The epistle opened by a half-satirical account of the London season then nearly drawing to its close, in which various characters and incidents I have not placed before my readers, but all well known to me, were touched with that quiet, subdued raillery she excelled in. The flirtations, the jiltings, the matches that were on or off, the rumoured duels, debts, and difficulties of every one we were acquainted with, were told with a most amusing smartness—all showing, young as she was, how thoroughly the wear and tear of fashionable life had invested her with the intricate knowledge of character, and the perfect acquaintance with all the intrigues and byplay of the world. 'How unlike Louisa Bellew!' said I, as I laid down the letter after reading a description of a manoeuvring mamma and obedient daughter to secure the prize of the season, with a peerage and some twenty thousand pounds per annum. It was true they were the vices and the follies of the age which she ridiculed; but why should she have ever known them? Ought she to have been conversant with such a state of society as would expose them? Were it not better, like Louisa Bellew, to have passed her days amid the simple, unexciting scenes of secluded life, than to have purchased all the brilliancy of her wit and the dazzle of her genius at the price of true womanly delicacy and refinement? While I asked and answered myself these questions to the satisfaction of my own heart, I could not dismiss the thought, that amid such scenes as London presented, with such associates as fashion necessitated, the unprotected simplicity of Miss Bellew's character would expose her to much both of raillery and coldness; and I felt that she would be nearly as misplaced among the proud daughters of haughty England as my fair cousin in the unfashionable freedom of Dublin life.

I confess, as I read on, that old associations came crowding upon me. The sparkling brilliancy of Julia's style reminded me of the charms of her conversational powers, aided by all the loveliness of her beauty, and all that witchery which your true belle of fashion knows how, so successfully, to spread around her; and it was with a flush of burning shame on my cheek I acknowledged to myself how much her letter interested me. As I continued, I saw O'Grady*s name, and to my astonishment found the following:—

'Lady Charlotte came back from the duke's ball greatly pleased with a certain Major of dragoons, who, among his other excellent qualities, turns out to be a friend of yours. This estimable person, whose name is O'Grady, has done much to dissipate her ladyship's prejudices regarding Irishmen—the repose of his manner, and the quiet, unassuming, well-bred tone of his address being all so opposed to her preconceived notions of his countrymen. He dines here twice or thrice a week, and as he is to sail soon, may happily preserve the bloom of his reputation to the last. My estimate of him is somewhat different. I think him a bold *effronté* kind of person, esteeming himself very highly, and thinking little of other people. He has, however, a delightful old thing, his servant Corny, whom I am never tired of, and shall really miss much when he leaves us.

'Now as to yourself, dear cousin, what mean all the secret hints and sly looks and doubtful speeches about you here! The mysteries of Udolpho are plain reading compared to your doings. Her ladyship never speaks of you but as "that poor boy," accompanying the epithet with the sigh with which one speaks of a shipwreck. Sir George calls you John, which shows he is not quite satisfied about you; and, in fact, I begin to suspect you must have become a United Irishman, with "a lady in the case." Yet even this would scarcely demand one half the reserve and caution with which you are mentioned. Am I indiscreet in saying that I don't think De Vere likes you? The Major, however, certainly does; and his presence has banished the lordling, for which, really, I owe him gratitude.'

The letter concluded by saying that my mother had desired her to write in her place, as she was suffering from one of her nervous headaches, which only permitted her to go to the exhibition at Somerset House; my father, too, was at Woolwich on some military business, and had no time for anything save to promise to write soon; and that she herself, being disappointed by the milliner in a new bonnet, dedicated the morning to me, with a most praiseworthy degree of self-denial and benevolence. I read the signature some half-dozen times over, and wondered what meaning in her own heart she ascribed to the words, 'Yours, Julia.'

'Now for O'Grady,' said I, breaking the seal of the Major's envelope.

'My dear Jack,—I was sitting on a hencoop, now pondering on my fortunes, now turning to con over the only book on board—a very erudite work on naval tactics, with directions how "to moor a ship in the Downs"—when a gun came booming over the sea, and a frigate with certain enigmatical colours flying at her main-top compelled the old troop-ship we were in to back her topsails and lie to. (We were then steering straight for Madeira, in latitude———, longitude the same—our intention being, with the aid of Providence, to reach Quebec at some remote period of the summer, to join our service companies in Canada.) Having obeyed the orders of H.M.S. *Blast*, to wait until she overtook us—a measure that nearly cost us two of our masts and the cook's galley, we not being accustomed to stand still, it seemed—a boat came alongside with the smallest bit of a midshipman I ever looked at sitting in the stern-sheets, with orders for us to face about, left shoulder forward, and march back to England, where, having taken in the second battalion of the Twenty-eighth, we were to start for Lisbon.

'I need not tell you what pleasure the announcement afforded us, delighted as we were to exchange tomahawks and bowie-knives for civilised warfare, even against more formidable foes. Behold us then in full sail back to old England, which we reached within a fortnight—only to touch, however, for the Twenty-eighth were most impatiently expecting us; and having dedicated three days to taking in water and additional stores, and once more going through the horrible scene of leave-taking between soldiers and their wives, we sailed again. I have little inclination to give you the detail, which newspapers would beat me hollow in, of our march, or where we first came up with the French. A smart affair took place at daybreak, in which your humble servant, to use the appropriate phrase, "distinguished" himself—egad! I had almost said "extinguished"; for I was shot through the side, losing part of that conjugal portion of the human anatomy called a rib, and sustaining several other minor damages, that made me appear to the regimental doctor a very unserviceable craft for his Majesty's service. The result was, I was sent back with that plaster for a man's vanity, though not for his wounds, a despatch-letter to the Horse Guards, and an official account of the action. As nothing has occurred since in the Peninsula to eclipse my performance, I continue to star it here with immense success, and am quite convinced that with a little more loss I might have made an excellent match out of the affair.

'Now to the pleasant part of my epistle. Your father found me out a few evenings since at an evening party at the Duke of York's, and presented me to your lady-mother, who was most gracious in her reception of me; an invitation to dinner the next day followed, and since, I have spent almost every day at your house. Your father, my dear Jack, is a glorious fellow, a soldier in every great feature of the character; you never can have a finer object of your imitation, and your best friend cannot wish you to be more than his equal. Lady Charlotte is the most fascinating person I ever met; her abilities are first-rate, and her powers of pleasing exceed all that ever I fancied even of London fashionables. How you could have left such a house I can scarcely conceive, knowing as I do something of your taste for comfort and voluptuous ease. Besides, *la cousine*, Lady Julia—Jack, Jack, what a close fellow you are! and how very lovely she is! she certainly has not her equal even here. I scarcely know her, for somehow she rather affects hauteur with my cloth, and rarely deigns any notice of the red-coats so plentifully sprinkled along your father's dinner-table. Her kindness to Corny, who has been domesticated at your house for the last five weeks, I can never forget; and even he can't, it would appear, conjure up any complaint against her. What a testimony to her goodness!

'This life, however, cannot last for ever; and as I have now recovered so far as to mount a horse once more, I have applied for a regimental appointment. Your father most kindly interests himself for me, and before the week is over I may be gazetted. That fellow De Vere was very intimate here when I arrived; since he has seen me, however, his visits have become gradually less frequent, and now have almost ceased altogether. This, *entre nous*, does not seem to have met completely with Lady Julia's approval, and I think she may have attributed to me a circumstance in which certainly I was not an active cause. However happy I may feel at being instrumental in a breach of intimacy between her and one so very unworthy of her, even as a common acquaintance, I will ask you, Jack, when opportunity offers, to put the matter in its true light; for although I may, in all likelihood, never meet her again, I should be sorry to leave with her a more unfavourable impression of me than I really deserve.'

Here the letter broke off; but lower down on the paper were the following lines, written in evident haste, and with a different ink:—

'We sail to-night. Oporto is our destination. Corny is to remain behind, and I must ask of you to look to him on his arrival in Dublin. Lady Julia likes De Vere, and you know him too well to permit of such a fatal misfortune. I am, I find, meddling in what really I have no right to touch upon; this is, however, *de vous à moi*. God bless you.—Yours ever, Phil o'Grady.'

'Poor Phil!' said I, as I laid down the letter; 'in his heart he believes himself disinterested in all this, but I see plainly he is in love with her himself.' Alas! I cannot conceive a heavier affliction to befall the man without fortune than to be thrown among those whose prospects render an alliance impossible, and to bestow his affections on an object perfectly beyond his reach of attainment. Many a proud heart has been torn in the struggle between its own promptings and the dread of the imputation, which the world so hastily confers, of 'fortune-hunting'; many a haughty spirit has quailed beneath this fear, and stifled in his bosom the thought that made his life a blessed dream. My poor friend, how little will she that has stolen away your peace think of your sorrows!

A gentle tap at my door aroused me from my musings. I opened it, and saw, to my surprise, my old companion Tipperary Joe. He was covered with dust, heated, and travel-stained, and leaned against the door-post to rest himself.

'So,' cried he, when he had recovered his breath, 'I'm in time to see you once more before you go! I run all the way from Carlow, since twelve o'clock last night.'

'Come in, my poor boy, and sit down. Here's a glass of wine; 'twill refresh you. We 'll get something for you to eat presently.'

'No, I couldn't eat now. My throat is full, and my heart is up here. And so you are going away—going for good and all, never to come back again?'

'Who can say so much as that, Joe? I should, at least, be very sorry to think so.'

'And would you, now? And will you really think of ould Ireland when you 're away? Hurroo! by the mortial, there's no place like it for fun, divilment, and diversion. But, musha, musha! I'm forgettin', and it's gettin' dark. May I go with you to the packet?'

'To be sure, my poor boy; and I believe we have not many minutes to spare.'

I despatched Joe for a car while I threw a last look around my room. Sad things, these last looks, whether bestowed on the living or the dead, the lifelike or the inanimate! There is a feeling that resembles death in the last glance we are ever to bestow on a loved object. The girl you have treasured in your secret heart, as she passes by on her wedding-day, it may be happy and blissful, lifts up her laughing eyes, the symbol of her own light heart, and leaves in that look darkness and desolation to you for ever. The boy your father-spirit has clung to, like the very light of your existence, waves his hand from the quarterdeck, as the gigantic ship bends over to the breeze; the wind is playing through the locks your hand so oftentimes has smoothed; the tears have dimmed his eyes, for, mark t he moves his fingers over them—and this is a last look. My sorrow had no touch of these. My eye ranged over the humble furniture of my little chamber, while memories of the past came crowding on me—hopes that I had lived to see blighted, daydreams dissipated, heartfelt wishes thwarted and scattered. I stood thus for some minutes, when Joe again joined me.

Poor fellow! his wayward and capricious flights, now grave, now gay, were but the mockery of that sympathy my heart required. Still did he heal the sadness of the moment. We need the voice, the look, the accent of affection when we are leaving the spot where we have once been happy. It will not do to part from the objects that have made our home, without the connecting link of human friendship. The hearth, the roof-tree, the mountain, and the rivulet are not so eloquent as the once syllabled 'Good-bye,' come it from ever so humble a voice.

Farewell to Tipperary Joe.

The bustle and excitement of the scene beside the packet seemed to afford Joe the most lively gratification; and, like the genius of confusion, he was to be seen flitting from place to place, assisting one, impeding another, while snatches of his wild songs broke from him every moment. I had but time to press his hand, when he was hurried ashore amongst the crowd; and the instant after the vessel sheered off from the pier, and got under way. The poor boy stood upon a block of granite, waving his cap over his head. He tried a faint cheer, but it was scarcely audible; another, it too failed. He looked wildly around him on the strange, unknown faces, as if a scene of desolation had fallen on him, burst into a torrent of tears, and fled wildly from the spot. And thus I took my leave of Ireland.

At this period of my narrative I owe it to my reader—I owe it to myself—to apologise for the mention of incidents, places, and people that have no other bearing on my story than in the impression they made upon me while yet young. When I arrived in Ireland I knew scarcely anything of the world. My opportunities had shown me life only through the coloured gloss of certain fashionable prejudices; but of the real character, motives, and habitual modes of acting and thinking of others, still more of myself, I was in total ignorance. The rapidly succeeding incidents of Irish life—their interest, variety, and novelty—all attracted and excited me; and without ever stopping to reflect upon causes, I found myself becoming acquainted with facts. That the changeful pictures of existence so profusely scattered through the land should have made their impression upon me is natural enough; and because I have found it easier and pleasanter to tell my reader the machinery of this change in me than to embody that change itself, is the reason why I have presented before him tableaux of life under so many different circumstances, and when, frequently, they had no direct relation to the current of my own fate and the story of my own fortunes. It is enough of myself to say, that, though scarcely older in time, I had grown so in thought and feeling. If I felt, on the one hand, how little my high connections and the position in fashionable life which my family occupied availed me, I learned, on the other, to know that friends, and stanch ones, could be made at once, on the emergency of a moment, without the imposing ceremony of introduction and the diplomatic interchange of visits. And now to my story.

CHAPTER XLVII
LONDON

It was late when I arrived in London and drove up to my father's house. The circumstances under which I had left Ireland weighed more heavily on me as I drew near home, and as I reflected over the questions I should be asked and the explanations I should be expected to afford; and I half dreaded lest my father should disapprove of my conduct before I had an opportunity of showing him how little I had been to blame throughout. The noise and din of the carriages, the oaths and exclamations of the coachmen, and the uproar of the streets turned my attention from these thoughts, and I asked what was the meaning of the crowd.

'A great ball, sir, at Lady Charlotte Hinton's.'

This was a surprise, and not of the pleasantest. I had wished that my first meeting with my father at least should have been alone and in quietness, where I could fairly have told him every important event of my late life, and explained wherefore I so ardently desired immediate employment on active service and a total change in that career which weighed so heavily on my spirits. The carriage drew up at the instant, and I found myself once more at home.

What a feeling does that simple word convey to his ears who knows the real blessing of a home—that shelter from the world, its jealousies and its envies, its turmoils and its disappointments; where, like some landlocked bay, the still, calm waters sleep in silence, while the storm and hurricane are roaring without; where glad faces and bright looks abound; where each happiness is reflected back from every heart and ten times multiplied, and every sorrow comes softened by consolation and words of comfort! And how little like this is the abode of the great leader of fashion; how many of the fairest gifts of humanity are turned back by the glare of a hundred wax-lights, and the glitter of gilded lackeys; and how few of the charities of life find entrance where the splendour and luxury of voluptuous habits have stifled natural feeling, and made even sympathy unfashionable!

It was not without difficulty I could persuade the servants, who were all strangers to me, that the travel-stained, dusty individual before them was the son of the celebrated and fashionable Lady Charlotte Hinton, and at length reach my room to dress.

It was near midnight. The rooms were filled as I entered the drawing-room. For a few moments I could not help feeling strongly the full influence of the splendid scene before me. The undoubted evidences of rank and wealth that meet the eye on every side in London life are very striking. The splendour of the women's dress, their own beauty, a certain air of haughty bearing peculiarly English, a kind of conscious superiority to the rest of the world mark them; and in their easy, unembarrassed, steady glance you read the proud spirit of Albion's 'haughty dames.' This alone was very different from the laughing spirit of Erin's daughters, their *espiègle* looks and smiling lips. The men, too, were so dissimilar—their reserved and stately carriage, their low voices, and deferential but composed manner contrasting strongly with Irish volubility, quickness, and gesticulation. I stood unnoticed and alone for some time, quietly observant of the scene before me; and as I heard name after name announced, many of them the greatest and the highest in the land, there was no semblance of excitement as they entered, no looks of admiring wonder as they passed on and mingled with the crowd. This showed me I was in a mighty city, where the chief spirits that ruled the age moved daily before the public eye; and again I thought of Dublin, where some third-rate notoriety would have been hailed with almost acclamation, and lionised to the 'top of his bent.'

I could remember but few of those around, and even they had either forgotten me altogether, or, having no recollection of my absence, saluted me with the easy nonchalance of one who is seen every evening of his life.

'How are you, Hinton?' said one, with something more of warmth than the rest. 'I have not met you for some weeks past.'

'No,' said I, smiling. 'I have been nearly a year from home.'

'Ah, indeed! In Spain?'

'No, in Ireland.'

'In Ireland? How odd!'

'Who has been in Ireland?' said a low, plaintive voice. Turning round as she spoke, my lady-mother stood before me. 'I should like to hear something—— But, dear me, this must be John!' and she held out her jewelled hand towards me.

'My dear mother, I am so happy to see you look so very well——'

'No, no, my dear,' said she, sighing, 'don't speak of that. When did you arrive? I beg your Royal Highness's pardon, I hope you have not forgotten your protege, my son.'

I bowed reverently as a large, full, handsome man, with bald head and a most commanding expression, drew himself up before me.

'No, madam, I have not forgotten him, I assure you!' was the reply, as he returned my salute with marked coldness, and passed on.

Before Lady Charlotte could express her surprise at such an unlooked-for mark of displeasure, my father, who had just heard of my arrival, came up.

'Jack, my dear fellow, I am glad to see you. How large you have grown, boy, and how brown!'

The warm welcome of his manly voice, the affectionate grasp of his strong hand, rallied me at once, and I cared little for the looks of king or kaiser at that moment. He drew his arm within mine, and led me through the rooms to a small boudoir, where a party at cards were the only occupants.

'Here we shall be tolerably alone for a little while, at least,' said he; 'and now, my lad, tell me everything about you.*

In less than half an hour I ran over the principal events of my life in Ireland, omitting only those in which Miss Bellew bore a part. On this account my rupture with Lord de Vere was only imperfectly alluded to; and I could perceive that my father's brow became contracted, and his look assumed a severer expression at this part of my narrative.

'You have not been very explicit, Jack, about this business; and this it is which I am really uneasy about. I have never known you do a mean or a shabby thing; I will never suspect you of one. So, now, let me clearly understand the ground of this quarrel.'

There was a tone of command in his voice as he said this which decided me at once, and without further hesitation I resolved on laying everything before him. Still, I knew not how to begin; the mention of Louisa's name alone staggered me, and for a second or two I stammered and looked confused.

Unlike his wonted manner, my father looked impatient, almost angry. At last, when seeing that my agitation only increased upon me, and that my difficulty grew each moment greater, he looked me sternly in the face, and with a voice full of meaning, said—

'Tell me everything! I cannot bear to doubt you. Was this a play transaction?'

'A play transaction! No, sir, nothing like it.'

'Was there not a bet—some disputed wager——mixed up in it?'

'Yes, there was a wager, sir; but— —'

Before I could conclude, my father pressed his hand against his eyes, and a faint sigh broke from him.

'But hear me out, sir. The wager was none of mine.' In a few moments I ran over the whole circumstances of De Vere's bet, his conduct to Miss Bellew, and my own subsequent proceedings; but when I came to the mention of O'Grady's name, he stopped me suddenly, and said—

'Major O'Grady, however, did not approve of your conduct in the affair.'

'O'Grady! He was my friend all through it!'

My father remained silent for a few minutes, and then in a low voice added—

'There has been misrepresentation here.'

The words were not well spoken when Lord Dudley de Vere, with my cousin Lady Julia on his arm, came up. The easy nonchalance of his manner, the tone of quiet indifference he assumed, were well known to me; but I was in nowise prepared for the look of insufferable, patronising impertinence he had now put on.

My cousin, more beautiful far than ever I had seen her, took off my attention from him, however, and I turned with a feeling of half pride, half wonder, to pay my respects to her. Dressed in the most perfect taste of the fashion, her handsome features wore the assured and tranquil expression which conscious beauty gives. And here let no inexperienced observer rashly condemn the placid loveliness of the queen of beauty, the sanctioned belle of fashionable life. It is, indeed, very different from the artless loveliness of innocent girlhood; but its claim is not less incontestable. The features, like the faculties, can be cultivated; and when no unnatural effort suggests the expression, who shall say that the mind habitually exercised in society of the highest and most gifted circle will not impart a more elevated character to the look than when the unobtrusive career of everyday life flows on calm and unruffled, steeping the soul in a dreary monotony, and calling for no effort save of the commonest kind.

Julia's was indeed splendid beauty. The lustrous brilliancy of her dark-blue eyes was shaded by long, black lashes; the contour of her cheeks was perfect; her full short lips were slightly, so slightly curled, you knew not if it were no more smile than sarcasm; the low tones of her voice were rich and musical, and her carriage and demeanour possessed all the graceful elegance which is only met with in the society of great cities. Her manner was most frank and cordial; she held out her hand to me at once, and looked really glad to see me. After a few brief words of recognition, she turned towards De Vere—

'I shall ask you to excuse me, my lord, this set. It is so long since I have seen my cousin.'

He bowed negligently, muttered something carelessly about the next waltz, and with a familiar nod to me, lounged away. O'Grady's caution about this man's attentions to Julia at once came to my mind, and the easy tone of his manner towards her alarmed me; but I had no time for reflection, as she took my arm and sauntered down the room.

'And so, *mon cher* cousin, you have been leading a very wild life of it— fighting duels, riding steeplechases, breaking your own bones and ladies' hearts, in a manner exceedingly Irish?' said Julia with a smile, into which not a particle of her habitual raillery entered.

'From your letters I can learn, Julia, that a very strange account of my doings must have reached my friends here. Except from yourself, I have met with scarcely anything but cold looks since my arrival.'

'Oh, never mind that; people will talk, you know. For my part, Jack, I never will believe you anything but what I have always known you. The heaviest charge I have heard against you is that of trifling with a poor girl's affections; and as I know that the people who spread these rumours generally don't know at which side either the trifling or the affection resides, why, I think little about it.'

'And has this been said of me?'

'To be sure it has, and ten times as much. As to your gambling sins, there is no end to their enormity. A certain Mr. Rooney, I think the name is, a noted play-man——'

'How absurd, Julia! Mr. Rooney never played in his life; nor have I, except in the casual way every one does in a drawing-room.'

'*N'importe*—you are a lady-killer and a gambler. Now as to count number three—for being a jockey.'

'My dear Julia, if you had seen my steeplechase you 'd acquit me of that.'

'Indeed, I did hear,' said she roguishly, 'that you acquitted yourself admirably; but still you won. And then we come to the great offence—your quarrelsome habits. We heard, it is true, that you behaved, as it is called, very honourably, etc; but really duelling is so detestable——'

'Come, come, fair cousin, let us talk of something besides my delinquencies. What do you think of my friend O'Grady?'

I said this suddenly, by way of reprisal; but to my utter discomfiture she replied with perfect calmness—

'I rather was amused with him at first. He is very odd, very unlike other people; but Lady Charlotte took him up so, and we had so much of him here, I grew somewhat tired of him. He was, however, very fond of you; and you know that made up for much with us all.'

There was a tone of sweetness and almost of deep interest in these last few words that made my heart thrill, and unconsciously I pressed her arm closer to my side, and felt the touch returned. Just at the instant my father came forward accompanied by another, who I soon perceived was the royal duke that had received me so coldly a few minutes before. His frank, manly face was now all smiles, and his bright eye glanced from my fair cousin to myself with a quick, meaning expression.

'Another time, General, will do quite as well, I say, Mr. Hinton, call on me to-morrow morning about ten, will you? I have something to say to you.'

I bowed deeply in reply, and he passed on.

'And let me see you after breakfast,' said Julia, in a half-whisper, as she turned towards De Vere, who now came forward to claim her for the waltz.

My father, too, mixed with the crowd, and I felt myself alone and a stranger in what should have been my home. A kind of cold thrill came over me as I thought how unlike was my welcome to what it would have been in Ireland; for although I felt that in my father's manner towards me there was no want of affection or kindness, yet somehow I missed the exuberant warmth and ready cordiality I had latterly been used to, and soon turned away, sad and disappointed, to seek my own room.

CHAPTER XLVIII
AN UNHAPPY DISCLOSURE

'What!' cried I, as I awoke the next morning, and looked with amazement at the figure which waddled across the room with a hoot in either hand—'what! not Corny Delany, surely?'

'Ugh! that same,' said he, with a cranky croak. 'I don't wonder ye don't know me; hardship's telling on me every day.'

Now really, in vindication of my father's household, in which Sir Corny had been domesticated for the last two months, I must observe that the alteration in his appearance was not exactly such as to justify his remark; on the contrary, he had grown fatter and more ruddy, and looked in far better case than I had ever seen him. His face, however, most perseveringly preserved its habitual sour and crabbed expression, rather increased, than otherwise, by his improved condition.

'So, Corny, you are not comfortable here, I find?'

'Comfortable! The ways of this place would kill the Danes! Nothing but ringing bells from morning till night; carriages drivin' like wind up to the door, and bang, bang away at the rapper; then more ringing to let them out again; and bells for breakfast and for luncheon and the hall dinner; and then the sight of vitals that's wasted—meat and fish and fowl and vegetables without end. Ugh! the Haythins, the Turks! eating and drinking as if the world was all their own.'

'Well, apparently they take good care of you in that respect'

'Devil a bit of care; here it's every man for himself. But I'll give warning on Saturday; sorrow one o' me 'll be kilt for the like of them.'

'You prefer Ireland, then, Corny?'

'Who said I did?' said he snappishly; 'isn't it as bad there? Ugh, ugh! the Captain won't rest aisy in his grave after the way he treated me—leaving me here alone and dissolate in this place, amongst strangers!'

'Well, you must confess the country is not so bad.'

'And why would I confess it? What's in it that I don't mislike? Is it the heap of houses and the smoke and the devil's noise that's always going on that I'd like? Why isn't it peaceful and quiet like Dublin?'

And as I conversed further with him, I found that all his dislikes proceeded from the discrepancy he everywhere discovered from what he had been accustomed to in Ireland, and which, without liking, he still preferred to our Saxon observances—the few things he saw worthy of praise being borrowed or stolen from his own side of the Channel And in this his ingenuity was striking, insomuch that the very trees in Woburn Park owed their goodness to the owner having been once a Lord Lieutenant in Ireland, where, as Corny expressed it, 'devil thank him to have fine trees! hadn't he the pick of the Fhaynix?'

I knew that candour formed a most prominent feature in Mr. Delany's character, and consequently had little difficulty in ascertaining his opinion of every member of my family; indeed, to do him justice, no one ever required less of what is called pumping. His judgment on things and people flowed from him without effort or restraint, so that ere half an hour elapsed he had expatiated on my mothers pride and vanity, apostrophised my father's hastiness and determination, and was quite prepared to enter upon a critical examination of my cousin Julia's failings, concerning whom, to my astonishment, he was not half so lenient as I expected.

'Arrah, isn't she like the rest of them, coorting one day with Captain Phil, and another with the young lord there, and then laughing at them both with the ould duke that comes here to dinner! She thinks I don't be minding her; but didn't I see her taking myself off one day on paper—making a drawing of me, as if I was a haste! Mayhe there's worse nor me,' said the little man, looking down upon his crooked shins and large knee-joints with singular complacency; 'and mayhe she'd get one of them yet.' À harsh cackle, the substitute for a laugh, closed this speech.

'Breakfast on the table, sir,' said a servant, tapping gently at the door.

'I'll engage it is, and will be till two o'clock, when they'll be calling out for luncheon,' said Corny, turning up the whites of his eyes, as though the profligate waste of the house was a sin he wished to wash his hands of. 'That wasn't the way at his honour the Jidge's; he'd never taste a bit from morning till night; and many a man he 'd send to his long account in the meantime. Ugh! I wish I was back there.'

'I have spent many happy days in Ireland, too,' said I, scarce following him in more than the general meaning of his speech.

A fit of coughing from Corny interrupted his reply, but as he left the room I could hear his muttered meditations, something in this strain: 'Happy days, indeed! A dacent life you led! tramping about the country with a fool, horse-riding and fighting! Ugh!'

I found my cousin in the breakfast-room alone; my father had already gone out; and as Lady Charlotte never left her room before three or four o'clock, I willingly took the opportunity of our *tête-à-tête* to inquire into the cause of the singular reception I had met with, and to seek an explanation, if so might be, of the viceroy's change towards me since his visit to England.

Julia entered frankly and freely into the whole matter, with the details of which, though evidently not trusting me to the full, she was somehow perfectly conversant.

'My dear John,' said she, 'your whole conduct in Ireland has been much mistaken— —'

'Calumniated, apparently, were the better word, Julia,' said I hastily.

'Nay, hear me out. It is so easy, when people have no peculiar reasons to vindicate another, to misconstrue, perhaps condemn. It is so much the way of the world to look at things in their worst light, that I am sure you will see no particular ingenuity was required to make your career in Dublin appear a wild one, and your life in the country still more so. Now you are growing impatient; you are getting angry; so I shall stop.'

'No, no, Julia; a thousand pardons if a passing shade of indignation did show itself in my face. Pray go on.'

'Well then, when a young gentleman, whose exclusive leanings were even a little quizzed here—there, no impatience!—condescends at one spring to frequent third-rate people's houses; falls in love with a niece, or daughter, or a something there; plays high among riotous associates; makes rash wagers; and fights with his friends, who endeavour to rescue him— —'

'Thank you, Julia—a thousand thanks, sweet cousin! The whole narrative and its author are palpably before me.'

A deep blush covered her cheek as I rose hastily from my chair.

'John, dear John, sit down again,' said she, 'I have only been in jest all this time. You surely do not suppose me silly enough to credit one word of all this?'

'It must have been told you, however,' said I, fixing my eyes on her as I spoke.

The redness of her cheek grew deeper, and her confusion increased to a painful extent, as, taking my hand in hers, she said in a low, soft voice—

'I have been very, very foolish; but you will promise me never to remember—at least never to act upon—the— —'

The words became fainter and fainter as she spoke, and at last died away inaudibly; and suddenly there shot across my mind the passage in O'Grady's letter. The doubt once suggested, gained strength at every moment: she loved De Vere. I will not attempt to convey the conflicting storm of passion this thought stirred up within me.

I turned towards her. Her head was thrown gently back, and her deep-blue lustrous eyes were fixed on me as if waiting my reply. A tear rolled heavily along her cheek; it was the first I ever saw her shed. Pressing her hand to my lips, I muttered the words, 'Trust me, Julia,' and left the room. 'Sir George wishes to see you, sir, in his own room,' said a servant, as I stood stunned and overcome by the discovery I had made of my cousin's affection. I had no time given me for further reflection as I followed the man to my father's room.

'Sit down, Jack,' said my father, as he turned the key in the door. 'I wish to talk to you alone here. I have been with the duke this morning; a little explanation has satisfied him that your conduct was perfectly irreproachable in Ireland. He writes by this post to the viceroy to make the whole thing clear, and indeed he offered to reinstate you at once—which I refused, however. Now to something graver still, my boy, and which I wish I could spare you; but it cannot be.'

As he spoke these words he leaned his head in both his hands, and was silent. A confused, imperfect sense of some impending bad news almost stupefied me, and I waited without speaking. When my father lifted up his head his face was pale and care-worn, and an expression such as long illness leaves had usurped the strong and manly character of his countenance.

'Come, my boy, I must not keep you longer in suspense. Fortune has dealt hardly with me since we parted. Jack, I am a beggar!'

A convulsive gulp and a rattling sound in the throat followed the words, and for a second or two his fixed looks and purple colour made me fear a fit was approaching. But in a few minutes he recovered his calmness, and proceeded, still with a broken and tremulous voice, to relate the circumstances of his altered fortune.

It appeared that many British officers of high rank had involved themselves deeply in a loan to the Spanish Government, under the faith of speedy repayment. The varying chances of the Peninsular struggle had given this loan all the character of a gambling speculation, the skill in which consisted in the anticipation of the result of the war we were then engaged in. My father's sanguine hopes of ultimate success induced him to enter deeply into the speculation, from which, having once engaged, there was no retreat. Thousand after thousand followed, to secure the sum already advanced; and at last, hard pressed by the increasing demands for money, and confident that the first turn of fortune would lead to repayment, he had made use of the greater part of my cousin Julia's fortune, whose guardian he was, and in whose hands this trust-money had been left My cousin would come of age in about four months, at which time she would be eighteen; and then, if the money were not forthcoming, the consequences were utter ruin, with the terrific blow of blasted character and reputation.

There was a sum of ten thousand pounds settled on me by my grandfather, which I at once offered to place at his disposal.

'Alas, my poor fellow! I have advanced already upwards of thirty thousand of Julia's fortune! No, no, Jack, I have thought much over the matter; there is but one way of escaping from this difficulty. By disposing of these bonds at considerable loss, I shall be enabled to pay Julia's money. This will leave us little better than above actual want; still, it must be done. I shall solicit a command abroad; they'll not refuse me, I know. Lady Charlotte must retire to Bath, or some quiet place, which in my absence will appear less remarkable. Strict economy and time will do much. And as to yourself, I know that having once learned what you have to look to I shall have no cause of complaint on your score; the duke has promised to take care of you. And now my heart is lighter than it has been for some months past.'

Before my father had ceased speaking the shock of his news had gradually subsided with me, and I was fully intent on the details by which he hoped to escape his embarrassments. My mother was my first thought. Lady Charlotte, I knew, could never encounter her changed condition; she was certain to sink under the very shock of it. My father, however, supposed that she need not be told its full extent; that, by management, the circumstances should be gradually made known to her; and he hoped, too, that her interest in her husband and son, both absent from her, would withdraw her thoughts in great measure from the routine of fashionable life, and fix them in a channel more homely and domestic.

'Besides,' added he, with more animation of voice, 'they may offer me some military appointment in the colonies, where she could accompany me; and this will prevent an exposure. And, after all, Jack, there is nothing else for it.' As he said this he fixed his eyes on me, as though rather asking than answering the question.

Not knowing what to reply, I was silent.

'You were fond of Julia, as a boy,' said he carelessly.

The blood rushed to my cheek, as I answered, 'Yes, sir; but—but——'

'But you have outgrown that?' added he, with a smile.

'Not so much, sir, as that she has forgotten me. In fact, I believe we are excellent cousins.'

'And it is not now, my dear boy, I would endeavour to make you more to each other. What is not a union of inclination shall never be one of sordid interest. Besides, Jack, why should we not take the field together? The very thought of it makes me feel young enough!'

I saw his lip quiver as he spoke; and unable to bear more, I wrung his hand warmly, and hurried away.

CHAPTER XLIX
THE HORSE GUARDS

I will not say that my reverse of fortune did not depress me; indeed, the first blow fell heavily; but that once past, a number of opposing motives rallied my courage and nerved my heart. My father, I knew, relied on me in this crisis to support his own strength. I had learned to care less for extravagant habits and expensive tastes, by living among those who accorded them little sympathy and less respect. Besides, if my changed career excluded me from the race of fashion, it opened the brilliant path of a soldier's life before me; and now every hour seemed an age, until I should find myself among the gallant fellows who were winning their laurels in the battlefields of the Peninsula.

According to the duke's appointment of the preceding evening I found myself, at ten o'clock punctually, awaiting my turn to be introduced, in the ante-chamber of the Horse Guards. The room was crowded with officers in full dress. Some old white-haired generals of division had been coming daily for years past to solicit commands, their fitness for which lay only in their own doting imaginations; some, broken by sickness and crippled with wounds, were seeking colonial appointments they never could live to reach; hale and stout men in the prime of life were there also, entreating exchanges which should accommodate their wives and daughters, who preferred Bath or Cheltenham to the banks of the Tagus or the snows of Canada. Among these, however, were many fine soldierlike fellows, whose only request was to be sent where hard knocks were going, careless of the climate and regardless of the cause. Another class were thinly sprinkled around—young officers of the staff, many of them delicate, effeminate-looking figures, herding scrupulously together, and never condescending, by word or look, to acknowledge their brethren about them. In this knot De Vere was conspicuous by the loud tone of his voice and the continued titter of his unmeaning laugh. I have already mentioned the consummate ease with which he could apparently forget all unpleasant recollections, and accost the man whom he should have blushed to meet. Now he exhibited this power in perfection; saluting me across the room with a familiar motion of his hand, he called out—

'Ah, Hinton, you here, too? Sick of Ireland; I knew it would come to that. Looking for something near town?'

A cold negative, and a colder bow, was my only answer.

Nothing abashed by this—indeed, to all seeming, quite indifferent to it" he continued—

'Bad style of thing, Dublin; couldn't stand those con-founded talkers, with their old jokes from circuit. *You* were horribly bored, too; I saw it.'

'I beg, my lord,' said I, in a tone of seriousness, the best exchange I could assume for the deep annoyance I felt—'I beg that you will not include me in your opinions respecting Ireland; I opine we differ materially in our impressions on that country, and perhaps not without reason too. These latter words I spoke with marked emphasis, and fixing my eyes steadily on him.

'Very possibly,' lisped he, as coolly as before. 'I left it without regret; you apparently ought to be there still! Ha, ha, ha! he has it there, I think.'

The blood mounted to my face and temples as I heard these words, and stepping close up beside him, I said slowly and distinctly—

'I thought, sir, that one lesson might have taught you with whom these liberties were practicable.'

As I said thus much the door opened, and his grace the Duke of York appeared. Abashed at having so far forgotten where I was, I stood motionless and crimson for shame. Lord Dudley, on the contrary, bowed reverently to his Royal Highness, without the slightest evidence of discomposure or irritation, his easy smile curling his lip.

The duke turned from one to the other of us without speaking, his dark eyes piercing, as it were, into our very hearts. 'Lord Dudley de Vere,' said he at length, 'I have signed your appointment. Mr. Hinton, I am sorry to find that the voice I have heard more than once within the last five minutes, in an angry tone, was yours. Take care, sir, that this forgetfulness does not grow upon you. The colonel of the Twenty-seventh is not the person to overlook it, I promise you.'

'If your Royal Highness——'

'I must entreat you to spare me any explanations. You are gazetted to the Twenty-seventh. I hope you will hold yourself in readiness for immediate embarkation. Where's the detachment, Sir Howard?'

'At Chatham, your Royal Highness,' replied an old officer behind the duke's shoulder. At the same moment his grace passed through the room, conversing as he went with different persons about him.

As I turned away, I met Lord Dudley's eyes. They were riveted on me with an expression of triumphant malice I had never seen in them before, and I hurried homeward with a heart crushed and wounded.

I have but one reason for the mention of this trivial incident. It is to show how often the studied courtesy, the well-practised deception, that the fashion of the world teaches, will prevail over the heartfelt, honest indignation which deep feeling evinces; and what a vast superiority the very affectation of temper confers, in the judgment of others who stand by the game of life and care nothing for the players at either side. Let no one suspect me of lauding the mockery of virtue in what I say here. I would merely impress on the young man who can feel for the deep sorrow and abasement I suffered the importance of the attainment of that self-command, of that restraint over any outbreak of passion, when the very semblance of it insures respect and admiration.

It is very difficult to witness with indifference the preference of those we have once loved for some other person; still more so, when that other chances to be one we dislike. The breach of affection seems then tinctured with a kind of betrayal; we call to mind how once we swayed the temper and ruled the thoughts of her who now has thrown off her allegiance; we feel, perhaps for the first time too, how forgotten are all our lessons, how dead is all our wonted influence; we remember when the least word, the slightest action, bent beneath our will; when our smile was happiness and our very sadness a reproof; and now we see ourselves unminded and neglected, and no more liberty to advise, no more power to control, than the merest stranger of the passing hour. What a wound to our self-love!

That my cousin Julia loved De Vere, O'Grady's suspicions had already warned me; the little I had seen of her since my return strengthened the impression, while his confident manner and assured tone confirmed my worst fears. In my heart I knew how utterly unworthy he was of such a girl; but then, if he had already won her affections, my knowledge came too late. Besides, the changed circumstances of my own fortune, which must soon become known, would render my interference suspicious, and consequently of no value; and, after all, if I determined on such a course, what allegation could I bring against him which he could not explain away as the mere levity of the young officer associating among those he looked down upon and despised?

Such were some of my reflections as I slowly returned homewards from the Horse Guards. As I arrived, a travelling-carriage stood at the door; boxes, imperials, and cap-cases littered the hall and steps; servants were hurrying back and forward, and Mademoiselle Clémence, my mother's maid, with a poodle under one arm and a macaw's cage in the other, was adding to the confusion by directions in a composite language that would have astonished Babel itself.

'What means all this?' said I. 'Is Lady Charlotte leaving town?'

'Miladi va partir——'

'Her ladyship's going to Hastings, sir,' said the butler, interrupting. 'Dr. T——-has been here this morning and recommends an immediate change of air for her ladyship.'

'Is Sir George in the house?'

'No, sir, he's just gone out with the doctor.'

Ah, thought I, this then is a concerted measure to induce my mother to leave town. 'Is Lady Julia at home?'

'Yes, sir, in the drawing-room.'

'Whose horse is that with the groom?' 'Lord Dudley de Vere's, sir; he's upstairs.' Already had I turned to go to the drawing-room, when I heard these words. Suddenly, a faint, half-sick feeling came over me, and I hastened upstairs to my own room, actually dreading to meet any one as I went. The blank future before me never seemed so cheerless as at that moment—separated, without a chance of ever meeting, from the only one I ever really loved; tortured by my doubts of her feeling for me (for even now what would I not have given to know she loved me!) my worldly prospects ruined; without a home; my cousin Julia, the only one who retained either an interest in me or seemed to care for me, about to give her hand to the man I hated and despised. 'How soon, and I shall be alone in the world!' thought I; and already the cold selfishness of isolation presented itself to my mind.

A gentle tap came to the door. I opened it; it was a message from Lady Charlotte, requesting to see me in her room. As I passed the door of the drawing-room I heard Lady Julia and Lord de Vere talking and laughing together. He was, as usual, 'so amusing,' as my mother's letter called him— doubtless, relating my hasty and intemperate conduct at the Horse Guards. For an instant I stopped irresolute as to whether I should not break suddenly in, and disconcert his lordship's practical coolness by a disclosure: my better reason prevented me, and I passed on. Lady Charlotte was seated in a deep arm-chair, inspecting the packing of various articles of toilette and jewelry which were going on around her, her cheek somewhat flushed from even this small excitement.

'Ah, dearest John, how d'ye do? Find a chair somewhere, and sit down by me; you see what confusion we 're in. Dr. Y—— found there was not an hour to spare; the heart he suspects to be sympathetically engaged—don't put that Chantilly veil there, I shall never get at it—and he advises Hastings for the present. He's coming with us, however—I'll wear that ring, Clémence—and I must insist at his looking at you. You are very pale to-day, and dark under the eyes; have you any pain in the side?'

'None whatever, my dear mother; I'm quite well.'

'Pain is, however, a late symptom; my attack began with an—a sense of—it was rather—— Has Bundal not sent back that bracelet? How very provoking! Could you call there, dear John?—that tiresome man never minds the servants—it's just on your way to the club, or the Horse Guards, or somewhere.'

I could scarce help a smile, as I promised not to forget the commission.

'And now, my dear, how did his grace receive you? You saw him this morning?'

'My interview was quite satisfactory on the main point. I am appointed to the Twenty-seventh.'

'Why not on the staff, dear John? You surely don't mean to leave England! Having been abroad already—in Ireland I mean—it's very hard to expect you to go so soon again. Lady Jane Colthurst's son has never been farther from her than Knightsbridge; and I'm sure I don't see why we are to be treated worse than she is.'

'But my own wish——'

'Your own wish, my dear, could never be to give me uneasiness, which I assure you you did very considerably while in Ireland. The horrid people you made acquaintance with—my health, I'm certain, could never sustain a repetition of the shock I experienced then.'

My mother leaned back and closed her eyes, as if some very dreadful circumstance was passing across her memory; and I, half ashamed of the position to which she would condemn me, was silent.

'There, that aigrette will do very well there, I'm sure. I don't know why you are putting in all these things; I shall never want them again, in all likelihood.'

The depressed tone in which these words were spoken did not affect me much; for I knew well, from long habit, how my mother loved to dwell on the possibility of that event, the bare suggestion of which, from another, she couldn't have endured.

Just at this moment Julia entered in her travelling dress, a shawl thrown negligently across her shoulders.

'I hope I have not delayed you. John, are we to have your company too?'

'No, my dear,' said my mother languidly, 'he's going to leave us. Some foolish notion of active service——'

'Indeed!' said Julia, not waiting for the conclusion of the speech— 'indeed!' She drew near me, and as she did so her colour became heightened, and her dark eyes grew darker and more meaning. 'You never told me this!'

'I only knew it about an hour ago myself,' replied I coolly; 'and when I was about to communicate my news to you I found you were engaged with a visitor—Lord de Vere, I think.'

'Ah, yes, very true; he was here,' she said quickly; and then perceiving that my eyes were fixed upon her, she turned her head hastily, and in evident confusion.

'Dear me, is it so late?' said my mother with a sigh. 'I have some calls to make yet. Don't you think, John, you could take them off my hands? It's only to drop a card at Lady Blair's; and you could ask if Caroline 's better—though, poor thing, she can't be, of course; Dr. Y—— says her malady is exactly my own. And then if you are passing Long's, tell Sir Charles that our whist-party is put off—perhaps Grammont has told him already. You may mention to Saunders that I shall not want the horses till I return; and say I detest greys, they are so like city people's equipages; and wait an instant'—here her ladyship took a small ivory memorandum tablet from the table, and began reading from it a list of commissions, some of them most ludicrously absurd. In the midst of the catalogue my father entered hastily with his watch in his hand.

'You'll be dreadfully late on the road, Charlotte; and you forget Y—— must be back here early to-morrow.'

'So I had forgotten it,' said she with some animation; 'but we're quite ready now. Clémence has done everything, I think. Come, John, give me your arm, my dear: Julia always takes this side. Are you certain it won't rain, Sir George?'

'I really cannot be positive,' said my father, smiling.

'I'm sure there's thunder in the air,' rejoined my mother; 'my nerves would never bear a storm.'

Some dreadful catastrophe in the West Indies, where an earthquake had swallowed up a whole population, occurred to her memory at the instant, and the possibility of something similar occurring between Seven Oaks and Tunbridge seemed to engross her entire attention. By this time we reached the hall, where the servants, drawn up in double file, stood in respectful silence. My mother's eyes were, however, directed upon a figure which occupied the place next the door, and whose costume certainly was strangely at variance with the accurate liveries about him. An old white greatcoat with some twenty capes reaching nearly to the ground (for the garment had been originally destined for a much larger person), a glazed hat fastened down with a handkerchief passed over it and tied under the chin, and a black-thorn stick with a little bundle at the end of it were his most remarkable equipments.

'What is it? What can it be doing there?' said my mother, in a Siddons tone of voice.

What is it?

'What is it? Corny Delany, no less,' croaked out the little man in the crankiest tone of his harsh voice. 'It's what remains of me, at laste!'

'Oh, yes,' said Julia, bursting into a laugh, 'Corny's coming as my bodyguard. He'll sit in the rumble with Thomas.'

'What a shocking figure it is!' said my mother, surveying him through her glass.

'Time doesn't improve either of us,' said Corny, with the grin of a demon. Happily the observation was only heard by myself. 'Is it in silk stockings I'd be trapesing about the roads all night, with the rheumatiz in the small of my back! Ugh! the Haythina!'

My mother was at length seated in the carriage, with Julia beside her — the hundred and one petty annoyances to make travelling uncomfortable, by way of rendering it supportable, around her; Corny had mounted to his place beside Thomas, who regarded him with a look of as profound contempt as a sleek, well-fed pointer would confer upon some mangy mongrel of the roadside; a hurried good-bye from my mother, a quick, short glance from Julia, a whisper lost in the crash of the wheels — and they were gone.

CHAPTER L
THE RETREAT FROM BURGOS

Few men have gone through life without passing through certain periods which, although not marked by positive misfortune, were yet so impressed by gloom and despondence that their very retrospect is saddening. Happy it is for us that in after days our memory is but little retentive of these. We remember the shadows that darkened over the landscape, but we forget in great part their cause and their duration, and perhaps even sometimes are disposed to smile at the sources of grief to which long habit of the world and its ways would have made us callous.

I was almost alone in the world—bereft of fortune, separated irrevocably from the woman I loved, and by whom I had reason to think my affection was returned. In that home to which I should have looked for fondness I found only gloom and misfortune—my mother grown insensible to everything save some frivolous narrative of her own health; my father, once high-spirited and freehearted, care-worn, depressed, and broken; my cousin, my early playfellow, half sweetheart and half sister, bestowing her heart and affections on one so unworthy of her. All lost to me—and at a time, too, when the heart is too weak and tender to stand alone, but must cling to something, or it sinks upon the earth, crushed and trodden upon.

I looked back upon my past life, and thought over the happy hours I had spent in the wild west, roaming through its deep valleys and over its heath-clad mountains. I thought of her my companion through many a long summer day by the rocky shore, against which the white waves were ever beating, watching the sea-birds careering full many a fathom deep below us, their shrill cries mixing with the wilder plash of the ever-restless sea—and how we dreamed away those hours, now half in sadness, now in bright hope of long years to come, and found ourselves thus wandering hand in hand, loved and loving; and then I looked out upon the bleak world before me, without an object to win, without a goal to strive at.

'Come, Jack,' said my father, laying his hand on my shoulder, and startling me out of my reverie, 'one piece of good fortune we have had. The duke has given me the command at Chatham; some hint of my altered circumstances, it seems, had reached him, and without my applying, he most kindly sent for me and told me of my appointment. You must join the service companies of the Twenty-seventh by to-morrow; they are under sailing-orders, and no time is to be lost. I told his grace that for all your soft looks and smooth chin there was no lack of spirit in your heart; and you must take an eagle, Jack, if you would keep up my credit.'

Laughingly spoken as these few words were, they somehow struck upon a chord that had long lain silent in my heart, and as suddenly awoke in me the burning desire for distinction, and the ambitious thirst of military glory.

The next evening at sunset the transport weighed anchor and stood out to sea. A slight breeze off shore and an ebb-tide carried us gently away from land; and as night was falling I stood alone, leaning on the bulwarks, and looking fixedly on the faint shadows of the tall chalk-cliffs, my father's last words, 'You must take an eagle, Jack!' still ringing in my ears, and sinking deeply into my heart.

Had my accidents by flood and field been more numerous and remarkable than they were, the recently-told adventures of my friend Charles O'Malley would prevent my giving them to the public. The subaltern of a marching regiment—a crack corps, it is true—I saw merely the ordinary detail of a campaigning life; and although my desire to distinguish myself rose each day higher, the greatest extent of my renown went no further than the admiration of my comrades that one so delicately nurtured and brought up should bear so cheerfully and well the roughings of a soldier's life; and my sobriquet of 'Jack Hinton, the Guardsman,' was earned among the stormy scenes and blood-stained fields of the Peninsula.

My first experiences of military life were indeed but little encouraging. I joined the army in the disastrous retreat from Burgos. What a shock to all my cherished notions of a campaign! How sadly different to my ideas of the pride, pomp, and circumstance of glorious war! I remember well we first came up with the retiring forces on the morning of the 4th of November. The day broke heavily; masses of dark and weighty clouds drifted across the sky. The ground was soaked with rain, and a cold, chilling wind swept across the bleak plain, and moaned dismally in the dark pine-woods. Our party, which consisted of drafts from the Fiftieth, Twenty-seventh, and Seventy-first regiments, were stationed in a few miserable hovels on the side of the highroad from Madrid to Labeyos. By a mistake of the way we had missed a body of troops on the preceding day, and were now halted here in expectation of joining some of the corps retiring on the Portuguese frontier. Soon after daybreak a low rumbling sound, at first supposed to be the noise of distant cannonading, attracted our attention; but some stragglers coming up soon after, informed us that it proceeded from tumbrels and ammunition-waggons of Sir Lowry Cole's brigade, then on the march. The news was scarcely communicated, when the head of a column appeared topping the hill.

As they came nearer, we remarked that the men did not keep their ranks, but strayed across the road from side to side; some carried their muskets by the sling, others on the shoulder; some leaned on their companions, as though faint and sick; and many there were whose savage looks and bloated features denoted drunkenness. The uniforms were torn and ragged; several of the men had no shoes, and some even had lost their caps and shakos, and wore handkerchiefs bound round their heads. Among these the officers were almost undistinguishable; fatigue, hardship, and privation had levelled them with the men, and discipline scarcely remained in that disorganised mass. On they came, their eyes bent only on the long vista of road that lay before them. Some, silent and sad, trudged on side by side; others, maddened by drink or wild with the excitement of fever, uttered frightful and horrible ravings. Some flourished their bayonets, and threatened all within their reach; and denunciations of their officers and open avowals of desertion were heard on every side as they went. The bugle sounded a halt as the column reached the little hamlet where we were stationed; and in a few seconds the road and the fields at either side were covered with the figures of the men, who threw themselves down on the spot where they stood, in every posture that weariness and exhaustion could suggest.

All the information we could collect was that this force formed part of the rear-guard of the army; that the French under Marshal Soult were hotly in pursuit, having already driven in the cavalry outposts, and more than once throwing their skirmishers amongst our fellows. In a few minutes the bugle again sounded to resume the march; and however little disposed to yield to the dictates of discipline, yet old habit, stronger than even lawless insubordination, prevailed; the men rose, and falling in with some semblance of order, continued their way. Nothing struck me more in that motley mass of ragged uniform and patched clothing than the ferocious, almost savage, expression of the soldiers as they marched past our better equipped and better disciplined party. Their dark scowl betokened deadly hate; and I could see the young men of our detachment quail beneath the insulting ruffianism of their gaze. Every now and then some one or other would throw down his pack or knapsack to the ground, and with an oath asseverate his resolve to carry it no longer. Some even declared they would abandon their muskets; and more than one sat down by the wayside, preferring death or imprisonment from the enemy to the horrors and severities of that dreadful march.

The Highland regiments and the Guards alone preserved their former discipline; the latter, indeed, had only lately joined the army, having landed at Corunna a few weeks previously, and were perfect in every species of equipment. Joining myself to a group of their officers, I followed in the march, and was enabled to learn some tidings of my friend O'Grady, who, I was glad to hear, was only a few miles in advance of us, with his regiment.

Towards three o'clock we entered a dark pine-wood, through which the route continued for several miles. Here the march became extremely difficult, from the deep clayey soil, the worn and cut-up road, and more than all the torrents of rain that swept along the narrow gorge, and threw a darkness almost like night over everything. We plodded on gloomily and scarcely speaking, when suddenly the galloping of horses was heard in the rear, and we were joined by Sir Edward Paget, who, with a single aide-de-camp, rode up to our division. After a few hurried questions to the officer in command, he wheeled his horse round, and rode back towards the next column, which, from some accidental delay, was yet two miles in the rear. The sound of the horse's hoofs was still ringing along the causeway, when a loud shout, followed by the sharp reports of pistol-firing, mingled with the voice. In an instant all was as still as before, and save the crashing of the pine-branches and the beating rain, no other sound was heard.

Our conjectures as to the cause of the firing were just making, when an orderly dragoon, bareheaded and wounded, came up at the top of his horse's speed. The few hurried words he spoke in a half-whisper to our commanding officer were soon reported through the lines. Sir Edward Paget, our second in command, had been taken prisoner, carried away by a party of French cavalry, who were daring enough to dash in between the columns, which in no other retreat had they ventured to approach. The temerity of our enemy, added to our own dispirited and defenceless condition, was the only thing wanting to complete our gloom and depression, and the march was now resumed in the dogged sullenness of despair.

Day followed day, and all the miseries of our state but increased with time, till on the morning of the 17th the town of Ciudad Rodrigo came in view, and the rumour spread that stores of all kinds would be served out to the famished troops.

By insubordination and intemperance we had lost seven thousand men since the day the retreat from Burgos began, and although neither harassed by night marches nor excessive journeys, losing neither guns, ammunition, nor standards, yet was the memorable document addressed by Wellington to the officers commanding divisions but too justly merited, concluding in these words:—

'The discipline of every army, after a long and active campaign, becomes in some degree relaxed; but I am concerned to observe that the army under my command has fallen off in this respect to a greater degree than any army with which I have ever been, or of which I have ever read.'

CHAPTER LI
A MISHAP

If I began my career as a soldier at one of the gloomiest periods of our Peninsular struggle, I certainly was soon destined to witness one of the most brilliant achievements of our arms in the opening of the campaign of 1813.

On the 22nd of May the march began—that forward movement, for the hour of whose coming many a heart had throbbed, and many a bosom beat high. From Ciudad Rodrigo to the frontier our way led through the scenes of former glory; and if the veterans of the army exulted at once again beholding the battlefields where victory had crowned their arms, the new soldiers glowed with ambition to emulate their fame. As for myself, short as the period had been since I quitted England, I felt that my character had undergone a very great change; the wandering fancies of the boy had sobered down into the more fixed, determined passions of the man. The more I thought of the inglorious indolence of my former life, the stronger was now my desire to deserve a higher reputation than that of a mere lounger about a court, the military accompaniment of a pageant. Happily for me, I knew not at the time how few opportunities for distinction are afforded by the humble position of a subaltern; how seldom occasions arise where, amid the mass around him, his name can win praise or honour. I knew not this; and my reverie by day, my dream by night, presented but one image—that of some bold, successful deed, by which I should be honourably known and proudly mentioned, or my death be that of a brave soldier in the field of glory.

It may be remembered by my reader that in the celebrated march by which Wellington opened that campaign whose result was the expulsion of the French armies from the Peninsula, the British left, under the command of Graham, was always in advance of the main body. Their route traversed the wild and dreary passes of the Tras-os-Montes, a vast expanse of country, with scarcely a road to be met with, and but few inhabitants; the solitary glens and gloomy valleys, whose echoes had waked to no other sounds save those of the wild heron or the eagle, were now to resound with the thundering roll of artillery waggons, the clanking crash of cavalry columns, or the monotonous din of the infantry battalions, as from sunrise to sunset they poured along—now scaling the rugged height of some bold mountain, now disappearing among the wooded depths of some dark ravine.

Owing to a temporary appointment on the staff, I was continually passing and repassing between this portion of the army and the force under the immediate command of Lord Wellington. Starting at daybreak, I have set off alone through these wild untravelled tracts, where mountains rose in solemn grandeur, their dark sides wooded with the gloomy cork-tree, or rent by some hissing torrent whose splash was the only sound that broke the universal silence—now dashing on with speed across the grassy plain, now toiling along on foot, the bridle on my arm—I have seen the sun go down and never heard a human voice, nor seen the footsteps of a fellow-man; and yet what charms had those lonely hours for me, and what a crowd of blissful thoughts and happy images they yet bring back to me! The dark glen, the frowning precipice, the clear rivulet gurgling on amid the mossy stones, the long and tangled weeds that hung in festoons down some rocky cliff, through whose fissured sides the water fell in heavy drops into a little basin at its foot—all spoke to me of the happiest hours of my life, when, loved and loving, I wandered on the livelong day. How often, as the day was falling, have I sat down to rest beneath some tall beech, gazing on the glorious expanse of mountain and valley, hill and plain, and winding river—all beneath me; and how, as I looked, have my thoughts wandered away from those to many a far-off mile; and then what doubts and hopes would crowd upon met Was I forgotten? Had time and distance wiped away all memory of me? Was I as one she had never seen, or was she still to me as when we parted? In such moments as these how often have I recurred to our last meeting at the holy well—and still, I own it, some vague feeling of superstition has spoken hope to my heart, when reason alone had bid me despair.

It was at the close of a sultry day—the first of June; I shall not readily forget it—that, overcome by fatigue, I threw myself down beneath the shelter of a grove of acacias, and, tethering my horse with his bridle, fell into one of my accustomed reveries. The heat of the day, the drowsy hum of the summer insects, the very monotonous champ of my horse, feeding beside me—all conspired to make me sleepy, and I fell into a heavy slumber. My dreams, like my last-waking thoughts, were of home; but, strangely enough, the scenes through which I had been travelling, the officers with whom I was intimate, the wild guerilla chiefs who from time to time crossed my path or shared my bivouac, were mixed up with objects and persons many a mile away, making that odd and incongruous collection which we so often experience in sleep. A kind of low, unbroken sound, like the tramp of cavalry over grass, awoke me; but still, such was my drowsiness that I was again about to relapse into sleep, when the sound of a manly voice, singing at the foot of the rock beneath me, fully aroused me. I started up, and, peeping cautiously over the head of the cliff, beheld to my surprise and terror a party of French soldiers stretched upon the greensward around a fire. It was the first time I had ever seen the imperial troops, and notwithstanding the danger of my position, I felt a most unaccountable longing to creep nearer and watch their proceedings. The sounds I had heard at first became at this moment more audible; and on looking down the glen I perceived a party of about twenty dragoons cantering up the valley. They were dressed in the uniform of the Chasseur Légers, and in their light-blue jackets and silvered helmets had a most striking and picturesque effect.

La Vivandière

My astonishment at their appearance was not diminished by the figure who rode gaily along at their head. She was a young and pretty-looking girl, dressed in a blue frock and jean trousers; a light foraging-cap, with the number of the regiment worked in silver on the front, and a small canteen suspended from one shoulder by a black belt completed her equipment. Her hair, of a glossy black, was braided richly at either side of her face, and a couple of bows of light blue attested a degree of coquetry the rest of her costume gave no evidence of. She rode *en cavalier*; and the easy attitude in which she sat, and her steady hand on the bridle, denoted that the regimental riding-school had contributed to her accomplishments. I had heard before of the Vivandières of the French army, but was in nowise prepared for the really pretty figure and costume I now beheld.

As the riding-party approached, the others sprang to their feet, and drawing up in line performed a mock salute, which the young lady returned with perfect gravity; and then, carelessly throwing her bridle to the one nearest, she dismounted. In a few moments the horses were picketed; the packs were scattered about the grass; cooking utensils, provisions, and wine were distributed; and, amid a perfect din of merry voices and laughter, the preparations for dinner were commenced. Mademoiselle's part, on the whole, amused me not a little. Not engaging in any of the various occupations about her, she seated herself on a pile of cavalry cloaks at a little distance from the rest, and taking out a much-worn and well-thumbed-looking volume from the pocket of her coat, she began to read to herself with the most perfect unconcern of all that was going on about her. Meanwhile the operations of the *cuisine* were conducted with a despatch and dexterity that only French soldiers ever attain to; and, shall I confess it, the rich odour that steamed upwards from the well-seasoned *potage*, the savoury smell of the roast kid, albeit partaking of onions, and the brown breasts of certain *poulets* made me wish heartily that for half an hour or so I could have changed my allegiance, converted myself into a *soldat de la garde*, and led Mademoiselle in to dinner.

At length the party beneath had arranged their meal upon the grass; and the corporal, with an air of no inconsiderable pretension, took Mademoiselle's hand to conduct her to the place of honour at the head of the feast—calling out as he did, 'Place, Messieurs, place pour Madame la Duchesse de—de——'

'N'importe quoi,' said another; 'the Emperor has many a battle to win yet, and many a kingdom and a duchy to give away. As for myself, I count upon the *bâton* of a marshal before the campaign closes.'

'Have done, I beg you, with such folly, and help me to some of that *salmi*,' said the lady, with a much more practical look about her than her expression a few moments before denoted.

The feast now progressed with all the clatter which little ceremony, hearty appetites, and good-fellowship produce. The wine went round freely, and the *qui propos*, if I might judge from their mirth, were not wanting; for I could but catch here and there a stray word or so of the conversation.

All this time my own position was far from agreeable. Independent of the fact of being a spectator of a good dinner and a jolly party while famishing with hunger and thirst, my chance of escape depended either on the party moving forward, or being so insensible from the effects of their carouse that I might steal away unobserved. While I balanced with myself which of these alternatives was more likely, an accident decided the question. My horse, who up to this moment was grazing close beside me, hearing one of the troop-horses neigh in the valley beneath, pricked up his ears, plunged upwards, broke the bridle with which I had fastened him, and cantered gaily down into the midst of the picketed animals. In an instant every man sprang to his legs; some rushed to their holsters and drew forth their pistols; others caught up their sabres from the grass; and the young lady herself tightened her girth and sprang into her saddle with the alacrity of one accustomed to moments of danger. All was silence now for a couple of minutes, except the slight noise of the troopers engaged in bridling their horses and fixing on their packs, when a loud voice called out, '*Voilà!*; and the same instant every eye in the party was directed to my shako, which hung on a branch of a tree above me, and which up to this moment I had forgotten. Before I could determine on any line of escape, three of the number had rushed up the rock, and with drawn sabres commanded me to surrender myself their prisoner. There was no choice; I flung down my sword with an air of sulky resignation, and complied. My despatches, of which they soon rifled me, sufficiently explained the cause of my journey, and allayed any apprehensions they might have felt as to a surprise party. A few brief questions were all they put to me; and then, conducting me down the cliff to the scene of their bivouac, they proceeded to examine my holsters and the flaps of my saddle for any papers which I might have concealed in these places.

'Eh, bien! mon colonel,' said the leader of the party, as he drew himself up before me, and carried his hand to his cap in a salute as respectful and orderly as though I were his officer, 'what say you to a little supper ere we move forward?'

'There's the bill of fare.' said another, laughing, as he pointed to the remnant of roast fowls and stewed kid that covered the grass.

I was too young a soldier to comport myself at the moment with that philosophic resignation to circumstances which the changeful fortunes of war so forcibly instil, and I merely answered by a brief refusal, while half unconsciously I threw my eyes around to see if no chance of escape presented itself.

'No, no,' cried the corporal, who at once read my look and its meaning; 'don't try *that*, or you reduce me to the extremity of trying *this*,' patting, as he spoke, the butt of his carbine with an air of easy determination there was no mistaking.

'Let me rather recommend Monsieur le Capitaine to try this,' said the Vivandière, who, unperceived by me, was all this while grilling the half of a *poulet* over the embers.

There was something in the kindness of the act, coupled as it was with an air of graceful courtesy, that touched me; so, smothering all my regretful thoughts at my mishap, I summoned up my best bow and my best French to acknowledge the civility, and the moment after was seated on the grass beside Mademoiselle Annette, discussing my supper with the appetite of a man whose sorrows were far inferior to his hunger.

As the moon rose, the party, who evidently had been waiting for some others they expected, made preparations for continuing their journey, the first of which consisted in changing the corporal's pack and equipments to the back of my English thoroughbred, his own meagre and raw-boned quadruped being destined for me. Up to this instant the thought of escape had never left my mind. I knew I could calculate on the speed of my horse; I had had some trials of his endurance, and the only thing was to obtain such a start as might carry me out of bullet range at once, and all was safe. Now this last hope deserted me, as I beheld the miserable hack to which I was condemned; and yet, poignant as this feeling was—shall I confess it?— it was inferior in its pain to the sensation I experienced as I saw the rude French soldier, with clumsy jack-boots and heavy hand, curvetting about upon my mettlesome charger, and exhibiting his paces for the amusement of his companions.

The order was now given to mount, and I took my place in the middle file—the dragoons on either side of me having unslung their carbines, and given me laughingly to understand that I was to be made a riddle of if I attempted an escape.

The long months of captivity that followed have, somehow, I cannot at all explain why, left no such deep impression on my mind as the simple events of that night. I remember it still like a thing of yesterday. We travelled along the crest of a mountain, the valley lying in deep, dark shadow beneath; the moon shone brightly out upon the grey granite rocks beside us; our pace was sometimes pushed to a fast trot, and then relaxed to a walk, the better, as it appeared to me, to indulge the conversational tastes of my escort than for any other reason. Their spirits never flagged for a moment; some jest or story was ever going forward—some anecdote of the campaign, or some love adventure, of which the narrator was the hero, commented on by all in turn with a degree of sharp wit and ready repartee that greatly surprised me. In all these narratives Mademoiselle played a prominent part, being invariably referred to for any explanation which the difficulties of female character seemed to require, her opinion on such points being always regarded as conclusive. At times, too, they would break forth into some rude hussar song, some regular specimen of camp lyric poetry, each verse being sung by a different individual, and chorussed by the whole party in common. I have said that these trifling details have left a deep impression behind them. Stranger still, one of those wild strains haunts my memory yet; and strikingly illustrative as it is, not only of those songs in general but of that peculiar mixture of levity and pathos, of reckless heartlessness and deep feeling so eminently French, I cannot help giving it to my reader. It represents the last love-letter of a soldier to his mistress, and runs thus:—

LE DERNIER ADIEU DU SOLDAT

I

'Rose, l'intention d'la présente
Est de t' informer d'ma santé.
L'armée française est triomphante,
Et moi j'ai l'bras gauche emporté.
Nous avons eu d'grands avantages;
La mitraille m'a brisé les os,
Nous avons pris arm's et baggages;
Pour ma part j'ai deux bals dans l'dos.

II

'J' suis à l'hôpital d'où je pense
Partir bientôt pour chez les morts.
J' t'envois dix francs qu' celui qui me panse
M'a donnés pour avoir mon corps.
Je me suis dit puisq'il faut que je file,
Et que ma Rose perd son épouseur,
Ça fait que je mourrai plus tranquille
D'savoir que j'lui laiss' ma valeur.

III

'Lorsque j'ai quitté ma vieil l'mère,
Elle s'expirait sensiblement;
A rarrivée d'ma lettre j'espère
Qu'ell' sera morte entièrement;
Car si la pauvre femme est guérite
Elle est si bonne qu'elle est dans le cas
De s' faire mourir de mort subite
A la nouvelle de mon trépas.

IV

'Je te recommand' bien, ma p'tit' Rose,
Mon bon chien; ne l'abandonn' pas;
Surtout ne lui dis pas la chose
Qui fait qu'il ne me reverra pas —
Lui qu' je suis sûr se fait une fête
De me voir rev'nir caporal;
Il va pleurer comme une bête,
En apprenant mon sort fatal.

V

'Quoiqu' ça c'est quelqu' chose qui m'enrage
D'être fait mourir loin du pays —
Au moins quand on meurt au village,
On peut dire bonsoir aux amis,
On a sa place derrière l'église
On a son nom sur un' croix de bois,
Et puis on espèr' qu' la payse
Viendra pour prière quelque fois.

VI

'Adieu, Rose I adieu! du courage!
A nous r'voir il n' faut plus songer;
Car au régiment où je m'engage
On ne vous accorde pas de congé.
Via tout qui tourne =! j' n'y vois goutte!
Ah, c'est fini! j' sens que j' m'en vas;
J' viens de recevoir ma feuill' de route;
Adieu t Rose, adieu! n' m'oubli' pas.'

Fatigue and weariness, that seemed never to weigh upon my companions, more than once pressed heavily on me. As I awoke from a short and fitful slumber the same song continued; for having begun it, somehow it appeared to possess such a charm for them they could not cease singing, and the

'Adieu! Rose, adieu! n' m'oubli' pas,'

kept ringing through my ears till daybreak.

CHAPTER LII
THE MARCH

Such, with little variety, was the history of each day and night of our march—the days usually passed in some place of security and concealment, while a reconnaissance would be made by some three or four of the party; and, as night fell, the route was continued.

One incident alone broke the monotony of the journey. On the fourth night we left the mountain and descended into a large open plain, taking for our guide the course of a river which seemed familiar to my companions. The night was dark; heavy masses of cloud concealed the moon, and not a star was visible; the atmosphere was close and oppressive, and there reigned around a kind of unnatural stillness, unbroken by the flow of the sluggish river which moved on beside us. Our pace had been a rapid one for some time; and contrary to their wont the dragoons neither indulged in their gay songs nor merry stories, but kept together with more of military precision than they had hitherto assumed. I conjectured from this that we were probably approaching the French lines; and on questioning the corporal, was told that such was the case.

A little after midnight we halted for a few moments to refresh the horses. Each man dismounted, and stood with his hand upon the bridle; and I could not but mark how the awful silence of the hour seemed to prey upon their spirits as they spoke together in low and broken whispers, as if fearful to interrupt the deep sleep of Nature. It was just then that every eye was directed to a bright star that burst out above the horizon, and seemed to expand gradually into a large mass of great brilliancy, and again to diminish to a mere speck—which it remained for some time, and then disappeared entirely. We continued gazing on the dark spot where this phenomenon had appeared, endeavouring by a hundred conjectures to explain it. Wearied at length with watching, we were about to continue our journey, when suddenly from the quarter from where the star had shone a rocket shot up into the dark sky and broke into ten thousand brilliant fragments, which seemed to hang suspended on high in the weight of the dense atmosphere. Another followed, and another; then, after a pause of some minutes, a blue rocket was seen to mount into the air, and explode with a report which even at the distance we stood was audible. Scarcely had its last fragments disappeared in the darkness when a low rumbling noise, like the booming of distant thunder, seemed to creep along the ground. Then came a rattling volley, as if of small-arms; and at last the whole horizon burst into a red glare, which forked up from earth to sky with a crash that seemed to shake the very ground beneath us. Masses of dark, misshapen rock sprang into the blazing sky; millions upon millions of sparks glittered through the air; and a cry, like the last expiring wail of a drowning crew, rose above all other sounds—and all was still. The flame was gone; the gloomy darkness had returned; not a sound was heard; but in that brief moment four hundred of the French army met their graves beneath the castle of Burgos, which in their hurried retreat they had blown up, without apprising the troops who were actually marching beneath its very walls.

Our route was now resumed in silence; even the levity of the French soldiers had received a check; and scarcely a word passed as we rode on through the gloomy darkness, anxiously looking for daybreak, to learn something of the country about us.

Towards sunrise we found ourselves at the entrance of a mountain pass traversed by the Ebro, which in some places almost filled the valley, and left merely a narrow path between its waters and the dark cliffs that frowned above. Here we proceeded—sometimes in single file; now tracing the signs of the retreating force which had just preceded us, now lost in astonishment at the prodigious strength of the position thus abandoned. But even these feelings gave way before a stronger one—our admiration of the exquisite beauty of the scenery. Glen after glen was seen opening as we advanced into this wide valley, each bearing its tributary stream to the mighty Ebro—the clear waters reflecting the broken crags, the waving foliage, and the bright verdure that beamed around, as orange-trees, laurels, and olives bent over the current, or shot up in taper spires towards the clear blue sky. How many a sheltered nook we passed, with an involuntary longing to rest and linger among scenes so full of romantic beauty! But already the din of the retreating column was borne towards us on the breeze, the heavy, monotonous roll of large guns and caissons; while now and then we thought we could catch the swell of martial music blending through the other sounds. But soon we came up with waggons carrying the wounded and sick, who, having joined by another road, had fallen to the rear of the march. From them we learned that the King of Spain, Joseph himself, was with the advanced guard, and that the destination of the forces was Vittoria, where a junction with the *corps darmée* of the other generals being effected, it was decided on giving battle to the Anglo-Spanish army.

As we advanced, our progress became slower and more difficult; close columns of infantry blocked up the road, or dense masses of cavalry, with several hundred led horses and baggage mules, prevented all chance of getting forward. Gradually, however, the valley widened, the mountain became less steep; and by evening we reached a large plain, closed towards the north-east by lofty mountains, which I learned were the Pyrenees, and beheld in the far distance the tall spires of the city of Vittoria. Several roads crossed the plain towards the city, all of which were now crowded with troops—some pressing on in the direction of the town, others taking up their position and throwing up hasty embankments and stockades. Meanwhile the loaded waggons, with the spoil of the rich convents and the royal treasure, were seen wending their slow way beneath the walls of Vittoria on the road to Bayonne, escorted by a strong cavalry force, whose bright helmets and breastplates pronounced them Cuirassiers de la Garde. The animation and excitement of the whole scene was truly intense, and as I rode along beside the corporal, I listened with eagerness to his account of the various regiments as they passed hither and thither and took up their positions on the wide plain.

'There, look yonder,' said he, 'where that dark mass is defiling beside the pine wood! See how they break into parties; watch them, how they scatter along the low bank beside the stream under shelter of the brushwood. There were eight hundred men in that battalion: where are they now? All concealed—they are the tirailleurs of the army; and see on that low mound above them where the flag is flying—the guns are about to occupy that height. I was right, you see; there they come, six, seven, eight pieces of heavy metal. *Sacrebleu!* that must be a place of some consequence.'

'What are the troops yonder with the red tufts in their caps, and scarlet trousers?'

'*Ah, parbleu!* your countrymen will soon know to their cost: they are the Infanterie de la Garde. There's not a man in the column you are looking at who is not *decoré*.'

'Look at this side, monsieur! See the Chasseurs à Cheval,' said Annette, putting her hand on my arm, while her bright eyes glanced proudly at the glittering column which advanced by a road near us—coming along at a sharp trot, their equipment clattering, their horses highly conditioned, and the splendid uniform of light blue and silver giving them a most martial air.

'Bah!' said the corporal contemptuously, 'these are the dragoons to my taste.' So saying, he pointed to a dark column of heavy cavalry, who led their horses slowly along by a narrow causeway; the long black horse-hair trailed from their dark helmets with something of a gloomy aspect, to which their flowing cloaks of deep blue added.

'The Cuirassiers de Milhauds. But look—look yonder! *Tonnerre de ciel!* see that!'

The object to which my attention was now directed was a park of artillery that covered the whole line of road from the Miranda pass to the very walls of Vittoria.

'Two hundred, at least,' exclaimed he, after counting some twenty or thirty of the foremost. '*Ventre bleu!* what chance have you before the batteries of the Guard?'

As he spoke, the drums beat across the wide plain; a continuous dull roll murmured along the ground. It ceased; the trumpets brayed forth a call; a clanging crash followed, and I saw that the muskets were brought to the shoulder, as the bayonets glanced in the sun and the sharp sabres glittered along the squadrons. For a second or two all was still, and then the whole air was rent with a loud cry of '*Vive le Roi!*' while a mounted party rode slowly from the left, and entering one of the gates of the city disappeared from our sight. Night was now beginning to fail, as we wended our way slowly along towards the walls of Vittoria—it being the corporal's intention to deliver his prisoner into the hands of the *état major* of Marshal Jourdan.

CHAPTER LIII
VITTORIA

What a contrast to the scene without the walls did the city of Vittoria present! Scarcely had we left behind us the measured tread of moving battalions, the dark columns of winding cavalry, when we entered streets brilliantly lighted. Gorgeous and showy equipages turned everywhere; music resounded on all sides; servants in splendid liveries made way for ladies in all the elegance of evening dress, enjoying the delicious coolness of a southern climate at sunset; groups of officers in full uniform chatted with their fair friends from the balconies of the large majestic houses; the sounds of gaiety and mirth were heard from every open lattice, and the chink of the castanet and the proud step of the fandango echoed around us.

Women, dressed in all the perfection of Parisian coquetry, loitered along the streets, wondering at the strange sights the Spanish city afforded — themselves scarcely less objects of wonder to the dark-eyed senoras, who, with close-drawn mantillas, peered cautiously around them to see the strangers. Young French officers swaggered boastfully about with the air of conquerors, while now and then some tall and swarthy Spaniard might be seen lowering with gloomy frown from under the broad shadow of his sombrero, as if doubting the evidence of his own senses at seeing his native city in the occupation of the usurper.

In the open plazas, too, the soldiers were picketed, and stood in parties around their fires, or lay stretched on the rich tapestries they had carried away as spoils from the southern provinces. Cups and goblets of the rarest handiwork and of the most costly materials were strewn about them. The vessels of the churches; the rich cloths of gold embroidery that had decorated the altars; pictures, the *chefs-d'oeuvre* of the first masters — all were there, in one confused heap, among baskets of fruit, wine-skins, ancient armour, and modern weapons. From time to time some brilliant staff would pass, usually accompanied by ladies, who seemed strangely mixed up with all the military display of the scene.

My guide, after conversing for a few moments with a *sous-officier* of his regiment, turned from the Plaza into a narrow street, the termination to which was formed by a large building now brilliantly lit up. As we approached, I perceived that two sentries were on guard at the narrow gate, and a large banner, with the imperial 'N' in the centre, waved heavily over the entrance. 'This is *le quartier général,* said the corporal, dropping his voice respectfully, as we drew near. At the same instant a young officer, whose long plume bespoke him as an aide-de-camp, pushed past us; but, turning hastily round, said something I could not catch to the corporal. 'Bien, mon lieutenant,' said the latter, carrying his hand to his shako. 'Follow me, monsieur,' said the officer, addressing me, and the next moment I found myself in a large and richly furnished room, when having motioned me to be seated, he left me.

My meditations, such as they were, were not suffered to be long, for in a few seconds the aide-de-camp made his appearance, and with a low bow requested me to accompany him.

'The general will receive you at once,' said he.

I eagerly asked his name.

'Le Général Oudinot.'

'Ah, the Marshal?'

'No; his brother. I perceive you are a young soldier; so let me give you a hint. Don't mind his manner; "c'est un brave homme" at bottom, but'—the loud burst of laughter from a room at the end of the corridor drowned the conclusion of his speech, and before I had time for another question the door opened, and I was introduced.

In a small but richly furnished chamber sat four officers round a table covered with a magnificent display of silver cups and plate, and upon which a dessert was spread, with flasks of French and Spanish wine, and a salver holding cigars; a book, apparently an orderly book, was before them, from which one of the party was reading as I came in. As the aide-de-camp announced me they all looked up, and the general, for I knew him at once, fixing his eyes steadily on me, desired me to approach.

As I obeyed his not very courteous order, I had time to perceive that the figure before me was that of a stout, square-built man of about fifty-five or sixty. His head was bald; his eyebrows, of a bushy grey, were large and meeting. A moustache of the same grizzly appearance shaded his lip, and served to conceal two projecting teeth, which, when he spoke, displayed themselves like boar's tusks, giving a peculiarly savage expression to his dark and swarthy countenance. The loose sleeve of his coat denoted that he had lost his left arm high up; but whenever excited, I could see that the short stump of the amputated limb jerked convulsively in a manner it was painful to look at.

'What, a deserter! a spy! Eh, what is it, Alphonse?'

The aide-de-camp, blushing, whispered some few words rapidly, and the general resumed—

'Ha! Be seated, monsieur.' The officers of the imperial army know how to treat their prisoners; though, *pardieu*, they can't teach their enemies the lesson! You have floating prisons, they tell me, in England, where my poor countrymen die of disease and starvation. *Sacré Dieu!* what cruelty!'

'You have been misinformed, General. The nation I belong to is uniformly humane to all whom chance of war has made its prisoners, and never forgets that the officers of an army are gentlemen.'

'Ha! what do you mean?' said he, becoming dark with passion, as he half rose from his seat; then, stopping suddenly short, he continued in a voice of suppressed anger, 'Where are your troops? What number of men has your Villainton got with him?'

'Of course,' said I, smiling, 'you do not expect me to answer such questions.'

'Do you refuse it?' said he, with a grim smile.

'I do distinctly refuse,' was my answer.

'What rank do you hold in your service?'

'I am but a subaltern.'

'*Tenez!*' said another of the party, who for some time past had been leisurely conning over the despatches which had been taken from me, 'You are called "capitaine" here, monsieur.'

'Ha! ha! What say you to that?' cried the general exultingly. 'Read it, Chamont.'

'"The despatches which Captain Airey will deliver——"

Is it not so?' said he, handing me the paper.

'Yes,' said I coolly; 'he is the senior aide-de-camp; but being employed on General Graham's staff, now occupied in the pursuit of your army——'

'*Mille tonnerres!* Young man, you have chosen an unsuitable place to cut your jokes!'

'Sa Majesté le Roi,' said an aide-de-camp, entering hastily, and throwing the door open to its full extent; and scarcely had the party time to rise when the Emperor's brother appeared.

Of the middle size, pale, and with a thoughtful, expressive countenance, Joseph Bonaparte's appearance was much in his favour. His forehead was lofty and expansive, his eye large and full, and the sweet smile which seemed the gift of every member of the family he possessed in perfection. After a few words with General Oudinot, whose rough manner and coarse bearing suffered no change by his presence, he turned towards me, and with much mildness of voice and courtesy of demeanour inquired if I were wounded. On hearing that I was not, he expressed a hope that my captivity would be of brief duration, as exchanges were already in progress. 'Meanwhile,' said he, 'you shall have as little to complain of as possible.'

As he concluded these few but to me most comforting words, I received a hint from the aide-de-camp to withdraw, which I did, into an adjoining room. The same aide-de-camp by whom I had hitherto been accompanied now joined me, and, slapping me familiarly on the shoulder, cried out—

'*Eh, bien!* I hope now you are satisfied. Joseph is a fine, generous fellow, and will take care not to forget his promise to you. Meanwhile, come and take a share of my supper.'

He opened a door in the wainscot as he spoke, and introduced me into a perfectly-fitted-up little boudoir, where a supper had been laid out for him. Another cover was soon provided for me, and in a few minutes we were seated at table, chatting away about the war and the opposing armies, as though instead of partisans we had merely been lookers-on at the great game before us. My companion, though but a year or two older than myself, held the grade of colonel, every step to which he won at the point of his sword; he was strikingly handsome, and his figure, though slight, powerfully knit. As the champagne passed back and forward between us, confidences became interchanged, and before midnight sounded I found my companion quite familiar with the name of Louisa Bellew, while to my equal astonishment I was on terms of perfect intimacy with a certain lovely marquise of the Chaussée d'Antin. The tinkle of a sharp bell suddenly called the aide-de-camp to his legs; so drinking off a large goblet of cold water, and taking up his chapeau, he left the room.

I now threw myself back into my chair, and, tossing off a bumper of champagne, began to reason myself into the belief that there were worse things even than imprisonment among the French. Flitting thoughts of the past, vague dreams of the future, confused images of the present, were all dancing through my brain, when the door again opened, and I heard my companion's footsteps behind me.

'Do you know, Alphonse,' said I, without turning in my chair, 'I have been seriously thinking of making my escape? It is quite clear that a battle is not far off; and, by Jove! if I only have the good fortune to meet with your *chef d état major*, that savage old Oudinot, I'll pledge myself to clear off scores with him.'

A half chuckle of laughter behind induced me to continue:—

'That old fellow certainly must have risen from the ranks—not a touch of breeding about him. I'm certain his Majesty rated him soundly for his treatment of me, when I came away. I saw his old moustaches bristling up; he knew he was in for it.'

A louder laugh than at first, but in somewhat of a different cadence, induced me to torn my head, when what was my horror to see before me, not my new friend the aide-de-camp, but General Oudinot himself, who all this time had been listening to my polite observations regarding his future welfare! There was a savage exultation in his look as his eye met mine, and for a second or two he seemed to enjoy my confusion too much to permit him to break silence. At last he said—

'Are you on parole, sir?'

'No,' I briefly replied, 'nor shall I be.'

'What, have I heard you aright? Do you refuse your parole?'

'Yes; I shall not pledge myself against attempting my escape the very first opportunity that offers.'

'Indeed,' said he slowly, 'indeed! What is to become of poor General Oudinot if such a casualty take place? But come, sir, I have his Majesty's orders to accept your parole; if you refuse it, you are then at *my* disposal. I have received no other instructions about you. Yes or no—I ask you for the last time.'

'No! distinctly no!'

'C'est bien; holla, garde! numéro dix et onze.'

Two soldiers of the grenadiers, with fixed bayonets, appeared at the door; a few hurried words were spoken, the only part of which I could catch was the word *cachot* I was at once ordered to rise; a soldier walked on either side of me, and I was in this way conducted through the city to the prison of the gendarmerie, where for the night I was to remain, with orders to forward me the next morning at daybreak, with some Spanish prisoners, on the road to Bayonne.

CHAPTER LIV
THE RETREAT

My cell, for such it was, although dignified with the appellation of chamber, looked out by a small window upon a narrow street, the opposite side to which was formed by the wall of a churchyard pertaining to a convent. As day broke, I eagerly took my place at the casement to watch what was going on without; but except some bareheaded figure of a monk gliding along between the dark yew avenues, or some female in deep mourning passing to her morning's devotions beside the grave of a relative, I could see nothing. A deep silence seemed to brood over the city, so lately the scene of festivity and mirth. Towards four o'clock, however, I could hear the distant roll of drums, which gradually extended from the extreme right to the left of the plain before the town; then I heard the heavy monotonous tramp of marching, broken occasionally by the clank of the brass bands of the cavalry, or the deep sullen thunder of the artillery waggons as they moved along over the paved roads. The sounds came gradually nearer; the trumpets too joined the clamour with the shrill reveille, and soon the streets towards the front of the prison re-echoed with the unceasing clatter of troops moving forward. I could hear the voices of the officers calling to the men to move up; heard more than once the names of particular regiments, as some distinguished corps were passing. The music of the bands was quick and inspiriting; and as some popular air was struck up, the men would break forth suddenly into the words, and the rough-voiced chorus rang through the narrow streets, and fell heavily on my own heart as I lay there a prisoner. Hour after hour did this continue, yet the silence behind remained as unbroken as ever; the lonely churchyard, with its dark walks and sad-looking trees, was still and deserted. By degrees the din in front diminished; regiments passed now only at intervals, and their pace, increased to a run, left no time for the bands; the cavalry, too, trotted rapidly by, and at last all was still as in the gloomy street before me.

It was now eight o'clock, and no summons had yet come to me, although I had heard myself the order for our marching on the Bayonne road by sunrise. The prison was still as the grave; not a step could I hear; not a bolt nor a hinge creaked. I looked to the window, but the strong iron grating that defended it left no prospect of escape; the door was even stronger, and there was no chimney. The thought occurred to me that the party had forgotten me, and had gone away with the other prisoners. This thought somehow had its consolation; but the notion of being left to starve came suddenly across me, and I hastened to the window to try and make myself known to some chance passer-by.

Just then the loud boom of a gun struck upon my ear; another followed, louder still; and then a long heavy crashing noise, which rose and fell as the wind bore it, told me that the work of death had begun. The sound of the large guns, which at first came only at intervals, now swelled into one loud continuous roar, that drowned all other noise. The strong frames of the windows shook, and the very ground beneath my feet seemed to tremble with the dreadful concussion of the artillery; sometimes the din would die away for a few seconds, and then, as the wind freshened, it would swell into a thunder so loud as to make me think the battle was close to where I stood. Hour after hour did this continue; and now, although the little street beside me was thronged with many an anxious group, I no longer thought of questioning them. My whole soul was wrapped up in the one thought—that of the dreadful engagement; and as I listened, my mind was carrying on with itself some fancied picture of the fight, with no other guide to my imaginings than the distant clangour of the battle. Now I thought that the French were advancing, that their battery of guns had opened; and I could imagine the dark mass that moved on, their tall shakos and black belts peering amidst the smoke that lay densely in the field. On they poured, thousand after thousand; ay, there goes the fusilade—the platoons are firing. But now they halt; the crash of fixing bayonets is heard; a cheer breaks forth; the cloud is rent; the thick smoke is severed as if by a lightning flash; the red-coats have dashed through at the charge; the enemy waits not; the line wavers and breaks; down come the cavalry, like an eagle on the swoop! But again the dread artillery opens; the French form beneath the lines, and the fight is renewed.

The fever of my mind was at its height. I paced my room with hurried steps, and springing to the narrow casement, held my ear to the wall to listen. Forgetting where I was, I called out as though at the head of my company, with the wild yell of the battle around me, and the foe before me.

Suddenly the crowd beneath the window broke; the crash of cavalry equipments resounded through the street, and the head of a squadron of cuirassiers came up at a trot, followed by a train of baggage-waggons, with six horses to each; the drivers whipped and spurred their cattle, and all betokened haste. From the strength of the guard and the appearance of the waggons, I conjectured that they were the treasures of the army—an opinion in which I was strengthened by the word 'Bayonne' chalked in large letters on a chest thrown on the top of a carriage. Some open waggons followed, in which the invalids of the army lay, a pale and sickly mass; their lack-lustre eyes gazed heavily around with a stupid wonder, like men musing in a dream. Even they, however, had arms given them, such was the dread of falling into the hands of the guerilla bands who infested the mountain passes, and who never gave quarter even to the wounded and the dying.

The long file at length passed, but only to make way for a still longer procession of Spanish prisoners, who, bound wrist to wrist, marched between two files of mounted gendarmes. The greater number of these were mountaineers, guerillas of the south, condemned to the galleys for life, their bronzed faces and stalwart figures a striking contrast to their pale and emaciated companions, the inhabitants of the towns, who could scarce drag their weary limbs along, and seemed at every step ready to sink between misery and privation. The ribald jests and coarse language of the soldiers were always addressed to these, there seeming to be a kind of respect for the bolder guerillas even in the hour of their captivity. The tramp of led horses, the roll of waggons, the cracking of whips, mingled with the oaths of muleteers and the fainter cries of the sick, now filled the air, and only occasionally did the loud cannonade rise above them. From every window faces appeared, turned with excited eagerness towards the dense crowds; and though I could perceive that inquiries as to the fate of the day were constantly made and answered, my ignorance of Spanish prevented my understanding what was said.

The noise in front of the prison, where the thoroughfare was wider and larger, far exceeded that around me; and at last I could hear the steps of persons marching overhead, and ascending and descending the stairs. Doors clapped and slammed on every side; when, suddenly, the door of my own cell was shaken violently, and a voice cried out in French, 'Try this; I passed twice without perceiving it.' The next moment the lock turned, and my room was filled with dragoons, their uniforms splashed and dirty, and evidently bearing the marks of a long and severe march.

'Are you the Guerilla Guiposcoa de Condeiga?' said one of the party, accosting me, as I stood wrapped up in my cloak.

'No; I am an English officer.'

'Show your epaulettes, then,' said another, who knew that Spanish officers never wore such.

I opened my cloak, when the sight of my red uniform at once satisfied them. At this instant a clamour of voices without was heard, and several persons called out, 'We have him! here he is!' The crowd around me rushed forth at the sound; and following among them I reached the street, now jammed up with horse and foot, waggons, tumbrels, and caissons—some endeavouring to hasten forward towards the road to Bayonne; others as eagerly turned towards the plain of Vittoria, where the deafening roll of artillery showed the fight was at its fiercest. The dragoons issued forth, dragging a man amongst them whose enormous stature and broad chest towered above the others, but who apparently made not the slightest resistance as they hurried him forward, shouting, as they went, '*A la grand' place!—à la place!*'

It was the celebrated Guerilla Guiposcoa, who had distinguished himself by acts of heroic daring, and sometimes by savage cruelty towards the French, and who had fallen into their hands that morning. Anxious to catch a glance at one of whom I had heard so often, I pressed forward among the rest, and soon found myself in the motley crowd of soldiers and townspeople that hurried towards the Plaza.

Scarcely had I entered the square when the movement of the multitude was arrested, and a low whispering murmur succeeded to the deafening shouts of vengeance and loud cries of death I had heard before; then came the deep roll of a muffled drum. I made a strong effort to press forward, and at length reached the rear of a line of dismounted dragoons who stood leaning on their carbines, their eyes steadily bent on a figure some twenty paces in front. He was leisurely employed in divesting himself of some of his clothes, which, as he took off, he piled in a little heap beside him; his broad guerilla hat, his dark cloak, his sheep's-wool jacket slashed with gold, fell one by one from his hand, and his broad manly chest at last lay bare, heaving with manifest pride and emotion, as he turned his dark eyes calmly around him. Nothing was now heard in that vast crowd save when some low, broken sob of grief would burst from the close-drawn mantillas of the women, as they offered up their heartfelt prayers for the soul of the patriot.

A low parapet wall, surmounted by an iron railing, closed in this part of the Plaza, and separated it from a deep and rapid river that flowed beneath—a branch of the Ebro. Beyond, the wide plain of Vittoria stretched away towards the Pyrenees; and two leagues distant the scene of the battle was discernible, from the heavy mass of cloud that lowered overhead, and the deep booming of the guns that seemed to make the air tremulous.

The Spaniard turned his calm look towards the battlefield, and for an instant his dark eye flashed back upon his foes with an expression of triumphant daring, which seemed as it were to say, 'I am avenged already!' A cry of impatience burst from the crowd of soldiers, and the crash of their firelocks threatened that they would not wait longer for his blood. But the guerilla's manner changed at once, and holding up a small ebony crucifix before him, he seemed to ask a moment's respite for a short prayer.

The stillness showed his request was complied with; he turned his back towards the crowd, and placing the crucifix on the low parapet, he bent down on both his knees, and seemed lost in his devotions. As he rose I thought I could perceive that he threw a glance, rapid as lightning, over the wall towards the river that flowed beneath. He now turned fully round; and unfastening the girdle of many a gay colour that he wore round his waist, he threw it carelessly on his left arm; and then, baring his breast to the full, knelt slowly down, and with his arms wide apart called out in Spanish, 'Here is my life! come, take it!' The words were scarcely uttered, when the carbines clanked as they brought them to the shoulder; the sergeant of the company called out the words, '*Donnez!*' a pause—'*Feu!*' The fusilade rang out, and as my eyes pierced the smoke I could see that the guerilla had fallen to the earth, his arms crossed upon his bosom.

A shriek wild and terrific burst from the crowd. The blue smoke slowly rose, and I perceived the French sergeant standing over the body of the guerilla, which lay covered with blood upon the turf. A kind of convulsive spasm seemed to twitch the limbs, upon which the Frenchman drew his sabre. The rattle of the steel scabbard rang through my heart; the bright weapon glanced as he raised it above his head. At the same instant the guerilla chief sprang to his legs; he tottered as he did so, for I could see that his left arm hung powerless at his side, but his right held a long poniard. He threw himself upon the Frenchman's bosom; a yell followed, and the same moment the guerilla sprang over the battlements, and with a loud splash dropped into the river beneath. The water had scarce covered his body, as the Frenchman fell a corpse upon the ground.

A perfect roar of madness and rage burst from the French soldiers, as, rushing to the parapet, a hundred balls swept the surface of the river; but the tall reeds of the bank had already concealed the bold guerilla, whose left arm had received the fire of the soldiers, who now saw the meaning of that quick movement by which he had thrown his girdle around it. The incident was but the work of a few brief moments; nor was there longer time to think on it, for suddenly a squadron of cavalry swept past at the full speed of their horses, calling out the words, 'Place there! Make way there in front! The ambulance! the ambulance!'

A low groan of horror rose around; the quick retreat of the wounded betokened that the battle was going against the French; the words 'beaten and retreat' reechoed through the crowd; and as the dark suspicion crept amid the moving mass, the first waggon of the wounded slowly turned the angle of the square, a white flag hanging above it. I caught but one glance of the sad convoy; but never shall I forget that spectacle of blood and agony. Torn and mangled, they lay an indiscriminate heap—their faces blackened with powder, their bodies shattered with wounds. High above the other sounds their piercing cries rent the air, with mingled blasphemies and insane ravings. Meanwhile the drivers seemed only anxious to get forward, as, deaf to every prayer and entreaty, they whipped their horses and called out to the crowd to make way.

Escape was now open; but where could I go? My uniform exposed me to immediate detection; should I endeavour to conceal myself, discovery would be my death. The vast tide of people that poured along the streets was a current too strong to stem, and I hesitated what course to follow. My doubts were soon resolved for me; an officer of General Oudinot's staff, who had seen me the previous night, rode up close to where I stood, and then turning to his orderly, spoke a few hurried words. The moment after, two heavy dragoons, in green uniform and brass helmets, came up, one at either side of me; without a second's delay one of them unfastened a coil of small rope that hung at his saddle-bow, which with the assistance of the other was passed over my right wrist and drawn tight. In this way, secured like a malefactor, I was ordered forward. In vain I remonstrated; in vain I told them I was a British officer; to no purpose did I reiterate that hitherto I had made no effort to escape. It is not in the hour of defeat that a Frenchman can behave either with humanity or justice. A volley of *sacrés* was the only answer I received, and nothing was left me but to yield.

Meanwhile the tumult and confusion of the town was increasing every minute. Heavy waggons inscribed in large letters, 'Domaine extérieure de sa Majesté l'Empereur,' containing the jewels and treasures of Madrid, passed by, drawn by eight and sometimes ten horses, and accompanied by strong cavalry detachments. Infantry regiments, blackened with smoke and gunpowder, newly arrived from the field, hurried past to take up positions on the Bayonne road to protect the retreat; then came the nearer din and crash of the artillery as the French army were falling back upon the town.

Scarcely had we issued from the walls of the city when the whole scene of flight and ruin was presented to our eyes. The country for miles round was one moving mass of fugitives; cannon, waggons, tumbrels, wounded soldiers, horsemen, and even splendid equipages were all mixed up together on the Pampeluna road, which lay to our right. The march was there intercepted by an overturned waggon; the horses were plunging, and the cries of wounded men could be heard even where we were. The fields at each side of the way were soon spread over by the crowd, eager to press on. Guns were now abandoned and thrown into ditches and ravines; the men broke their muskets, and threw the fragments on the roadside, and vast magazines of powder were exploded here and there through the plain.

But my attention was soon drawn to objects more immediately beside me. The Bayonne road, which we now reached, was the last hope of the retiring army. To maintain this line of retreat strong detachments of infantry, supported by heavy guns, were stationed at every eminence commanding the position; but the swooping torrent of the retreat had left little time for these to form, many of whom were borne along with the flying army. Discipline gave way on every side; the men sprang upon the waggons, refusing to march; the treasures were broken open and thrown upon the road. Frequently the baggage-guard interchanged shots and sabre-cuts with the infuriated soldiers, who only thought of escape; and the ladies, who but yesterday were the objects of every care and solicitude, were hurried along amid that rude multitude—some on foot, others glad to be allowed to take a place in the ambulance among the wounded, their dresses blood-stained and torn, adding to the horror and misery of the scene.

Such was the prospect before us. Behind, a dark mass hovered as if even yet withstanding the attack of the enemy, whose guns thundered clearer and clearer every moment. Still the long line of wounded came on—some in wide open carts, others stretched upon the gun-carriages, mangled and bleeding. Among these my attention was drawn to one whose head having fallen over the edge of the cart was endangered by every roll of the heavy wheel that grazed his very skull. There was a halt, and I seized the moment to assist the poor fellow as he lay thus in peril. His helmet had fallen back, and was merely retained by the brass chain beneath his chin; his temples were actually cleft open by a sabre-cut, and I could see that he had also received some shot-wounds in the side, where he pressed his hands, the blood welling up between the fingers. As I lifted the head to place it within the cart, the eyes opened and turned fully upon me. A faint smile of gratitude curled his lip; I bent over him, and to my horror recognised in the mangled and shattered form before me the gallant fellow with whom the very night before I had formed almost a friendship. The word 'cold,' muttered between his teeth, was the only answer I could catch as I called him by his name. The order to march rang out from the head of the convoy, and I had barely time to unfasten my cloak and throw it over him ere the waggon moved on. I never saw him after.

A squadron of cavalry now galloped past, reckless of all before them; the traces of their artillery were cut, and the men, mounting the horses, deserted the guns, and rode for their lives. In the midst of the flying mass a splendid equipage flew past, its six horses lashed to madness by the postillions; a straggling guard of honour galloped at either side, and a grand *écuyer* in scarlet, who rode in front, called out incessantly, 'Place, place, pour sa Majesté!' But all to no purpose; the road, blocked up by broken waggons, dense crowds of horse and foot, dead and dying, soon became impassable. An effort to pass a heavily-loaded waggon entangled the coach; the axle was caught by the huge waggon; the horses plunged when they felt the restraint, and the next moment the royal carriage was hurled over on its side, and fell with a crash into the ravine at the roadside. While the officers of his staff dismounted to rescue the fallen monarch, a ribald burst of laughter rose from the crowd, and a pioneer actually gave the butt of his carbine to assist the king as, covered with mud, he scrambled up the ditch. I had but an instant to look upon his pale countenance, which even since the night before seemed to have grown many years older, ere I was myself dragged forward among the crowd.

Darkness now added its horror to the scene of riot and confusion. The incessant cries of the fugitives told that the English cavalry were upon them; the artillery came closer and closer, and the black sky was traversed by many a line of fire, as the shells poured down upon the routed army. The English guns, regardless of roads, dashed down on the terrified masses, raining balls and howitzer-shells on every side. Already the cheers of my gallant countrymen were within my hearing, and amid all the misery and danger around me my heart rose proudly at the glorious victory they had gained.

Meanwhile my escort, whose feeling towards me became more brutal as their defeat was more perceptible, urged me forward with many an oath and imprecation. Leaving the main road, we took the fields, already crowded with the infantry. At last, as the charges of the English came closer, my escort seemed to hesitate upon being any longer burdened by me, and one, after interchanging some angry words with his companion, rode off, leaving me to the care of him who passed the cord round my wrist. For a second or two this fellow seemed to waver whether he might not dispose of me more briefly, and once he half withdrew his pistol from the holster, and turned round in his saddle to regard me more steadily. A better feeling, however, gained the mastery; the hope, too, of promotion, could he bring in an officer his prisoner, had doubtless its share in his decision. He ordered me to jump up behind him, and, dashing spurs into his troop-horse, rode forward.

I have, perhaps, lingered too long in my recollections of this eventful night; it was, however, the last striking incident which preceded a long captivity. On the third day of the retreat I was joined to a band of Spanish prisoners marching towards Bayonne. Of the glorious victory which rescued the Peninsula from the dominion of the French, and drove their beaten armies beyond the Pyrenees, or of the great current of events which followed the battle of Vittoria, I do not purpose to speak. Neither will I trouble my reader with a narrative of hardship and suffering; it is enough to mention that my refusal to give my parole subjected me in all cases to every indignity. Wearied out at length, however, I accepted this only chance of rendering life endurable; and on reaching Bayonne I gave my word not to attempt my escape, and was accordingly separated from my companions in misfortune, and once more treated as a gentleman.

The refusal to accept 'parole,' I learned afterwards, was invariably construed by the French authorities of the day into a direct avowal not only to attempt escape by any means that might present themselves, but was also deemed a rejection of the hospitality of the country, which placed the recusant beyond the pale of its courtesy. No sooner had I complied with this necessity—for such it was—than I experienced the greatest kindness and politeness in every quarter. Through every village in the south, the house of the most respectable inhabitant was always opened to me; and with a delicacy it would be difficult to match elsewhere, although the events of the Spanish war were the subjects of general interest wherever we passed, not a word was spoken nor a hint dropped before the 'prisoner' which could in the slightest degree offend his nationality or hurt his susceptibility as an enemy.

I shall now beg of my reader to pass over with me a long interval of time, during which my life presented nothing of interest or incident, and accompany me to the environs of St. Omer, where, in the commencement of the year 1814 I found myself domesticated as a prisoner of war on parole. During the long period that had elapsed since the battle of Vittoria, I had but once heard from home. Matters there were pretty much as I had left them. My father had removed to a colonial appointment, whence he transmitted the rich revenues of his office to my mother, whose habitual economy enabled her to dispense hospitality at Bath, much in the same kind of way as she had formerly done at London. My lovely cousin—in the full possession of her beauty and a large fortune—had refused some half-dozen brilliant proposals, and was reported to have an unswerving attachment to some near relative—which happy individual, my mother suggested, was myself. Of the Bellews, I learned from the newspapers that Sir Simon was dead; and Miss Bellew, having recovered most of the great estates of her family through the instrumentality of a clever attorney (whom I guessed to be my friend Paul), was now the great belle and fortune of Dublin. I had frequently written home, and once or twice to the Rooneys and the Major, but never received any answer; so that at last I began to think myself forgotten by every one, and dreamed away my life in a state almost of apathy—dead to the exciting events of the campaign, which, even in the seclusion where I lived, were from time to time reported. The brilliant march of our victorious troops through the Pyrenees and the south of France, Nivelle, Orthez, and Toulouse, I read of as people read of long past events. Life to me appeared to have run out; and my thoughts turned ever backward to the bright morning of my career in Ireland—my early burst of manhood, my first and only passion.

The old royalist seigneur upon whom I was billeted could evidently make nothing of the stolid indifference with which I heard him and his antiquated spouse discuss the glorious prospect of a restoration of the Bourbons: even the hope of liberty was dying away within me. One ever-present thought had damped all ardour and all ambition—I had done nothing as a soldier; my career had ended as it begun; and, while others had risen to fame and honour, *my* name had won nothing of distinction and repute. Instead of anxiously looking forward to a meeting with Louisa Bellew, I dreaded the very thoughts of it. My mother's fashionable *morgue* and indifference I should now feel as a sarcasm on my own failure; and as to my cousin Julia, the idea alone of her raillery was insufferable. The only plan I could devise for the future was, as soon as I should recover my liberty, to exchange into some regiment in the East Indies, and never to return to England.

It was, then, with some surprise and not much sympathy that I beheld my venerable host appear one morning at breakfast with a large white cockade in the breast of his frock-coat, and a huge white lily in a wineglass before him. His elated manner and joyous looks were all so many riddles to me; while the roll of drums in the peaceful little town, the ringing of bells, and the shouts of the inhabitants were all too much even for apathy like mine.

'What is the *tintamarre* about?' said I pettishly, as I saw the old gentleman fidget from the table to the window and then back again, rubbing his hands, admiring his cockade, and smelling at the lily, alternatively.

'Tintamarre!' said he indignantly, 'savez-vous, monsieur? Ce n'est pas le mot, celui-là. We are restored, sir! we have regained our rightful throne! we are no longer exiles!'

'Yes!' said the old lady, bursting into the room, and throwing herself into her husband's arms, and then into mine, in a rapture of enthusiasm—'yes, brave young man! to you and your victorious companions in arms we owe the happiness of this moment. We are restored!'

'Yes! restored! restored!' echoed the old gentleman, throwing open the window, and shouting as though he would have burst a blood-vessel; while the mob without, catching up the cry, yelled it louder than ever.

'These people must be all deranged,' thought I, unable to conjecture at the moment the reasons for such extravagant joy. Meanwhile, the room became crowded with townspeople in holiday costume, all wearing the white cockade, and exchanging with one another the warmest felicitations at the happy event.

I now soon learned that the Allies were in the possession of Paris, that Napoleon had abdicated, and the immediate return of Louis xviii. was already decided upon. The trumpets of a cavalry regiment on the march were soon added to the uproar without, accompanied by cries of 'The English! The brave English!' I rushed to the door, and to my astonishment beheld above the heads of the crowd the tall caps of a British dragoon regiment towering aloft. Their band struck up as they approached; and what a sensation did my heart experience as I heard the well-remembered air of 'Garryowen' resound through the little streets of a French village!

'An Irish regiment!' said I, half aloud.

The word was caught by a bystander, who immediately communicated it to the crowd, adding, by way of explanation, 'Les Irlandois! oui, ces sont les Cossaques d'Angleterre.'

I could not help laughing at the interpretation, when suddenly my own name was called out loudly by some person from the ranks. I started at the sound, and forcing my way through the crowd I looked eagerly on every side, my heart beating with anxiety lest some deception might have misled me.

'Hinton! Jack Hinton!' cried the voice again. At the head of the regiment rode three officers, whose looks were bent steadily on me, while they seemed to enjoy my surprise and confusion. The oldest of the party, who rode between the two others, was a large swarthy-looking man, with a long drooping moustache, at that time rarely worn by officers of our army. His left arm he wore in a sling; but his right was held in a certain easy, jaunty manner I could not soon forget. A burst of laughter broke from him at length, as he called out—' Come, Jack, you must remember me!' 'What!' cried I,' O'Grady! Is it possible?' 'Even so, my boy,' said he, as throwing his reins on his wrist he grasped my hand and shook it with all his heart. 'I knew you were here, and I exerted all my interest to get quartered near you. This is my regiment—eh?—not fellows to be ashamed of, Jack? But come along with us; we mustn't part company now.'

Amid the wildest cries of rejoicing and frantic demonstrations of gratitude from the crowd, the regiment moved on to the little square of the village. Here the billets were speedily arranged; the men betook themselves to their quarters, the officers broke into small parties, and O'Grady and myself retired to the inn, where, having dined *tête-à-tête*, we began the interchange of our various adventures since we parted.

CHAPTER LV
THE FOUR-IN-HAND

My old friend, save in the deeper brown upon his cheek and some scars from French sabres, was nothing altered from the hour in which we parted; the same bold, generous temperament, the same blending of recklessness and deep feeling, the wild spirit of adventure, and the gentle tenderness of a child were all mixed up in his complex nature, for he was every inch an Irishman. While the breast of his uniform glittered with many a cross and decoration, he scarcely ever alluded to his own feats in the campaign; nor did he more than passingly mention the actions where his own conduct had been most conspicuous. Indeed, there was a reserve in his whole manner while speaking of the Peninsular battles which I soon discovered proceeded from delicacy towards me, knowing how little I had seen of service owing to my imprisonment, and fearing lest in the detail of the glorious career of our armies he might be inflicting fresh wounds on one whose fortune forbade him to share in it. He often asked me about my father, and seemed to feel deeply the kindness he had received from him when in London. Of my mother, too, he sometimes spoke, but never even alluded to Lady Julia; and when once I spoke of her as the protector of Corny, he fidgeted for a second or two, seemed uneasy and uncomfortable, and gave me the impression that he felt sorry to be reduced to accept a favour for his servant, where he himself had been treated with coldness and distance.

Apart from this—and it was a topic we mutually avoided—O'Grady's spirits were as high as ever. Mixing much with the officers of his corps, he was actually beloved by them. He joined in all their schemes of pleasure and amusement with the zest of his own buoyant nature; and the youngest cornet in the regiment felt himself the Colonel's inferior in the gaiety of the mess as much as at the head of the squadrons.

At the end of a few days I received from Paris the papers necessary to relieve me from the restraint of my parole, and was concerting with O'Grady the steps necessary to be taken to resume my rank in the service, when an incident occurred which altered all our plans for the moment, and, by one of those strange casualties which so often occur in life, gave a new current to my own fate for ever.

I should mention here, that, amid all the rejoicings which ushered in the restoration, amid all the flattery by which the allied armies were received, one portion of the royalists maintained a dogged, ungenial spirit towards the men by whom their cause was rendered victorious, and never forgave them the honour of reviving a dynasty to which they themselves had contributed nothing. These were the old *militaires* of Louis xviii.—the men who, too proud or too good-for-nothing to accept service under the Emperor, had lain dormant during the glorious career of the French armies, and who now, in their hour of defeat and adversity, started into life as the representatives of the military genius of the country. These men, I say, hated the English with a vindictive animosity which the old Napoleonists could not equal. Without the generous rivalry of an open foe, they felt themselves humbled by comparison with the soldiers whose weather-beaten faces and shattered limbs bore token of a hundred battles, and for the very cause, too, for which they themselves were the most interested. This ungenerous spirit found vent for itself in a thousand petty annoyances, which were practised upon our troops in every town and village of the north of France; and every officer whose billet consigned him to the house of a royalist soldier would gladly have exchanged his quarters for the companionship of the most inveterate follower of Napoleon. To an instance of what I have mentioned was owing the incident which I am about to relate.

To relieve the ennui of a French village, the officers of the Eighteenth had, with wonderful expenditure of skill and labour, succeeded in getting up a four-in-hand drag, which, to the astonishment and wonder of the natives, was seen daily wending its course through the devious alleys and narrow streets of the little town, the roof covered with dashing dragoons, whose laughing faces and loud-sounding bugles were all deemed so many direct insults by the ill-conditioned section I have mentioned. The unequivocal evidences of dislike they exhibited to this dashing 'turn-out' formed, I believe, one of its great attractions to the Eighteenth, who never omitted an occasion, whatever the state of the weather, to issue forth every day, with all the noise and uproar they could muster.

At last, however, the old *commissaire de police*, whose indignation at the proceeding knew no bounds, devised an admirable expedient for annoying our fellows—one which, supported as it was by the law of the country, there was no possibility of evading. This was to demand the passport of every officer who passed the *barrière*, thus necessitating him to get down from the roof of the coach, present his papers, and have them carefully conned and scrutinised, their *visés* looked into, and all sorts of questions propounded.

When it is understood that the only drive led through one or other of these barriers, it may be imagined how provoking and vexatious such a course of proceeding became. Representations were made to the mayor ever and anon, explaining that the passports once produced no further inconvenience should be incurred; but all to no purpose. Any one who knows France will acknowledge how totally inadequate a common-sense argument is in the decision of a question before a government functionary. The mayor, too, was a royalist, and the matter was decided against us.

Argument and reason having failed, the gallant Eighteenth came to the resolution to try force; and accordingly it was decided that next morning we should charge the *barrière* in full gallop, as it was rightly conjectured that no French employé would feel disposed to encounter the rush of a four-in-hand, even with the law on his side. To render the *coup de main* more brilliant, and perhaps, too, to give an air of plausibility to the infraction, four dashing thoroughbred light chestnuts—two of the number having never felt a collar in their lives—were harnessed for the occasion. A strong force of the wildest spirits of the regiment took their places on the roof; and amid a cheer that actually made the street ring, and a tantarara from the trumpets, the equipage dashed through the town, the leaders bounding with the swingle-bars every moment over their backs. Away we went, the populace flying in terror on every side, and every eye turned towards the *barrière*, where the dignified official stood, in the calm repose of his station, as if daring us to transgress his frontier. Already had he stepped forward with his accustomed question. The words, 'Messieurs, je vous demande,' had just escaped his lips, when he had barely time to spring into his den as the furious leaders tore past, the pavement crashing beneath their hoofs, and shouts of laughter mingling with the uproar.

The Four-in-hand.

Having driven for a league or so at a slow pace, to breathe our cattle, we turned homewards, rejoicing in the success of our scheme, which had fully satisfied our expectations. What was our chagrin, however, as we neared the *barrière*, to discover that a strong force of mounted gendarmes stopped the way, their drawn sabres giving us plainly to understand the fate that awaited our horses if we persisted in our plan! What was to be done? To force a passage under the circumstances was only to give an opportunity to the gendarmerie they were long anxious for, to cut our whole equipage in pieces. To yield was the only alternative; but what an alternative!—to be laughed at by the whole town on the very day of our victory!

'I have it!' said O'Grady, who sat on the box beside the driver—'I have it, lads! Pull up when they tell you, and do as they direct.'

With some difficulty the four dashing nags were reined in as we came up to the *barrière*; and the commissaire, bursting with passion, appeared at the door of the lodge, and directed us to get down.

'Your passports will avail little on the present occasion,' said he insolently, as we produced our papers. 'Your carriage and horses are confiscated. St. Omer has now privilege as a fortified town. The fortresses of France enforce a penalty of forty thousand francs——'

A burst of laughter from the bystanders at our rueful faces prevented us hearing the remainder of the explanation. Meanwhile, to our horror and disgust, some half-dozen gendarmes, with their long caps and heavy boots, were crawling up the sides of the drag, and taking their seats upon the top. Some crept into the interior, and showed their grinning faces at the windows; others mounted into the rumble; and two more aspiring spirits ascended to the box, by one of whom O'Grady was rudely ordered to get down, a summons enforced by the commissaire himself in a tone of considerable insolence. O'Grady's face for a minute or two seemed working with a secret impulse of fun and devilment which I could not account for at such a moment, as he asked, in a voice of much humility—

'Does Monsieur the Commissaire require me to come down?'

'Instantly,' roared the Frenchman, whose passion was now boiling over.

'In that case, gentlemen, take charge of the team.' So saying, he handed the reins to the passive gendarmes, who took them, without well knowing why. 'I have only a piece of advice,' continued Phil, as he slowly descended the side—'keep a steady hand on the near-side leader, and don't let the bar strike her; and now, good-bye.'

He flourished his four-in-hand whip as he spoke, and with one tremendous cut came down on the team, from leader to wheeler, accompanying the stroke with a yell there was no mistaking. The heavy carriage bounded from the earth as the infuriated cattle broke away at full gallop. A narrow street and a sharp angle lay straight in front; but few of those on the drag waited for the turn, as at every step some bearskin shako shot into the air, followed by a tall figure, whose heavy boots seemed ill-adapted for flying in. The corporal himself had abandoned the reins, and held on manfully by the rail of the box. On every side they fell, in every attitude of distress. But already the leaders had reached the corner; round went the swingle-bars, the wheelers followed, the coach rocked to one side, sprang clean off the pavement, came down with a crash, and then fell right over, while the maddened horses, breaking away, dashed through the town, the harness in fragments behind them, and the pavement flying at every step.

The immediate consequences of this affair were some severe bruises, and no small discouragement to the gendarmerie of St. Omer; the remoter ones, an appeal from the municipal authorities to the Commander-in-chief, by whom the matter was referred for examination to the Adjutant-General. O'Grady was accordingly summoned to Paris to explain, if he could, his conduct in the matter. The order for his appearance there came down at once, and I, having nothing to detain me at St. Omer, resolved to accompany my friend for a few days at least, before I returned to England. Our arrangements were easily made; and the same night we received the Adjutant-General's letter we started by post for Paris.

CHAPTER LVI
ST. DENIS

We were both suddenly awakened from a sound sleep in the *calèche* by the loud cracking of the postillion's whip, the sounds of street noises, and the increased rattle of the wheels over the unequal pavement. We started up just as, turning round in his saddle and pointing with his long whip to either side of him, the fellow called out—

'Paris, Messieurs, Paris! This is Faubourg St. Denis; there before you lies the Rue St. Denis. *Sacristi!* the streets are as crowded as at noonday.'

By this time we had rubbed the sleep from our eyelids and looked about us, and truly the scene before us was one to excite all our astonishment. The Quartier St. Denis was then in the occupation of the Austrian troops, who were not only billeted in the houses, but bivouacked in the open streets—their horses picketed in long files along the *pavé*, the men asleep around their watch-fires, or burnishing arms and accoutrements beside them. The white-clad cuirassier from the Danube, the active and sinewy Hungarian, the tall and swarthy Croat were all there, mixed up among groups of peasant girls coming in to market with fowls and eggs. Carts of forage and waggons full of all manner of provisions were surrounded by groups of soldiers and country-people, trading amicably with one another as though the circumstances which had brought them together were among the ordinary events of commerce.

Threading our way slowly through these, we came upon the Jager encampment, their dark-green uniform and brown carbines giving that air of *sombre* to their appearance so striking after the steel-clad cuirassier and the bright helmets of the dragoons. Farther on, around a fountain, were a body of dismounted dragoons, their tall colbacks and scarlet trousers bespeaking them Polish lancers; their small but beautifully formed white horses pawed the ground, and splashed the water round them, till the dust and foam rose high above them. But the strangest of all were the tall, gigantic figures, who, stretched alongside of their horses, slept in the very middle of the wide street. Lifting their heads lazily for a moment, they gazed on us as we passed, and then lay down again to sleep. Their red beards hung in masses far down upon their breasts, and their loose trousers of a reddish dye but half concealed boots of undressed skin. Their tall lances were piled around them; but these were not wanting to prove that the savage, fierce-looking figures before us were the Cossacks of the Don, thus come for many a hundred mile to avenge the slaughter of Borodino and the burning of Moscow. As we penetrated farther into the city, the mixture of nation and costume became still more remarkable. The erect and soldierlike figure of the Prussian; the loose, wild-eyed Tartar; the brown-clad Russian, with russet beard and curved sabre; the stalwart Highlander, with nodding plume and waving tartan; the Bashkir, with naked scimitar; the gorgeous hussar of Hungary; the tall and manly form of the English guardsman—all passed and repassed before us, adding, by the babel of discordant sound, to the wild confusion of the scene.

It was a strange sight to see the savage soldier from the steppes of Russia, the dark-eyed, heavy-browed Gallician, the yellow-haired Saxon, the rude native of the Caucasus, who had thus given themselves a rendezvous in the very heart of European civilisation, wandering about—now stopping to admire some magnificent palace, now gazing with greedy wonder at the rich display of some jeweller, or the costly and splendid dresses which were exhibited in the shop windows; while here and there were gathered groups of men whose looks of undisguised hate and malignity were bent unceasingly upon the moving mass. Their *bourgeois* dress could not conceal that they were the old soldiers of the Empire—the men of Wagram, of Austerlitz, of Jena, and of Wilna—who now witnessed within their own capital the awful retribution of their own triumphant aggressions.

As the morning advanced the crowds increased, and as we approached the Place du Carrousel, regiments poured in from every street to the morning parade. Among these the Russian *garde*—the *Bonnets d'or*—were conspicuous for the splendour of their costume and the soldierlike precision of their movements, the clash of their brass cymbals and the wild strains of their martial music adding indescribably to their singular appearance. As the infantry drew up in line, we stopped to regard them, when from the Place Louis Quinze the clear notes of a military band rang out a quick step, and the Twenty-eighth British marched in to the air of 'The Young May Moon.' O'Grady's excitement could endure no longer. He jumped up in the *calèche*, and, waving his hat above his head, gave a cheer that rang through the long corridor beneath the Louvre. The Irish regiment caught up the cry, and a yell as wild as ever rose above the din of battle shook the air. A Cossack picket then cantering up suddenly halted, and, leaning down upon their horses' manes, seemed to listen; then dashing spurs into their horses' flanks they made the circuit of the Place at full gallop, while their 'Hurra!' burst forth with all the wild vehemence of their savage nature.

'We shall get into some precious scrape with all this,' said O'Grady, as, overcome with laughing, he fell back into the *calèche*.

Such was my own opinion; so telling the postillion to turn short into the next street we hurried away unperceived, and drove with all the speed we could muster for the Rue St. Honoré. The Hôtel de la Paix fortunately had room for us; and ordering our breakfasts we adjourned to dress, each resolving to make the most of his few hours at Paris.

I had just reached the breakfast-room, and was conning over the morning papers, when O'Grady entered in full uniform, his face radiant with pleasure, and the same easy, jaunty swagger in his walk as on the first day I met him.

'When do you expect to have your audience, Phil?' said I.

'I have had it, my boy. It's all over, finished, completed. Never was anything so successful I talked over the old Adjutant in such a strain, that, instead of dreaming about a court-martial on us, the worthy man is seriously bent on our obtaining compensation for the loss of the drag. He looked somewhat serious as I entered; but when once I made him laugh, the game was my own. I wish you had seen him wiping his dear old eyes as I described the covey of gendarmes taking the air. However, the main point is, the regiment is to be moved up to Paris, the commissaire is to receive a reprimand, our claim for some ten thousand francs is to be considered, and I am to dine with the Adjutant to-day and tell the story after dinner.'

'Do you know, Phil, I have a theory that an Irishman never begins to prosper but just at the moment that any one else would surely be ruined.'

'Don't make a theory of it, Jack, for it may turn out unlucky. But the practice is pretty much what you represent it. Fortune never treats people so well as when they don't care a fig about her. She's exactly like a lady patroness—confoundedly impertinent if you'll bear it, but all smiles if you won't. Have you ever met Tom Burke—"Burke of Ours," as they call him, I believe, in half the regiments in the service?'

'No, never.'

'Well, the loss is yours. Tom's a fine fellow in his way; and if you could get him to tell you his story—or rather one of his stories, for his life is a succession of them—perhaps you would find that this same theory of yours has some foundation. Well pick him up one of these days, and I'll introduce you. But now, Jack, I have a piece of news for you. What do you think of it, my lad?—Lady Charlotte Hinton 's at Paris.'

'My mother here? Is it possible?'

'Yes. Her ladyship resides No. 4 Place Vendôme, opposite the Hôtel de Londres. There's accuracy for you.'

'And who is with her? My father?'

'No. The General is expected in a few days. Lady Julia, I believe, is her only companion.'

There was a kind of reserve suddenly in O'Grady's manner as he mentioned this name, which made us both pause for a few seconds. At length he broke the awkwardness of the silence by saying, in his usual laughing way—

'I contrived to pick up all the gossip of Paris in half an hour. The town is full of English—and such English too! The Cossacks are civilised people, of quiet, retiring habits, compared to them. I verily believe the French are more frightened by our conviviality than ever they were by the bayonets of the Allies. I'm dying to hear your lady-mother's account of everything here.'

'What say you, then, if you come along with me? I 'm becoming very impatient to see my people once more. Julia will, I 'm certain, be very amusing.'

'Ah, and I have a debt of gratitude in that quarter,' said O'Grady hesitatingly. 'Lady Julia was so very kind as to extend her protection to that old villain Corny. I cannot for the life of me understand how she endured him.'

'As to that,' said I, 'Julia has a taste for character; and not even the Chevalier Delany's eccentricity would pain her. So let's forward.'

'Did I tell you that De Vere is here?' said O'Grady.

'No; not with my friends, I trust?'

'On the contrary, I ascertained that he does not visit at Lady Charlotte's. He is attached to Lord Cathcart's embassy; he's very little in society, and rarely to be seen but at the salon, where he plays tremendously high, loses every night, but reappears each day with a replenished pocket. But I intend to know the secret of all this, and of many other matters, ere long. So now let us proceed.'

CHAPTER LVII
PARIS IN 1814

If the strange medley of every nation and costume which we beheld on entering Paris surprised us, how much greater was our astonishment when, having finished a hurried breakfast, we issued forth into the crowded streets! Here were assembled, among the soldiers of every country, visitors from all parts of Europe, attracted by the novel spectacle thus presented to them, and eager to participate in the pleasures of a capital whose rejoicings, so far from being checked by the sad reverse of fortune, were now at the highest pitch; and the city much more resembled the gay resort of an elated people than a town occupied by the troops of conquering enemies. The old soldier of the Empire alone grieved in the midst of this general joy; with the downfall of Napoleon died his every hope. The spirit of conquest, by which for so many years the army had been intoxicated, was annihilated by the one line that signed the treaty of Fontainebleau. Thus among the gay and laughing groups that hurried onward might now and then be seen some veteran of the Old Guard scowling with contemptuous look upon that fickle populace, as eager to celebrate the downfall as ever they had been to greet the glory of their nation.

Nothing more strikingly marked the incongruous host that filled the city than the different guards of honour which were mounted at the several hotels where officers and generals of distinction resided. At this time the regulation was not established which prevailed somewhat later, and gave to the different armies of the Allies the duty of mounting all the guards in rotation. Thus at one door might be seen the tall cuirassier of Austria, his white cloak falling in heavy folds over the flank and haunches of his coal-black horse, looking like some Templar of old; at another the plumed bonnet of a Highlander fluttered in the breeze, as some hardy mountaineer paced to and fro, his grey eye and stern look unmoved by the eager and prying gaze of the crowd that stopped to look upon so strange and singular a costume. Here was the impatient schimmel of some Hungarian hussar pawing the ground with restless eagerness, as his gay dolman slashed with gold glittered in the sun. The Jager from Bohemia, the deadly marksman with the long rifle, the savage Tartar of the Ukraine devouring his meal on his guard, and turning his dark suspicious eye around him, lest every passer-by might mean some treachery—all denoted that some representative of their country dwelt within; while every now and then the clank of a musket would be heard, as a heavy *porte cochere* opened to permit the passage of an equipage, as strange and as characteristic as the guard himself. Here would issue the heavy waggon of some German prince, with emblazoned panels and scarlet hammer-cloth, the horses as fat and lethargic as the smoking and moustached figure they were drawing; there was a low drosky of a Russian, three horses abreast, their harness tinkling with brass bells as the spirited animals plunged and curvetted along. The quiet and elegant-looking phaeton of English build, with its perfection of appointment, rolled along with its deep woody sound beside the quaint, old-fashioned *calèche* of Northern Germany, above whose cumbrous side-panels only the heads of the passengers were visible. Nor were the horsemen less dissimilar; the stately Prussian, with his heel *à plomb* beneath his elbow; the Cossack, with short stirrups, crouched upon his horse's mane; the English horse artilleryman powdering along with massive accoutrements and gigantic steed; the Polish light cavalry soldier, standing high in his stirrups, and turning his restless eye on every side—all were subjects for our curiosity and wonder.

The novelty of the spectacle seemed, however, to have greatly worn off for the Parisians, who rarely noticed the strange and uncouth figures that every moment passed before their eyes, and now talked away as unconcernedly amid the scene of tumult and confusion as though nothing new or remarkable was going on about them—their very indifference and insouciance one of the strangest sights we witnessed.

Our progress, which at the first was a slow one, ceased entirely at the corner of the palace, where a considerable crowd was now collected. Although we asked of the bystanders, no one could tell what was going forward; but the incessant roars of laughter showed that something droll or ridiculous had occurred. O'Grady, whose taste in such matters would suffer no denial, elbowed his way through the mob, I following as well as I was able. When we reached the first rank of the spectators, we certainly needed no explanation of the circumstances to make us join in the mirth about us.

It was a single combat of a very remarkable description. A tall Cossack, with a long red beard now waving wildly on every side, was endeavouring to recover his mutcka cap from a little decrepit old fellow, from whom he had stolen a basket of eggs. The eggs were all broken on the ground; and the little man danced among them like an infuriated fiend, flourishing a stick all the while in the most fearful fashion. The Cossack, whose hand at every moment sought the naked knife that was stuck in his girdle, was obliged to relinquish his weapon by the groans of the mob, who unequivocally showed that they would not permit foul play, and being thus unarmed, could make nothing of an adversary whose contemptible appearance caused all the ridicule of the scene. Meanwhile the little fellow, his clothes in rags, and his head surmounted by a red Cossack mutcka, capered about like nothing human, uttering the most frightful sounds of rage and passion; at length, in a paroxysm of fury, he dealt the tall Cossack a rap on the temples which made him reel again. Scarcely had the blow descended, when, stung by the insult and the jeers of the mob, the enraged savage grasped his knife; with one spring he pounced upon the little man; but as he did so a strong hand from behind seized him by the collar, and with one tremendous jerk hurled him back upon the crowd, where he fell stunned and senseless.

Corny's combat with the Cossack.

I had only time to perceive that it was O'Grady who had come to the rescue, when the little old fellow, turning fully round, looked up in his protector's face, and, without evincing any emotion of surprise or wonder or even of gratitude, croaked out—

'And it's standin' looking on ye wor all the time, and I fighting my sowle out! Ugh! bad luck to service! Look at my coat and small-clothes! Ay, you might laugh, ye grinning bastes as ye are—and a basket of fresh eggs in smithereens, and this Friday!'

The convulsions of laughter which this apparition and the speech excited prevented our hearing more. The mob, too, without understanding a word, were fully sensible of the absurdity of the scene, and a perfect chorus of laughter rang through the street.

'And my elegant beaver, see it now!' said Corny—for we hope our reader recognises him—as he endeavoured to empty the batter from his head-piece, and restore it to shape. 'Ugh! the Haythins! the Turks! see now, Master Phil, it's warning I'm giving you this minit—here, where I stand. May the divil—— Ah, if ye dare, ye eternal robber!' This elegant exordium was directed to the poor Cossack, who, having regained his feet, was skulking away from the field, throwing as he went a lingering look at his red cap, which Mr. Delany still wore as a spoil of his victory.

We now made our way through the crowd, followed by Corny, whose angry looks on every side elicited peals of laughter; and thus accompanied we approached the massive *porte cochère* of a large hotel in the Place Vendôme, where a Swiss, in full costume of porter, informed us that Lady Charlotte Hinton resided. While I endeavoured to pass on, he interposed his burly person, informing me, in very short phrase, that her ladyship did not receive before four o'clock.

'Arrah, hould your prate!' cried Corny; sure it's the woman's son you're talking to. Two pair of stairs to your left hand, and the first door in the passage. Look at the crowd there, the lazy craytures! that has nothing better to do than follow a respectable man. Be off! bad luck to yez! ye ought to be crying over the disgrace ye're in. Be the light that shines! but you desarved it well.'

Leaving Corny to his oration before the mob, of which, happily for the safety of his own skin, they did not comprehend one word, I took the direction he mentioned, and soon found out the door, on which a visiting card with my mother's name was fastened.

We were now introduced into a large and splendidly furnished saloon, with all that lightness and elegance of decoration which in a foreign apartment is the compensation—a poor one sometimes—for the more comfortable look of our English houses. The room was empty, but the morning papers and all the new publications of the day were scattered about with profusion. Consigning my friend for a short time to these, I followed the *femme de chambre*, who had already brought in my card to my mother, to her ladyship's dressing-room. The door was opened noiselessly by the maid, who whispered my name. A gentle 'Let him come in' followed, and I entered.

A Cutting reception

My mother was seated before a glass, under the hands of a coiffeur, and dared not turn her head. As I approached she reached me her hand, however, which having kissed dutifully, I drew my chair, and sat down beside her. 'My dear boy!' said she, as her eyes turned towards me, and a tear fell from the lid and trickled down her cheek. In spite of the unnatural coldness of such a meeting, the words, the accents, and the look that accompanied them came home to my heart, and I was glad to hide my emotion by again pressing my lips to her hand. Having kindly informed me that the ceremony she was then submitting to was imperative, inasmuch as if she had not M. Dejoncourt then, she could not have him at all—that his time was so filled up, every moment of it, from eight in the morning till eleven at night, that the Emperor Alexander himself couldn't obtain his services, if he wished for them—she proceeded to give me some details of my father, by which I could learn that the change in his circumstances had never been made known to her, and that she had gone on since we last met in her old career of extravagance and expense, the indulgence of which, and the cares of her ever-declining health, having given her abundant occupation.

As I looked at her beautiful features and delicately fair complexion, upon which time had scarcely laid a touch, I sighed to think at what a frightful sacrifice of feeling, of duty, and of happiness, too, such loveliness had been purchased. If the fine pencilling of that brow had never known a wrinkle, the heart had never throbbed to one high or holy thought; if the smile sat easily on the lip, it was the habitual garb of fashionable captivation, and not the indication of one kind thought or one affectionate feeling. I felt shocked, too, that I could thus criticise my mother; but in truth for a minute or two I forgot she was such.

'And Julia,' said I, at length—'what of her?'

'Very handsome indeed—strikingly so. Beulwitz, the emperor's aide-de-camp, admires her immensely. I am sincerely glad that you are come, dear John. You know Julia's fortune has all been saved: but of that another time. The first point now is to secure you a ticket for this ball; and how to do it, I'm sure I know not.'

'My dear mother, believe me I have not the slightest desire——'

'How very unkind you are to think we could separate from you after such an absence! Besides, Julia would be seriously offended, and I think with cause. But the ticket—let's consider about that. Dejoncourt, is it true that the Princesse de Nassau was refused a card for the ball?'

'Oui, miladi. The King of Prussia has sent her one of his, and is to take her; and Madame la Duchesse de St. Bieve was so angry at being left out that she tried to get up an alarm of conspiracy in the *faubourg*, to prevent the sovereigns from going.'

'But they will go, surely—won't they?'

'Ah, to be sure. *Pardieu*, they would say to-morrow that they had been omitted too, if they didn't appear.'

'What are we to do?' said her ladyship with energy. 'Grammont can be of no use here; for unfortunately these people are not French.'

'What then,' said I, 'is it some of the crowned heads who are the entertainers?'

'Oh, no! Indeed, I don't know who they are; nor do I know any one who does. The only fact of importance is that this is their third *fête*—the first two were the most brilliant things ever given in Paris; that the Emperor of Russia always dances there; that the King of Prussia makes his whist-party; that Blucher takes the head of one of the supper-tables; and, in a word, Talleyrand himself has employed more diplomacy to secure an extra ticket than he has often dispensed in carving out a new monarchy.'

My mother handed me a splendidly embossed card, as she spoke, upon which, in letters of pale burnished gold, were inscribed the following words: 'Madame de Roni, née Cassidy de Kilmainham, prie honneur,' etc. A burst of laughter at the absurdity of the title stopped my reading further.

'She's an Italian, possibly,' said my mother.

'I should think not,' I replied; 'the "née Cassidy de Kilmainham" smacks of something nearer home. What think you of Ireland?'

'Ireland! Are these people Irish?' said she, starting with horror at the thought. 'I trust, my dear John, you would not think it proper to jest on such a subject.'

'My dear mother, I never heard of them before; the only thing that strikes me is the name. "Cassidy" is assuredly more Milesian than Roman.'

'But she has birth—that's certain,' replied my mother proudly.

Not caring to argue the point, which after all resolved itself into the question that the lady was the child of somebody, and that somebody was called 'Cassidy,' I began to meditate on the singularity of such a phase in life as the entertainers of sovereigns, kaisers, kings, princes, archdukes, and ambassadors being a person utterly unknown.

'But here's Grammont,' said my mother, as a gentle tap was heard at the door and the Count entered—the only change in his appearance since last I saw him being the addition of another cordon to his blue coat, and a certain springiness in his walk, which I afterwards remarked as common among all the returned *émigrés* at the restoration.

'Que diable faut il faire,' said the Count, entering, 'with this Madame de Roni? She refuses all the world. Ah, Jack, *mon cher*, how do you do?—safe and sound from all the perils of these terrible French, who cut you all to pieces in the Peninsula? But only think, *miladi*, no card for la Duchesse de

Tavenne; Madame de Givry left out! *Sapristi!* I hope there is nothing against *ce pauvre* Roi de Prusse.'

'Well, and here is John,' said my mother; 'what are we to do about him?'

My renewed disclaimer of any wish in the matter was cut short by a look of reproof, and I waited the whole discussion with patience.

'Never was there such a difficulty,' said the Count, musing. 'There is certainly nothing to be done through the worthy husband of Madame. Dejoncourt and two or three more gave him a *diner en gourmand* at Very's, to seduce him; and after his fifth flask of champagne he frankly confessed he was sorry he could not return their civilities as he wished. I 'll entertain you here, and have Blucher and Platon, Fouché, and any one else you like to meet you. I'll introduce you to old Prussia and the Czar whenever you please; you shall have permission to shoot at Fontainebleau any day you mention; but as to Madame de Roni, she is devilish exclusive. I really cannot manage that for you.'

'I wish you could prevail on yourself to be serious,' said my mother, in nowise pleased with the jocular spirit the Count's anecdote had excited. 'But here is Julia—what does she advise?'

As my mother spoke, the door opened, and my cousin appeared. Her figure had more of the roundness of womanhood, and her face, though paler, was fuller, and its expression had assumed a more decided character than when I last saw her. Her winning smile and her graceful carriage were all unchanged; and her low soft voice never struck me as more fascinating than when she held out her hand and said—

'My dear cousin, how happy it makes me to see you again!'

Her dark-blue eyes were tearful as she spoke, and her lip—that haughty lip—trembled. A strange wild thrill crept through my heart as I pressed her hand within both of mine—a vague feeling which I dared not suffer to dwell in my mind, and yet feared lest when it should depart that I had lost my chance of happiness. Yes, there are times when a man without the admixture of any coxcombry in the feeling, without a particle of vanity— nay, with a deep sense of his own unworthiness—can ask himself, 'Does this woman like me?' And at such moments, if his own heart give not the ready answer, it were far better that he sought not the reply from his reason.

It was only when my mother asked, for the second time, what was to be done about John's ticket, that Julia seemed aware of the question—a slight, a very slight, curving of her lip showing the while the sense she entertained of such an inquiry after long years of separation; and at last, as if unable to repress the indignation of the moment, she said abruptly—

'But, of course, as we shall not think of going tonight——'

'We not go! Eh, *pardieu!* why not?' said the Count.

'The Colonel below-stairs begs to say that he will call somewhat later,' said the *femme de chambre* at this juncture.

'The Colonel! Whom does she mean?'

'Oh, my friend O'Grady. Poor fellow! I have been forgetting him all this while. So allow me to join him, and we'll wait for your appearance in the drawing-room.'

'I remember him perfectly,' said my mother—'an agreeable person, I think. So take Julia and the Count with you, and I'll follow as soon as I can.'

Julia blushed deeply, and as suddenly grew pale again as my mother spoke. I knew that she had always treated my friend with hauteur and reserve, without any assignable reason, and had long determined that when an opportunity arose I would endeavour to get rid of the unjust impression she had somehow conceived of my warmest, truest friend. This was not, however, the time for explanations; and I merely said, as I offered my arm—

'Poor O'Grady has been badly wounded; but I think he's now getting on favourably.'

She said something in reply, but the words were lost in the noise of descending the stairs. Just as we reached the landing I caught a glimpse of my friend issuing from the *porte cochère*, and only in time to call him by his name—

'Holloa, Phil! Don't go away.'

As he turned back towards the drawing-room, he cried out—

'It's only this instant, Jack, I remembered how very awkward it was of me to come here with you at this hour. You have, of course, so much to say and hear after your absence—'

The sight of my fair cousin cut short his speech, as she stood near the door with her hand out to receive him. As O'Grady took her taper fingers within his own, there was an air of cold distance in his manner that actually offended me. Bowing deeply, he said a few brief words in a tone of gravity and stiffness quite unusual with him; and then, turning to Grammont, he shook the Count's hand with a warmth and cordiality most markedly different. I only dared to glance at Julia; but as I did so I could mark an expression of haughty displeasure that settled on her brow, while her heightened colour made her turn away towards the window.

I was myself so much annoyed by the manner in which O'Grady had received advances which I had never seen made to any one before, that I was silent. Even Grammont saw the awkwardness of all parties so much in need of his intervention that he at once opened the whole negotiation of the ball to O'Grady, describing with a Frenchman's volubility and sarcasm the stratagems and devices which were employed to obtain invitations, the triumph of the successful, the despairing malice of the unfortunate—heightening his narrative by the mystery of the fair hostess, who, herself unknown and unheard of till now, was at this moment at the pinnacle of fashion, dictating the laws and distributing the honours of the beau monde to the greatest sovereigns of Europe.

'She is very beautiful, no doubt?' asked O'Grady.

'Oui, pas mal,' said Grammont, with that all-explaining shrug of the shoulders by which a foreigner conveys so much.

'Very rich, perhaps?'

'Millionaire!' said the Frenchman, in a tone of exultation that bespoke his full acquiescence in that surmise at least.

'And her rank?'

'Ah, I don't read riddles. All I know is, her house is the best thing at Paris; she has secured old Cambaceres' *chef de cuisine*; has bought up the groom of the chambers of the ex-Emperor; keeps an *estafette* going on the Strasbourg road for *pâtés de foie gras*; and is on such terms with the sovereigns that she has their private bands to play at all her parties. Que voulez-vous?'

'Nothing more, indeed!' said O'Grady, laughing. 'Such admirable supremacy in the world of *bon ton* it would be rank heresy to question further, and I no longer wonder at the active canvass for her invitations.'

'Oui, parbleu!' said the Frenchman gaily. 'If Monsieur the Comte d'Artois does not exert himself, people will be more proud of a ticket to these balls than of the Croix de St. Louis. For my own part, I think of wearing mine over the cordon.'

As he spoke, he flourished his card of invitation in the air, and displayed it in his bosom.

'Madame de Roni, née Cassidy de Kilmainham,' said O'Grady, bursting into a perfect roar of laughter. 'This is glorious, Jack! Did you see this?'

'See! eh? to be sure; and what then?'

But O'Gradys mirth had burst all bounds, and he sat back in an arm-chair laughing immoderately. To all our questions he could give no other reply than renewed bursts of merriment, which, however enjoyed by himself, were very provoking to us.

'He knows her,' whispered Grammont in my ear; 'be assured he knows Madame.'

'Jack, where shall we meet in half an hour?' said Phil at length, jumping up and wiping his eyes.

'Here, if you like,' said I. 'I shall not leave this till you return.'

'Be it so,' said he; and then with a bow to my cousin and an easy nod to Grammont, O'Grady took his hat and departed.

Grammont now looked at his watch, and remembering some half-dozen very important appointments, took his leave also, leaving me once more, after so long an interval, *tête-à-tête* with Julia.

There were so many things to talk over since we had met, so many reminiscences which each moment called up, that I never thought of the hours as they ran over; and it was only by Lady Charlotte's appearance in the drawing-room that we were apprised it was already past four o'clock, and that the tide of her morning visitors would now set in, and break up all hopes of continuing our colloquy.

'Where is your friend?' said my mother, as she carried her eyes languidly round the spacious apartment.

'Gone some hours ago; but he promised to take me up here. We shall see him soon, I suspect.'

'Colonel O'Grady,' said a servant; and my cousin had just time to leave the room by one door as he entered by another.

Advancing to my mother with a manner of respectful ease which he possessed in perfection, O'Grady contrived in a few brief words to resume the ground he had formerly occupied in her acquaintance, throwing out as he went an occasional compliment to her looks, so naturally and unaffectedly done as not to need acknowledgment or reply, but yet with sufficient *empressement* to show interest.

'I have heard since my arrival that you were interested about this ball, and took the opportunity to secure you some tickets, which, though late, some of your friends may care for.'

He presented my mother as he spoke with several blank cards of invitation, who, as she took them, could not conceal her astonishment nor repress the look of curiosity, which she could scarcely repel in words, as to how he had accomplished a task the highest people in Paris had failed in. I saw what was passing in her mind, and immediately said—

'My mother would like to know your secret about these same cards, O'Grady; for they have been a perfect subject of contention here for the last three weeks.'

'Her ladyship must excuse me—at least for the present—if I have one secret I cannot communicate to her,' said O'Grady, smiling. 'Let me only assure her that no one shall know it before she herself does.'

'And there is a secret?' said Lady Charlotte eagerly.

'Yes, there is a secret,' replied O'Grady, with a most ludicrous gravity of tone.

'Well, at least we have profited by it, and so we may wait in patience. Your friend Colonel O'Grady will give us the pleasure of his company at dinner, I hope,' continued my mother, with her most winning smile.

O'Grady declined, having already accepted the invitation of the Adjutant-General, but begged he might be permitted to join our party at the ball—which being graciously acceded to by my mother, we both made our bows, and sauntered out to see more of the sights of Paris.

'Come, Phil,' said I, when we were once more alone, 'what is the secret? Who is Madame de Roni?'

'Not even to you, Jack,' was his answer, and we walked on in silence.

CHAPTER LVIII
THE RONI FÊTE

There is no epidemic more catching than excitement. The fussy manner and feverish bustle of the people about you are sure, after a time, to communicate themselves to you—the very irritation they create being what the physicians call a predisposing cause. I became an illustration in point, as the hour of this ball drew nigh. At first I could not but wonder how in the midst of such stupendous events as were then taking place—in the heart of a city garrisoned by an enemy, with everything that could wound national pride and offend national honour—even French levity could raise itself to the enjoyment of fashionable frivolity; but by degrees the continual recurrence of the subject familiarised my mind to it" wearing off my first and more natural impressions, and at last I began, like my neighbours, not only to listen with patience, but even to join in the various discussions with animation and interest.

No sooner had the report gained currency that Lady Charlotte was in possession of blank invitations, than our hotel was besieged by half Paris—the unfortunate endeavouring, by every species of flattery and every imaginable stratagem, to obtain tickets; the lucky ones all anxious to find out the mystery of her ladyship's success, which at first seemed almost incredible. The various surmises, guesses, hints, allusions, and subterfuges which followed one another in rapid succession, as this motley mob of fashionables came and went, and went and came again, amused me considerably—the more so, perhaps, as the occasion called into full play all my cousin Julia's powers of flippant raillery and sarcasm, both of which she exercised without scruple, but never within range of discovery by any of her victims.

Everything gave way to the convenience of this splendid *fête*. The eight o'clock dinner was anticipated by full two hours; no other subject of conversation was ever broached by the company; and at nine the carriages were ordered to the door, it being wisely calculated that if we reached our destination at eleven we should esteem ourselves fortunate.

How often, as the dashing equipage whirls past to some scene of pleasure, where beauty and rank and riches await the sated votary of fashion, will the glare of the carriage-lamps fall upon the gloomy footway, where, wet and weary, some melancholy figure steals along with downcast head and plodding step, his thoughts turned ever to some accustomed scene of wretchedness, where want and misery, disease, neglect, decay, all herd together, and not even hope can enter! The poor man, startled, looks up; the rich one, lolling back upon his easy cushion, casts a downward glance; their eyes meet—it is but a second; there is no sympathy between them—the course of one lies north, the other south. Thus at each moment did my sad heart turn away from all the splendour of the preparation about me, to wonder with myself how even for an instant I could forget my own path in life, which, opening with every prospect of happiness, yet now offered not a hope for the future. Between these two alternate states the hours crept on. As I sat beside Julia in the carriage, I could not but mark that something weighed also on her spirits. More silent than usual, she replied, when spoken to, with effort; and more than once returned wrong answers to my mother, who talked away unceasingly of the ball and the guests.

It was near midnight when we drove into the large archway of the Hôtel de Rohan, where Madame de Roni held her court. Brilliantly lighted with lamps of various colours, the very equipages were made a part of the spectacle, as they shone in bright and changeful hues, reflected from gorgeous housings, gilded trappings, and costly liveries. A large, dark-coloured travelling-carriage, with a single pair of horses, stood in the corner of the court, the only thing to distinguish it being two mounted light dragoons who waited beside it, and a chasseur in green and gold uniform who stood at the door. This simple equipage belonged to the King of Prussia. Around on every side were splendidly appointed carriages, glittering with emblazonry and gilding, from which, as the guests descended and entered the marble vestibule, names of European celebrity were called out and repeated from voice to voiqe along the lofty corridors. Le Prince de Schwartzenberg, Count Pozzo di Borgo, Le Duc de Dal-berg, Milord Cathcart, Le Comte de Nesselrode, Monsieur Talleyrand de Perigord, with others equally noble and exalted, followed in rapid succession.

Our turn came at last; and as we reached the hall we found O'Grady waiting for our arrival.

'There's no use in attempting to get forward for some time,' said he; 'so follow me, and I'll secure you a more comfortable place to wait in.'

As he spoke he passed through the hall, and, whispering a few words to a servant, a door was opened in the wainscot, admitting us to a small and neatly-fitted-up library, where a good fire and some easy-chairs awaited us.

'I see your surprise,' said O'Grady, as my mother looked about her with astonishment at his perfect acquaintance with the whole locality; 'but I can't explain—it's part of my secret. Meanwhile, Jack, I have another for your ear,' said he, in a low whisper, as he drew me aside into a corner. 'I have made a very singular discovery, Jack, to-day, and I have a notion it may lead to more. I met, by accident, at the Adjutant-General's table, the brother of a French officer whose life I saved at Nivelle; he remembered my name in a moment, and we became sworn friends. I accepted his offer of a seat in his carriage to this ball, and on the way he informed me that he was the chief of the secret police of Paris, whose business it is to watch all the doings of the regular police and report upon them to Fouché, whose spies are in every salon and at every dinner-table in the capital I have no time at present to repeat any of the extraordinary stories he told me of this horrible system; but just as we entered the courtyard of this hotel, our carriage was jammed up in the line and detained for some minutes. Guillemain suddenly let down the glass, and gave a low, peculiar whistle, which, if I had not been paying considerable attention to everything about him, might have escaped my notice. In about a minute after a man, with a hat slouched over his face, and a large cravat covering his mouth, approached the carriage. They conversed together for some time, and I could perceive that the new-comer spoke his French in a broken manner and with a foreign accent. By a slight movement of the horses one of the lamps threw the light full upon this man's face; I fixed my eyes rapidly on him, and recognised—whom, think you? But you'd never guess: no other than your old antagonist, Ulick Burke!'

'Ulick Burke! You must have been mistaken.'

'No, no. I knew him at once; the light rested on him for full five minutes, and I had time enough to scan every feature of his face. I could swear to the man now. He left us at last, and I watched him till he disappeared among the crowd of servants that filled the courtyard.'

'"That's one of your people," said I carelessly, as Guillemain drew up the glass, and sat back in the carriage.

'"Yes, and a thorough scoundrel he is—capable of anything."

'"He's not French," said I, with the same indifference of manner I had feigned at first.

'Guillemain started as I spoke; and I half feared I had destroyed all by venturing too much. At length, after a short pause, he replied: "You're right, he's not French; but we have them of all nations—Poles, Swedes, Germans, Italians, Greeks. That fellow is English."

'"Say Irish, rather," said I, determining to risk all, to know all.

'"You know him, then?" said Guillemain hurriedly; "where did you see Fitzgerald?"

'"Fitzgerald!" said I, repeating the name after him; and then affecting disappointment, added, "That's not the name."

'"Ha! I knew you were mistaken," said Guillemain, with animation; "the fellow told me he defies recognition; and I certainly have tried him often among his countrymen, and he has never been detected. And yet he knows the English thoroughly and intimately. It was through him that I first found out these very people we are going to."

'Here, Jack, he entered upon a long account of our worthy hosts, who with great wealth, great pretensions, and as great vulgarity came to Paris some weeks ago in that mighty flood of all sorts of people that flocked here since the peace. Their desire to be ranked among the fashionable entertainers of the day was soon reported to the minister of police, who, after considering how far such a house might be useful, where persons of all shades of political opinion might meet—friends of the Bourbons, Jacobites, Napoleonists, the men of '88, and the admirers of the old *régime*—measures were accordingly taken that their invitations should go out to the first persons in Paris, and, more still, should be accepted by them.

'While these worthy people are therefore distributing their hospitalities with all the good faith imaginable, their hotel is nothing more nor less than a *cabinet de police*, where Fouché and his agents are unravelling the intrigues of Paris, or weaving fresh ones for their own objects.'

'Infamous system! But how comes it, Phil, that they have never discovered their anomalous position?'

'What a question, Jack! Vulgar pretension is a triple shield that no eye can pierce; and as you know the parties——'

'Know them! no, I never heard of them before.' 'What, Jack! Is your memory so short-lived? And yet there was a pretty girl in the house who might have rested longer in your memory.'

The announcement of Lady Charlotte and my cousin's names by the servant at the foot of the stairs broke up our conference; and we had only time to join our party as we fell into that closely-wedged phalanx that wound its slow length up the spacious staircase. O'Grady's last words had excited my curiosity to the highest pitch; but as he preceded me with my mother on his arm, I was unable to ask for an explanation.

At last we reached the ante-chamber, from which a vista of salons suddenly broke upon the view; and although anticipating much, I had formed no conception whatever of the splendour of the scene before me. More brilliant than noonday itself, the room was a blaze of wax-lights; the ceilings of fretted gold and blue enamel glittered like a gorgeous firmament; the walls were covered with pictures in costly frames of Venetian taste. But the decorations, magnificent and princely as they were, were as nothing to that splendid crowd of jewelled dames and glittering nobles, of all that was distinguished in beauty, in rank, in military glory, or in the great contest of political life. Here were the greatest names of Europe—the kings and princes of the earth, the leaders of mighty armies, the generals of a hundred battles; here was the collective greatness of the world, all that can influence mankind—hereditary rank, military power, stupendous intellect, beauty, wealth—mixing in the vast vortex of fashionable dissipation, and plunging into all the excesses of voluptuous pleasure. The band of the Imperial Guard stationed near the staircase were playing with all the delicious softness of their national instrument—the Russian horn—a favourite mazurka of the emperor as we entered, and a partial silence reigned among the hundred listeners.

O'Grady conveyed my mother through the crowd to a seat, where, having placed my cousin beside her, he once more came near me.

'Jack,' whispered he, 'come a little this way.' He drew aside a curtain as he spoke, and we entered a boudoir, where a buffet of refreshments was placed. Here the scene was ludicrous in the extreme, from the incongruous mixture-of persons of so many nations and languages who were chatting away and hobnobbing to one another in all the dismembered phrases of every tongue in Europe; loud laughter, however, poured from one corner of the room, whither O'Grady directed his steps, still holding my arm. A group of Cossack officers in full scarlet costume, their loose trousers slashed with gold embroidery and thrust into wide boots of yellow leather, stood in a circle round a person whom we could not yet perceive, but who, we were enabled to discover, was exercising his powers of amusement for this semi-savage audience, whose wild shouts of laughter broke forth at every moment. We made our way at length through the crowd, and my eyes at last fell upon the figure within. I stared; I rubbed my eyes; I actually began to doubt my very senses, when suddenly turning his joyous face beaming with good-humour towards me, he held forth his hand and called out, 'Captain, my darling, the top of the morning to you. This beats Stephen's Green, doesn't it?'

Mr Paul Rooney and his Cossack Friends

'Mr. Paul Rooney!' said I.

'No, no! Monsieur de Roni, if you please,' said he, again breaking out into a fit of laughing. 'Lord help you, man, I've been christened since I came abroad. Let me present you to my friends.' Here Paul poked a tall Cossack in the ribs to attract his attention, and then pointing to me, said: 'This is Captain Hinton; his name's a poser—a cross between chincough and a house-key. Eh, old fellow?'

A Tartar grin was the reply to this very intelligible speech; but a bumper of champagne made everything comprehensible between them. Mr. Rooney's hilarity soon showed me that he had not forgotten his native habits, and was steadily bent upon drinking glass for glass with his company, even though they only came in detachments. With Bashkir chiefs, Pomeranian barons, Rhine graafs, and Polish counts he seemed as intimate as though he had passed as much of his time in the Caucasus as the Four Courts, and was as familiar with the banks of the Don as ever he had been with those of the Dodder.

'And is it really our old friend Mrs. Paul who entertains this host of czars and princes?'

'Is it really only now that you've guessed it?' said O'Grady, as he carried me away with him through the salon. 'But I see Lady Charlotte is amongst her friends, and your cousin is dancing; so now let's make the most of our time. I say, Jack, your lady-mother scarcely supposes that her host is the same person she once called on for his bill. By Jove, what a discovery it would be to her! and the little girl she had such a horror of is now the belle of Paris. You remember Louisa Bellew, don't you? Seven thousand a year, my boy, and beauty worth double the money. But there she is, and how handsome!'

As he spoke, a lady passed us leaning on her partner's arm, her head turned slightly over her shoulder. I caught but one glance, and as I did so, the rushing torrent of blood that mounted to my face made my very brain grow dizzy. I knew not where I stood. I sprang forward to speak to her, and then became rooted to the ground. It was she, indeed, as beautiful as ever; her pale face wore the very look I had last seen the night I saved her from the flood.

'Did you observe her companion?' said O'Grady, who fortunately had not noticed my confusion. 'It was De Vere. I knew he was here; and I suspect I see his plans.'

'De Vere!' said I, starting. 'De Vere with Miss Bellew! Are you certain?'

'Quite certain; I seldom mistake a face, and his I can't forget. But here's Guillemain. I'll join you in a moment.'

So saying, O'Grady left my side, and I saw him take the arm of a small man in black, who was standing at a doorway. The rush of sensations that crowded on me as I stood there alone made me forget the time, and I knew not that O'Grady had been above half an hour away when he again came to my side.

'How the plot thickens, Hinton!' said he, in a low whisper. 'Only think, the villain Burke has actually made the hand and fortune of that lovely girl the price of obtaining secret information from De Vere of the proceedings of the British embassy. Guillemain did not confess this to me; but he spoke in such a way, that, with my knowledge of all the parties, I made out the clue.'

'Burke! but what influence has he over her?'

'None over her, but much over the Rooneys, whom, independent of threats about exposing their real condition in life, he has persuaded that such a marriage for their ward secures them in fashionable society for ever. This with Paul would do nothing; but Madame de Roni, as you know, sets a high price on such a treasure. Besides, he is in possession of some family secret about her mother, which he uses as a means of intimidation to Paul, who would rather die than hurt Miss Bellew's feelings. Now, Jack, De Vere only wants intellect to be as great a scoundrel as Master Ulick, so we must rescue this poor girl, come what will.'

'We must and we will,' said I, with a tone of eagerness that made O'Grady start.

'Not a moment is to be lost,' said he, after a brief pause. 'I 'll try what can be done with Guillemain.'

An opening of the crowd as he spoke compelled us to fall back, and as we did so I could perceive that an avenue was made along the room.

'One of the sovereigns,' whispered O'Grady.

I leaned forward, and perceived two aides-de-camp in green uniform, who were retreating step by step slowly before some persons farther back.

'The Emperor of Russia,' whispered a voice near me; and the same instant I saw the tall and fine-looking figure of Alexander, his broad massive forehead, and frank manly face turning from side to side as he acknowledged the salutations of the room. On his arm he supported a lady, whose nodding plumes waved in concert with every inclination of the Czar himself. Curious to see what royal personage shared thus with him the homage of the assembly, I stooped to catch a glance. The lady turned — our eyes met; a slight flush coloured her cheek as she quickly moved her head away. It was Mrs. Paul Rooney herself! Yes, she whom I had once seen with an effort subdue her pride of station when led in to dinner by some Irish attorney-general, or some going judge of assize, now leaned on the arm of an emperor, and divided with him the honours of the moment!

While O'Grady sought out his new friend, the minister of police, I went in search of my mother and Lady Julia, whom I found surrounded by a knot of their own acquaintances, actively engaged in surmises as to the lady of the house — her rank, fortune, and pretensions. For some time I could not but feel amused at the absurd assertions of many of the party, who affected to know all about Madame de Roni and her secret mission at Paris.

'My dear John,' said my mother in a whisper, 'you must find out all about her. Your friend, the Colonel, is evidently in the secret. Pray, now, don't forget it. But really you seem in a dream. There's Beulwitz paying

Julia all the attention imaginable the entire evening, and you've never gone near her. Apropos, have you seen this ward of Madame de Roni? She is very pretty, and they speak of her as a very suitable person.' (This phrase was a kind of cant with my mother and her set, which expressed in brief that a lady was enormously rich and a very desirable match for a man with nothing.) 'I forget her name.'

'Miss Bellew, perhaps,' said I, trembling lest any recollection of ever having heard it before should cross her mind.

'Yes, that's the name; somehow it seems familiar to me. Do you know her yet, for my friend Lady Middleton knows every one, and will introduce you?'

'Oh, I have the pleasure of being acquainted with her already,' said I, turning away to hide my confusion.

'That's quite proper,' said her ladyship encouragingly. 'But here she comes; I think you must introduce me, John.'

As my mother spoke, Louisa Bellew came up, leaning on a lady's arm. A moment's hesitation on my part would have only augmented the embarrassment which increased at every instant; so I stepped forward and pronounced her name. No sooner had the words 'Miss Bellew' escaped my lips than she turned round; her large full eyes were fixed upon me doubtingly for a second, and her face grew deep scarlet, and then as suddenly pale again. She made an effort to speak, but could not; a tottering weakness seemed to creep over her frame, and as she pressed her companion's arm closely I heard her mutter—'Oh, pray move on!'

'Lady Charlotte Hinton—'Miss Bellew,' said the lady at her side, who had paid no attention whatever to Louisa's agitated manner.

My mother smiled in her sweetest manner, while Miss Bellow's acknowledgments were made with the most distant coldness.

'My son had deemed himself fortunate enough to be known to you,' said Lady Charlotte.

Miss Bellew became pale as death; her very lips were bloodless, as with a voice tremulous with emotion, she replied—

'We were acquainted once, madam; but——'

What was to be the remainder of the speech I know not, for as the crowd moved on she passed with it, leaving me like one whose senses were forsaking him one by one. I could only hear my mother say, 'How very impertinent!' and then my brain became a chaos. A kind of wild reckless feeling, the savage longing that in moments of dark passion stirs within a man for some act of cruelty, some deed of vengeance, ran through my breast. I had been spurned, despised, disowned by her of whom through many a weary month my heart alone was full. I hurried away from the spot, my brain on fire. I saw nothing, I heeded nothing, of the bright looks and laughing faces that passed me; scornful pity and contempt for one so low as I was seemed to prevail in every face I looked at. A strange impulse to seek out Lord Dudley de Vere was uppermost in my mind; and as I turned on every side to find him, I felt my arm grasped tightly, and heard O'Grady's voice in my ear—

'Be calm, Jack, for heaven's sake! Your disturbed looks make every one stare at you.'

He drew me along with him through the crowd, and at length reached a card-room, where, except the players, no one was present.

'Come, my dear boy, I saw what has annoyed you.'

'You saw it!' said I, my eyeballs straining as I spoke.

'Yes, yes; and what signifies it? So very handsome a girl, and the expectation of a large fortune, must always have followers. But you know Lady Julia well enough— —'

'Lady Julia!' repeated I, in amazement.

'Yes. I say you know her well enough to believe that Beulwitz is not exactly the person— —'

A burst of laughter at his mistake broke from me at the moment; but so wild and discordant was it that O'Grady misconstrued its meaning, and went at some length to assure me that my cousin's affection for me was beyond my suspicion.

Stunned by my own overwhelming sorrow, I felt no inclination to undeceive him, and let him persist in his error without even a word of reply.

'Rouse yourself, Jack,' said he, at length. 'This depression is unworthy of you, had you even cause for grief. There's many a heart heavier than your own, my boy, where the lip is smiling this minute.'

There was a tone of deep affliction in the cadence of his voice as these words fell from him, and he turned away his head as he spoke. Then rallying in an instant, he added—

'Do you know, our dear friend Mrs. Paul has scarcely ventured to acknowledge me to-night, and I feel a kind of devilish spirit of vengeance working within me in consequence. To out me! I that trained her infant mind to greatness; that actually smuggled for her a contraband viceroy, and brought him alive into her dominions! What dire ingratitude! Come, what say you to champagne?'

He poured me out a large glassful as he spoke, and, filling his own, called out, laughing—

'Here, I give you a toast—"La Vendetta!" eh, Jack? Corsican vengeance on all who maltreat us!'

Glass after glass followed; and I felt my brain, instead of being excited, grow calmer, steadier; a firm and determined resolution usurped the flitting thoughts and wandering fancies of before.

'They're moving towards the supper-room,' said O'Grady, who for some time past had talked away, without my paying any attention to what he said.

As we descended the stairs, I heard my mother's carriage announced, and could just see her and my cousin handed to it by some Austrian officers as we entered the supper-room.

The incessant crash and din of the enormous banquet-ing-room, its crowd and heat, its gorgeous table-equipage and splendid guests, were scarce noticed by me as I followed O'Grady half mechanically towards the end of the room. For some time I remained stupidly unconscious of all around; and it was only after a very considerable time that I descried that immediately in front of where we stood Mrs. Paul Rooney was seated—the Emperor of Russia on her right, the King of Prussia on her left hand; Swartzenburg, Blucher, Talleyrand, Nesselrode, and many others equally distinguished occupying places along the board. Her jocund laugh and merry voice, indeed, first attracted my attention.

'By Jove! she does it admirably,' said O'Grady, who for full five minutes had been most critically employed scrutinising Mrs. Paul's manner. 'Do you remark the tact with which she graduates her attentions to the emperor and the king? And look at the hauteur of her bearing to old Blucher! But, hush! what's coming?'

A kind of suppressed murmur buzzed along the crowded room, which, subsiding into a dead silence, the Emperor Alexander rose, and addressing the guests in a few but well-chosen words in English, informed them he had received permission from their amiable and captivating hostess to propose a toast, and he took the opportunity with unqualified delight to give the health of 'the Prince Regent.' A perfect thunder of applause acknowledged this piece of gracious courtesy, and a 'hip! hip! hurrah!' which astonished the foreigners, shook the very roof. While the deafening shouts rose on every side, Mrs. Paul wrote a line with her pencil hastily on her card, and turning round gave it to a Cossack aide-de-camp of the emperor to deliver into Mr. Rooney's hands. Either from the excitement of the moment or his imperfect acquaintance with English, the unlucky Cossack turned for an explanation towards the first British officer near him, who happened to be O'Grady.

'What does this mean?' said he in French.

'Ah,' said Phil, looking at it, 'this is intended for that gentleman at the foot of the table. You see him yonder—he's laughing now. Come along, I'll pilot you towards him.'

Suspecting that O'Grady's politeness had some deeper motive than mere civility, I leaned over his shoulder and asked the reason of it.

'Look here,' said he, showing me the card as he spoke, on which was written the following words: 'Make the band play "God Save the King "; the emperor wishes it.'

'Come with us, Jack,' whispered O'Grady; 'we had better keep near the door.'

I followed them through the dense crowd, who were still cheering with all their might, and at last reached the end of the table, where Paul himself was amusing a select party of Tartar chiefs, Prussian colonels, Irish captains, and Hungarian nobles.

'Look here,' said Phil, showing me the card, which in his passage down the room he had contrived to alter, by rubbing out the first part and interpolating a passage of his own; making the whole run thus—

'Sing the "Cruiskeen Lawn"; the emperor wishes it.'

I had scarcely time to thrust my handkerchief to my mouth and prevent an outbreak of laughter, when I saw the Cossack officer present the card to Paul with a deep bow. Mr. Rooney read it—surveyed the bearer; read it again—rubbed his eyes, drew over a branch of wax-candles to inspect it better, and then, directing a look to the opposite extremity of the table, exchanged glances with his spouse, as if interrogating her intentions once more. A quick, sharp nod from Mrs. Paul decided the question thus tacitly asked; and Paul, clearing off a tumbler of sherry, muttered to himself, 'What the devil put the "Cruiskeen Lawn" into his Majesty's head I can't think; but I suppose there's no refusing.*

A very spirited tapping with the handle of his knife was now heard to mix with the other convivial sounds, and soon indeed to overtop them, as Paul, anxious to fulfil a royal behest, cleared his throat a couple of times, and called out, 'I'll do the best I can, your Majesty'; and at once struck up—

> *'Let the farmer praise his grounds,*
> *Let the huntsman praise his hounds,*
> *And talk of the deeds they had done;*
> *But I more blest than they — —'*

Here Paul quavered, and at last the pent-up mirth of the whole room could endure no more, but burst forth into one continuous shout of laughter, in which kings, dukes, ambassadors, and field-marshals joined as loudly as their neighbours. To hear the song was utterly impossible; and though from Mr. Paul's expanded cheeks and violent gesticulation it was evident he was in full chant, nothing could be heard save the scream of laughing which shook the building—an emotion certainly not the less difficult to repress, as Mrs. Paul, shaking her hand at him with passionate energy, called out—

'Oh, the baste! he thinks he's on circuit this minit!' As for myself, half choking and with sore sides, I never recovered till I reached the street, when O'Grady dragged me along, saying as he did so—

'We must reach home at once. Nothing but a strong alibi will save my character.'

CHAPTER LIX
FRESCATI'S

I was not sorry when I heard the following morning that my mother would not appear before dinner-hour. I dreaded the chance of any allusion to Miss Bellow's name requiring explanation on my part; and the more so, as I myself was utterly lost in conjectures as to the reason of her singular reception of me.

Julia, too, appeared more out of spirits than usual She pleaded fatigue; but I could see that something lay heavily on her mind. She conversed with evident effort, and seemed to have a difficulty in recalling her faculties to the ordinary topics of the day. A thought struck me that perhaps De Vere's conduct might have given cause for her depression; and gradually I drew the conversation to the mention of his name, when I soon became undeceived on this point. She told me with perfect unconcern how my father had tracked out the whole line of his duplicity and calumny regarding me, and had followed the matter up by a representation to the duke at the head of the army, who immediately commanded his retirement from the Guards. Later on, his family influence had obtained his appointment as *attaché* to the embassy at Paris; but since their first rupture he had discontinued his visits, and now had ceased to be acknowledged by them when they met.

My cousin's melancholy not being then attributable to anything connected with De Vere, I set myself to work to ascertain whence it proceeded; and suddenly the thought struck me that perhaps my mother's surmise might have some foundation, and that Julia, feeling an affection for me, might have been hurt at my evident want of attention towards her since we met.

I have already begged of my reader to separate such suspicions from the coxcombry of the lady-killer, who deems every girl he meets his victim. If I did for a moment imagine that my cousin liked me, I did so with a stronger sense of my own unworthiness to merit her love than if I myself had sought her affection. I had felt her superiority to myself too early in life to outlive the memory of it as we grew older. The former feeling of dread which I entertained of Julia's sarcasm still lived within me, and I felt keenly that she who knew the weaknesses of the boy was little likely to forget them in reflecting over the failures of the man; and thus, if she did care for me, I well knew that her affection must be checkered by too many doubts and uncertainties to give it that character of abiding love which alone could bring happiness. I perceived clearly enough that she disliked O'Grady. Was it, then, that, being interested for me, she was grieved at my great intimacy with one she herself did not admire, and who evidently treated her with marked coldness and reserve?

Harassed with these suspicions, and annoyed that those I had hoped would regard each other as friends avoided every opportunity of intimacy, I strolled forth to walk alone, my mind brooding over dark and disagreeable images, and my brain full of plans all based upon disappointed hopes and blighted expectations. To my mother's invitation to dinner for that day O'Grady had returned an apology; he was engaged to his friend M. Guillemain, with whom he was also to pass the morning; so that I was absolutely without a companion.

When first I issued from the Place Vendôme, I resolved at all hazards to wait on the Rooneys, at once to see Miss Bellew, and seek an explanation, if possible, for her manner towards me. As I hastened on towards the Chaussée, however, I began to reflect on the impropriety of such a course, after the evident refusal she had given to any renewal of acquaintance. 'I did know Mr. Hinton,' were the words she used—words which, considering all that had passed between us, never could have been spoken lightly or without reason. A hundred vague conjectures as to the different ways in which my character and motives might have been slandered to her occupied me as I sauntered along. De Vere and Burke were both my enemies, and I had little doubt that with them originated the calumny from which I now was suffering; and as I turned over in my thoughts all the former passages of our hatred, I felt how gladly they would embrace the opportunity of wounding me where the injury would prove the keenest.

Without knowing it, I had actually reached the street where the Rooneys lived, and was within a few paces of their house. Strangely enough, the same scene I had so often smiled at before their house in Dublin was now enacting here—the great difference being, that instead of the lounging subs, of marching regiments, the swaggering cornets of dragoons, the overdressed and underbred crowds of would-be fashionables who then congregated before the windows or curvetted beneath the balcony, were now the generals of every foreign service, field-marshals glittering with orders, powdered diplomatists, cordoned political writers, savants from every country in Europe, and idlers whose *bons mots* and smart sayings were the delight of every dinner-table in the capital; all happy to have some neutral ground where the outposts of politics might be surveyed without compromise or danger, and where, amid the excellences of the table and the pleasures of society, intrigues could be fathomed or invented under the auspices of that excellent attorney's wife, who deemed herself meanwhile the great attraction of her courtly visitors and titled guests.

As I drew near the house I scarcely ventured to look towards the balcony, in which a number of well-dressed persons were now standing chatting together. One voice I soon recognised, and its every accent cut my very heart as I listened. It was Lord Dudley de Vere, talking in his usual tone of loud assumption. I could hear the same vacant laugh which had so often offended me; and I actually dreaded lest some chance allusion to myself might reach me where I stood. There must be something intensely powerful in the influence of the human voice, when its very cadence alone can elevate to rapture or sting to madness. Who has not felt the ecstasy of some one brief word from 'lips beloved,' after long years of absence; and who has not experienced the tumultuous conflict of angry passions that rise unbidden at the mere sound of speaking from those we like not? My heart burned within me as I thought of her who doubtless was then among that gay throng, and for whose amusement those powers of his lordship's wit were in all likelihood called forth; and I turned away in anger and in sorrow.

As the day wore on I could not face towards home. I felt I dare not meet the searching questions my mother was certain to ask me; nor could I endure the thought of mixing with a crowd of strangers, when my own spirits were hourly sinking. I dined alone at a small *café* in the Palais Royal, and sat moodily over my wine till past eleven o'clock. The stillness of the room startled me at length, and I looked up and found the tables deserted; a sleepy waiter lounged lazily on a bench, and the un-trimmed candles and disordered look of everything indicated that no other guests were then expected.

'Where have they gone to?' said I, curious to know what so suddenly had taken the crowd away.

'To Frescati's, monsieur,' said the waiter; 'the salon is filling fast by this time.'

A strange feeling of dislike to being alone had taken hold on me, and having inquired the way to the Rue Richelieu from the servant, I issued forth.

What a contrast to the dark and gloomy streets of Paris, with their irregular pavement, was the brilliantly lighted vestibule, with its marble pillars and spacious stair rising gracefully beyond it, which met my eyes as I entered Frescati's! Mingling with the crowd of persons who pressed their way along, I reached a large antechamber where several servants in rich liveries received the hats and canes of the visitors who thronged eagerly forward, their merry voices and gay laughter resounding through the arched roof.

As the wide doors were thrown open noiselessly, I was quite unprepared for the splendour of the scene. Here were not only officers of rank in all the gala of their brilliant uniforms, and civilians in full dress, shining in stars and decorations, but ladies also, with that perfection of toilette only known to Parisian women, their graceful figures scattered through the groups, or promenading slowly up and down, conversing in a low tone; while servants passed to and fro with champagne and fruit-ices on massive silver salvers, their noiseless gesture and quiet demeanour in perfect keeping with the hushed and tranquil look of all around. As I drew closer to the table I could mark that the stillness was even more remarkable; not a voice was heard but of the croupier of the table, as with ceaseless monotony he repeated: 'Faites le jeu, messieurs! Le jeu est fait. Noir perd, et couleur gagne.

Rouge perd, et la couleur——' The rattle of the rake and the chink of the gold followed, a low muttered 'Sacre!' being the only sound that mingled with them.

But I could mark, that, although the etiquette of ruin demanded this unbroken silence, passion worked in every feature there. On one side was an old man, his filmy eyes shaded by his hand from the strong glare of wax-lights, peering with eagerness and tremulous from age and excitement as the cards fell from the banker's hands, his blanched lips muttering each word after the croupier, and his wasted cheek quivering as the chances inclined against him. Here was a bold and manly face, flushed and heated, whose bloodshot eye ranged quickly over the board, while every now and then some effort to seem calm and smile would cross the features, and in its working show the dreadful struggle that was maintained within. And then again a beautiful girl, her dark eye dilated almost to a look of wild insanity, her lips parted, her cheeks marked with patches of white and red, and her fair hands clenched, while her bosom heaved and fell as though some pent-up agony was eating at her very heart.

At the end of the table was a vacant chair, beside which an officer in a Prussian uniform was standing, while before him was a small brass-clasped box. Curious to know what this meant, I turned to see to which of those about me I might venture to address a question, when suddenly my curiosity became satisfied without inquiry. A loud voice talking German with a rough accent, the heavy tramp of a cavalry boot clanking with large spurs, announced the approach of some one who cared little for the conventional silence of the rooms; and as the crowd opened I saw an old man in blue uniform, covered with stars, elbow his way towards the chair. His eyebrows of shaggy grey almost concealed his eyes as effectually as his heavy moustache did his mouth. He walked lame, and leaned on a stick, which, as he took his place in the chair, he placed unceremoniously on the table before him. The box, which was opened the moment he sat down, he now drew towards him, and plunging his hand into it drew forth a handful of napoleons, and, without waiting to count, he threw on the table, uttering in a thick guttural voice the one word 'Rouge.' The impassive coldness of the croupier as he pronounced his habitual exordium seemed to move the old man's impatience, as he rattled his fingers hurriedly among the gold and muttered some broken words of German between his teeth. The enormous sum he betted drew every eye towards his part of the table—of all which he seemed totally regardless, as he raked in his winnings, or frowned with a heavy lowering look as often as fortune turned against him. Marshal Blucher—for it was he—was an impassioned gambler, and needed not the excitement of the champagne, which he drank eagerly from time to time, to stimulate his passion for play.

As I turned from the *rouge et noir* table, I remarked that every now and then some person left the room by a small door, which, concealed by a mirror, had escaped my attention when I entered. On inquiry I found that this passage led to a secret part of the establishment, which only a certain set of players frequented, and where the tables were kept open during the entire day and night. Curious to see the interior of this den of greater iniquity, I presented myself at it, and on opening found myself in a narrow corridor, where a servant demanded my billet. Having informed him that I was merely there from motives of curiosity, I offered him a napoleon, which speedily satisfied his scruples. He conducted me to the end of the gallery, where, touching a spring, the door opened, and I found myself in a room considerably smaller than the salon, and, with the exception of being less brilliantly lighted, equally splendid in its decorations. Around on all sides were small partitions, like the cells in a London coffee-house, where tables were provided for parties to sup at. These were now unoccupied, the greater attraction of high play having drawn every one around the table, where the same monotonous sounds of the croupier's voice, the same patter of the cards, and the same clinking of the gold continued unceasingly. The silence of the salon was as nothing to the stillness that reigned here. Not a voice save the banker's was ever heard; each player placed his money on the red or black square of the table without speaking, and the massive rouleaus were passed backwards and forwards with no other sound save the noise of the rake. I remarked, too, that the stakes seemed far heavier;

crumpled rolls of *billets de banque* were often thrown down, and from the muffled murmur of the banker I could hear such sums as 'seven thousand francs,' 'ten thousand francs,' called out.

It was some time before I could approach near enough to see the play; at last I edged my way to the front, and obtained a place behind the croupier's chair, where a good view of the table was presented to me. The different nations, with their different costumes, tongues, and expressions so strangely congregated, were a study that might have amused me for a long time, had not a chance word of English spoken close by me drawn off my attention.

Immediately in front, but with their backs towards me, sat two persons, who seemed, as was often the habit, to play in concert. A large heap of gold and notes lay before them, and several cards, marked with pin-holes to chronicle the run of the game, were scattered about. Unable to see their faces, I was struck by one singular but decisive mark of their difference in condition and rank. The hands of one were fair and delicate almost as a woman's—the blue veins circling clearly through them, and rings of great price and brilliancy glittering on the fingers; those of the other were coarse, brown-stained, and ill cared for—the sinewy fingers and strong bony knuckles denoting one accustomed to laborious exertions. It was strange that two persons, evidently so wide apart in their walks in life, should be thus associated; and feeling a greater interest from the chance phrase of English one of them had dropped, I watched them closely. By degrees I could mark that their difference in dress was no less conspicuous; for although the more humble was well and even fashionably attired, he had not the same distinctive marks which characterised his companion as a person of class and condition. While I looked, the pile of gold before them had gradually melted down to some few pieces; and as they bent down their heads over the cards, and concerted as to their play, it was clear that by their less frequent ventures they were becoming more cautious.

'No, no I' said he, who seemed to be the superior, 'I'll not risk it.'

'I say yes, yes!' muttered the other, in a deeper voice; 'the *rouge* can't go on for ever: it has passed eleven times.'

'I know,' said the former bitterly; 'and I have lost seventeen thousand francs.'

'*You* have lost!' retorted the other savagely, but in the same low tone; 'why not *we*? Am *I* for nothing in all this?'

'Come, come, Ulick, don't be in a passion!'

The name and the tone of the speaker startled me. I leaned forward; my very head reeled as I looked. It was Lord Dudley de Vere and Ulick Burke.

The rush of passionate excitement that ran through me for a minute or two, to be thus thrown beside the two only enemies I had ever had, unnerved me so far that I could not collect myself. To call them forth at once, and charge them with their baseness towards me; to dare them openly, and denounce them before that crowded assembly—was my first rapid thought. But from this wild thrill of anger I was soon turned, as Burke's voice, elevated to a tone of passion, called out—

'Hold! I am going to bet!'

The banker stopped; the cards still rested in his hands.

'I say, sir, I will do it,' said Burke, turning to De Vere, whose cheek was now pale as death, and whose disordered and haggard air was increased by his having torn off his cravat and opened the collar of his shirt. '*I* say I will; do *you* gainsay me?' continued he, laying on the words an accent of such contemptuous insolence that even De Vere's eye fired at it. 'Vingt mille francs, noir,' said Burke, placing his last billet on the table; and the words were scarce spoken when the banker cried out—

'Noir perd et passe.'

A horrible curse broke from Burke as he fixed his staring eyeballs on the outspread cards, and counted over the numbers to himself.

'You see, Burke,' said De Vere.

'Don't speak to me, now, damn you!' said the other, with clenched teeth.

De Vere pushed back his chair, and rising, moved through the crowd towards an open window. Burke sat with his head buried between his hands for some seconds, and then starting up at the banker s call, cried out—

'Dix mille, noir!'

A kind of half-suppressed laugh ran round the table at seeing that he had no funds while he still offered to bet. He threw his eyes upon the board, and then as quickly turned them on the players. One by one his dark look was bent on them, as if to search out some victim for his hate; but all were hushed. Many as reckless as himself were there, many as utterly ruined, but not one so lost to hope.

'Who laughed?' said he in French, while the thick veins of his forehead stood out like cordage; and then, as none answered to his challenge, he rose slowly, still scowling with the malignity of a demon.

'May I have your seat, monsieur?' said a dapper little Frenchman, with a smile and a bow, as Burke moved away.

'Yes, take it,' said he, as lifting the strong chair with one hand he dashed it upon the floor, smashing it to pieces with a crash that shook the room.

The crowd, which made way for him to pass out, as speedily closed again around the table, where the work of ruin still went forward. Not a passing glance was turned from the board to look after the beggared gambler.

The horrible indifference the players had shown to the sufferings of this wretched man so thoroughly disgusted me that I could no longer bear even to look on the game. The passion of play had shown itself to me now in all its most repulsive form, and I turned with abhorrence from the table.

My mind agitated by a number of emotions, and my heart now swelling with triumphant vengeance, now filled with pity for the sake of him who had ruined my fortunes for ever, I sat in one of the small boxes I have mentioned, which, dimly lighted, had not yet been sought by any of the players to sup in. A closely drawn curtain separated the little place I occupied from the adjoining one, where from time to time I heard the clink of glasses and the noise of champagne corks. At first I supposed that some other solitary individual had established himself there to enjoy his winnings or brood over his losses, when at last I could hear the low muttering of voices, which ere long I recognised as belonging to Burke and De Vere.

Burke, who evidently from his tone and manner possessed the mastery over his companion, no longer employed the insulting accents I had witnessed at the table; on the contrary, he condescended to flatter—affected to be delighted with De Vere's wit and sharpness, and more than once insinuated that with such an associate he cared little what tricks fortune played them, as, to use his own phrase, 'they were sure to come round.'

De Vere's voice, which I could only hear at rare intervals, told that he had drunk deeply, and that between wine and his losses a kind of reckless desperation had seized him, which gave to his manner and words a semblance of boldness which his real character lacked completely.

When I knew that Burke and De Vere were the persons near me, I rose to leave the spot; the fear of playing the eavesdropper forbade my remaining. But as I stood up, the mention of my name, uttered in a tone of vengeance by Burke, startled me, and I listened.

'Yes,' said he, striking his hand upon the table, and confirming his assertion with a horrible oath. 'Yes; for him and through him my uncle left me a beggar. But already I have had my revenge; though it shan't end there.'

'You don't mean to have him out again? Confound him, he's a devilish good shot; winged you already—eh?'

Burke, unmindful of the interruption, continued—

'It was I that told my uncle how this fellow was the nephew of the man who seduced his own wife. I worked upon the old man so that he left house and home, and wandered through the country, till mental irritation, acting on a broken frame, became fever, and then death.'

'Died—eh? Glorious nephew you are, by Jove! What next?'

'I'll tell you. I forged a letter in his handwriting to Louisa, written as if on his death-bed, commanding as his last prayer that she should never see Hinton again; or if by any accident they should meet, that she should not recognise him nor know him.'

'Devilish clever, that; egad, a better martingale than that you invented a while ago. I say, pass the wine! red fourteen times—wasn't it fourteen?—and if it had not been for your cursed obstinacy I'd have backed the red. See, fifty naps! one hundred, four, eight, sixteen, thirty-four, or six—which is it? Oh, confounded stupidity!'

'Come, come, Dudley! better luck another time. Louisa's eyes must have been too kindly bent on you, or you 'd have been more fortunate.'

'Eh, you think she likes me?—Capital champagne that!—I always thought she did from the first. That's what I call walking inside of Hinton. How he'll look! Ha! ha! ha!'

'Yes, how he'll look!' echoed Burke, endeavouring to join the laugh. 'But now one thing is yet wanting.'

'You mean those despatches,' replied De Vere suddenly. 'You always come back to that. Well, once for all, I say no!'

'Just hear me, Dudley! Nothing is easier; nothing incurs less risk.'

'Less risk! what do you mean? No risk for me to steal the papers of the embassy, and give them to you to hand over to that scoundrel at the head of the secret police? Devilish green I may be, but not so green as that, Master Burke!'

'Guillemain will give us forty thousand francs. Forty thousand! with half that, and your luck, De Vere, we'll break every bank in Paris. I know you don't wish to marry Louisa.'

'No; hang it, that's always the wind-up. Keep that for the last throw, eh?—There's heavy play there; see how silent they are.'

'Ay; and with forty thousand francs we might join them,' said Burke, as if musing; 'and so safely it may be done.'

'I say no!' replied De Vere resolutely.

'What do you fear? Is it me?'

'No, not you! I believe you are true enough. Your own neck will be in the rope too; so you'll say nothing. But I won't do it!—pass the champagne!— there's something so devilish blackguard in stealing a man's papers.'

Burke started, as if the tones of his companion's voice had stung him like an adder.

'Have you thought over your present condition?' said Burke firmly. 'You have not a guinea left; your debts in Paris alone, to my knowledge, are above forty thousand francs!'

'I'll never pay a franc of them—damned swindlers and Jew money-lenders!' was the cool reply.

'Might not some scrupulous moralist hint there was something blackguard in that?' said Burke, with slow and distinct articulation.

'What!' replied De Vere; 'do you come here to tutor me—a low-bred horse-jockey, a spy? Take off your hands, sir, or I'll alarm the room; let loose my collar!'

'Come, come, my lord, we're both in fault,' said Burke, smothering his passion with a terrible effort; 'we of all men must not quarrel. Play is to us the air we breathe, the light we live in. Give me your hand.'

'Allow me to draw on my glove first,' said De Vere, in a tone of incomparable insolence.

'Champagne here!' said Burke to the waiter as he passed, and for some minutes neither spoke.

The clock chimed a quarter to two, and Burke started to his feet.

'I must be going,' said he hastily; 'I should have been at the Porte St. Martin by half-past one.'

'Salute the Jacobite Club, *de ma part*,' said De Vere, with an insulting laugh, 'and tell them to cut everybody's throat in Paris save old Lafitte's; he has promised to do a bill for me in the morning.'

'You'll not need his kindness so soon,' replied Burke, 'if you are willing to take my advice. Forty thousand francs——'

'Would he make it sixty, think you?'

'Sixty!' said Burke, with animation; 'I'm not sure, but shall I say for sixty you'll do it?'

'No, I don't mean that; I was only anxious to know if these confounded rigmaroles I have to copy sometimes could possibly interest any one to that amount.'

Burke tried to laugh, but the hollow chuckle sounded like the gulping of a smothering man.

'Laugh out!' said De Vere, whose voice became more and more indistinct as his courage became stronger; 'that muttering is so devilish like a spy, a rascally, low-bred— —'

A heavy blow, a half-uttered cry, followed, and De Vere fell with a crash to the floor, his face and temples bathed with blood, while Burke, springing to the door, darted downstairs and gained the street before pursuit was thought of. A few of the less interested about the table assisted me to raise the fallen man, from whose nose and mouth the blood flowed freely. He was perfectly senseless, and evinced scarcely a sign of life as we carried him downstairs and placed him in a carriage.

'Where to?' said the coachman, as I stood beside the door.

'I hesitated for a second, and then said, 'No. 4 Place Vendôme.'

CHAPTER LX
DISCLOSURES

I have more than once heard physicians remark the singular immunity a fool's skull seems to possess from the evil effects of injury—as if Nature, when denying a governing faculty, had, in kind compensation, imparted a triple thickness to the head thus exposed. It is well known how among the educated and thinking classes many maladies are fatal which are comparatively innocuous among those whose hands alone are called on to labour. A very ingenious theory might be spun from this fact, to the manifest self-gratulation of foxhunters, sailors, gentlemen who assault the new police, tithe-proctors, and others. For the present I have no further use for the remark than as it bore upon the head-piece of Lord Dudley de Vere, whose admirable developments had received little or no damage from the rude assault of his companion. When he awoke the next morning, he was only aware that something unusual had occurred; and gradually by 'trying back' in his sensations, he remembered every particle that took place—had the clearest recollection of the 'run upon red'; knew the number of bottles of champagne he had partaken of; and was only puzzled by one thing— what could possibly have suggested the courage with which he confronted Burke, and the hardihood that led to insulting him. As to any awkwardness at being brought home to the house of the person he had himself so ill-treated, he never felt anything approaching to it; the extent of his reasoning on this point only went to his satisfaction that 'some one' took care of him, and that he was not left to lie on the floor of the salon.

This admirable philosophy of De Vere served in a great measure to relieve me from the constraint I felt in presenting myself before him, and soon put me perfectly at my ease in our interview. After learning, that, except some headaching sensations, the only inconvenience he experienced was an unconquerable thirst, I touched lightly on the cause of his misfortune; when, what was my astonishment to discern that he not only did not entertain a particle of ill-will towards the man who had so brutally ill-treated him, but actually grew warm in his panegyric of Burkes consummate skill and address at play—such qualities in his estimation being well worthy to cover any small blemishes of villainy his character might suffer under.

'I say, don't you think Burke a devilish sharp fellow? He's up to everything, and so cool, so confoundedly cool! Not last night, though; no, by Jove! he lost temper completely. I shall be marked with that knock, eh? Damn me, it was too bad; he must apologise for it. You know he was drunk, and somehow he was all wrong the whole evening; he wouldn't let me back the "rouge," and such a run—you saw that, I suppose?'

I assented with a nod, for I still hesitated how far I should communicate to him my knowledge of Burke's villainy towards myself.

'By-the-bye, it's rather awkward my being here; you know your people have cut me. Don't you think I might get a cab to bring me over to the Rue d'Alger?'

There was something which touched me in the simplicity of this remark, and I proceeded to assure him that any former impressions of my friends would not be remembered against him at that moment.

'Oh, that I'm sure of; no one ever thinks it worth while to bear malice against a poor devil like me. But if I'd have backed the red——'

'Colonel O'Grady is in the drawing-room,' said a servant in a low voice to me at this instant; and leaving Lord Dudley to speculate on the contingencies of his having 'backed the red,' I joined my friend, whom I had not seen on the previous day. We were alone, and in ten minutes I explained to him the entire discovery I had fallen upon, concealing only my affection for Louisa Bellew, which I could not bring myself even to allude to.

'I see,' said Phil, when I concluded—'I see you are half disposed to forgive De Vere all his rascality. Now, what a different estimate we take of men! Perhaps—I can't say—it is because I am an Irishman, but I lean to the bold-faced villain Burke; the miserable, contemptible weakness of the one is far more intolerable to me than the ruffian effrontery of the other. Don't forget the lesson I gave you many a year ago: a fool is always a blackguard. Now, if that fellow could see his companion this minute, there is not a circumstance he has noticed here that he would not retail if it bore to your disadvantage. Untouched by your kindness to him, he would sell you—ay, to the very man you saved him from! But, after all, what have we to do with him? Our first point is to rescue this poor girl's name from being ever mixed with his; anything further is, of course, out of the question. The Rooneys are going back: I saw Paul this morning. "The Cruiskeen Lawn" has been their ruin. All the Irish officers who had taken Madame de Roni for an illustrious stranger have found out the true scent; and so many distinguished persons are involved in the ridicule of their parties that the old *chef de police*, my friend, has sent them a private order to leave Paris in a week. Paul is in raptures at it. He has spent eighteen thousand in two months; detests the place; is dying to be back in Dublin; and swears that except one Cossack officer he hasn't met a pleasant fellow since he came abroad.'

'And Mrs. Paul?'

'Oh, the old story. I put Guilemain up to it, and he has hinted that the Empress of Russia has heard of the Czar's attentions; that there's the devil to pay in St. Petersburg; and that if she doesn't manage to steal out of Paris slyly, some confounded boyard or other will slip a sack over her head and carry her off to Tobolsk.

Elizabeth and the Exiles has formed part of her reading, and Madame de Roni will dream every night of the knout till she reaches her dear native land.—But now to business. I, too, have made my discoveries since we met. De Vere's high play has been a matter of surprise to all who know him. I have found out his secret—he plays with forged *billets de banque*.'

'And has the wretched fellow gone so far as this?'

'He doesn't know it; he believes that the money is the proceeds of bills he has given to Burke, who affects to get them discounted. See here—here are a handful of their notes. Guillemain knows all, and retains the secret as a hold over Burke, whose honesty to himself he already suspects. If he catch him tripping——'

'Then——'

'Why, then, the galleys for life. Such is the system; a villain with them is worthless if his life isn't at their disposal Satan's bond completely—all, all. But show me De Vere's room, and leave me alone with him for half an hour. Let us then meet at my hotel, and concert future measures.'

Having left O'Grady with De Vere, I walked out upon the boulevards, my head full of the extraordinary facts so suddenly thronging one upon the other. A dash of hope, that for many a day had not visited me, was now mingled through all my meditations, and I began to think that there was yet a chance of happiness for me.

I had not gone many paces when an arm was thrust into mine, and a hearty chuckling laugh at the surprise rang in my ear. I turned: it was Mr. Paul Booney, taking his morning's promenade of Paris, and now on his way home with an enormous bouquet for Madame, which she had taught him to present to her each day on her appearing in the drawing-room.

'Ah, Captain, the very man I wanted! We haven't had a moment to ourselves since your arrival. You must come and take a bit of dinner with us to-day—thank Heaven, we've no company! I have a leg of pork, smuggled into the house as if it was a bale of goods from Alexandria; nobody knows of it but myself and Tim.'

'Tim! why, have you brought Tim to Paris?'

'Hush!' said he in a low, cautious voice; 'I'd be ruined entirely if Madame was to find him out. Tim is dressed like a Tartar, and stands in the hall; and Mrs. Rooney believes that he never heard of a civil bill in his life. But here we are.'

So saying, he opened a small wicket with a latchkey, and led me into a large and well-trimmed garden, across which we walked at a rapid pace, Paul speculating from the closed shutters of his wife's room that he needed not have hurried home so fast.

'She's not down yet—one o'clock as I'm a sinner! Come along and sit down in the library; I'll join you presently.'

Scarcely had Paul left the room when I began to think over the awkwardness of my position should I meet Miss Bellew. What course to follow under the circumstances I knew not; when just at the moment the door opened, and she entered. Not perceiving me, as I stood in a deep window-recess, she drew a chair to the fire and sat down. I hardly ventured to breathe. I felt like one who had no right to obtrude himself there, and had become, as it were, a spy upon her. A long-drawn breath burst from me; she started up. I moved slightly forward, and stood before her. She leaned her hand upon the arm of the chair for support; her cheek grew deadly pale, and a tremulous quiver shook her lip.

'Mr. Hinton,' she began; and then as if the very sound of her voice had terrified her, she paused. 'Mr. Hinton,' resumed she, 'I am sure—nay, I know—if you were aware of the reasons of my conduct towards you, you would not only acquit me of all blame, but spare me the pain of our ever meeting again.'

'I know them—I do know them,' said I passionately. 'I have been slandered.'

'No, you do not, cannot know what I mean,' interrupted she. 'It is a secret between my own heart and one who is now no more.'

The last words fell from her one by one, while a single tear rolled from her eyelid and trickled along her cheek.

'Yes, yes, Louisa; I do know it—I know all. A chance has told me how your dear father's name has been used to banish me for ever from your sight; how a forgery of his handwriting——'

'What! who could have told you what my father's last note contained?'

'He who wrote it confessed it in my hearing—Ulick Burke. Nay, I can even repeat the words' But as I spoke, a violent trembling seized her; her lips became bloodless; she tottered, and sank upon the chair. I had only time to spring forward and catch her in my arms, and her head fell heavily back, and dropped on my shoulder.

I cannot, if I would, repeat the words which in all the warm eloquence of affection I spoke. I could mark by her heightened colour that the life-blood again coursed freely in her veins, and could see that she heard me. I told her how through every hardship and suffering, in all the sorrow of disappointed ambition, in the long hours of captivity, my heart had ever turned to her; and then, when we did meet, to see her changed!

'But you do not blame—you cannot blame me if I believed——'

'No, if you tell me now that but for this falsehood you have not altered; that your heart is still as much my own as I once thought it.'

A faint smile played on her lips as her eyes were turned upon me; while her voice muttered—

'And do you still love me?'

I pressed her hand to my lips in rapture, when suddenly the door opened and Paul Rooney rushed in.

'Another candidate for the leg of—— Eh! what's this?' said he, as I rose and advanced to meet him; while Louisa, blushing deeply, buried her head in her hand, and then starting up, left the room.

'Captain, Captain,' said Paul gravely, 'what does this mean? Do you suppose that because there is some difference in our rank in life, that you are privileged to insult one who is under my protection? Is it because you are the Guardsman and I the attorney that you have dared to take a liberty here which in your own walk you couldn't venture on?'

'My dear Mr. Rooney, you mistake me sadly.'

'If I do not mistake you, I'll put a hole in your body as sure as my name's Paul,' was the quick reply.

'You do, then, and wrong me to boot. I have been long and ardently attached to Miss Bellew. From the hour I met her at your house I loved her. It is the first time we have met since our long separation: I determined it should not be lost. I've asked her to be my wife.'

'You have! And what does she say?'

'She has consented.'

'Rum-ti-iddity, iddity!' said Paul, snapping his fingers, and capering about the room like a man deranged. 'Give me your hand, my buck! I 'd rather draw the settlements, so help me, than I 'd see the warrant to make me Master of the Rolls. Who 'd say there isn't luck in a leg of pork? She's a darling girl; and beautiful as she is, her looks isn't the best of her—an angel as sure as I am here! And look here'—here he dropped his voice—'seven thousand a year, that may be made nine! Hennessy's farm is out of lease in October; and the Cluangoff estate is let at ten shillings an acre. Hurroo! maybe I won't be drunk to-night; and bad luck to the Cossack, Tartar, Bohemian, or any other blackguard I'll let into the house this day or night! Sworn, my lord.'

After some little discussion, it was arranged that if Louisa would give her consent to the arrangement, the marriage should take place before the Rooneys left Paris. Meanwhile, Paul agreed with me in keeping the whole matter a perfect secret from everybody, Mrs. Rooney herself included. Our arrangements were scarcely completed when O'Grady appeared. Having waited for me some time at his hotel, he had set out in search of me.

'I'm your man to-day, Paul,' said he. 'You got my note, I suppose?'

'All right,' said Mr. Rooney, whose double secret of the marriage and the leg of pork seemed almost too much for him to bear.

'I suppose I may tell Phil,' said I in a whisper.

'No one else,' said Paul, as we left the house, and I took O'Grady's arm down the street.

'Well, I have frightened De Vere to some purpose,' said O'Grady. 'He has made a full confession about Burke, who was even a deeper villain than we supposed. What do you think? He has been the spy of the Bonapartist faction all this time, and selling old Guillemain as regularly as the others. To indulge his passion for play, he received the pay of four different parties, whom he pitted against one another exactly as he saw proper. Consummate clever scoundrel!—he had to deal with men whose whole lives are passed in the very practice of every chicanery and deceit, and yet he has jockied them all. What a sad thing to think that such abilities and knowledge of mankind should be prostituted to the lowest and most debasing uses; and that the sole tendency of such talent should be to dishonour and disgrace its possessor! Some of his manufactured despatches were masterpieces of cleverness.'

'Well, where is he now? Still in Paris?'

'No. The moment he had so far forgotten himself as to strike De Vere, he forged a passport and returned to London, carrying with him hosts of papers of the French authorities, which to our Foreign Office will be very acceptable. De Vere meanwhile feels quite at his ease. He was always afraid of his companion, yet can't forgive him his last indignity.

'No! A blow!'

'Not at all; you mistake. His regrets have a different origin. It is for not backing the "rouge" that he is inexorable towards him. Besides, he is under the impression that all these confessions he has been making establish for him a kind of moral insolvency act, by which he is to come forth irresponsible for the past, and quite ready to contract new debts for the future. At this moment his greatest point of doubt consists in whether he should marry your cousin, Lady Julia, or Miss Bellew; for, in his own phrase, "he must do something that way to come round."'

'Impudent scoundrel!'

'Fact, I assure you; and so easy, so unaffected, so free from embarrassment of any kind is he, that I'm really quite a convert to this modern school of good manners, when associating with even such as Burke conveys no feeling of shame or discomfort. More than could be said some forty years ago, I fancy.'

It was the hour of my mother's morning reception, and we found the drawing-room crowded with loungers and fashionable idlers, discussing the news of the day, and above all the Roni *fête*, the extraordinary finale to which gave rise to a hundred conjectures—some asserting that Monsieur de Roni's song was a violent pasquinade against the Emperor Alexander; others, equally well informed, alleging it was the concerted signal for a general massacre of the Allies, which was to have begun at the same moment in the Rue Montmartre. She is a Bonapartist, a Legitimist, a Neapolitan, an Anversoise,' contended one after another—my only fear being that some one would enlighten the party by saying she was the wife of an Irish attorney. All agreed, however, she was *bien mauvais ton*; that her *fête* was, with all its magnificence, anything but select; her supper superb, but too crowded by half; and, in fact, that Madame Roni had enjoyed the pleasure of ruining herself to very little other purpose than that of being generally ridiculed and laughed at.

'And this niece, or ward, or whatever it is—who can tell anything of her?' said my mother.

'Ah, *pardieu!* she's very handsome,' said Grammont, with a malicious smile.

'Perfect,' said another; 'quite perfect; but a little, a very little too graceful Don't you think so?'

'Why what do you mean?' said Lady Charlotte, as her eyes sparkled with animation at the thought of a secret.

'Nothing,' replied the last speaker carelessly; 'except that one always detects the *danseuse*. She was thinner when I saw her at Naples.'

I whispered one word—but one—in his ear, and his face became purple with shame and confusion.

'Eh, what is it?' said my mother eagerly. 'John knows something of her too. John, dearest, let us hear it?'

'I am in your ladyship's debt as regards one secret,' said O'Grady, interrupting; 'perhaps I may be permitted to pay it on this occasion. The lady in question is the daughter of an Irish baronet, the descendant of a family as old as any of those who now hear me. That baronet would have been a peer of the realm had he consented to vote once—but once—with the minister, on a question where his conscience told him to oppose him. His refusal was repaid by neglect; others were promoted to rank and honours before him; but the frown of a minister could neither take away the esteem of his country nor his own self-respect. He is now dead; but his daughter is the worthy inheritor of his virtues and his name. Perhaps I might interest the present company as much in her favour by adding, she possesses something like eight thousand per annum.'

'Two hundred thousand *livres de rente!* said Grammont, smacking his lips with astonishment, 'and perfectly insensible to the tone of mockery in which O'Grady's last words were spoken.

'And you are sure of all this?' said my mother.

O'Grady bowed deeply, but without speaking, while his features assumed an expression of severe determination I had never witnessed before. I could not help remarking, that, amid the dismay such an announcement created in that gossiping and calumnious assembly, my cousin Julia's eyes shone with an added lustre, and her whole face beamed with a look of proud and exalted beauty.

This was now the time to tell O'Grady my secret; and drawing him towards a window, I said—

'Phil, I can wait no longer—you must hear it. I'm going to be married.'

The words had not left my lips, when O'Grady started back, his face as pale as death, and his whole frame trembling with eagerness. By a violent effort, however, he rallied; and as he clutched my arm with his fingers, he said—

'I must be going; these good people have made me forget an appointment. Make my respectful homage to her ladyship—and the bride. I shall see you before I leave.'

'Leave! Why, where are you thinking of going?'

'To India.'

'To India!' said Julia, starting round as he spoke.

'To India!' said I, in amazement.

He nodded, and turning quickly round, left the room.

I hastened after him with all my speed, and dashing downstairs was making for the *porte cochère*, when a shadow beside the doorway caught my eye. I stopped. It was O'Grady; he was leaning against the wall, his head buried in his hands. A horrible doubt shot through my heart. I dared not dwell upon it; but rushing towards him, I called him by his name. He turned quickly round, while a fierce, wild look glistened in his eyes.

'Not now, Hinton, not now!' said he, motioning me away with his hand; and then, as a cold shudder passed over him, he drew his hand across his face, and added in a lower tone, 'I never thought to have betrayed myself thus. Good-bye, my dear fellow, good-bye! It were better we shouldn't meet again.'

'My dearest, best friend! I never dreamed that the brightest hour of my life was to throw this gloom over your heart.'

'Yes, Jack,' said he, in a voice low and broken, 'from the first hour I saw her I loved her. The cold manner she maintained towards me at your father's house——'

'In my father's house! What do you mean?'

'When in London, I speak of—when I joined first—your cousin—'

'My cousin!'

'Yes, Lady Julia. Are you so impatient to call her wife that you will not remember her as cousin?'

'Call her wife! My dear boy, you're raving. It's Louisa Bellew!'

'What! Is it Miss Bellew you are to marry?'

'To be sure——'

But I could not finish the sentence, as O'Grady fell upon my shoulder, and his strong frame was convulsed with emotion.

In an instant, however, I tore myself away; and calling out, 'Wait for me, O'Grady!' I rushed upstairs, peeped hastily into the drawing-room, and then hurrying along the corridor opened a door at the end. The blinds of the windows were down, and the room so dark that I could scarcely perceive if any one were there had not my steps been guided by a low sob which I heard issue from the end of the sofa.

'Julia,' said I, rushing forward—'Julia, my dearest cousin! this is no time to deceive ourselves. He loves you—loved you from the first hour he met you. Let me have but one word. Can he, dare he hope that you are not indifferent to him? Let him but see you, but speak to you. Believe me, you have bent a heart as proud and haughty as your own; and you will have broken it if you refuse him. There, dearest girl—— Thanks! my heart's thanks for that!'

The slightest pressure of her taper fingers sent a thrill through me, as I sprang up and dashed down the stairs. In an instant I had seized O'Grady's arm, and the next moment whispered in his ear—

'You 've won her!'

CHAPTER LXI
NEW ARRIVALS

Mr. Paul Rooney's secret was destined to be inviolable as regarded his leg of pork; for Madame de Roni, either from chagrin or fatigue, did not leave her room the entire day. Miss Bellew declined joining us; and we sat down, a party of three, each wrapped up in his own happiness in a degree far too great to render us either social or conversational It is true the wine circulated briskly, and we nodded pleasantly now and then to one another; but all our efforts to talk led to so many blunders and cross answers that we scarcely ventured on more than a chance phrase or a good-humoured smile. There were certainly several barriers in the way of our complete happiness, in the innumerable prejudices of my lady-mother, who would be equally averse to O'Grady's project as to my own; but now was not the time to speculate on these, and we wrapped ourselves up in the glorious anticipation of our success, and cared little for such sources of opposition as might now arise. Meanwhile, Paul entered into a long and doubtless very accurate statement of the Bellew property, to which, I confess, I paid little attention, save when the name of Louisa occurred, which momentarily aroused me from my dreaminess. All the wily stratagems by which he had gained his points with Galway juries, all the cunning devices by which he had circumvented opposing lawyers and obtained verdicts in almost hopeless cases, however I might have relished another time, I only now listened to without interest, or heard without understanding.

Towards ten o'clock I received more than one hint from O'Grady that we had promised to take tea at the Place Vendôme; while I myself was manoeuvring to find out, if we were to adjourn for coffee, what prospect there might be of seeing Louisa Bellew in the drawing-room.

It was in that dusky twilight we sat, a time which seems so suited to the quiet enjoyment of one's claret with a small and chosen party; where intimacy prevails sufficiently to make conversation more a thing of choice than necessity; where each man can follow out his own path in thought and only let his neighbour have a peep here and there into his dreamings, when some vista opens, or some bold prospect stretches away. Next to the blazing fire of a winter's hearth, this is the pleasantest thing I know of. Thus was it, when the door opened, and a dusky outline of a figure appeared at the entrance.

'Is Master Phil here?' said a cranky voice there was no mistaking as Mr. Delany's.

'Yes, Corny. What's wrong? Anything new?'

'Where's the Captain?' said he in the same tone.

'I'm here, Corny,' said L

'Well, there's them looking for you without,' said he, 'that'll maybe surprise you, pleasant as ye are now.'

A detestable effort at a laugh here brought on a fit of coughing that lasted a couple of minutes.

'Who is it?' said I. 'Where are they?'

A significant gesture with his thumb over his shoulder was the only reply to my question, while he barked out, 'Don't you see me coughing the inside out o' me?'

I started up, and without attending to Paul's suggestion to bring my friends in, or to O'Grady's advice to be cautious if it were Burke, hurried outside, where a servant of the house was in waiting to conduct me.

'Two gentlemen in the drawing-room, sir,' said he, as he preceded me down the corridor.

The next instant the door opened, and I saw my father, accompanied by another person, who being wrapped up in travelling equipment, I could not recognise.

'My dear father I' said I, rushing towards him, when suddenly I stopped short, as I perceived that instead of the affectionate welcome I looked for he had crossed his hands behind his back, and fixed on me a look of stern displeasure.

'What does this mean?' said I, in amazement; 'it was not thus I expected——'

'It was not thus I hoped to have received my son,' said he resolutely, 'after a long and eventful separation. But this is too painful to endure longer. Answer me, and with the same truth I have always found in you—is there a young lady in this house called Miss Bellew?'

'Yes, sir,' said I, and a cold perspiration broke over me, and I could scarcely support myself.

'Did you make her acquaintance in Ireland?'

'Yes, sir.'

'Did you at that time use every effort to win her affections, and give her to understand that she had yours?'

'Yes, sir,' said I more faintly than before, for already some horrible doubt was creeping on my mind.

'And have you now, sir,' continued he, in a voice elevated to a higher pitch—'have you now, sir, when a prospect of a richer alliance presents itself, dishonoured yourself and my name, by deserting the girl whose affections you have so gained?'

'No, sir! that is untrue.'

'Stop, young man! I have one at hand this moment who may compel you to retract your words as shamefully as you have boldly said them. Do you know this gentleman?'

'Father Loftus!' said I, starting back with astonishment, as the good priest unfolded a huge comforter from his throat, and stood forth.

'Yes, indeed! no other,' said he, in a voice of great sadness; 'and sorry I am to see you this way.'

'You, surely, my dear friend,' said I—'you cannot believe thus harshly of me?'

'If it wasn't for your handwriting, I'd not have believed the Pope of Rome,' was his reply, as he wiped his eyes. 'But there it is.'

So saying, he handed to me, with trembling fingers, a letter, bearing the Paris postmark.

I tore it open, and found it was written in my own name, and addressed to Father Loftus, informing him of my deep regret that, having discovered the unhappy circumstance of her mother's conduct, I was obliged to relinquish all thoughts of an alliance with Miss Bellow's family, whose connection with my own had been so productive of heavy misfortune. This also contained an open note, to be handed by the priest to Miss Bellew, in which I was made formally to renounce her hand, for reasons in the possession of Father Loftus.

In a second the truth flashed across me from whom this plot proceeded; and scarcely permitting myself time to read the letter through, I called out—

'This is a forgery! I never wrote it, never saw it before!'

'What!' said my father, starting round, and fixing his eye on the priest.

'You never wrote it?' echoed Father Tom. 'Do you say so? Is that your word as a gentleman?'

'It is,' said I firmly. 'This day, this very day, I have asked Miss Bellew to be my wife, and she has consented.'

Before my father could seize my hand, the good priest had thrown his arms round my neck and given me an embrace a bear might have envied. The scene that followed I cannot describe. My poor father, quite overpowered, sat down upon a chair, holding my hand within both his; while Father Tom bustled about the room, looking into all the glass and china ornaments for something to drink, as his mouth, he said, was like a lime-burner's hat. The honest fellow, it appeared, on receiving the letters signed with my name, left his home the same night and travelled with all speed to London, where he found my father just on the eve of leaving for Paris. Very little persuasion was necessary to induce him to continue his journey farther. On their arrival at Paris they had gone to O'Grady's hotel, where, securing Corny*s services, they lost not a moment in tracking me out in the manner I have mentioned.

O'Grady's surprise was little inferior to my own, as I introduced General Hinton and Father Loftus. But as to Mr. Rooney, he actually believed the whole to be a dream; and even when candles were brought, and he had taken a patient survey of the priest, he was far from crediting that my parent was not performed by deputy, till my father's tact and manner convinced him of his mistake.

While the priest was recounting some circumstances of his journey, I took occasion to tell my father of O'Grady's intentions regarding Julia, which with all the warmth of his nature he at once responded to; and touching his glass gaily with Phil's, merely added, 'With my best wishes.' Poor O'Grady caught up the meaning at once, and grasped his hand with enthusiasm, while the tears started to his eyes.

It would lead me too far, and perhaps where the goodnature of my reader might not follow me, were I to speak more of that happy evening. It is enough to say that Father Loftus won every moment on my father, who also was delighted with the hearty racinees of honest Paul. Their stores of pleasantry and fun, so new to him, were poured forth with profusion; and a party every member of which was more disposed to like one another and be pleased, never met together.

I myself, however, was not without my feeling of impatience to reach the drawing-room, which I took the first favourable opportunity of effecting— only then perceiving that O'Grady had anticipated me, having stolen away some time before.

CHAPTER LXII
CONCLUSION

It would be even more wearisome to my reader than the fact was worrying to myself, were I to recount the steps by which my father communicated to Lady Charlotte the intended marriages, and finally obtained her consent to both. Fortunately, for some time previous she had been getting tired of Paris, and was soon brought to suppose that these little family arrangements were as much 'got up' to afford her an agreeable surprise and a healthful stimulant to her weak nerves as for any other cause whatever.'

With Mrs. Rooney, on the other hand, there was considerable difficulty. The holy alliance she had contracted with the sovereigns had suggested so much of grandeur to her expectations that she dreamed of nothing but archdukes and counts of the empire, and was at first quite inexorable at the bare idea of the *mésalliance* that awaited her ward. A chance decided what resisted every species of argument. Corny Delany, who had been sent with a note to Mr. Rooney, happened to be waiting in the hall while Mrs. Rooney passed out to her carriage escorted by the 'Tartar' of whom we have already made mention. Mrs. Rooney was communicating her orders to her bearded attendant by a code of signals on her fingers, when Corny, who watched the proceeding with increasing impatience, exclaimed—

'Arrah, can't you tell the man what you want? Sure, though you have him dressed like a wild baste, he doesn't forget English.'

Caught a Tartar

It is a Tartar!' said Mrs. Rooney, with a contemptuous sneer at Corny and a forbidding wave of her hand ordaining silence.

'A Tarther! Oh, blessed Timothy! there's a name for one that comes of dacent people! He's a county Oarlow man, and well known he is in the same parts. Many a writ he served—eh, Tim?'

'Tim!' said Mrs. Rooney, in horror, as she beheld her wild-looking friend grin from ear to ear, with a most fearful significance of what he heard.

'It wasn't my fault, ma'am, at all,' said the Tartar, with a very Dublin accent in the words; 'it was the master made me.'

What further explanation Tim might have afforded it is difficult to say, for Mrs. Rooney's nerves had received too severe and too sudden a shock. A horrible fear lest all the kingly and royal personages by whom she had been for some weeks surrounded might only turn out to be Garlow men, or something as unsubstantial, beset her; a dreadful unbelief of everything and everybody seized upon her, and quite overcome, she fainted. O'Grady, who happened to come up at the instant, learned the whole secret at once, and with his wonted readiness resolved to profit by it. Mrs. Paul returned to the drawing-room, and ere half an hour was fully persuaded that as General Hinton was about to depart for Ireland as Commander of the Forces, the alliance was on the whole not so deplorable as she had feared.

To reconcile so many conflicting interests, to conciliate so many totally opposite characters, was a work I should completely have failed in without O'Grady's assistance. He, however, entered upon it *con amore*; and under his auspices, not only did Lady Charlotte receive the visits of Father Tom Loftus, but Mr. Paul became actually a favourite with my cousin Julia; and, finally, the grand catastrophe of the drama was accomplished, and my lady-mother proceeded in all state to wait on Mrs. Rooney herself, who, whatever her previous pretensions, was so awed by the condescension of her ladyship's manner that she actually struck her colours at the first broadside.

Weddings are stupid things in reality, but on paper they are detestable. Not even the *Morning Post* can give them a touch of interest. I shall not, then, trouble my reader with any narrative of white satin and orange-flowers, bouquets, breakfasts, and Bishop Luscombe; neither shall I entertain him with the article in the French *Feuilleton* as to which of the two brides was the more strictly beautiful, and which more lovely.

Having introduced my reader to certain acquaintances—some of them rather equivocal ones, I confess—I ought perhaps to add a word of their future fortunes.

Mr. Ulick Burke escaped to America, where, by the exercise of his abilities and natural sharpness, he accumulated a large fortune, and distinguished by his anti-English prejudices, became a leading member of Congress.

Of Lord Dudley de Vere I only know that he has lived long enough, if not to benefit by experience, to take advantage of Lord Brougham's change in the law of imprisonment for debt. I saw his name in a late number of the *Times*, with a debt of some fifteen thousand annexed to it, against which his available property was eleven pounds odd shillings.

Father Loftus sleeps in Murranakilty. No stone marks his resting-place; but not a peasant's foot, for many a mile round, has not pressed the little pathway that leads to his grave, to offer up a prayer for a good man and a friend to the poor.s

Tipperary Joe is still to be met on the Kilkenny road. His old red coat, now nearly russet colour, is torn and ragged; the top-boots have given place to bare legs, as well tanned as their predecessors; but his merry voice and cheerful 'Tally-ho!' are still as rich as of yore, and his heart, poor fellow! as light as ever it was.

Corny Delany is the amiable proprietor of a hotel in the neighbourhood of Castlebar, where his habitual courtesy and amenity are as conspicuous as of yore. He has requested me to take this opportunity of recommending his establishment to the 'Haythins and Turks' that yearly perform tours in his vicinity.

The Rooneys live, and are as hospitable as ever. I dare not venture to give their address, lest you should take advantage of the information.

O'Grady and his wife are now at Malta.

Jack Hinton and his are, as they have every right to be—

Your very grateful and obedient Servants.

My dear Friends,—You must often have witnessed, in the half-hour which preludes departure from a dinner-party, the species of quiet bustle leave-taking produces. The low-voiced announcement of Mr. Somebody's carriage, the whispered good-night, the bow, the slide, the half-pressed finger—and he is gone. Another and another succeed him, and the few who linger on turn ever towards the opening door, and while they affect to seem at ease, are cursing their coachman and wondering at the delay.

The position of the host on such an occasion is precisely that of the author at the close of a volume. The same doubts are his whether the entertainment he has provided has pleased his guests; whether the persons he has introduced to one another are mutually satisfied. And, finally, the same solitude which visits him who 'treads alone some banquet-hall deserted' settles down upon the weary writer who watches one by one the spirits he has conjured up depart for ever, and, worse still, sees the tie snapped that for so long a period has bound him to his readers; and while they have turned to other and newer sources of amusement, he is left to brood over the time when they walked together, and his voice was heard amongst them.

Like all who look back, he sees how much better he could have done were he again to live over the past. He regrets many an opportunity of interesting you lost for ever, many an occasion to amuse you which may never occur again. It is thus that somehow—insensibly, I believe—a kind of sadness creeps over one at the end of a volume; misgivings as to success mingle with sorrows for the loss of our accustomed studies; and, altogether, the author is little to be envied, who, having enjoyed your sympathy and good wishes for twelve months, finds himself at last at the close of the year at the limit of your kindness, and obliged to say 'Good-bye,' even though it condemns him to solitude.

I did wish, before parting with you at this season, to justify myself before you for certain things which my critics have laid to my charge; but on second thoughts I have deemed it better to say nothing, lest by my defence against manslaughter a new indictment should be framed, and convict me of murder.

Such is the simple truth. The faults, the very great faults, of my book I am as well aware of as I feel myself unable to correct them. But in justice to my monitors I must say, that they have less often taken me up when tripping than when I stood erect upon good and firm ground. Yet let me be grateful for all their kindness, which for critics is certainly long-lived; and that I may still continue for a season to enjoy their countenance and yours is the most sincere desire of your very devoted servant,

Harry Lorrequer.

P.S.—A bashful friend desires an introduction to you. May I present Tom Burke, of Ours? H. L.